Catrin
COLLIER

A Silver Lining
Spoils of War

Catrin Collier was born and brought up in Pontypridd. She lives in Swansea with her husband, three cats and whichever of her children choose to visit. Her latest novel in Orion paperback is *Finders & Keepers*, and her latest novel in hardback, *Tiger Bay Blues*, is also available from Orion. Visit her website at www.catrincollier.co.uk.

By Catrin Collier

HISTORICAL

Hearts of Gold
One Blue Moon
A Silver Lining
All That Glitters
Such Sweet Sorrow
Past Remembering
Broken Rainbows
Spoils of War
Swansea Girls
Swansea Summer
Homecoming
Beggars & Choosers
Winners & Losers
Sinners & Shadows
Finders & Keepers
Tiger Bay Blues

CRIME (*as Katherine John*)

Without Trace
Midnight Murders
Murder of a Dead Man
By Any Other Name

MODERN FICTION (*as Caro French*)

The Farcreek Trilogy

Catrin
COLLIER

A Silver Lining
Spoils of War

A Silver Lining
First published in Great Britain by Century in 1994

Spoils of War
First published in Great Britain by Century in 2000

This omnibus edition published in 2009
by Orion Books Ltd
Orion House, 5 Upper St Martin's Lane
London WC2H 9EA

An Hachette UK company

A CIP catalogue record for this book is available from the British
Library.

ISBN 9781407221021

Printed in Great Britain by Clays Ltd, St Ives plc

www.orionbooks.co.uk

A Silver Lining

For all the refugees who came to the valleys in search of a new life, especially my mother, Gerda Jones, née Salewski.

Chapter One

OIL LAMPS GLOWED, a straggling line of beacons wavering in the damp wind that whistled and tore through the sodden canvas that tented the market stalls. The cobbled gangway between the trestles that lined Market Square was far too narrow to accommodate the swell of late-night shoppers who spilled continuously into the area from both sides of the town. And not only the town: the lilting speech of those who lived in the multi-stranded valleys above Pontypridd could be heard mingling with the sharper, more commercial accents of the traders and the softer intonations of the townsfolk who were attempting to push their way through the jammed throng.

The air, even beneath the canvas shroud, was thick, heavy with moisture; the atmosphere rich with the eye-stinging pungency of paraffin oil, the sour odour of unwashed clothes, and the reek of seasonal nips of whisky and brandy wafting on the tides of the traders' breath as they called their wares.

'Last chance for a bargain before Father Christmas comes down the chimney to burn his bum on hot ashes tonight, love. Come on, two a penny. You won't find cheaper anywhere.' A tall, thin man with a pockmarked face, shabby clothes and military bearing held up a pair of unevenly hemmed, coarsely woven handkerchiefs.

'Not today, thanks.' Alma Moore tucked her auburn curls beneath her home-knitted tam without relinquishing her hold on the cloth purse that contained her wages from both the tailor's shop where she worked mornings, and the café where she waitressed most nights and week-ends. Once she'd secured her hair she thrust her purse deep into her pocket, burying it securely beneath her hand.

Nearly all the money she carried was earmarked for necessities – rent, coal, and paying something off the 'tab' on their endless bill in the corner shop. She knew if she spent the remainder on Christmas cheer for her mother and herself, there'd be nothing left for coals or food at the end of the week. But then – she gripped her purse so tightly that the edges of the coins cut into the palm of her hand – it *was* Christmas. And if she couldn't treat her mother to a little luxury at Christmas, what did she have to look forward to?

Using her shoulder as a wedge, she nudged and jostled through the dense crowd until she reached an alleyway fringed by an overspill of stalls that led off Market Square. Two minutes later she was outside the old Town Hall that housed the indoor second-hand clothes market. She forged ahead towards Horton's stall.

'Come for your mam's coat?' Seventeen-year-old Eddie Powell, resplendent in an almost new blue serge suit which had been knocked down to him in two days' work in lieu of wages, smiled at her. It was a smile she didn't return. She couldn't forget that it had been Eddie's sixteen-year-old sister Maud who'd captured the heart – and hand – of Ronnie Ronconi, her ex-employer and ex-boyfriend of more than four years.

'The coat, and—' she pulled her purse from her pocket – 'I was hoping you'd have a good woollen scarf to go with it. Real wool, mind. None of your cotton or rayon mixes.'

'We've sets of matching gloves and scarves. All brand spanking new,' Eddie suggested eagerly, scenting a sale in the air. 'Boss bought them in as specials for Christmas. So many customers came asking he looked around for a supplier. We don't get many second-hand accessories.' He was proud of the 'trade' word he'd heard Wilf Horton mention and had never used himself before now. He picked up a woollen bundle from the top of an enormous, roughly crafted pine chest behind him. 'Just feel the quality in this. Go on, feel.' He thrust the grey cloth into Alma's blue face. 'It's the best machine knit you'll find anywhere,' he continued, still imitating his boss's sales patter. 'A lot smoother than anything that comes off your mam's needles, and pure wool. Soft wool,' he said persuasively. 'Not the scratchy kind that brings you up in red bumps.'

Alma reached out with chilled fingers and tentatively rubbed the cloth.

'That's a real crache scarf, just like the nobs on the Common wear.' Eddie leaned over the counter and she jumped back warily as his mouth hovered close to hers. 'You won't find finer than that, not even in there.' He pointed down the lane where the gleaming electric lights of the Co-op Arcade cast strange elongated patterns over the shiny black surfaces of the pavements behind the stalls. 'Or even at Gwilym Evans',' he added recklessly, conjuring images of the silver and gold tinsel-bedecked windows of the most exclusive and expensive shop Pontypridd had to offer. 'Go on, take it. Try it. Wrap it around your neck. Think what that will do for your mam on a cold winter's night,' he concluded on a hard-sale note, his mind fixed on the shilling bonus Mr Horton had promised him if the takings outside of what had been 'put by' on penny a week cards, topped fifteen pounds that day.

Alma didn't need the sales pitch. She was already envisaging her mother wrapped snugly in the scarf and their old patched quilt, sitting next to the kitchen stove which was blasting out heat in imagination as it was never allowed to do in the cold reality of frugal coal rations. Her mother deserved warm clothes. Particularly on the four days a week she economised by not setting a match to the stove.

'There's gloves and hat to match. All the same quality.' He rubbed his frozen hands together and danced a jig. Centre doorway might be a good spot from a trade point of view, but it played hell with his circulation.

Alma extricated a glove from the bundle Eddie pushed towards her. She pulled the woollen fingers, stretching them, looking for dropped stitches, signs of unfinished seams or loose knitting. There were none. Then she picked up the second glove.

'This one is bigger than the other.' She held up the offending garment. 'And the wool is different. It's coarser, greasier.'

'Then try these.' Eddie reached behind him and withdrew a pair of gloves from another bundle.

'They're two right gloves.' Costly experience had taught Alma every trick the market boys with their second-quality wares had to offer.

'How about this set, then?' Undeterred, Eddie opened the chest and produced a new pack from its depths. Hat, scarf and gloves were stitched together with huge tacking stitches in thick brown twine. Alma carefully loosened the threads and went through each piece. She put the hat and gloves to one side but held up the scarf.

'Dropped stitch in this.'

'Then swap it with the other one.' Eddie's patience was wearing thin; he'd just caught sight of his boss eyeing him suspiciously from the other side of the stall in a way he wouldn't have if Alma had been old, or ugly.

'Colour's not the same.'

'Tell you what.' Eddie glanced over his shoulder to make sure no one was listening. 'I'll knock it down to you at a special price.'

'What kind of special price?'

'For you, two bob the lot. Hat, scarf and gloves.'

'Two bob!' Alma tossed the bundle aside in disgust. 'It's not worth that. Besides . . .' she dangled the promise of extra trade. 'It wouldn't leave me enough to pick up the coat I've put by, or buy the jumper my mam needs.'

'You've come for your coat, Alma?' Wilf pushed Eddie out of his way. 'Mrs Edwards needs seeing to, boy,' he ordered brusquely. 'She's after a suit for her son, and she wants you to try the jacket to check the size.'

4

'Right away, Mr Horton.' Eddie wasn't sorry to leave Alma. She might be a looker, but she was nineteen; far too old for him, and boy, was she fussy! No wonder Ronnie had taken off for Italy with Maud.

'You looking for something beside your coat, Alma?' Wilf lifted the tips of his fingers to his wrinkled, red-veined face, and blew on them.

'I'd like to buy my mother a scarf, gloves, and if I've enough money left over, a jumper, Mr Horton.'

'Right, let's see what I can do for you.' He bent beneath the counter and rummaged among the boxes under the trestles.

'I'd like the jumper to be the same quality as this, please.' Alma held up the only perfect scarf Eddie had shown her.

'You know what to look for. This suit you?' He held up a mass of purple, green and red wool. 'Colours ran in the dye batch, but they didn't affect the quality. It's lamb's-wool like the scarf. I'll be with you now Edith!' he shouted to a woman who was pushing a man's shirt under his nose.

'I want it for a present, Mr Horton,' Alma retorted icily.

'That's what I thought. It's warm and your mam wouldn't know the difference,' he said bluntly, too pre-occupied with the buying potential of the customers pressing around his stall to concern himself with Alma's sensitivity.

'My mother might be blind, Mr Horton, but that doesn't mean I'd allow her to walk around looking like something the cat dragged in.'

'Suit yourself. That one I can do for one and six. Perfect like this—' he tossed an emerald green pullover at her – 'I can't do for less than five bob, and then I'd be robbing myself. Got your card for the coat?' Wilf turned his back on Alma and took the shirt from Edith. 'A shilling to you love, and seeing as how it's Christmas I'll throw in a hanky for free. How's that for a bargain?'

'I'll take it, Wilf.' The woman opened her purse as Wilf

5

threw the shirt and handkerchief at Eddie to be wrapped in newspaper.

Mesmerised, Alma stared at the jumper. It was such a deep, beautiful green. A jumper like that could make even the old black serge skirt she was wearing look good. She brushed her hand lightly against the surface; it was softer than any wool she'd ever touched. But five shillings! Reluctantly she dropped the jumper on to the counter, and picked up the one that looked as if it had been attacked by a colour-blind artist. Wilf Horton was right: the colouring hadn't affected the quality. She pulled her card out of her pocket and looked at it. Not that she needed to. She knew exactly how much she owed.

'Coat was ten bob, less . . .' Wilf took Alma's card and peered short-sightedly at the numbers scrawled on it. 'Fifteen weeks at sixpence a week. That leaves half a crown Alma. What do you want to do about the jumper?'

Alma heard the clock on St Catherine's strike the half-hour. Tina Ronconi was covering a double station of tables in the café, but Tina wouldn't be able to do that for long. Christmas Eve was always busy, and she still had to buy the other things on her list. She clutched the scarf and fingered the multicoloured pullover.

'How much for everything?' She comforted herself with the thought that it cost nothing to ask.

'This pullover, the scarf, hat and gloves?'

'The lot.'

'You broken a set there?' Wilf looked suspiciously at the garments she was holding.

'The gloves that went with this scarf were odd.'

'Call it five bob with what you owe on the coat.'

'I don't want charity,' Alma snapped, pride stinging.

Wilf sighed. You just couldn't win with some people. It was open knowledge in the town that Alma Moore and her mother had lived hand to mouth since Ronnie Ronconi had left Pontypridd for Italy. Alma couldn't even afford bargain prices, but she wasn't past holding up business to haggle, and now, when he was offering her

6

goods at a loss just to get rid of her, she wouldn't take them.

'That's my price, take it or leave it.'

'She'll take it. And the green jumper.'

Alma whirled round to see Bobby Thomas, who collected her rent, holding a ten-bob note high in his hand. Hot, rum-laden breath wafted into her face as she nodded briefly before turning back to Wilf. Anxious to avoid a scene she pulled out her purse. 'I'll take everything except the green jumper, Mr Horton,' she said hastily, fear of Bobby and the propositions he'd put to her every rent day since Ronnie had left making her reckless. She dug into her purse and produced a couple of two-shilling pieces, and four joeys.

'Eddie, wrap for the lady!' Wilf ordered.

'And the green jumper.'

Wilf looked from Bobby to Alma, wondering if Alma had found herself a new fancy man. If so, the few people who bothered to talk to her now would soon stop. Bobby Thomas had a wife born and bred in East Street, who was five months gone in the family way.

'Thank you Mr Horton. Hope your wife likes the jumper, Bobby,' Alma said loudly for Wilf Horton's benefit as she walked away from the stall. She pretended not to hear Bobby calling out, asking her to wait. The last thing she needed was to get involved in a conversation with a drunk on the market. With Ronnie gone from Pontypridd people were saying enough about her as it was.

Trying to concentrate on the task in hand, Alma fought her way from the clothes to the butcher's market. Her mother had scraped together the ingredients for a cake weeks ago, but they hadn't been able to run to what was needed for a pudding. There was no way she could afford a chicken, and now that Ronnie had left she wouldn't be getting one as a Christmas bonus as she had done in previous years. Christmas! Her mother was looking forward to it because it was the only day of the year Alma didn't have to work, but what was the point in celebrating when they couldn't even afford to buy themselves a decent Christmas dinner? Clutching the carrier bag Eddie had given her in one hand, and fingering her lighter, slimmer purse with the other, she pictured the coins in her mind's eye. Sixpence for a tree. That had to be bought no matter what, and sweets to hang among the old paper decorations, made and carefully treasured from year to year. It didn't matter that her mother couldn't see the tree, she would be able to smell it. She wondered how many boiled sweets she would get from Mrs Walker's stall for sixpence. Then there was fruit. Two of those bright paper-wrapped oranges, two apples and some nuts: that would be at least another fourpence. She was already into next week's rent money, and that was without meat.

'Bag of ends for fourpence! Come on Missus, just what you need for Boxing Day when your old man is growling with his belly stretched by Christmas dinner.' William Powell, Maud Powell's cousin – Alma felt surrounded by Powells, she couldn't seem to get away from them no matter which way she turned – was standing on a box behind Charlie the Russian's butcher's stall.

'How about it, Alma?' he shouted. 'Bag of ends for fourpence?'

'What's in it?' she demanded sceptically.

William balanced the bag precariously on his outstretched palm and peered theatrically inside. 'Now what do I see?' he mused in a loud voice as he gathered a hushed crowd around the stall. 'I see two neck of lamb chops . . .' he looked up and beamed at a plump, toothless old woman who'd pushed her way to the front, 'a pair of sweetbreads. Just what you need to get yourself going, eh, Mrs Jones?' he winked impudently, a dark curl falling low over his forehead.

'Come home with me and I'll show you what I need to get myself going, Willie Powell!' she chuckled throatily.

'Willie! Willie! I'm not sure you know me well enough to call me Willie . . .'

'Get on with it,' a man shouted impatiently.

'On with what, Ianto? Courting May Jones here?' He held up his hand to silence the raucous crowd. 'The remainder of what's in this bag, is a . . . a . . .' he opened his dark brown eyes wide as he scanned his expectant audience. 'Mystery,' he hissed in a stage whisper. 'And one that will only be solved after you've dug in your pockets.'

Alma opened her purse. She wasn't going to get cheaper this side of the nine o'clock bell, and she couldn't wait.

'I'll take a bag, please, Charlie.' She thrust a three-penny bit and a penny at William's boss, a stocky, broad-built, muscular man with white-blond hair and possibly the palest skin in the valleys. She'd always thought of Charlie as tall, but now, seeing him standing next to William she realised that he was a good three or four inches shorter than William's six feet two.

He picked up a bag from the back of the row laid out on the slab behind him. 'Keep it separate from the rest of your shopping. The blood will stain everything it touches,' he warned in a guttural accent that sounded exotic to ears accustomed to the Welsh lilt. 'And Merry Christmas.'

'Merry Christmas to you, Charlie.'

'Catch!'

A soft parcel wrapped in newspaper flew through the air, landing on top of the bag Charlie had given her. She peeled back a corner of the paper and saw shining green wool.

'Happy Christmas, Alma.' Bobby Thomas was already out of reach, separated from her by the mass of bargain hunters homing in on the offer on Charlie's stall. 'I'll be around to pick up my present in the New Year,' he leered over the heads of the crowd.

'I don't want this . . .'

It was too late. Bobby had his back to her and was half-way through the door. She'd never catch up with him

9

now. A sick feeling stole over her as she stared at the parcel. She could throw it away, but if she did it would only get picked up by someone who might or might not keep it. And if they didn't, where would they take it? To the police station? Without a name or address, the constables wouldn't be able to return it to Bobby. She could take it back to Wilf Horton but there was no guarantee that he'd be seeing Bobby either. Either way it was doubtful Bobby Thomas would get to hear of her gesture, and come next rent day he'd turn up on her doorstep to claim the 'present' he expected in return.

She'd begun to dread rent days since Ronnie had left. Bobby had taken to lingering in their kitchen, making lewd suggestions, and when she'd threatened to report him to her landlord he'd pointed out that he was the one with position and standing in the town, not her.

Rage at the gossips who'd destroyed her reputation vied with an anger directed against Bobby as she thrust the parcel under her arm and struggled out of the crowd into the haberdashery, toy and sweet market.

'Christmas bag do you, Alma?' Mrs Walker asked, as Alma hesitated before her stall.

'How much?'

'Threepence for two giant coconut ice sticks, a bag of toffee scrapings, assortment of boiled sweets and liquorice laces. Sixpence for a bigger helping of everything except the coconut ice sticks, plus four chocolates.'

Alma's mouth watered at the prospect of chocolates, but she remembered the extravagance Bobby had driven her into at Horton's stall. 'Threepenny bag, please.'

'Seeing as how it's you, and Christmas, I'll do the sixpenny offer for fivepence,' Mrs Walker offered temptingly.

Alma hesitated. It *was* Christmas Eve. Perhaps a customer would leave a tip. One of the bus crew perhaps . . . 'I'll take it,' she answered impulsively. 'Thank you Mrs Walker, and a Merry Christmas.'

'And a Merry Christmas to you, dear. Remember me to

your mother.' She handed over a paper cone of confectionery.

Pushing the sweets deep into the carrier bag of clothes, Alma turned on her heel and elbowed her way to the fruit market. Picking a stall that sold Christmas trees as well as fruit, she negotiated the price for the lot down to ninepence. If she didn't spend another penny, she'd be able to pay the rent – just. She blanched at the thought of the grocer's bill they'd run up in Hopkins' corner shop. If she didn't settle something off it soon, they'd lose their credit. She really needed a Christmas tip. St Catherine's clock struck again as she left the indoor market for Taff Street. She'd better get a move on or there'd be no Christmas tips to pick up.

'Want me to take some of that home for you, Alma?' Iorwerth Hopkins, the son of Edna who ran the shop near the house she shared with her mother in Morgan Street, held out his hand for the tree.

'That would be good of you, Iorwerth. It would save me carting it to the café.' She smiled as she suddenly thought of a solution to her problem. 'You know Bobby Thomas don't you, Iorwerth?'

'Yes,' he answered suspiciously in a tone that said knowing and liking were two different things.

'He dropped this at Wilf Horton's stall.' She handed him the newspaper-wrapped jumper. 'It's his wife's Christmas present. I don't know where he lives so I was going to leave it at the police station, but it would be better if you could take it to his wife.'

'They live in Bassett Street. I'll drop it in to her when I take Madge home.'

'Thanks a lot, Iorwerth.' She breathed easier. 'You've taken a load off my mind. I hope it isn't far out of your way.'

'Not far. Have you met Madge?'

'I don't think so,' Alma murmured absently, offloading her tree on to him.

'Madge, come over here!'

A pretty girl with dark hair and eyes and a glowing complexion left a queue at a fruit stall, sidled up to Iorwerth and smiled shyly at Alma.

'Madge and I are getting married in the New Year,' Iorwerth announced proudly from behind the Christmas tree.

'Congratulations.' Alma almost choked on the word. Most days she was too busy scraping a living to think about love, marriage, how much Ronnie had meant to her, or how empty her life had now become. She smiled hollowly at the couple as she dumped the remainder of her packages into Iorwerth's arms. Why did everything, especially lack of money and Ronnie's absence from her life, seem so much worse just because it was Christmas?

The room was an unprepossessing place in which to spend Christmas Eve. High-windowed, its bare walls were painted sickly hospital shades of dark green and rancid cream that appeared to have been selected to blend with the complexions of the most diseased patients imaginable. But as delivery rooms went, it was no better, and no worse, than the ones Bethan Powell had worked in as a trainee midwife in the Graig Hospital in Pontypridd. Simply a dismal, uninspiring place in which to make an entry into the world.

'Darling, are you all right?' Andrew, her husband of three months hovered ineffectually at the foot of the iron bedstead, an anxious frown creasing his handsome face.

'Of course she's not all right!' Lettie the cockney nurse snapped tartly. 'Men!' she grinned sympathetically at Bethan as she took her pulse. 'They get us into these states and then have the nerve to ask if we're all right.'

'I'm fine,' Bethan smiled weakly, valiantly trying to ignore the discomfort of the thin mattress and rickety bedsprings. 'Really, it's not that bad.'

'Not yet it's not,' the nurse agreed. 'But believe you me, it's going to get a lot—'

'. . . worse before it gets better,' Bethan finished for her.

The phrase was one she'd used often enough herself during deliveries.

'Midwives! They always make the worst patients. Wouldn't you agree, Doctor John?'

Andrew smiled vaguely, too preoccupied with Bethan's pain to follow Lettie's conversation.

'I'm only half a trained midwife,' Bethan corrected, gasping as another pain gathered inside her.

'And it looks as though you're going to be too busy for a while to see to the other half. Doctor John?' Lettie looked enquiringly at Andrew. 'Do you intend to deliver your baby yourself?'

'No. Doctor Floyd's coming in,' Andrew replied quickly, deferring to his immediate superior.

'Then it's time I called him. You'll be all right for five minutes?' she asked Bethan.

'Ten if you can't reach him.' Bethan continued to smiled with clenched teeth.

'I'll reach him.' Lettie marched out of the room, closing the door behind her.

'Are you really coping?' Andrew grasped Bethan's hand as he sat on the bed beside her.

'You're the doctor. You tell me.' Her smile deteriorated into a grimace as yet another pain sliced through her abdomen. Sharper and more intense, it made her feel as though she were being torn in two. 'I never minded this happening to anyone else,' she joked feebly.

'Neither did I.' He enclosed her hand within both of his. 'If you want me I'll be just outside the door.'

'Coward!'

'Absolutely.' He squeezed her hand mutely. The door opened and the nurse returned.

'Doctor Floyd's coming, and you,' she glared at Andrew, 'can get off that bed when you like. I shouldn't need to remind you, of all people, of the rules.' Andrew rose quickly.

Lettie studied Bethan for a moment. 'Doctor John, if

you're not here in a medical capacity, I think it's time you left.'

'Midwives are the same the world over,' he complained. 'Bossy.'

Bethan wasn't fooled by his mild protest. She read the relief in his eyes as he walked to the door.

'See you later, Mrs John,' he whispered as he disappeared into the corridor.

'Husbands! When the going gets rough they cut and run, even doctors,' Lettie Harvey said in a voice loud enough to carry outside. 'Now look at what I've brought you. A nice smart hospital-issue gown, the absolute latest in maternity wear.'

Bethan struggled to sit up but another pain prevented her. The nurse pressed her gently back on to the bed. Laying her hand firmly against Bethan's abdomen she pulled out her watch and timed the contraction. 'Nice and regular now, Mrs John, it won't be much longer.'

'Thank you,' Bethan murmured, drifting helplessly as the pain ebbed. The bare light bulb wavered overhead. The atmosphere was tainted by a strong smell of disinfectant and rubber from the sheeting she was lying on. She stared blankly at the ceiling. It was meshed with a myriad hairline cracks. She traced their origins, following them backwards and forwards, her mind meandering through black and crimson tunnels of pain as a dense cloud floated towards her. It drifted slowly, gradually sinking over her. Soft, warm, it obliterated everything from view.

'Mrs John! Bethan! Bethan . . .'

'What's the problem?' Andrew's voice, rough with concern, penetrated her consciousness. A face loomed overhead, bushy eyebrows and curling grey hair above a white mask.

'You'll soon be all right, Mrs John. We're just taking you to somewhere more comfortable.'

She tried to say she was quite comfortable where she

was, but her mouth was dry and her lips refused to open when she tried to speak. A damp-stained ceiling flowed rapidly overhead. She saw Andrew, wide-eyed, white-faced, his back pressed against the tiled wall of the corridor. A different room flooded around her, bright with lights and the silver glint of chrome. Again the pungent nauseating odour of rubber assailed her nostrils and she plunged downwards, swinging backwards and forwards . . . backwards and forwards . . . backwards and forwards . . . clinging for dear life to a thin, stretched, bouncing, strand of rubber.

Fear clawed at her throat as she realised that her tenuous grip on the elastic frond was all that kept her from falling into the black abyss that lapped at her feet. The rubber band lengthened . . . snapped . . . and she hurtled helplessly downwards.

'Bethan, can you hear me?'

She struggled to open her eyes. A mask pressed over her face, white gauze tented over a metal frame. She could smell iron as well as chloroform. Chloroform! Sweet, overpoweringly soporific chloroform – Andrew had been using chloroform the first time she'd seen him, when she'd been asked to assist him in that dingy, delivery room off the maternity ward in the Graig Hospital.

A pain pierced the numbing effect of the anaesthetic, shattering the sides of the abyss into a million crimson fragments.

'Andrew,' she moaned.

'I'm here, darling. Right here.'

'No!' she screamed as loudly as she could. 'No!' She thrashed her arms wildly as agonising pain after pain pierced her body. It was worse than anything she'd ever experienced – she knew only that she wanted it to end, whatever the price. She should never have allowed Andrew to make love to her. He had made her pregnant and then left her – alone. No, not alone. Not entirely alone. She'd turned to her hidden comfort: the bottle of brandy she'd secreted behind the drawer in her dressing table away from her mother and sister's prying eyes. At first she'd believed that brandy could make anything go away but then she'd learned that it couldn't help with the things that mattered, only the unimportant things, like blotting out the here and now.

It hadn't taken away the baby – or brought Andrew back when she'd needed him most, but he'd come later . . .

'Andrew!' she screamed again into the black void only to hear her cry fall unanswered, on deaf unhearing ears.

'We're going to have to use forceps.'

'There's something seriously wrong, isn't there?' Andrew's voice, sharp, anguished, echoed outside the darkness that had closed around her again.

'There's nothing wrong. Nothing at all, darling. How could there be when you came back for me. I left Pontypridd. Went to London with you.'

She spoke but he didn't hear. Warm, opiate-seasoned tides washed over her, filtering out the pain. She wanted to think of something pleasant. Not the time Andrew had left her. A day when she had been happy. Her wedding! Here, in London, away from family and friends – no, not all her friends. Laura and Trevor had stood behind them, happy honeymooners, married for almost two weeks. She'd worn the indigo dress and dark green coat Andrew had insisted on buying her although it had taken almost every penny of his spare money.

'I do.' Andrew looking at her, love etched in his deep brown eyes. 'That's it, Mrs John. You're not going to get away from me now. Not ever again.'

His lips warm, moist, closing over her own as he carried her over the doorstep of the beautiful, modern flat he'd rented.

Her protest. 'We have to save . . .'

'For a rainy day? It'll never get any wetter than it is

now. Another year or two and we'll be rolling in it. I'll be a senior doctor, and you'll be a mother.'

Her Aunt Megan had said the same thing. 'The rainy day is now.'

But it hadn't been. Not for Megan. The rain had turned into a cloudburst the day the police took her Aunt Megan away for handling stolen goods. Megan who had meant so much to her – the only woman apart from her dead grandmother who'd been kind to her when she was small – was serving ten years' hard labour.

'Mrs John? Mrs John? Bethan? Come on now. Wake up, it's time to wake up.'

There was a baby crying. She could hear its wail: weak, resentful.

'Mrs John? Bethan?'

Andrew's voice, harsh and bitter. 'Take it away before she sees it.'

'It!' Her baby? She made an effort, swam upwards towards the light. Fought to open her eyes. They hurt so. Every part of her hurt. She felt as though she'd been trampled on by an army of miners wearing hobnailed boots.

'My baby?'

Andrew looked at her. Doctor Floyd stood next to him. Both had pulled down their masks, and both were wearing gowns.

'You're doing fine, Mrs John. We'll just make you comfortable, then you can sleep.' Lettie bustled around the bed.

'My baby?'

Andrew turned away. Doctor Floyd was kinder.

'He has a few problems, Mrs John. Nothing for you to worry about. I've sent for a paediatrician. Don't concern yourself. All that can be done for him will be. You have to concentrate on yourself. Get well and strong for your husband.'

She couldn't see Andrew's face. His back was still

turned to her and he was looking out through the door. The wail grew fainter. She closed her eyes. Don't concern yourself? With her own baby?

It was all her fault. When Andrew had left her she'd tried to murder the poor mite even before it was born. But the drunken fall down the stone steps of the Graig Hospital hadn't worked, nor had the brandy and boiling foot-bath. Not mercifully quickly they hadn't.

Chapter Two

IT WAS WARM in the tailor's shop despite the frost that iced the window panes. Warm, with the oppressive heat that only a paraffin stove in an ill-ventilated room emits. Mary Morris nudged her neighbour and they both looked across the large central cutting table littered with cloth scraps, pins, chalk and wooden measuring poles, to where Alma Moore sat crouched over a treadle sewing machine.

Alma's light auburn curls fell forward, covering most of her face, but what little skin could be seen was deathly pale. Her lips were as bloodless as her cheeks, and every minute or two her hands slipped beneath the bed of the sewing machine and the trouser leg she was stitching to clutch her abdomen.

'What did I tell you?' Mary whispered knowingly to Freda. 'She's in the family way. No doubt about it.'

'Something wrong, Mary?' Mostyn Goldman, the tailor who owned the shop, glanced up from the corner nearest to the stove where he was shaping felt pads on a dummy's shoulders, a skilled task he never entrusted to any employee.

'Nothing, Mr Goldman. Nothing at all,' Mary answered innocently with a snide smile on her face, and a sly peep at Freda.

Alma had noticed the two women watching her and exchanging glances. Unnaturally high colour flooded into her cheeks as she rose hastily from her chair and dashed out of the workshop.

'What's up with her?' Mostyn enquired sternly. The first rule on the list pinned above the door was that no one could leave the shop without asking his permission. It was a rule none of the women had dared flout before.

'Up with her?' Freda who was younger, sillier, and plainer than Mary, giggled archly.

'If there is anything wrong with Alma she hasn't told us about it, Mr Goldman,' Mary chipped in, giving Freda a warning look.

'Well, get on with your work,' he ordered curtly. 'Don't turn every little thing into an excuse to down tools and gossip!' He glared at George, his young nephew and apprentice, as well as the two women. Mary and Freda bent their heads and carried on diligently with their buttonholing while George tailor-tacked a paper pattern on to a bed of cloth. Mostyn laid down his shears, stretched his cramped fingers, and walked over to the window. The tailor's shop was long and narrow with two windows, both small, set either end of the room. One overlooked Taff Street, hardly bustling, although most of the shops were open in the hope of attracting some Boxing Day trade; the other framed a dingy, high-walled, concreted back yard. Mostyn walked to the window that gave a view of the yard. He stared at the ragged planked door of the ty bach, the 'little house' that held the WC, watching for Alma to emerge. Despite the cold, beads of perspiration blossomed on her forehead, and her hand shook as she latched the door. He turned his back on the glass and glared at his workforce.

'I'll be in the stockroom if anyone wants me.' Mostyn Goldman never allowed customers into the tailor's shop itself, so all fitting was done in a cubicle that fronted the storeroom where he kept his bales of cloth. The communal stock and fitting-room door was barely four feet away from the shop, and well within earshot.

He walked on to the landing, but instead of opening the fitting-room door, he tiptoed lightly down the bare wooden stairs along the stone-flagged passageway that ran the length of the building, and into the yard where Alma was washing under the outside tap. She had screwed her handkerchief into a ball and was rubbing it over her forehead.

'Sorry, Mr Goldman,' she said contritely as soon as she saw him. 'It's just that I felt so awful. I had to—'

'What's the matter with you?' He peered suspiciously into her face.

'It must be something I ate,' she replied, clinging to the tap for support. 'Yesterday. You know what Christmas is like. Too much rich food,' she began, remembering the ridiculously large bundle of meat Charlie had handed her in exchange for her fourpence. There had been two thick pork, not lamb, chops in the bag, as well as half a pound of sausages and a slice of liver. If her mother hadn't been so excited at the prospect of cooking real meat for once instead of tripe and scraps, she would have kept them and thrown them back in Charlie's face. Living hand to mouth had made her overly sensitive to anything that smacked of charity.

Mostyn Goldman eyed Alma's slender figure critically. He was past fifty, a grandfather with a wife who'd long since run to fat, but he could still remember the times when his wife, pale and trembling, had run to the ty bach as a result of eating too much rich food. He had three strapping sons to show for her upsets, but they had all been born safely within wedlock, unlike any brat Alma Moore would carry. And the last thing he was prepared to risk was a scandal that might affect his depression-depleted business with the upright chapel and church-going citizens of Pontypridd's elite, or 'crache', as they were known in the town.

'You'd better go home,' he ordered abruptly realising that he'd been staring at her.

'There's no need, Mr Goldman,' Alma protested, thinking of her outstanding tab in the corner shop.

'You can't work the way you are. I won't run the risk of anyone vomiting in the workroom with all that expensive cloth lying about. Besides . . .' he looked pointedly at her cold, clammy hands, '. . . you'll more than likely stain any cloth you work on with your sweat.'

'Then I'll come in same time tomorrow, Mr Goldman,'

she broke in as a ghastly suspicion formed in her mind. 'I'm sure I'll be right as rain after a lie down,' she added as convincingly as she could. She hesitated as she counted off the chimes on the church clock. It was only ten o'clock. Mostyn Goldman wouldn't pay her for four hours' work when she had barely completed two.

'I've been meaning to talk to you for some time.' Mostyn stepped back out of the yard into the marginally less freezing air in the passage. Averting his eyes he evinced a sudden interest in a block of peeling plaster on the wall. 'What with the slump, the crache patronising the big tailors in Cardiff who can afford to undercut small operatives like me because they buy their cloth in bulk, and even the town's businessmen making a good suit last two years instead of one, trade's not been what it was.'

'But the depression can't last for ever Mr Goldman?' A chill rivulet of fear ran down Alma's spine. Losing her credit in the corner shop would be devastating; losing a vital chunk of her weekly wage, catastrophic.

'Business doesn't warrant our present level of staffing,' he proclaimed pompously. 'I've been meaning to lay someone off, and it makes sense to lay off the part-timer.' He thrust his hand into his trouser pocket. 'When business picks up, I'll let you know.'

'Mr Goldman?' She searched her mind feverishly for something to make him change his mind, but no phrases came. 'Please, Mr Goldman,' she repeated lamely.

'Here. That's a full week's wage.' He grasped her fingers and dropped two half crowns into her palm. 'I know you've only done two and a half days with it being Christmas, but we'll call the extra a bonus, shall we?' He smiled without meeting her panic-stricken gaze.

'Mr Goldman?'

'Take care of yourself, Alma. You haven't left anything upstairs, have you?'

'No, but Mr Goldman . . .'

'In that case there's no need for you to come up again.'

'You'll let me know?'

'Know?' he repeated blankly, pausing for a moment with one foot on the bottom stair.

'When the work picks up?'

'Of course.'

His heavy tread thundered overhead as she reached for her threadbare navy blue mac, thrust her arms into the sleeves and fumbled in the pocket for her comb. She rarely carried any money to work, there was no need when she lived only ten minutes' walk away. But she had money now. She opened her hand and stared at the half-crowns. She could pay off the grocer's bill, but then what would she do for rent next week? It would be a struggle to make ends meet on the seven shillings she earned in Ronconi's working Saturdays, Sundays, and five nights. The Ronconis were opening a new café soon and she had been promised a full-time job there, but would it come soon enough to keep her and her mother out of debt, and more important still, out of the workhouse?

Damn Mostyn Goldman and his cold-blooded talk of staffing levels! Fury coursed fiercely through her as she walked towards the front door for the last time. She slammed it behind her, her mouth acrid with the taste of unshed tears. The gossips were busy shredding her reputation, she'd lost her job, and she couldn't even see a way to fight back.

The nagging ache in her stomach getting stronger and more unbearable with each passing minute, she stumbled along the icy pavement. The sound of tapping fingers on glass rattled above her. She looked up. Freda and Mary were watching her from the window. She longed to wipe the smug expression off both their faces. They had never liked her. A horrible suspicion crossed her mind. Had they said something about her to Mr Goldman? Mary had been trying to get her niece a job in the sweatshop for years and Mr Goldman's reasoning about the effects of the depression didn't hold water when she remembered that orders fell off every year around Christmas time. Mary wiggled her fingers and Alma saw red. Resorting to sheer childishness she stuck her tongue out. Mary and Freda finally withdrew from the window, and she walked away, dragging one foot in front of the other, the unremitting pain making her dizzy and faint. Gathering the remains of her strength she headed towards the grey concrete and red-brick YMCA building intending to cut up the side-street alongside it on to Gelliwastad Road, and through the network of alleyways and terraces behind it to Morgan Street.

A horde of boys dressed in rugby strip and boots donated by the town's chamber of trade thundered down the stone steps of the building, charged across the road and around the corner past the old bridge, heading for the park gates. Of course! Boxing Day rugby match! She rested for a moment, allowing them to pass. William Powell waved to her as he ran alongside his cousin Eddie. William thickset, heavier than Eddie, but both of them tall and good-looking, with black hair and brown eyes; and behind them sixteen-year-old Angelo Ronconi, swarthy with flashing dark eyes, curly hair, and olive skin that instantly, and painfully, reminded her of his brother, Ronnie.

The overcast sky, the frosted grey pavement, the ring of boot studs on concrete as the boys dashed past in their white strip swirled around her. She made a conscious effort and took a deep breath. Her lungs craved oxygen but there wasn't any in the air. Only pain – thick red pain.

'Are you all right, Miss Moore?'

She focused on the startlingly white blond hair and deep blue eyes of Charlie.

'Quite well, thank you,' she answered stiffly, swaying on her feet.

'You don't look well to me.' He caught her elbow in the palm of his hand.

'Don't you dare touch me!' The stream of boys slowed their pace. Some were staring but suddenly she didn't give a toss about them – or anyone. Everyone in the town thought the worst of her, so what did it matter how she behaved?

'I was only trying to help,' he complained mildly.

'I've seen how you try to help,' she countered acidly. 'When I buy fourpennyworth of meat from a butcher I expect just that. Not a charity handout that's more than any normal family can eat in a month of Sundays.'

'But Miss Moore . . .'

She didn't wait to hear what the 'but' was. Wrenching her elbow out of his supporting hold she strode round the corner and up the hill. Sustained by anger she managed to ignore her pain until she turned into a small grimy street hemmed in on both sides by narrow terraced cottages. Morgan Street – home. An inviting image of her bed hovered tantalisingly in her mind. At that moment all she wanted was to lie down and close her eyes against the world, but even as the desire formulated itself her fingers closed around the unaccustomed weight of the two half-crowns in her pocket. There was something she had to do first, before she lost, or was tempted to spend, her unaccustomed riches.

She halted outside the first stone house in the terrace. Inside, a table had been pushed close to the sooty window of the front parlour. Dusty packets of tea, dried peas, sugar, and four small pyramids of tins were displayed against a background of deep blue sugar paper. Two of the tins contained luxurious corned beef, the others held the more everyday tomatoes, beans and sardines. At the very front, within easy view of even the smallest child, lay a large open cardboard box jammed with wooden twigs of liquorice chews, farthing 'dabs', halfpenny everlasting strips, toffee and coconut scrapings, and sherbet screws.

Pushing open the warped wooden door she walked over the uneven flags of the passage and turned into the front-room shop that was dominated by a rough, waist-high counter. There was room enough – just – to stand in front of it and study the goods ranged on the shelves behind.

'Don't normally see you in here at this time of day, Alma.' Edna Hopkins wrapped a wafer-thin slice of cheese she had just cut for Lilian Bartlett, the only other customer in the shop.

'Come to settle our tab, Mrs Hopkins.' Alma looked round for something to lean against. There was nothing but the wall behind the door.

'Well that's welcome news.' Edna lifted a child's red-covered exercise book from the deep wooden tray that served as a till. 'I wish all our customers were as prompt.' She gave Mrs Bartlett a sideways glance.

'Three and six, I think.' Alma took the two half-crowns from her pocket and pushed them over the counter.

'Come into a fortune, Alma?' Lilian Bartlett joked as Mrs Hopkins pencilled a large cross over the page and extracted the change from her box.

'Hardly,' Alma closed her eyes for a moment as another pain gripped her abdomen.

'You look peaky, love. Are you all right?'

'No. I think I've eaten something.'

'Always the same at Christmas,' Edna interrupted as she replaced the red book. 'Stuff ourselves silly with things we can't afford the rest of the year only to suffer for it for days afterwards.'

'That's it,' Alma agreed as she pocketed her money. 'And thank your Iorwerth for me will you please, Mrs Hopkins. It was good of him to carry my tree and parcels back from the market.'

'Think nothing of it, love. He's always looking for an excuse to flex those muscles of his. Especially in front of Madge.'

'She seems a nice girl.' Alma bit her lip to stop herself from crying out.

'That she is. He's done well for himself there.'

'Nice to see someone happy.' There was an unmistakable edge to Alma's voice: she wondered if Mrs Hopkins would have made her as welcome if she'd been the one Iorwerth had brought home.

Lilian nodded knowingly as Alma made her way unsteadily out of the shop. 'She *is* looking peaky. Did you know about that one and Ronnie Ronconi? . . .' her penetrating voice followed Alma to her own house, but by

26

then she was too ill to care what was being said.

She turned the knob, taking care not to kick the rotten panel on the bottom of her door. It needed replacing, but the last time she had tackled Bobby Thomas about it he had told her in no uncertain terms that the rot was due to her neglect, and all tenants had a responsibility to keep their houses in good decorative order, which meant painting them at least once every two years. The price paint was, he might as well have suggested her financing the redecoration of the Town Hall.

Keeping her coat on, she walked down the bare, cheerless passage. Pushing aside the curtain that hung in place of a door, she went into the kitchen. If there was any residue of Christmas warmth, she couldn't feel it. The room was cold and uninviting. Her mother had economised again by not lighting the kitchen stove. The table had been cleared of their breakfast things, and a clean cloth laid; the floor swept, and the rag rug shaken. It had probably cost her mother a few knocks and all morning to complete the simple tasks, but she knew it was useless to remonstrate. Her mother would only deliver her standard martyred reply: 'If you stop me doing what little I can, I may as well lie down in my box now. At least then I'll no longer be a burden to you.'

Her mother's chair, the only chair in the house that boasted a cushion, was cold. She opened the door to the washhouse and called out, 'Mam!' There was no point in looking in the tiny parlour. The three-piece and piano her mother had bought with her father's first year's wages had long since been sold to pay pressing bills. She went into the back yard and opened the door to the ty bach. Another griping pain came and she fell in front of the thunderbox. She retched, but there was nothing left in her stomach except bitter green bile. As she lay on the stone floor she heard her mother's voice echoing over next door's wall. She should have known. Betty Lane made a point of asking her mother over on days when their chimney failed to smoke. There was always an excuse – her mother was needed to unravel old sweaters for wool so that larger striped ones could be re-knitted for Betty's eight growing children, or to tell stories to keep the little ones amused while Betty coped with the family wash or the baking. Alma was grateful because it meant her mother could sit in the warm, but that didn't stop the imitation of charity from hurting.

She returned to the house and walked up the stairs to her bedroom. The temperature was no warmer than outside. Condensation on the window had dripped into icicles that hung like stalactites from the sash. The water in the jug on the rickety chair she used as a washstand had frozen, and even the bowl she washed in was fringed with hard, beaded droplets.

Her entire wardrobe of waistcoat and skirt, second white blouse and 'best' summer sprigged cotton dress hung from bent wire hangers hooked on to the curtain rail behind the old chintz curtains her mother had bought years ago from Wilf Horton.

She laid her coat over the patchwork quilt that her mother had stitched eight years ago. It was the last thing she had made before losing her sight, and Alma thought of it as a patchwork of her life. In the centre were the thin cotton pastel squares of her baby dresses, stitched double thickness for extra strength. Around them were six large pieces of rich red velvet, all that remained of the only party dress she could remember, which her mother had made from her own 'best' pre-marriage dance dress. Then came circles of navy cut from her school gymslips interspersed with the white of old sheets and blouses, and the green and gold striped silk lining from the only suit her father had ever owned. He had been killed in a pit accident when she was three years old, but the suit hadn't been unpicked until four years ago; her mother couldn't bring herself to take the shears to it before then. Alma had asked her to, time and again, because she had wanted to remodel the cloth into a skirt and waistcoat, the same skirt and waistcoat that now hung from her curtain rail.

Next to her bed was a wooden orange crate she'd begged from the market and covered with a tablecloth the Ronconis had discarded because it had one too many cigarette burns. She had darned the burns and used the cloth to conceal her underclothes and jumpers. Two pictures were pinned to the faded blue paper that covered the walls. One was of her and Ronnie. The photograph had been taken in the café by Bruno the cook just before he had left Wales for Italy. The other had been cut from an illustrated magazine: a highly coloured portrait of an idyllic rural summer scene complete with lurid yellow sun, improbably blue sky, white-tipped mountain peaks and greener grass on the lower slopes of the hills than she had ever seen on the slag heaps of Wales. She had cut it out before Maud Powell had come between her and Ronnie, because she had associated the scene with Italy – the land of Ronnie's birth.

She stretched out her hand intending to tear down both pictures, but another pain came. Aching at first, it soon honed itself into a sharp, agonising point. Without bothering to undress she crawled into bed, leaving the quilt and coat on top of the blanket. She closed her eyes and tried to conjure images of a blissful world where young girls were allowed to have stomach cramps without everyone assuming they were pregnant. And where Ronnie waited for her just over the horizon with open arms, a smile on his face and no Maud Powell at his side. But no matter how she concentrated she failed to picture him. His features blurred into indistinct shadows, replaced by the grinning, lecherous face of Bobby Thomas.

Boxing Day found Charlie Raschenko confused and disorientated. It was a Wednesday, a market day only marginally less important than Saturday, yet it would have been ridiculous for him to have opened up his stall because most of his customers had bought enough meat on Christmas Eve to see them through to the following

Friday; and those who hadn't, wouldn't have any money left from Christmas to spend anyway.

He'd whiled away the morning hunched in his overcoat watching his fellow lodger William play rugby in the park, and trying to stem his irritation with Alma Moore for creating a scene outside the YMCA. He usually succeeded in containing his emotions, priding himself on never feeling very much of anything. Anger, irritation, displeasure, or happiness – especially happiness, because that sooner or later gave rise to memories. Bitter experience had taught him that they inevitably led to pain. No, it was better to live life as it came. One day at a time.

Still trying to forget Alma's outburst he'd returned to Graig Avenue with William and Eddie Powell for a midday dinner of Christmas leftover 'fry-up'. Afterwards he tried to spend the holiday the way he usually spent Sundays; and as he never attended chapel – much to his landlady's disgust – that meant passing the hours playing chess and reading.

But this Boxing Day was different to a Sunday, when everything in the town except the Italian cafés was closed. Before the dishes were cleared from the table, William and Eddie disappeared to a special showing of *Song of Freedom* featuring Paul Robeson, in the White Palace. And Diana Powell, William's sister, wasn't around; she was working at her job in the sweet shop in High Street. It would have been madness for her boss to have closed it with all the Christmas pennies burning holes in small children's pockets.

Charlie's only consolation was that his landlord Evan Powell, who 'called' the streets on a rag and bone cart, was at a loose end too. It was his landlady, Elizabeth Powell's habit to sit in the icy front parlour reading the Bible after she had cleared and washed the Sunday dishes, and she took advantage of the extra holiday to do the same. As soon as she left the warm back kitchen, Charlie went into the downstairs 'front' room he lodged in and returned

30

with a long, flattish wooden box, crudely varnished with alternating dark and light squares. Lifting the catch he opened it out on the table and removed the chess pieces carefully, handling them as though they were delicate, precious objects, not roughly carved chunks of stained wood. He set up the board on the side of the table closest to the stove, and Evan joined him.

An hour and one game later, Evan had smoked half the pipe tobacco his son and nephew had bought him for Christmas, and shared all of the chocolate that Diana had given him with Charlie. The room was warm from the kitchen stove, and fragrant with the smell of pine logs and the chicken soup Elizabeth was simmering from the carcass of their Christmas dinner. Both men were content and pleasantly drowsy when their peace was shattered by a knock that echoed down the passage from the front door. The knock in itself was bizarre, as all the Powells' friends and neighbours simply walked into the house. Evan opened the kitchen door and shouted irritably down the passage, but not soon enough. Elizabeth had put aside her Bible with a martyred sigh and opened the door.

'Doctor Lewis?' She successfully concealed her surprise. Trevor Lewis, the young local doctor, had been a friend of their eldest daughter, Bethan before she had left Pontypridd for London.

'Is Mr Powell home, Mrs Powell?'

She inclined her head. 'In the kitchen.'

'I wonder if I might have a word with both of you?'

'Yes of course. Come in.' Elizabeth stood aside to allow him to enter the house. She was curious to know the reason for his visit, but not curious enough to ask.

'Dr Lewis. Nice to see you,' Evan extended his hand hospitably. 'Would you like some tea?'

'Nothing, thank you, I've just had my dinner.'

'Shouldn't we sit in the parlour, Evan?' Elizabeth reprimanded.

'It's freezing in there.' Evan opened the door to the back kitchen. Charlie had already packed away his chess set.

'Please Charlie, don't leave on my account,' Trevor said politely.

Charlie merely smiled before he left. Elizabeth walked in. She'd combed her short straight hair and pulled the creases from her skirt.

Trevor turned to face them. Thin, tall, and despite the efforts of his wife Laura, always slightly unkempt, he usually managed to look cheerful. Today was different. His cheeks seemed unnaturally hollow, his spirit crushed by the news he was carrying. 'Mrs Powell, I think you should sit down.' He looked into their faces. He couldn't keep them in suspense any longer. 'Andrew telephoned and asked me to come here. Bethan's baby was born early yesterday morning. A boy.' He took a deep breath. 'I'm sorry, there's something wrong with him. We call it cerebral palsy. It's impossible for any doctor to determine at this early stage just how badly he's affected.' He threw them the sop of vain hope of limited damage, just as he had done to Andrew earlier.

'You're telling us that Bethan's child, our grandchild, is a cripple?' Elizabeth turned a stony face to his.

'Cripple isn't a word I'd choose, Mrs Powell.'

'How's Bethan?' Evan's voice was quiet, restrained.

'She's fine.' Trevor was glad of an opportunity to turn the conversation away from the baby. 'She's upset of course, but physically she's fine. Andrew told me to tell you they'll write soon.' He twisted the brim of his hat in his hands. 'I'm sorry I can't stay. I've promised to call in on a patient.'

'Thank you for coming to tell us yourself.' Evan opened the door. Elizabeth still sat, sphinx-like in front of the fire.

'Goodbye, Mrs Powell.' If she heard Trevor she gave no sign of it.

'I'll see you out.' Evan followed him into the passage and closed the door behind them.

'If there's anything I can do for Mrs Powell . . .' Trevor ventured, concerned by Elizabeth's unnatural composure. She'd always struck him as a cold woman. But surely no one could be as indifferent to the plight of a first grandchild as she appeared to be.

'I'll send for you, Doctor Lewis.'

'I could come tomorrow. After I've finished in the hospital.'

'There's no need.' Evan didn't trust himself to say more. His thoughts were with his eldest daughter. Alone in a hospital bed in an impersonal, unsympathetic cry. Too far for him to visit. But no, she wasn't alone. She had a baby to care for. A baby that would be a burden to her for the rest of its life. He didn't spare a thought for her husband. The responsibility of caring for children, especially ones that 'weren't right', always fell squarely on the mother.

Trevor turned right at the foot of the steps to Evan's house, and walked up Graig Avenue towards the patch of scrubland that marked the beginning of the mountain. Regretting the impulse that had led him to leave his car, he turned up the collar on his thin raincoat and tried to ignore the hailstones bouncing off his back. He had walked to the Avenue via his garden, stepping over the wall straight on to the mountain. He had lied to Evan: there was no patient waiting for him. Barring an emergency, he was free for the rest of the day, but he didn't want to go home. Not yet. He didn't want to face Laura. He felt helpless, ill-equipped to deal with her misery, as well as his own.

Andrew and Bethan were their closest friends, and he valued their friendship, particularly that of Bethan, for whom he had a very definite soft spot. Andrew – well, Andrew was Andrew. Everything had always come easy to him. He had been born into a comfortable moneyed home. He hadn't had to fight for a thing in his life. Charming, good-looking, easygoing, generous to a fault, Andrew's good points were enough to make everyone, or at least almost everyone, forgive his occasional irresponsibility, thoughtlessness and selfishness. Still, Trevor couldn't help wondering how Andrew would cope with misfortune of such a magnitude.

He stumbled over a stone into a freezing puddle that covered his shoe. Icy water seeped through the patches on his sole as he asked himself the terrible question, 'How would I cope if it was Laura who'd given birth to a child with palsy?' He shuddered. Feeling the need to touch wood he found a pencil in his pocket and gripped it tightly. It was the ultimate irony, he thought bitterly. Giving a man arrogant enough to call himself healer a child who could not be healed.

He recalled the pitiful scraps of humanity that lay in the cots of J ward in the Graig hospital. Babies abandoned to workhouses and institutions by parents who could not cope with the physical demands or emotional pressures of bringing up a child whose disability made it an outcast. But then, perhaps those who had been through the experience knew best. Perhaps institutions offered the only solution for parents and child alike. He himself had counselled enough women facing the problem with cold logic, telling them that in time they would have other children who had the right to demand all of their attention, not the little that could be spared from caring for a member of the family who would never be able to care for itself. Reassuring them with the official maxim that institutions, not homes, were the best place for those born damaged.

He had said it, and often, but a visit to J ward invariably shook his faith. He had never discussed the matter with Andrew, but couldn't help wondering if Andrew felt the way he did. And if he did, where did that leave Andrew's son – and Bethan?

Much as he liked Andrew he suspected that his friend would try to ignore the problem – and the child. And that would mean Bethan coping with everything on her own, without any support. If only Pontypridd were closer to London!

He kicked a stone across the sodden, muddied grass of the mountainside. The hailstones had turned to an icy

34

rain that teemed down relentlessly, soaking through his worn mac into the wool of his sweater. He didn't care. He looked up. The rock the Graig children called the slide gleamed, shining and grey on an outcrop of stone-spattered mountainside ahead. He resolved to walk there. Sit on it for a while and think.

He and Laura had been married for three months, and already she'd had three disappointments. She wanted a child much, much more than he did. He was happy with things the way they were and only wished she could be as content with him as he was with her. Change, as Andrew and Bethan were undoubtedly learning, was not always for the better. And there was no guarantee that a child born perfect would remain so. He'd never forgotten the pain of watching his sick, worn-out mother nursing one of his younger brothers through the final stages of meningitis. His feeling of helplessness then had been the driving force that had sustained him through the lean, and often lonely, years when he had studied medicine alongside those born better heeled and better connected.

He sat on the rock and looked over the town spread out below him, but his thoughts remained with Bethan. Was she lying in a hospital bed this very minute, blaming herself for her son's misfortune? Knowing Bethan, she would be. Punishing herself by recalling every mouthful of every bottle of brandy she had drunk during the early stages when she didn't know she was pregnant and believed that Andrew had abandoned her. Reliving every blow she had taken when she had fallen down the steep stone staircase of the maternity block of the Graig Hospital in a drunken stupor. Would Andrew have the sense to take her hand, hold it, look into her eyes and tell her – sincerely – that it would have happened anyway? That her son's flaws were none of her doing?

Trevor made a fist and slammed it impotently and painfully into the rockface beside him. Nursing his bruised fingers he stared at the grey waterlogged sky, tears mingling with the icy raindrops that fell on his cheeks.

Chapter Three

'Alma. Are you up there?'

'Yes. I'll be down now, Mam.' Although she hadn't slept, Alma was reluctant to leave her bed. Despite the chill in the air, it was warm beneath the quilt and coat. The pain in her stomach had subsided while she'd remained quietly curled in the foetal position on her mattress, but the memory of the agony remained, and she was wary that movement would precipitate its return. She crossed her fingers tightly, hoping that news hadn't travelled out of Goldman's about her losing her job. She didn't want to tell her mother, not yet. And not until she had to. Her mother already lived in terror of the paupers' ward in the Graig workhouse. Better she leave the house every morning as usual and use the time to hunt for work. The unemployment register in the town was overflowing with girls her age only too willing to take any job they could get, but armed with a reference from the Ronconis she might pick up something if she wasn't too fussy about money.

She put one foot on the floor, wincing as the pain returned to knife viciously at her stomach. Doubled up in agony she looked down at her skirt and saw, even in the half-light of the street lamp that filtered through her window, that it was hopelessly crumpled. She pulled down hard on the hem, smoothed the front panel with her fingers and checked the buttons on her blouse. Picking up her mac from the bed, she felt in the pockets for her comb. After tugging it blindly through her curls she poured water from the jug into the bowl and splashed her face, dried herself hastily with the towel that hung on the back of the chair and made her way downstairs.

The first thing she noticed when she entered the kitchen was that the stove was lit.

'We have a visitor.' Her mother stood nervously in front of the dresser, cups and saucers in hand.

'So I see.'

Mr Parry, the chapel minister, made a point of calling in on Mrs Moore whenever he was in the Morgan Street area, but despite his outwardly solicitous attitude towards her mother's welfare, Alma found it difficult to remain in the same room with the man, let alone be polite. Four years ago when she had begun working Sundays in Ronconi's café, he'd come to the door backed by a full complement of deacons, to tell her that she was no longer welcome among the congregation of the faithful. Distraught by the ostracism the decree implied, her mother had pleaded with them to reconsider their decision. She couldn't bear to think of her only daughter being denied, not only entry to chapel services, but also the social life that was an important part of chapel membership. The afternoon teas, evening concerts, drama and youth clubs, not to mention the annual outing to the seaside, had been closed to Alma from that day on. At the time Alma had borne the ban with equanimity, upset more for her mother than herself. She'd had Ronnie then, and believed, really believed, she needed no one else.

'Alma.' The minister acknowledged her presence with a brief nod of his long thin head.

'Mr Parry.' She couldn't bring herself to enquire after his health.

'Your mother tells me you've been in bed,' he commented critically.

'I was tired,' she replied shortly.

'A girl of your age shouldn't be tired.'

'I think that depends on how much work a girl of my age does.' She wondered how any man, let alone a chapel minister, could live and work in an area like Pontypridd without realising just how close to the bone most people lived. In winter there was little else for her to do except sleep between shifts at the tailor's and the café, especially on days when the stove wasn't lit.

'I didn't think that either of your jobs was particularly taxing.' The minister was sitting in her mother's chair, which he had pulled as close to the stove as was physically possible without actually moving into the hearth. 'If you don't mind me saying so Mrs Moore, this room is quite chilly.' He glanced accusingly at Alma as though she were to blame.

'This house is difficult to heat,' Lena acknowledged in a small voice.

Alma gritted her teeth, loathing her mother's deferential tone.

'Mrs Parry has found that draughtproofing the windows with rolls of newspaper helps enormously.' He imparted his wife's discovery as though they should be humbly grateful for such largesse.

'Our house is cold, Mr Parry, because we have precious little to burn, although I notice Mam always seems to find a few coals whenever you visit.'

'Alma, please!' her mother begged.

'There's many that find life hard these days, Alma,' he countered testily. 'Instead of looking for more, you should give daily thanks for what you already have. A kind and loving mother, a roof over your head—'

'If we've a roof over our head it's no thanks to anyone except ourselves!'

The minister shook his head. 'Unfortunately that is the kind of remark I've come to expect from you, Alma, since you embraced pagan ways. You have strayed far from the path on which you were brought up. I can only repeat what I have had cause to say on more than one occasion before now. I visit this house purely to see your mother, and I don't think it's unreasonable of me to expect politeness from you while I'm here.'

'Alma, please say you're sorry to Mr Parry.' Lena wrung her hands in her apron before opening up the hotplate to boil the kettle.

'I am sorry, Mr Parry.' Alma gave the apology in a tone that even her mother with her acute hearing couldn't fault, but she stared at the minister coolly as she lifted the lid on the saucepan simmering on the second hob. Her mother had made a thin soup from the chop bones and peelings of the Christmas vegetables. She picked up one of the bowls set on the warming rack above the stove and ladled out a tiny portion.

'Would you like some broth?' her mother ventured to the minister when she heard Alma replace the lid on the pot.

'No thank you, Mrs Moore. I've satisfied the inner man well over the festive season. I was at the workhouse yesterday, to help serve the paupers their dinners, and I have to say that the town did them proud. You should have seen the decorations, the table, the linen, the variety of meats,' he eulogised, hearing no humour in the words he used to a blind woman. 'There was a choice of roast pork, chicken or beef, three vegetables and all the trimmings—'

'I take it there was enough left over to feed the crache who'd been doling out their annual allowance of charity?' Alma couldn't resist the gibe. It was a tradition in the workhouse that the poor were served their Christmas dinners by the town's councillors and well-to-do businessmen.

'I won't deny we had a fair meal. But we hardly took food out of the paupers' mouths. I doubt that any of them could have managed another morsel.'

'If you'd given them a couple of hours I'm sure they would have, bearing in mind their diet the rest of the year.'

'I take it you think they're hard done by?' The minister raised his voice as though he was sermonising in chapel. 'These people aren't deserving of Christian charity or pity. Having contributed nothing to the town, they throw themselves on the parish demanding to be clothed, warmed and fed. They don't spare a thought for the decent, hard-working, thrifty people who find themselves having to work all the harder to keep the workhouse doors open. The inmates are nothing more than idle layabouts who've never done a day's work, or saved a farthing in their lives. And instead of punishing them for their laziness and lack of prudence as we should, what do we do? We give them Christmas presents,' he answered quickly, lest Alma interrupt. 'There wasn't a man yesterday who didn't get his ounce of tobacco, or a woman who didn't get a bar of chocolate and an orange. And as if that isn't enough, we feed them first-class food. The meal I saw yesterday was as good as you'll get for half a crown in the New Inn any day of the week.'

'Workhouse inmates don't get Christmas dinner every day of the week,' Alma pointed out.

'You will take a cup of tea with us, won't you Mr Parry?' Lena broke in hastily as the kettle began to boil.

'I don't think so, but thank you for offering, Mrs Moore.'

'Please don't go on my account. I have to be on my way.' Alma rose from the table.

'In that case, perhaps just one cup, Mrs Moore.'

Lena went to the pantry to get the sugar and milk, hoping Alma wouldn't say any more than had already been said.

Alma carried her soup bowl into the washhouse and managed to tip most of what little she'd taken down the sink without her mother hearing.

'Don't wait up for me.' She kissed her mother on the cheek as she prepared to leave. She said no goodbye to the minister.

The last thing she saw as she allowed the curtain to swing down over the doorway was the Christmas tree she'd set up in the alcove next to the stove. Christmas had only been yesterday, yet already it seemed like months ago. The sweets and fruits she'd bought had all disappeared from the boughs and the presents she'd wrapped for her mother had gone from underneath it. It looked ragged and forlorn, and she made a mental note to take it down as soon as she returned.

She smiled as she recalled the expression on her mother's face when she'd handed her two of the four chocolates she'd bought. Her mother had loved the coat, but Alma had learned as a child that it was the little things that made Christmas memorable. Upstairs she had a new jumper. Not the green lamb's-wool she'd coveted on Wilf's stall, but a grey one that her mother had re-knitted her from her father's last remaining garment.

As she closed her front door she thought of the picture the minister had painted of the workhouse Christmas. An abundance of food and presents! If it really was that marvellous why hadn't people been queuing up to admit themselves to the dreaded building?

Exhausted by the long walk to the Tumble, Alma paused for a moment outside Ronconi's café. Through the fog of condensation that misted the windows she could see shadows at virtually every table. Didn't people have anywhere else to go on Boxing night?

The thought of spending the evening ahead ferrying teas and snacks in the hot, crowded, noisy atmosphere loomed, an awful task, but with her morning job gone, the last thing she could afford was the luxury of illness. She laid her hand on the door and pushed.

'You look dreadful, Alma,' Tina Ronconi greeted her tactlessly as she walked behind the counter to hang up her coat. 'You feeling all right?'

'Just something I ate over Christmas,' Alma mumbled as she tied her apron around her waist.

A crash of dishes resounded from the kitchen, followed by the sound of Tony Ronconi's voice raised in anger.

'I take back everything I ever said about Ronnie before he went to Italy,' Tina whispered as she slid a hot pie out of the steamer on to a plate. 'Tony's ten times worse than Ronnie ever was. All he does is pick – pick – pick, from first thing in the morning till last thing at night. Finding fault with everything, and right in nothing, especially the things I do,' she added, raising her voice in the hope that her complaint would carry as far as the kitchen.

'It's a lot to take on a place like this when you're only nineteen. He's just a bit unsure of himself.' Alma stepped smartly aside as Tony barged out of the kitchen. 'I'll start clearing the tables in the back.' She picked up a tray.

'Thank you Alma,' Tony said loudly in a voice directed at his sister. 'I'm glad to see that at least one person around here knows how to work.'

Charlie and William were sitting in the back room drinking tea and playing dominoes with a few of the boys from the Graig. The dominoes were an innovation. On Sundays they risked playing cards, even if it was illegal.

'Alma, how about another tea?' Glan Richards, the Powells' next-door neighbour shouted.

'Oxo for me, Alma.'

'Pie and chips for me, love,' a tram driver called out as he passed her on his way to the table next to the fire.

Half an hour later the pain in Alma's stomach had grown, intensifying until it invaded every aspect of her entire being, mind as well as body. By then Tina was working flat out manning the till and serving the tables in the front room because Tony was too busy screaming at their younger brother, Angelo, in the kitchen to concern himself with what was happening in the café.

As fast as Alma cleared dirty dishes and wiped down the tables, new customers filled them.

'Looks like the whole town has come out for an airing tonight,' Tina grumbled as Alma opened the glass case on the counter and removed a Chelsea bun. 'So much for Tony's quiet Boxing night.'

'Miss, Miss we'll have two teas and two scones.'

Alma recognised the voice and glanced across the room. Mary Morris and Freda from the tailor's shop were sitting at one of her tables in the back, but they were shouting at Tina.

'Workmates throwing their weight around?' Tina raised her eyebrows as she clanged the till shut.

'Ex-workmates,' Alma replied through clenched teeth as she reached for the butter dish. 'And don't you serve them. I'll get around to them in my own good time.'

'You lose your job?'

Alma didn't reply. She finished buttering the Chelsea she had cut open and carried it through to William.

'You want to order?' She stood in front of Freda and Mary's table.

'Yes, but we don't want to be served by you.' Mary pitched her voice high enough to reach all the corners of the café.

'In that case perhaps you'd better go elsewhere.' A thick red mist of anger began to cloud Alma's vision.

'I think the manager will have something to say about one of his waitresses talking to a customer like that!' Mary countered indignantly.

William scraped his chair noisily over the tiled floor, sat back, and stared belligerently at Mary. He regarded the Ronconi café as his second home and everyone who worked in it as his friend. If a man insulted Alma he would have waded in, fists flying; but women were different, and he hesitated, not quite certain how to react. Charlie, who was sitting next to him, laid down the domino he was about to add to the snake angled across the table, and turned his chair until he, too, faced Mary.

'What's going on here?' Tina, hearing the word 'manager', abandoned the till and her tables and positioned herself protectively beside Alma.

'My friend and I,' Mary simpered in a false 'refined' voice, 'do not want to be served by the likes of her.' She pointed her finger at Alma.

'Tough,' Tina snapped. 'She's the waitress here. If you don't like it, you can lump it.'

Tony hearing his sister's voice raised in an anger that surpassed his own decibel level, left the kitchen and barged into the back room, towel and spatula in hand.

43

'I could hear you in the kitchen, Tina . . .'

'These ladies,' Tina almost spat the word as she indicated Mary and Freda, 'don't want to be served by our waitress.'

Alma retreated from the table and leaned white-faced against the wall close to William's chair.

'Miss Moore has been a waitress here for many years,' Tony began evenly. 'She is perfectly competent to deal with—'

'It's not her competency but her morals we're calling into question,' Mary snapped self-righteously. 'Decent women have the right to object to being served by someone who's carrying a . . . a . . .' she faltered, lowering her eyes while glancing slyly beneath her eyelashes to make sure she held the attention of everyone in the room '. . . a bastard,' she divulged triumphantly to the hushed café, revelling in the consternation she was creating. 'And if *you* aren't prepared to take our complaint seriously then we'll just have to take our custom elsewhere. Freda?' Pulling the lapels of her coat high around her throat she rose majestically from her seat. 'We may be the first, but I promise you, Mr Ronconi,' she swept the skirt of her coat from her chair, 'we won't be the last women of the town to refuse to eat here.'

Confused, Tony turned, just in time to see Alma collapse. Charlie dived out of his chair and caught her, but not before she hit her head on the kerb of the tiled hearth.

'I've got her.'

Alma recognised Charlie's accent. She opened her eyes briefly and stared up into the Russian's deep blue eyes. The last thing she was aware of before plunging into unconsciousness was his strong arms wrapped around her body.

'Run up to Graig Street and get Doctor Lewis,' Charlie ordered Tony as he took control of the situation. 'You've got the keys to the Trojan?'

'I have but . . .' Tony's cheeks reddened as he squirmed

in embarrassment. He didn't want to look ridiculous in front of the entire clientele of the café by admitting that he'd never got the hang of driving the van.

'Here, give them to me,' William shouted impatiently, holding out his hand as he stared at Alma's deathly pale face, now streaked by a single scarlet ribbon of blood trickling from her temple down to her chin.

'They're behind the counter.'

William ran to get them. Neither Charlie nor Tony thought to ask where he'd learned to drive.

'Is there anywhere private I can take her?' Charlie demanded as customers strained their necks in an effort to get a good look at what was going on.

'Upstairs,' Tony suggested, as Mary and Freda banged the front door behind them.

'Over here, Charlie.' Tina lifted the flap on the counter and preceded Charlie up the narrow flight of stairs. The air was freezing, musty with disuse. There was no electricity on the first floor of the café. The only light that illuminated the upper staircase came in from the street lamp outside, through the window of a landing littered with cardboard boxes and catering tins of coffee, beans and cocoa. Tina had to put her shoulder to the door before it finally grated over the damp, swollen floorboards.

'Put her on the bed. I'll get a glass of water.' Tina disappeared back down the stairs.

Charlie laid Alma on the bed, but as the cover felt damp he shrugged his shoulders out of his jacket and lifted Alma again to wrap it around her. He stared at the cheap flowered cotton curtains hanging limply at the window and the paper dangling loosely from the walls. The floorboards were bare, and apart from the bed and a single chair the room was empty. A stub of candle, glued by a puddle of wax to a saucer, balanced on the seat of the chair. He reached into his pocket for a box of matches.

'Ronnie?'

Charlie struck the match and held it to the wick. It flared briefly before settling into a small flame that

45

scuppered low, finally dying in a draught that blew in from the door.

'It's Charlie,' he answered softly.

'What happened?' Alma tried to sit up. Reaching out frantically she clutched at Charlie's shirt-sleeve before falling back on to the bed with a moan.

'You fainted. Try and rest.'

'You don't understand. I've got to work,' she insisted hysterically. 'You can't stop me. I need the job . . .'

'Has she come round?' Tina reappeared in the doorway with a glass of water.

'I'm fine. I . . .'

'You're not fine,' Tina answered without realising Alma was raving. 'You can't work like that, and I can't breathe in here. This room smells like a tomb. I don't think anyone's been up here since Ronnie left,' Tina said, anxiety making her even more tactless than usual. She handed Charlie the glass, walked over to the window and wrenched down the sash. 'I know it's freezing outside,' she babbled, 'but then it's freezing in here too, so I don't suppose it will make any difference to you, Alma.'

Neither Alma, nor Charlie who was busy with the candle, answered her. The second flame he'd nurtured flickered weakly as he sat beside Alma on the bed, propped her against his chest and held the glass to her lips.

'You're going to be fine, Alma. Isn't she, Charlie?' Tina demanded.

Charlie sensed that Tina was looking for reassurance, but he had never lied in his life, and wasn't about to begin now. He brushed Alma's hair away from her clammy forehead and pulled his jacket closer round her shoulders. Alma writhed in his arms but didn't open her eyes.

Tina crept closer and he handed her the glass.

'If you see to Alma, I'll wait outside.' Shivering in his thin shirt and waistcoat he left the room and sat on the top stair, conscious that it wasn't right for a man to be in a bedroom – any bedroom – with a woman who wasn't his wife.

'Has she come round yet?' Tony called from the kitchen as he heard Charlie's measured tread on the rickety floor.

'Not really,' Charlie answered.

'Tell Tina to stay with her. We'll manage somehow until Trevor gets here.'

Charlie settled his back against the cold wall and waited. Tina glanced at him from time to time, glad not to be alone with the unconscious Alma. His pale face and athletic body reminded her of the picture postcards of marble statues her Italian relatives sent her father on his birthday. She could read nothing in the dispassionate set of his features, but inside Charlie's head, thoughts and emotions spiralled and whirled like dead leaves in an autumn wind.

It had been a long, long time since he, Feodor Raschenko (in his thoughts he always referred to himself by his Russian name, never the nickname that had been bestowed on him in Pontypridd market), had held a woman. He was still young. Only twenty-eight, but sometimes, surrounded in his working and lodging life by younger men like William and Eddie Powell, he felt like a grandfather.

He'd compartmentalised his life into sections: the proscribed past, and the allowable present. (He *never* attempted to forecast what the future might hold.) The problems of childhood, adolescence and early manhood paled into insignificance when set against the traumatic events that had marked his entry into Russian adult life. Afterwards had come the numb, desensitised years of exile. Five long years during which he had tried valiantly, with varying degrees of success, not to feel anything of a remotely emotional or personal nature.

And now – now – the simple act of carrying a sick woman up a staircase had reminded him that life didn't have to be cold and solitary. That human existence could encompass warmth, physical contact with people – and even – the possibility hovered tantalisingly, almost beyond his present conception – a relationship with a woman.

He looked into the bedroom. Tina was sitting on the bed. All he could see of Alma was a mass of red hair lying on the pillow, the same hair that had flowed over his arm when he had carried her up the stairs. Perhaps that was it! The combination of red hair and green eyes. Nothing more. A passing physical resemblance. An attraction that was not born of his feelings for Alma, but Masha . . . Masha . . .

'Charlie?'

The shadowy figure of Trevor Lewis stood before him on the staircase. 'William tells me Alma collapsed.'

'Yes. I'm sorry, I'm in your way,' Charlie apologised, rising quickly.

'Hello Charlie.' Trevor's wife Laura, who had been a Ronconi before her marriage, acknowledged him before following her husband into the room. 'I'll take over here, Tina, you go and help Tony downstairs,' Laura Lewis murmured in her brisk no-nonsense nursing voice. Charlie waited for Tina, then followed her down the stairs into the café where Tony's raised voice and Angelo's intensified crashing of pots and pans testified to the chaos that the temporary shortage of staff had created.

'It's appendicitis and mild concussion,' Trevor announced through the open door at the foot of the stairs.

'That isn't too bad, is it?' Tina enquired uneasily from behind the counter.

'I don't think the mild concussion will present much of a problem, and appendicitis is usually straightforward,' Trevor agreed, 'but Alma's appendix is on the point of bursting. I'm going to have to operate right away.'

'Here?'

Even Trevor smiled at the panic on Tony's face. 'Not in that bedroom, with only the stub of a candle for light and the wind whistling in and flapping the wallpaper! But I could move her into the kitchen. You do have a scrub-down table and sharp knives to hand?'

'You're joking?' Tony wasn't absolutely sure, even after the smile.

'My car's outside. I'll take her up to the cottage hospital. I'll need help to carry her downstairs,' Trevor frowned, thinking of the narrow staircase.

'I'll carry her down for you Doctor Lewis.' Wanting to help, but uncertain how, Charlie had been hovering close to the counter.

'She has to be held steady,' Trevor warned.

'He took her up there without any trouble,' Tina replied for him.

'Then if you'll be kind enough, Charlie. The sooner we get started, the sooner I can operate.'

'Someone's going to have to tell Alma's mother.' Tina hoped it would be her. High drama was infinitely preferable to the boredom of waiting at tables.

'I'll go,' William offered. 'If I take the Trojan I can drive Mrs Moore to the hospital.'

'There won't be anything for her to do there,' Trevor protested. 'Better you stay with her until it's all over. I'll call in and see her on my way back.'

'A woman should go with him,' Tina pressed urgently. 'Mrs Moore will need some sympathy . . .' A fleeting expression of annoyance crossed Tony's face and Tina fell silent. Ever since her family had detected the signs of budding mutual infatuation between her and William Powell, her father and brothers had dedicated themselves to keeping the pair of them apart.

'If Charlie comes with me to the hospital, Laura can go with William to Mrs Moore's.' Trevor's attention was fixed on Charlie as he walked slowly down the stairs with Alma, still wrapped in his coat, in his arms.

'She's just regained consciousness.' Laura followed Charlie into the café.

'Go with William to her mother's house.' Trevor gave

his wife an absentminded peck on the lips much to the delight of the customers. 'You'll know what to say to her.' He held the door open for Charlie to carry Alma outside.

'I can't go to hospital,' Alma protested vehemently as Charlie deposited her gently on the back seat of Trevor's car before walking around and climbing in next to her.

'I don't think you have any choice in the matter, young lady.' Trevor extracted the starting handle from beneath the seat and handed it to Tony, who was fussing round them. 'You're very ill, and you'll be even worse if we don't sort you out – and quickly.'

The cottage hospital on the Common was a long, low, colonial-type structure built on the top of the hill that overlooked the town. Flanked by the big semis and detached houses of the crache it was high enough, and far enough away from the collieries to ensure a plentiful supply of good clean air – a commodity often in short supply in Pontypridd.

'I haven't paid a subscription to the Cottage,' Alma gasped, biting her lip and grasping Charlie's hand in an effort to control the pain.

Trevor turned the corner by the old bridge, pointed his ancient car up the hill and pressed the accelerator down to the floor. 'You pay me my penny a week.'

'Yes, and the penny a week for the Graig Hospital, but I've never been able to afford the guinea a week for the Cottage,' she repeated dogmatically, wondering why Trevor was finding it so difficult to understand. 'I should go to the workhouse.'

'There's a better operating theatre in the Cottage than the Graig. Your father was a miner, wasn't he?'

'The union membership doesn't cover widows and orphans my age and we're—' she clutched Charlie's hand again, crushing his fingers as the pain became almost too great to bear.

'Yes it does,' Trevor contradicted flatly turning a sharp

left through the gates of the hospital.

'Are you sure?' Alma's eyes were rolling and she could only speak in short staccato gasps, yet her primary concern was still money.

'You have my word. You will not get a bill either for the hospital or my services. Is that good enough for you?' Trevor wrenched the handbrake of the car. 'Can you manage?' he asked Charlie.

Charlie nodded, lifted Alma out of the car and followed Trevor up a short flight of steps on to a veranda and through a pair of glassed wooden double doors into the foyer. A nurse stepped briskly out of an adjoining room. The expression of annoyance on her face was replaced by a smile when she saw Trevor.

'Doctor Lewis,' she curtsyed to him as he explained the situation and called for a trolley and porter.

A few seconds later Charlie laid Alma on the trolley and watched as Trevor, the nurse and a porter wheeled it down a corridor that led to the hidden recesses of the hospital. Left to his own devices he paced across the hallway. Trying to ignore the overpowering smell of disinfectant, he hesitated below a brass plaque that commemorated the opening of the hospital. Concerned only for Alma, Trevor had disappeared without a word, and Charlie was uncertain whether he was expected to wait or not.

A clock set high on the wall in front of the window of the closed office ticked on. Five . . . ten minutes passed. He shivered, realising he was in his waistcoat and shirt-sleeves. Alma had still been wrapped in his jacket when he had laid her down on the trolley. The nurse who had greeted Trevor walked back down the corridor, smiled at Charlie then turned a corner and entered one of the rooms.

He turned his back on the plaque and continued to pace up and down, swinging his arms in an effort to ward off the cold, and, with nothing else to do, he began to think . . . and remember . . .

*

'It was on the point of bursting, but it stayed in one piece until I dropped it in the kidney dish, thank God. So that minimises the risk of infection. Lucky she fainted when she did, and Tony had the sense to send for me.' Trevor handed Charlie his jacket.

'Then she is going to be all right?'

'Thanks to all of you, yes I think so,' Trevor hazarded cautiously. 'Although it's early days and the wound may get infected yet. She'll have to stay in here for at least three weeks, and even then it'll be a couple more weeks before she'll be up to doing anything strenuous.'

'That's going to hit her hard. I've heard money is very tight in that household.'

'It's tight everywhere,' Trevor commented philosophically as he rolled down his cuffs. 'Want to come with me to see her mother?'

Charlie shook his head. 'I don't want to intrude.'

'Then I'll drop you off in town. Perhaps you could call into the café and tell them how she's going. Oh, and you'd better warn Tony that he's going to have to find a replacement waitress for a month or so, but I wouldn't mention that until you're half-way out of the door if I were you. You know what his temper is like.'

Chapter Four

'YOU REALLY ARE a terrible patient.' Tina reached out to the bedside locker and filched a strawberry cream from the box of chocolates she had ostensibly brought for Alma.

'How can you expect me to lie here doing nothing when there's no one at home to take care of my mother?'

'I told you,' Tina gave a sigh of exasperation as her fingers strayed into the box again, 'Mrs Lane next door is keeping an eye on her and the house. Not that it needs it,' she added. 'Your mother is a marvel at housework. When I saw her scrubbing your kitchen and washhouse floors I would never have guessed she was blind.'

'You don't understand. Even if Mam *is* coping at home, I still need to work. The bills won't stop coming in just because I'm lying here.' Alma tossed restlessly on the bed.

'Laura's seeing to all your bills,' Tina blurted out thoughtlessly as she studied the illustrations on the inside of the chocolate-box lid.

'Seeing to them! With what?'

'Money, I should imagine. I haven't heard of anyone taking buttons yet.'

'And how on earth am I supposed to pay her back?'

'By putting in extra hours at the café when you're well?' Tina suggested casually. 'Oh and by the way, Eddie Powell was asking after you. I think he's sweet on you.'

Alma wasn't to be put off by tales of Eddie Powell. 'I'm fit enough to leave here now . . .'

'You most certainly are not.' Trevor Lewis strode down the centre of the ward, his white doctor's coat flapping around his lean figure. He smiled and nodded to the occupants of the other beds in the women's ward as he headed towards Alma. 'After three weeks of complete bed rest it'll be as much as you can do to stagger to the bathroom.'

'I walked there just fine this morning.'

'I don't doubt you did, but as it's only one hour into the first afternoon I'll talk to you again tonight.'

'I still don't see why I can't go home. I can rest just as well there.'

'I've yet to meet the woman who can rest in her own home without bobbing up and down every five minutes to see to something,' Trevor replied tactfully. He had visited Alma's house several times during the past three weeks, and had seen for himself exactly how bare and comfortless it was. He knew himself precisely what it meant to live out every day fighting a constant shortage of coal and food; and as a doctor, the last thing he was prepared to do was discharge Alma Moore into a cold, hungry home, where she'd be looking for paid work before her operation scar had time to heal. 'You're here for at least one more week, Madam, whether you like it, or not.'

Alma's mouth set in a grim line as she turned her face to the wall. Pity and charity! Since she'd collapsed in the café they greeted her at every turn. She knew from what her mother had told her during her Sunday and Wednesday visits, that she had practically moved in with Betty Lane next door, supposedly 'to help out with the children'. She also knew that Laura Lewis called in every day to check that her mother was all right and had everything she needed. The kindness of neighbours and friends was proving very hard to take, particularly as she knew it was extremely unlikely she'd ever be able to reciprocate their favours.

'Laura'll be here in a minute with your mother.' Trevor picked up Alma's chart from the foot of her bed and studied it.

'See, you can stop worrying, we have everything under control,' Tina mumbled, her mouth full of chocolate cream.

'Including the disposal of any sweets that the patient is

given?' Trevor lifted an eyebrow. 'Did you remember to bring in two boxes, one for yourself and one for Alma?'

Tina stuck a chocolate-coated tongue out at him.

'Only thinking of your figure, dear sister-in-law,' he teased.

Alma looked towards the door. Leaning heavily on Laura's arm, her mother was walking slowly down the central aisle between the beds. Dressed in the second-hand coat, woollen hat, scarf and gloves Alma had given her for Christmas, she was carrying a brown string carrier bag.

'Here we are, Mrs Moore.' Laura led Alma's mother towards the chair Tina had vacated, and lined her up in front of the seat. 'You can sit here, right next to Alma's bed.'

Alma reached out and placed her mother's hand on the edge of the seat; only then did Lena Moore gingerly lower herself.

'Doctor Lewis tells me you're feeling better, Alma?' She felt for the bed and deposited her carrier bag on it.

'I'm fine.' Alma forced herself to sound bright and cheerful.

Using Alma's voice as a guide, Lena leaned forward and fumbled for her daughter's hand: 'Are you really?' she whispered intensely.

'Of course,' Alma reassured her, taking her hand.

'Tina and I have to visit the men's ward,' Laura said as she tapped her sister's arm. 'Our uncle was brought in last night.'

'Oh dear, nothing serious I hope.' Mrs Moore lifted her face in Laura's direction.

'He chopped his hand when he was chopping chips in his café last night,' Tina explained, gathering her coat and handbag from the floor. 'But it's all right. My cousin fished his finger out of the fat fryer.'

'You'll have to excuse Tina, Mrs Moore,' Laura apologised, as she kicked her sister's shin. 'She has a peculiar sense of humour.'

'Have you brought him a box of chocolates as well, Tina?' Trevor replaced Alma's chart on the rail at the foot of her bed.

'Of course,' Tina retorted. 'See you later, Alma.'

'I'll be back before visiting ends to fetch you, Mrs Moore,' Laura called over her shoulder as they walked away.

'Thank you,' Mrs Moore answered as she heard their footsteps echo down the ward. 'Mrs Lewis is a lovely person, and so kind,' she enthused as she turned her back to Alma. 'And you really are better, aren't you? I can hear it in your voice.'

'I can get out of bed whenever I feel like now.'

'Don't forget to take it slowly,' her mother cautioned. 'Doctor Lewis told me how ill you'd been. He said that even when you come home you are on no account to work for at least two weeks, and that's in the house, let alone outside work.'

'We'll see how I feel, Mam.'

'At least two weeks. He warned me of serious consequences if you don't heed his advice, Alma.' To Lena Moore the words of ministers and doctors were sacrosanct. Both professions she placed in a social stratum only marginally lower than God.

'I'd be bored silly at home all day.' Alma forced a laugh. 'You know what I'm like Mam, I can't sit still for a minute.'

'Well, for once you're going to have to.' Her mother opened the carrier bag and lifted out a clean nightdress. 'Besides, there's nothing for you to do at home. Mrs Lewis has seen to everything. The rent, the bills, the shopping – she even got that nice young man who works for the foreign butcher in the market – what's his name?'

'William Powell,' Alma said suspiciously.

'That's him. She even got him to put a load of coals into the coal-house for me.'

'And you let him? What did you pay him with?'

'It's all right Alma,' her mother smiled. 'Mrs Lewis is

paying for everything out of the insurance you took out in work in case you got sick. She's been collecting your full wages. And not just the café wages. It's twelve shillings, the same as it would be if you'd been able to carry on with both jobs. Although no one from Goldman's been near the house to ask after you. That's not very neighbourly of them I must say. You see, you don't have to worry about a thing. These last two weeks I've even been able to put a little aside. By the time you come out we'll have a few shillings spare. Maybe enough to buy a length of pretty cotton so you can sew yourself a new summer dress.'

Alma lay back on her pillows listening to her mother's tales of how marvellous everything was at home, and saying little except the odd 'yes' or 'no'. She knew her mother had been worried sick about her. Now, for the first time in almost three weeks, relief was evident in the relaxed lines of Lena Moore's face and voice. The last thing she could do was shatter her mother's illusions.

She'd wondered just how Laura had managed to get her mother to accept charity. Now she knew. Insurance! How would her mother feel if she told her there was no insurance. That there never had been. That even if such a policy existed, she'd never had money enough to spare to subscribe to one.

Bethan hovered at the 'dining end' of the one-reception, two-bedroomed flat, or 'apartment' as Andrew liked to call it. She checked the table in a desultory, absentminded fashion, straightening knives and forks that were already beautifully regimented, patting the bunch of violets she'd arranged in her smallest, prettiest crystal vase – a wedding present from Laura and Trevor – passing time while she waited, half in anticipation, half in fear, for the sound of Andrew's key in the door.

She'd taken a great deal of trouble with the table, using the best damask tablecloth that Andrew's sister Fiona and brother-in-law Alec had given them as a belated wedding present. She'd spent half an hour that afternoon polishing the silver cutlery that Andrew's parents had sent, along with a fine set of Doulton china, from Harrods. She could accuse them of antagonism towards her, but never meanness. Fiona, Alec, Laura, Trevor and Andrew's parents – the only thing on the table she could honestly say was the product of their own taste was the posy she'd bought from the flower seller outside their block of flats.

Andrew wouldn't have approved of her going downstairs with the baby in her arms. It upset him to think of people looking at the child. One glance in the shawl or under the hood of the pram he'd asked her to keep raised in all weathers would be enough for anyone to see that something was wrong with little Edmund. Even the baby's name wasn't right. Before the birth they'd decided if the child was a boy they'd name him Evan after her father, and if it was a girl, Isobel after Andrew's mother. But then, before the birth they'd both hoped that the baby would help to heal the rift that had existed between their families ever since she'd run off to London to be with Andrew. Andrew's parents had never really forgiven her for being a miner's daughter and six months pregnant with Andrew's child when they'd married, and her parents had never forgiven Andrew for making her pregnant in the first place.

She wandered into the inner hall and peeped through the open door of the darkened nursery she and Andrew had lavished a great deal of money, time and trouble on before the baby's birth – and a room Andrew hadn't entered since the day she'd carried Edmund into it.

The baby lay on his back, eyes closed. She listened hard. His breathing was soft, regular. It sounded so . . . so normal. If *only* she hadn't drunk so much brandy. She was a nurse: she knew full well that alcohol taken in excess in pregnancy leads to complications and birth palsy in infants. And then to go and fall down the stairs of the Graig Hospital in a drunken stupor – and afterwards . . .

She closed her eyes tightly, gripped the door and swallowed hard. Little Edmund was the way he was because she'd tried to kill him before he even had a chance of life. She had never thought of him as an individual – a living, breathing being in his own right – until Andrew had returned to Pontypridd and talked about the baby they were about to have. So much guilt – hers and hers alone – and poor, innocent Edmund was paying the penalty.

How could she forgive herself! Not only for what she'd done to Edmund, but for the pain she'd caused Andrew. He'd hardly said a word to her beyond the brief exchanges that have to be made since she'd defied him and brought Edmund home from hospital against his express wishes. He had pleaded with her to leave the child in the nursery at the hospital until he was old enough to go into an institution – if he lived that long.

Perhaps it was the brutal honesty of Andrew's final remark that decided her, activating the stubborn streak she'd inherited from her grandmother. If Edmund was going to have a short life she owed it to him to make it a happy one. She didn't need her nurse's training to see just how frail the baby was. His legs and arms were paralysed. His oversized head lolled alarmingly on his thin neck. And worst of all, the only response he made to her ministrations was ceasing to cry when she fed him.

Before she brought Edmund home, before the crushing silence had settled between her and Andrew, he'd tried to talk to her about suitable places for children like Edmund. He had shown her photographs of institutions that had been set up in converted manor houses with beautiful gardens. But her time in the Graig workhouse had taught her the exact worth of beautiful gardens. Most patients were never allowed to walk in them, or touch the flowers. The closest they got to the manicured lawns was to look at them through glass windows.

The unwritten rule in the medical world was that inmates of institutions had to be kept indoors, segregated from 'normal' people lest the sight of them offend and upset. She recalled the rows of utility iron cots in the depressing, green-painted rooms of J ward in the Graig; the listless babies too used to neglect even to whimper, because they knew that crying wouldn't bring attention. She'd tried to make Andrew understand how she felt, taking all the blame squarely on herself, but none of her efforts had lessened his shame at the son they had produced, or his determination to remove all trace of the child from their lives as soon as possible.

She went into the bedroom they shared and glanced at the alarm clock. Not quite seven. She tiptoed back into the hall, and took one last look into the cot before closing the door.

Edmund was generally very good and had begun to sleep through until six in the morning. It was just as well; it irritated Andrew beyond measure when she left their bed to see to him.

Pulling her small, entirely useless 'fancy' lace-trimmed apron tight at the waist she checked her reflection in the hall mirror. She'd had no trouble in regaining her figure after the baby's birth. In fact she was probably too thin. She'd lost all appetite when Andrew had insisted on her taking salts to dry up her milk so Edmund could be bottle-fed. She stared at her eyes, rubbing the taut skin beneath them as though she could wipe away the dark shadows. Not wanting to get out her lipstick, in case Andrew noticed and made a comment about her 'dressing up' in the house, she bit her lips to make them redder, and patted her hair, which was neatly waved just the way her Aunt Megan had taught her to do it. She hesitated, impulsively returned to the bedroom to put one more dab of essence of violets behind her ears, then went into the tiny kitchen to check on the meal.

The potato soup was simmering on the gas stove. It was so much easier to cook with gas. She felt guilty just thinking of her mother and all the women on the Graig who had to cope with temperamental coal-fired ovens. The choice at home at this time of day would have been scorched or tepid soup. The only way to gently warm a saucepan was on the rack above the stove that was used for dishes.

Tomorrow morning there'd be no oven to rake out or blacklead, only the living-room fireplace to clean. The work in the flat was nothing compared to the work of keeping house in Graig Avenue. Perhaps that was part of the trouble. If she had more to do, she'd have less time to think. The only person other than Andrew and the doctors she'd talked to since leaving hospital was the flower seller. They had a telephone, but she knew no one in London except Andrew's sister Fiona; no one in Pontypridd, apart from Andrew's parents and Laura, had a telephone in the house. She was afraid of Fiona's sophistication, and she worried too much about the cost of the call to telephone Laura. Her only contact with her family was through the post, and she was finding it increasingly difficult to write about things that mattered, like the baby. Instead she filled the pages of her letters with questions about what they were doing, and descriptions of the park across the road. But then, considering the state of little Edmund, perhaps it was just as well that most of her family had proved poor correspondents, except of course her mother. And she gained as little information or comfort from her mother's cold epistles as her mother probably did from her own unsatisfactory communications.

She opened the door of the oven to check on the dinner, then went through the menu in her mind. She'd made the dessert – 'dessert', not afters, she had to be careful not to revert to the vocabulary of her home because she sensed it annoyed Andrew – of apple jelly and cheese creams earlier, and they were now cooling on the marble slab in the pantry.

A perfect meal – and all of it copied from the *Complete Illustrated Cookery* that her brothers had saved up and bought for her from a *News of the World* offer. All she needed was someone to eat it. The clock chimed the quarter-hour and she shuddered. Andrew was coming home from the hospital later and later, and that was something else that had to be her fault. He couldn't bear to watch her give Edmund his last feed. He was right. She was being selfish in refusing to give up the baby. As he had said in an angry outburst before she had left the hospital, 'How can people be expected to trust a doctor who's produced a son like Edmund?'

Tears burned her eyes at the thought of handing her son over to strangers who wouldn't recognise the difference between a cry that denoted a serious need, and one that didn't. She stood staring at her wavering reflection in the uncurtained, blackened window, trying to remember all the arguments Andrew had put forward.

Every doctor who had seen Edmund, including Andrew, predicted an early death for the child. They said it was for the best; but none of their predictions had assuaged her guilt, or prevented her from loving the poor mite.

Dr Floyd had told her to forget the baby and concentrate on having another. But how could she? Edmund was nearly two months old and Andrew still treated her as though she had the plague, sticking rigidly to his half of the bed, wearing pyjamas, when he had always slept naked. She knew that at the back of his mind, and hers, lay the thought that there was no guarantee that another baby would either help her to forget their first-born, or be any more whole and perfect than its brother.

She dried her tears and checked the clock again. Half-past seven. If he didn't come soon the meal would be spoiled. Perhaps he was already seeking solace in someone else's arms. He was very good-looking, and used to girls flinging themselves at him the way they had in Pontypridd. A sudden picture filled her mind of Andrew, his arms wrapped around a slim, blonde nurse.

'Good evening.'

She started at the sound of his voice. 'I'm sorry, I was miles away. I didn't hear you come in,' she said nervously, aware that she was saying too much, too quickly. 'The meal's ready whenever you are.' She hesitated, hoping he'd kiss her; even a meaningless touch on the cheek would be a step in the right direction.

'I'll wash my hands.' The apologetic tone in her voice, her eagerness to please, set his teeth on edge. He fought the urge to lash out and shake her. Why didn't she ask him where he'd been until now as any normal wife would do? Alec said Fe gave him hell if he was as much as ten minutes late. Instead, all he got was longsuffering martyrdom wrapped in a coating of sugar-sweet bright-ness. Why didn't she shout at him? Reproach him for his failure to come to terms with their child's disability? Tantrums and screaming matches would be more honest than this ridiculous pretence of blissful domesticity.

In the bathroom he washed his hands, deliberately replacing the immaculately folded towel at an angle. He picked up the tooth-powder and scrubbed his teeth, hoping to rid his mouth of the taste of the half a pint of beer and the cigar he'd spun out in the bar round the corner from the hospital. Only a few short weeks ago he'd rushed home at the end of every shift, literally counting the minutes until he could be with Bethan. Now he was the last out of the pub, staying on with the widowers and bachelors, who had no reason to leave until their clubs began to serve dinner.

If only she'd allow him to put the child elsewhere. The whole time he was home he was conscious that in the next room lay a mockery of humanity, a living reminder of his failure to look after her when she'd needed him most. If he hadn't left her alone when he had, she wouldn't have been working, and she wouldn't have fallen down the stairs of the hospital. Complications might not have arisen in labour – why hadn't he demanded a Caesarean earlier? He should have known her pains were more severe than normal labour pains from the start. A Caesarean would have been better for Edmund. He would have been born perfect . . .

He shut his mind against a heart-wrenching image of

him and Bethan with a beautiful, flawless child. His superiors had sympathised, told him that Edmund's condition was simply one of those medical 'accidents' that happened from time to time. Oxygen starvation during a difficult delivery. No one's fault. But cold, medical logic didn't stop him looking for a scapegoat, or finding one in himself.

He left the bathroom. Bethan had served the soup. It was steaming in a tureen in the centre of the table.

'Shall I dish out for you?' she asked, instantly angry with herself for saying 'dish out' instead of serve.

'I'll do it myself,' he said gruffly. Ladling the smallest possible portion on to his plate he sat down and began to eat. In silence. There didn't seem to be any safe topic left for them to discuss. If he asked about her day he'd run the risk of her telling him, and he didn't want to hear how she'd coped with their son. Not now. Not ever.

'How nice of you to call, Mrs Lewis. Alma dear, it's Mrs Lewis,' Lena Moore called from the kitchen into the washhouse where Alma was leaning on the stone sink peeling potatoes.

'I'll be there now.' Alma dropped her knife into the dirty water, went outside to rinse her hands under the tap, and returned to the kitchen, drying her hands on her apron as she walked.

'Would you like a cup of tea, Laura?' she asked, grateful that the oven was lit so she could offer. The coal stocks William had brought had lulled her mother into a false sense of security and she'd insisted on lighting the stove every day since Alma had come home from hospital.

'That would be nice, thank you.' Laura set her basket on the floor. 'I've brought you some fruit from the market.' She lifted half a dozen brown paper bags from the top of her basket and laid them on the table.

'Thank you. That really is very good of you,' Alma's mother chattered gratefully. 'As you well know, Alma isn't up to carrying anything heavy like shopping yet, and

64

I won't be going into town until Mrs Lane takes me on Saturday morning.' Lena picked up the kettle from the hearth and walked slowly but surely out into the yard. She filled it at the outside tap. Turning, she hesitated for a moment on the threshold of the washhouse. The onset of her blindness had brought with it a heightened sensitivity to the atmosphere people carried with them and she sensed strain between her daughter and Laura.

'I'll do it, Alma,' she murmured as Alma held out her hand to take the kettle when she finally returned to the kitchen. She picked up the iron hook they used to lift the hotplate and set the kettle to boil. 'I'm sorry Mrs Lewis, I hope you'll excuse me.' She scooped her knitting from the table. 'I was just on my way to see Mrs Lane next door. I promised to show her a cable stitch she needs to make up a sweater for her youngest.'

'In that case I'll see you next time Mrs Moore.' Laura reached out and touched the old woman's hand as she confidently walked the six paces along the passage to the front door.

'Sit down,' Alma invited as the door closed. She indicated the most comfortable chair, the rickety wooden upright that sported a home-made cushion padded with old shredded stockings.

'You're not overdoing it, are you?' Laura asked critically, looking Alma over with a professional eye. 'You have to remember that you only came out of hospital three days ago.'

'I'm fine,' Alma snapped.

Laura sat down and stared at the kettle hissing on the stove.

'I'm feeling fine,' Alma repeated, conscious of having spoken sharply.

'I'm glad to hear it.'

Alma poured a little hot water into the teapot, swirled it round and took it into the washhouse to empty it down the sink. Busying herself on her return, she refused to meet Laura's searching looks. She spooned tea into the pot, filled it and took two cups and saucers from the dresser.

'I've just come from the new café,' Laura volunteered.

'When will it be opening?'

'The way it's looking now the builders will be working there for at least another month.'

'Ronnie promised me a full-time job there when it opened. Head waitress.' Alma felt as though she was demeaning herself by begging for a position.

'There will be a job of one sort or another for you as long as the Ronconis run cafés,' Laura promised quietly.

'I was hoping there would, but after . . . well after what happened that night with Mary and Freda I wasn't too sure.' Alma's voice trailed away as she poured the tea. It was difficult to look Laura in the eye.

'Alma . . .'

'I've been wanting to talk to you,' Alma interrupted. Thrusting her hand into the pocket of her skirt she pulled out a piece of paper and handed it to Laura.

'What's this?' Laura unfolded it.

'A list of everything I owe you for the bills you've paid, and the money you gave my mother when I was in hospital. I make it two pounds seventeen and eightpence.'

Laura glanced down at the list. Alma had left out nothing. Four weeks' rent at nine shillings a week, two hundredweight of coal, four weeks' groceries from the corner shop. Even the fruit and chocolates Tina had taken into hospital had been added to the list.

'Look Alma—'

'No, you look!' Alma's green eyes blazed fiercely in the thin light that filtered into the room from the back yard. 'They're my bills. Mine and my mother's. Have you any idea how it makes me feel to have you pay them?'

'Alma, we employ you. We're your friends,' Laura protested.

'Friend or not I intend to pay you back. Every penny,' she mumbled.

'You don't have to.'

'Yes I do,' Alma countered, swallowing her tears.

'Alma, no matter how good you think you feel now, you're still recovering from a serious operation. You need to give yourself time. You're not fit for work.'

'If Tony'll have me I intend to go back tonight.'

'Alma please . . .'

'This—' Alma opened a drawer in the table and lifted out a small cloth purse. She emptied it and coins fell into a noisy heap on the table next to Laura. They represented the sum total of her and her mother's savings. All the pennies her mother had scrimped from the 'insurance' money Laura had given her – 'is the first instalment on what I owe.'

'I can't leave you penniless.'

'We can get credit in the shop at the end of the street until Saturday. And I can start back to work tonight. Can't I?' Alma's face was a study in determination and defiance.

Laura made no move to pick up the money.

'I can have my job back, can't I?' Alma repeated, raising her eyes.

'We had to do some reorganising after you left,' Laura murmured evasively. 'We don't need anyone out front any more, but Tony really could do with some help in the kitchen. If you take the job it'll be at a higher hourly rate because there won't be any tips.'

'I'm a waitress, not a kitchen hand.'

'It will only be for a short while.'

'You're afraid someone else will make a scene, like Mary and Freda?'

'There's no sense in meeting trouble half-way.'

'But you're still prepared to employ me?' Alma's heart pounded erratically. Laura couldn't let her go. She just couldn't . . .

'Speaking as a nurse, I'd rather you didn't go back for at least another week.'

'My mother and I need the money.'

'Alma please. Let us help you. You've worked for us

for a long time. I thought we were friends.'

'I won't take charity.'

'If you won't take help from us, you and your mother are going to end up in the workhouse,' Laura stated bluntly.

'If we do end up there it won't be for the want of trying to find work.'

'Alma, be realistic. If you go back to work tonight you could collapse again. And then where will you and your mother be?'

'I won't collapse.'

'Ronnie would never forgive me if he knew that I'd allowed you to go back to work straight after an operation.' If she hadn't been so desperate to make Alma see sense Laura would never have used her eldest brother's name.

'Is that why you want to help me? Because I was your brother's fancy woman?'

The silence in the kitchen closed in unbearably. Laura stood up and picked up her basket.

'I'll tell Tony to expect you tonight.'

'Take the money.'

'No. I'd rather you paid me back all at once.'

'That could take time.'

'I can wait.'

Laura walked towards the curtain that screened off the passage. 'You will come to us if you need help?' she pleaded one last time.

'Thank you for the offer, but I'll manage,' Alma replied stubbornly.

'I would never have moved you out of the café into the kitchen if I'd had any choice. You do know that, don't you?'

'I know what everyone in the town is saying about me.' Alma's cheeks flamed crimson but she still looked Laura in the eye.

'Alma, all this gossip started when Ronnie left you to marry Maud. As Ronnie isn't here, the rest of the family

68

have to bear some responsibility for what's happening to you,' Laura said finally, weary of diplomacy and mincing words.

'No they don't.' Alma lifted her eyes to meet Laura's. 'If I've lost my reputation, it's my own fault. No one else's. And I'll sort things out my own way without charitable handouts. From anyone!'

Chapter Five

'NO ONE ELSE is sitting down.'

'What everyone else does is no concern of yours. I'm the manager of this café, and if you want work, the only job I have on offer is vegetable preparation. And from now on that's done sitting down.' Tony dumped a chair in front of the wooden preparation table. 'Are you going to make a start or not?'

'Yes,' Alma answered sullenly, pulling the chair towards her.

'Here's your knife. There's the potatoes.' Tony pointed to the massive stone sink at the end of the table that Angelo had filled with half a hundredweight of potatoes.

'Thank you.' Alma didn't even try to keep the sarcasm from her voice.

'You feel the slightest bit ill, you go home.'

'I feel fine.'

'Angelo,' he shouted to his brother who was browning toast over a gas flame.

'I'll keep my eye on her.'

When Tony had started to work in the family's cafés, it had been Alma, not his older brother Ronnie, who had shown him the ropes and eased him into the café routine, and he was embarrassed at having to play the part of boss to her kitchen maid now. Banging the door behind him, he returned to the café. It was a Saturday night, the busiest of the week and his sisters, Tina and Gina, were dashing back and forth between the tables and the counter like yo-yos. Neither of them was as skilful at waitressing as Alma, and he picked up murmurs of discontent as the girls slopped coffee and tea into saucers, and beans off plates as they dumped them down in front of the customers.

'Gina! Tina!' He called them to the counter.

'I *am* sorry. The management appears to be having a crisis,' Tina apologised to the bus crew she was about to serve.

'More haste, less speed,' Tony hissed as his sisters approached him.

'What?' Gina asked blankly.

'Both of you are rushing it. You're slopping up, not serving the customers' orders. They're not happy.'

'We're run off our feet and you call us over to tell us that?' Tina stared at him in disbelief.

'I overheard someone complaining.'

'Someone will always complain. If you hire waitresses who look like Anna May Wong and sing like Judy Garland they'll still find something to gripe about,' Gina said mutinously.

'That's not the attitude . . .' Tony began.

'Well, clever clogs, seeing as how you know all about attitudes as well as waiting tables, you can damn well run this place yourself.' Tina pulled the bow on the back of her apron, whipped it off and handed it together with her notebook to her brother.

'Don't be stupid,' Tony growled. 'And don't use language like that. I just thought you should know they're moaning.'

'Well let them moan,' she raised her voice. 'If they don't like the way Gina and I wait tables, they shouldn't have kicked up such a bloody fuss about Alma.'

'Come on now, who'll offer me twopence for this? There's got to be two full pounds in weight here.' William Powell held a sheet of newspaper piled high with creamy folds of tripe above his head so even those at the back of the crowd who'd gathered around Charlie's stall could see what he was auctioning. 'Did I hear anyone say twopence?'

'Penny,' a woman shouted from the centre of the throng.

'Penny-halfpenny,' another called.

'It's yours.' William wrapped the newspaper around the tripe and glanced down at the remaining meat on the display slab. Unlike some of the other butchers on the market, Charlie insisted on clearing his stall of stock every night. Opening as they did only on Wednesdays, Fridays and Saturdays he liked to start every trading day with fresh meat, which he spent Mondays, Tuesdays and Thursdays preparing in the slaughterhouse.

William shivered in the icy draught of the constantly opening door as he debated which of the remaining bundles to auction next.

'What about those chop bones?' Viv Richards, Evan Powell's next-door neighbour pushed his way to the front. 'You ever going to hold them up?'

William looked at what was left. Four beef hearts, three shin bones splattered with a few meat scrapings, and the single heap of small, splintered chop bones Viv wanted. With luck, they'd be able to pack up in another ten minutes. 'OK, Viv, how much you prepared to give me?'

'A penny.'

'I'll give you a penny-farthing,' a woman elbowed Viv aside.

'Penny halfpenny.'

'Twopence.'

At a nod from Charlie, who knew just how little meat there was on the bones, William knocked them down to Viv. 'Now who'll give me a shilling for a beef heart?'

It was a procedure they went through every Saturday night after nine o'clock 'auction bell', and every Saturday night the hearts were knocked down for tenpence. Very occasionally the last straggler was lucky enough to get a misshapen one for eight or ninepence, but never less. There was good eating in a beef heart, and everyone knew it. Sunday dinner for the family, and afterwards, thinly sliced, it provided sandwich fillings for the week for those fortunate enough to be working.

While William sold off the remaining meat Charlie lifted the lid on the meat safe and checked the shelves. They were bloodstained, but empty. Taking the zinc buckets from beneath the counter, he left the stall in William's charge while he prepared for the nightly scrub-down. Two plump women, dressed in the white overalls and caps of the cheese and bacon stalls, were gossiping as they filled their buckets in the market wash house, and Charlie held back, waiting politely, and silently for them to finish.

'It's right, I tell you,' one said to the other. 'The Ronconis have put her to work out of sight in the kitchen because she's expecting. It's all over town, and Ronnie Ronconi married to Maud Powell and in Italy. Well that's one poor bastard that will never see its father. You can be sure of that. Do you know Mostyn Goldman sacked her?'

'No!' the other gasped.

'Well he had to, didn't he. It's what the Ronconis would have done if they could have, but then seeing as how Ronnie's responsible they couldn't.'

'Why not?' The question was a valid one. Paternity suits were difficult to prove at the best of times, and even if the judge was satisfied, with the father in Italy it would be well nigh impossible to extract the one or two shillings a week Alma could hope to be awarded.

'Gossip!' The woman nodded her head sagely. 'Well would you want to eat there, knowing they'd abandoned their own flesh and blood, even if it will be born the wrong side of the blanket?'

'There's plenty that won't want to eat there knowing a woman like her is working in the back.'

'You're right.' The tap was turned off and the full bucket exchanged for an empty one. 'But then, it's her mother I feel sorry for. Blind or not, she'll never be able to hold her head up in this town again. I can't think what the girl was thinking of.'

'That's obvious isn't it? The café. If she'd caught

Ronnie she'd never have had to look for food for herself and her mother again.'

'Well from what I've seen lifting your skirt leads more often to the workhouse than to wedding rings. But it's a shame to think she'll take her mother down with her. Lena McIver was a smart girl in her day, but then she would go and marry a Moore. Good-looking fellows the Moores, but none of them lived long. Weak chests,' the woman nodded sagely.

'I thought Lena's husband died in the pit.'

'He did, but if he hadn't he wouldn't have lasted long. Not with the Moore chest.'

With the second bucket full, the two women turned around. They paled at the sight of Charlie.

'Mrs Rees. Mrs Pickering.' He nodded to them as he stepped forward with his own buckets. The women continued to talk, even before they'd moved out of earshot.

'He's always so quiet.'

'Sneaking around . . .'

'Never know when he's there . . .'

'Sly, like all foreigners.'

Wilf Horton turned up with a bucket and stood beside Charlie. 'Bloody dog messed up the front of my stall,' he complained. 'Just when I sent the boy off to the night safe.'

'That's always the way it is,' Charlie sympathised as he stood back from the water splashing up from his bucket.

'Bloody dogs. Oughtn't to be allowed . . .'

'Tell me, Mr Horton,' Charlie interrupted. 'Do you happen to know who owns that empty shop by the fountain?'

'Which empty shop?' Wilf growled. 'If you ask me, Taff Street has more empty shops than full ones. Ponty looks more like a ghost town every day.'

'The shop that used to sell china.'

'Meakins' shop. Little wonder he pulled out, what with people cutting back to the bone. Not many have food

74

these days, so there's no point in them buying plates. He's taken a stall on the outside market now. Less working days, less money, but then there's less overheads and—'

'Did he own the shop?' Charlie pressed.

'Does any trader own a shop in this one-horse town?' Wilf retorted, using a phrase from a Western he'd watched in the Palladium. 'That place is one of Fred the Dead's.'

'Thanks, Wilf.' Charlie swung the heavy buckets easily into his hands and left the washroom for his stall.

'Looks like that's about it for the day,' William greeted Charlie on his return. The last few customers were wandering between the stalls as they finally made their way outside. Like chickens searching for grubs they darted their heads first one way, then the other, scanning the counters in search of edible leftovers which the traders might be prepared to give away.

'Missus . . . hey Missus!' Charlie shouted to a woman who was bundled up in a grey ragged blanket tied with a length of twine at what passed for her waist. 'Do you want some bones for your dog?' he asked when he caught her attention.

She nodded, flaccid lips trembling around her toothless gums. He wrapped the shin bones and one small heart, all that was left on the counter, in newspaper, and handed them to her. She ran off clutching them close to her chest.

'You know old Patsy hasn't got a dog.' Will tipped soda into one of the buckets.

'Start with the meat safe.'

'You could have sold that heart back to the slaughterhouse for dog meat,' Will grumbled as he tossed a cloth into the hot water.

'It's not worth it for what we'd get.'

'It would have been enough for a pint. You're a soft touch Charlie and everyone around here knows it . . .'

He looked up from the counter he was wiping down. Charlie wasn't listening. He'd picked up the wooden box that contained the day's takings, and pulled out the notebook he kept in his shirt pocket. Piles of farthings, halfpennies, pennies, threepences, and silver sixpences were mounting up on the shelf at the back of the stall. Alongside them lay a few florins and half-crowns. There was even a ten-bob note, but only one.

'We do all right, Charlie?' William asked.

'All right,' Charlie agreed as he handed William his half a crown wages. They'd taken nearly ten pounds, six pounds of which was earmarked to buy the next stock of meat. His boss, the Cardiff butcher who owned the stall, paid him on a commission basis on trading days. Today's share would amount to twelve shillings, a good average for a Saturday. It made up for the weekdays when the stall was closed and he cut meat in the slaughterhouse on Broadway, for which he only got paid two and six a day, the same as William. Most weeks he cleared one pound ten shillings after he'd paid his lodge and expenses. He had a lot to be grateful for. There were plenty worse off than him, and because he had no wife or children to keep, he'd managed to save over a hundred pounds. Enough to rent a shop and employ someone to run it for a couple of months until the profits started coming in.

He poured the day's takings into a cloth bag and tucked it inside his shirt, tightening his belt so it nestled against his chest. Then he bent over his notebook, concentrating hard as he jotted down a set of figures. William watched him as he wrote, wondering just when he was going to lend a hand with the clearing up. Eventually Charlie straightened up, tore a page out of his notebook, and folded it carefully into his shirt pocket.

'Lock up for me.' He tossed his keys at William.

'You trust me?' William asked facetiously.

'Not entirely, but then once the knives are locked into the meat safe, there's not a lot worth stealing. You will clean the knives properly before you put them away?'

'Don't I always?'

'When I watch.' Charlie smiled one of his rare wry smiles.

'Thanks a lot. May I ask where you're off to that's so important?'

'The New Inn.' Charlie took off his blue-striped apron and white overalls. Straightening his tie, he slipped on his jacket and coat.

'Drinking with the crache. The rest of us not good enough for you now?'

'Something like that,' Charlie murmured as he left.

William bent his head and attacked the wooden chopping block with a wire brush. Experience had taught him that if Charlie didn't want to talk about his business, there was no power on God's earth that would make him.

Charlie found the undertaker, Fred Jones, known in the town as 'Fred the Dead' standing at the bar of the 'Gentleman's Only' in the New Inn. People who knew insisted Fred was over forty, but it was difficult to tell his exact age as unlike most men in Pontypridd, he'd worn well and was always immaculately groomed. His fair hair was styled matinée-idol fashion and creamed with expensive preparations. The suits he sported on his thickset, bull-necked frame were well cut, spotless, crisp and new. Mostyn Goldman's wares were not for Fred. He patronised a Cardiff tailor and set aside a day every spring and autumn just to travel there to be measured.

Fred had left Pontypridd as a young man to join the Indian army, and in ten years had worked his way up to the rank of Drill Sergeant. He'd left only when his father, still known in the town as 'Big Fred the Dead' had died. 'Little Fred', as no-one now dared call him to his face, had kept his healthy-looking tan and his military bearing. No one ever tangled willingly with him.

He employed three men and had sons of working age who helped him in the business of undertaking and property rental that he'd inherited from his father, but he still 'walked out' ahead of the hearse at all of the funerals 'F. Jones and Son' arranged. And it was nearly always Fred himself who made the first personal call, and laid out the bodies of the crache who had money enough to purchase the best that his firm had to offer.

Charlie ordered a pint of beer. Sipping it, he moved along the bar until he stood alongside Fred, who, foot on brass rail, arm extended, was holding forth on the depression and its causes to Ben Springer who owned a shoe shop in town. When Fred finally paused to finish his drink, Charlie stepped forward.

'Another, Mr Jones?'

The undertaker eyed Charlie suspiciously before replying. 'I don't mind if I do. Double brandy.'

Charlie ordered the brandy. He stuck to his beer; it had been a long time since he'd eaten, and he needed to keep a clear head. At least for the next half-hour.

'I know you,' Fred said as he picked up the glass the barman handed him. 'You're that foreign butcher who works the market.'

'I am.'

'Don't know why we have to import foreigners to run the town's businesses when there's so many local lads out of work,' Ben Springer grumbled nastily, aggrieved that he hadn't been included in the round of drinks.

'I manage the stall for a Cardiff butcher,' Charlie explained. 'It's not mine.'

'And I suppose you think that makes it all right. But it's still a job you've taken from those that need it.'

'Is the brandy all right, Mr Jones?' Charlie asked, turning his back on Ben Springer.

'Fine.' Fred drained his glass and motioned to the barman to refill it and pour Charlie another beer.

'Could I have a word with you in private, Mr Jones?' Charlie asked.

Fred led the way to a table in a secluded corner. New Inn prices were too steep for all but a handful of people in the town, and the bar wasn't crowded, even on a Saturday night.

'What are you after?' Fred asked bluntly as soon as they were seated.

'I'd like to know what rent you're asking for your shop in Taff Street.'

'I own a lot of shops in Taff Street. Which one you after?'

'The one at the bottom of Penuel Lane that used to be a china shop.'

'Good spot that, next to the entrance to the fruit market.' Fred picked up his replenished brandy glass and sipped it. 'You know an opportunity when you see it, young man. You after it for yourself?'

'I'll be employing others to run it.'

'And what would you be selling. Meat?'

'No. Fancy goods,' Charlie replied vaguely.

'You'd have to sell a lot of those to pay the rent I'm asking. That's an expensive shop you're looking at there. It's even got a nice little flat above it. Did you know that?'

'Yes. That's one of the reasons I'd like it. But if the rent is too much for the profit margin I expect to be making, I'll look elsewhere.' Charlie finished his first pint and picked up the one Fred had bought him. 'I counted thirty-five empty shops in town this morning.'

'Not all of them have backyards, or living accommodation above.'

'Not all of them have high rents either.'

Fred narrowed his eyes. 'What are you prepared to pay?'

'No more than a pound a week.'

'That's scandalous.'

'Not for a five-year lease.'

'You're not lacking in confidence, I'll say that for you.'

'Two hundred and sixty pounds over five years, for a shop that was probably only worth three hundred and fifty pounds before the depression, looks a pretty good option to me.'

'There'll be no let-out clause in the lease,' Fred warned. 'I'll have it sewn up tighter than my wife's corsets.'

'I won't sign unless there's an option to buy at the end of the five years. I understand that's usual practice.'

'Do you now.' Fred fingered his chin thoughtfully as he drained his glass. 'All right, I don't see any problem with that. Option to buy at the going rate five years hence.'

'At one hundred pounds.'

'That's daylight robbery!'

'You'll be getting three hundred and sixty pounds for a rundown shop that wouldn't fetch a hundred and fifty if it was put on the open market now.'

'I'm in no hurry to sell.'

Charlie finished his second glass and left his chair.

'Where are you going?'

'To see the solicitor Mr Spickett Monday morning. He's acting for the estate that owns the shop next to the Park Hotel.'

'My shop's by the entrance to the fruit market.'

'The one by the Park Hotel is close to the Taff Street park gates, it will get a fair amount of casual trade in the summer.'

'Mine will get it all the year round.'

'Word will soon get about. People will always go where there's a bargain to be had.'

'Tell you what.' Fred signalled to the barman to fill his own glass and Charlie's again. 'I'll give it to you for two hundred at the end of the lease.'

'I offered a hundred.' Charlie ignored the beer the barman carried to their table.

'A hundred and fifty.'

'One hundred and twenty-five, and that's my final offer.'

The undertaker stared into the Russian's cold blue eyes and saw the man meant exactly what he'd said.

'I'll get my solicitor to draw up the papers tomorrow.'

'In the meantime if you wouldn't mind signing this.' Charlie pulled the piece of paper he'd torn from his notebook out of his pocket and pushed it over the table. Only then did he pick up his glass.

'What's this?'

'Details of our agreement.'

Fred peered at the figures. 'Lease at fifty-two pounds a year, payable quarterly . . . you said nothing about quarterly!'

'Standard business practice.'

'Comes to something when a foreigner tells a man what's standard business practice in his own country.' There was a trace of humour in Fred's voice that had been absent from Ben Springer's. 'Buying at one hundred and twenty-five pounds . . . you had it all worked out before you walked in here!'

'I worked out what I could afford beforehand. Yes.'

'Even if I sign this, it wouldn't be witnessed, so it wouldn't be legal.'

'No,' Charlie acceded. 'But it would be legal enough to make a fuss should you try to pull out tomorrow morning.'

'What did your family do in Russia? Horse-trading?'

'Something along those lines,' Charlie agreed mildly.

Fred removed a fountain pen from his top pocket, and signed his name at the foot of the page. 'How soon do you want to be in?'

'Monday morning.'

'This week coming?'

Charlie nodded. 'There's some work that needs doing.'

'How do you know?'

'I took a good look before the china people moved out.'

'Snooping?'

'I used to deliver meat for Mrs Meakins.'

'I'm not paying out any money for repairs. You take the place as you find it.'

'That's why I knocked you down on price.' Charlie finished his beer. 'If I'm going to own the place eventually, I'd like to see the job done properly.'

'Ever had the feeling you've been had?' Fred muttered to the barman as he pushed his glass across the bar after Charlie left.

'Every night I work in this place, sir.' The barman

pulled the brandy bottle from beneath the counter.

As Fred picked up his refilled glass he smiled. At least he'd managed to rent his empty shop, which was more than the poor sod who owned the shop next to the Park Hotel had done.

William had never been in the market so late. If there were things that needed doing that warranted staying behind for more than half an hour, Charlie inevitably saw to them, an arrangement that suited William admirably. After all, Charlie was the one who managed the business. He was only the paid help, although he was more than prepared to put in whatever effort was needed. He was grateful to Charlie for employing him, grateful that he had somewhere to go six days a week, unlike his cousin Eddie who worked for Wilf Horton every Wednesday and Saturday and tried to make up the money he earned by helping his father out on the cart. It was an open secret between the men in the household that Evan and Eddie didn't bring in enough money tatting to keep one of them, let alone two.

After putting on his coat and cap, William slammed the wooden shutters that Charlie had hinged across the stall, secured the padlock and breathed a sigh of relief hoping that he'd thought of everything. Knives . . . emptying buckets . . . oh well, what wasn't done, wasn't. He was damned if he was going to open the shutters again. He glanced at the clock over the door. Ten o'clock. Too late to do anything except go to Ronconi's, drink chocolate, and hope that Tina would evade her brother's eagle eye long enough for them to exchange a word or two.

Hands in pocket, coat buttoned high against the wind, he whistled the opening bars of '*You were temptation*' as he walked towards the side door.

'Will?'

'Vera?' he stared at a girl he last remembered as a ragged, grubby ten-year-old who'd lived a couple of doors down from him in Leyshon Street. He looked up at the stall. 'You working for old George now?'

'He's left me to lock up and I can't lift the shutters. You wouldn't give me a hand would you?'

'For you, Vera, anything,' he winked. Pushing his cap to the back of his head he picked up the first of the square wooden shutters, which unlike those around Charlie's stall, needed to be hoisted up and slotted into place at the front of the counter.

'Where's George then?' he asked as he heaved the last into place.

'It's Saturday night,' she said disparagingly.

'Don't tell me, he's playing cards in the back room of the Queen's.'

'You've got it.'

'Bit unfair, leaving you to do all the work.' William secured the bar across the shutters and slipped on the open padlock. 'There, all done.' He turned and smiled at her. Vera was a couple of years younger than him. Sixteen, if he remembered rightly, the same age as his sister Diana; but he didn't recall her being as pretty as she was now. Her wild, unkempt matted curls had been tamed, and there was no sign of the spots that had earned her the nickname of Nettles. Her dark brown hair was neatly waved and glossy. It framed an oval face with a beautiful peaches-and-cream complexion that showed off her brow-shaped mouth and large brown eyes to fine advantage. But he didn't waste too much time looking at her face. Her figure had filled out, and his glance lingered on the full, rounded breasts, clearly outlined beneath her thin cotton overall. If she had anything on underneath, it certainly didn't show, and he admired her capacity to withstand the cold. He was shivering through the thick layers of his jacket and coat.

'George has left me to lock up four Saturdays running,' she grumbled. 'He never used to before we were married.'

'You married George Collins?' William couldn't keep the shock from his voice. George Collins was fat, bald . . . old. He had to be at least fifty.

'He's a good man, and he takes care of me. I want for nothing.' She might have been repeating a lesson she'd learned by heart, and William realised this wasn't the first time she'd had to defend her marriage. 'He was my father's oldest friend and when Dad died . . .'

'I heard about that. I'm sorry. And I'm sorry we lost touch after you moved from Leyshon Street.'

'Mam says we should never have moved. The house we rented in Wood Road was bigger, but Mam says there's no people in Ponty like the neighbours we had on the Graig.'

'So how long you been married?'

'Four months. George is so kind, and not only to me. He helps my mam out too. She's still got five at home, and it's been hard on her since Dad died. George's money makes all the difference . . .' she stopped suddenly, realising she was saying far too much.

'Who would have thought it,' William said tactlessly. 'Little Vera and old George.'

'I'm not little Vera any more, and George is not that old,' she countered indignantly. But her protest didn't fool William. He noticed her bottom lip tremble.

'Obviously not in the way that matters, seeing as how he married you,' William consoled clumsily.

'Thanks for the shutters.'

'Any time.' He took a step forward, but something made him turn back. Vera was holding on to the padlock she'd fastened, sobs shaking her shoulders, tears pouring down her cheeks.

'Hey. Come on,' William put his hand on her arm. 'Whatever it is, it can't be that bad.'

'I'm just being silly,' she wiped her eyes with the back of her hand, but tears still clung to her eyelashes. For the first time William saw that she wasn't simply pretty. She was beautiful. She even looked good when she cried, unlike his sister Diana, whose nose always turned bright red. 'Come on, I'll walk you home,' he offered.

'George's house is on the Parade, and I know you still

live on the Graig. I saw Diana and Tina Ronconi waiting in the queue to get into the pictures. George lets me go to the Palladium with my sister every week, because he doesn't like the pictures. Diana told me that you were both living with your aunt and uncle now after . . .'

'Come on. Pick up your coat. If we don't make a move we're going to be landed with the job of locking the whole market.' The last thing William wanted was to get caught up in a discussion on the events that had led to his mother's imprisonment.

'Do you remember all those picnics we had over Shoni's pond?' Vera asked as they walked out of Market Square into Taff Street. 'That time you and your cousin Haydn fell in when you tried to catch fish. You said you were going to cook them over the fire we'd lit on the bank.'

'Just as well it was the wrong time of year for tadpoles,' he said carelessly. 'I have a feeling they wouldn't have been very tasty.'

'And then there was that time you hid Miss Jones's glasses in Sunday School, and tied Mrs Edwards's cat—'

'How long have you been working on George's stall?' William didn't enjoy talking about his childhood in Leyshon Street. It reminded him of home, of his mother, and he had never really come to terms with the thought of her locked up in Cardiff prison day after day.

'Since two weeks before we got married.'

'I can't get over you and George.' He shook his head as they rounded the corner by the old bridge. 'I always used to think that you and Jimmy . . .'

'Jimmy's in Cornwall. When he couldn't get a job around here he went to the Labour Exchange and they found him a place on a farm. He wrote to me once or twice, he seems to like it there.'

'Jimmy would. He was only happy when he was outside on the mountain. Remember that time he tried to ride one of Jones's cows in Penycoedcae.' They both laughed as they turned into the Parade.

'I don't think you should walk me to the door,' she said falling serious.

'Why not?'

'I'm a married woman now, and well, it's George. You see he can be a bit jealous.'

'After you've only been married four months?'

'It's my fault,' she said earnestly, looking around to make sure the street was deserted. 'I'm so much younger than him, and as he says, I always want to be off doing things that married women shouldn't. Like going to the pictures. And dancing . . . I really miss those dances in the Catholic Hall in Treforest. Do you?'

'I still go to them.' William looked into her eyes, shining with reflected lamplight, and recalled one evening when he and Tina had managed to evade her brothers and they'd gone round the back of the hall only to see Jimmy and Vera, and to quote Tina afterwards, 'not just kissing'.

'Oh it is good talking to you about the old days,' she cried.

'Vera, you sound as if you're a hundred years old, not sixteen.'

'Married to George sometimes I feel I am a hundred. Look,' she glanced up and down the street again. 'How about if you go down the lane and come into the house the back way? I'll leave the door open in the wall so you'll know which house it is, and I'll pull the kitchen curtains and stand in front of the window so there'll be no mistake. That way we can have a cup of tea. Talk some more . . .'

'I thought you said George is the jealous type.'

'He is. But the card game in the Queen's never finishes before three in the morning. I should know,' she added bitterly. 'He plays there four times a week.'

'I don't know . . .'

'Come on, Will,' she coaxed. 'It's been so good talking to you, and the fire will be banked up. My mother sees to that. She lays out a little supper too.' She touched his hand with the tips of her gloved fingers and his mouth went dry. He loved Tina Ronconi. But then Vera knew

86

that, and she *was* lonely. A cup of tea, a chat, a sandwich – what could be more innocent?

'All right.'

'It's the sixth house down from this end. Give me five minutes and I'll open the door to the lane.'

'Five minutes,' he echoed. If it was all so innocent, why was he perspiring when the air temperature was barely above freezing?

The first thing William noticed as he crept after Vera through the darkened washhouse into the brilliantly lit back kitchen was that she had changed out of her cotton overalls into the same kind of silk dressing gown he'd seen Myrna Loy swanning around in on the screen in the White Palace. It was cream coloured, pulled in at the waist by a belt that Vera had tied *very* tightly. It clung to the contours of her body, leaving absolutely nothing to his imagination, and once again he was left with the uncomfortable feeling that she was wearing very little, if anything, beneath it.

'I've put the kettle on. Why don't you sit down.' She closed, and locked the washhouse door behind him. He looked round the room. The furniture was oak, old but good; the covers on the easy chairs and the lino on the floor new. The bright, clean and long-piled hearth-rug clearly hadn't seen much coal dust.

'George said I could change anything I liked in the house. He buys me whatever I ask for in the way of furniture, and, as you can see, clothes.' She fingered the skirt of her dressing gown, pulling it wide to display an expanse of smooth white thigh that sent William's pulse soaring. 'But then I don't see much point in change simply for the sake of change, do you?'

'No,' he agreed thickly, without the faintest idea what she was talking about. He was totally preoccupied with the sight of her long, slim legs, and her full breasts. Were they really that shape? Or was she wearing something that made them point upwards?

'I know this furniture is old-fashioned, but George is very fond of it. It was his mother's. She only died last year.'

'He wasn't married before?' By concentrating on a print of Jesus recruiting the fishermen of Galilee that hung over the mantelpiece, William just about managed to get the gist of Vera's last sentence.

'George,' she laughed, clearly amused by the notion. 'Good Lord, no! My father always used to say that George was a born bachelor. Here, there's a gap in the curtains. I'd better close them in case someone sees you.'

'What if George just walks in?' William asked nervously, suddenly wishing he'd turned a deaf ear to her invitation.

'He won't. I've locked the front and back doors and bolted them from the inside. No one can walk in.'

'Won't that make him suspicious?' William's breath quickened as she leaned across his chair.

'Not George. I always lock them in the evening when he's not at home. He calls me a scaredy cat, but I don't care. It feels so lonely here. Just me rattling around this big house. I get afraid. After living in a houseful of people all my life I'm not used to being by myself.' She leaned back for a moment, studied the curtains, then reached out again. The ends of her silk belt fell across William's face, and as he brushed them aside he caught a heady whiff of rose-scented perfume.

'Don't you like being tickled?' she teased, falling forward, laughing, on to his lap.

'That depends on who's doing the tickling,' he whispered, his voice thickening to a hoarse whisper as the weight of her thighs pressed down on his.

'How about if we try this instead.' Locking her arms around his neck she pulled his head close to hers and kissed him. A deep, long-drawn-out, sensual kiss that sent his senses reeling.

He pushed her away. 'Vera, we shouldn't be doing this.' He couldn't believe what he was saying. Here he was in a warm room with a practically naked, and it seemed all too willing, woman on his lap. She'd assured him there was no likelihood of their being disturbed and he was running scared. Was there something wrong with him? After all wasn't this every boy's dream? According to his cousin Eddie it was. Eddie was three years younger than him, and over a year ago he'd been boasting of his fleshy experiences with a naked chorus girl. The sum total of William's expertise was two quick kisses stolen from Tina Ronconi on the one occasion she'd escaped her brothers' vigilance.

But then, experience wasn't what mattered. At least that's how he, and his equally unworldly cousin Haydn, had consoled one another. It was the woman who was important. And he loved Tina. He'd told her as much. But . . .

'Will,' Vera slipped from the chair and knelt on the floor in front of him, her hands still resting lightly in his lap. 'You have no idea what it's like for me. You see, George . . .' her eyes looked at him, enormous, trusting pools of innocence. 'He's . . . he . . .' tears welled into her eyes once more, all the more poignant and pathetic for the dignified silence in which they fell.

'He what, Vera?' She looked so young, practically a child. She couldn't possibly have any idea what she was doing to him; what powers of restraint he was having to call upon as her fingers played restlessly against the front panel of his trousers.

'I expected so much when we married,' she murmured softly. 'I knew he was old, of course, but at the time that seemed to make it all the more exciting. I thought he'd be experienced. That he'd know what to do. I was even looking forward to it in a funny kind of way. You know what I mean, half frightened, half curious, not really knowing what to expect. But all he did on our wedding night, all he ever does—' a faint blush stole over he cheeks and she averted her gaze, staring down at the floor – 'is undress me. Then when I'm completely naked . . .' she looked at him again, 'I mean completely naked, he makes me lie down and he looks at me. Sometimes he touches me,' she took William's hand and pressed it against her breast, 'here, and—' she slid his fingers down over the silk to the top of her thighs – 'here. It's awful. Sometimes on a Sunday he won't allow me to dress at all. He even makes me cook and eat the dinner with no clothes on. And all he ever does is look and stroke. In the same way you'd pet a cat. Nothing more – nothing normal. You have no idea how it upset me at first. For weeks I could not stop crying. My mam doesn't know what goes on behind our curtains, but she did think that something was wrong. But when I tried to tell her about it, she wouldn't listen. All she did was remind me that I had made a promise in chapel to obey George, and that meant in every way. I went to the doctor and tried to talk to him, but he said it was my husband's right to do whatever he wanted with me, and my duty to put up with it. Then I saw my married sister. She said it shouldn't be like that. That there was something more. Much, much more.'

She lay back on the hearth-rug, watching him as he watched her. Then slowly, very slowly, she undid the knot on her dressing-gown belt. Sighing, she parted the two panels of silk.

Heart pounding, paralysed, William felt a certain sympathy with George. He couldn't have moved at that moment to save his life. He had been right. She was wearing nothing underneath the gown. And she was beautiful. Very beautiful. He gazed, mesmerised by the first naked female form he had seen off a picture postcard. Her breasts did point upwards, her skin was white, so fine there wasn't a single blemish to mar the perfection. He coloured as she looked up at him, then very slowly, quite deliberately she parted her thighs.

The word 'shameless' sprang to mind as he tried, and failed, to stop himself from staring. Then he remembered the life she led with her old, perverted husband, and felt ashamed of himself. George obviously thought no more of

Vera than the boys did of the women who posed naked for the photographs that were handed around the gym's changing room to the accompaniment of sniggers.

'Will.' She lifted her arms. 'Please. Show me that some men can do more than look.'

The next instant he was on top of her, his hands exploring every inch of her body, his fingers probing, lingering over the soft skin of her nipples, plunging down between her thighs. She moaned, and he moved back, tearing off his own clothes. His last thought, as he thrust into her, was of Tina. It was better for Tina, for both of them, that he went to their marriage bed with some experience. And with Vera married he wasn't taking any risks. None at all.

Chapter Six

HUDDLED INTO THEIR winter coats and stamping their feet in an effort to keep warm, Charlie and Evan shuffled impatiently along the line of men waiting to go in through the door of the New Town Hall.

'Mind how you go in there, Evan,' Constable Huw Davies, his sister-in-law Megan Powell's brother, called out as they inched their way past the group of policemen who had gathered in front of the closed box-office.

'I always do, Huw.' Evan raced up the wide stone steps and down the long, sloping corridor that led into the packed hall.

Unlike variety shows, the seats had been taken on a first-come first-served basis, and although Evan and Charlie had left Graig Avenue at five for the six o'clock political meeting, it obviously hadn't been early enough.

'Here?' Evan suggested, pointing to a bank of four seats still vacant in the centre of the last row of the stalls. Charlie nodded.

'Didn't expect to see you here, Charlie,' Billy Morris, a miner who had been on Evan's 'gang' when they'd worked in the Maritime pit, commented as Charlie slid into the seat beside him. 'After all, this isn't your fight, or even your country.'

'I said I'd be here.' Charlie's voice was ominously restrained.

'Looks like all the men on the Graig and half the men in the town are here,' Evan chipped in.

'Most of them wondering what a man's got to say that's worth paying a hundred pounds instead of the usual ten to rent this place on a Sunday night.' Billy pulled out his tobacco tin and filched a cigarette paper from his top pocket.

'Red Dai's stirring it up down the front.' Evan shifted in his seat, searching for a comfortable position for his long legs.

'The only thing he's likely to stir up is trouble.' Charlie looked around. It was obvious that the audience wasn't in an attentive frame of mind. He glanced behind him, wondering how many more people would be allowed in. Uniformed constables were filing in through the door, forming a line that effectively sealed off the back of the hall. A protesting voice that echoed in from the corridor outside was silenced as the door slammed. Metal bolts grated home, sealing in the audience.

Charlie glanced uneasily at Evan. The icy relationship between Evan and his wife had deteriorated even further since Trevor Lewis had brought them the news of their grandchild's condition. Usually calm and equitable in the face of whatever misfortune life threw at him, Evan had withdrawn into a morose brooding mood that no one, not even Eddie, William or Diana had been able to penetrate.

The hubbub of voices died as the side door nearest to the stage opened, and another small army of men, this time dressed entirely in black, began to enter.

'Good God, there's got to be close on a hundred of them,' Billy gasped as the door finally shut behind the blackshirts who'd lined up facing the audience in front of the stage.

'What's the matter, Mosley?' Red Dai, who'd picked up his nickname because of his loyalty to the Communist party, heckled. 'Scared to face us without a bodyguard?' he jeered at the empty stage.

The blackshirts snapped smartly to attention, their stern, set features glaring beneath their peaked caps towards a point somewhere at the back of the hall. Charlie turned again. The constables, arms folded, truncheons hooked at their belts, were staring impassively back.

The stage curtains were already open. A grey backcloth had been draped over the back wall and a row of chairs was ranged before it. In front of these stood a box-like stand, topped by a microphone. Muffled clankings and high-pitched screeches resounded from the orchestra pit.

'What the hell does he want a bloody orchestra for?' Billy bawled. 'Is he going to do a tap dance?'

Charlie didn't answer. He had a very real sense of foreboding. The tense atmosphere had heightened until it smouldered, an emotionally charged time-bomb. The first heated exchange would probably set it off.

The blackshirts stood at ease to a shouted command from their unit commander. They were an impressive sight. Not one of them under six feet, they were smartly turned out in brushed black shirts fastened by gleaming, polished buttons. They paraded in glaring contrast to the unemployed, shabbily dressed, Communist and Socialist miners who had queued since midday to pack the front rows of the stalls.

Half a dozen men, also in black shirts and trousers, walked on to the stage. A man Evan recognised as Mosley from newspaper photographs stepped forward and the orchestra struck up the opening bars of 'God Save the King'.

'That's not our bloody national anthem!' Dai yelled from the front row. 'Come on boys, let's give them ours.' He stepped forward, turned his back to the stage and waved his arms in the air. The audience, who had determinedly and quite deliberately sat through the orchestral overture of 'God Save the King', rose to a man and soon 'Land of my Fathers' echoed to the rafters, drowning out the strains of the orchestra and the Fascist voices.

Charlie, whose hearing was more acute than most, heard the sergeant behind him murmur, 'Steady lads.' He turned his head. The older policemen like Huw Griffiths were still standing sedately by, truncheons dangling from their belts. The younger ones were not so cool and composed. Most had unclipped their weapons and were holding them in both hands.

'It's just a singing contest, boys,' the sergeant muttered as the audience paused for breath between the first and second verses. 'You've seen them often enough in the bandstand in Ponty Park. Just think of it as the chapel versus the working men's club choir.'

Huw Griffiths nudged a rookie who'd stepped out of line, and Charlie watched as the boy retreated into the shadows at the back of the hall. The blackshirts stopped singing. Even the orchestra gave up trying to compete half-way through the second verse, but the men on stage remained on their feet waiting patiently for the audience to finish. The impromptu choristers, triumphant in their victory, sang their hearts out when they reached the final lines, raising the roof and deafening those, who like Charlie, didn't know the Welsh words.

Afterwards, the silence brought an uneasy sense of anti-climax. The singers shuffled awkwardly on their feet and looked to Dai for leadership.

He bowed, shouted, 'Well done boys!' and returned to his seat. Everyone in the auditorium followed suit, but Mosley wasn't a party leader for nothing. He stepped up to the microphone, and waited centre stage for absolute quiet.

'Ladies . . .'

'There are no ladies here,' Billy yelled. 'We've more bloody sense than to let them loose near a man like you. They'd skin you alive.'

A burst of laughter rocked the auditorium, and again Mosley waited for quiet.

'Gentlemen . . .'

'Why are we here, listening to the likes of him in a Town Hall that's been built with blood money earned on the backs of men who've given their lives for coal?' Dai shouted.

'He's right,' another echoed. 'No blackshirt's got a right to come here. There's nothing that he or any of his henchmen could say that would interest us.'

A crescendo of voices joined in from the auditorium.

'Everyone has the right to free speech,' Evan was on his feet shouting as loud as any of them. 'Without it—'

'Without it he'd be put in a camp where his bloody mate Hitler is starving and beating the Communists and Jews in Germany,' a voice to Evan's left screamed.

'What about the Jews, Mosley?' Dai taunted.

'Fascism means taking a pride in your country. It means a rebirth of nationalism . . .'

'It means torturing Jews!' Dai stepped threateningly towards the stage and a blackshirt grabbed him by the collar. The whole of the front row surged forward.

'Break it up!' The sergeant's voice carried above the hubbub as he used the loud-hailer he'd kept hidden at his feet. 'Break it up.'

The blackshirt reluctantly released his hold on Dai's collar. A dozen policemen moved down the central aisle and motioned Mosley's bodyguard to the side of the hall. Half of them moved, dragging their heels to the accompaniment of boos and jeers from the angry crowd.

'You're not wanted here. Any of you,' Billy yelled as the first of the line drew alongside the back row. 'Why did you bother to come?'

'You want jobs don't you?' the blackshirt shouted back in a cockney accent. 'A vote for Fascism is a vote for prosperity. Work, houses and cars for all those who are prepared to graft—' Boos interrupted his impromptu speech. He waited until they died down. 'What's the matter?' he mocked as soon as he could make himself heard. 'Are the miners of South Wales afraid of hard work? Is that why you're not even prepared to listen to what we have to say?'

'You bastard! What do you know about hard work? You ever been underground?' Billy vaulted over his seat and dived forward in a rugby-style tackle. Catching the blackshirt off guard, he head-butted him in the chest, bowling him over. Pressing his advantage he thumped his fists into the soft part of the man's stomach. Seeing the mass of blackshirts closing in behind Billy, Evan leaped over the back of his seat. Charlie tried to follow, but found himself jammed in by a solid wall of policemen surging forward from the back.

The sight of one of their own in difficulties enraged the blackshirts. Billy was felled to his knees by a well-aimed kick to the back of his leg. Evan reached him just in time to see a uniformed bodyguard swing a punch at Billy's head. All the pent-up anger and frustration of the past months exploded as Evan looked into the small eyes, pursed lips and fat face of the blackshirt.

An ardent Communist who had never missed a meeting except for those that had coincided with his shifts when he had been working, Evan fervently believed that the miners of Wales had suffered nothing but injustice at the hands of the English government for years. The pit closures had sapped pride, broken spirits and brought poverty, starvation rations, cold, the means test and the very real threat of the workhouse, to his own and every miner's family in the valleys. He was angry with everyone and everything: the government, for allowing the valleys to suffer; the town councillors who had rented Mosley the Town Hall, allowing him to spread his filthy creed in Pontypridd; his wife for her constant sighs of martyrdom and for blaming him for the joyless, daily grind of their existence; and a fate that had brought sorrow to his beloved daughter at what should have been the happiest time of her life. His temper snapped. He could do nothing to ease the greater miseries of his life, but he could do something about the bastards who were moving in on Billy.

He arced his fist wide, intending to land the blackshirt immediately behind Billy a punch on the nose. A young policeman, also seeing the threat to Billy, moved in on the blackshirt, pulling him aside just in time to receive the full force of Evan's blow on his temple.

Apart from four porters who'd called in for beans on toast before their late shift in the workhouse, Ronconi's café was empty, unimaginable on any normal Sunday evening. Tony paced restlessly from the counter to the kitchen and back, checking the stock of pies, pasties and Welsh cakes, chivvying Alma to peel more chips, hoping they'd have enough food to meet the demand of the rush he expected at the end of the meeting. He'd just picked up a clean, boiled rag to polish the steam urn when Eddie Powell burst through the door.

'Is Dad or Charlie here?' Eddie's collar was turned up in an attempt to disguise his boxing strip, but it was obvious from the way his coat flapped loosely around him that he had very few clothes on underneath it.

'No. Why, is the meeting over?'

'There's no getting near the Town Hall, Eddie.' William ran in behind him. 'The police have blocked off Market Square.'

'What's happening?' Tony asked.

'Wyn Rees couldn't get into the Town Hall earlier, so he and a couple of the boys hung around outside for a while,' William explained. 'The sergeant moved them on when they sent up to the police station for reinforcements, so Wyn and the others called into the gym . . .'

'Then trouble's broken out.'

'And my father and Charlie are in the middle of it.' Shivering, Eddie pushed his hands into his pockets as he sat down on the nearest chair.

'Both of them have got enough sense to stay out of any punch-ups.' Tony poured two teas and carried them over to Eddie's table. 'Which is more than I can say for you. I don't know about your mam, Eddie, but mine would kill me for walking around with no clothes on like that.'

'I was sparring when Wyn came in. I grabbed my trousers and coat and came here hoping to find Dad.' Eddie took the tea and sipped it.

'And I was playing cards in the changing rooms,' William complained. 'Wyn couldn't have picked a worse moment. I was just about to take a tanner off Dai Pickles—'

'Eggs and vinegar pickles?' Tony referred to the trader who sold eggs and vinegar on the streets of the town from the back of a horse-drawn cart.

'That's the one, and he can well afford a tanner.'

Eddie looked through the window and down the deserted street. 'You haven't seen anyone from the meeting then, Tony?'

'No one's been in here. It's been dead all night.'

'What do you think?' Eddie looked at William. 'Go back to Market Square?'

'I can't see the coppers changing their minds about letting us through so there's no point.'

'Well I'd best go back to the gym and dress. I can't go around like this all night.' Eddie finished his tea and pushed his chair beneath the table.

'Not if you don't want to get arrested.' Tony picked up the empty cup. 'That'll be a penny.'

'For what?'

'The tea.'

'I thought . . .'

'You thought I was running a charity shop?'

Eddie put his hand into his pocket only to realise he'd left his money, along with the rest of his clothes, in the gym. 'Will?' He appealed to his cousin.

'What am I, a bloody bank?' Will grumbled.

'I'll give it back.'

'The question is when.'

Eddie opened the door to the café. 'Crowd coming,' he shouted excitedly as a solid tide of men, flanked on both sides by police, marched up the centre of the bridge below the New Theatre.

'Are Uncle Evan and Charlie with them?' William joined him in the doorway.

'Some hope of seeing them in the middle of that lot, even if they are.'

'What's been happening, Uncle Huw?' Will shouted to Huw Griffiths.

'What we expected, a bust-up.' Huw Griffiths stood back from the crowd of marching men, close to the café door. 'We're escorting everyone from out of town to the station before any more heads get broken.' He nodded to one of the younger constables who moved into the middle of the road and directed the marching men to the right, into station yard.

'Have you seen Dad or Charlie?' Eddie asked.

'I saw them, but I've no idea where they are now.' Huw pushed back his helmet to reveal a massive, swollen bruise on his forehead.

'I bet that hurts,' Tony said as he joined them.

'It does, but not as much as the one I gave back.'

'To one of Mosley's blackshirts?' Will asked.

'To your next-door neighbour Viv Richards who was throwing out punches alongside them,' Huw answered sourly. 'That little fracas has really sorted out the black from the white sheep of this town.'

Andrew paused before his apartment. He bent his head and stared at the door for a moment before fumbling for his keys. It took him a full minute to find the right one. Lurching forward, he attempted to insert it into the lock. He missed – tried – and failed again. A door opened behind him. His neighbour peeped through the crack, her sleep-numbed face topped by a garish pink and green chiffon scarf wrapped round a mass of iron curlers.

'Good evening,' he slurred, his voice thickened by beer and whisky. The door slammed. 'Bloody neighbours,' he muttered without really knowing what he was saying. The truth of the matter was, even in his fuddled state he did care what the neighbours thought of him. But then London wasn't Pontypridd. No one ever spoke, not even to pass the time of day. Never said as much as 'Hello', 'Good morning' or 'Good-night'. The only consolation was they probably didn't speak to each other either. But then who would want to speak to him, he thought despondently, if they knew about his son.

Pushing a vision of the baby from his mind he swayed on his feet and squinted at his door again. It seemed to be moving. Normally he stuck to one, or at the most two beers in an evening, but this evening the pace had been set by his colleagues and he had found it difficult to resist the pressure to join in their rounds. They'd gone out to celebrate someone's impending marriage. He scarcely knew the bridegroom, but that didn't matter. It had seemed a good idea to go with the crowd after work instead of going home to Bethan.

He dived forward, dropping the coat which he had folded and slung over one shoulder. This time, more by luck than judgement, the key homed into the lock. He turned it and the door swung open. Scraping his coat from the floor he fell into the hallway. Switching on the light, he looked out to make sure he'd left nothing behind, then pulling out his key he unintentionally slammed the door noisily behind him.

He stood for a moment bracing himself, expecting a wail from the baby. When none came, he breathed a sigh of relief and opened the door to the living room. It was in darkness. He switched on the lamps and looked around. The fire had been banked down for the night and the guard hooked into place. The hearth was swept clean, the tiled fireplace sparkling, the cushions plumped up on the sofa. A vision of perfect domestic bliss; not much evidence of the luxury that came with the kind of wealth he aspired to, but all order and cleanliness. Damn Bethan for making him feel guilty, even now when he was falling down drunk!

He threw his coat and hat on the sofa and backed out of the door, hitting his shoulder painfully on the jamb. Cursing, he went into the bathroom, reached for the tooth mug and dropped it. It shattered on the tiled floor. He salvaged his toothbrush from the mess, rinsed it under the tap and scrubbed his teeth. He ran a sink full of cold water and plunged his face into it, soaking the front of his hair, but it didn't do any good. The room still revolved around him when he pulled out the plug.

Bethan lay in bed and listened to Andrew moving around the flat. From the curses and sounds of shattering glass she knew something was wrong. When he'd telephoned earlier to say he'd be late, he'd mentioned something about a stag party, but she didn't even recognise the name of the groom, and she'd realised then that he was simply making excuses again. It hurt knowing that he'd rather spend an evening with strangers than with her, but she hadn't protested. Merely told him to have a good time. After he'd hung up, she scraped the dinner she'd prepared into the bin and went to bed. Not that she'd slept. Dr Floyd, Andrew's superior, had also telephoned earlier in the evening to ask if she'd decided where to put the baby. If she hadn't, he knew of a suitable place in the West Country, and could arrange an introduction to the matron. Uncertain whether or not Andrew had spoken to Dr Floyd, she'd thanked him for his concern, told him the situation would soon be resolved and hung up. But as she listened to Andrew retching in the bathroom she knew it wasn't going to be resolved soon – or ever – unless she did something to resolve it.

She left the bed and wrapped her blue silk dressing gown around herself. Heart pounding, she padded softly towards the bathroom. Andrew hadn't closed the door. He was sitting on the side of the bath, the shattered mug on the floor at his feet, his head in his hands, tears oozing between his fingers.

She stepped back quickly, and went into the kitchen. Filling the kettle she put it on the gas stove to boil, then ground a handful of coffee beans. It was later than she'd thought. Three in the morning. Andrew was on duty at eight, and he'd have to be sober by then. The door swung open and she started, almost dropping the coffee pot.

'I was making you some coffee,' she said apologetically. 'I thought you'd need it.'

'You don't have to wait hand and foot on me.' He kicked out a chair from beneath the kitchen table and sat on it.

'I know, it's just that—'

'You think I'm incapable?'

'No.' Her hand shook as she emptied the drawer of the grinder into the coffee pot. She looked at him and realised that as the result of his anger, or his retching, or possibly a combination of both, he wasn't as drunk as she'd thought. 'We need to talk, Andrew,' she said, grasping the opportunity.

'There's no point. You know my feelings about the—'

'I'm sorry,' she broke in hastily, not wanting to hear the cold, clinical adjectives he used to describe her son. 'Please, I just need more time.'

'I could give you all the time in the world, it wouldn't make any damned difference!'

The kettle hissed on the stove. She didn't answer him because she knew he was right. Time wouldn't make any difference. In fact it would probably only serve to strengthen the bond that had grown between her and the baby.

Andrew sat back and stared at her. It was the first time he'd looked at his wife, really looked at her, since the day the baby had been born. The light silk gown clung to her waist and hips, flaring out around her legs. The creamy lace collar highlighted what little colour there was in her face. Her dark hair gleamed, waved, shining and freshly brushed. He could even smell her perfume. She certainly hadn't let herself go, he allowed grudgingly, as he felt the faint stirrings of a desire that had lain dormant for what suddenly seemed like far too long. She looked clean, wholesome – and so very different from the grubby, peroxide blonde showgirls who had joined his party for supper.

He reached out and pulled her close to him. Her dressing gown brushed against his cheek as he clung to her. Emotions he'd held in check since the baby's birth flooded back, liberated by a sudden, overwhelming pang of pure lust. He was beset by an uncontrollable urge to lose himself and all his problems in her; yet at the same time he felt an acute sense of loss for the warm, loving familiarity he associated with the old pre-maternal

Bethan. Feelings he sensed were now beyond recapture.

'We had so much,' he rose and caressed her face, cradling it close to his chest. 'Don't destroy it, darling. Please, I need you . . .'

The warmth of his fingers seared her flesh through the light silk. She had prayed that he would come to her for months, never dreaming that it would be like this, with him pleading – and half drunk.

'I'm . . .' she looked down into his deep brown eyes and the pain she saw mirrored in their depths touched a raw nerve of conscience. He closed his mouth over hers. She steeled herself to return his kiss, suppressing her revulsion at the smell of stale tobacco smoke and beer that clung to his breath.

'Bethan,' he murmured when he finally released her. 'It could always be like this, if only . . .'

The hiss of the kettle turned to a high-pitched whistle. She broke away from him, not wanting to hear his 'if onlys', wishing with all her might that their problems would fade away, but knowing they wouldn't. Not until she finally gave in and handed her son over to an institution.

She switched off the gas and poured boiling water into the coffee pot. She sensed Andrew watching her, but she couldn't, simply couldn't, bring herself to look at him. As soon as she'd made his coffee she returned to the bedroom, closing the door behind her before getting into bed.

She needed time to think, to prepare herself for the arguments she knew he'd confront her with in the morning, but he gave her no time. He followed her, slumped on the edge of the bed and stripped off his clothes. He tumbled down beside her and planted a kiss on her cheek. She opened her arms to him, hoping he wouldn't say any more. It was easier to cope without words.

What followed wasn't lovemaking. Not on her part. It was grim, mechanical, loveless sex. She sensed Andrew was using her to forget his problems, just as he'd used drink earlier. It was as simple as that. She knew as he pierced her body with his own that he would never have contemplated making love to her if he had been sober. That it was a combination of the drink and some other woman, probably a nightclub dancer or singer who had momentarily aroused his interest, that she had to thank for his attentions.

Andrew fell asleep while he was still on top of her. She rolled him over. He lay on his back, arms outstretched, insensible to her presence and to the world. She envied him his unconsciousness as she lay quietly beside him, remembering . . . and thinking.

In the hours that followed, somewhere high above the clouds that blanketed London, dawn broke. The gloom in the bedroom lightened from dark to pale grey. Indistinct shapes of bedroom furniture crystallised and became recognisable.

Bethan turned on her side and watched her husband as he slept. His handsome features relaxed, his lips slightly parted, his hair ruffled, falling low over his forehead. Drunk, careless of her feelings, too weak to cope with their child – she loved him with all her heart. Would always love him. But she also loved another. One who had no one else, and who needed her more.

Chapter Seven

'WHAT DO YOU reckon?' Viv Richards paced the cell in the basement of Pontypridd police station where he, Evan, Billy and Charlie had been held for the past two hours. 'Charge us, or let us off with a caution?'

Neither Evan Powell nor Billy answered him. Billy sat slumped in the corner, nursing his battered head in his hands. Evan was kneeling on the stone floor next to the bunk on which the police had dumped Charlie's semi-conscious figure.

'Well they can't do much to us, can they?' Viv argued. 'After all it was provocation. It would have been a peaceful meeting if it hadn't been for the police.'

'The police? It was those bloody blackshirts,' Billy began heatedly.

'Considering no one was listening to what they had to say . . .'

'They have nothing to say that's of any interest to us in the valleys.'

'Of course they do!' Viv contradicted him vehemently. 'We're working men with no work, aren't we? There were enough of those in Germany before Herr Hitler took over and look at the difference Fascism has made to their lives. We won the Great War, but they're the ones with the work, houses and if what I've heard is right, even cars. You won't find any bloody means tests, starvation wages or depression over there!'

'We'll have less of that language or you'll be facing more than one charge, Richards,' a constable's voice blasted into the cell from the corridor outside.

'If life's so grand over there, why don't you . . . go and

live there?' Billy demanded irately, only just stopping himself from swearing.

'I would if I could . . .'

'Doctor!' the same officious voice announced sharply as a key grated the lock. Evan looked up to see Doctor John, Bethan's father-in-law, follow a constable into the cell.

'Everyone who's fit outside,' the constable said gruffly.

Viv Richards immediately stepped out into the corridor. The doctor walked over to Billy and prodded a swollen cut above his eye.

'Does that hurt?'

'Yes.'

'And this?'

'Yes.'

'Follow my finger with your eyes.'

'Nothing seriously wrong with this one,' Doctor John pronounced a few moments later.

'Outside,' the constable commanded.

'Mr Powell, isn't it?' Evan heard the contempt in the doctor's voice.

'It is,' Evan lifted his chin defiantly.

'Are you hurt?'

'Just bruised.' Evan rose stiffly to his feet. The full force of one of the blackshirt's punches had landed on his chest. Every time he breathed he felt as though a knife was being twisted between his ribs.

'Strip off and I'll take a look.'

'It's nothing.' Evan would rather put up with his discomfort than submit to an examination by the man.

'Then outside,' the constable directed brusquely.

'I'm concerned about my friend,' Evan protested.

'He's the only one not facing any charges,' the constable volunteered to the doctor.

'Don't worry, Mr Powell. I'll take care of him,' Doctor John reassured him coldly.

Hearing voices, Charlie opened his eyes. He looked at Evan.

'Tell the family where I am,' Evan whispered as the

constable gripped the top of his arm ready to haul him away. 'All of them. And tell them not to worry,' he added wryly, remembering the punch he had let fly which had floored the young copper.

It was as much as Charlie could do to nod agreement as he swung his legs to the floor.

'Charlie?' Tony stared in horror at the apparition hovering in the doorway of the café. One sleeve of the Russian's overcoat was hanging off, attached to the shoulder only by the lining. A white bandage, only marginally lighter in colour than his face, was wrapped low around his forehead, completely covering his left eye. Dried blood streaked his blond hair and the left-hand side of his face, his lower lip was split and swollen, the shredded skin already turning a dark, bruised blue.

'Are Eddie and William here?' he mumbled, looking around the café with his uncovered eye.

'They're in the back. They've been looking for you. Alma!' Tony called out urgently as Charlie walked unsteadily forward.

'Bloody hell, what happened to you?' William dropped the cards he was holding in a fan, face up on the table much to Glan Richards's delight.

'Here, sit down.' Eddie pulled a chair out close to the fire. 'Can I get you something?' Wanting to ask after his father, but afraid of the answer he'd get, he tried to remember what Charlie preferred. 'Tea? Coffee?'

'I think he needs something stronger than tea.' Tony appeared with a small glass of amber-coloured liquid. Alma followed with a bowl of cold water and a cloth.

'I'm all right.' Despite his protestation Charlie took the glass Tony offered.

'Where's Uncle Evan?' William asked.

'And my father?' Glan Richards demanded.

'They're holding six men including Evan and Mr Richards until the magistrates' court opens tomorrow morning. They were about to charge them when they let me go.' Charlie jerked his head to one side as Alma dabbed at the dried blood on his cheek.

'I'm only trying to clean it up, it's still bleeding,' she protested.

'That's because the doctor reopened it when he dressed it,' Charlie replied, pain making him even terser than usual.

Rebuffed, she wrung the cloth out and handed it to him. All she could think of was the gossip, and her outcast status. Feeling more like a leper than ever, she picked up the bowl and returned to the kitchen.

'What are they charging them with?' Glan asked.

'No doubt we'll find out tomorrow.'

'What happened?' William demanded, wanting to hear all the gory details.

'There was a fight.'

'You don't have to tell me. Red Dai started it.' Glan clenched his fists as though he was ready to take on the entire Communist party single-handed.

'Billy did when he attacked a blackshirt.'

'Billy from Dad's gang?'

Charlie nodded. 'The other blackshirts moved in—'

'And of course everyone went to Billy's aid,' William chimed in derisively. 'Even Uncle Evan who'd normally walk a mile out of his way to avoid a fight. And he calls me hot-headed.'

'Did Dad get hurt?' Now it was Eddie who looked as though he was ready to take on the world.

'No, but he hit a policeman.'

'A policeman?'

'He meant to hit a blackshirt,' Charlie explained briefly.

'And my father?' Glan persisted, wishing anyone other than Charlie was sitting there. It was easier to get money out of the dole than words out of Charlie.

'I only know they're holding him.'

'What will they do to Dad, Charlie?' Eddie ventured, dreading the answer. 'They can't put him away, can they?'

'I don't know Eddie,' Charlie replied slowly. 'I really don't know.'

At half-past five the milk cart rattled past the apartment block and the baby began to whimper. Bethan had been lying in bed, awake, waiting for the cry. Carefully, so as not to disturb Andrew, she stole from between the sheets and out of the bed. Picking up her nightdress and dressing gown from the floor she crept into the bathroom to wash her hands before making up the baby's feed. She put the kettle on to boil, then went into the nursery. He was lying just as she'd left him the night before, on his back in the bottom of the cot, his eyes open but unfocused as he made the soft mewing noises that normally preceded his cry.

She lowered the side of the cot and lifted him out, cuddling him close as she laid a rubber sheet over his eiderdown. Despite Edmund's lack of response she took her time over changing him: tickling his tummy, kissing his hand, reciting the same nursery rhymes and Welsh words of endearment that her grandmother had sung to her. When she'd finished she picked him up again and left him to kick on the floor while she took the soiled nappy to the bucket she kept outside on the balcony. After washing her hands yet again, she returned with his bottle and settled into the comfortable rocking chair that she and Andrew had bought together in that happier time, when it had not occurred to either of them that the child they were expecting would be born any way other than perfect.

The baby fell asleep in her arms before he finished half of the four ounces of milk. Usually she left him, but today was different. The events of the night preoccupied her. The late-night conversation and the lacklustre sex that had followed made her strangely reluctant to face Andrew. So for once she remained in her chair, quietly rocking the sleeping baby, wishing some miracle could make him well and strong.

At six o'clock the baby went rigid in her arms. She knew what to do. Fighting the urge to panic she rushed into the bathroom and ran a sinkful of warm water. She plunged him into it, clothes and all, careful to hold his head above the water.

'Convulsions?'

She didn't look away from Edmund, but she was conscious of Andrew standing behind her.

'Yes,' she admitted.

'You want me to look at him?'

'No. This always works.'

'He might need an injection of morphine.'

'They're never bad enough for that.'

'Then this isn't the first?'

'I mentioned them to the paediatrician when I took Edmund back to the hospital for his check-up,' she replied defensively.

'If you hadn't been a nurse you would have had to give him up at birth. You do know that, don't you?'

'But I am a nurse. And these convulsions are not that bad . . .'

'They're not good either, Bethan. Neither is his prognosis. When will you listen to sense?'

'Andrew please, we've been through all this before.' Tears fell from her eyes into the water that lapped around the relaxing figure of the baby.

'And we'll continue to go through it until you make the right decision. For his—' he pointed to the baby – 'welfare as well as your own. Tonight,' he insisted firmly, 'when I come home we'll discuss it. No more excuses, no more putting off what has to be done. You'll make your choice of place. God only knows I've brought enough brochures home. And when you've decided, we'll take him there. Together.'

He turned on his heel and returned to their bedroom. She lifted Edmund from the sink on to her lap, pulled out the plug and wrapped a towel round him. Retreating to the nursery she undressed and dried him, covering him with a thick, clean towel and blanket. She sought the sanctuary of the rocking chair, holding the baby close while she listened to Andrew moving around in their bedroom.

Obviously he hadn't gone back to sleep. When the alarm clock rang at six-thirty it was promptly switched off. She heard his footsteps in the small hall as he went to run his bath. She followed his movements in her mind's eye as he washed, shaved, dressed, combed his hair and splashed cologne on his chin; all the small routine tasks she had loved to watch when they had first been married.

She waited for him to go into the kitchen. Normally she would have cooked him bacon, eggs and toast by now. Before the baby had been born, this had been one of her favourite times of the day. They had sat and talked while Andrew ate. Discussing everything – and nothing in particular: the headlines in the paper, childhood reminiscences, amusing stories about his patients and the internal politics of the hospital he worked in. But they hadn't enjoyed a breakfast like that in months. Since the birth of the baby he had taken to eating in a silence she hadn't found the courage to brave.

Eventually the front door banged. A pang of guilt beset her as she realised he had left without eating anything. But still she lingered in the chair. Andrew might have forgotten something, he might return . . . The minutes ticked by. Five . . . ten . . . only then did she rise and return her sleeping child to his cot with an anxious check, just to make sure he was breathing.

She picked up the half-finished bottle and went into the kitchen. The coffee she had made the night before stood, cold and untouched in the pot. She emptied it down the sink. She had to think, plan out exactly what she was going to do. She tidied the kitchen and walked through the small inner hallway. The doors to all the rooms except the baby's were open. She saw their unmade bed, a thin patina of dust on the linoleum beneath it. The fire had gone out in the living room and the hearth was covered with ashes and coal dust. She couldn't leave the flat untidy for Andrew to return to after a hard day's work. That simply wouldn't be fair. But it would mean her catching a later train and not getting home until late in the evening . . .

Home – a train journey away. Money! Everything she had was in her purse. Seventeen shillings and sixpence housekeeping that was supposed to last her until Friday. Third class to Pontypridd was at least twice that amount. She could hardly go around the transport cafés looking for a lift with the baby. All the bank and cheque books were in Andrew's name.

Her heart sank at the thought of having to stay here until Andrew came home to coldly, calmly and logically discuss the removal of Edmund from their daily lives. She must have something she could sell or pawn. Her wedding ring caught the light, gleaming on her left hand. She could hardly carry a baby home without a ring, but she did have a gold and blue enamelled antique locket that Andrew had given her. It had cost twenty pounds, and she loved it, not because it had been expensive and was the only piece of good jewellery she possessed, but because Andrew had given it to her before she had become pregnant. If she pawned it, she could lose it for ever, but she consoled herself with the thought that she could send the ticket to Andrew. If it meant as much to him as it did to her he would redeem it; if it didn't, then it might be as well that she had no tangible memento of their early relationship. Either way, she had no choice. She couldn't stay here knowing how much the baby's presence upset Andrew, any more than she could abandon Edmund.

Still in her nightdress and dressing gown she picked up a duster and mop and attacked the bedroom. Stripping the bed, she cleaned the room thoroughly before remaking the mattress with fresh sheets. Filling the bath with water and soapsuds she threw the sheets and all the white washing she could find into it and left them to soak. Then she tackled the feeding bottles. It was a long journey from Paddington to Pontypridd: it might mean six or even more hours travelling. She had four bottles, and to be on the safe side she decided to fill them all.

The baby woke again at eight, taking her completely by surprise. She was on the balcony, pegging the sheets, nappies and collars on the washing line and hadn't realised it was so late. Not only had she finished the washing, she had also laid the fire in the living room. All that Andrew need do when he came home was put a match to it.

She lifted Edmund's small tin bath into the larger bath and filled it, deciding to wash him before giving him his feed. She splashed water over his fingers and toes and told him about the trip they were about to make as he lay back listless and unresponsive on her arm. Another four ounces of milk and she could have her own bath, and begin packing.

As she lifted down her old cardboard suitcase from the top of the wardrobe she remembered Andrew's dinner. He would be hungry when he came home. She ran to the pantry. There was a cold meat and potato pie she had made yesterday for his supper. If she peeled some fresh vegetable to go with it he could eat that. She looked along the shelves: a madeira cake and half a loaf of bread, fresh fruit, butter in the butter dish – he had enough to see him through tonight and knowing Andrew, he'd make other arrangements tomorrow, with his sister Fiona, or with one of the clubs his colleagues belonged to.

Packing didn't take long. Setting aside one of her three sets of underclothes and the coat and dress Andrew had bought for her wedding outfit, which she intended wearing, all she had left to fold in the suitcase was a blue serge skirt, a white blouse, her remaining underclothes and her old ringed black velvet dance dress. She looked at the two maternity dresses in the wardrobe. Deciding they could be cut down, she tossed them into the case. There was still room for a dozen of the baby's nappies and his spare towel. She closed the case and looked around for something to pack the baby's clothes in. There were only

Andrew's leather suitcases and she didn't want to take anything of his, so she settled on a roomy shopping bag. Carrying it into the baby's bedroom she folded the contents of his chest of drawers into it.

She bathed, dressed, combed her hair, and put on a little make-up, then prowled restlessly around the flat, checking for dust with her finger, making doubly sure that everything was neat and tidy. Finally she stood in the middle of the living room, holding her hat and coat, imagining Andrew walking through the door. Would he call her name? Look for her? Would he open the door to the baby's room, the room he hadn't entered since Edmund had occupied it? Would he wonder where she was? Miss her even?

She went to the sideboard drawer and pulled out the writing pad she used to write her letters home. Opening her handbag she took out the fountain pen her father had bought her the day she'd passed her eleven-plus and been accepted for grammar school. He had been so proud of her then. If only he were here now, to hug her, and tell her that she was doing the right thing. She poised the nib over the pad, and her mind went blank. It was ridiculous. She and Andrew were married, had made a child together, she loved him. There had to be something she could say. She began to write

Dear Andrew
There is a meat pie in the oven that can be heated up, and vegetables prepared on the stove. All you have to do is light the gas. I'm sorry I'm not here, but I am taking the baby home with me for a while. Should you want to get in touch you can write to me at my father's house. Please don't follow me, it's probably best that we both have some time away from one another to think things out.
I love you.
Bethan

The baby began to cry. Bethan laid the pad with her

note turned uppermost in the centre of the table and went to him. She fed and changed him, dressing him in a warm set of hand-knitted clothes that Laura had made, the only present anyone had sent her after he had been born. Wrapping him in the bedclothes from the cot she tucked him into his pram and wheeled him through to the outer hall. She laid the shopping bag at his feet, put on her coat and hat, and picked up her suitcase and handbag.

Her wedding ring was on her finger, her locket safely tucked in its box in her handbag. She was ready. The clock in the living room struck the hour. If she was to reach home today she'd better get going. She wheeled the pram through the front door and closed it behind her. She looked at the keys in her hand, then pushed them through the letterbox. There was no turning back. Not now.

'Six months' hard labour.'

'What?' Eddie turned his shocked face to Huw Griffiths.

'The magistrates' verdict. The others got six months for assault, your father got the same with hard labour because he hit a policeman as opposed to a blackshirt.'

'How come they've been sentenced already?' Eddie demanded. 'I thought the courts didn't open until ten o'clock.'

'They were expecting trouble, so they convened at six to deal with the cases from the Town Hall.'

'Where's Dad now?' Eddie asked.

'Waiting to be taken to Cardiff prison.'

'Can we see him?' Charlie spoke slowly. His head was still aching from the pounding he'd received the day before.

'Officially the answer's no, but I'll see what kind of a mood the Super's in.' Huw left the high counter in the reception area of the police station, and disappeared into the back. He emerged a few moments later. 'Super says you can have five minutes. But I warn you, the Black Maria's expected any minute, and when it comes you'll have to go.' He opened the flap in the counter, and Charlie stepped back to allow Eddie through first. They didn't have far to walk. Evan, Billy and Viv Richards were sitting in a row with three others on a hard bench in the corridor outside the reception room, their wrists linked together with cuffs, a policeman on guard duty beside them.

'Evan?'

Evan looked up. He tried to smile when he saw Charlie and Eddie behind Huw.

'You're the last people I expected to see,' Evan murmured. 'Not that I didn't hope you'd come.' He rose to his feet, but the handcuffs hampered the movement of his arms.

'No touching the prisoner,' the duty constable commanded sharply.

'Sorry, my fault.' Evan sank back down on the bench.

'Dad we'll get a solicitor . . . we'll . . .' Eddie clenched and unclenched his hands. Used to settling his problems with his fists, he felt helpless in the presence of so many policemen.

'You'll do no such thing, boy. No sense in throwing good money away.' He looked past Eddie to Charlie. 'There's nothing to be done. I hit him, I pleaded guilty, and the least I can do now is take my punishment like a man.'

'But Dad . . .'

'Six months will soon pass. You'll tell everyone I'm fine?'

'Everyone,' Eddie echoed dully, not realising his father was speaking to Charlie.

'All the family?' Evan repeated.

'I'll tell them,' Charlie promised.

'How is Elizabeth taking it?'

'Mam, like all of us thought you were only going to be kept in overnight,' Eddie murmured miserably.

'Then she's going to have to wait a while before giving me what for. That's almost worth serving six months' hard labour.' Evan smiled wryly. 'And you,' he nodded to his son. 'No late nights for six months. You take the cart out every day, rain or shine, and make enough to keep the mortgage paid. Nothing else matters, do you hear me? We'll be all right as long as we keep a roof over our heads.'

'I'll try, Dad.'

'Don't worry,' Charlie pushed his hands deep into his pockets. 'I'll see it's paid.'

'With *my* money,' Evan insisted. 'You're a good mate, Charlie, but we've borrowed too much off you already.'

'You've always paid me back.'

The steel double doors at the end of the corridor opened. The duty constable stepped out and pegged them against the outside wall. A van drew close to the opening, obliterating the small square of grey concrete yard and blue sky. The back door of the van opened from the inside and another constable stepped out.

'Move along there. Look sharp.'

Eddie stared at the steel cage inside the van; at the utility metal benches bolted to the floor either side of the back.

'Time you were gone.' Huw Griffiths laid a hand on Eddie's shoulder.

'We'll visit you, Dad. Just as soon as we're able,' he called out as Evan shuffled into the van with the others.

'Don't worry about me. Just keep the bills paid.'

'Someone's going to have to tell Mam,' Eddie said as he and Charlie walked outside into the thin, early spring sunshine.

'It would be best coming from you.'

'But you'll be with me?'

'If you want.'

'Not now.' Eddie balked at the idea of walking back up the Graig hill to tell his mother the news. He would have nothing to do for the rest of the day except sit around the house and listen to her moans. 'Later. I'll take out a cart . . .'

'They'll have all gone for the day.' Charlie led the way across the road and down the Co-op Arcade.

'The best rigs will have,' Eddie conceded. 'But if I take out whatever's left I can stick close to home. Do Maesycoed. Anything I make has got to be better than nothing.'

'It'll have to be better than sixpence or you'll be worse off,' Charlie pointed out practically. 'And your mother won't be very happy if she finds out about your father from someone else.'

'She won't. No one else knows except us.'

'It'll soon be all over town.'

'I may stop off home for dinner.'

Seeing that Eddie wasn't to be dissuaded, Charlie put his hand in his pocket. 'Here's sixpence,' he said, handing Eddie the rental money for the cart.

'It's all right, I've got some left from the money I get for cleaning the gym.'

'You sure?'

'I'm sure. You going back to the slaughterhouse?'

'I've some business to see to first.' Charlie turned left at the foot of the arcade. 'Are you all right?'

'I'm fine.'

Eddie thought about the look on his father's face as they had led him away. Despite Charlie's support he had never missed his brother and sisters so much. Seventeen years of age, an experienced boxer who had the reputation for never turning down or backing away from a fight, he was still absolutely terrified of facing his mother's wrath alone.

Chapter Eight

'YOU DON'T SEEM to know what to do with yourself, Vera.' Mondays had been special to George Collins since he was seventeen and his father had died, forcing him to take over the family business. It was his only real day of rest, one on which he didn't even have to go to chapel. A day which set him up for the busy week ahead. He worked from dawn until after nine on market days running his cheese stall, and delivering dairy goods to the valley corner shops in his van on the others. Monday he could put his feet up, read his library books, have a sort through his stamp collection, or play with the train set he had bought himself for his fortieth birthday and hadn't dared look at since Vera had moved into the house, lest she mock his childishness.

'I'm bored, George,' Vera complained, swinging her long legs over the arm of the easy chair she was sitting in. She screwed the top back on a bottle of nail varnish. Blowing on her fingers she wiggled them in front of his eyes. 'Scarlet passion, do you like it?'

'Very nice.' He pushed his glasses further up his nose and returned to his stirring tale of a shootout in downtown Dodge City.

'George?'

'Yes?' He wrenched himself away just as the hero had been forced to pull out his gun in response to the villain's threatening behaviour towards the schoolmarm.

'Take me somewhere.'

'You mean a ride. Out in the van?'

'I don't like the van,' she sighed impatiently. 'I wish we had a car.'

'We'll be able to afford one soon, if we're careful with money,' he said tersely.

'Well it's not very nice for me, is it? Sitting up on display in the front seat of a van for all the world to see. I don't know why you had to buy a van instead of a car in the first place.'

'I bought it to make deliveries, Vera. I need the loading space in the back.'

'I suppose you do.' She stood up, turned her back to him, and looked out of the window. 'It's chilly in here.' She walked over to the fire and lifted her skirt to her thighs, warming the backs of her legs in front of the flames.

'We could go up to Llanwonno for a walk. It's a quiet run and there won't be many around to see you sitting in the van. It's a pretty place.' He gave up on his book and shut it. 'Mother liked going there. There's a pretty church, old too, and some of the tombstones—'

'I don't want to see tombstones, George.' Vera plucked her skirt higher so he could see the fine lace that trimmed the legs of her French silk knickers. 'I want to see life while I'm still young enough to enjoy it.'

'If it was summer we could go to Barry, or Porth-cawl . . .' his voice tailed away. She *was* his wife, and they were alone. But after his mother's puritanical propriety he found Vera's blatant exhibitionism embarrassing.

'But it's not summer, George.'

'No I suppose it isn't.' He swallowed hard as she adjusted a stocking top. 'I know, how about we go down to Cardiff? I could buy you tea in the Lyons.'

'And take me to the shops?' she asked excitedly.

'If you want to,' he agreed doubtfully. Vera certainly wasn't the manager his mother had been. He hadn't saved a penny of his weekly income since the day they'd married. He'd even had to dip into his hard-earned capital, and that worried him. The van wouldn't last for ever. And he really ought to invest in one of those new cool-boxes to keep the stock fresh, and then there was that car she was always on about . . .

'There's a darling spring outfit advertised in the *South Wales Echo*. It's London made. You can see it in the cut of the cloth. Real crache. Real style. Howell's are stocking it . . .'

He blanched. Howell's was the most expensive shop in Cardiff. He couldn't understand why Vera didn't buy her clothes in the Co-op. His mother had, and everyone had always said she was a smart woman. Everyone, that is, except Vera. The first thing she'd done after they'd got married was give his mother's entire wardrobe to her mother. And although he couldn't be sure, he had his suspicions that some of the clothes had ended up on Wilf Horton's stall.

'. . . and it's only eight pounds, George.'

'Eight pounds!'

'You *do* want your wife to look nice, don't you George?' She leaned forward and twiddled her fingers in the short hair at the nape of his neck.

'Of course I do.' He couldn't resist her, that was the problem. He left his chair and slipped his hands around her waist.

'Not now, George. Not if we're going to Cardiff. Besides, you know I don't like you touching me in the kitchen. What if one of the neighbours looks in through the window?'

'I know,' he sighed. Twice in four months. All the touching she'd allowed him. Still, he had to be patient. She *was* very young. He had no right to expect too much. Not all at once. And perhaps if he bought her the outfit . . .

'Where did you spring from?' Elizabeth asked her daughter as Bethan walked into the kitchen carrying her baby.

'The station.' Bethan laid Edmund down on the easy chair closest to the stove.

'You travelled up on the train today?'

'All day, and it feels like weeks,' Bethan answered wearily.

'How did you get up here from the station?'

'I walked as far as Laura and Trevor's. He was in, so he brought me up in the car.'

'You called in on them before coming here?'

'The pram wouldn't fit in the station taxi. Trevor only just got it into his boot, and then he couldn't close it.'

'I can see you're used to London ways, thinking nothing of throwing your money away on a taxi. I only wish I had a shilling for every time I had to push a pram up and down that hill, and not with just one tired baby in it either.'

Bethan was too tired to snipe back. It had taken longer than she'd expected to find a pawn shop willing to give her anything for her locket, and even then she'd had to settle for six pounds, not the ten she'd hoped for. She had caught the eleven o'clock train out of London but it had been delayed in Reading, and having to change in Bristol had seemed like the last straw. She had spent an hour huddled on a bench close to the fire in the ladies' waiting room waiting for the next train to Cardiff. And there she'd had to change, not only trains but platforms, humping the pram and suitcase up and down two flights of stairs with the help of a passing stranger.

She had negotiated the top step of the Rhondda and Pontypridd platform just in time to see the engine steaming gently out of the station. She had felt like screaming, but forced to accept the inevitable, she had wheeled the pram into yet another miserable 'Ladies Only' waiting room, and fed and changed Edmund while waiting.

Exhausted and reckless enough to order a taxi when she finally reached Pontypridd, she had almost resorted to tears when the pram refused to fit into the cab. Strapping her suitcase to the pram handle with the belt from her dress, she balanced the shopping bag and pushed the pram up the Graig hill, practically falling into Laura's arms when she reached Graig Street. And despite the stew and sympathy Laura and Trevor had fed her, she still felt on the verge of collapse.

'I expect you could do with a cup of tea?' Elizabeth moved slightly so she could sneak a look into the bundle of shawl and blankets Bethan had set on the chair, but all she could make out was the top of a small head covered in light, downy hair.

'Tea would be nice,' Bethan murmured, sitting down.

'You staying long?'

'For a while.'

'Something wrong between you and Andrew?' Elizabeth asked bluntly.

'No. I just wanted to come home for a few days. London isn't like Pontypridd. It's noisy. There's no fresh air there. I felt as though I couldn't breathe.'

'Well, if it's fresh air you want there's plenty of that around here, but precious little else is being given away for nothing. I hope you can support yourself while you're here. Your father still doesn't bring in enough to keep the house going.'

'I can support myself and the baby.' Bethan looked down at her wedding ring and wondered what she'd get for it in Arthur Faller the pawnbroker's in Pontypridd.

'Elizabeth!'

'That's Mrs Richards from next door. I don't doubt she saw you coming in here and wants a look at the baby. Being the way he is I'd keep him covered up if I were you,' Elizabeth advised. She opened the passage door and called down to her neighbour, 'Come in.' That in itself was a novelty on the Graig where most of the neighbours were in and out of each other's back kitchens at all hours of the day and night. It was a practice Elizabeth had actively discouraged, and as a concession her neighbours generally came no further than the hall unless they knew Evan was in.

'What do you think?' Mrs Richards walked into the kitchen. She paused, taken aback by the sight of Bethan sitting with the baby on her lap in Evan's chair, but she wasn't to be put off her stride by asking questions that could wait. 'They tried our men early this morning. They all got six months, your Evan and my Viv included.'

'Six months?' Elizabeth echoed uncomprehendingly. Charlie had told her Evan was being kept in the cells overnight so the police could get to the bottom of what had happened in the Mosley meeting. She'd assumed he'd witnessed a fight, nothing more.

'Not that my Viv got hard labour, mind.' Mrs Richards folded her arms across her ample bosom. 'Your Evan did. But then he hit a policeman.'

'My father hit a policeman?' This time it was Bethan who was shocked.

'Oh Elizabeth,' Mrs Richards flopped her ample body down on the nearest chair. 'What are we going to do?' she wailed theatrically.

'At least your Glan is in work,' Elizabeth said acidly, her thoughts turning to money. They had just about scraped by on what Evan brought in from his carting round. How on earth was she going to manage with just the lodgers' money coming in?

'Do you want to see the costume and hat on me?'

'Seeing as how I've paid for them, I suppose I may as well.'

George was angry. His wallet was twenty, not eight pounds, lighter because Vera had seen a hat, shoes, handbag, gloves and bracelet that she'd wanted every bit as much as the costume. She'd pleaded so eloquently he hadn't really minded. Not when he was handing the money over, but then he'd turned just in time to see one of the male floorwalkers looking up Vera's skirt as he bent to pick up the handkerchief she'd dropped at his feet. And as if that hadn't been enough, Vera had stepped quite deliberately forward, in his opinion, to give the man an even better view. There'd been no question of tea in Lyons. He'd felt like hitting Vera for the first time in his married life. Restraining himself, he'd frogmarched her to the van, pushed her inside and driven straight home. And even now the minx had the gall to behave as though nothing had happened.

'Why don't you come up to the bedroom, George?' Vera called out seductively as she climbed the stairs. Despite her brave front, she realised she'd gone too far. It wasn't like George to sulk for so long.

'You come down here,' he replied gruffly, returning to his seat in the kitchen and his book.

'I'll only be a minute.'

She thought rapidly as she closed the curtains in the bedroom. Her mother had promised to leave an Irish stew and an apple tart in the pantry. All she had to do was warm them up in the oven. She was absolutely hopeless at all things domestic, a fact she only managed to keep from George with the complicity of her mother. All the cooking and cleaning in the household was done by her mother in exchange for a more than generous remuneration. But judging by the look on George's face, it was going to take a lot more than an Irish stew and apple tart to make him happy this time.

She stripped down to her stockings, suspender belt and French knickers. Slipping on the formal tailored jacket and skirt, she admired her profile in the cheval glass. The suit was pale grey with navy blue edging. 'Very chic,' she murmured repeating a phrase the salesgirl had used. She balanced the hat on her head, picked up her new handbag and gloves, slipped on her shoes and walked down the stairs.

'What do you think?' She paraded in front of George.

'All right.' He barely glanced up from the page.

'George.' She went to him, took his book from his hands and sat on his lap. 'Please, don't be a grumplestilskin,' she pleaded in a squeaky childish voice that had charmed him when she'd been younger.

'I've every right to be furious,' he replied refusing to be mollified.

'Not over this outfit. It will last for years and years . . .'

'Have you made tea?'

'Irish stew and apple tart. They're in the pantry. I'll put them in the oven now. They only need warming up.'

'When did you make them?'

'This morning. When you were putting the coal in,' she lied.

He looked over her head trying to ignore the warmth of her body on his lap. She might be a spendthrift, but at least she managed to keep the house clean and decent food on the table, he decided grudgingly. Pity she couldn't keep away from other men.

'George.' Her lips pouted very close to his. 'George, please don't be angry. I didn't know that man was looking up my skirt. Honestly!'

'But you should have realised . . .'

'You know how trusting I am. I expect all men to be like you, George.' She wriggled on his legs until her skirt rode high over her thighs. It was going to crease, but her mother could always iron it. She saw him staring at the expanse of white flesh above her stocking top. 'See what I mean, George,' she cooed. 'Most men would be taking advantage of me by now. You never have. And you're the only man I've ever really known. If I'm too trusting it's your fault.'

'You got a petticoat on?'

'I wore a thick flannel one to Cardiff. I had to take it off to try this on. The skirt wouldn't have hung right with it underneath.' She moved again, slipping precariously. He put his hand on her hip to catch her before she fell.

'You're not wearing any bloomers either,' he said accusingly.

'Yes I am. I'm wearing the silk ones my sister gave me for Christmas. See.' Like a little girl showing off, she lifted her skirt above her waist.

'Vera . . .' he babbled, aroused beyond logic.

'Do you want your Irish stew now, George?' she asked innocently.

'I think I want something else.'

She hung her head modestly.

'I *am* your husband Vera,' he reminded her.

'Of course you are, George. And I promised to obey

you. It's just that I don't like you talking about anything . . . like that.'

'Nor should any decent woman,' he reassured her as she climbed from his lap. 'Vera?'

'Yes George,' she murmured as she preceded him up the stairs.

'Do you think you could take all your clothes off this time?'

'Oh George.'

He felt an absolute brute as he heard a tremor in her voice. 'It doesn't matter.' He resigned himself to having to deal with her modesty.

'Well, perhaps if you switch the light out, George,' she agreed meekly as she turned back the blankets on the bed.

Elizabeth sat on one of the hard, upright kitchen chairs, her hands clasped together on the table, knuckles white with strain.

'I'll never be able to hold my head up in this town again. And to think my own son allowed Maggie Richards to be the one to tell me! Why didn't Eddie come back this morning? That was the least he could have done.'

'Mrs Richards has only just heard about the sentence, and her husband's involved just as much as Dad. Perhaps Eddie didn't find out anything this morning, and maybe he still doesn't know,' Bethan suggested mildly, her sympathies lying entirely with her brother. If she had been given the choice between carrying news of her father's trial and imprisonment to her mother, or running off to wherever Eddie was hiding, she knew which she would have chosen.

'Eddie must have known about the sentence,' Elizabeth protested. 'He and Charlie left here at seven for the police station.'

'It's possible the court hadn't finished by then—'

'Then they should have gone on to the court!'

Knowing there'd be no reasoning with Elizabeth in her present mood, Bethan opened the kitchen door and went down the passage. The pram and her suitcase were still outside under the bay window where she had left them. The bag containing the baby's things was just inside the front door. Edmund needed to be changed and fed, and his bottles were dirty. The soiled nappies from the journey were wrapped in a rubber sheet. So much had to be done, and she was absolutely and completely exhausted.

'You've always taken your father's and the boys' part against me,' Elizabeth said angrily when Bethan returned to the kitchen with the shopping bag.

'Mam, we won't know anything for certain until Eddie comes home.' She glanced at the baby to make sure he was in no danger of rolling off the chair, then she picked up the kettle.

'I suppose you want tea? A time like this and all you can think about is your stomach.'

'The baby needs changing and feeding. I need boiling water to wash his bottles.'

'There's plenty in the boiler in the stove, but then, I suppose that won't be good enough for you.'

'I'd prefer it on the boil,' Bethan said. 'It sterilises better.'

'There's no bed made up for you,' Elizabeth announced, almost triumphantly. 'Diana's in your old room.'

'Then I'll share with her.'

'You and the baby?' Elizabeth scorned. 'I can't see Diana being enamoured with the thought of sharing with a baby that cries every four hours.'

'He's slept right through for the last month.' Bethan struggled to keep her temper in check.

'I suppose Diana could move back into the box room. But don't expect me to start changing bedclothes around at this time of day.'

'If there's a bed in the box room I'll make it up as soon as I've seen to the baby.'

'There's nowhere for him to sleep, either down here or

up there,' Elizabeth persisted, venting her frustration on her daughter. 'I kept the cot you all slept in as babies, but your father threw it out when he cleared the box room so Diana could move into the house.'

'I have a pram,' Bethan said coldly, more angry with Elizabeth's indifference towards Edmund than with the cold reception she was extending towards her.

'A pram? How big a pram? One of those ridiculous coach jobs that will scratch all the paintwork in the hall, I suppose.'

'It is big,' Bethan conceded.

'Where is it now?'

'Outside the front door.'

'For all the neighbours to see that you've left your husband and come running home. As if they won't have enough to talk about with your father's doings.'

'I haven't left Andrew,' Bethan remonstrated.

'Well I know the neighbours around here, Miss, even if you don't. And that's what they'll be saying, especially with you producing a child like that . . .'

'I'll see to the bottles.'

Not trusting herself to remain in the same room as her mother a moment longer, Bethan carried her bag into the washhouse. She didn't know what she'd expected when she'd run home on impulse. Her thoughts had all been centred on her father; his strength, his support. Now that he wasn't here and she was faced with her mother's carping about everything from her father to their lack of money, she didn't know what to do, or where to turn. She only knew she was too drained to spare a thought for the appalling predicament her father was in, let alone cope with what was expected of her. Even the simple, mechanical things like seeing to the baby, feeding him, bathing him, washing his clothes, loomed over her, chores that demanded far more energy than she possessed.

She rinsed out the bottles with cold water and left them to soak, delaying her return to the kitchen until the mounting steam began to rattle the kettle lid. Thankfully there was no sign of her mother, and when she heard a creak overhead she assumed that Elizabeth had taken refuge in her bedroom. The baby was lying where she had left him on the chair. The one good thing about having a child like Edmund, she thought bitterly, was he always stayed where he was put.

She washed and scalded the bottles and made up two feeds before venturing back down the passage and opening the front and parlour doors. Moving her mother's prized octagonal mahogany table aside, she wheeled her pram into the parlour and dumped her suitcase next to it. One thing at a time ... wash ... change ... feed and afterwards if there was time before she had to begin all over again – rest.

'Beth? Is that really you?' Eddie flicked on the light as he walked into the kitchen. Bethan started, clutching the baby closer to her. He wailed and Eddie smiled.

'I knew it had to be you when I saw the pram and suitcase in the parlour. Did you come because of Dad? How did you know about it? How did you get here so quickly? It's great to see you, sis.' Eddie's questions tumbled out faster than she could answer them. She looked past him at the old, grease-stained clock on the wall. The hands pointed to eight o'clock. She had slept for over an hour.

'Where's Mam?' Eddie asked, noticing the empty table and stove. Mindful of her duty towards her lodgers, his mother always had tea cooked and ready, and the table laid when they came in.

'She went upstairs after Mrs Richards told us that Dad had been sentenced to six months' hard labour.' The nap had restored Bethan enough for her to appreciate the full enormity of her father's plight. 'Is she right Eddie? Is Dad in gaol?'

He nodded, pulled a chair out from under the table and sat down. He wanted to move closer to the fire, but he'd just spent the last hour offloading his day's pickings in the rag-sorting sheds down Factory Lane, and an itch told him that he was probably carrying an unwelcome boarder that would just love the upholstery.

'What did he do?' Bethan demanded. 'Mrs Richards said something about Dad hitting a policeman, but I can't see him doing anything like that.'

'He did,' Eddie said shortly. 'He and Charlie went to a Mosley meeting yesterday—'

'And they got into a fight?'

'With Mosley's blackshirts. According to Charlie a policeman got between Dad and one of the thugs. He took the full force of a blow Dad intended to land on the Fascist. The last thing Dad said to me this morning was to tell everyone that he's all right. That he'll be fine, and six months will soon pass.'

'Then you knew about the sentence this morning?'

Eddie nodded sheepishly. 'If I'd known Mam would take to her bed I might have come back. But you know what she can be like, Beth.'

'I know.'

'But even so, it's not like Mam not to have tea ready.'

'No it isn't. Perhaps she went to sleep. Either way I don't think we should disturb her. There's bound to be something in the pantry that I can cook.'

'Give me ten minutes to wash and change, and I'll mind the little fellow for you while you sort it out.'

'Would you? You know he's delicate?'

'Trevor told me.'

'And you're not afraid of nursing him?'

'Of course not. I'm looking forward to getting to know him. After all he is my nephew.'

Eddie was bewildered by the expression on Bethan's face. He wasn't to know that it was the first time anyone had offered to hold the baby for her since the day she'd left the maternity ward.

Bethan opened the pantry door and switched on the light. Everything was neat, orderly and immaculate, just as she'd expected. The Welsh maxim, 'She was so clean you could eat off her floor' had always applied to her mother's housekeeping. As a child, equating love and warmth with the slightly chaotic domestic disorder of her Aunt Megan's home, she had often wished that her mother hadn't been quite so obsessive about the house. It might have made for a happier childhood but now, when she was about to make a meal, in what felt like a strange house, she was grateful for her mother's strict regimentation.

She opened the meat safe and peered inside: two breasts of lamb, already boned, rolled and larded, were stacked on a soup plate. As they'd take at least two hours to cook and everyone was expected home within the next half-hour she assumed that the news about her father had done the unthinkable – made her mother forget her duty as a housewife. She sniffed the meat and put it aside; it would keep until tomorrow. Behind the lamb she found two strings of sausages hanging on a hook. Hoping her mother wasn't keeping them for the lodgers' breakfast she took them out and looked around for something she could cook with them.

Elizabeth had always preferred to go without rather than risk wastage of food. And with money being short, her pantry was under a tighter and sparser control than Bethan remembered. Half a sack of potatoes, one of carrots, a slab of margarine, a pound of butter, a full milk jug, a loaf of uncut bread and a three-inch crust of another, a dozen eggs, two cake tins, one of Welsh cakes, one of scones, bags of flour, and sugar, packets of tea and cocoa, a row of pots of home-made blackberry jam, two dripping pots, one with pale skimmings of the best quality, the other speckled with the brown jelly that settled on the bottom, which her mother used as a sandwich spread.

'How does toad-in-the-hole sound to you?' Bethan called to her brother, settling on something that wouldn't require too much effort.

'Sounds fine.'

Lifting down the ingredients Bethan stepped back into the kitchen.

'Who's a fine fellow then. Look at me. Come on, look. Say hello. I'm your uncle.' Eddie was holding the baby firmly upright in his two hands, supporting Edmund's lolling head with his outstretched fingers as he dangled him on his knee.

Bethan almost dropped the mixing bowl in amazement. 'I had no idea you were good with babies,' she commented.

'Which proves you don't know everything about me.' Eddie tucked the baby into the crook of his arm and started tickling him gently under the chin. 'Joey Rees always gets me to look after his granddaughter when he brings her down the gym.'

'A baby? In the gym?' Bethan smiled at the notion as she broke an egg into the bowl.

'Joey has no choice but to bring her. His son gassed himself when the means test people refused to give him any money until he'd sold off his radio and furniture. A week later his son's widow ran off with a commercial salesman and left the baby with a neighbour. Joey's wife died years ago, so Joey had to either take in his granddaughter or put her in the workhouse.'

'How old is she?' Bethan asked.

'Eighteen months. And she's so bright for a dot of her age. You should see her spar . . .'

'Spar! Don't tell me you lot are teaching her to box?'

'Of course. What else do you expect us to teach her in a gym?'

Bethan shook her head in despair as she began beating the batter.

'I'm home, and I'm starving. Charlie worked every last ounce of sweat out of me today.' William slammed the front door and walked down the passage into the kitchen.

'Good God!' He stared in amazement at Bethan who stood, dressed in her mother's overall, at the kitchen table. 'When did the wind blow you in, Beth?'

'A couple of hours ago.'

'And this is my little nephew?' He walked across to Eddie and joined him in tickling the baby.

'He can't be your nephew, you're not my brother,' Bethan pointed out tartly.

'He'll forgive you for not having the sense to be born into the right family. Won't you, butch?' William addressed the baby gravely. 'Take a good long look at your Uncle William now. I'm easy to remember. I'm the handsomest one you'll see around here.'

Eddie snorted. Bethan cut the sausages, laid them in her mother's biggest baking tin and poured the batter over them. Despite her exhaustion she was content for the first time in months. Who would have thought that the boys, of all people, would have accepted her son so completely, and unquestioningly? The front door opened and closed again, quietly this time, and Diana, closely followed by Charlie walked in, bringing with them the cold, fresh smell of rain and the outside.

'Bethan!' Diana wrapped her arms around her cousin and hugged her tightly. 'It's great to see you. I was so upset when Will stopped off to tell me about Uncle Evan. Is there anything I can do to help?' she asked scanning the cooking debris on the table. 'Where's Aunt Elizabeth?'

'Upstairs resting,' Bethan replied, 'I'm afraid tea's going to be late.'

'And this is your baby. Here, you haven't got a clue, Eddie Powell.' Diana lifted the baby gently from Eddie's arms, and stood in front of the stove swaying from side to side as she rocked him in her arms.

A lump rose in Bethan's throat as she carried the dirty mixing bowl into the washhouse. Used to Andrew regarding the baby as a disgrace, she was now finding it hard to accept everyone's support.

'Is there anything I can do to help, Bethan?' Charlie, who'd hung back while Diana had greeted her, stepped into the washhouse.

'Nothing thanks, Charlie,' Bethan answered, struggling to keep the emotion from her voice.

'I could wash that for you.'

'It can wait until I do the dishes.' She turned and smiled at him, reassured by the solid strength that radiated from his heavily muscled, blessedly familiar figure. Charlie had once told her that neither she nor anyone else in Pontypridd could depend on him. That he was a drifter, a wanderer, 'here today, gone tomorrow'. But she was astute enough to realise that although that might be the way he saw himself, he was in reality very different. For as long as she'd known him he'd been there, quietly but staunchly lending his strength and support to his friends in times of need. It had been Charlie who'd helped William pick up the pieces after William's mother, her Aunt Megan, had been jailed. Charlie, who'd given William a job when he needed one. Charlie who'd lent her father the money he needed to start his rag and bone round. 'It's good to see you,' she said, meaning it.

'It's good to see you too,' he replied giving her one of his rare smiles.

'I'm off then!'

Bethan looked into the kitchen. Her mother was standing in the open doorway. The warm air of the kitchen was blowing out around her into the passage as a freezing cold draught whistled in from the rest of the unheated house. Standing in the open doorway of the kitchen was a cardinal sin Elizabeth would have taken anyone else severely to task over.

'Mam, where are you going?'

'I'm leaving, and I won't be back.'

For the first time Bethan noticed that her mother was dressed in her old grey coat, the only coat she remembered seeing her wear. Her black felt hat and the jet-headed pin she had inherited from her own mother were in her hands. Her handbag and a battered brown leather suitcase that had seen better days stood at her feet. Elizabeth jammed her hat on her head, skewering it firmly in place with the pin. 'I'm leaving,' she repeated in a voice pitched perilously close to hysteria. 'I wasn't brought up to criminal dealings. My father was a minister of God. He would turn in his grave if he could see just how low his daughter has been brought by the man she was blind and foolish enough to marry.'

'But where will you go at this time of night?' Bethan ventured practically, unnerved by the peculiar look in her mother's eyes. Elizabeth was inevitably cutting and dismissive of any behaviour that deviated from her own rigid standards. But she had always behaved rationally. Bethan felt as though the woman in front of her was a stranger. A ranting, wild-eyed stranger.

'I am going to throw myself on the mercy of my Uncle John Joseph Bull in the hope that he doesn't close his door against me in my hour of need.'

'Mam, you know what he's like,' Eddie protested.

'I *do* know what he's like,' she shouted, turning viciously on Eddie. 'He's unlike you. He's a minister of God. A good Christian, God-fearing man who knows the path of righteousness. He would never allow the Devil to lead him astray as your father has done. He—'

'Mam, it's late. Why don't you stay here just for tonight,' Bethan pleaded. 'We'll have tea soon. You can get a good night's rest, then if you still want to go, I'll take you to Uncle Bull's first thing in the morning.'

'I won't spend another night under the roof of a disciple of the Devil. My family warned me. So help me God, Uncle Joseph himself told me the day I married your father that it would come to this. And he was right. I sacrificed the best years of my life to that man. Bore his children, reared them, and look at my reward! You've all ignored my teachings to follow in your father's evil ways. Every one of you. Haydn, my eldest son, the one I had such hopes for. Did he enter the ministry as I brought him up to do? Oh no, not him! He had to go "on stage". Singing, dancing like a fool for the amusement of those who know no better than to watch the antics of a half-wit. Consorting with naked women—'

'Mam!' Bethan interjected.

'And you can talk, Miss, or is it Mrs now? Your child bears the hallmark of God's punishment for your sins. The retribution of the Lord may be slow in coming, but it comes, and when it does it is always just. You may count on that.'

'Mam, that's a cruel thing to say.' Eddie was on his feet, fists clenched.

'You dare talk to me about cruelty? You, whose only thoughts are of money and how to get it by beating people to a pulp. I wouldn't be surprised if even Maud's lung sickness stems from the rottenness that abounds in this family. Look where she is now, living in a heathen land among papists . . .'

'If you're set on going Mam, I'll carry your case.' Seething with barely suppressed anger, Eddie stepped forward and picked up his mother's bags.

'I can go alone.'

'Not at this hour of the night you can't.' Eddie glanced at Bethan and knew the same thought was in both their minds. John Joseph was as hard and unforgiving as their mother. If he refused to open his door, Elizabeth would be left on the streets of the Rhondda too late to catch the last bus back to Pontypridd. And it was a very long walk from the Rhondda to the Graig.

'I could go down to the café and ask Tony if I can borrow the Trojan,' Will offered.

'You will do no such thing,' Elizabeth retorted. 'As if it isn't bad enough that the whole town knows about my disgrace.'

Turning up the collar on his coat, Eddie walked to the front door with the case.

Elizabeth looked at her daughter. 'Goodbye,' she said sternly. 'Don't forget to tell your father what I've said. I will never set foot in this house again as long as I live. My only desire is to never clap eyes on him again. He has burdened this camel with the final back-breaking straw. I have made my last sacrifice for him.' She walked away stiffly. Bethan stood and watched her go. The door closed. It was left to Diana to break the silence.

'Here.' She handed William the baby.

'I don't know what to do with a baby,' he objected.

'Time you learnt.' She picked up the toad-in-the-hole and put it in the oven. 'Have you made up beds for yourself and the baby, Beth?'

'No. I fell asleep earlier and I didn't get around to doing them.'

'Well there's no time like the present. Charlie lay the table please, and keep an eye on the tea, or is it supper now. What do you say we make up your parents' bed with clean sheets Beth, seeing as how the room's empty now?'

Chapter Nine

'WHAT ABOUT EDDIE?' Diana protested as Bethan cut the toad-in-the-hole into four and shared it among them, giving herself the smallest portion.

'There's nothing worse than a meal like this that's been kept warm for hours. The pudding part turns to leather. I'll make him an omelette when he gets back.'

As Diana cut into the crisp batter and well-browned sausages she tried to think of something she could say to lighten the atmosphere. Elizabeth's outburst had affected them all. Except perhaps Charlie, who sat eating his meal as self-possessed and remote as ever.

'Will, do you remember seeing a cot when Uncle Evan and Eddie cleared the box room for me?' Diana asked her brother, finally settling on a safe topic.

'I wasn't around when they cleared it,' William replied.

'I'm sure there was one,' Diana mused. 'I'm not happy with the idea of you sharing your bed with the baby, Beth.' She sliced her sausage daintily into small pieces as she spoke. 'I know you. You'll be so afraid of rolling on him during the night, you won't close your eyes. And by the look of you you haven't had a good night's sleep in months.'

'I sleep well enough. And we'll manage. I think he's as worn out by the travelling as I am.' Bethan looked across to where Edmund lay on her father's easy chair, held securely in place by a makeshift contraption William had ingeniously constructed out of cushions and the kitchen stool.

'I wonder if they put it in the loft.'

'What?' William shovelled the last of the food on his plate into his mouth. The hollow in his stomach after a hard day's work had been a great deal larger than either the toad or the hole. He looked around hopefully for signs of something sweet and substantial. Fruit pie or jam roly-poly and custard, perhaps?

'The cot of course,' Diana answered irritably.

'I'll climb up the attic when we've finished eating and take a look.'

'As long as you're careful,' Bethan warned.

'You remember the time Haydn and Eddie fell through the rafters?'

'They told my mother they were looking for treasure. She wasn't very amused. It cost a fortune in plasterboard to repair the ceiling to my bedroom,' Bethan explained to Diana and Charlie.

'I'll go up there if you like,' Charlie offered.

'Thank you.'

'That's great, Beth. You let him go not me,' William grumbled.

'He's lighter on his feet than you,' Diana pointed out.

'He may be lighter on his feet but he's heavier overall.'

Despite Diana's brave attempts, the mood remained strained. Exhaustion coupled with the emotional upset of her mother's leaving had made Bethan lightheaded, and when Diana suggested, to William's chagrin, that she clear the dishes, Bethan was happy to take her up on the offer. She changed Edmund and gave him his last feed while William and Charlie went rummaging upstairs. William emerged triumphant ten minutes later, with cobwebs in his hair, dust streaked down his nose and a large parcel wrapped in an old sheet.

'We've put the big cot in your dad's bedroom, Bethan,' he said, self-consciously omitting Elizabeth's name. 'It was in pieces so Charlie's screwing it together. But look what else I found.' He pulled the sheet back to reveal a beautiful hand-carved oak cot. Set low on wide bowed rockers it had high sides and an overhanging fretwork canopy to shield the precious occupier from draughts.

'Mam Powell's old family cot!' Bethan exclaimed in

delight. 'I'd forgotten all about it. I remember you sleeping in it and Diana, and Maud. Mam Powell told me her grandfather carved it for her mother when she was born.'

'Then it must be a fair old age now.' William held it up to the light and looked it over with a keen eye. 'The wood's split in one or two places, but there's nothing serious that I can see. A clean-up, oiling, a bit of polish, a good dry-out in front of the fire and it will be as good as new. In fact if I get to work on it right away you'll probably be able to use it tomorrow.'

'The perfect day cot for down here. Will, you're a genius.' Bethan was so pleased she kissed him on the cheek.

'No slop please.' He made a wry face as he rubbed the spot she'd kissed with his handkerchief. 'You're a married woman now, and I'm a very handsome eligible bachelor. What *would* cashmere coat say if he could see you?'

Bethan fell silent. The cot wasn't the only thing she'd forgotten about. The nickname her brothers and William had bestowed on her husband held just the right ring of valley contempt for the crache. Exactly the kind of contempt the younger male Powells had reserved for Andrew.

'Will the other cot need airing?' Diana asked as she walked in from the washhouse with the dishcloth in her hand.

'It's painted iron. Does that need airing? It's certainly cold enough.'

'Iron doesn't need airing, you fool.'

'The mattress will though. It's been wrapped in rubber sheeting, but it still feels damp to me.'

'Of course it's damp,' Diana countered impatiently. 'It's been in the attic, you stupid boy.'

'I am neither a boy nor stupid . . .'

'Did you bring the mattress downstairs?' Bethan asked tactfully in an attempt to divert her cousins' attention.

'No, I couldn't carry it and this at the same time.'

William set the cot down on the hearth-rug.

'I'll go up and take a look at it.' Diana opened the door.

'I didn't mean for you to go running about,' Bethan protested. 'You've been working all day.'

'You sit there and feed the baby,' Diana smiled. 'You look very pretty, like an advertisement for motherhood.'

An hour later Diana had organised everything. Both cots had been washed and disinfected, inside and out. The mattress Elizabeth had so carefully stored in rubber sheets had been placed in front of the stove to air. Diana had made up the baby's bed, substituting a folded bolster for the mattress, and using pillowcases instead of sheets.

'It's only for one night,' she told Bethan as she came downstairs with the slop bucket. 'And now everything's ready, I suggest you take yourself and your baby up the wooden hill and get a good night's sleep.'

'I should wait for Eddie to get back.'

'I'll wait up for Eddie.'

'But you've got work in the morning.'

'One late night isn't going to kill me. Go on, off with you.'

'I really should talk to Eddie.'

'The kind of talking you two have to do is probably best left until morning. Neither of you can set the world, or your mam and dad, to rights tonight.'

'Yes mother,' Bethan joked, relieved to offload her problems on to Diana's willing shoulders for one night.

'See you in the morning.' Diana took the baby's bottle from Bethan's hand. 'I'll wash this, and in case you start looking for it, I've carried your case upstairs. All you have to do is undress and get into bed.'

Bethan glanced at the clock as she left her chair. It was half-past nine, way past the bedtime hour she had made Edmund adhere to in London. 'Thanks a million, Diana. What would I do without you?' she murmured, exhaustion and emotion making her tearful.

'You'd be just fine,' Diana retorted firmly. 'Everything will seem a whole lot better in the morning, Beth. You'll see.'

'It can't be any worse, and that's for sure,' William muttered darkly from behind the detective novel Evan had borrowed from the Central Lending Library.

Charlie sat quietly in one of the easy chairs until Bethan went upstairs, then he walked down the hall and picked up his coat from a hook behind the front door.

'Pint in the Graig?' Will asked, looking up from the book he was only half reading, in the hope Charlie would ask him along. Normally he would have gone down the gym with Eddie, not to box, but for company and a card game. No one had the money to do very much on a week night and it was easy for boredom to set in. But he knew better than to try to go anywhere with Charlie uninvited.

'Just a walk,' Charlie answered flatly as he went outside. He closed the door behind him and stood on the doorstep for a moment. It was a cold, crisp, clear night. Stars shone down, glittering spangles in a navy blue velvet sky. A sharp new moon silvered gossamer wisps of clouds as they drifted slowly across its pitted surface. The perfect night for a walk. After the strain of the day, Charlie had a sudden craving for clean, fresh air.

Reaching into his pocket for a cigarette, he descended the steps and walked out on to the unmade road. Iced by a thin layer of frost, the bare earth crunched beneath his feet as he turned right towards the end of the Avenue and the beginning of the mountain. If it hadn't been for the glow of the street lamps and the distant whine of a bus battling to climb up the Graig hill he could have been the last man left on earth. The thought wasn't an unpleasant one.

The front windows of the houses he passed were shrouded in darkness. Everyone in Graig Avenue lived out their waking lives in the warmth of their back kitchens, leaving bedtime and their freezing bedrooms until the last possible moment. He bent his head and struck a match. Inhaling deeply on the strong tobacco, he climbed towards the crest of the mountain. He had always sought peace and solace in nature rather than the company of other men, and after witnessing Elizabeth's savage outburst he felt he didn't have to justify his preference to himself, or others, ever again.

As his eyes grew accustomed to the darkness, his pace quickened. He reached a large flat stone lightly padded by coarse, wiry whinberry plants. It made the ideal seat. Wrapping his arms around his knees, he propped his chin on his hands and continued to smoke. Below him, lit by street and kitchen lamps, lay the backs of the houses that ribboned the lower slopes of the Graig. The cubes of coalhouses and ty bachs, divided by garden walls and fogged by smoke from low-built chimneys, stood in regimented rows. An ex-miner walked into a backyard in Danygraig Street. Charlie knew he'd worked on the coal-face by the sound – a foul, lung-wrenching cough that could never ruffle the surface of the thick layer of dust that had settled on his chest. He counted himself fortunate that he hadn't had to resort to making a living in the pits.

If only he could be sure he was doing the right thing. Opening the shop meant working for himself, tying himself to a building, putting down roots, making himself responsible for the welfare and well-being of others. Something he had sworn he would never do again. And he didn't have to look far for the motive that had caused him, if not to forget, then at least to set aside his promise to himself.

Alma? He pictured her slim figure bending, swaying to avoid people as she walked through the crowded market. She reminded him of reeds wavering in the winds that had blown around a lake, where – 'back home'? He had to stop thinking of back home. He had no home now.

He shivered and pulled the lapels of his coat high around his neck, wishing he'd brought his muffler. Winters had been cold in Russia too. But not damp. Never damp, with this insidious chill that permeated the bones and joints, making the middle-aged creak like ninety-year-olds. Would that happen to him if he remained in Pontypridd?

No matter how he tried to look at it, one of the reasons for renting the shop and setting up in business was Alma. Ever since he'd held her in his arms he hadn't been able to stop thinking about her. The gossip he'd overheard in the market worried him. He knew just how harsh and unforgiving a face the town could present to a girl who'd lost her reputation. He'd seen it with Bethan Powell before Andrew John had come back to Pontypridd to get her. How much closer had the loss of her morning job put Alma to the breadline? Was she really making ends meet?

Strange, when she'd been Ronnie Ronconi's girl he'd scarcely given her a second thought. She'd simply been the pleasant waitress who'd served him every time he went into the café. After Ronnie left he'd noticed she'd lost weight, looked ill, but her plight hadn't really touched him. Not until the night she'd collapsed.

He wanted to offer Alma a full-time job in his shop. Afraid that something might go wrong, he'd put off approaching her until everything was signed and sealed, but as of that morning the place was his. He was stuck with it – but what if she wouldn't work for him? There were plenty of others who would jump at the chance. The problem was, another girl wouldn't be the same as Alma.

Charlie tried to examine his motives objectively. Didn't he simply want to make some money to put behind him against – against what? The time he returned to Russia? There was no going back. He had known that the day he'd jumped ship in Cardiff docks. But it wasn't as if he was thinking of settling down with the girl. He had, after all, only signed a lease. It was simply a matter of getting the shop on its feet. Six months, a year at the most, then if he wanted to he could sell it as a going concern, and sign the lease over at a profit. He had checked that the solicitor had put a transfer clause into the document. William was a good lad, a bit headstrong but he was a hard worker. If he signed the business over to William, he'd get his money back – eventually.

So what was he worried about? He didn't have to

stay in Pontypridd one day longer than he wanted to. There was nothing more to keep him in Wales today than there had been yesterday. Nothing except a reed–slim girl with red hair, witching green eyes, and pride enough to hold her head high, even when the whole town condemned her for falling in love with a man who had deserted her.

He dropped his cigarette and trod on it. If he wasn't careful Alma Moore could become a problem. But then, he hadn't offered her the job yet, and when he did there was a chance she might not take it. But if she did? The little devil voice echoed in his mind as he rose stiffly to his feet and descended the hill. If she did, he'd have to watch himself, that was all. He had survived eight years without getting too close to people. He could survive a few years more until – when?

The future loomed cold, empty, terrifying in its grey solitude. He shivered. He hadn't allowed himself to think about where he was going for eight long years. He dare not break that habit. Not now.

Graig Avenue was still peaceful and deserted. Charlie walked swiftly and quietly close to the high wall that enclosed the back gardens of Phillips Street. Pausing outside the door of the house opposite the Powells' he listened. A dog barked in the distance. Boots rang over the paved area around the corner in Llantrisant Road. Even if whoever was making the noise was turning into Graig Avenue, he still had a few minutes. Pressing down the latch he stepped down into the back garden of the first house in Phillips Street and closed the door quickly behind him. He walked down the well-trodden centre path that bisected the tiny area, negotiated a narrow flight of steps and lowered himself into a small enclosed yard. To his left, fine threads of light peeped between the folds of a pair of unusually thick curtains. In front of him the greyish white paint of the washhouse door glimmered in the darkness. He knocked before opening it.

'Mrs Pugh, Miss Harry,' he called so they wouldn't be alarmed. 'It's Charlie.'

The kitchen door opened and a cloud of warmth gusted out to greet him. Phyllis Harry, middle height, thin faced, appeared in the doorway. She smiled as she ran her fingers through her greying, mousy hair.

'Come in, Charlie. It's good to see you. Can I get you a cup of tea?'

'No thank you, Miss Harry.' He followed her into Rhiannon Pugh's kitchen, ducking his head below the low lintel of the washhouse door. The room was bright and cosy, a hard-working poor woman's room, glowing with multicoloured rag rugs, hand-knitted cushion covers and patchwork curtains. A cardboard box of home-made rag dolls and knitted animals stood in the corner.

'Charlie.' Rhiannon Pugh, well into her seventies and crippled by arthritis and bronchitis, nodded to him. Charlie looked from her to Phyllis and saw they already knew what he had come to tell them.

'Mr Roberts from next door called in this morning. He told us that Evan has been sentenced to six months' hard labour.'

'I saw Evan before they took him away. He told me to tell you he's fine, and six months will soon pass.'

'Typical Evan,' Phyllis smiled as she shook her head fondly.

'It will be hard on Elizabeth,' Rhiannon wheezed. Much as she loved Phyllis, who was more like a daughter than a lodger, she couldn't resist reminding her that the love of her life and father of her child also had a wife.

'She has taken it hard,' Charlie agreed shortly without elaborating.

'Will you be walking through?' Phyllis asked. Rhiannon had lived all her live in Phillips Street, and to spare her neighbours the long walk around Vicarage Corner allowed her house to be used as a thoroughfare between Graig Avenue and the streets below her own. It was a shortcut that had served Phyllis well. It was impossible to watch the front and back doors of the house at the same time, and even the most determined gossip had been unable to hazard a guess as to the identity of the father of her child.

'If that's all right with you, Mrs Pugh,' Charlie said, thinking that a beer with a whisky chaser drunk in the warm, masculine atmosphere of the bar of the Graig Hotel would go down extremely well.

'I'll see you out.' Phyllis closed the kitchen door behind her as she led the way to the front of the house.

'Miss Harry . . .'

'Phyllis.' She had told Charlie to call her by her Christian name at least a dozen times, but he never did.

'If you and the boy need anything, you will ask me?'

Phyllis looked at him proudly. 'We're fine Charlie, but thank you for the offer.'

Charlie'd had enough of stubborn Welsh pride in one day to last him a lifetime. He put his hand in his pocket and pulled out a ten-pound note. It was one of five he'd taken out of the bank to buy essential building materials and stock for his shop, and represented a tenth of his capital. 'Evan asked me to give you this.'

Phyllis stared at it in disbelief. 'Where did Evan get ten pounds from?' she demanded suspiciously.

'He's been saving. He wanted you to have it.'

'Not his wife?' Phyllis asked wryly.

'Eddie can keep the business going and the bills paid until Evan gets out.'

'I suppose he can.' Phyllis didn't want to take the money, but she had little choice. The savings she'd put by in the Post Office during twenty years of work as a cinema usherette in the White Palace were almost at an end. Now that Evan was out of reach he wouldn't be able to pay her the five shillings he had slipped her every week without fail since their son's birth. And although Rhiannon was very generous, her widow's pension didn't go far.

Charlie thrust the note into her hand.

'Will you be seeing him?'

'I hope to.'

'Thank him for me, and explain why I won't visit.'

'I will.'

'I'd write, only it might cause complications. They do open letters addressed to prisoners, don't they?'

'Probably.'

'You'll call in again?' she pressed, reluctant to let him go. He was a link, albeit a tenuous one, with Evan. And she was dreading the next six months without Evan Powell's nightly visits.

'Yes. You may see Bethan walking through,' he added, remembering that Bethan had often stopped to talk to Phyllis even when others had passed by.

'Bethan's home?' Phyllis smiled broadly. 'Tell her to call in when she has time.'

'I will. Goodnight.'

Charlie walked down the front steps and along the road towards the Graig hotel. He wondered why life in the Welsh valleys always had to be so complicated. It had been a great deal simpler in his home village in Russia. When Igor the bootmaker had left his attractive, shrewish wife for a plain, but gentle and kind widow, no one had blamed him. The gossips had targeted the shrew, not the widow, and he was sure if Evan made a similar move he would receive the same absolution from his neighbours. Elizabeth Powell's character was well known on the Graig, and Graig people were more inclined to sympathise with a man's ungodly mistress than a hard, unforgiving saint of a wife.

If he'd been offered the choice of living with Elizabeth or Phyllis he knew which he'd prefer. It was strange: physically the two women weren't dissimilar. Poverty had drawn the same angles and thin, spare features into Phyllis's frame as Elizabeth's, but their characters couldn't have been more unalike. Phyllis Harry's wasted cheeks and tired eyes radiated a warmth and compassion that Elizabeth was incapable of feeling. A warmth all the Powells could benefit from, especially Bethan.

*

Head down, a woollen scarf wrapped high around her neck and a cotton one tied cornerwise over her hair to protect it from the rain, Alma walked quickly down the dark street. The road gleamed like polished pewter and the fine drizzle haloed the lamplights, but Alma was too nervous to appreciate the beauty of the scene. She had never liked walking through the town late at night, but now that the gossips were shredding her reputation she hated it even more. What if someone should recognise her? Say something to her face? Or start denouncing her as Freda and Mary had done? A scene late at night in town was bound to be heard by the people who lived above their shops.

She slowed her steps as she heard the ringing of a pair of heels on the pavement and looked nervously over her shoulder. Blank panes of glass gleamed from the darkened shop windows. All she could hear was the pulsating drumbeat of blood in her veins, and the sound of her own laboured breath. She fought to subdue panic, straining her eyes as she peered into a cluster of shadows in the doorway of Heath's piano shop. Were they really shadows? Or a tall man wearing a trilby? She stepped up her pace, the throbbing of her heartbeat vying with the tapping of her steps on the pavement.

If Tony had mastered driving the Trojan she would have swallowed her pride and asked him to give her a lift home as Ronnie had done every night she had worked late. It was barely five minutes' drive in the slow, lumbering van, but a good fifteen minutes on foot. She had a sudden, very real picture of herself sitting in the van next to Ronnie, his left hand resting on her knee, a cigarette dangling carelessly from his lips. It conjured up memories of sweet, loving intimacy. But even if Tony had mastered driving the van, he might not want to take her home. Particularly if his parents were aware of the gossip.

What she hated most about Ronnie's desertion was that she'd been left with no real friend to turn to. Ronnie had been everything to her: lover, friend, holder of her deepest, and most private secrets. Now there was only her mother, who had been more burden than help to her for the last few years. She pulled herself up sharply; how could she ever consider her mother a burden? If she was in trouble, it was her own stupid fault. If she had no friends, it was because she had relied on Ronnie too much – for everything. Even now she had him to thank for her job, the food on her table and the roof over her head. Laura would never have helped her when she'd been in hospital if it hadn't been for Ronnie. If only she didn't miss him so much! His physical presence, his caustic wit, sarcastic repartee, but most of all the close, loving, physical relationship they had shared. It was hard for her to remember, even now when he was in Italy married to Maud, that she had loved him so much more than he had loved her.

The clock on St Catherine's struck twelve as she reached the corner by the YMCA building. She had to stop thinking about Ronnie. The past was past. She had more immediate problems to solve, like how to keep the worst of the gossip from her mother, and how to pay the bills on half a wage. She'd started back to work; that was the first positive step. Laura had said something about more money but she hadn't said how much more, and like a fool Alma hadn't thought to ask. She had to start saving as well to pay Laura what she owed, but how could she?

Her mother's pension of five shillings a week didn't even cover the rent. And now she was down to eight shillings – maybe nine if Tony was generous – a week. Where could they cut back? A cheaper house? They didn't come much cheaper than Morgan Street. Coals? Her mother usually only lit the range three days a week and they needed it to cook on. Clothes? They only bought them now as presents on birthdays and at Christmas. Food? It had to be food, but it was difficult to see where . . .

'Walk you round the corner, Alma?'

She whirled round. Bobby Thomas was standing behind her.

'You been following me, Bobby?' she demanded.

'Would I do a thing like that?'

'Yes.'

'You were going my way so I thought I'd just check to make sure you get home all right.'

'I'm fine thank you,' she said icily, walking on.

'Proper Miss Hoity Toity, aren't you?' He took hold of her arm. She struggled to free herself from his grip but he propelled her across the road.

'If you don't let go of me, now, this minute, I'll scream,' she threatened.

'What and wake up all the good people who are asleep in their beds? You don't want to do that, Alma. It would only give them something else to say about you.'

'I don't know what you mean.'

'Don't play the wide-eyed innocent with me.' He kept a firm grasp on her arm above her elbow as they walked up the hill towards Morgan Street. 'Mary and Freda have been telling everyone in town about you.'

'Telling them what?'

'As if you didn't know! How about it, Alma? I might not have a café, but I do have a lot of other things to offer.'

'How about you let go of me?' she said coldly, still trying to shrug off his grip.

'I'm Fred Jones's right-hand man,' he whispered. 'I can always put a word in if you can't make your rent.'

'My rent is paid up to date.'

'Only because your old boyfriend's sister has been paying it. Sooner or later she's going to get tired of forking out for someone else's bills. Take my word for it.' His hand travelled up to her chin as he pulled down the scarf she had wound around her throat. 'What you need, Alma, is a bit of security.' He caressed the nape of her neck with his thumb and forefinger. 'I'd be only too happy to look after you.'

'I can look after myself.'

'Not that well from what I've heard. Come on Alma,' he wheedled. 'You've put a smile on a few fellows' faces, what's one more? You'll not find me ungrateful, I promise.'

'And what would your wife say if she could hear you now, Bobby Thomas?' Unequal to struggling against his strength she finally stopped walking and faced him, hoping to shame him into leaving her alone.

'What the eye don't see, the heart don't grieve. Now how about you invite me in for a quick cup of tea. Your mam's gone to bed.' He nodded towards the dark windows in her house lower down the street.

'There's no point in lighting lamps for the blind.'

'She's always in bed by nine. I know. I collect the rent, remember.'

'I wouldn't invite you over our front doorstep if you were the last man on earth.'

'That's because you don't know me yet the way I'd like you to.' He inched his hand inside the top of her coat.

'Let go of me, or I swear to God I'll scream loud enough to bring the police running.'

'Well if you're prepared to risk it.' He heaved her towards him, tearing the buttons from her coat. He bent his head to kiss her but she turned aside, and his lips brushed wetly against her hair. 'A few liberties are nothing to a girl like you.' He thrust his hand inside her open coat and squeezed her breast. 'After all it's not as if I'm going to get you in the family way, you're already there. Come on, ten minutes with me will clear your rent for a week.'

She thrust her hand into his thinning hair, gripped and yanked hard.

'Ow!' he yelped. 'You little bitch . . .'

She kicked his shin, turned and ran towards her front door. For the first time in her life she bolted it behind her, but she could still hear him calling after her.

'You turn your rent in just one hour late, and you'll find out what's what, Alma Moore. Just one hour late and you'll wish you'd come crawling to me when you had the chance.'

'Alma,' her mother's querulous voice floated down the stairs.

'Coming, Mam.' She straightened her coat, too flustered to remember that her mother couldn't see it, and climbed the stairs, feeling her way in the darkness. 'Can I get you anything?' She pushed open the door to her mother's bedroom.

'You all right Alma? I heard shouting.'

'I'm fine, Mam.' She struggled to keep her voice calm and even, knowing that her mother was sensitive to the slightest tremor.

'Was there someone out there with you?'

'Only Bobby Thomas the rent man.'

'We don't owe anything do we?' Mrs Moore asked anxiously.

'Nothing,' Alma replied firmly. 'If you don't want anything I'll go to bed, Mam. I'm tired.'

'Alma, are you in the family way?'

'No!'

'Mrs Lane told me you were. She heard it in the shop tonight. She said she thought she ought to tell me before someone else did. I would have rather heard it from you.'

'I'm sorry people are telling you lies, Mam. But I promise you, I'm not anything of the kind.'

'Then why are people saying that you are?'

'Because I was ill. Because I went into hospital, and,' she took a deep breath, 'because Ronnie Ronconi has gone to Italy.'

'But Alma you can't just let people say what they like about you. You've got to do something. Otherwise your reputation—'

'Mam if you can think of something I can do, I'll do it,' Alma interrupted angrily.

'Ronnie Ronconi — you didn't do anything you shouldn't have with him, did you? I warned you how dangerous talk can be to a young girl like you, with no father to care for her. If men think you're not a decent woman they'll try to take advantage . . . they'll . . .'

'I'm beginning to find out just what *they'll* do, Mam.'

'I suppose there's nothing you can do except brazen it out.' Lena Moore's voice was tired, resigned, tremulous with unshed tears. 'I only hope the minister doesn't get to hear any of this.'

'I couldn't give a damn if he does.'

'Alma, your language. If you talk like that no wonder people are gossiping. They say there's no smoke without fire. Mr Ronconi never did anything to you, did he? I mean . . .'

'He never did anything to me that I didn't want him to,' Alma interrupted shortly.

'What kind of an answer is that?'

'Whatever he did, it's not important now. He's gone and he won't be back.'

'Well I suppose there's nothing for it. I'll have to stand by you no matter what. A lot wouldn't. Mrs Higgins down the road had her daughter put away for less.'

'I know, Mam.'

Alma stood in silence for a moment listening to the mattress creak and groan as her mother turned over.

'There never was any insurance money, was there?' her mother whispered as she settled back on her pillows.

'No there wasn't,' Alma admitted harshly.

'Then how are we going to live?'

'As best we can, Mam.' Alma closed the door and went into her own bedroom. 'As best we can,' she repeated as she arranged the threadbare curtains over her window.

Chapter Ten

'DON'T WORRY, SIS, we'll manage somehow, we always do.' Evan pinched Bethan's cheek gently as she scooped fried bread on to his plate.

'I wish I could be as optimistic as you. You sure Mam didn't say any more to you last night?'

'Not a word. I told you, she wouldn't even sit next to me on either of the buses. I carried her case to Uncle Joe's door for her. She rang the bell, he opened it, they went inside, and that's the last I saw of her. No goodbye, nothing.'

'You sure he didn't throw her out later?'

'I waited ten minutes. Any longer and I would have missed the last bus home. Look Beth, we'll manage without Mam. We'll be fine.'

'It's not us I'm worried about.'

'After what she said to you about the baby, you're worried about Mam?'

She tried to smile at him as she sat on the chair that had been hers. What was it her grandmother used to say? 'Count your blessings.' Well she'd better start now.

The first night without Elizabeth had gone remarkably peacefully, and already she could detect an absence of strain without her mother's presence lying like a frost over the household. Even the morning rush had gone well. Will, Diana and Charlie had raced around the kitchen like whirlwinds while she'd fed the baby, making their own breakfasts, cleaning their shoes, and all in a mad dash that would have had her mother shouting at them a dozen times over about opening doors, causing draughts and carrying dirt through to the kitchen from the outside yard.

'Well even if we're going to be "all right" I still need to know what the bills are on this place if I'm going to manage the money,' she said at last. 'Do you know what the mortgage is?'

'Seventeen bob a week.'

'Seventeen shillings! But Dad's been paying it off for years and his father before him.'

'He remortgaged it to buy out his mother and brother, and . . .' Eddie concentrated intently on the bread on his plate, slicing it into small triangles.

'And?' Bethan demanded.

'You're not to tell a soul this.' Eddie looked over his shoulder, even though he'd heard the others leave for work. 'He borrowed another twenty a while back. I only know about it because he dropped the papers when he was climbing down from the cart one day. I salvaged them out of the gutter for him.'

'And you didn't ask what he needed that kind of money for?'

'Come on, Beth. Would you have?'

'Was he in trouble of any kind? Had he been backing horses?'

'Dad!'

'It must have gone somewhere!'

'Wherever it went, there wasn't any obvious sign of it that I could see.'

'How much have you and Dad been clearing on the round?' she enquired, giving up on the subject.

'Thirty bob in a good week. Twenty to twenty-five shillings on the not so good.'

'Is that all?' Andrew gave her a pound a week house-keeping, and she hadn't had to pay rent or electricity out of that.

'Don't forget we've got nineteen shillings a week coming in from the lodgers. Charlie and Will pay seven and six each and Diana pays four shillings. She pays less because she used to help Mam with the housework.'

Bethan did some rapid calculations in her head.

Looking on the black side, if Eddie only brought in a pound, she'd have one pound one and sixpence a week to feed four adults and one baby, and that was without taking things like coal and electricity into consideration. She'd never do it. What had she been thinking of when she'd decided to come home? The only money she had, or was likely to have for some time, was in her purse. And that wouldn't be enough to keep her and Edmund for more than a month. If her father had been around it might have been different, but she could hardly expect her brother to support her.

'Post.' Eddie mopped up the last drops of grease with his bread before going to the door. He returned with two letters. 'Bloody electricity bill,' he swore.

'We'll have less of that language in the house, thank you.'

'Since when have you taken after Mam? Here, there's one for you.' He tossed a white envelope with a London late-evening postmark on to her lap. 'You didn't say how long you'd be staying Beth,' he probed as she stared at the handwriting. She'd know it anywhere as Andrew's.

'Mm . . . oh as long as you need me, I suppose.'

'Have you left him?' Eddie asked earnestly.

'Who?' she replied unthinkingly as she ripped the envelope open with her thumbnail.

'Cashmere coat.'

'Do you know I'd forgotten about that nickname until Will mentioned it last night.' She looked up. Eddie was watching her. In London it had been easy to ignore her brother's antagonism towards Andrew, but here it wouldn't be so simple. 'No, I haven't left him,' she answered.

'Then when are you going back?'

'When I've sorted a few things out.'

'Powell family things, or John family things?'

'Bit of both I suppose.' She glanced across to the little cot, bright and gleaming with polish, snugly furnished with an assortment of crocheted woollen blankets Diana had unearthed from the deepest recesses of her mother's ottoman. 'We've got a few problems,' she admitted reluctantly.

'Little ones by the look of it,' he said astutely, following her line of vision.

'It's nothing we can't work out. And,' she laid her hand over his, 'it is good to be home, and with you.'

'Don't try to soft-soap me, Beth. It won't wash. Good God is that the time! If I don't get a move on I'll miss the good rigs in Factory Lane again. See you, sis.'

'Don't forget to find out about prison visiting times if you can,' she shouted as he picked up his boots and tore down the passage.

'I won't. Bye.'

The door closed and she was alone. Blessedly, wonderfully alone. Broke, and a burden on her family. She pulled out two pieces of paper from the envelope. Andrew hadn't written her a long letter. In fact it was more of a note.

Dear Bethan,
You're probably right about us needing to take a break from one another. I'll send you one of these every month.
Take care of yourself,
Love Andrew.

The second piece of paper was a cheque for five pounds. Her pride told her to send it back. But if she did, what would she and the baby live on? Besides, he'd written that he'd loved her, hadn't he?

'I'm no builder, Charlie, but even I can see it's in a bad way in places.' William looked up at the ceiling of the largest room over the shop. Charlie had opened it up with a key he'd signed for at the solicitor's. 'Roof must have gone. That's more than just the damp of disuse coming in there.' William pointed to a corner where dark green patches were sprouting mould.

'The floorboards are sound.' Charlie stamped his feet

as he walked across the empty room.

'The windows haven't seen a lick of paint in years.'

Charlie fingered the blackened sash. 'But the wood's still solid. There's no sign of rot.'

'You thinking of renting this, then?' William was used to Charlie's mysterious ways, but even he had been a little bewildered by his boss's insistence on viewing the shop as soon as they'd finished for the day in the slaughterhouse.

'Yes.'

'Going to do it up yourself?'

'Not the roof.' Charlie pushed up the window and sat on the windowsill. Leaning out backwards, he looked up at the slates.

'But you'll paint the inside?'

'There's nothing here that you and I can't manage.' Charlie ducked back inside and slammed the window shut. 'I may even get Eddie to help.'

'Why this shop, Charlie?' William asked as he followed Charlie into a tiny, dark kitchen at the back. 'The town's full of places in better nick than this.'

'The solicitor handling them wouldn't drop the price.'

'And Fred the Dead gave you a good deal!' William exclaimed sceptically. Fred's reputation for driving a hard bargain was legendary.

'Eventually,' Charlie replied vaguely.

'I suppose it could be a good spot for trade,' William admitted grudgingly as they walked out on to a small landing and opened the doors to three other rooms. Two were as small, and as they were built at the back of the building, as dark as the kitchen. The third was a bathroom with a sink, bath and toilet, all in need of a good scrub.

'My godfathers. A bathroom!' When Charlie made no comment, William went to the front window again and looked down on the shuttered entrance to the fruit market.

'You'll get the town as well as the market traffic,' he commented, 'and depending on your prices, the idlers hanging around the fountain.'

'Do you want to manage this place?'

'This shop?'

'What do you think we've been talking about?'

'You've signed the lease?'

'Yesterday.'

'You bought it?'

'Sort of. It will be mine in five years.'

'What happens if you don't make a go of it?'

'I'll be broke.'

'I don't know the town can stand another butcher's shop,' William said doubtfully. 'It's getting hard enough on the market with most people only being able to afford the odd half-pound of tripe or brains.'

'It's not going to be a butcher's shop. At least, not like the one on the market.' Charlie led the way down the stairs and into the shop.

'Then what are you going to sell?' William asked, irritated at having to drag every word out of Charlie.

'Cooked meats. Meat pies and pasties. Sausage rolls, brawn, cold tongue, slices of stuffed belly pork, cooked beef and chicken. And every day of the week, not just market days.'

'There isn't another shop in Ponty that specialises in savoury baking,' William said thoughtfully.

'Exactly. And although people can't afford a joint of meat, most will be able to afford a slice or two if it's ready cooked, and cold enough to slice thin. We have lots of shops like that in Russia. They did well, even when people had very little money.'

'So that's why you wanted this place. Because it was a bakery years ago.'

Charlie opened a door in the back wall behind the counter. Two huge black iron ovens faced him; in front were three zinc-coated tables and two wooden ones. There were even dusty mixing bowls on the open wooden shelves, and rows of grimy metal utensils.

'They went bankrupt,' he explained. 'Fred Jones was the main creditor.'

'And he didn't think it was worth emptying this place before renting it to Meakins. Charlie you're a genius.'

'Not a word about what we're going to sell to anyone,' Charlie warned, well acquainted with Will's garrulous tongue.

'Not until we open. You crafty old devil,' William looked at the counter, which despite the years spent displaying china still showed the grey residue of old flour mixed with dust in the cracks around the glass front and marble serving slabs.

'Then you'll manage the shop?'

'Of course. Thank you for asking, but I warn you now I'm no cook.'

'I want you to sell, not cook. I have someone else in mind for that.'

'But what about the stall? I won't be able to do the two. Or are you giving that up?'

'Not for the moment.'

'You'll never manage it on your own.'

'I'll get Eddie to help.'

'He won't like that. He'll miss the cart.'

'He can still take that out on the days I don't need him.'

'But you'll be cutting more meat than ever in the slaughterhouse.'

'*We'll* be cutting more meat,' Charlie corrected. 'I forgot to tell you, the manager of this shop works long hours. He has to start work in the slaughterhouse at five in the morning, and doesn't finish in the shop much before eight at night.'

After a discussion on priorities, Charlie and William set about scrubbing down the ovens and water boilers in the old bakehouse kitchen. Although Charlie began with a better will and more energy than William it soon became obvious that his mind wasn't on the task. His hand slowed as he rubbed the brown patina of rust from the ironwork. He paused frequently, staring into space as he visualised

Alma dressed in a white overall and hat, moving around the kitchen as it would look once he'd transformed it. She would be busy cooking, cleaning, lifting trays out of the oven on to the tables, smiling at him as he worked alongside her, in that same distant, preoccupied way she had once smiled at Ronnie Ronconi. Perhaps she'd talk to him as they worked – but what about? Trade in the shop. The weather? If she learned to trust him, something more personal? What had he talked about with Masha when they had sat side by side in front of the stove every night after the day's work? Everything and nothing. The past – the future. His grandfather's funeral, what their unborn children would look like . . .

'Know anything about cooking meats then, Charlie?' William asked after he'd watched Charlie idle away a good ten minutes of working time.

'A little.' Charlie reluctantly faced the stove again.

'Seems to me you've got to know more than a little to cook on the scale you've been talking about.'

'You're right.' Charlie dropped his scouring pad on to the stove, and went to the tap. He turned it on but no water came out.

'Stopcock's off,' William informed him as Charlie stared blankly at the dry tap.

Charlie bent below the sink and turned the small wheel set there. Water gushed fiercely downwards, splashing out of the sink over his neck.

'Not with it are you, mate? You feeling all right after that blow to the head?'

'I'm fine. I have to see someone.' Charlie unfastened his overall, now stained with black filth from the cooker as well as dried blood from the slaughterhouse.

'Want me along?' William asked hopefully, fed up with scrubbing at the rusted ironwork.

'No.'

William watched as Charlie rubbed the dirt from his square, capable hands in the stream of water that flowed into the sink. When they were as clean as he could get them, he replaced the collar and tie he'd removed before starting work, and buttoned his waistcoat and jacket. Taking a comb out of his pocket he flicked his thick blond hair straight back from his forehead before putting on his overcoat. William had observed Charlie transform himself from worker into well-dressed businessman many times, and never ceased to marvel at how he could do it so proficiently without the aid of a mirror.

'You've got a big black smut on the end of your nose.'

Charlie removed a spotless white linen handkerchief from the breast pocket of his jacket and rubbed at his nose.

'Fooled you,' William laughed as he turned the pad of wire wool over in his hand.

'Keep working. I won't be long.'

'Give her my love.'

'Who?' Charlie paused by the door and looked back.

'Whoever she is. It must be love, I've never seen you so half-soaked before.'

'If it's love, you're looking at it,' Charlie said unsmilingly, indicating the shop as he closed the door.

'As if you could be in love with this bloody filthy place,' William muttered, staring miserably at the thick layer of grime that coated everything in sight, and wishing that Vera would walk through the door.

Charlie turned left and headed towards the Fairfield end of town.

'You moving in next door then, Charlie?'

'Yes.' Charlie paused in front of Frank Clayton's radio shop, the one shop in town that was always bursting at the seams with people, who, unfortunately for Frank, only came to listen to his radios and radiograms, not to buy them.

'Meat won't go down well here,' Frank warned sternly. 'It's one thing for people to come across pig's heads and tripe in the butcher's market where they expect to find such things, quite another for them to see offal in a window next to a luxury goods shop like mine.'

'I expect they'll get used to it, Mr Clayton.'

'In summer you'll bring nothing but smells and flies around here. It'll be unhygienic. Don't intend to do your killing out the back in the yard, do you?'

'No, Mr Clayton.' Charlie smiled wryly. Frank Clayton knew as well as him that if he tried to slaughter anything at the back of the shop the authorities would close him down overnight.

'Well I'm telling you now, the first whiff of a stink that upsets one of my customers, and I'll be reporting you to the Public Health.'

'I wouldn't have it any other way, Mr Clayton.' Charlie placidly tipped his hat.

'Bloody foreigners,' Frank swore to his son, inadvertently slamming the door in a customer's face as he retreated inside his shop. 'You'd think we'd have the sense to keep them out of this country. Instead what do we do? We let them in, give them the best shops in the prime trading positions, allow them to make money off the backs of people who were born and bred here and can ill afford to keep body and soul together as it is. Our own starve, while the likes of Russian Charlie grow fat. You mark my words lad, that man'll be riding around in a car soon if he isn't stopped.'

Outwardly oblivious to the town's interest in his affairs Charlie carried on walking down Taff Street, tipping his hat to customers and acquaintances, nodding gravely to the traders who were standing on their doorsteps looking out for potential customers. He turned the corner by the YMCA building, and a few moments later found himself the other side of Gelliwastad Road. He remembered someone saying the night Alma had been taken into hospital that she lived in Morgan Street, and although he'd never had cause to go into that area, he found it without too much trouble.

Though it hadn't rained that day, the unmade stretch that separated the double terrace of houses was covered with a thick layer of sticky mud, peppered with surprisingly deep puddles. Ducking his head to avoid hitting a washing line laden with sheets stretched between the houses, he almost fell over two small street urchins who were sailing newspaper 'ships' across an unwholesome-looking 'sea' speckled with mountainous islands constructed from stones and rubbish.

'Haven't seen you around here before, Mister.' The boy was thin, ragged and small. He was dressed in patched grey short trousers, and a jersey that was more holes than wool; his feet and legs were bare. His sharp, ferret-like face looked older than Charlie would have expected to see on a child of his size.

'That's because I haven't been here before.'

'You don't talk as though you come from round here either.' The second boy was as emaciated and threadbare as the first, and his hands and face were encrusted with thick brown running sores.

'That's because I come from another country.' Charlie pulled two halfpennies from his pocket and held them high, just out of the boys' reach. 'Can you tell me where Alma Moore lives?'

'My mam says she's a tart. You one of her fancy men?'

The boy with the sores wasn't interested in scandal. His attention was firmly fixed on Charlie's money. 'Over there, Mister.' He jumped up and snatched the coins from Charlie's hand. Holding them out of his friend's reach, he pointed to a house with a dilapidated front door.

Trying to avoid the mud by stepping carefully around the puddles, Charlie walked towards it. Seeing no knocker, he tapped lightly on the door.

'Come in.'

He pushed gingerly at the wood around the knob. The door opened into a cold passageway, floored in well-scrubbed, almost white flagstones, amazingly free from the taint of the mud that coated the street. He scraped his shoes on a sacking mat, and seeing a door to his left he pushed it. It swung open to reveal a bare room: no rug, furniture, nothing except a pair of faded curtains hanging at the window. He closed the door and walked down the passage. A piece of sheeting at the far end twitched aside and Alma's face, drained of colour by her vivid red hair and bright green eyes, peered suspiciously at him.

'Charlie? You're the last person I expected to see.' For the first time she wished she could call him by something other than the nickname that served him as both Christian and surname. 'Charlie' seemed appropriate enough in the café, particularly when he sat with the boys like Glan, William and Eddie, but here, in her own home, it sounded insulting and disrespectful. 'Won't you come in?' She pulled back the curtain.

'Thank you.' The smell of soapsuds and washing soda assailed his nostrils. Then he picked up on something else; something he recognised from the last year he had spent in Russia. Cold, clean poverty. The kind of poverty that is spawned when proud people try to hang on to their sense of decency in the face of overwhelming odds. He shivered involuntarily as he entered the chill atmosphere of the kitchen. It was colder than the street, with a damp, wintry frostiness that had been stored in the unheated stone walls of the old house for years.

Flustered, Alma pulled the chair with the cushion into the centre of the room. 'Won't you sit down?'

He took the seat she offered.

'I'd like to offer you tea, but I'm afraid I can't. Today's my day for cleaning out the range, and we don't have a gas stove, so I can't boil water.'

He glanced at the range. The brass fenders and rails were brightly polished, the ironwork newly blackleaded. It was spotless and, he suspected, ready for lighting, if there had been any coal.

'Would you like a biscuit?' Alma opened a tin that contained three oatmeal biscuits that were left from the trayful her mother had made when the stove had last been lit.

'No thank you.'

'You look better than you did on Sunday.'

'I'm fine.' He fingered the plaster that had replaced the bandage on his head.

She stood in front of him, wiping her hands on her apron, feeling unsettled and awkward, wishing he'd say whatever he'd come to say, then go away and leave her in peace.

'I heard you lost your job in the tailor's,' he said apprehensively, wary of provoking a scene.

'That's old news,' she retorted.

'Are you looking for full-time work?'

'Of course. It's impossible for my mother and me to live on what I bring in working in the café.'

'That's what I thought. I'm opening a shop.'

'I don't think I'd be able to run a shop,' she broke in swiftly. 'You saw what happened in the café.'

'I wasn't going to ask you to run it.l I already have a manager. What I need is someone to supervise the cooking.'

'Cooking? You're opening a café then?'

'No. A cooked meats shop.'

She laughed mirthlessly as she waved her hand around the sparsely equipped and furnished kitchen, 'I know very little about cooking the kind of meat you'd find in a shop.'

'You can read, write and follow a recipe, can't you?'

'Yes, but—'

'It will be quite straightforward. Cooking, pressing, pickling, curing, potting, collaring, smoking and boiling meats,' Charlie recited, automatically going through the full range he had envisaged stocking and selling. 'Slicing them when they're cold. Making faggots, croquettes, pies, pasties, rolls and brawn from offcuts and offal. Arranging everything on display plates ready for sale.'

'But I've never done any cooking professionally.' Alma could have kicked herself. Here was Charlie offering her an opportunity to make ends meet and she was putting obstacles in his path.

'I've seen you in the café. Like all good workers you learn fast. Ronnie . . . the Ronconis,' he amended diplomatically, 'have always thought a lot of you. You're conscientious, honest, not afraid of hard work, and—' he turned to face her – 'I thought you might like to leave the café.' He didn't elaborate on his reasons for coming to that conclusion. Colour flooded into her cheeks as he continued. 'I was hoping to turn the Ronconis' loss to my gain.'

'But I—'

'I'm not afraid of the gossips,' he said simply. 'Do you want the job or don't you?'

She remained silent, wondering if Charlie realised the importance most people in Pontypridd attached to the rumours being spread about her. What was it her mother had said? 'No smoke without fire.' Her presence could result in a boycott of Charlie's shop, but she needed full-time work.

'I'm not having a baby, Charlie,' she said at last, lifting her chin defiantly, her green eyes glittering antagonistically.

'I never thought you were. Do you want the job, or not?'

'You really don't give a damn about gossip, do you?' she asked incredulously.

'I don't have to listen to it.' He rose from his seat unable to stand the cold a moment longer without moving. 'My father always used to say that the best and most loyal workers are the ones who need the money the most, and from what I can see, you need the money,' he said with devastating simplicity. He walked over to the window that overlooked the tiny back yard. 'There is one problem, however.'

'What?' She steeled herself, half expecting him to make the same obscene overtures that Bobby had.

'Anything to do with cooking demands an early start. I was thinking of five at the latest. Four would be better. That would give us a couple of hours to do the cooking and set out the counter before the first customers come in at six. You could probably finish by midday as there'd only be the shop to run after that, but it would mean that you couldn't work late nights at the café.'

'I could if I had a rest in the afternoon.'

'I'd rather you didn't. Tired staff are inefficient. And as I'd be paying you a pound a week . . .'

'A pound a week?' Her eyes grew round in disbelief.

'It's not as generous as it sounds. I'd be taking eight shillings back for the rent and meat allowance.'

'You mean you want me to live in this shop of yours?'

'There's three rooms, a small kitchen and a bathroom on the second floor. I'm happy living on the Graig, but I can't afford to leave the place empty, and as you'd have an early start every morning it would make sense for you to live on the premises.'

'Let's get this straight.' Alma stiffened her back and looked him straight in the eye. 'You're offering me twelve shillings a week, meat and rent paid . . .'

'And electricity and fuel.'

'This shop of yours has electricity, even upstairs?'

'Even upstairs,' he echoed drily.

'You want to give me all that for eight hours' work a day?'

'It will be for six days a week,' he reminded her. 'Early closing on Thursday won't affect the cooking you'll have to do. If anything, there might be more as we'll have the weekend rush ahead of us. And I'll expect you to do all the cleaning. The shop and bakehouse as well as the flat and stairs.'

'I've already been accused of being the kept woman of one businessman in town. I'm not about to move on to another,' she snapped.

'Take it or leave it.' He met her look of suspicion with equanimity. 'The job is there if you want it. If you turn it down I'll advertise it in the Labour Exchange.'

'You'd offer the same pay and conditions to anyone?'

'They go with the job.'

'How do I know you don't want anything else from me?'

'You don't.' He crossed the room and pulled aside the curtain. 'Let me know what you decide. I hope to have the shop open and trading within the month. That only gives you a week to make up your mind.'

Chapter Eleven

Andrew passed his neighbour on the communal staircase. It was the same woman who'd spied on him the night he'd come home drunk. He recognised the sharp, beaky features beneath the glossy waved hair and thick bright red lipstick. Her Eau-de-Cologne wafted around him, the clip of her heels on the marble treads of the stairs resounded in his ears, a door opened and closed, there was quiet, and she was gone. She had looked right through him. Either her eyesight was failing, or she had seen him and hadn't felt the need to acknowledge his presence. But then, neither had he attempted to acknowledge hers. He should be proud of himself, he decided sourly: he had taken the first major step towards becoming a Londoner.

He let himself into the apartment, threw his coat and hat on the empty table in the living room and walked through to the kitchen. Dirty glasses and plates were stacked haphazardly in the sink just as he'd left them that morning. The remains of the pie Bethan had left for him days ago stood congealing and mouldy in a Pyrex dish. He scraped the remains into the waste bin. Was he hungry? Most people ate at this time of day. He did, because it was expected of him. He came home, sat down and ate the meal his wife had prepared and cooked. Only now there was no wife. And because there was no wife, he had bypassed the bachelors and dubious attractions of their company for the first time in months to come straight home from the hospital. If Bethan had still been in London he would be in the pub now, nursing his half-pint, trying to make it last until the stragglers from his group left to dine in their clubs.

He opened the pantry door: half a loaf of rock-hard bread, a tray of eggs, a vegetable rack filled with potatoes, and the yellowed leaves of a cabbage of advancing age. A bowl of wrinkling apples. He picked one up and bit into it. It would do for now. He would have a bath, listen to the radio. There was a play due to be transmitted at half-past eight that someone had mentioned at the lunch table. Afterwards he could go to the Italian restaurant round the corner. He couldn't afford to make a habit of it, but just this once wouldn't hurt. Tomorrow he'd ask around the hospital, find out what the clubs charged for membership and dinner. He would explain that Bethan had returned to Wales to sort out a problem with her family. It was truth – of a sort.

In the bathroom he stripped off and ran a bath. When he opened the linen basket he was mildly surprised to find it crammed full of his dirty clothes. Yet another tangible reminder of Bethan's flight, and yet another domestic problem he'd have to tackle himself. Bethan had made a point of washing their clothes daily, even before she'd had the baby's nappies to deal with.

Suddenly and furiously aware of her absence, from the apartment and from his life, he sat on the edge of the bath and thought about what he was doing. Immersing himself in domestic trivia so he wouldn't have to dwell on the defection of his wife, or the child that suffered because of his shortcomings. What had been the use of all the study, all the training when he hadn't been able to lift a finger to help his own family? His superior had stopped him again today to assure him that no one was to blame, least of all himself. But then that was easy for Doctor Floyd to say. He hadn't had to watch impotently while his wife had fought to bring a child who was already half dead into the world. Why hadn't he demanded a Caesarean when things had first begun to go wrong?

He shuddered, damning himself for going over the events of that day yet again. It was no use. What was done, was done. The child had been a hopeless case from the start because he had failed Bethan at the birth – and before. Compounding neglect with negligence. She had deserved better. Much better.

An image of her invaded his mind. Smiling, laughing, her brown eyes shining with the sheer pleasure of life, as they had done the first time he had danced with her. If she had listened to him and placed the child in the care of professionals it could be like that again. Both of them happy, free to enjoy their marriage and all the attractions London had to offer.

Overwhelmed by a sudden acute sense of loss, he forgot his anger for a moment, and remembered how much he missed that young, beautiful, smiling Bethan. The pain of separation was intense, the dependency it suggested terrifying to one who had always prided himself on cool self-sufficiency, especially in matters of the heart.

If she truly loved him she would have been happy to have given the child up instead of deserting him, leaving him to fend for himself in this empty apartment. Was she trying to make him more aware of the love and passion they had once shared? Didn't she already know how he felt? Even the note she'd left, which he had read and reread until he had memorised every line, had ended 'Love Bethan'. Did she really love him – or were they simply idle words written out of habit? He had never received a letter from her before. Not even a note, so he had no way of knowing.

He still loved her. With a love he had tried to deny once before, only to cause both of them misery and heartache. But now the situation was reversed. It was he who needed her, and she who had walked away. Why hadn't she seen his need, his desire for her . . . for happiness. Why had she persisted in taking everything they had and throwing it away?

The baby had come between them, and would always lie between them. A child he couldn't bear to look at. And while she insisted on keeping it there was no hope of them picking up the threads of their life. Couldn't she see that she wouldn't have to do it alone? He would support her every step of the way. Together they would walk the long, flower-bordered drive of the gabled Tudor manor house Doctor Floyd had given him photographs of. The door would open, they'd be shown inside. A white and blue gowned nurse would be waiting in an ante-room to take the bundle Bethan carried in her arms. They would walk back down the drive together arm in arm: Bethan would be free from burden for the first time in five months. And so would he. He would no longer have to face a daily reminder of the guilt he carried.

The picture he'd painted was vivid, real; so real that tears started in his eyes when he looked around the bathroom and realised he'd been daydreaming. He took off his watch. He was hungry. Tonight he could drive to the fish and chip shop down the road and he could eat in the restaurant tomorrow. He wouldn't have to ask about clubs until the day after. Two days could change a great deal – perhaps even Bethan's mind. Tomorrow he might return from work to find her here. Then he wouldn't have to ask about clubs at all.

He switched off the taps and stepped into the bath. As the water flowed around him he began to relax. It was only a matter of time. She had written that she loved him. She'd be back. Wouldn't she?

'Rent man.'

Alma's hands turned clammy when she heard Bobby's clumsy footsteps in the passageway. She jumped from her chair, dropping her library book and the blanket she'd been huddling under. She was alone in the house. Her mother was out, shopping with Betty Lane. She wouldn't have put it past Bobby to wait for them to leave; it was common knowledge in the street that Mrs Lane took her mother down to the post office every Thursday to cash her pension. From there they went to Betty's sister's house for tea. What had started as a favour had become a weekly routine since Alma's stay in hospital. One for which Alma was grateful. After a culmination of minor incidents of the Mary and Freda type she had stopped walking out with her mother, and rarely by herself, unless it was absolutely necessary. Especially in broad daylight.

In fact she never went anywhere now except the café, and she had taken to walking as much of the way down the quieter Gelliwastad Road as was possible. 'Decent' women, especially chapelgoers would cross the road when they saw her approaching, and despite Tony and Laura's stout denials, she knew that trade in the café was suffering. She might be out of sight in the kitchen, but she certainly wasn't out of the minds of the townsfolk. She had even heard mutterings among her neighbours in Morgan Street about disgraced girls who were brazen enough to show themselves in public. She would have been only too delighted to keep herself hidden behind the walls of her home, if only she could have thought of some other way of earning money.

'Rent's due.' Bobby pulled back the curtain and grinned at her. Leaving the blanket and library book where they lay on the floor, she shrank back towards the washhouse door.

'I don't get paid until tonight.'

'Is that so?' He stepped into the room, kicking aside the book and blanket with the toe of his muddy boot.

'You can pick it up from me in Ronconi's tonight. I'll be there from six o'clock on.' She could have swallowed her tongue. Now he knew what time her shift started.

'The last thing I want to do on a Friday night is visit a temperance bar.'

'If you give me your address I'll bring it round to your house first thing tomorrow,' she pleaded, resolving to ask Tony if he'd pay her on Thursday nights in future. Far better to risk upsetting Tony than Bobby.

'I'm disappointed in you, Alma. I thought you'd remember our little chat about keeping your rent book up to date.'

'I do. And I've always paid on time before.'

'This is how it starts.' He walked over to the mantelpiece and picked up a framed photograph of her father. 'With one slip. Pay late once and it's easier to pay late the next time, and the next, until before you know it you've missed a week. Then one week becomes two . . .'

'Not with me. Please Bobby . . .' she began, hoping he'd leave without making a scene, or worse still, attempting to touch her.

'Oh it's "please Bobby" now, is it?' he smiled unpleasantly. 'Come down off our high horse now we can't pay our rent, have we, Miss Hoity Toity?'

'I told you. You'll get it tomorrow,' she repeated harshly, trying not to think about what her mother was spending in town.

'Alma?' He replaced the photograph and drew closer to her. Reaching out, he fingered one of her red curls. Stretching and pulling it between his fingers, he stroked her cheek. She recoiled, crashing into the washhouse door.

'I said you'd have it tomorrow.'

'I could give you longer,' he murmured.

'Get out.' Her voice rose precariously.

'Alma.' His face was close to hers. Very close. His tongue slicked wetly across his lips.

'If you don't get out now I'll scream for Mr Lane,' she threatened, fumbling blindly behind her for the knob of the door.

'I'm terrified. Do you mean that the wheezing old geezer from next door is actually likely to burst in here to . . . to what, Alma?' He frowned in feigned perplexity. 'Protect your virtue?' he suggested. 'Even you have to admit it *is* somewhat tarnished. I don't think there's a man or woman in Pontypridd who'd believe anything you have to say about a situation like this. Let's be practical.' He walked to the chair, sat down and propped his boots on the polished brass rail of the fender. 'How many years did you work for Ronnie Ronconi getting paid for more than your waitressing? You did well for yourself there, Alma.

That is until a decent girl caught his eye and he took himself a wife.'

'I said you'd have your money.'

'Come on, Alma, don't play games with me. Everyone knows how destitute you are. You could barely make ends meet when you earned money from two jobs. Not that I've heard anyone blaming Goldman for sacking you. After all, he can't afford to have any gossip, either about his business or himself. He's a family man, with a wife. Unlike Tony Ronconi who's only a kid and not at all worldly wise. Not yet.'

He sat forward, eyeing her up and down as he tapped a cigarette from a packet he'd taken from the top pocket of his tweed sports coat. 'But then I'd bet a pound to a penny that you'd be only too willing to educate him in the ways of the world . . . for a consideration. Always supposing of course that he doesn't mind taking up with his brother's cast-offs.'

'You foul . . .'

'I'm only spelling out what people are thinking about you, Alma. But as I said before, I can help you. In the same way Ronnie Ronconi did.' He paused for a moment, giving her the opportunity to speak. When she didn't he continued. 'You're an attractive woman. Bit thin for my taste, but then that'll soon alter. And when it does no one will be around to make the kind of offer I'm making to you. Make hay while the sun shines as they say, and seeing as how I happen to know that your mother won't be back for a while how about showing me the upstairs . . .'

She turned abruptly and pulled up the sash on the kitchen window, breaking her fingernails as she did so.

'Mr Lane!' she yelled.

'Tomorrow morning, no later than ten. I'll be here. If you haven't the money I'll be in the bailiffs' office first thing Monday morning, and then it'll be time for you to walk up the Graig.' Bobby rose to his feet, kicked the chair into the hearth and left the room.

Trembling, Alma sat at the table and sank her head on

to her arms. What was she doing? A theatrical bout of self-pity was a luxury she couldn't afford. Especially now. Opening the drawer in the rickety table she removed a stub of pencil and an old paper bag, and frantically began to jot down figures. She had been putting off this task for far too long, terrified of what her calculations might reveal.

Tony was paying her eight shillings a week. Her mother had five shillings a week pension. The rent was nine shillings. The doctor and the hospital took another penny a week each, and that was something she dare not cut back on, not with her mother growing frailer every passing year. Although they only lit the stove three days a week, a shilling went on coals. Soap was ninepence, washing blue a penny. Her mother paid eightpence a week burial insurance so there'd be enough for a decent funeral for herself and mourning clothes for Alma. That was something else they had to keep paying: her mother was terrified of the prospect of a pauper's grave. Tenpence went on a beef heart, the only meat they ate all week. A loaf of bread a day and marge to put on it took another two and sixpence. Tea worked out at elevenpence halfpenny. Milk came to a shilling . . . she was over eighteen shillings and that was without potatoes, fruit, vegetables, jam, flour, sugar, lard . . . With only thirteen shillings a week coming in they had to cut back. But where?

She owed Laura nearly three pounds, and their tab at Hopkins' corner shop stood at ten shillings. She took a deep breath. Bobby was right. They were getting deeper and deeper into debt and she could take one of two ways out. On the basis of the figures she'd just worked out, if she opted for the workhouse they might as well walk out of the house and up to Courthouse Street tonight. There was no need even to pack a bag. They wouldn't be allowed their own things. Her mother would have to wear the grey uniform of the women's geriatric ward, and she would be set to scrubbing floors in the coarse overalls of the women's ward until they found her outside domestic work. Either way she probably wouldn't be allowed to see her mother except on high days and holidays ever again.

And the alternative? It was merely a question of who she preferred: Charlie or Bobby? After all, as Bobby had so crudely put it, it wouldn't be that big a step to take. She had played the part of the fancy woman already, she thought resentfully, remembering Ronnie Ronconi and the French letters he had bought to use in the cold bedroom above the café, before Maud Powell had come on the scene. But it had been different with Ronnie. She couldn't even remember deciding to sleep with him. It had just happened as a natural result of the passion he had engendered within her. She had lived for the moments when she and Ronnie had been alone, naked in one another's arms . . . But now there was no Ronnie, only Bobby Thomas, married, his breath and clothes smelling of drink.

Bobby's sly insinuations and leering looks unnerved and frightened her. At least Russian Charlie was clean, and the wages he offered meant she and her mother could leave worries about rent and Morgan Street behind them. If he kept his word about the meat, fuel and rent it would also mean that in time she would be able to pay off every penny they owed.

Charlie would probably call into the café some time over the weekend. She resolved to ask Tony to tell him to wait for her after work. The sooner she took him up on his offer the better. And if he expected her to sleep with him as part of the arrangement, what did it matter? One man couldn't be that different from another.

William was the first tradesman into the butchers' market on Friday morning. For three weeks, ever since Charlie had picked up the key to the shop, he seemed to have done nothing but work. Scrub, clean and paint until late at night after his stints in the slaughterhouse. Run the stall single-handed while Charlie negotiated meat at wholesale prices, or checked out the cost of repairing the roof. He'd even put four extra hours in at the slaughterhouse late last night to help Charlie cut all the meat they needed for the weekend so Charlie could take this morning off to meet the builder he'd finally chosen to carry out the repairs.

It had been hard work, but it had been worth it. At least it enabled him to steal an extra ten minutes in bed.

He dumped the pig he was carrying, feet down. Propping its back against the side of the closed shutters, he pulled Charlie's keys out of his overall pocket and heaved on the padlock. He glanced down the aisle of stalls, peering into the dairy market in the hope of catching a glimpse of Vera. He'd spent the last four Saturday nights on the hearth-rug in her kitchen, and was already shivering in anticipation. The hands of the clock over the door pointed to five. Another forty-one hours and he'd be there.

He spent all his waking hours thinking about Vera, and the things they did to one another. She was even beginning to haunt his dreams, naked except for creamy silk stockings and a white satin and lace suspender belt, her breasts beautifully, deliciously bare, her arms extended, waiting to accept his embrace, her thighs parted – ready. Last night he'd woken to find Eddie pounding him viciously in the chest, telling him to stop moaning, or else.

'Will.'

'Good God, where did you spring from?' His mouth went dry as he stepped closer to the shutters, shielding her with his body to minimise the risk of anyone seeing them.

'I came in through the clothes market.' She smiled coyly, looking up at him from beneath lowered lashes with an expression that sent his pulse rate soaring. 'George thinks I'm having breakfast with my mother. He had to drive up to the farm because he sold out of clotted cream yesterday. He won't be here for at least another half-hour. No one will.'

William forgot all the promises he'd made to Charlie

about jointing carcasses and preparing the stall. He wanted Vera. Now. This minute. He couldn't wait until Saturday night. He looked around. Someone was moving down in the second-hand clothes market, but they were too far away to see anything.

'Quick.' He unlocked the shutters and pulled her towards him. 'Crawl in there before anyone sees you.'

Vera needed no second bidding. Dropping to her hands and knees she crept through the gap in the side of the boards. William relocked the shutters and after a second check, ducked beneath the shutters himself. Pushing the door shut, he wedged it with his foot.

'You are clever. No one would know we're here,' Vera giggled. Her voice sounded eerie in the darkness. All he could see were one or two cracks of grey light through chinks in the thick wooden shutters. The smell was overpowering: washing soda and stale meat, strongly and improbably perfumed with attar of roses, Vera's favourite scent, or so she had told him three times before he'd finally taken the hint and gone out and bought her a bottle.

'Ssh!' he commanded, suddenly terrified as footsteps echoed towards them. They halted just outside the stall. He could even hear someone breathing. As he crouched there, quivering in the darkness, he cursed the madness that had overtaken him. If George tore the shutters open above their heads now, what could he say?

'I dropped my keys and Vera was helping me find them?' Or, 'We're playing hide and seek, do you want a game?'

After an eternity, whoever it was moved, walking with sluggish steps towards the dairy market. William breathed again. He opened his mouth ready to tell Vera to go, then felt her fingers working to unfasten the buttons on his overall. Seconds later they were at his fly. She pulled him on top of her. He fell forward, but was careful to keep the soles of his feet firmly against the half-door let into the side of the stall. She'd hitched the skirt of her overall high, and as he slid his hand between her stockinged legs he realised she wasn't wearing any underclothes. She moaned softly, shifting beneath his weight.

'No noise,' he hissed into where he thought her ear should be. 'For God's sake, no noise.'

He didn't enjoy what followed. Fearful of every footfall, every bang of neighbouring shutters opening. And when it was over and he crawled outside to check the lie of the land he saw that his overall was covered with sawdust.

'Been rolling around in the hay, Will?' Eddie laughed as he carried a bucket of water over to Wilf Horton's stall.

'Dropped my keys,' he shouted back. As soon as Eddie'd gone he whispered to Vera. 'Out now. Quick.'

She tripped over her high-heeled shoes as she emerged.

'Your overall is filthy,' he groaned as she struggled to her feet.

'Thank you for helping me up, Mr Powell,' she said in a loud voice as Mrs Walker passed them. 'It was stupid of me to trip. And I think you're right. I will have to go home to change.'

Ostensibly unlocking the stall, he watched as she tottered away. The seams of her stockings were crooked. There was a ladder in the back of her heel, and her white overall was covered in black smuts and sawdust; but dirty and dishevelled, she still exuded sex as she swung her hips enticingly, allowing the cloth to flow over thighs he alone among the men in the market knew were naked. As he lusted after her retreating figure he vowed never again to take such a risk. Saturday nights with George down the road in the Queen's were dangerous enough; Charlie's stall on a Friday morning was sheer lunacy.

He folded back the shutters and clipped them to the sides of the stall. He opened the meat safe, and taking out the largest knife went to get the pig. He stared in disbelief at the vacant space where he had left it. Panic-stricken, he walked around the stall. It was nowhere to be seen.

Feeling sick, he locked himself behind the counter and began to unpack the safe of the meat they'd prepared the night before. A whole pig represented three trading days' profits. Charlie would kill him. Particularly now when the shop was taking every penny of his spare cash. It would take a month of overtime and working for nothing to pay Charlie back. And he hadn't even been able to take a good look at Vera.

'Here you are, Alma, your wages. You wanted them a day early.'

'For the rent, yes. Thanks Tony.' She took the three half-crowns and sixpence he handed her and secreted them in her purse.

'You managing all right?' he asked, thinking she looked even paler and thinner in the face than usual.

'I'm managing fine,' she answered quickly. Too quickly, judging by the fleeting expression of concern that crossed his face. 'See you usual time tomorrow.' She put on her coat, checked her tam was straight in the mirror that hung behind the counter and went out. It was raining heavily again, she noticed miserably as she hesitated to tie a headscarf over her hat. Putting her head down into the wind, looking neither to the left nor right, she began to walk.

It was the tail end of a long, hard week. She had waited impatiently for Charlie to appear in the café. Tony had begun to give her odd looks when she came in every night asking the same question. 'Has Charlie been in?' No one had seen him, or, for that matter, William or Eddie Powell around anywhere except the market for two weeks. And tonight had been the last straw. Glan Richards had overheard her asking Tina about Charlie yet again, and shouted through to the kitchen from the café 'Will I do?' The cheap gibe had earned him a laugh, and done nothing to increase her self-respect, or standing with the Ronconis. Rightly or wrongly, she was beginning to feel they would be happy to show her the door as Mostyn

Goldman had done. Whatever strings were attached to Charlie's offer of a job and accommodation, she now saw it as the only escape from the deepening pit of debt. But no matter how she tried to explain or dismiss his absence to herself, Charlie's disappearance from his usual haunts worried her. She lacked the courage to go looking for him in the market, and couldn't understand why he had forsaken the café, unless . . . unless he had taken her less than enthusiastic response to his offer as a refusal. She could well be building her future on a job Charlie had already given to someone else. And if he had? What would she do then?

It had taken her entire wages and the remnants of her mother's pension to pay off last week's rent, less one and six that despite all her efforts she had failed to raise. Terrified of what Bobby might do, she had tried to cover the difference by pawning the blankets and pillows off her bed, but Arthur Faller had refused to take them, saying they were too worn. She was dreading tonight, or tomorrow morning at the latest, when she would have to sit her mother down and explain exactly how things stood. She had to put a stop to the Lane children's daily trips to the corner shop to pick up her mother's bread, marge, tea and sugar. Every morning this week she had listened while her mother have given them her order, and every morning she had clenched her fists and grit her teeth dreading their return, waiting for them to say, 'Sorry Auntie Moore, but Mrs Hopkins says your tab's full, and we can't bring you anything else until it's paid off.'

Food – she wished she could stop thinking about it. It had become an obsession since the beginning of last week when she'd cut down severely on her own meals in the hope of making a saving on their grocery bill. She limited herself to half a piece of bread and margarine at breakfast, half at dinner and half before she went to work in the café. But she'd waited in vain for the hunger pangs to subside as her stomach shrank. If anything, the pangs had begun to dominate her waking thoughts, not to mention her sleeping ones. Last night she'd dreamed of cream cakes and chocolates like the ones she drooled over every time she passed the display window of St Catherine's café in the Arcade. She had even caught herself looking longingly at the scrapings left on the plates that came into the kitchen to be washed. It was just as well that she spent most of her time on vegetable preparation, not dish-washing or cooking, otherwise she might be tempted to put more than the odd lump of raw carrot or raw potato in her mouth when she could be sure Angelo and Tony weren't looking. But no matter how she cut back, the bill in the corner shop mounted alarmingly higher with every passing day, and the rent loomed too. They formed a double-edged sword of Damocles, poised, ready to fall at any moment and wreak destruction on what little remained of their home.

She had to talk to her mother first thing in the morning. But it would help if her bad news could be softened by some good. If only she'd been able to see Charlie first and be sure of the job – perhaps if she sent one of the Lane children to him with a note? The market opened very early . . .

A cat-call echoed across the empty street. Terror prickled down her spine as she remembered Bobby and his foul propositions. Staring at the pavement and walking in the shadow of the buildings, she hurried forward. It had been twelve o'clock when she had left the café. The pubs had disgorged their last customers over an hour ago. No one but shift workers and the police should be on the streets now, and of course tramps. She wasn't sure who she was most afraid of meeting, Bobby or a tramp.

She glanced furtively over her shoulder. If it hadn't been for the whistling cat-call she could have sworn that the street was empty. Perhaps it *was* a tramp? Like the awful hobo she had seen in the American second feature that had played with *The Scarlet Pimpernel*. It had been over six months since she had treated herself to a visit to the cinema, but she could recall every detail, not only of the main film, but also of the short, cartoon, second feature and newsreel. And that tramp had terrified her. He had broken into the heroine's house, tied up her mother, eaten everything in the kitchen and then climbed the stairs to the heroine's bedroom . . .

Her thoughts froze as she heard it again: a mocking sound that set the hairs on the back of her neck crawling. It seemed to come from up ahead. The ornate fountain? She darted into a doorway and studied the grey stone edifice. A figure swayed out from behind it. Stumbling clumsily, it staggered towards her.

'Rent day tomorrow.'

'I know, Bobby.' Quickening her pace she dodged him and crossed to the left-hand side of the road. To her dismay he followed.

'You want me to reduce it for you?'

'No thank you, Bobby.' If she remained polite, carried on walking, he might leave her alone.

'Go on, you know you can't pay. The reduction I'm offering would be more than worth your while.' He reached out and clasped her arm.

'You'll get your rent!' She snatched her arm away but he lurched forwards. Wrapping both his arms around her waist he fell on top of her, dragging them both to the ground.

'Let me go!' She fought with every ounce of strength she could muster, kicking out at his legs, lashing him with clenched fists. He rolled on top of her and started to laugh, with the inane cackle of the truly drunk.

She heaved him off and attempted to rise, but his hand had closed like a steel vice round her right wrist, pinning it to the pavement.

'If you don't let me go, Bobby, I'll scream. And after last time you know I will,' she hissed, terror muting her voice to a whisper.

He struggled to his knees and peered up and down the

deserted street. 'I don't see anyone who'll hear you, so go ahead,' he slurred. He sat back on his heels, his eyes rolling as he strained to focus on her. 'Come on, Alma,' he wheedled. 'Be a sport. You know you want it. Everyone knows girls like you miss it when it's taken off them suddenly. After all, how long is it since Ronnie Ronconi left? Five . . . six months?' He tried to dive on top of her again, but she moved quicker than he did, rolling away from him at the last moment. He landed heavily on his knees.

'Alma!' he chanted, laughing again as he closed his fingers even tighter around her wrist and carried her hand to his mouth. 'Alma . . .'

Desperate to get away, she sank her teeth as hard as she could into the soft fleshy part of his hand below the thumb.

'You cow!' He released his grip just long enough for her to regain her feet. She raced forward and he flung himself after her in a rugby tackle. She crashed heavily to the ground, and this time she did scream. Long, loud and clearly, a piercing echo that resounded around the deserted buildings as her head and chest connected painfully with the pavement.

An explosion of black burst in her brain. Through a thick mist she watched helplessly while Bobby, still laughing, locked his hands around her ankles and dragged her by her legs along the pavement into the doorway of Heath's piano shop.

'Leave me alone!' She struggled to pull her clothes down, conscious he was able to look up her skirt. 'Leave me—'

A hand materialised above Bobby's head. Even in her confused state she realised it couldn't be Bobby's because both of his gripped her ankles. She watched spellbound as luminous white fingers sank into Bobby's black curls. His head jerked back sharply, his grasp on her ankles relaxed, then finally loosened. He rose slowly, infinitely slowly into the air above her, like a marionette being manipulated by a dark, shadowy puppeteer. He swung away, his legs dangling ineffectually above the ground.

Heaving for breath and shaking in terror, Alma crawled to the display window of the shop behind her. She tried to stand, but a sharp pain in her ribs felled her to her knees. The pane of glass at her back shuddered in its frame as she stumbled against it. The fingers had formed a fist. It connected with Bobby's jaw and he shot backwards, landing with a dull thud on the ground beside her.

The only silhouette that remained standing was thickset, stocky, with wide shoulders and a cap pulled down low over its face, but she could see the white blond hair escaping its confines.

Chapter Twelve

'ARE YOU ALL right?' Charlie was bending over her, his hand extended. She took it and tried to pull herself up, but she tumbled back again, sliding weakly over the tiled floor of the piano shop porchway.

'I . . . I . . .'

The dark street whirled in a kaleidoscope as he scooped her into his arms and carried her through the open doorway of the shop next door.

'I was working late. I heard a noise outside,' he explained as he looked around for somewhere to put her.

The shop was no longer the series of grimy, filthy rooms Charlie had shown to William. The walls, floors and work surfaces were clean and shining; the atmosphere eye-stinging, redolent with the mixed odours of paint, varnish and turpentine. In the corner was a pile of dustsheets, dry, if none too clean. He lowered Alma gently on to them, but she locked her hands around his neck, clinging to him, refusing to allow him to move away from her.

'You're safe here with me, I promise you,' he murmured soothingly, recognising the terror in her eyes. He reached around to the back of his neck and prised her fingers apart. Then he went into the kitchen to fetch his coat. 'You're shivering.' He laid it over her.

'You always seem to be coming to my rescue.' She tried to smile but a grimace froze on her lips as pain shot through her head.

'You're hurt.' He returned to the kitchen and looked around. He and William had worked hard to clean the place up but there was precious little in it that was any use to him now. He spotted two mugs they'd used to drink lemonade because they hadn't wanted to waste coal by lighting the stove just to make tea. Lifting one down from the window-sill, he rinsed it under the tap and filled it with cold water. As an afterthought he pulled a clean handkerchief out of his overall pocket and soaked that as well before returning to Alma in the shop.

Sitting on the floor next to her and propping her against his chest he helped her to drink. Still dizzy and disorientated she hung on to him in an effort to steady herself. Charlie gently but firmly disentangled himself from her grasp, and placed the wet handkerchief over an angry red mark on her forehead.

'Your skin isn't broken, only swollen,' he reassured her.

She held the handkerchief over her temple. It was cool, although it smelt nauseatingly of paint.

'This is your shop?'

'Yes.'

'You were painting it now, at this time of night?'

'I hope to open next month, and as I work most days that only leaves the evenings.'

'Is that why you haven't been in the café?'

He nodded.

'I tried to get a message to you about the job,' she mumbled. She closed her eyes. Everything was swimming around her in a turgid, chemically tainted atmosphere.

'You're all right now,' he said, and for the first time in her life she actually believed the platitude. She leaned against him and allowed herself to relax. He smelt clean. A strange combination of bleach, soda and honestly won sweat. She would be able to stand him touching her. But not Bobby. *Never* Bobby. She opened her eyes and lifted her face to his, expecting a kiss. Charlie looked at her for a moment, then moved away.

'I'll be back in a moment.'

'Don't leave me,' she pleaded, hysteria mounting at the thought of being left alone.

'I have to go outside.'

She watched, feeling very small, alone and abandoned as he went to the door.

The pavement outside his shop was empty. He looked into the doorway of the piano shop. That too was empty. Whoever had attacked Alma hadn't stayed around. He returned to the shop, this time closing and locking the door behind him. Alma was still lying, white, frightened and tearful where he had left her on the dustsheets, his coat spread over her like a blanket.

'I'll lock you in and get the police. I won't be long.'

'No.' Her hand shook as she put the mug of water he'd given her on the floor.

'The next person he attacks might not be as lucky as you.'

'He won't attack anyone else.' She wanted him to come to her and take her in his arms, so she could feel warm, secure and comfortable again.

'Do you know who he is?'

'Yes.' Charlie was keeping his distance. Did that mean he didn't like her? But he'd offered her a job. Too confused to analyse the situation, she only knew that for the first time since Ronnie had left her for Maud, she had felt safe in a man's arms. She even felt safe now. Charlie's presence in the room was enough, even when he wasn't physically close to her. 'He's my rent man,' she replied, wanting to explain everything. Suddenly it seemed very important that Charlie knew the truth, not the rumours being spread about her. 'Since I lost my morning job in the tailor's I've had trouble paying my bills. He wants me to make up the difference with something other than money,' she said baldly.

'He attacked you. He deserves to be punished.'

'By who? The police couldn't care less about people like me.'

'He broke the law.'

'A law that says everyone should pay their debts. All he'd have to say is he threatened me with the bailiffs for not paying my rent and I attacked him.'

'I saw different.'

'He'd only make even more trouble for me if I went to the police. Please, my mother and I are lucky to have a roof over our heads as it is. Can't we just drop the subject?'

'How much do you owe him?'

'Why do you want to know?' she demanded, suddenly suspicious. A few moments ago she would have done anything he'd wanted her to, but that had been when he'd held her in his arms. Now, as he interrogated her across the empty shop, he didn't seem to be the same man. Was he going to proposition her, coldly, unemotionally as Bobby had? Other women got caresses, kisses and promises. Was there something about her that made all men want to treat her like a worthless slut?

'If you're going to work for me, I should know what trouble I'm taking on.'

'Damned sure I'm going to take the job, aren't you?' She closed her eyes, wishing the ground would swallow her up. Charlie was her only hope of leading a decent life. He'd saved her from Bobby and his odious intentions, and here she was throwing the opportunity he offered back in his face.

'No,' he answered quietly.

'Tomorrow I'll owe two shillings and sixpence on my rent,' she capitulated. 'But as well as the rent, there's our tab in Hopkins' shop. It'll only be a matter of time before they stop our credit, and as if that's not enough, I owe Laura two pounds seventeen shillings and eightpence.' Tears started in the corner of her eyes. The whole lot didn't amount to five pounds. But on an income of thirteen shillings a week it might as well have been fifty-five.

'You can move in here as soon as you like.'

'If I do, I suppose I could sign notes . . .'

'I'll lend you what you need to settle your debts against your future earnings.' Charlie still made no attempt to move from the door.

'Why would you do that?'

'You are going to work for me aren't you?' he asked, weary of fencing words.

'That still doesn't explain why you'd want to help me beforehand.'

'I told you last time I saw you. You're a good worker.'

'And because I jumped in Ronnie Ronconi's bed you want me to jump in yours?' She was glad she'd found the courage to ask the question outright. For once in her life everything was open and above board.

'The last thing I want or need at the moment, Miss Moore, is a woman in my bed. But thank you for the offer.'

She had expected a reply along the lines of, 'Seeing as how you brought up the subject, I'll take you up on that.' His rebuff left her speechless.

'I'll lend you ten pounds. That should be enough to cover your debts and keep you and your mother until you get your first wage packet from this shop.'

'I don't need that much.'

'Let's say ten pounds just to be on the safe side. That way you can pay off everything you owe and have a little to spare. You can pay me back at two shillings a week.'

'But that will take me—' her head ached as she frantically added up the figures – 'a year to pay back, and that's without interest.'

'There won't be any interest, now, if you feel up to it, I'll take you home.' He walked towards her and gently pulled back the handkerchief. A huge lump had broken out on the surface of her forehead. Red and swollen, it looked extremely painful.

'That hurts,' she protested.

'I'm not surprised. But better out than in.'

'What do you mean?'

'If the swelling occurs on the inside it can cause dangerous pressure, which could do considerable damage.'

'I didn't know that.' She bit her lip hard.

'Can you walk?' he asked, aware of how the sight of the two of them, alone in his shop at this time of night, could be misconstrued.

'I think so.' She rose stiffly to her feet. 'Here's your coat.'

'Keep it around your shoulders. It's cold outside.'

He didn't offer her his arm, but he watched carefully as she stumbled to the door. He switched off the light and locked the door behind her.

'I hate owing anyone money,' Alma murmured as he walked alongside her up Taff Street.

'You seem to have little option at the moment.'

'When I'm straight, I'm going to save every penny I can so I'll never get in this mess again,' she said vehemently. The effort of speaking made her feel dizzy again and she clutched at Charlie's arm. He lent her his support, but she still felt a distance she was convinced hadn't existed earlier when he'd carried her into the shop. She glanced up at his face. His eyes didn't even seem to be focused on the surroundings. They were looking inward with an expression that further chilled her icy body.

She wasn't to know that he was back in another time, another place. Walking out on a cold night just like this one, with a young girl clinging to his arm. One who, like her, had red hair and deep green eyes that a man could look into and lose his soul.

'What are you thinking about, Feo?'

She had been wearing a thick black wool coat and a bright red hand-knitted scarf. He'd had to bend down to kiss the tip of her frozen nose.

'You're not my mother,' she'd protested.

'I don't want to be your mother. But I want to make sure that you're around to share that future I've been dreaming about.'

'When we'll have our own house . . . just like my brother Dmitri and his wife,' she began, laughing at him a little.

'Not like Dmitri. Ours will be grander.'

'Grander?'

'Grander,' he repeated, refusing to acknowledge her scepticism. 'It will have a veranda downstairs and a balcony upstairs that you'll be able to sit out on and pick cherries from the trees that I'll plant all around the garden. There'll be stoves in all the rooms, not just the kitchen, with flues going up into the bedrooms to keep them warm.'

'I won't need flues. I'll have the feather bed my grand-mother is making us, and,' she arced her eyebrows, 'you to keep me warm Feo.'

Her smile bewitching, mischievous. Her lips beneath his, warm, enticing.

'Masha . . .'

'The others won't be back from my uncle's name day for hours. The barn is warm, we could go in for just a little while.'

'Don't you know what you're doing to me?'

'Spring will soon break, then we'll be married.'

'A few weeks.'

'In which to practise.'

'Masha!' He'd pretended to be shocked.

'Come on Feo, you're wasting time. The barn is dry . . .'

Dry and warm, just as she'd promised. Smelling of hay and the chickens that nested between the bales. And her hair, sweet, fragrant loosed from the bond of the net she wore. He wanted no woman in his bed. None except Masha . . .

'This is it?'

Charlie looked about him and realised Alma had led him to her front door.

'Thank you for walking me home.' She removed her arm from his and handed back his coat. 'Won't you come inside?'

'I don't think so. It's very late.'

She hesitated, her hand on the doorknob.

'Are you afraid to go in?' he asked intuitively.

'I know it's silly of me. It's just that Bobby collects my rent. He knows where I live.'

'Do you want me to check your house?'

Although he'd visited her before, she was torn between a desire to keep her poverty private, and her fear of Bobby. The fear won. 'Please, come in, just for a moment.' She opened the door and walked down the passage. Charlie closed the door behind him and instinctively reached out and felt for an electric light switch, then he saw the faint, brief flare of a match, followed by the soft glow of a candle through the thin curtain up ahead. Alma pushed aside the curtain, and he followed her into the kitchen.

'The back door is in the washhouse.' She lit another stub of candle from the flame of the one she held in her hand.

He took the candle she offered, lifted the latch and checked the washhouse thoroughly before opening the back door and looking into the yard, outhouse and coalhouse.

'Nothing out there. Do you want me to bolt the door?'

'Please.'

He did as she asked, then followed her back into the cold kitchen.

'I'll stay here while you check the upstairs,' he said, handing her the candle.

Charlie stood, gazing out of the small kitchen window, listening to her footsteps as they echoed over the flagstones in the passage. They paused for a moment, and he heard her checking the empty front room before walking up the uncarpeted staircase.

After Russia he'd believed himself immune to the wretchedness poverty trailed in its wake. Now he knew he wasn't. The house even smelt of poverty, an odour compiled from shame and the humiliation of not having two halfpennies to rub together. The last time he'd stood in the kitchen he'd noticed only the obvious: the lack of fire, cushions, rugs, small comforts that those who had the luxury of work took for granted. Now he had time to study the room at length without Alma's eagle eye watching him, he was appalled by its bleakness.

The battered and patched tin bucket in front of the stove contained barely half an inch of small coal. There was no sign of wood, only newspapers. The scrubbed surfaces of the pine-topped deal table and breadboard were devoid of the smallest crumb. He couldn't even smell food, and he had a shrewd suspicion that if he were to open the doors of the pantry and dresser they'd be bare. If any mouse was foolhardy enough to enter this house it would probably starve to death along with the occupants. The dresser held two cups, two saucers and two plates, if there had been more he didn't doubt they'd been sold or pawned. A single clean but patched saucepan hung upside down on the drying rack above the cold stove. Even the stub of candle Alma had lit was the last on the mantelpiece. A framed photograph stood incongruously next to it. Pushing the candle closer, he studied it.

'My father.'

Alma was standing in front of the curtain.

'He died when I was small. Pit accident.' She walked over to the photograph and picked it up. 'What I hate more than anything is not being able to remember him. Only the funeral, and my mother crying. Endlessly crying.'

He reached inside his shirt and took out the bag he kept his takings in. Carrying them and the stub of candle over to the table he counted out five pounds.

'That's for the rent and the corner shop. I'll stop by tomorrow with another five.'

He replaced the bag inside his shirt and slipped his arms into the sleeves of his coat. It smelt of the household soap she used and the cooking he associated with Ronconi's café.

'I don't need this much,' she protested as she looked

down at the mixed silver and ten-shilling note on the table.

'Take it. I'll see you tomorrow and we'll make arrangements for you to move into the flat above the shop. Don't forget to bolt the door behind me.'

She followed him but he stepped outside without a backward glance. She had been prepared to sleep with him. He'd rejected her, yet he'd given her money. The thought that floated uppermost in her mind as she rammed the bolt home on the door as that at least the women in station yard had the satisfaction of knowing that they'd earned their money.

It was strange how soon life, any life, eventually becomes a routine, Bethan thought as she carried buckets of water from the boiler in the stove to the enormous tub in the washhouse to do the weekly wash. She had been home for over five weeks and already it felt as though she and Edmund had never lived anywhere else. Strange too how, as if by tacit agreement, no one in the house ever brought up the subject of her mother.

Eddie had made a point of going calling for rags in the Rhondda the morning after Elizabeth Powell's departure, and on his return had mentioned that he had seen Elizabeth beating John Joseph's mats on his washing line. Eddie hadn't attempted to speak to his mother, but then neither had she said a word to him, although she must have heard the sound of his horn. From that scant piece of information Bethan presumed that Elizabeth had found a home with her uncle. The following day she wrote her mother a letter telling her that she and Eddie were going to try and keep the home going between them. Elizabeth had never replied, and as the household slipped easily and effortlessly into a new routine that eventually became an established pattern of life, Elizabeth became, if not exactly forgotten, at least relegated to a past that seldom warranted a thought, let alone a mention.

William, Eddie and Diana became more talkative in the

days following Elizabeth's dramatic exit and, although none of them tried to analyse their feelings, they all felt as though a smothering, suffocating fog had been blown from the house. Charlie alone remained as taciturn and preoccupied as ever, but Bethan put that down to the problems connected with opening his shop coupled with the financial loss of a whole pig. She'd lent William ten shillings to cover his carelessness, all that she could afford, but she knew that it went nowhere towards compensating Charlie for the loss of his unsold stock.

Despite Evan's absence which affected them all, William and Eddie took to whistling as they went about their chores. They filled the coal bucket, cleared the ashes from the stove and carried the vegetable peelings up to the compost heap at the top of the garden without Bethan ever having to nag for their help as Elizabeth had frequently resorted to doing. They also took to cleaning their shoes over old newspaper in the washhouse instead of the cold yard, ferrying cups of tea up to her and Diana in their bedrooms first thing in the morning, and dunking the biscuits Diana made in the evenings in their tea instead of nibbling them dry. Small things Elizabeth would have severely disapproved of and put a stop to at once.

Bethan knew that although the fabric of the house in Graig Avenue remained unchanged, there were subtle differences in the household as she ran it that her mother would have condemned as examples of degenerate, ungodly behaviour. For example, not one of them had set foot in a chapel since Elizabeth had left. Bethan had used the baby's condition as an excuse, but the boys and Diana hadn't even felt the need to fabricate one. Instead, for the boys and Charlie, Sunday had become a day for working on the shop, something they had the good sense to do quietly, concentrating on cleaning and decorating the back rooms where they couldn't be seen by the chapel contingent. For Diana and Bethan it became a day for reading, playing cards, and catching up with the hundred and one small jobs neither of them ever seemed to find time to do in the week.

If Bethan wasn't happy, she was at least contented, and for that she was grateful. Generally too busy to think about Elizabeth, or even her father, she only had cause to remember them when she dusted their wedding photograph which had been kept out of sight in the sacrosanct front parlour for as long as she could remember. But strangest of all was the way she had managed to banish all thoughts of Andrew from her mind, at least during her waking hours. Last Friday another money order had been delivered by the postman, accompanied by a brief note: 'Hope you are well. Best wishes, Andrew.' She had sent him the pawn ticket for her pendant with a brief explanation, finishing with the line, 'I am well', and although he hadn't asked after his son, 'Edmund is well too. Thank you for the money. Bethan.'

But in the cold, early hours of the morning she truly did miss him. She lay awake in her parents' great bed yearning for his presence with a fervour that could only have been soothed by his touch. It was then, when she watched the moon shining down on the back garden through the crack in the curtains as she listened to Edmund's slow, quiet breathing, that she remembered. The good times! There had been so many of them. When she had first met Andrew and gone out with him, when she had left Pontypridd to be with him in London. And the last days of her pregnancy when he had cared for her so tenderly and solicitously, in fact right up to the moment of Edmund's birth.

Pushing the memory of that painful moment from her mind she picked up half of the pile of sheets and pillowcases she had stacked on the floor and threw them into the tub. Five beds and a cot made for a lot of washing. And afterwards there'd be the boys' shirts and long johns, and her and Diana's petticoats and blouses, the baby's nightdresses, and if the water was still warm and clean enough, Charlie and William's butchers' overalls. They were so soiled she set them in a bucket of soda to soak overnight and washed them out separately before dumping them in with the rest of the wash prior to boiling and starching.

Bethan picked up the wooden dolly and started pounding. Her new maxim in life was quite simple: keep busy, take each task, and day, as it came. By the time she had cleaned the house, cooked the food, done the washing and shopping with the baby in a shawl wrapped Welsh fashion around him and her, so no one could take more than a sly peek at him, there wasn't much time left for thinking – all she had to do was try to find a way to sleep at night. If she succeeded in that, there would be no time for complex desires or introspection.

The dolly slipped in her wet hand and water slopped on to the flagstoned floor. She smiled, imagining the scolding Elizabeth would have doled out, as she tossed the floorcloth over the sudsy mess.

'Bethan! Bethan!'

'Mrs Richards, I'm in the washhouse,' she answered. Much as she appreciated the love and support of her family around her, she resented the interference of the neighbours more than ever after London, and Mrs Richards was by far and away the worst culprit. Annoying Bethan constantly by referring to Edmund as 'that poor mite', she was always trying to peek into the cot as though the child was an exhibit in a freak show.

'Bethan, what do you think?' Mrs Richards burst open the door to the washhouse. 'I saw Billy's wife down the market and . . .' she paused for breath as she laid her loaded shopping basket on the floor at her feet.

'And?' Bethan prompted as she concentrated on her washing.

'And she told me they're allowing visitors into Cardiff this Sunday. Your dad is in Cardiff?'

'Yes,' Bethan replied shortly.

'I thought they might have put him somewhere else, what with him getting hard labour and everything.' She made it sound a far deeper disgrace than mere prison. 'Where was I? Oh yes, visiting. Well I stopped off to get a message to my Glan in the workhouse. Of course we'll be going along with Billy's wife and his old mother, and I thought I should come right up here and tell you. You'll have to get a message to your mam, wherever she is.' She looked slyly at Bethan. 'I mean she'll want to see him, won't she? It being over a month since they were sent down,' she babbled, not really knowing, but guessing the cause of Elizabeth's flight from her home of over twenty years.

'This Sunday you say, Mrs Richards.' Bethan pulled the cumbersome free-standing mangle closer to the tub. 'What time?'

'Two o'clock. It's the first time anyone in our family has visited a prison, but it isn't for you, is it? Your Aunt Megan has been there quite a while now. Over a year?'

'William and Diana go to see their mother as often as they can,' Bethan said flatly in an attempt to shame Mrs Richards out of her tactless cross-examination.

'According to what Billy's wife told me, we won't be able to take much in for them. A few bits of food, that's all. They won't let them wear their own clothes or read anything except the one letter a month. They even cut up any cakes you bake, but at least we'll be able to see how they are for ourselves, won't we?'

'Thank you for calling in.' Bethan heaved the first of the sheets up to the mangle with the end of the wooden dolly. 'If you'll excuse me, I must get on with this before the baby wakes for his next feed.'

'Oh, bless him too, the poor little mite. Will you be going to see your dad?' Mrs Richards made no attempt to pick up her basket.

'Probably. I'll have to talk it over with my brother.'

'Oh yes of course, Eddie. It must be hard for you at a time like this not to have Haydn around. Such a nice sensible boy, Haydn. But then you must be missing your husband too. I was only saying to our Glan the other day what a good-looking young man Doctor John is. Will we be seeing him soon?'

'Possibly,' Bethan replied shortly, heaping the first sheet into the sink and starting to wring the second.

'Oh and I almost forgot in my hurry to tell you about the prison . . .' Mrs Richards leaned back against the wall, still hoping that Bethan would invite her to have a cup of tea so she could get a good look at the baby. A lot of people were wondering what he looked like, and as next-door neighbour, she thought it only fitting she should be the one to tell them. 'I heard down Griffiths' shop that Rhiannon Pugh's not expected to last the night. The poor old thing's done for. According to the doctor she's just plain worn out. But then, that's what comes of having the likes of Phyllis Harry in the house. Rhiannon's run herself ragged looking after Phyllis's bastard . . .'

'Rhiannon has been ill for years,' Bethan interposed quickly. She'd had a soft spot for Phyllis since the days when Phyllis had worked as an usherette in the White Palace and turned a blind eye to younger brothers and sisters who'd been smuggled into the back row of the chicken run through toilet windows; and she was very fond of Rhiannon, who had offered her tea and Welsh cakes – flat cakes baked on a griddle – every time she had used her house in Phillips Street as a short cut on the way to school, town and, later, to her work in the Graig Hospital.

'I know Rhiannon has been ill for years, but the Good Lord would have spared her for a bit longer if it hadn't been for all that worry over Phyllis. And now there's no saying what will happen to Phyllis and the boy. The house is rented in Rhiannon's name and I can't see Fred the Dead passing the rent book over to an unmarried mother, even if Phyllis could afford to keep it on, which I doubt she can.' Mrs Richards crossed her arms as though defying Bethan to tell her any different.

'She'll manage somehow, Mrs Richards, most of us do.'

'We manage. But the question is will we continue to

manage inside or outside the workhouse?'

'Let's hope it will be outside, for all of us.' Bethan dumped the last of the sheets into the water.

'So I pray to God every night.' Mrs Richards stooped and picked up her basket, finally accepting that she was not going to get a cup of tea, or a peek at the baby. 'I suppose it's time I went next door to start on my own washing. You've no idea of the state my Glan gets that porter's uniform of his into.'

'It's a nice drying day,' Bethan commented, hoping to finally edge Mrs Richards out. 'I'll see you to the door.'

'I know the way, dear. You stay and finish what you're doing.'

'No trouble, and thank you for the news about the prison.' Bethan followed Mrs Richards into the kitchen, positioning herself so as to ensure that Mrs Richards couldn't see Edmund. She opened the door. 'Thank you for calling in.'

'See you on Sunday then?'

'Perhaps.'

Mrs Richards walked down the Powells' front steps reflecting that although Elizabeth had left Graig Avenue, the welcome in her house was as cold as it had ever been.

Bethan rushed through her washing in record time, finishing it just before the baby woke for his feed. Eddie sometimes came home for dinner if he was calling the streets anywhere near home, but because she wanted him to come that particular day, he didn't show his face, and the bread and Welsh cakes she'd baked that morning remained locked in their tins in the pantry.

At two o'clock she picked up the spare bottle and nappy she had packed into a string carrier bag, put on her coat and hat and wrapped the baby and herself in a shawl. As an afterthought she filled an empty tin with her cakes and Diana's biscuits. She glanced around the kitchen before she left. It wasn't as smart or modern as the London flat, but it had been her home as a child, and it had become home again, providing a safe haven when she had needed one. It looked shabby and worn, but also clean, and cosy with the stove belching out heat. The warm, welcoming smell of fresh baking lingered in the air. She imagined the boys and Diana walking in, and the thought occurred to her that she didn't know how long she was going to be. She took a pencil from the marmalade jar on the windowsill and the back of one of Andrew's envelopes and scribbled, 'In Rhiannon's with Phyllis. Bethan.'

'Rent.' Bobby swaggered through the shabby door of Alma's house, purposely kicking the bottom panel as he went. It splintered from its supporting nails and fell in three large pieces on to the flagstones. Glancing up from the wreckage, he saw Alma standing in front of the curtained doorway of the kitchen, her green eyes contemptuous as she held out her rent book at arm's length.

'It's all there, folded inside. A ten-shilling note and a sixpence. Nine shillings for this week, plus the one and six I owe from last week.'

'It'll cost another ten shillings to mend this door. A pound for a new one if it can't be fixed.'

'You broke it. You pay.' For the first time she noticed the deep black and purple bruise that spread from his chin along his jawline up to his left ear. There was a cut on his eye too. She could see its bloody jagged edge beneath the plaster that was covering his left eyebrow.

'That rain guard fell off when I opened the door because you haven't given it a single lick of paint in the last ten years.'

'It was fine until you kicked it.'

'I say otherwise, and seeing as how the landlord pays me to check the houses and collect the rent I know who he'll believe.'

'Not after last night.'

'What happened last night, then?' He stared at her cockily as he wrenched the rent book from her outstretched hand.

'You know as well as I do.'

'I know nothing.'

'The mess on your face tells a different story.'

Bobby pushed past her, slamming her into the wall with his shoulder as he pulled back the curtain and walked into the kitchen. He laid the rent book down on the table and took a fountain pen from his pocket. He unscrewed the top with a flourish.

Although he had taken his time, waiting until he'd seen Alma's mother walk off to the market clinging to Mrs Lane's arm, he looked over his shoulder as he signed the book, just to make sure the house was really deserted. After last night he didn't entirely trust Alma not to have someone lying in wait.

'You Charlie the Russian's bit on the side then now?' he taunted after he'd ensured they were alone. 'Is that where this—' he stuffed the money that had been folded into her rent book into a bag – 'came from?'

'It's my money.'

'Not honestly earned I'll be bound, unless of course,' he sniggered, 'you count lying on your back working.'

She went to the window and opened it wide, letting in a draught of freezing air. 'Just sign the rent book and go, Bobby,' she said loudly.

'Or what?' Secure in the knowledge that not only was Mrs Lane out, but Mr Lane had taken advantage of his wife's absence to walk around the corner to visit the illicit bookie shop, he pushed his face close to Alma's. 'Or you'll go whining to your foreign friend and ask him to work me over again? Well, have I got news for you. I know a lot of funny people in this town, and Russian Charlie had better watch his back.'

'You touch him and I'll go straight to the police.'

'And tell them what? That I turned down your offer to pay the rent without handing over any money?' He caught her hair and twisted her head back. Planting his wet, greasy lips over hers, he kissed her. She kicked him on the shins and he yelped. This time she was quicker than him, fleeing down the passage and out through the front door before he managed to retrieve his pen from the table. She stood outside, trembling, waiting for him to leave. He followed her, kicking aside the pieces of wood then opening the door as wide as it would go.

'You'd better watch your Ps and Qs,' he warned softly as he walked into the street. 'You can start by having this door repaired,' he added in a louder voice. 'And if it isn't done by next week, I'll see you out of here for neglecting the terms of your lease.'

'You try that and I'll tell your wife all about you, Bobby Thomas,' Alma screamed after him, silencing the children who were playing in the street. 'And don't you come knocking at my door any more for the rent either. I'm walking up to Maesycoed to pay it to Mr Jones direct. And I'm telling him why.'

Chapter Thirteen

P HYLLIS WAS UPSTAIRS, sitting watching at Rhiannon's deathbed with her small son playing at her feet, when she heard Bethan call her name softly in the downstairs passage. She rose quietly from her chair and picked up her son. He looked anxiously up into her face from large brown frightened eyes as she smoothed the hair away from Rhiannon's face. He didn't understand what was happening, only that his mother and Mamgu were very quiet, and Mamgu didn't get out of bed or want to play with him any more.

'I heard about Rhiannon. I came as soon as I could. Can I look after the little one for you?' Bethan asked as Phyllis walked down the stairs.

Phyllis bit her lip in an effort to hold back her tears. Her shame at bearing a bastard had led her to expect ostracism, and the indifference she had affected after his birth had frustrated the efforts of even the most determinedly helpful of the women in the street.

'Please. You know that if my Aunt Megan were here, she'd be with you.' Bethan put a finger from her free hand into Phyllis's son's hand. He took it and smiled.

The smile decided Phyllis. Since Rhiannon had taken to her bed two days ago, she had felt more alone than she had ever done in her entire life. With Rhiannon lying unconscious, having to be washed, fed and changed as though she were a helpless baby, and without Evan's daily visits she had felt cut off from and neglected by the world.

'Thank you.' She set her son down on the floor close to Bethan.

Bethan held out her hand to him. 'What's his name?'

'Brian. I named him after my father,' Phyllis said as the child tottered unsteadily towards the kitchen door.

'Come on Brian, you can help me make some tea.' Bethan hesitated for a moment. 'Is there anyone I should send for, Phyllis?'

'Rhiannon has no family left.'

'What about you?'

'Charlie,' Phyllis said decisively without thinking who she was speaking to. 'Please, send for Charlie. He'll know what to do.' She turned and walked back upstairs.

Bethan was totally bewildered. If anyone had asked, she would have said that Charlie and Phyllis didn't even know one another. Keeping a firm grip on Brian's hand she opened the front door and walked out on to the top step. A ragged collection of boys were playing football with a tin can lower down the street. Three young girls were walking up and down following the game, taking it in turns to push a battered old pram containing a small baby. Cheaper and more readily available than a doll, Bethan thought wryly. She stared at the boys, hoping to see one she recognised, but it was difficult. A few months away in London and none of the faces looked familiar. Finally she settled on one she thought she recalled from Eddie's schooldays.

'Martin Gibbs?'

'That's not Martin, Nurse Powell. That's his brother Michael,' one of the young girls, dressed in a cotton dress that was too thin for the cold weather assured her knowledgeably.

'Run and get him for me would you please?'

'Our mam told us not to play near this house,' one of the girl's playmates commented gravely to Bethan. 'She said that old Mrs Pugh is dying and she deserves a bit of peace before she goes, without us yelling in the street outside.'

'She is dying,' Bethan murmured softly, clutching Brian's hand all the harder. 'And I'm sure she's grateful to you for keeping quiet.'

'You want me, Nurse Powell?' The boy Bethan thought was Martin ran towards her.

'I'd like you to run an errand for me.' Bethan pulled her purse out of her coat pocket.

'Down the shop?'

'No, down the market. You'd better tell your mam where you're going.'

'She's out gossiping, she won't miss me.'

'There's no one in your house?'

'My dad.'

'Then tell him.' She produced a penny. 'You can have this, and two more when you come back.'

His eyes grew round. Threepence was birthday money for a child on the Graig.

'I'll go with him, Missus.'

'And me.'

'And me . . .'

'Just you.' Bethan handed the penny to the boy. 'You know Charlie's stall in the meat market?'

'Course I do. Everyone knows Russian Charlie.'

'Ask him to . . . tell him . . .' Bethan thought for a moment, wondering how best to phrase Phyllis's message. 'Tell him Mrs John needs him in Rhiannon Pugh's house. And tell him it's urgent.'

Phyllis sat on one side of Rhiannon Pugh's bed holding her withered hand, and Bethan sat on the other. Bethan had helped Phyllis to change the old lady's bed earlier and remake it with rubber draw-sheets and the deep blue satin coverlet that had been kept for 'best'. Now it lay over the smoothed sheets and blankets, and the frail figure of the old lady who'd treasured it all her married life. Phyllis had hung the unbleached linen shroud and white stockings that Rhiannon had stitched against this day over the central mirror of the dressing table. The old lady had asked her to remove the garments from her chest when she had taken to her bed, and had also extracted a promise from Phyllis that she would dress her in them before the undertaker placed her in her coffin. In front of the grave clothes stood a blue vase inscribed with gold lettering that read, 'A present from Porthcawl'. It was filled with daffodils that Charlie had brought up from the market, a gesture that had amazed both Phyllis and Bethan. Neither of them had ever considered the Russian thoughtful before; although as Bethan watched him stand impassively at the foot of the bed next to the door, arms folded as he kept silent vigil with them, and remembered some of the things he had done for her family over the past three years she realised it was an adjective he well deserved.

He had arrived on Rhiannon's doorstep with the flowers in his hand and Trevor Lewis in tow. Respecting Phyllis's need to be with the old lady, Trevor had examined Mrs Pugh in her presence, shaking his head gravely as he tucked his stethoscope into his bag.

Bethan had given him tea afterwards, and he had taken the opportunity to check Edmund over, and to chastise her for not coming to visit him and Laura more often. She promised to do so as soon as time allowed, and he left, muttering something about coming back later. Diana had arrived at Rhiannon's door within five minutes of coming home from work and reading Bethan's note. Sizing up the situation, she took Edmund off Bethan's hands and went home to make Eddie and William's supper. Bethan washed the endless empty cups dotted around Rhiannon's kitchen, bathed Brian in Rhiannon's enormous stone sink, and put him to bed in the big double bed he shared with his mother.

Sensing something was wrong, Brian listened intently while Bethan sung him a lullaby, accepted her good-night kiss without a murmur, snuggled down with a knitted rabbit and fell quietly asleep, which was probably as well, because for the first time in his life his mother didn't come to kiss him goodnight.

Once Brian was asleep, Bethan's evening became a marathon of making endless cups of tea, ferrying them to Phyllis and Charlie upstairs . . . and waiting. And at eleven o'clock all was much as it had been when Bethan had arrived at two in the afternoon. Rhiannon hadn't stirred. Her eyelids hadn't even flickered when Bethan and Phyllis remade her bed around her. The cheese sandwiches Bethan had made stood, curling and untouched where she had left them on Rhiannon's dressing table at six o'clock. Phyllis hadn't drawn any of the curtains all day, and as dusk fell Charlie lit one of the stubs of candle on the dressing table. As in most of the houses on the Graig, Rhiannon's electrical lights only extended as far as the downstairs rooms.

The candle flickered, silence reigned, and the old tin alarm clock that had woken Rhiannon's husband every day of his working life continued to tick away the final minutes of Rhiannon's life.

Charlie watched the light of the candle flicker across the old woman's face and remembered another deathbed. It had been spring then too. But not a damp cold spring like this. Dry days had burst sunny and warm, melting snows into lifegiving water, coaxing buds to unfurl on the trees. And the curtains in the death room had been kept open so the occupant could see the apple-blossom cloud, pink and fragrant on the branches outside the window.

He remembered the fragile weight of his grandfather's wasted hand in his. 'It is your time now, Feodor. Enjoy it. Enjoy it while you can. Every minute, boy. Life is wonderful. But for me now, it is over.'

He stepped from the doorway towards the bed. He trod softly, and if the rickety floorboards hadn't creaked beneath his weight Bethan wouldn't have noticed he'd moved. She shook herself from her reverie and watched as he laid his hand lightly on Rhiannon's neck, just as a doctor would have done. The action was so fluid, so natural, she didn't even think about it.

'She's gone,' he murmured, wrapping his arm around Phyllis's shoulder. Phyllis turned to him and he helped her to her feet. She stood there, head buried in his chest while Bethan went to Rhiannon. Charlie was right: the spirit that had animated the frail bundle of bones had left.

'It's not right,' Phyllis sobbed. 'Saying nothing . . . going without a word, like that . . .'

Bethan recalled some of the deaths she had witnessed as a nurse. Deaths lacking in dignity where people had gone out fighting, rattling and screaming to the last.

'It's the kindest way, Phyllis,' she said quietly. 'Believe me, it's what I want for myself, and I'm sure it's what Rhiannon would have wanted if she'd been given the choice.'

Phyllis stifled her sobs, gripped Charlie's shoulders, and turned round to face Bethan. 'You'll help me lay her out?'

'I'd be honoured.' Bethan looked at Charlie.

'I'll go downstairs and bring up some hot water. Then I'll walk to the Graig Hotel and telephone Doctor Lewis.' He glanced at the clock. It had stopped. He pulled out his pocket watch. 'Half-past eleven. Rhiannon died at half-past eleven?'

Phyllis nodded. Picking up the grave clothes she held them tightly in her hands. Suddenly they seemed to be all she had left.

At midnight, Trevor Lewis arrived in response to Charlie's telephone call. A few minutes after he'd signed the death certificate in Rhiannon's bedroom, there was a knock at the front door.

'I called the undertaker,' Trevor explained apologetically to a startled Phyllis. 'I thought you'd need a coffin.'

Phyllis took one of Rhiannon's cold hands in her own and kissed it as Charlie went down to open the door. Outwardly Phyllis was composed, but inwardly she was desperately trying to cling to what little routine remained of her life. As long as the old lady lay here in her own bed she was at least an integral part of the household. Coffins had no part to play in life. They belonged to cemeteries, to the ceremonies that underlined the finality of the ultimate separation.

Phyllis realised that once Rhiannon was removed from this bed, she would never again see the woman who had been more of a mother to her than her own. She would be on her own, as she had never been before. Alone with sole responsibility for her son; the prospect terrified her.

'I wasn't sure which model you wanted. I've brought a standard pine with wooden fittings to be getting on with. If you want it replaced with mahogany and brass . . .' Fred Jones's voice floated up the stairs. Charlie murmured a reply, too low for Bethan and Phyllis to hear.

'If it's all right with you we'll set it up in place now, then carry the body down. I take it, she is in one of the bedrooms?'

Phyllis and Bethan considered Fred Jones's voice loud and insensitive for a house of death, but experience had taught the undertaker that it was easier to be misunderstood when you spoke in hushed tones.

Charlie looked at the narrow stairwell and nodded agreement. While he rearranged Rhiannon's heavy old Victorian furniture in the front parlour, the undertaker brought in trestles and set them up in pride of place in the centre of the room. After Charlie had given him a hand to carry in the coffin, he fussed around, inching the supports first one way, then the other in order to give anyone looking in from the passage the best possible view of the coffin, and its contents.

'Not that I suppose there'll be that many who'll come in to look at her,' Fred asserted when everything had been arranged to his satisfaction. 'From what I hear they led a quiet life in this house.'

In the end it was Charlie who carried Rhiannon's body, wrapped in the best bedcover, down the stairs, and Phyllis aided by Bethan who arranged the cheap machined cotton frill around the old lady's face and shroud.

'She looks peaceful, doesn't she?' Phyllis asked, seeking confirmation.

'I hate to get down to brass tacks at a time like this,' Fred interrupted in a rasping voice, before either Bethan or Charlie could answer. 'But the sooner the business side is tied up to everyone's satisfaction, the sooner you can get on with your mourning.'

'Can't it wait?' Phyllis pleaded as she folded Rhiannon's fingers around the gold crucifix her husband had bought to celebrate the birth of their only son over sixty years ago.

'I'll sit with Rhiannon while you talk to Mr Jones,' Bethan interposed, knowing how important 'corpse sitting' was to the women of the Graig, especially during the first night after death.

Phyllis reluctantly returned Rhiannon's hands to the coffin, and with one final backward glance, left the parlour. Trevor, Fred Jones and Charlie filed solemnly after her into the kitchen. Without thinking, Phyllis filled the kettle, put it on the stove to boil and counted heads. She went to the open-shelved dresser and lifted down three of Rhiannon's 'best' blue and gold cups and saucers for the men, then three more, one for herself, one for Bethan, and one for Rhiannon. When she'd realised what she'd done, the tears began to flow again. Charlie took the last cup gently from her trembling hands and replaced it on the shelf.

'I take it Mrs Pugh was insured?' It was after twelve. Fred had downed several brandies in the New Inn, and all he wanted now was his bed. Preferably warmed by the plump body of his wife. He resented being called out on a Saturday night. Any other night of the week he didn't mind, but a Saturday night was special. He found himself wondering, not for the first time, why people couldn't die during respectable daylight hours, say between eight in the morning and six in the evening.

'She was.' Phyllis dried her tears and set about spooning pungent black tea-leaves from Rhiannon's old tin caddy into the pot.

'Now, about the funeral . . .' He removed a notebook covered in shiny black cloth from his pocket and licked the lead on the pencil that had been tucked into its spine.

Phyllis stared at the book. She had only ever seen red notebooks before. Even the manager of the White Palace had carried a red one. She wondered if black ones were produced specially for undertakers.

'. . . how many cars besides the hearse?'

'Just one,' she answered instantly and decisively, much to Trevor and Charlie's admiration.

'One mourners' car. That's all? You sure?'

'There's no family, only me. Rhiannon had no one.' Phyllis picked up the boiling kettle and poured water into the brown china teapot.

'But there'll be friends and neighbours,' Fred urged softly.

'Who'll make their own way to Glyntaff.' Trevor had taken to calling Fred in on his final visit to a patient, to ensure that none of Fred's subtle pressure was exerted on families at a time when they were least able to cope with it.

The undertaker debated whether or not to press the point, and decided against it. Jones & Sons might be the biggest undertakers in town, but they weren't the only ones. 'I'll put you down for a hearse and one car. Grave?'

'She wants . . . wanted,' Phyllis corrected herself sharply as she handed out filled teacups, 'to be buried with her husband and her son. It is a grave for three. Rhiannon bought the plot in Glyntaff cemetery when they were killed in the pit accident.'

'I'll need the grave number.' He looked up from his notebook. Phyllis pulled out a bundle of papers neatly tied with black satin. 'These are the grave papers.'

He squinted at them and took down the number. 'There'll still be costs, you know,' he sniffed. Russian Charlie had made the decision that a standard pine coffin with wooden furniture would do without even consulting Phyllis, although heaven only knew where he fitted into the household. And with only one car and a hearse, and no new plot pickings were going to be slim – very slim indeed. The next thing they'd be saying was they wanted to cut back on flowers. 'The grave has to be opened so you'll still have to pay for the gravediggers' time. Twice. Once to open, and once to close the plot. I take it there will be a new engraving to be put on the headstone?'

'Only the date of death. Rhiannon put on her name, date of birth and "beloved wife of" when her husband died. How much will it all come to, Mr Jones?'

'Well it seems that you want a simple funeral, but even so, all things considered you won't get much change out of thirty pounds.'

'That will be fine, Mr Jones.' Phyllis breathed a sigh of relief. Rhiannon's insurance would come to exactly that sum, and in addition she had taken a penny a week policy out on her landlady's life which would pay her five pounds. More than enough for flowers and black mourning clothes for herself and her son, and extra tea and cake for the mourners.

'The insurance will cover all the costs?' the undertaker asked prudently.

'It will. Please go ahead and make the arrangements.'

Trevor handed Phyllis his empty cup. 'Well if you'll excuse me I must be going. There's a case of bronchitis I promised to visit in Penycoedcae last thing tonight. But I can call in again on my way down the hill.'

'There's no need, Doctor Lewis,' Phyllis said as she left her chair.

'Then I'll be back in the morning.'

'Thank you for everything you did for Rhiannon, Doctor Lewis, and thank you for coming out so late.'

'If it wasn't for the sad circumstances I'd say it was always a pleasure to visit this house.' He gripped Phyllis's hand firmly. 'Remember, if you need me for anything, just send. Any time, day or night.'

'I must be off too.' Fred scribbled a final line in his notebook and snapped it shut.

Charlie walked both men to the door. Trevor hung back for a moment to hand Charlie a small packet when the undertaker was outside and out of earshot.

'She'll probably insist on sitting up all night. If you stir this into her tea, she'll sleep. Don't worry, she won't taste it, and there's no after-effects.'

Charlie pocketed the envelope.

'Strange set-up back there,' Fred commented as Trevor walked past his hearse on the way to his car.

'In what way?' Trevor asked warily.

'Russian Charlie being there. You think he fathered her bastard?'

'I have no idea, Mr Jones,' Trevor replied frostily.

'Could be. She's a bit long in the tooth and thin in the face, but I'll say this much for her, she's not a bad-looking woman considering her age.'

Charlie walked back into the silent house and glanced into the parlour. Phyllis was sitting on one of the high-backed, heavily carved, Rexine-covered chairs. Bethan was standing behind her. The main light had been switched off, the thick green plush curtains were drawn, but the women had lit two red candles that had stood in Rhiannon's brass candlesticks on her mantelpiece for years; possibly saved for this very night. They had placed them on a small octagonal table at the head of the coffin. The flames flickered, creating shadows that danced and bowed in every corner of the room, lending the scene the sepia and gold effect of a Rembrandt.

Charlie stood and watched for a moment. Bethan was holding Phyllis's hand, but the older woman had clearly withdrawn into a world of private grief. In the kitchen the pot of tea was still warm, and Charlie poured out three cups. Stirring the powder Trevor had given him into one, he carried it into the parlour.

'Thank you. Both of you.' Emerging from her misery Phyllis took the cup Charlie handed her and wrapped her freezing fingers round it. A fire hadn't been lit in the parlour since the day of Rhiannon's husband's funeral. It was a perfect temperature for corpses but uncomfortable for the living. 'I don't know what I would have done without you,' Phyllis continued.

'You would have managed.' Bethan took her cup from Charlie. 'People always do when they have no choice.'

'It's easier when you have someone to help.'

'There's nothing more you can do tonight. Why don't you go to bed and try to get some sleep while you can?' Bethan suggested.

'I don't think I could sleep. Besides, my place is here.'

'I'll stay with Rhiannon tonight,' Bethan offered.

'No, it's all right, really . . .'

'You have a few more days to say your goodbyes. Why don't you sit in the kitchen for a while? Eat something. I doubt if you've eaten all day.'

'I haven't,' Phyllis admitted.

'I'll make you some fresh tea and toast,' Bethan offered.

Phyllis suddenly realised that she wasn't the only one who hadn't eaten for hours. 'I'll go and make us all something,' she said and finally left her chair.

'I'll sit with Rhiannon.'

It didn't occur to either of the women to consider Charlie's suggestion odd.

Phyllis found two toasting forks, Bethan opened the door to the stove and they set about making toast. As soon as the first piece was ready Bethan buttered it and handed it to Phyllis, who sat back in her easy chair to eat it. Her eyes closed before she'd finished chewing the second bite. Bethan plumped up a patchwork-covered cushion, pushed it beneath Phyllis's head and lifted her feet on to an ancient beadwork stool. The knitted blanket Rhiannon had used to cover her arthritic knees was still folded on her chair. Bethan tucked it around Phyllis's slumped figure.

'I've made you some toast and tea.' Bethan stood in the doorway of the parlour.

'Is Phyllis asleep?' Charlie asked.

Bethan nodded. 'In the kitchen.'

'I'll carry her upstairs.'

'You'll risk waking her,' Bethan warned.

Phyllis didn't wake. Charlie laid her next to her son,

and Bethan, who'd followed him, slipped off Phyllis's shoes and draped the bedcover around her.

'You eat and I'll sit with Rhiannon for a while,' Bethan whispered as they reached the foot of the stairs.

'If we leave the door open we'll be able to see the candles from the kitchen.'

'And that's all that matters?'

'I don't think Rhiannon is likely to tell us any different.'

In all of the four years she had been acquainted with him, Bethan had never known Charlie to be flippant or make light of any situation, but that didn't stop her from scrutinising him as they went into the kitchen. He took off his coat. Hanging it on the back of a chair he rolled up his sleeves and went outside to wash his hands and face.

'Remind me to replace the food I've used tomorrow,' Bethan's voice was soft, low, although there was no real need to whisper.

'You won't need reminding.' He sat down and took a piece of toast.

'No I suppose I won't.' She looked across the table as she poured out fresh tea for both of them, and smiled, suddenly blessing Charlie's presence here, in this house of death; his solid dependability and his habit of saying very little, but always what was short, important and to the point. 'Now that the worst is over why don't you go home and get some sleep?' she suggested.

'It's all right, I'll stay with you.'

'You'll be exhausted tomorrow.'

'Tomorrow's Sunday.'

'What about the stall?'

'It's too late to worry about that now. What William hasn't done will have to wait until Monday. Let's just hope he hasn't lost another pig.'

'Will you sack him if he has?'

'Maybe.' She still couldn't detect any trace of humour in his voice. He sat back and drank his tea. Bethan thought of all the times she'd sat in this kitchen as

Rhiannon's guest, talking to her, eating her Welsh cakes . . .

'It's strange to think I won't see her any more when I walk through here on my way to town,' Bethan said.

'Rhiannon?'

'Yes.' She pushed the plate with the remaining slices of toast over to him. 'Everything seems to be changing so quickly, and I'm powerless to stop it. I go away, come back and nothing is the same. My father's gone—'

'He'll be back soon.'

'And my mother?'

Charlie didn't answer that question.

'And it's not as if it's just Rhiannon and my father. It's Haydn and Maud as well. I turn my back for five minutes and the whole family splits up. Nothing will ever be the same again.'

'You grew up, left home and had a family of your own,' he pointed out logically.

'I suppose I did.' She was ashamed of the bitterness she could hear creeping into her voice. She felt as though she was condemning and betraying her own son simply for being born.

It was most peculiar, sitting here, in another woman's kitchen across the table from Charlie, she was thinking – and talking about more important things than she had ever dared to discuss with Andrew. Perhaps it was Charlie's undemanding, uncritical presence. His habitual silences had taken a great deal of getting used to, but now she was grateful for them.

Charlie lit a cigarette and moved from the table to one of the easy chairs. 'The candles are still lit,' he said.

'Corpse lights. We used to watch their flames flickering through the shadows of drawn curtains when we were children. My grandmother told us that they were lit to guide the soul to heaven. All it had to do was follow the line of the smoke.'

'That's a nice thought.'

'When my grandmother died and I sat up with her, I

222

watched the candles burn in my Aunt Megan's back bedroom for hours. I really felt as though I was watching her soul leave for a better place.'

'I wish I'd had the same thought when my grandfather died.' It was the first time she'd heard Charlie mention his family, and she waited, hoping he'd say more. He left his chair and opened the door to the stove. The fire was burning low. He picked up the tongs and heaped half a dozen large lumps of coal from the bucket into the embers.

'Russia is not so different from Wales.' He was speaking so quietly she had to strain to catch his voice. 'Not when it comes to matters of death. The corpse is watched. Everyone in the village comes into the house to view the body and pay their respects before the burial.' He replaced the tongs, closed the oven door, looked up and gave Bethan a rare smile. 'The village gossips count the funeral carriages, the cost of the headstone and the widow's clothes.'

'You have gossips in Russia too?'

'People may speak different languages and wear different clothes, but from what I've seen they're much the same the world over.'

'They weren't in London.'

'No gossips?' He brushed his hands through his thick hair and for the first time she noticed the layers of fair hairs on his lower arms.

'No gossips,' she repeated firmly. 'I would have been happy to have met just one. I would have had someone other than Andrew and myself to talk to.'

'Is that why you came back? Because you were lonely?'

'That and . . .' she faltered as she realised what she was saying, and who she was saying it to. If her father had been home she would have talked to him. As he wasn't, why not talk to Charlie? After all, she could be sure that her confidences would go no further. '. . . and the baby. Everyone in London wanted me to put him in an institution,' she stated harshly.

'A workhouse?' She had just told him that no one had talked to her in London. It didn't take a lot to deduce who the 'everyone' was.

'It would have been a workhouse in all but name. I just couldn't do it. I couldn't . . .'

'I can understand that.'

'You can?'

'I think that children like Edmund need their parents even more than healthy ones.'

'What happens to them in Russia?'

'Oh we have institutions in Russia too. Perhaps even more than here. It is peculiar, I've never really thought of it before. The well-educated people always send their crippled children to institutions, but not the peasants. They keep their children with them no matter how they turn out.'

'I don't suppose it matters so much on a farm. They won't get pointed or stared at, or disgrace the family.' She could hear resentment in her voice, but was powerless to stop it from surfacing.

'We don't have farms like you do here. Not family farms. We have collectives. It's something like a village,' he tried to explain, regretting the impulse that had led him to talk about his homeland because it brought memories only too vividly to the forefront of his mind. 'Everyone lives in one area and they all work the land, take what they need and the rest of the produce is sent off to the cities.'

'Then you can have more than one family living there?'

'Hundreds on the larger ones.'

A farm to Bethan was one of the hill farms on Penycoedcae or over in Maesycoed. She couldn't imagine a farm big enough to hold hundreds of families. 'Did you live on a farm?'

'No, but I grew up in a village that had many farmers.'

'And it became a . . . a collective?'

'Not exactly.' Charlie retreated into his shell. He wasn't ready to talk about his past, but didn't want to rebuff Bethan. He hadn't talked to anyone like this since Evan had been sent to jail, and he hadn't realised just how much he'd missed him. He returned to the easy chair and lit another cigarette. 'Have you heard about my shop?'

'I've heard about nothing else for weeks from Will.'

'I hope to open the doors next week. That way we can start trading, and hopefully making some money to offset my outlay.'

'William told me there's a flat with a bathroom upstairs.'

'Yes.'

'Are you moving in there?' She dreaded his reply. Money wasn't a problem at the moment. Between the lodgers' rent money, the little that Eddie brought in, and her pound a week they were managing. But she knew that without her money her father would be hard pushed to meet the mortgage, and the loss of Charlie's would be almost as disastrous. He was that rare being in Pontypridd: a lodger with a steady job who was also easygoing, and always ready to lend a hand. There were women who'd throw their husbands out of the house to make room for a steady, sober man like Charlie.

'No.' He looked at her in bewilderment, and she was relieved to see that the thought of leaving the Avenue hadn't crossed his mind.

'I'm glad to hear it. We'd hate to lose you.'

'If you want me to go . . .'

'I'd hate for you to go. We need you, Charlie, and I don't mean your money. With Dad away I don't know what we'd do without you. At times like this, for example.'

'I've asked Alma Moore if she'll work in the shop. In the back, superintending the cooking. I was hoping she and her mother would live in the flat.'

'You're going to rent the flat to Alma Moore?'

'She's always been a good worker for the Ronconis, I thought I could do worse.'

'You could do a lot worse,' Bethan said thoughtfully,

recalling the rumours Diana had talked about, 'but then, from what little William's told me about the flat, so could she.'

'I don't suppose you'd call into the shop and give me your opinion on what we've done so far and what needs doing before I open the doors?'

'I don't know anything about shops.'

'You do from a customer's point of view. I don't even know how many chairs I should have for shoppers to sit on.'

'If there's room, at least three.'

'Why three?'

'One for tired invalids, one for ladies who think they're important and one for children to climb on.'

'I wouldn't have thought of that.'

'Don't underestimate the children. They'll drag their parents into any shop where there's a chance of a free taste of food.'

'That's something else I hadn't thought of. It could prove expensive,' he mused, visualising slices of his best ham cut up into thin slivers as 'tasters' and disappearing down the throats of the town's half-starved urchins.

'What are you going to be selling?'

'Cooked meats, pies . . .'

'Pastry stars.'

He looked at her uncomprehendingly.

'Get whoever does the cooking for you to make shapes out of the leftover pastry. If you really want to attract a crowd, mix some stale leftover cheese with it. Lots of shops do them in London.'

'Cheap giveaway.'

'Provided you don't try to feed the town.'

'Thanks for the tip, but you'll still call into the shop?'

'As soon as I get a chance.'

'I'd better get back to the front parlour before Phyllis wakes up and finds Rhiannon alone.' He picked up his coat from the chair. Tucking it under one arm he pulled down his shirt-sleeves and buttoned them up.

'And I'd better clear the dishes.' She brushed past him as she went to the kitchen window and pulled the curtains open. A pale light shone low over the garden, peeling back the darkness from the ground. 'Another hour and dawn will break.'

'You've seen in the dawn before?'

'Often when I was working in the hospital.'

'Of course. I forgot you worked nights as a nurse.'

'I'd almost forgotten it myself.'

'I used to watch the dawn break over the sea when it was my turn to take watch. It's different out there. At least when it's not raining. Colder, clearer and brighter than it is on land, especially in the North Sea.'

'Were you a sailor long?'

'A while,' he answered evasively.

'In between living in Russia and here?'

'Yes.' He shrugged his coat over his massive shoulders and stepped into the hall. 'I'll close this door behind me. It's getting colder and you'll need to keep the heat in. Phyllis and the little one will be waking up soon.'

Bethan opened the drawer at the bottom of the stove. It was choked with white-hot, powdery ash. As she went out to the washhouse to look for the ash bin she wondered how well one human being ever really knew another. Particularly where a man like Charlie was concerned.

Chapter Fourteen

THEY STARTED ARRIVING before dawn. Small children, shabbily and inadequately dressed in torn jerseys, faded shorts and cotton skirts, knocked Rhiannon's front door and handed over plates of Welsh cakes and fruit cakes that were more flour and fat than fruit, with whispers of 'Mam says she's very sorry, and she'll be over later.'

Bethan stacked the cakes on plates in the pantry and marvelled at the speed of the Graig grapevine. Either Trevor had let something slip at the house of the bronchitis patient, or a neighbour had seen the undertaker's hearse and spread the word. It soon seemed as though every family on the Graig knew that Rhiannon had passed on. At eight o'clock the women began to arrive, and the gifts of food from their meagre stores mounted. Those who hadn't lit their stoves that day brought pots of home-made blackberry jam and cold bowls of 'cawl' made with the cheapest, scraggiest of scrag ends of lamb, 'to be heated up later to save the poor girl cooking at a time like this'.

By the time Phyllis had roused, washed and dressed herself and her son, the callers had begun to arrive in earnest. Bethan and Charlie took it in turns to corpse-sit and make tea, trying to look as though they were listening attentively as the neighbours repeated the same trite phrases over and over again.

'So sorry to hear the news.' 'But then she was a good age, wasn't she?' 'How old was she, by the way?' 'Would have been eighty next month!' 'Well then, that's all any of us can really expect, isn't it?'

Even the women who had shunned Phyllis came, but

they took care to make it abundantly clear that they called only out of respect for Rhiannon. The cakes in the pantry were brought out, cut and distributed on Rhiannon's best china plates. Brian, totally bewildered by the influx of alien people into his home, sat on his own small chair in the corner next to the stove, solemnly eating cake for breakfast and pocketing the halfpennies handed to him by one or two of the women who had working husbands. He knew from the quiver in his mother's voice and the tears that hovered perilously close to the surface of her red-rimmed eyes that he had to be extra good, so he bravely concealed his excitement at the very first money he'd ever owned.

'Well, I am sorry to hear the news and no mistake. Mind you, not that it's unexpected, but you must be devastated all the same.' Mrs Richards walked into the kitchen through the washhouse door just as Myra Jones, Phyllis's next-door neighbour was leaving, and just in time to take possession of the easy chair. Now she was enthroned as though she had taken root. 'Is there anything I can do to help?' she asked Phyllis, who sat white faced and drawn in the chair opposite.

'Not really, Mrs Richards,' Phyllis replied softly. 'Bethan and Charlie have done everything.'

'Well they won't be here to help this afternoon, but then neither will I,' Mrs Richards announced. She glanced at the women crowded into the room in the hope that someone would ask why she wouldn't be around. When no question came she volunteered the information in a piercing voice that made Bethan cringe. 'It's prison visiting. The first since they sentenced my Vivian and Evan Powell. Martyrs, that's what they are. Martyrs to the Communist cause,' she repeated, conveniently forgetting her husband's Fascist leanings, which would gain her no sympathy in this company.

'Bethan, you must be exhausted, and you must have things to do at home.' Phyllis followed Bethan as she went to fill the kettle and get away from the chattering throng in the kitchen. 'Thank you for all you've done. I don't know how I would have managed without you.'

'I will go now if you don't mind,' Bethan said wearily. 'But I'll be back tonight, and in the meantime I'll send Diana over.'

'There's no need . . .'

'You're going to need someone to organise that lot for you,' Bethan jerked her head towards the kitchen door. 'And I can't think of anyone better than Diana. She's her mother's daughter in more ways than one. If anyone can get Mrs Richards off the topic of her Viv, and out of that chair, it's Diana.' Bethan was cheered by the sight of a tight smile crossing Phyllis's face. It wasn't much, but it was the first sign of animation since Rhiannon had died.

There was barely time for Bethan to wash and change herself and the baby before they had to leave for Cardiff. She stumbled down the Graig hill between Charlie and Eddie like a sleepwalker, wondering how she had ever managed to work a full night shift in the Graig Hospital when she had been doing her midwifery, and then go out all day with Andrew. All she wanted now was to put her feet up. Even the prospect of a bus seat seemed like deep luxury, but because it was a Sunday with an uncertain local service they had to walk down to Broadway to be sure of getting a connection.

Edmund, normally so placid, became fretful as a cold wind whistled up the Cardiff Road and through the inadequate cover of the shelter. When the bus finally came, the only seats available were the hard wooden slatted ones at the back that were usually reserved for labourers dressed in their working clothes. They jolted painfully over every pot-hole in the road between Pontypridd and Cardiff, and long before they reached Taffs Well Bethan would have believed anyone who told her that the bus company had switched to wooden tyres to save money.

The closer they drew to Cardiff the more peevish the baby became. Worried in case he was sickening for something, Bethan became irritable herself. Eddie took Edmund from her to give her a break, and jiggled him up and down in his arms, but the child refused to be placated, and Bethan greeted the conductor's bell with heartfelt relief when they finally reached the stop closest to the prison. They walked up the road in silence, then Bethan stopped, stunned by the number of people who were standing outside waiting to go in. Mrs Richards and her son Glan must have caught an earlier bus, for they were well up the front of the queue. Behind them pale-faced mothers coped as best they could with children that ranged from clinging, whining babies to fully grown boys and girls who were passing the time by fighting and spitting at one another. Old women stood patiently in line as they dabbed at their eyes and noses with damp, grubby handkerchiefs. Young men, hands thrust deep in trouser pockets, talked loudly amongst themselves and tried to look nonchalant, as though visiting prison was nothing special, simply an everyday event in their lives and nothing to be ashamed of.

'Ten minutes to wait,' Eddie murmured as they halted at the end of the queue.

'Yoo-hoo! Bethan! Eddie! Charlie!' Mrs Richards waved vigorously from the head of the line.

'I'll kill that woman one of these days,' Eddie muttered darkly.

'They'll want to search us before they'll let us in,' Charlie warned.

'You've visited prison before?' Bethan asked.

'With Diana and William. They'll go through everything you've brought for Evan as well.'

'It's only tobacco and Welsh cakes.'

'They'll still want to examine them.'

A grating of bolts galvanised everyone. A small wooden door set in the left-hand side of one of the two massive wooden doors that closed off the prison yard opened, and an acid-faced, black-suited warder stepped over the wooden stoop on to the pavement.

'Form an orderly queue there. Step lively,' he shouted, and the ragged crowd of visitors lined up in tight formation.

'The sooner we do as he asks, the sooner we'll get in,' Eddie suggested hopefully, pushing into line.

Charlie, who knew better, stood protectively at Bethan's side. The warder watched as they waited what seemed like hours, although the hands on Charlie's pocket watch ticked off only five minutes. Finally the warder capitulated and allowed the first half a dozen people through the door.

The queue shuffled forward with interminable slowness. Bethan fixed her attention on the door and waited. She wasn't sure what she expected to see inside. To be shown straight into a room where her father would be sitting, waiting for them perhaps? A clean, bright airy room like the waiting room in the workhouse which was always being painted by the inmates in order to make a good impression on any influential visitors? Would she be allowed to hug her father? Hold his hand? Hand him the baby?

A second warder appeared in the gateway and ushered the small group that they were a part of into a bleak, empty, stone-lined ante-room to the left of the gate. A barred iron door crashed shut behind them, penning them in like sheep. Frustrated and disappointed she had to stand and wait again, trying to make sense of the noises that she could hear from the open yard she had caught a glimpse of on her way through the door.

A series of 'Move along there', 'What's this then?' and 'You can go' couched in brusque, masculine tones echoed into the room. After another ten minutes of frustrating inactivity the door finally opened and they were herded along a path that cut a straight line between raised flowerbeds adorned with the shrivelled, spidery arms of hibernating plants.

'Move along there.'

Charlie drew close to Bethan. Taking her arm he

steered her across an open yard hemmed in by the towering grey blocks of the prison.

'All bags, parcels and gifts for the prisoners to be left here.'

Bethan shivered despite the thick flannel shawl that was wrapped around the baby and herself. The yard was more sheltered than the pavement, but it was still icy with the chill of an atmosphere that was rarely, if ever, touched by the warmth of the sun. Charlie guided her and Eddie towards one of four tables set out in the bleak courtyard, and they stood in line yet again, waiting while the warders tore open the bundles and parcels of those in front of them.

Bethan watched as the warders broke a fruit cake into crumbs, turned a bible upside down and shook it until the pages fluttered free of the spine, and spread the contents of a tobacco tin so thinly over a sheet of white paper that half the strands were lost in the breeze that fluttered, trapped between the walls of the buildings.

'Your baby, Miss?'

Bethan stared uncomprehendingly at the hatchet-faced warder facing her.

'It's Mrs! Mrs John. Her husband's a doctor so you'd better watch your mouth,' Eddie snarled angrily.

'Didn't mean anything by the remark, son,' the warder said easily.

'And I'm not your son either.'

'Eddie, it's all right. They're just doing their job,' Charlie interrupted smoothly, realising that although Bethan and Eddie were both intimidated by the uniformed men and bleak surroundings, they were coping in very different ways. Bethan had sought refuge in silence and Eddie was, as usual, trying to conceal his feelings behind a front of open aggression.

'Your baby, madam,' the officer repeated with elaborate courtesy. 'I have to check his shawl and his clothes. Sorry, it's customary procedure.'

'Can't we go inside? He isn't well and it's freezing out here.'

'I'll be as quick as I can.'

Bethan reluctantly unwound the shawl and handed it to the man. He held it by the corner and shook it, while she opened her coat and pushed the baby inside, close to her shivering body.

'I'm sorry, madam, but I have to check the baby's clothes as well. You can keep hold of him.'

Bethan held out Edmund and the man ran his fingers over his tiny frame.

'Now you, madam.'

'Here, give the baby to me.' Charlie retrieved the shawl from the warder and wound it inexpertly around the baby, who'd begun to whimper. The warder ran his hands down the sides of Bethan's coat and asked her to empty her pockets. She laid a comb, handkerchief and sixpence in change on the table.

'You can go the other side of the table, madam, but you'll have to wait while I examine your bag and parcels.'

Bethan took the baby from Charlie, and huddling in what little shelter the wall afforded, wrapped both herself and Edmund in the shawl. She soon saw that the warder had been quick with her. He certainly took his time over inspecting her handbag and Eddie and Charlie's clothes, asking them to empty shirt, trouser and coat pockets, as well as checking and double-checking the turn-ups on their trousers. The parcel Bethan had prepared for her father received his attention last of all. The Welsh cakes she had wrapped so carefully between layers of greaseproof paper in an old biscuit tin were emptied out and broken up, every single one of them, into three pieces.

'For God's sake what do you think we're going to hide in a Welsh cake?' Eddie complained bitterly.

'You'd be surprised, lad. You'd be surprised,' the warder echoed, totally unaffected by Eddie's irritation. He fingered the crumbs then scooped them back into the tin. He opened the tobacco, peeled back the outer covering and prodded the contents, before stripping away the gold leaf and shifting the brown strands from one side of the pack to the other.

'Prisoner visitors through the double doors and along the corridor on the right,' he barked when he was finally satisfied that the tobacco and cakes were what they appeared to be.

Charlie took Bethan's arm as they walked through a doorway flanked by two more warders. The corridor was painted dark green; the walls and tiled floor looked clean but the air stank of male sweat and stale urine. The passage opened out into a small hallway bisected by a row of desks. Two warders sat behind each one, bellowing the same questions as the visitors approached.

'Name? Age? Address? Name of prisoner to be visited?'

'Damn it all, anyone would think we were the ones who'd committed a crime,' Eddie said as they joined yet another column of shuffling people.

'No more than two visitors to a prisoner,' a warder said sharply to Bethan, Eddie and Charlie when they finally reached the end of their line.

'Does the baby count?' Eddie countered truculently.

'Infants under one year don't count as visitors,' the man replied, straight-faced.

'Can we change over after ten minutes?' Charlie asked, knowing full well from visits to Megan that changeovers were allowed.

'You'll have to keep an eye on the time yourself. Next.'

They walked down yet another corridor, where floor and walls bore the scratch marks of hours of scrubbing. The deeper they went into the building, the more over-whelming the stench became. This time the sickly smell was overlaid with an odour of cooking, predominantly cabbage. At the end of the corridor they walked into a huge echoing hall. And for the first time since she'd entered the confines of the prison Bethan saw the prisoners.

A barricade of wire mesh stretched from one side of the room to the other. Supported by huge iron poles it effectively sliced the room into two: the visitors' side, and the prisoners'. On the prisoners' side, the fence was separated into small cubicles by tall, narrow wooden frames. Rows of hard upright metal chairs were ranged on both sides of the mesh, all of them chained to the floor, and on the far side Bethan saw a mass of grey-suited, grey-faced men who looked as though the sun hadn't shone on them in years.

'Prisoner?'

'Powell. Evan Powell.' Bethan heard Charlie answer the man, and tried to smile as she scanned the expectant faces of the inmates. Her father was probably watching her now, trusting the visit to give him the strength he needed to carry on living in this dreadful place.

The warden looked down his list. 'Prisoner number . . . 46 . . .' Bethan didn't hear any more. At that moment she spotted her father, thinner, and paler than she remembered as he made his way towards the barricade of wire.

'There he is!' Eddie was there before her. Grabbing two chairs, he pushed one in front of her before taking the second for himself.

'Thank you for your letter. It's good of you to come.' Her father smiled, but the smile didn't fool Bethan. She knew him too well.

'You've been ill, Dad?' she asked.

'It was nothing. Just a dose of flu. They looked after me well enough. Put me in the Infirmary.' His smile broadened. 'I get six months' hard labour and I spend the first four weeks in the Infirmary. How's that for fiddling the system?'

'You don't look at all well to me.'

'I'm well enough,' he answered cheerfully. 'Really. It's not that bad in here. They've put me on light work in the library for the next two weeks because of the flu. I get three square meals a day, which is more than a lot of people get outside.'

'And the hard labour?' Eddie asked.

'They say even that isn't so bad. But look, you haven't come all this way to talk about my boring life in here. How are you getting on?'

'We're managing fine,' Eddie answered, trying to sound optimistic in response to a nudge from Bethan. 'I'm keeping the round going like you told me to. Bethan's running the house . . .'

'Helping your mam, Beth?'

Bethan and Eddie exchanged guilty looks.

'What's wrong?' Evan demanded.

'Nothing, Dad,' Eddie began. 'It's just that . . .'

'Mam walked out when she heard about your sentence.' Bethan was too fond of her father to lie to him. Especially now.

'Where's she staying?' No flicker of expression betrayed his emotions.

'I took her to Uncle John Joseph's,' Eddie said flatly.

'He's keeping her?'

'He must be, Dad. I've written to her a couple of times but she hasn't written back.'

'Perhaps it's just as well, Beth.' Evan pulled the dog-end of a hand-rolled cigarette from behind his ear. 'I think I'm a great disappointment to her.'

'She got a bit het up when she found out. Mrs Richards came round just after I arrived and told both of us.' Bethan tried to soften the blow.

'Maggie Richards as a messenger must have gone down like a lead zeppelin with Elizabeth,' Evan said.

'It will be different when you get out and go and see her yourself, Dad.' Eddie forced a smile.

'That's if I bother. I don't think there was much left between us other than habit.' Evan turned to his neighbour and lit his stub of cigarette from a glowing end. What he couldn't say to his children was that there had never been much of anything between him and their mother except for one night of drunken fumblings that would never have occurred if he hadn't quarrelled with his childhood sweetheart. The result had been a quick marriage and Bethan, and although he didn't regret any of his children, he did regret every one of the miserable years he had spent tied to Elizabeth.

'This is my grandson then, Beth?' He peered at the baby through the mesh.

'Yes.'

'Hold him up love so I can take a look at him.'

Bethan did as he asked. Although her father looked away quickly, it wasn't quite quick enough. She saw the expression of pity and something else . . . something she couldn't quite fathom in the depths of his eyes.

'We brought you some Welsh cakes and tobacco, Dad. They took them off us. Cut up the cakes into small pieces . . .'

'That's all right,' Evan reassured Eddie. 'They do that to everything that's brought in. Don't worry I'll get the crumbs later.'

'Charlie's with us. He's opening a shop and he's asked me to work for him a couple of days a week, but don't worry. I won't let it interfere with the round, and he's offering me more money and better hours than Wilf Horton. And Haydn's written. He's having a great time in Brighton with all those chorus girls . . .'

The precious minutes trickled past consumed by Eddie's account of domestic trivia. And all the time Eddie gabbled Bethan longed to tear down the wire cage, reach out and stroke her father's pale, thin cheeks and ask how he really was.

'. . . oh, and Rhiannon Pugh died last night.' Beset by an onset of mixed emotion that he didn't dare examine too closely, Eddie moved on from the family's doings to an account of events on the Graig.

'Rhiannon?'

'Yes, last night,' Eddie repeated, surprised by the earnest look on his father's face. He hadn't realised he was so fond of the old lady. Of course they all knew her, walking through her house every day, the way half the street did . . .

'Is anyone with Phyllis?' Evan broke in. Something in the tone of his voice made Bethan look up.

'Charlie and I stayed with her last night, Diana's with her now.'

'That's why they both look so tired,' Eddie chipped in.

'How's Phyllis coping?' Evan asked. 'She had no one to turn to except Rhiannon, you know. She relied on her for everything.'

'She's coping,' Bethan murmured, a ghastly suspicion forming in her mind. 'Obviously she's upset, but she's bearing up under the strain, all things considered.'

Eddie looked from his father to his sister then back again at Charlie, who was hovering close to the door. 'It's time we changed over, that's if you want a word with Charlie.' Much as he loved his father he was glad of an excuse to leave the unnatural situation.

'I'd appreciate the chance of a word with him. Thanks for coming, son. You look after your sister and the house, and remember what I said about the round?'

'Of course.' Eddie pushed back his chair. 'And you don't mind about me taking the job Charlie offered? Just a couple of days a week.'

'No, I think it's a good idea. I'm not a believer in turning down regular money, you know that.' Evan watched his son walk away. 'You haven't left that husband of yours have you, Beth?' he asked when they only had strangers around them.

'No. He sends me money every week,' she said proudly.

'Then how come he isn't with you?' Evan raised his eyes until they looked into hers.

'Because he's having trouble coming to terms with Eddie. He wants to put him away.'

'And you don't?'

'He needs me,' she said simply.

'It must be a hard choice to make.'

'It doesn't have to be made at the moment,' she said practically. 'Not when I'm needed at home.'

'As long as you don't use our troubles as an excuse to run away from your own.'

'I'll try not to, Dad.' She sensed Charlie's presence behind her. 'Look after yourself.'

'I'm not about to get up to much in here love. Take care.'

Bethan nodded as she turned her back on the wire mesh and walked towards her brother. She could hear her father whispering to Charlie: low, solemn words that were too softly spoken to be deciphered, even if she'd been in a mood to do so. She was preoccupied with the strange look on her father's face when he had asked after Phyllis Harry. She remembered other things that had puzzled her. The way Phyllis had accepted Charlie's presence in the house as natural. The way she had leant on him, done everything he had suggested calmly, unquestioningly. And Phyllis's small son had such beautiful dark eyes and black curly hair, so different from Phyllis's fair hair and grey eyes – and so like her father's and Eddie's.

'You'll come again, next month?'

She turned. Her father's face was pressed against the wire, the forbidding presence of a warder behind him. Charlie hadn't had very long with him after all.

'As soon as they let us, Dad,' she called back. 'I promise.'

'I still don't understand why he's prepared to lend you the money to pay our rent and shop bill. It doesn't seem right to me.' Lena Moore sniffed as Alma ladled out a small tin of tomatoes on to two pieces of toast. As it was Sunday Alma had insisted on lighting the stove. For a few hours at least.

'I told you, Mam, he wants me to work for him,' Alma explained testily.

'If the wages he's promised you are straight and above board and all he expects from you is a week's worth in exchange, he can get any one of a number of girls with the money he's offering. So why you?'

'I've already answered that question, Mam,' Alma said impatiently. 'He's seen me work in the café and he thinks I'm a good worker—'

'And he's heard something of your reputation with the men?'

240

'It's not like that, Mam. Not with Charlie.'

'How do you know? Anything could happen once we're under his roof and in his power.'

'It won't. If you must know, I asked him outright if there was going to be any funny business and he said no.'

'What did you expect him to say? This whole arrangement doesn't sound right to me, Alma. It's too good to be true, and everyone is going to say so.'

'I've no choice but to take Charlie up on his offer.' Alma pushed a knife and fork into her mother's hand and guided her to her customary place at the table. 'If I hadn't, we would have already been put on the street by the bailiffs.'

'The chapel and the minister would never allow it to come to that, Alma. My father was a deacon . . .'

'The chapel's done precious little to help us until now. I can't see the minister or the deacons putting themselves out just because the bailiffs move in.'

'Of course they would help us. Look at what they did for poor old Mrs Edwards. They paid her house-keeper's wages when she was dying.' Her mother cut into the tomatoes and toast and ferried a forkful to her mouth.

'Poor old Mrs Edwards let it be known that she was leaving that great big house of hers to the chapel. They won't help us because there's nothing in it for them,' Alma commented caustically as she sat down by her mother.

'You're bitter because they banned you, Alma. But even if I say it myself, you were in the wrong. You work on the Lord's day of rest . . .'

'. . . to put food on this table. If I didn't we wouldn't even be able to afford this magnificent Sunday dinner.' Although she was hungry, Alma pushed her tomatoes aside in disgust.

'You don't even try to understand them, Alma. That's your trouble. They've been good to me over the years, particularly when your grandfather died. I wish he'd lived longer. Things wouldn't have come to this pass if he'd still been alive. He would never have allowed you to work on a Sunday for a start.'

'Rich, was he?' Alma enquired. She had heard the same stories before, many times, and steeled herself for the inevitable repetition.

'Only in a spiritual sense. You could have learned a lot from his example, Alma. He was religious, but forgiving and understanding as well. I upset him so much when I married your father. He tried, but no matter what he said, I wouldn't even listen. Now I know he was right. You've only got to look around this house to see how right he was.'

'My father kept us well enough until he was killed.'

'But he didn't really provide for us, and that's just what my father was worried about. I never understood until it was too late and I was left to bring you up on five shillings a week. But it's not just that.' Her mother reached across the table and laid her work-roughened hand over Alma's. 'It's these rumours. They would never have started if you'd done what the minister and deacons wanted. You should have listened to them, walked your grandfather's way as the minister wanted instead of . . .'

'Becoming a streetwalker!'

'Alma, how could you?'

'What, put the congregation's thoughts into words?'

'I'd rather you weren't beholden to any man,' her mother said sternly, suddenly finding her voice. 'This Russian? Who is he? Where does he come from? We don't know anything about him. Why is he living here instead of his own country? For all you know he could be a thief or a murderer.'

'The fact is, Mam, I can't see any other way I can support us.' Alma left the table and scraped her toast and tomatoes into the slop bucket.

'So in spite of everything I've said, you still intend to go ahead and work for him?'

'To keep a roof over our heads and food on the table. Yes.'

'Can't you see it should be this roof, Alma? Not his. People will talk.'

'Then let them. I won't be held responsible for their filthy minds.'

'I wish you wouldn't—'

Alma tried to block out the rest of her mother's speech as she left the kitchen. The biggest problem of all was that her mother was voicing her own doubts and fears. But she had made her decision. Anything Charlie offered her had to be better than Bobby Thomas or the workhouse. Didn't it?

Chapter Fifteen

'I MISSED YOU LAST Saturday night.'

'George insisted on staying with me until we closed, then he walked me home before going to the Queen's,' Vera whispered as she pushed her bucket under the tap in the washroom of the market.

'Jealous?'

She nodded, not daring to turn round and face William lest someone see her.

'But he's leaving early tonight,' she mumbled. 'I overheard Albert from the bread stall asking him if he was going to the Queen's after work, and he said yes.'

'Then I can walk you home?' William's pulse raced at the thought.

'I don't know about that,' Vera leaned forward to check the level in the bucket. 'But . . .'

'Vera. How long is that water going to take?'

'Not long now, George.' She turned round and gave her husband a bright, artificial smile.

'Nice weather we're having for the time of year, Mr Collins,' William commented blithely.

'If you're a duck and like it wet,' he answered sullenly, eyeing his wife's shapely buttocks and legs as she bent over the pail. He really would have to have a word with her about the length of her overalls. They were far too short, and probably the reason she had a damned Powell sniffing around her like a dog after a bitch on heat. The Powell family always had produced men who'd been too good-looking for the peace of mind of fathers and husbands. He could remember William's father swaggering around town, attracting the attention of every girl for miles, never giving ordinary blokes like him a look in.

'Wet or not, it's warm enough to bring the customers out,' William smiled. 'Trade's up on the winter figures.'

'Maybe on the butchers' stalls, but not the dairy.' George turned from William to his wife. 'You can take that bucket over to the stall and start scrubbing, Vera,' he ordered sharply, making William's blood boil. 'I'll bring the other one over as soon as it's full.'

'Whatever you say George,' she answered meekly, picking up the bucket.

'My sister Diana often talks about Vera,' William ventured boldly. 'They were in school together. She's always admiring Vera's clothes.'

'And so she should, the price I pay for them,' George snapped. He stood back, arms folded, glaring at William. George Collins wasn't a tall man, five foot six inches at the most, but he was built like an ox, a good wrestler in his youth who still enjoyed a bout or two of arm-wrestling in the pub after the card game on a Saturday night. 'You taken over the Russian's stall now?'

'Only for today. He had to go to a funeral,' William explained, picking up his bucket.

'Rhiannon Pugh's?'

'That's right.'

'Heard he's doing all the sorting out for Phyllis Harry.'

'Him and my cousin Bethan,' William corrected, taking exception to George's tone. 'Mrs Pugh was good to us when we were children, and she had no family left.'

'So that's why he's doing it. As a favour,' George raised his eyebrows sceptically. He turned the water off and walked away without another word.

'Where have you been?' Eddie complained when William finally turned up.

'Waiting in the queue,' William moved to the left of the stall and began to scrub down the shelves. From there he could just about see the Collins' cheese stall.

'What about the shelves this side?' Eddie asked, his arm aching from scraping the wooden chopping block with a wire brush.

'You do those,' William answered flippantly. 'That's the way Charlie and I work it.' He braved a wink at Vera as George, dressed in his overcoat, walked out through the door.

'Seems a crazy way to me,' Eddie grumbled, picking up the second bucket.

'That's because you know nothing about working a butcher's stall.' William lifted down the box containing the money and counted it into piles. Noting the amount in a small book, he bagged it and thrust the bag into his shirt as Charlie always did. 'Finished?' he asked Eddie impatiently.

'Just about.'

'Then let's go.'

'To the café.'

'No.'

'You promised Charlie you'd give Alma that message.'

'Tell you what,' William handed Eddie his half-a-crown's wages plus an extra sixpence. 'You do it and I'll give you a tanner.'

'Why? What are you doing that's so important?'

'Man's work,' William said mysteriously as he locked the shutters.

'Who is she, Will?'

'Ask me no questions and I'll tell you no lies.'

'I bet Tina Ronconi will give me more than a tanner to find out.'

'You mention this to her and I'll regale Bethan with the full account of the chorus girl in Ponty Park as told by you. Noises and all.'

'You wouldn't?'

'Try me.'

William waited until Eddie was out of the door before sauntering past the cheese stall. Vera's shutters lay piled in a heap on the floor, exactly where they'd been the first time he'd noticed her.

'Want a hand with those, Vera?' he shouted.

'I'll give Mrs Collins a hand.' Carrie Hardy, a fishwife

with arms the size of hams rose from behind the counter and loomed over him. 'Mr Collins doesn't like young men hanging around his wife,' she said sharply. 'That's why I'm helping her.'

William looked over her head to where Vera stood, rolling her eyes heavenward.

'In that case I'll be off. Night, Mrs Hardy. *Mrs* Collins.' He touched his cap and kept on walking. A small boy caught up with him as he was kicking a path through the debris of the closed stalls in Market Square.

'Mister. Hey Mister! Lady told me to give you this. Said you'd give me a penny.'

William unfolded a scrap of the greaseproof paper George used to wrap his cheese in. The message had been scribbled in pencil and was difficult to read. He walked over to a lamp and held it up to the light.

Wait in the garden. I'll open the kitchen curtains when it's safe for you to come in.

He kissed the paper and tossed the boy a penny. She wouldn't have written if there'd been no chance of him seeing her. All he had to do was creep down the back lane into her garden and wait. A gust of wind blew through the square, snatching the paper from his hand. As he turned to retrieve it he saw the square solid form of Carrie Hardy marching alongside Vera's slender figure. Mrs Hardy had probably received orders from George to sit for a while with his wife. There was time enough for him to slip into the gym for a game of cards, or the Queen's . . . No – better not make it the Queen's, he thought, remembering George's card game – the Central for a pint. Which was it to be? Cards or beer? The beer won. Whistling, he went on his way.

Eddie pushed open the door to the café and looked inside. It was crowded, as it was every market night.

'Will not with you tonight, Eddie?' Tony asked.

'Not tonight.'

'More important fish to fry than he can find in here then?' Tony looked across at Tina who tossed her head haughtily as she loaded a tray with teas and coffees.

'He's seeing someone about business,' Eddie answered evasively. 'Any chance of a quick word with Alma?'

'She's in the back. Go on through.' Tony flipped up the hatch on the counter.

The kitchen was hot and steamy. Angelo, chef's hat pushed to the back of his head, was dipping a huge basket of chips into an open fat fryer. Alma was sitting on a stool as far away from him as she could get, buttering a stack of bread.

'Does Tony know you're in here?' Angelo asked.

'He knows. Charlie asked me to give Alma a message.'

'Charlie?' Hearing his name, Alma turned round and smiled, but her face fell when she saw Eddie.

'He couldn't come down himself. He had to see to Rhiannon Pugh's funeral.'

'The old lady who died on the Graig?'

'She didn't have anyone except her lodger, and it's a lot for her to manage on her own.'

Alma's back stiffened. She'd heard all about Phyllis Harry. Everyone in Pontypridd had. Phyllis had a reputation even worse than her own.

'Anyway, he said to tell you that if it's all right we'll move you into the shop tomorrow.'

'So soon?'

'If it's not all right it'll have to be Sunday or next Thursday. They're the quietest days for Will and me, and we're the ones Charlie hired to do the job.'

'I suppose we could move tomorrow,' Alma said doubtfully, angry with Charlie because he couldn't be bothered to come down and tell her himself. She wondered why he'd arranged Rhiannon Pugh's funeral for Phyllis Harry. Was he the father of Phyllis's son? Was that why he didn't want her in his bed? Well if it was, it suited her. She'd have everything she wanted, a job, a home, money enough to live on and to spare, and all without strings attached.

'Eight in the morning suit you?'

'We'll be ready.'

'See you.' Eddie was glad to return to the warmth and companionship of the café. The more he saw of Alma the less reason he could find for Charlie to employ her. The woman was so damned spiky and miserable all the time.

It was cold behind George Collins's shed. Very cold, and very dark. Ianto Douglas next door came out to use his ty bach, and Will crouched low, holding his breath. He'd lost all track of time. He'd been staring at the closed curtains for what seemed an eternity. If they opened now he'd be too bloody frozen to move, let alone do anything. A washhouse door banged open and closed again. Ianto going in. Then he heard it, the unmistakable sound of the Collins washhouse door opening.

'Will?'

'Vera, I'm bloody frozen.'

'Ssh. I know, petal, but that horrid Hardy woman won't budge. George made her promise to stay with me until he got home.'

'Damn, he is suspicious, isn't he?'

'I've fed her three sherries and she's fallen asleep. If we're quiet we can go in here.'

'The shed?'

'Ssh . . .' Vera slipped the latch, and Will followed.

'What if she comes out?'

'I'll say I was looking for my tennis racket. The club's opening tomorrow. Come on Will, quick.' She straddled him, pulling her skirt to her waist.

His hands encountered warm, naked flesh. 'Don't you ever wear any underclothes?' he asked.

'I froze all day in the market hoping we'd have an opportunity to sneak into your stall like last time, but George wouldn't let me out of his sight for a moment.' She pulled at his belt buckle. 'He delivers to the valleys tomorrow. He goes every Tuesday and Thursday, if we found somewhere, we could . . .'

'What about here?' he whispered, nuzzling her neck.

'Too dangerous in daylight. We're bound to be seen by one of the gossips. But everyone says you're going to be working on Charlie's new shop. Isn't there a room there we could slip off to now and again? After all, you've got to have a midday break.' She slid her hand down the front of his trousers. 'Ooh you are cold.'

'Bloody frozen.' He racked his brains, then remembered the wooden storage shed in the shop yard. Charlie had dismissed it as a space to store rubbish. 'There is somewhere,' he murmured, struggling to speak coherently as her fingers slid teasingly, tantalisingly, between his thighs. 'But we're going to have to be careful.'

'Very careful, darling,' she echoed as he pulled her downwards. 'Very careful indeed.'

Charlie watched Eddie and William as they carried the last load of Alma's furniture up the stairs into the flat, and shook his head in despair.

'Checked it for woodworm?' he shouted.

'All of it,' William called back. 'It's firewood but it's clean firewood.'

'Alma wouldn't come on the cart with us, she's walking down with her mother.' Eddie looked down at him from over the stairwell.

'All right,' Charlie said absently as he returned to the closed shop. He'd brought a dozen large cuts of meat in from the slaughterhouse in the hope that he'd be able to cook them in preparation for the opening he'd planned for Saturday morning, but so far all he had done was succeed in lighting the two ranges, and after piling the coals into both chambers, he'd resolved to check on the price of running and buying a gas oven with Tony Ronconi. It was going to take an awful lot of meat sales to cover the cost of cooking by coal.

'Charlie?'

'Bethan! You came,' he smiled and walked round the counter to meet her.

'I had to do some shopping anyway.'

'On half-day?'

'It's quieter.' She tucked the shawl closer around herself and the baby.

'As you can see, I took your advice.' He pulled a chair out.

'Three chairs.' She looked around the room, noting the dark brown painted woodwork which provided a pleasing contrast to the cream walls. 'I like it.'

'Really?'

'It looks nice and new and clean. Just the sort of place a well–to–do housewife would patronise to buy cooked food for her family. You out to attract the crache, Charlie?'

'Not only the crache.' The Welsh colloquialism rolled oddly off his Russian tongue. 'I'm after the whole town, especially the people living on the dole. I'm hoping even they will be able to afford a slice or two of what I'm selling.'

'If you keep your prices low enough, they will. Well, I approve of the shop part.' She left her chair and walked round the counter. 'Mind you, you could do with something interesting on the wall.'

'Interesting?'

'Pictures. Something to stimulate their imaginations.'

'Appetites would be better. I'll see if I can find any prints of food. Would you like to see the kitchen?' He opened the door behind the counter.

'Who cleaned the range?'

'The boys. Why, haven't they done it properly?'

'If I'd realised they could clean a range like this, I would have set them to work on the one at home.'

He laughed and Bethan smiled.

'The shop's going to work out, Charlie. You do know that, don't you?'

'I hope so, otherwise I'm going to lose all the money I

have, and even some I don't,' he added remembering the five-year lease he'd signed. The rent would have to be paid on that every quarter whatever happened. A frown creased his forehead, and on impulse Bethan went to him and kissed him on the cheek.

'That's for luck,' she murmured as the door opened and Alma walked in.

'Sorry, I didn't know anyone was here.' Embarrassed, Alma backed out of the door.

'I'm just going.' Bethan put her hand into her shopping bag. 'I brought you something for your new home. I hope you like it.'

'Thank you.' Alma took the parcel, but made no move to open it.

'See you teatime, Charlie?' Bethan said as she left.

'See you,' he smiled, turning to a sour-faced Alma.

Bethan woke in complete darkness. She blinked, disorientated, and for one blissful unknowing moment she fumbled in the bed alongside her, seeking the reassurance of Andrew's presence. Surrounded by deafening silence she waited for the traffic noise of London to reverberate through the window from the street outside. Then she remembered: she was back home. In her parents' bedroom in Graig Avenue.

Fighting panic rooted in a fear she couldn't identify, she lay back aware of the thunder of her heartbeat, waiting for a repetition of whatever it was that had woken her. Something was wrong! She *knew* it. She listened hard, all her senses on the alert. Somewhere towards the mountain end of the street a dog barked, closely followed by the spitting, snarling sounds of fighting cats. Then the springs creaked in her grandmother's old double bed in the room next door as Diana turned in her sleep. Either William or Eddie coughed in their bedroom. None of the noises was in the least out of the ordinary. But there *had* been something. She was certain of it.

She sat up, swung her legs out of bed, and reached for

the old grey dressing gown she had left at home when she had fled to London. Wool, even scratchy worn wool, was more serviceable in the unheated bedrooms of the Graig than the silk and lace négligé Andrew had bought for her to wear in their centrally heated flat.

Edmund grunted, a muffling, snuffling sound unlike his normal steady breathing. In one single painful instant she knew what had woken her. She leaped from the bed and ran towards the door, feeling with her outstretched hand for the light switch. She flooded the room with a harsh light that brought tears to her eyes. Without giving herself time to become accustomed to the glare she darted towards the cot and picked up her baby. His tiny body was hot, fiery to the touch, so much she almost dropped him from shock. Holding him close, she carried him over to her bed and laid him down on the patchwork cover. He was rigid, his eyes staring blindly up into the bright light, but for the first time since his birth she was oblivious to his discomfort. She pulled up his soft flannel nightgown and carried out the routine checks she'd been taught under the eagle eye of Sister Church, who'd trained her in midwifery and infant care on the maternity ward of the Graig Hospital.

She ran her fingers over his chest. There was no rash. His nappy was dry. Was he dehydrated? His temperature! Holding him in one arm she went to the marble-topped washstand, poured cold water from the jug into the washing bowl and tossed in a flannel. Stripping Edmund, supporting his back and head with her hands, she plunged him into the bowl. He cried briefly as the chill of the water lapped around him, but even after she'd sponged him down, the fever still burned, flushing his skin a deep, unhealthy pink. Wrapping him in the sheet from the bottom of his cot she carried him, wet as he was, to Eddie's door and banged on it.

'What?' a sleepy voice mumbled.

'Eddie, run down the hill and get Trevor Lewis for me.' A crash came from the other side of the door, followed by a series of thuds. Eddie peered out sleepily. He was dressed in rumpled pyjama bottoms, his chest bare, spattered with the black and purple bruises of punches from his sparring sessions in the gym.

'Edmund's ill,' she explained, holding the damp bundle towards him.

'I'll go now.'

'I'll go Eddie, you stay with Beth.' William appeared in the doorway behind him. He'd already pulled his trousers over his pyjamas and was fastening the buttons. He reached out to the bottom of the bed, picked up his working shirt and thrust his naked feet into his boots. As Bethan retreated into her bedroom, she heard him clattering down the stairs.

She was sponging the baby down a second time when Eddie appeared, half dressed, in her bedroom.

'He is going to be all right, isn't he, Beth?' he asked urgently, staring at the tiny white figure laid out on a towel on her bed.

'I hope so, Eddie,' she breathed fervently as the baby wailed weakly. 'I really hope so.'

Even as he turned to go downstairs to make her a cup of tea he knew. One look into her eyes had been enough.

William had never flown in an aeroplane. He'd gone up to the field in Penycoedcae one Sunday when one had landed and offered trips over the town for half a crown, but he hadn't had the money. Now, as he raced headlong down the Graig Hill speeding past sleeping houses and empty streets, his footfalls ringing out on the metalled surface of Llantrisant Road, he felt as though the sensation couldn't be that different. He was whirling past a familiar world made strange. All life seemed to be extinguished. No lights burned except for the street lamps, and apart from a couple of cats fighting on the roof of a cottage he didn't see a living soul. But it was only when he passed the darkened window of Griffiths' shop on the corner of Factory Lane that he began to wonder just what time it was.

He placed his hands on his knees, bent over and took four or five deep breaths before sprinting on. Past the fish and chip shop, past the Temple chapel round the corner into Graig Street, up and over the triangular patch of rough grass to Laura and Trevor's front door. He hammered on it without pausing to catch his breath. Then he leaned back against the wall, gasping for air as he waited for his head to stop swimming and his heartbeat to steady.

'I'm coming.' He heard Trevor's voice from the bedroom overhead, the click of the landing light, the creak of the stairs as Trevor descended. The front door opened wide. No cracks, or peering around corners for a doctor used to night calls.

'William. Come in while I get my bag.'

'It's Bethan's baby,' William wheezed.

Trevor had already pulled his trousers over his pyjamas, but hadn't bothered with a shirt. He was wearing a leather patched sports coat over his striped open-necked jacket. He picked up a bunch of keys from the hall table next to the telephone and threw them to William, who was still in the doorway.

'Open the car and get out the starting handle.' He went into the front parlour to fetch his bag.

A few moments later they were chugging steadily up the Graig hill.

'Did Bethan say what it is?' Trevor asked.

'No. She just said to get you right away. I didn't see the baby. She had it wrapped in a wet sheet.'

'Fever.' Trevor slammed the car down a gear to climb the steep area past the fish and chip shop.

William was out of the car before Trevor drew to a halt. He raced up the front steps, turned the key in the door and held it open. 'She's in the main bedroom. The door facing you at the top of the stairs.'

Swinging his brown leather bag Trevor took the stairs two at a time, passing Eddie on the landing. Bethan was in the doorway waiting to meet him. William noticed that she'd dressed, and brushed her hair back from her face.

'High temperature,' Bethan announced without bothering with polite preliminaries. 'I've given him two cold baths and sponged him down three times, but it hasn't had any effect.'

'Convulsions?' Trevor asked.

'Yes, but he's had those before,' she explained as he followed her into the bedroom and closed the door.

William trailed behind Eddie into the kitchen. The light was on and he glanced up at the clock. The hands pointed to half-past three. No wonder he was tired. He opened the oven door, raked up the coals, recklessly adding another two pieces so that the kettle Eddie had already filled would boil quickly. Taking the easy chair opposite Eddie's, he sat back and waited; still, silent and impotent like his cousin, as they listened to the quiet murmurs percolating through the floorboards of the bedroom above.

'What is it?' Bethan's voice pitched high in urgency although she knew it was impossible for Trevor to make a firm diagnosis on the basis of Edmund's symptoms.

'I don't know.' He bent over Edmund and studied him closely. 'Frankly, I haven't a clue,' he added, irritated by his inadequacy. 'You know as well as I do how susceptible to infection children with palsy are. This could be anything from—'

'I took him out today, to town. And last Sunday we went to Cardiff. It was cold. He must have caught a chill while we waited in one of the bus shelters . . .'

'This isn't the result of a chill, Bethan. It's a deep-seated infection,' he said authoritatively as he laid his hand lightly on Edmund's stomach.

'You can't be sure of that. You—'

'Stop beating yourself with the stick of bad motherhood,' he admonished her. 'No matter what precautions you took this was bound to happen sooner or later. Didn't the paediatrician in the Cross warn you about the increased risk of infections for a child with palsy?'

'Yes.'

'I could admit him to the Graig. It would give you a break. You could rest . . .'

'What treatment would you prescribe?'

'At this stage only observation. I don't know enough to order otherwise.'

'I'd rather keep him here.'

'I couldn't stop you, but it might be better for Edmund, and for you, to have a shift of fresh nurses on hand rather than one tired mother.'

'I'll cope and I'd rather keep him,' she said firmly.

'You sure?'

'Perfectly.'

He knew Bethan too well to argue. 'I'll call in again before I do my morning rounds in the hospital. You obviously remember the drill. Try to keep the temperature down, and pour as much fluid into him as he will take. If he goes into convulsions again, even mild ones, send for me. Immediately! Laura always knows where I am.'

'Thank you for coming, Trevor.' Bethan wrapped the baby in a clean linen sheet. Although he still needed to be kept cool it didn't seem right for him to lie naked in the cold bedroom.

'That's what doctors do,' he replaced his stethoscope in his bag. 'Come when they're called. But for all of our training we can't help every patient the way we would like to.' He looked at her closely. She appeared composed, in complete control. But he'd worked with Bethan; seen her struggle through emotional traumas that would have felled a lesser person, only to collapse later when she'd believed herself alone. 'Do you want me to telephone Andrew?'

She looked down at her baby. 'If you like,' she answered dully.

'Bethan, surely it would be easier if Andrew were here, facing this with you.'

She bit her lower lip and shook her head, neither agreeing nor disagreeing.

'It's none of my business but if this was my son I'd want to be with him.'

'*You* would Trevor,' she said quietly. 'But Edmund's not your son, he's Andrew's.'

'Bethan, I couldn't live with myself if I kept something like this from any father, let alone Andrew who's a good friend . . .'

'Do what you think is right, Trevor. You're the doctor.' She sat on the bed and moved Edmund on to her lap.

'Then you won't mind if I call him?'

'He won't come.'

Eddie barged into the silence that had fallen between them, carrying two cups of tea that had slopped into the saucers.

'Keep it warm. I'll be back at half-past six before I go into the hospital.' Trevor picked up his bag.

Eddie dumped both cups on the bedside table. 'I'll see you out.'

'The baby?' Eddie whispered as soon as they were down the steps out of Bethan's earshot.

Trevor faced Eddie squarely. There was something infinitely pathetic about the boy who'd been forced to carry a man's load that wasn't even his, far too soon in life.

'I don't know what's going to happen to the baby,' he answered with more truth than diplomacy. 'If you're the praying sort you might try that.'

'I don't go to church, only the gym,' Eddie retorted drily.

'Pity we can't put whatever Edmund's got into a punchbag and give it a bloody good pounding.' Trevor opened his car door. 'That way we'd both be doing something useful.'

'That's all she said, "Do whatever you think is right"?' Laura turned the rashers of bacon she was frying.

'That and "He won't come."'

'And are you going to telephone him?'

'What do you think?'

'I think it's too early in the morning to play guessing games.' She clamped the lid back on the pan to prevent the fat from spitting over the stove.

'Truth is, Laura, I don't know what to do. I realise Bethan doesn't want me to telephone Andrew, but I can't help thinking of him, alone in that flat of theirs in London. He must miss them terribly . . .'

'The only thing Andrew John would miss in life is a good time. And, as he's living alone, it's my guess he isn't missing a thing.'

'That's a hard thing to say about any man.'

'If we were talking about any man I'd agree with you, but we're not, we're talking about Andrew John.' She lifted three eggs from the bowl on the dresser and placed them next to the frying pan. 'He never gave Bethan, or the baby she was carrying, a second thought when his parents sent him off to London because they didn't fancy the daughter of an unemployed miner joining the family.'

'He came back for her. He married her,' Trevor protested as he went out to wash his hands.

'So he did, but he isn't looking after her and that poor child now. Seems to me that whenever life gets tough Andrew runs.'

'We don't know for certain that he's running this time.'

'If he's a caring husband and father what is he doing in London while Bethan is coping all alone here?'

'Probably coming to terms with having a son like Edmund.'

'That's exactly my point.'

'Don't we all try to run away from the unpleasant things in life?' Trevor put his hands around Laura's waist and kissed the back of her neck.

'You don't,' she snapped irritably as she lifted the lid of the pan and received a spit burn on her finger.

'There have been times when I've wanted to.'

'Like now?'

'I've never wanted to run from you. But then you've never made it that tough on me.'

'I could. Especially if you carry on dilly-dallying about picking up that telephone.'

Trevor looked into the frying pan. The bacon still needed another few minutes before it became crispy, and Laura hadn't even broken the eggs yet. He had no excuse. If he *was* going to telephone Andrew he might as well do it now and get it over with.

He went into the hall, picked up the receiver and dialled the operator. He had to wait three minutes for her to make the connection, and when she finally did, the telephone at the other end seemed to ring with a hollow note as though it was trying to tell him there was no one around to pick it up.

He imagined the empty rooms, immaculately and exquisitely furnished in the modern, art deco blond wood pieces Andrew admired. Then he looked at his watch. Six o'clock. He should have asked Bethan what time Andrew went to the hospital. He didn't even know what department Andrew worked in, or if he was on call. For all he knew Andrew could be on night shift in casualty.

'Hello.'

The voice didn't even sound like Andrew's. Perhaps the operator had connected him to the wrong number.

'Could I speak to Doctor Andrew John, please?'

'Speaking.' The voice was curt. Trevor was beginning to regret his decision.

'I didn't recognise your voice. It's Trevor here.'

'Something's wrong with Bethan?'

'No.' Trevor took a deep breath. 'The baby.'

'It's bad.' It wasn't a question.

'It looks it.'

'I'll telephone the Cross and see if they can get someone to take over my shift. I'll be there as soon as I can.'

The line went dead. Trevor looked at the receiver for a moment before replacing it.

'Well?' Laura asked.

'He said he'd be down as soon as the hospital got a replacement for him.'

'Let's hope he'll be of some use to Bethan when he gets here. Do you want your eggs with runny or hard yolks?'

Chapter Sixteen

BETHAN SAT ON the edge of her bed, watching and waiting. She heard the alarm go off in the room Eddie shared with William. It continued to ring, and she realised that both boys must have remained downstairs. Seconds later it was joined by the tinny, angry sound of Charlie's alarm in the front room below her, but that was silenced almost as soon as it began. Nerves stretched to breaking point, she left Edmund lying in the centre of her bed and walked across the landing to Eddie's room. The clock with its cracked face stood on a chair next to the bed. She picked it up and silenced it just as Diana's clock started clanging. She felt like screaming. The same number of alarms went off in the house every morning. Today was no different. She couldn't expect the world to stop just because Edmund was ill. Edmund! She returned to her bedroom and laid her hand, yet again, on the baby's forehead. Was it her imagination? No! He was definitely a little cooler. Just a little. Did this mean that he was going to get better or . . .

'I've brought you another tea, Beth.'

'Thanks.' She tried, and failed to smile at Eddie.

'Friday's always a lousy day on the round,' he said awkwardly. 'So I thought I'd stay here. There's one or two things I've been meaning to get around to for a while. The shed needs tidying, and if there's any leftover paint in there I might give the outside walls a coat. And then again, if I stay I could help you with the housework,' he offered. 'I've watched Mam clean and blacklead the stove often enough to be able to do it myself. I can carry the rugs out and beat them on the line, and although I might not be a great cook, I can do a decent fry-up at a push. Ask

Charlie if you don't believe me. It was me who took over the cooking when Mam had to see to Uncle Joe last autumn when he went down with an attack of pleurisy.'

'It would be good to have you close at hand, Eddie,' she replied. It would be useful to have someone she could send to fetch Trevor at a moment's notice.

'I'll go and see to the breakfasts.'

'I'll be down in a moment.'

'You bringing the baby downstairs?'

'I think I'll have to. I don't want to leave him up here all alone. Do me a favour, move the day cot from the corner by the stove to the back corner next to the dresser. His temperature's dropping, but I still don't want him to get overheated.'

'Wouldn't both of you be better off up here until it's quiet? You know what it's like with everyone back and forth to the washhouse, doors opening and closing and draughts whistling everywhere.'

'You sure you can manage the breakfasts?'

'I'll bring you up some of my toast and porridge,' he boasted, hoping Diana would have time to show him how to make porridge. The last time he'd had a go, William had asked if he was trying to invent a new cement.

'I'd rather eat in the kitchen after everyone's left.'

'Don't forget to drink your tea,' he reminded her.

Bethan drank her tea and fought the temptation to pick up Edmund and nurse him. When the cup was empty, she left the bed, switched off the light, drew the curtains and pulled down the sash as far as it would go. Was the sky lighter than usual over the mountain? Perhaps spring was turning into summer after all. She had a sudden yearning for the warmth of the sun and the brightness of midsummer flowers.

She listened to the sound of water splashing as Diana washed in the bedroom next to hers. She heard footfalls descending the stairs and Eddie's voice hushed and self-important as he told Charlie and Diana about the baby's illness. She blessed him for taking the task upon himself.

It was far easier to sit and watch her baby in the growing light, doing nothing in particular, than face the family with the news.

She held her breath so she could monitor the baby's. Laying her fingers lightly on his forehead she felt his temperature steadily continue to decline in the face of the cool breeze that blew in through the window. She pulled the cotton sheet around him, laid his thin woollen shawl lightly on top, and continued to watch and wait, holding her breath every time he breathed in, only exhaling when she was certain that he'd breathed out. Silently praying until he drew his next breath. Hoping against hope that there'd be another . . . and another . . . and another.

'It's bad then?' Diana stirred a handful of salt into the porridge pot.

'I think so,' Eddie replied uncertainly, superstitiously hoping he wasn't precipitating anything dreadful by putting his worst fears into words. 'Doctor Lewis said he'd call again before he begins work in the hospital.'

'You know what a heavy sleeper I am. You should have woken me,' Diana said reproachfully.

'I would have if there'd been anything for you to do.'

Diana laid a burn-scarred wooden board in the centre of the table, carried the porridge saucepan over to it, and left it steaming while she went to the dresser to fetch bowls.

'Bethan said she'd eat later, but it might be better to take it up to her while it's hot,' Eddie said thoughtfully.

'Let me make up the baby's bottle first. She won't eat until Edmund's fed.'

'Have you got time?'

'I'll make time.' She jangled the keys in her skirt pocket. 'The only people likely to complain if I open up five minutes late are the customers, and they can wait. Wyn's too busy with the other shop to worry about what I do with mine.'

'Lucky you, having an easygoing boss,' William joked

in a voice loud enough to carry back to Charlie, who was cleaning his shoes in the yard. 'Mine's a slave-driver.'

'Four beef carcasses chopped and jointed for the boss's Cardiff shops by ten,' Charlie ordered as he washed his hands under the running tap. 'Then you can start on the lambs and lights we'll need for the stall tomorrow. And this afternoon you can slice all the cooked meats in the shop, and boil up those hams I bought.'

'See what I mean?' William moaned to his sister. He was deliberately avoiding the subject of Bethan and her baby, although he felt their presence in the room above him as keenly as the rest of them. Clowning around and banter had always been his way of coping.

'I could send a message to Wyn. Perhaps his sister could take over the High Street shop just for today,' Diana began doubtfully.

'There's no need,' Eddie interjected. 'I've already told Beth that I'll stay home today and help her.'

'Help her by all means,' William said warily. 'But please don't cook tea. My stomach hasn't recovered from the last bacon you fried. As a substitute for shoe leather it might have had a future, but as bacon . . .'

'Oh God, who's that now?' Diana complained as there was a loud rapping on the door.

'The doctor probably.' Eddie pushed his spoon into his porridge and left his chair. 'I'll let him in.'

Diana mixed the baby's milk powder in boiling water. Leaving the bottle to cool she picked up her own breakfast.

'Yoo-hoo, it's only me.'

'Mrs Richards, at this hour. Pity help us,' Diana muttered as she swallowed the last of her tea.

'Sorry to come over so early, but I thought you'd like to know.' Mrs Richards gave Charlie an arch look as he sat at the table in his shirt-sleeves with his collar hanging loose around his neck. 'The bailiffs are round Phyllis Harry's. They're throwing her and that baby of hers out on the street. Fred the Dead waited until he made his money from the funeral, and not one day more. If you want my opinion, the man ought to be shot. Even if it is Phyllis Harry he's evicting.'

'Mam, I don't know why you want to see the minister. Every time you talk to him he upsets you.'

'I won't have anyone else telling him and the deacons what you've done, or where we're living.' Lena pulled her knitted hat firmly down over her head.

'Why? What's the difference? They've already forbidden me to enter the chapel, what else can they do?' Alma carried the new hand towels Bethan had bought her as a house-warming present from the kitchen into the bathroom.

'I need to talk over what you've done with someone I respect. I need to know what people will think of you . . .'

'Mam please, don't start that again.' Alma returned from the tiny bathroom to the equally small kitchen. 'Charlie has given me a job, and us a better roof over our head. There's no reason for people to talk. It's purely a business arrangement. He still intends to lodge with the Powells. He's happy there,' she emphasised, embroidering the brief conversations she'd had with Charlie.

'It's all very well for you to say he won't be living here. He'll be working downstairs every day. This is his flat, you're in his power. He can do whatever he wants with you . . .'

'Mam, you make him sound like Fu Manchu.'

Lena wasn't impressed by her daughter's attempt at humour. 'All I'm saying is that if the minister has a word with this new boss of yours, tells him what a decent girl you are, then he might be more inclined to stick to the bargain he's made.'

'The last thing I want is for anyone from the chapel to speak to him. Don't you see, it would ruin everything. Charlie overlooked a lot of gossip when he gave me this job.'

'But that still doesn't make moving in here right. Alma, please listen. My father was a deacon, well respected in the chapel. There are businessmen in the congregation. Some of them might be looking for help. Ben Springer who owns the shoe shop is always taking on girls. If I ask the minister to put in a word and Ben agrees, you could tell this man—'

'His name is Charlie,' Alma shouted angrily.

'What kind of a name is that! When I was a girl people called their employers sir. They showed respect.'

'Charlie's real name is unpronounceable, not that it matters. It isn't a person's name that's important, but the way they are; and I wouldn't work for that slimy toad Ben Springer if you paid me double wages, and neither will anyone else. That's why he's always looking for girls.'

'Working for a married man could go a long way to making you respectable again.'

'Respectable! Respectable! Is it respectable to live in the workhouse? Because that's where we'd be going if it was up to your damned minister.'

'Alma, your language,' Lena sat down heavily on the kitchen chair.

'When are you going to realise that the congregation of that chapel you think so much of would be quite happy to sit back and watch both of us be put out on the street. They wouldn't lift a finger to help. They'd enjoy it,' she added cruelly, wanting to make her mother face the facts. 'But if you want to, go and visit your minister. Just remember we don't have anywhere else to live, and this flat goes with the job I've taken.'

'You told me you'd paid the rent on Morgan Street until today,' her mother said.

'I have,' Alma agreed grimly. 'But that didn't stop Fred Jones from taking someone else's money from tomorrow. We couldn't go back to Morgan Street now even if I wanted to, which I don't. The house has already been let to someone else.'

*

'You can't walk through here.' Bobby Thomas fingered his bruises as he blocked the door set into the garden wall of Rhiannon's house when Charlie, flanked by William and Eddie, crossed Graig Avenue.

'I'd like to call in and see Miss Harry,' Charlie murmured softly. Eddie and William squared up threateningly behind his back.

'She's at the front of the house. If you want to see her you're going to have to walk round to Phillips Street.'

'Who says?' Eddie stepped in front of Charlie and thrust his nose close to Bobby's. Bobby didn't step back, he merely let out a long, low whistle that carried piercingly through the cool morning air. The garden door opened at his back and two more of Fred's rent collectors stepped out.

'We'll walk around, Eddie,' Charlie said evenly, tipping his cap to Bobby.

'But we've been walking through Mrs Pugh's house for—'

'It doesn't matter,' Charlie interrupted. 'We'll walk around now.'

William nudged his cousin in the back. 'The sooner we go the sooner we'll be there.'

Much as he saw the need to hurry, Charlie waited until he could be sure Eddie would follow. The three of them finally walked off down the rough road towards Vicarage corner.

'We saw them off,' Bobby laughed, crossing his arms over his chest.

'For the moment.' James, Fred's eldest son, leant against the wall wishing his father was around to see the havoc his eviction order was creating. But the one thing he had learned in the six months he had been working for the family firm was that his father was *never* around on eviction days. One of the perks of being boss was being able to stay away from the seamier side of working life.

'I can't believe that Fred Jones would put Phyllis out on

the street with Rhiannon only just in her grave.' Eddie burned with righteous indignation.

'Rumour was going around that Phyllis Harry's son is Fred's. His wife gave him an ultimatum Wednesday afternoon: either he put Phyllis out, or she left.'

'Where did you hear that?' Charlie asked.

'In the Central, Wednesday night. Williams the milk came in. He lives next door to the Joneses and when he left home to go out, Fred's wife was crying all over Mrs Williams telling her the story. Apparently Fred used to collect the rents in Phillips Street himself, just about the time Phyllis had to give up her job in the White Palace.'

'I didn't know you went to the Central,' Eddie said, kicking a stone across the road.

'Now and again,' William replied airily.

'Well you never said a word to me about it.'

'You weren't there to hear it when I got home. Sometimes I think you live in that bloody gym.'

Charlie quickened his pace. By the time they reached the Graig Hotel he was ahead of them. He paused on the corner of Llantrisant and Walters Roads and looked up the hill. The front door of Rhiannon's house was wide open, and a crowd had gathered. Two men were carrying out her prized china cabinet. Even from that distance he could hear the crashing and smashing of the ornaments it contained.

'The bastards haven't even emptied it.' Eddie clenched his fists.

Charlie sprinted up the hill, Eddie and William running behind him. A woman stepped out of the crowd and shook her fist furiously at Bobby, who had obviously walked through the house to face Charlie and the boys when they arrived.

'You and your boss will rot in hell for his, Bobby Thomas,' she screamed hysterically. 'You mark my words. God will see you rot in hell. Putting a woman and her baby out on the street like this.'

'You want to join her, Mavis?' Bobby asked. 'If you do, just carry on.'

'You wouldn't dare. I pay my rent on the nose, every week. I've got my rent book to prove it.'

'But your kids make a racket. Mr Jones's other tenants don't like it. And you and your old man are always at it, hammer and tongs. I keep a record of all the complaints I get on my round, Mavis. You live in a rented house. Mr Jones has every right to put you out if he sees fit.'

The woman fell silent. Phyllis sat hunched on a kitchen chair that stood incongruously at the foot of the steps, her little boy wrapped in a shawl on her lap. All that could be seen of him beneath the layers of cloth was his red, runny nose.

'Phyllis?' Charlie had to call her name twice before she answered him.

'We'll have to find somewhere for you to go.'

She looked up, recognised Charlie, and a torrent of words poured out on a tide of tears, washing away all pretence of stoicism.

'It's not as if it's just me and the baby, Charlie. It's Rhiannon's furniture and all her things,' she sobbed looking at Rhiannon's prized possessions scattered over the street.

'There's nothing in my front room,' Mavis announced with a defiant look at Bobby. 'We had to sell all our best sticks, even my grandmother's rugs, before they'd give us enough dole to feed the kids. You're welcome to use it.'

Charlie turned to William and Eddie. 'Get as much of this furniture off the street and into next door as you can,' he ordered.

'We'll help.' The cry came from a dozen people. Paralysed by a sense of impotence, they had stood idly by not knowing what to do or how to help. Despite Phyllis's outcast status, her plight had invoked their pity.

'Where you going, Charlie?' Eddie picked up Rhiannon's sewing box.

'I'm taking Phyllis and the baby to Bethan.'

'You do that,' Eddie shouted in a voice calculated to carry to Bobby Thomas. 'We can take them in, our house is our own. It's not rented off any man.'

'Take them through our house,' Mavis ordered, wrapping her arm around Phyllis and the baby.

'Thank you, Mrs Davies.' Charlie looked warily at two men who were carrying a chaise-longue down the steps.

'Charlie?' One of the bailiff's men stepped forward, mopping his sweating face with a handkerchief. Charlie recognised him as a miner who had once worked with Evan. 'I . . . we . . . none of us like doing this,' he said awkwardly. 'But we need the money and when all's said and done, a day's work is a day's work.'

'You don't have to explain anything to me,' Charlie said flatly.

'Well I just wanted to say, the lady's clothes, the baby's cot and his toys . . . Well the boys and me, we don't want to carry them out here.'

'Is it all right if some of the things are carried through the house up to the Powells' house in Graig Avenue, Mr Jones?' Charlie asked James, who was standing just inside the door.

James turned aside, feeling very sick and ashamed of himself. 'I'll get the men to do it, Charlie,' he mumbled. 'Just tell us which pieces you want.'

Belinda Lane led Alma's mother through the town towards Berw Road. Avenue might have been a more appropriate name, as all the houses were built on one side. The other side sloped down steeply towards the river. Close up the water was black, turgid with coal dust, but distance and the trees that grew along the banks lent the flow of water a certain enchantment, and the houses were sought after by those who couldn't afford the prices of the villas on the Common.

The minister's house was a brisk five-minute walk out of town, close to a large, pleasant, open green space. Belinda led Lena Moore carefully up the steep stone steps, knocked the door tentatively and waited. She had to knock a second time before they heard rubber-soled carpet slippers squeaking over the flagstoned passageway.

'I'll play on the green, Auntie Moore,' Belinda said nervously. 'You can call out when you want to leave. I'll hear you.' She'd been in the minister's house once and had hated the unnatural silence and the smell: a closed-in musty scent of damp plaster and books that reminded her of chapel, mixed together with beeswax polish and boiled fish.

'Mind you don't go far, Belinda.'

'I won't.' The girl skipped off.

The door opened and the minister's sister stood framed in the porchway. A tall, well-built God-fearing woman, she had devoted her life to the chapel and her brother. Regarding herself as the epitome of the women of the scriptures, she had little time or sympathy for those who, in her narrow opinion, had strayed from the path of righteousness, and had told Lena so, repeatedly.

'Mrs Moore.' She peered suspiciously at Lena. 'Did you want to see my brother?'

'I rather hoped I could,' Lena said apologetically. The minister's sister always made her feel nervous. 'But if it's not convenient . . .'

'It is rather early for a call. However, he's just finishing his breakfast, and if you'd care to wait in his study I'll see if he can spare you a moment or two.' Her voice told Lena exactly how much of a nuisance she was being.

The study was every bit as cold and cheerless as the kitchen in Morgan Street.

'Can I take your coat, Mrs Moore?'

'No thank you. I won't disturb the minister for long. I only need a minute of his time.'

'There's a chair behind you to your left. I'll just go and finish seeing to his breakfast.'

Lena stood in the doorway of the room and extended her hands. She took small steps, halting when her foot touched the chair. She crouched down, and felt for the seat and fell into the chair rather inelegantly, glad that no one was around to witness her fumblings. While she waited she amused herself by trying to recall the study. She could remember the house quite well from her frequent visits as a child, invited on the strength of her father's position as a deacon. There'd been Christmas tea parties with stewed tea and boiled fruit cake, Harvest Thanksgiving when the table had been laid with slabs of coarse brown bread and home-made sour milk cheese, and fund-raising coffee mornings which she had spent washing up with the 'girl' in the scullery.

'My brother will be with you in a moment, Mrs Moore.' Lena started, wondering how long the minister's sister had been in the room.

'Would you like a cup of tea?' she offered curtly.

'I've just had breakfast, but thank you.'

'As you wish.'

'Mrs Moore, this is a surprise!' The minister himself bustled in. Lena heard a chair creak as he sat down, then the door closed. She assumed his sister had shut it behind her.

'May I ask what brings you down here today, Mrs Moore?' the minister asked.

'Alma,' she admitted miserably.

'Your daughter.' He shook his head, then remembered that she couldn't see his gesture of disapproval. 'I might have known. What's the girl been up to now?'

'It's been hard since she lost her job in the tailor's shop.'

'That I can believe,' he said harshly. 'But then if what I've heard is right, she deserved to lose it. As you well know, I've little patience with the girl, but I must confess that after thinking it over I've come to the conclusion that perhaps Alma isn't the only one to blame for your troubles.'

Lena looked in the direction of his voice, and waited for more.

'As your father would no doubt have told you if he'd lived longer, you spoilt the girl when she was young. You allowed her to run wild.'

'I did the best I could,' she protested.

'I'm not saying you didn't,' he pursed his lips. 'All things considered I suppose we couldn't really expect any better. Your father told me a few things about your husband, and we must remember that Alma has her father's blood in her. But when I hear—'

'She's found herself another job,' Lena interrupted quickly. 'That's what I wanted to talk to you about.'

'What kind of job?'

'Working in a cooked meat and pie shop.'

'Serving?' he asked incredulously. 'A young girl who worked with Alma in the tailor's told me that decent women have refused to allow Alma to wait on them.'

'I'm sure that's not true,' Lena countered timidly. She'd never dared contradict Mr Parry before in her life.

'I assure you the girl is quite reliable, and respectable.'

'This job isn't behind the counter. It's in the back, cooking and baking,' Lena broke in, not wanting to hear any more about the 'girl' or what she'd said.

'I didn't know Alma had received training in domestic skills,' the minister commented drily.

'And because she'll be starting work really early every morning we've had to move into a flat over the shop,' Lena continued valiantly, sticking rigidly to the topic she wanted to discuss.

'Where is this shop?'

'On the corner between Taff Street and Penuel Lane, by the fountain. Opposite the entrance to the fruit market.'

'So you've left Morgan Street. You really should have let us know. One of the deacons could have wasted time looking for you.'

'Alma didn't tell me we were moving until late Wednesday night. I came as soon as I could.'

'You do realise that if Alma loses this job, you will both be out on the street,' he informed her coldly.

'That's what I came to talk to you about. I know my father always valued your advice, and I was hoping you could help us. I begged Alma not to give up the house in Morgan Street but she insisted we couldn't afford the rent without her money from the tailor's . . .'

'Am I right in thinking that the rent you will be paying for this flat will be deducted from your daughter's wages?'

'Yes.'

'Then what are you going to live on? Surely her earnings will barely cover the cost of the flat?'

'She's going to get ten shillings after the rent, coals and food are paid for.'

'She is going to be earning enough to cover all that by cooking?'

'It seems a lot to me, but then I've no idea of wages.'

'I have, and I'd like to know just what kind of duties warrant that level of salary. I am acquainted with many married men who bring home a good deal less.'

'But she insists it's straightforward work. Early start in the kitchen. Three to four o'clock most mornings, and then work through to midday. And because it's better pay than she's getting now, she won't have to work nights in the café. She said it will be a better life for both of us. It just doesn't sound quite right to me . . .'

'Or me. So why exactly have you come here?'

'I was hoping you could talk to her,' Lena pleaded. 'Make her see sense before it's too late.'

'But you've told me that you are already living in the flat tied to this job.'

'Yes,' Lena admitted miserably.

'Then it is too late. There's nothing I can do for you or your daughter now, Mrs Moore.'

'I suppose there isn't.' She gripped the arms of her chair tightly.

'Might I ask the name of the man Alma is working for?'

'I'm not sure. Alma calls him Charlie.'

'The foreign butcher on the market!'

'I think he's the one.'

'Another unmarried foreigner like the last. I feel for you in your sorrow, Mrs Moore.' He rose from his chair.

'But there is nothing I can do for you. I have my sister and her reputation to consider, so I'm afraid I am going to have to ask you to leave.'

'I'm sorry . . .'

'And until such time as you leave this man's house I'm afraid I will have to ask you to forgo attending chapel.'

'No!' This was one eventuality that hadn't occurred to Lena. Brought up to revere the chapel, she interpreted the minister's edict not only as social disgrace but also as eviction from heaven. 'Please . . .'

'It is not me you should be pleading with, Mrs Moore, but your daughter. How could you allow her to behave this way? Going from one man to another without a wedding ring in sight. All I can say is I'm glad your father isn't here to see what his granddaughter has become.'

Lena burst into tears.

'You had better get down on your knees and ask for God's forgiveness – but not in my chapel. I will pray for you. Goodbye Mrs Moore.'

Chapter Seventeen

CHARLIE STOOD BACK to allow Phyllis and her baby to walk into the house before him.

'I shouldn't be here. Not here. Of all the houses on the Graig . . .' For the first time in her life hysteria mounted as the finality of the move she was making hit her.

'You can sit in my room while I see Bethan,' Charlie said gently but firmly. He stepped ahead of her and led the way to his room, which was just in front of the kitchen. He ushered Phyllis in. 'I'll go and find Bethan. I won't be long.' He closed the door, leaving Phyllis and the baby alone.

The room was clean, orderly and sterile. A single bed with plain deal foot- and head-boards, neatly made, and covered by a smooth grey, blue and black piece of woven Welsh flannel, was pushed up against the wall to the right of the door. Opposite it a lavishly embroidered firescreen concealed the hearth of a polished iron firegrate, topped by a brass airing rail that hung just below the wooden mantelpiece. White-painted wooden planking doors fronted the alcoves, and Phyllis presumed they held Charlie's clothes and possessions.

The curtains were pulled wide in the bay window, giving a view of the garden wall of Rhiannon's house opposite, and the centre sash had been pulled down a couple of inches. The room was cold, but with the kitchen stove going full blast next door, not overly so. Phyllis pulled the checked flannel shawl closer around both herself and Brian as she sat on the only chair in the room. Placed in the exact centre of the bay window it faced inwards. She tried to imagine Charlie sitting here and doing . . . what? There were no books in evidence and she decided that they too must be in the cupboards. The bed, the chair, the firescreen and a small card table pushed up against the back wall facing her – there was nothing else. Even the mantelpiece was free of dust and photographs. Not even one of the dark, hurriedly developed snaps the beach photographers took in Barry Island and Porthcawl.

She looked around. The walls were papered in a busy rose trellis pattern that would have camouflaged any pictures. Not a single object gave a clue to Charlie's likes, dislikes or personality. She knew that he had lived with the Powells for nearly a year, and Megan Powell, Evan's sister-in-law, for two before that. Three years in Pontypridd, but he might well have moved in yesterday. She wondered if he was really close to anyone. Man or woman.

Man! Evan Powell. They frequently had a drink together, and Evan had told her how much he relied on Charlie's judgement and friendship. She shuddered as an image of Evan came to mind. She had promised herself that she would never lean on him, never demand anything of him, no matter what; and here she was, sitting helplessly while Charlie of all people pleaded with Evan's daughter to take her and her son in. She was reduced to begging charity from a woman who had more cause to dislike her than anyone, except perhaps Elizabeth. She sank back into the chair, clutched her baby and wondered if it would have been better to have walked down to the workhouse after all.

Bethan was still in her bedroom watching her baby when she heard Charlie's soft, muted voice floating up the stairs. She heard the door to his room open and close and wondered who he was talking to. When she heard footsteps on the stairs she stood up and smoothed her skirt with her hands. It had to be Trevor. Charlie hadn't come up since the day he'd moved into the house; he had no reason to. She opened her door, stepping back in amazement when she saw Charlie standing on the landing.

'I know your baby is very ill, and I'm sorry to disturb you, Bethan. But I need to talk to you. The bailiffs are putting Phyllis and her baby out on the street.'

'Bailiffs. But why?' She stared at him uncomprehendingly.

'Fred Jones wants her out now that Rhiannon is dead, and as the rent book was in Rhiannon's name they have the right to do it.'

'But the funeral was only the day before yesterday. There's all the furniture . . .'

'William and Eddie are carrying some of it next door. I hope you don't mind, I asked them to bring Phyllis's more personal possessions here.'

'Of course.' Bethan thought rapidly. 'The front parlour will need clearing—'

'I'll see to that,' Charlie broke in swiftly.

Bethan turned away, went to the bed and picked up Edmund. She laid his cheek against her own. He was still unnaturally warm, but not as hot as he had been in the night.

'Phyllis and the baby have nowhere to go.'

She had known what Charlie was going to say and had been prepared for it. 'This is my mother's as well as my father's house.'

She spoke so quietly Charlie had to strain to catch what she was saying. He cleared his throat awkwardly.

'When we were in prison, with your father, I thought you'd guessed.'

'I guessed all right. Only too well.'

'If you don't take her in no one else will. They're all too afraid of their landlord.'

'That's Phyllis's problem.'

'After nursing there you know better than anyone what it's like in the workhouse for an unmarried woman. Bethan please, can she stay here? Just until I can sort out something better?' he pleaded. 'She can have my bed. I'll sleep on the floor of Eddie and William's room.'

'How can you ask me, of all people, to take her in?'

'I'm asking because it's what your father would do if he were home.'

'Not if my mother were here.'

'But neither of them is, and Phyllis is downstairs—'

'You've brought her here!'

'She's in my room. She knows I've come upstairs to talk to you.'

'How could you put me in this position, Charlie!' She bit her lower lip in an attempt to contain her anger.

'Because I don't want to leave her nursing her baby in the street, surrounded by Rhiannon's furniture,' he said simply.

'But this, all of this,' she said wearily, glancing down at her baby, 'will just create more scandal and gossip. I . . .' her voice trailed miserably as she looked into Charlie's deep blue eyes. None of the contempt she felt for herself was mirrored in their patient depths. Here she was worrying about scandal and gossip, as if scandal and gossip would make any difference to her relationship with Andrew. Their marriage had fallen apart on the day Edmund was born. What did it matter if she took Phyllis in, or that Phyllis was her father's mistress? What did any of it matter?

Her thoughts went out to Phyllis and the solemnly beautiful little boy with the black curly hair just like Eddie . . . just like her father.

'Get the boys to clear the parlour for the things Phyllis wants to bring with her. She'll have to sleep with the baby in the box room for the time being. The furniture . . .'

'Don't worry about the furniture. I'll sort it out. Thank you, Bethan.'

She closed the door and sank back on the bed. Edmund had fallen asleep on her shoulder, and his small body felt limp and damp against hers. Had she done the right thing? Her father would undoubtedly think so, and thank her for it, but her mother would probably never speak to her again if she ever got to hear. But there were the boys. Haydn was away, but what if he should come home and find out? And Eddie, he was always too handy with his fists. How many fights would he feel honour bound to settle when the whole of the Graig found out who Brian Harry's father was, and began talking about it?

'Bethan says you're welcome to stay.' Charlie exaggerated the truth when he saw Phyllis sitting, like an anguished Madonna with her son on her lap, in the bay window of his room.

'She did? But . . .'

'She knows who fathered your child,' he interposed. 'Bethan's baby is very ill and she's waiting for the doctor, but she suggested that you and Brian sleep in the box room. I'm sorry, but Diana had to go to work. There's no one to help you make up the bed, or make you breakfast,' he apologised artfully, knowing that the best thing for her would be work.

'If someone could bring over the linen and my clothes, I'll make up the bed.' Now she was away from the street and prying eyes she couldn't bear the thought of going back.

'I'll see to it. Why don't you sit in the kitchen. It's warmer there.'

She picked up Brian and followed Charlie. One glance at the disorder in the room was enough. She took off her coat and shawl and sat the baby on the hearth-rug in front of the stove. He wailed and clutched at her leg.

'You've got to be good,' she said sternly, as she set about clearing the table of breakfast dishes. Something in the tone of her voice silenced him. Charlie disappeared into his room and returned with a wooden box. He knelt on the floor beside the baby, opened it and showed him the chess figures it contained. Phyllis realised that there were some personal things tucked away in the alcove cupboards after all.

'If those are valuable don't give them to him,' she warned. 'He's teething. He might bite them.'

'He wouldn't be the first child to cut his teeth on them.'
Charlie rose to his feet. 'I'll bring your clothes and linen
over. You'll let the doctor in when he calls?'

'I will.' Phyllis was already soaking the burnt porridge
saucepan in the washhouse.

Bobby Thomas was nowhere to be seen when James Jones
allowed Charlie to walk through Rhiannon's house. It
already had a deserted air, as if the occupants had moved
out months ago. The washhouse was empty. Two broken
dolly pegs lay abandoned in a corner. The big round
washtub had been carried into the back kitchen, and one
of the men was emptying the contents of the pantry into
it: dishes, plates, bowls, a bag of potatoes, a bread bin, a
crock with three eggs in it. The kitchen itself had already
been stripped. There was no sign of Rhiannon's table and
chairs, or the easy chairs with their bright patchwork
cushions. Even the curtains had been taken down. Charlie
walked through the passage. He glanced in at the two men
who were denuding the parlour of its pictures.

The crowd's mood wasn't quite so ugly now that
Phyllis had gone. Mavis had opened the doors of
Rhiannon's prized inlaid china cabinet and she and two
other women were removing the china, placing all the
pieces into baskets: whole pieces one side, broken pieces
the other.

'I'll get our Cath to fix them with good glue,' Mavis
explained when she saw Charlie walking down the steps.
'She's a dab hand at it. Artistic, like my father. It's in the
blood.'

'I'm sure Phyllis will be very grateful.'

'We've put the table, chairs, dresser and beds in Mrs
Davies's front room, Charlie,' Eddie said as he and
William scanned the pavement wondering what to take
next.

'Bethan's agreed to have Phyllis,' Charlie murmured in
a low tone as he stood close to the boys.

'Good for our Beth,' Eddie said loudly.

'Quiet!' Charlie said sharply. 'Now listen, both of you.' He looked around. 'See that blanket chest over there. Put all the clothes, sheets and blankets you can find into it and carry it into my room.'

'Your room?' William stared at him in amazement.

'There isn't space for anything that size in the box room, and we'll need the front parlour for Rhiannon's better pieces,' Charlie answered shortly, reading the expression on William's face and not liking what he saw. 'Phyllis can take what she wants out of it and carry it upstairs.'

'Beth's putting Phyllis and the baby in the box room?' Eddie asked.

'For the time being,' Charlie answered evasively. He looked round and saw the bailiff who had worked with Evan. 'Give us a hand to carry this china cabinet over the road?'

The man looked to James, who nodded.

'Be glad to, Charlie,' he replied.

'Just give us five minutes to make room for it in the house, then we'll be with you.'

'He *must* be,' Mrs Richards hissed, elbowing Mavis Davies out of the way, and peering into the washtub as the men carried it past her before dumping it on the pavement.

'Phyllis's little boy's got black hair and brown eyes, and Charlie's hair is as white as snow and his eyes are blue,' Mavis protested.

'But Phyllis Harry's father had dark eyes, and hair the colour of coal,' Mrs Richards reminded her. 'Phyllis got her colouring from her mother, God rest her soul, but black hair and dark eyes are in her blood. That child of hers could be a throwback to old Harry. Take my word for it.'

'Well, I suppose Charlie has taken charge here,' Mavis conceded reluctantly, not really wanting the paternity of Phyllis's child to be resolved. It had been a topic of great discussion with the gossips in the street, and once the mystery was solved it would lose all interest as a talking point.

'*And* seen Phyllis Harry all right,' Mrs Richards pronounced with a decisive nod of the head. 'Which he'd want to do if the baby was his, wouldn't he?'

'What I can't understand is why he didn't marry her. He can't be short of a few bob.'

'Men. They're all the same, have their fun then clear off first chance they get.'

'Then why is he helping her now?'

'Who knows? Perhaps he has a conscience. Mind you, I'm surprised at Bethan Powell taking her in.'

'Bethan Powell's taking her in?' The group of women all turned to Mrs Richards.

'Didn't you hear Charlie talking to the boys? I did,' she crowed. 'Bethan's putting her in the box room, and I must admit I never expected to see that. With her being married to a John, and a doctor and all. The Johns won't like the idea of someone like Phyllis and her bastard living under the same roof as their daughter-in-law and grandson.'

'Seems to me they don't like the idea of Bethan Powell as a daughter-in-law, or the idea of a grandson like the one they've been given, full stop,' Mrs Evans muttered as she passed them carrying a bundle of Rhiannon's curtains. 'If they did they would have come to see her by now. And there's been no car except Doctor Lewis's outside that house since the day she came back.'

'You can't expect the likes of Doctor John and his wife to come to the Graig,' Mrs Richards pronounced.

'Or the likes of Bethan Powell to go crawling to the Common crache,' Mavis countered.

'Eddie told me the baby's really ill,' Mrs Evans announced as William, Eddie and Charlie reappeared at the front of the house.

'Shame for her. She was such a nice girl too.'

'Well that's what you get for marrying above you,' Mrs Richards said enigmatically as the women went back to their fetching, carrying and sorting.

*

Trevor dropped his leather bag on to the floor next to the cot, opened it and removed his stethoscope.

'Sorry I'm late,' he apologised, as he sat beside the baby on the bed.

'Your other emergency?' she asked.

'Can't fool a nurse. You're just like Laura. How can you tell?'

'The expression in your eyes and around your mouth.'

'Mr Hughes died half an hour after I left here early this morning.'

'Poor you. You can't have had much sleep.'

'It happens. You must have found that out with Andrew.'

'Not really. It's different, working in a big London hospital. He does his twelve-hour shift then he comes home. That's it until the next shift. Occasionally the senior consultants get called out, but not the junior doctors like Andrew. There's always another one around who'll cover.'

'That must be nice for you. Able to make dinner knowing that Andrew will come home on time to eat it.' He warmed the disc of the stethoscope in his hands before laying it against Edmund's bare chest.

'It used to be,' she murmured absently as if talking about something that had happened a long time ago.

Concentrating on listening to the baby's heartbeat Trevor didn't hear her answer. He frowned, then he pressed his hand gently on Edmund's chest and abdomen. He picked him up, laid him across his knee and listened to his back.

'His temperature *has* dropped,' Bethan informed him eagerly as he removed the stethoscope from his ears.

'Slightly. But he has a chest infection, Beth.'

'Is it pneumonia?'

'I don't think so. Not yet.'

'What can I do?'

'Keep him in an even temperature. Get plenty of fluids

down him. Watch him. In short do all the things you are already doing.' He opened his bag wider and rummaged in its depths.

'It's bronchitis, isn't it?'

'Yes,' he said reluctantly. 'I wish you'd let me admit him to the hospital.'

'They wouldn't let me stay with him.'

'No, they wouldn't. But he'd be well looked after, I promise you.'

'No, Trevor. I know you're only trying to help, and thank you, but no.' Her reply was firm and final.

'I telephoned Andrew.' He rose wearily and looked at the bedside clock. Half-past nine. He should have been in the Graig Hospital at eight. Now he wouldn't finish on the wards much before three, and he'd still have all his house calls to make. Better to steal ten minutes as he drove down the Graig hill now, and warn Laura that he wouldn't be home for dinner, than incur her wrath when he turned up to a burnt dinner at teatime.

'Is Andrew well?' Bethan might have been enquiring after a stranger.

'I didn't think to ask and he didn't say. He told me to tell you he'll be here as soon as he finds someone to take over his shift in the hospital.'

Bethan picked up Edmund and wrapped him in the cool sheet again. 'Will it be all right if I take him downstairs to the kitchen? I have to do some work. Wash his bottles, make up his feeds. Make tea for everyone.'

'As long as you keep him out of strong direct heat.'

'I asked Eddie to move his cot to the corner next to the dresser in the far corner, opposite the stove.'

'That should be all right.' He picked up his bag. 'Beth,' he said, placing a hand on her shoulder. 'You don't have to be strong all the time. Let Andrew carry some of this load. He's obviously prepared to.'

She allowed herself the luxury of relaxing against Trevor's shoulder for a moment. The most marvellous thing about Trevor was his calm, steady reliability. She found herself envying Laura. Not her husband, but his dependability. Trevor would have accepted Edmund if he'd been his son, she was sure of it. She turned away and laid Edmund down in his cot.

'You don't understand, Trevor. Andrew doesn't want Edmund—'

'Of course he does,' he contradicted fiercely, loyal to his friend. 'You know what Andrew is, he's never been very good at expressing his feelings. Edmund's his son. He loves him, Beth, I'm sure of it, even if he hasn't told you in so many words.'

'The reason I'm here, not London, is that Andrew wanted to put him in an institution. Please, you will help me won't you? You won't let Andrew put Edmund in the Graig. You know as well as I do that they won't do anything there that I can't do for him here. Please, Trevor . . .'

'I'll try,' he promised, resolving to get Laura to call up as soon as possible. 'But Andrew's a doctor, Beth. He's going to think of both of you. And frankly I'm as worried about you as I am about the baby. You're white as a ghost, you're not resting properly. How long will it be before you fall ill too? Then we'll have both of you to look after.'

'There's a reason for that.' She looked up at him, her eyes dark-ringed, enormous in her pale face. 'I'm going to have another baby.' Her voice jerked as relief poured through her veins. It was wonderful to tell someone her secret.

'All the more reason to put the strain of nursing Edmund on to someone else.'

'No! And I don't want you to tell Andrew.'

'He doesn't know?'

'If he did he'd only use this baby as just one more excuse to put Edmund away. He'd say I couldn't look after two.'

'Edmund does need a lot of time and nursing,' Trevor reminded her.

'I don't want another child,' she said savagely. 'Not if it

287

means having to give up Edmund. You're just like Andrew. You don't understand.'

'I'm trying to, Beth.' He dropped his bag and sat next to her on the bed. 'I really am.'

'What a day,' William complained to Charlie as they walked along Taff Street. 'I seem to have been working forever. Humping all that furniture up and down steps. Chopping carcasses, cleaning the shop—'

'It was worth it,' Charlie interrupted. 'It's finally ready to open.'

'I still think you've spent far too much money fixing up the roof and painting the outside. The place is leasehold, for pity's sake.'

'A lease that's going to revert to me.'

'And that carpet you put down in the living room of the flat?'

'It was a bargain. Because Wilf doesn't normally deal in them he wanted to get it off his hands.' Charlie took a cigarette and offered one to William.

'How about we have tea in Ronconi's?' William suggested as they headed towards the Tumble.

'I think we should go home,' Charlie said, thinking about Phyllis, and Bethan's baby.

'I saw Diana when I bought those pies for our dinner. Told her not to wait for us. I knew you'd hold my nose to the grindstone until this hour. There's nothing we can do even if we do go back,' William said bluntly, not wanting to face the sick-room atmosphere of Graig Avenue. Not just yet. He knew Bethan's baby couldn't help being ill, and that Phyllis and her baby had to go somewhere, he just wished they hadn't had to come into his back kitchen. 'There's three women in the house and Eddie to run any errands. We'd only be in the way, particularly wanting tea.'

The prospect of a nice quiet meal in front of the fire in the back room of Ronconi's suddenly seemed very appetising and very pleasant to Charlie.

'All right,' he agreed.

'And seeing as how you squeezed every last ounce of work out of me today, I'm going to land you with the bill.'

'As long as you eat only one dinner,' Charlie warned as he pushed open the door to the café.

'Tony! Double portion of sausage, chips, beans and egg, four rounds of bread and butter and a mug of strong tea,' William shouted as he walked up to the counter. 'And he's paying,' he pointed to Charlie.

'That OK with you, Charlie?' Tony asked, pencil poised.

'Fine,' Charlie murmured.

'You having anything?'

'Single portion of sausage and chips, no beans, and one round of bread and butter. And tea.' Charlie looked around. The back room was hot, noisy and smoky.

'Pub crowd in there,' Tony warned, nodding towards the archway that separated the two rooms. 'If I were you I'd sit in here.'

'Good idea.' William took the table nearest to the stove, unwound his muffler and pulled the cap from his head. He caught sight of Tina Ronconi ferrying a plateful of chips and three teas out the back and winked at her.

'Leave those, Tina,' Tony ordered. 'I'll see to them.'

'It's only Bobby Thomas and his crowd,' she protested. 'I can handle them.'

'You don't have to while I'm here,' he answered brusquely. 'See to the orders I've written.' He took the tray from her hands and disappeared out the back.

'Do you need seeing to?' she asked, flirting outrageously with William.

'Depends what you have in mind.'

She looked at Tony's scribbles. 'Three sausage and chips coming up. Two on one plate.' She pushed the swing door open with her back and went into the kitchen shouting the order at Angelo.

Alma was at the sink washing dishes.

'Guess what?' Tina whispered as she crept up behind

her keeping half an eye on Angelo, who was as likely to order her back out to the café as Tony.

'What?' Alma whispered.

'Charlie's just come in.'

'Charlie?' Alma hoped he'd wait and walk her back to the flat. She wanted to discuss her mother's banning from chapel with him, and warn him that as well as making her mother hysterical it could adversely affect his trade. But most of all she wanted to hear his reassurance that, no matter what, the job would remain hers.

'And I saw Mrs Richards on the Graig hill when I walked down,' Tina continued. 'She told me that Charlie moved Phyllis Harry into the Powells' house earlier today when the bailiffs put her and her son out on the street. Mrs Richards said it was terrible until Charlie came and sorted everything out. Now everyone's saying that Phyllis's baby is his. After all, it's the first time he's ever put himself out for a woman.'

'Tina, where the hell are you? Charlie and Will are waiting for their tea.'

'Coming, Tony.'

'What do you think of that, eh?' Tina dug Alma in the ribs. 'Bet you'll never see your new boss in the same light again.'

Alma stared at the grey, soapy water. She felt as though someone had just hit the breath from her body, and she didn't know why. After all, it wasn't as though she cared for Charlie.

Bobby had been ugly drunk when he had come into the café, and the food had made no difference to either the drunkenness or the ugliness. His cronies, who appeared to be floating in a similar alcoholic haze, became quieter and quieter as the evening progressed, too wary of saying anything that was likely to make him even more aggressive. After a while Bobby's voice was the only one that could be heard. Loud, raucous, it held absolute sway in the tense atmosphere.

'I did debate whether to let them in,' Tony confided to Charlie and William as he refilled their teacups and carried them back to their table. 'I hoped the food would sober them up, but it doesn't seem to have had any effect.'

'You, Angelo and the girls couldn't have done much to stop them coming in,' Charlie pointed out logically. 'Looks like there's six . . .'

'Seven,' Tony corrected him.

'Those odds are way too high, even for me.' William let out a large satisfied burp as he ate the last of his sausage.

'Ronnie always tried to pacify rather than confront.' Concern creased Tony's forehead as he wished his older brother were here to advise him.

'Do you hear from Ronnie?' William asked, trying to take Tony's mind away from the troublesome group.

'Do you hear from Maud?'

'Two letters last week. One for Bethan redirected from London, and one for Uncle Evan and Aunt Elizabeth. Bethan's decided not to tell her that Uncle Evan's in jail.'

'Maud must write more than Ronnie. We've only had a card from him telling us they arrived safely. Did Maud say how Ronnie's liking it over there?'

'From what I saw she only wrote a lot of nonsense about Ronnie.'

'Mush?' Tony laughed.

'Mush and lovey-dovey,' William agreed, glancing slyly at Tina.

Bobby chose that moment to push aside the bead curtain that separated the front from the back room. He'd intended to leave for the Cross Keys pub on Broadway, but the sight of Charlie stopped him in his tracks.

'If it isn't my Russian friend.' He swaggered over to the table. Ignoring William and Tony, he pushed his bruised face close to Charlie's. 'See this!' he pointed to a cut above his left eye, 'and this!' His finger travelled across to a bruise on his cheekbone. 'Do you remember how I got them? I bloody well do.' He lunged forward but Charlie was on his feet and out of his chair before Bobby had time to form his hands into fists. The blow slammed into the back of Charlie's empty chair, splintering the bar between the uprights. 'You bloody coward!' Bobby hissed. He whirled round, but Charlie was heading towards the door in an attempt to draw Bobby outside and away from Tina, who was white with shock. Bobby moved swiftly after him. Wrapping his arm around Charlie's neck he pulled him back into the room towards the archway.

'I don't want to hurt you again,' Charlie gasped as he prised Bobby's arm away and thrust him into the thick of his friends, who were standing with bemused expressions on their faces. William stepped close to Bobby, fists clenched at the ready. Charlie shook his head, warning him and Tony to keep their distance. While the argument was just between Bobby and him there was hope that it could be taken outside.

'Bobby?' Alarmed by the noise, Alma had left the kitchen and was standing behind the counter next to Tina. 'Please . . .' she began, as he turned to face her.

'This is nothing to do with you, you little tart,' Bobby snarled. 'This is between me and Mr Big here, who thinks he can come to Ponty, throw his weight around and get away with it.' He dived head-first towards Charlie again. His head connected with Charlie's stomach. Winded, Charlie slammed back against the partition wall.

'This is my café and I order you to stop it. Now! Before I call the police.' Tony's command sounded ineffectual even to his own ears. He tried to push between Charlie and Bobby, but all he succeeded in doing was collecting a punch on the nose from one of Bobby's mates.

'Stay out of it!' the man yelled as blood poured from Tony's face.

Angelo vaulted over the counter and adopted the classic boxer's stance, right fist raised above left, but William caught him by the shoulder and thrust him towards the door.

'Police station, and quick,' William whispered to him.

Angelo took one look at the half-dozen men grouped in

the back room, and Charlie sandwiched between them and Bobby. Then he ran.

'Bobby, if you insist on having this out here and now, I think we should follow Marquess of Queensberry rules, don't you?' William tried his best to stop his hand from shaking as he held it up.

Bobby grunted something unintelligible as he stared belligerently at Charlie.

'Whatever's going on here is between Charlie and Bobby, right?' The most sober of Bobby's friends nodded assent and the others followed suit. 'In that case shouldn't this be taken outside before any more of the Ronconis' property is damaged?' William insisted.

Charlie looked at William. His attention was distracted just long enough for him to be caught unawares as Bobby slammed him against the back wall. Alma crammed her fingers into her mouth, but she still cried out as Charlie's back crashed into the hard surface with a sickening crunch.

The chimney in the back room hadn't been swept all winter so it was difficult to keep a fire burning without great clouds of soot falling, damping down the flames. Tony had banked up the wood, coal and paper with an icing of small coal and had left the poker wedged beneath it to create a through draught. Bobby saw the tip of the poker glowing red, dived forward and pulled it from the grate. Waving it in the air, he lurched towards Charlie.

'For Christ's sake, Bobby!' one of his cronies shouted. 'Think about what you're doing, man.'

'Thump me in the face, would you?' Bobby hissed, his face contorted with hatred. 'Smash me on the pavement, would you?'

'Bobby, put the poker down before someone gets hurt.' William's voice was calm, belying the fear that vibrated through his body.

'Will's right, Bobby. If you don't put it down someone will get hurt.' Alfie White, a friend of Bobby's that William recognised from schooldays, rashly put himself between Bobby and Charlie.

'Out of my way!' Demented with rage and drink, Bobby swished the red-hot end of the poker wildly in the air. Everyone's attention focused on the glowing arc of light that hovered in the centre of the room for a moment. The arc vanished as suddenly as it appeared. The poker fell and the searing smell of burning wool and flesh filled the café, closely followed by a long, loud bestial scream. Alf fell to his knees clutching his arm. William leaned forward and grabbed Alf's leg, dragging him into the front room. Tony locked his shoulder under Alf's, helped him to his feet, and steered him into the kitchen. Alf's moans filled the atmosphere, heightening the tension. The only one who appeared unaware of the noise was Bobby, who still circled threateningly around Charlie with the poker in his hand.

'Can't anyone do *anything*?' Alma pleaded hysterically. 'Please . . .'

Bobby turned and stared at her. His friends took the opportunity to move towards the door. One of them opened it and soon his footsteps could be heard pounding up Taff Street.

'Please?' Bobby mocked as he stepped closer to her with the poker. 'Please . . . Please *what*, Bobby?'

Charlie moved like lightning. Hurling himself between Bobby and Alma, he reached for the glowing end of the poker. Closing his fingers around it, he lifted it and lashed out. The steel handle sank into Bobby's fleshy stomach. As Bobby crumpled to his knees the smell of scorched flesh again permeated the air. Charlie turned and walked slowly into the back room. He didn't drop the poker until he reached the firegrate. As it clattered into the hearth William saw that the end was no longer glowing, but covered in a fine grey-white film of skin.

Chapter Eighteen

Andrew reached Cardiff station at nine o'clock in the evening. Refusing a porter's help, he carried his doctor's bag and small suitcase himself, walking briskly ahead of the crowd that surged away from the train, down the steep flight of stone steps and into the white-tiled tunnel that connected all the platforms. He reached the Rhondda Valley departure point just in time to hear a barely decipherable announcement that the train to the valleys had been delayed until nine forty-five. Tired, irritable, and unaccountably angry with the world in general, this came as the last straw. He took his luggage and stormed towards the refreshment room only to find the door bolted and the lights dimmed. He looked at the outside benches. The only unoccupied one was covered with black smuts. He dropped his bags on to it and patted his pockets in search of a cigarette. Finding one in a squashed packet in the breast pocket of his suit, he lit it with his lighter and inhaled deeply. Across the rails a huge billboard was dominated by the swashbuckling image of a sword-wielding pirate, dark-haired beautiful girl behind him, evil-faced villain in front. Below the picture in foot-high crimson letters was 'CAPTAIN BLOOD AT YOUR LOCAL PICTURE PALACE NOW'.

Whoever Captain Blood was, he envied him. His choices were simple and clear cut. All he had to do was draw his sword, fight evil and rescue the beautiful damsel in distress. If only the choices in his life were that easy to make.

As he drew on his cigarette again he wondered what exactly he was doing standing on this platform. Trevor Lewis had telephoned and he'd come running. For what?

To witness the death of a son he'd done his damnedest to ignore since birth? To comfort Bethan? If she'd really wanted him she would have telephoned him herself. It was hypocritical of him even to have left London. Trevor had once told him he always looked for the easy way out. Trevor had been right. He'd do anything to avoid direct emotional confrontation, and not only with Bethan. A brave man would have been honest when Trevor phoned, realising the futility of paying lip service to a dead marriage. Why didn't he turn round? Now! This minute. Walk down the steps to the London platform and take the first train back. The refreshment room might even be open over there. He could buy himself a hot cup of tea and a sandwich; perhaps there'd be a sleeper. The thought of stretching out and relaxing was very tempting. And in London he had work waiting. His patients needed him, even if his son and his wife didn't, and best of all, their ailments weren't the result of his neglect. On the wards of the Cross he was a healer, not the guilty party.

'Andrew. Andrew John! How marvellous. You're coming home? For good, I hope. All the young people have missed you. Especially in the tennis club. Anthea never stops talking about the good times she had when you were a member.'

'Mrs Llewellyn Jones.' Of all the people in Pontypridd the one he least wanted to see at that moment was Mrs Llewellyn Jones, the wife of the town's bank manager, and one of his mother's most patronising bosom friends. But well trained since childhood, he was too polite to allow his dislike of the woman to surface. Taking his cigarette from his mouth with his left hand, he extended his right.

'You *are* going home, Andrew?'

'Evidently.'

'Yes of course.' She laughed shrilly, attracting the attention of everyone on the platform. 'You could hardly be going anywhere else from this part of the station, could you?'

'I'd offer to buy you tea, but the refreshment room is closed.'

'So remiss of them. First they delay the train, then they close everything down. But what *can* you expect? The whole country has gone downhill. Just look at this station. No matter what time I travel, I've never once seen it in an acceptable state. Or anyone even attempting to clean it.'

'It's the trains,' he informed her gravely. 'Running on coal makes them very dirty.'

'I suppose it does,' she replied doubtfully, uncertain whether it was a joke, or not. 'But then it's not just this station, it's every public place,' she continued, repeating an observation that had been very well received by the Ladies' Section of the Pontypridd Golf Club. 'No one takes any pride in themselves or their work any more. You need look no further than your father-in-law,' she slipped in slyly. She paused, waiting for him to comment, but he remained obstinately silent.

'Well, the situation is so awkward, for *your* parents of course. As I said to your dear mother, sometimes the social gulf between the Common and the Graig simply isn't wide enough. Gossip travels all too quickly, and when he was sent to gaol . . .'

The news of Evan Powell's imprisonment came as a complete surprise to Andrew, but by dint of superhuman control he managed to keep the shock from registering on his face. Anger burned furiously, as he remained outwardly impassive. Why hadn't Bethan told him his father-in-law was in gaol? Why had she allowed him to find out like this? Didn't she love him? Didn't she consider him part of her family? Didn't she have any regard for his feelings at all?

'. . . well I mean to say it's hardly the sort of thing you want to broadcast around the town. That you're connected, even by marriage, to a man who's serving six months' hard labour for assaulting a police officer.' She looked up at Andrew, wondering why he didn't say something. Perhaps he didn't want to discuss his father-in-law in public, but then – she glanced around – it wasn't as if there was anyone who *mattered* near them. 'I met your wife that once when we dined with your parents. She did seem a very nice girl, but . . .'

'*But!*' There was always a 'but' with the Mrs Llewellyn Joneses of this world, Andrew reflected acidly.

'. . . it can't be at all *nice* for her having come from a family like that. My woman who comes in to do the heavy work does occasional ironing for Mrs Leyshon.' She smiled broadly at Andrew. 'You *must* know the Leyshons. They live in the house on the Graig,' she said as though there was only one. 'Danygraig House. From what I understand it's the only decent house on that hill. Not that I've ever been there,' she qualified, as though the Graig was in some way tainted. 'Well, my woman told me that Mrs Powell has moved out. Apparently she's living with her uncle, a minister, chapel of course, in the Rhondda, and who can blame her? It must be very difficult given the circumstances. Your wife is coping with the situation, I trust?'

'Yes,' Andrew answered shortly, not knowing whether his parents, let alone Mrs Llewellyn Jones, were aware that Bethan was in Pontypridd. If Mrs Llewellyn Jones's 'woman' was as much of a gossip as he suspected, they probably did. And that would give his father one more reason to be angry with him.

'As if she hasn't enough to do with the baby . . . poor little thing. Your mother told us all about it. So sad. Mr Llewellyn Jones and I were so sorry to hear—'

'Bethan is coping perfectly well. Thank you for your concern.' He dropped his cigarette and ground it to dust beneath the toe of his shoe.

'She's living in Pontypridd, and you're living in London now?'

Damn it. The woman did know.

'Temporarily.' He spat out the word as he fumbled in his pocket for another cigarette.

'I'm glad to hear it. Separation, no matter what the

cause, is never good for a marriage. But I suppose your wife felt obliged to go home after her father's disgrace. We can't always do what we want in life. Mr Llewellyn Jones did his duty and volunteered his services during the Great War. I hardly saw him for four years. He spent the duration in the Admiralty Office in London, you know.'

'It must have been a very harrowing time for both of you,' Andrew commented drily.

'Very,' she concurred, failing to see the irony in his remark. 'You staying in Pontypridd long?' she probed artlessly.

'Unfortunately not.'

'Then you are hoping to take Bethan back with you?'

'Eventually.'

'Your mother will be so pleased to see you. She doesn't say much, but I can tell,' she wagged her finger at Andrew as if he were a naughty schoolboy. 'She misses you dreadfully. You really should write or telephone home more often. I know you have a wife now, but you must spare an occasional thought for your mother. It's a sad fact of life that a mother can never entirely cut the bonds that bind her to her child, no matter how she may try. Take me and Anthea . . .'

Andrew didn't hear the story of Anthea's devotion. He was dwelling on his mother's sometimes irritating, always fussy, but undeniably deep and abiding love for him. Mrs Llewellyn Jones was right: the bonds of motherhood were never altogether severed, even in adulthood.

For the first time he realised the enormity of the demands he had made of Bethan. He saw their son as a reproach, a living reminder of his failure to look after both mother and son, but Bethan saw him as her child, and no mother would willingly give up her child. He had driven Bethan into choosing between Edmund and him, and she had chosen the most vulnerable. Knowing her as he did, how could he have expected her to have done otherwise?

He'd been a fool. Seeing an institution as an easy solution to the problem of the baby. Putting Edmund away would solve nothing for him or for Bethan. The baby was there. Would always be there. A part of both of them that Bethan would never willingly abandon to strangers. Maternal instinct had taken its powerful, insidious hold. He couldn't deny the strength of the bond between Bethan and the child, but he also knew that the blame he carried would never allow him to feel the same way.

'Why, here's our train at last.' Mrs Llewellyn Jones had to tap him on the arm with her umbrella before he saw the steam train pull in.

'Mrs Llewellyn Jones. Let me help you.' He took hold of her elbow and propelled her towards the door of a first-class carriage. Opening it, he pushed her inside. 'So nice to see you,' he murmured, smiling at her for the first time. 'Do give my regards to Anthea, and Mr Llewellyn Jones.'

'Won't you join me?' she asked, flustered by his sudden, unexpected attention. 'It would be *so* nice to continue our little chat. I haven't told you about Anthea's trip to France and her—'

'It will have to wait until some other time, I'm afraid. I only have a third-class ticket,' he lied as he went back to the bench to get his bags.

'Soon, I hope!' she shouted after him. 'Soon.'

'You want to prefer charges, Charlie?' Constable Huw Davies asked as Charlie sat slumped on a chair in the back room of the café, his arm extended across the table, lying on a bleached linen tea towel. Tina and Alma were sitting either side of him covering his hand with potato skins.

Charlie looked up at Alma. She shook her head. The movement was slight, so slight that anyone who hadn't been looking for it would have missed it. Charlie recalled her fear of attracting more slanderous gossip.

'No,' he answered between clenched teeth. For about ten minutes after he had gripped the poker and wrenched it out of Bobby's hands his whole arm had gone blessedly, blissfully numb but now it was returning, all too agonisingly, to life.

'Well I do,' Tony Ronconi declared angrily. 'Just look at the state of this place.'

'Criminal damage,' Huw wrote in his neat script in his notebook.

'And just think about the effect this is going to have on our custom once word gets out.'

'Violent, threatening behaviour,' Huw continued to write. 'I've got more than enough to keep him overnight. Can you call down the station tomorrow morning Tony. We'll try and get him before a magistrate then.'

'I'll be there.'

'You ought to go to hospital and get that hand seen to,' Huw said to Charlie.

'I'll take him,' Tony volunteered.

'I'll get the Trojan.' William was happy to have an excuse to leave the café. He didn't want to look at Charlie's hand, yet he couldn't look away. The fingers were flayed red raw, the palm was charred, blackened, the flesh hanging loose in long, thin, bloody shreds. And it seemed to have been in that state for hours. Huw had taken the names and addresses of Bobby's friends, told them they'd be called as witnesses, and warned them that if they didn't stay out of trouble it wouldn't be the witness box but the dock they'd be finding themselves in. When he finally allowed them to leave, they sloped off silently, grateful to Huw for allowing them to sleep in their own beds that night. Only Bobby remained in the café. Huw had handcuffed him to the brass rail in front of the counter, and he sat there, a glowering, threatening presence that William could quite cheerfully have knocked senseless.

'Alma, you come with us. Tina, you and Angelo close up. I think we've all had enough for one night.'

'Tina can go. I'll clear up here,' Alma volunteered.

'Sort it out amongst yourselves,' Tony said impatiently. 'It doesn't matter what you decide as long as we get away from here soon for Charlie's sake.'

'Boys!' Huw Davies greeted the reinforcements he'd sent Angelo to fetch from the station. 'We have one rather nasty drunk here who wants to take us up on our offer of free bed and breakfast.'

*

'Bethan?' Phyllis knocked timidly at the bedroom door. In response to Bethan's answering call she carried in a cup of tea. 'I've come to take down your supper dishes.' She looked at the tray Diana had brought up earlier. 'Oh, you haven't touched a thing!'

'I'm not hungry.' Bethan leaned over her son's cot so she wouldn't have to look Phyllis in the eye.

'I'm boiling water for his bottles now.'

'Thank you.'

'I can run the house for you until your baby is better, that's if you want me to of course,' she offered shyly. She watched as Bethan picked up her baby, waiting for her to answer. When she didn't, she continued. 'I want to say . . . want you to know,' she stammered clumsily, 'how grateful I am to you for taking me and my son in. I know it couldn't have been easy for you, especially as you're so crowded here already.'

'It's what my father would have wanted me to do,' Bethan said coldly, wishing Phyllis would go, and leave her in peace with Edmund.

'Thank you anyway.' Phyllis retrieved the tray and retreated downstairs.

Bethan felt guilty almost before Phyllis was out of the door. She should have made an effort, accepted Phyllis's gratitude more graciously. It was just that she felt so tired and drained. Far too exhausted to think about anything, or anyone other than Edmund. Later, when she didn't feel as though the world was crashing down around her shoulders she'd make a point of apologising for her coldness. But not now. Not when Edmund had to struggle so hard to take even the shallowest breath.

'What the hell happened to you?' Eddie demanded as

William ushered a bandaged, white-faced Charlie into the back kitchen.

'Ssh! Keep your voice down,' Diana ordered abruptly from the depths of the pantry where she was stacking newly washed dishes. 'Bethan's having a hard time nursing that baby as it is without you waking him every five minutes with your noise. What on earth . . .' She stepped out and put her hand to her mouth when she saw Charlie.

William took the burden of explanation upon himself, and while he talked, Phyllis set about making Edmund's bottles and putting the kettle back on the stove for tea.

'Is there anything we can do?' Diana asked, shocked by the size of the bandage on Charlie's arm.

'Make us both a cup of hot sweet tea to take away the shock, and if Uncle Evan's got something a bit stronger tucked away, so much the better.'

'There's a bottle of vodka in my room, Will.' Charlie rested his head wearily against the back of the easy chair. 'It's in the alcove to the right of the fireplace.'

'I didn't know you indulged,' William said, tearing himself away from the warmest spot in front of the stove.

'I don't. That's why I have a full bottle,' Charlie answered brusquely. His hand was painful despite the anaesthetic. And he wasn't at all happy with Doctor John's recommendation that he take at least two weeks off work, and refrain from cutting meat until the skin had completely healed, for the sake of both his customers' health and his own.

'Looks like I'll have to take over the stall and the slaughterhouse for a while,' William said returning with the bottle. He took a corkscrew and a set of six small glasses on a wooden stand from the dresser shelf.

'I can work one-handed,' Charlie growled.

'There's no need. Take a rest for once in your life. If you have to do something, you can take the money in the shop when it opens on Saturday. How much of this stuff do you put in a glass?' He pulled the cork that sealed the bottle.

'Fill it up, to the brim,' Charlie ordered, noting the size of the glasses.

'Anyone else?' William asked. 'Diana? Phyllis? Eddie?'

'Joey's arranged a sparring match for me tomorrow.'

'I'd prefer tea,' Phyllis said shyly.

'And so would I,' Diana snapped, concerned about Charlie.

'Would you take the baby's bottle upstairs, Diana?' Phyllis asked. 'I think his feed is about due.'

'Yes of course.' Diana stared at the tray Phyllis had brought down. 'I don't suppose she's eaten anything all day?' A knock at the door interrupted them.

'If that's Mrs Richards again, she can go to hell,' Eddie declared firmly.

'She never knocks, just walks in,' Diana pointed out.

'She knocked this morning,' Eddie said.

'Well I've had enough for one day,' William said. He handed Charlie a full glass of vodka and pulled Evan's chair close to the range for himself. 'Go and answer it, Di,' he ordered when a second knock sounded.

'What did your last slave die of?' Diana demanded.

'I've been working all day, and I've had a hard evening.'

'What the hell do you think I've been doing?' Diana picked up the baby's bottle.

Phyllis hoped they didn't expect her to open it. After the events of the morning it was much as she could do to face this roomful of people, let alone any others.

Eddie left his chair just as the front door opened.

'It's me Eddie,' Trevor called out as Eddie opened the kitchen door. He stood on the coconut mat and shook the rain from his coat.

'Hello Eddie,' Andrew said, following Trevor in.

'Bethan's upstairs,' Eddie informed him curtly. 'She hasn't left the bedroom all day.'

'I'll show Andrew the way,' Trevor said pleasantly. Eddie watched them climb the stairs, then retreated to the kitchen and slammed the door behind him.

'Who was it?' William asked.

'Bloody cashmere coat,' Eddie said angrily.

'That *is* his sick baby and wife upstairs,' William reminded him.

'I bloody well wish he'd never married her,' Eddie declared fervently. 'Bethan's troubles only started when she met him.'

Bethan was nursing the baby against her shoulder in the darkened bedroom, standing in front of the window. It wasn't much of a view in daylight, but darkness had softened the harsh aspect, shading broken walls and blanketing the evidence of poverty's dereliction with compassionate shadows. She looked out over the ty bach roof at her father's wire mesh dog run, the shed, the old stone wall that ran the width of the garden, dividing it from the lane behind, and beyond that the tops of the neighbours' chicken coops. High over everything a dark sliver of night sky, devoid of moon and stars, hovered above the crest of the blackened mountain.

Bethan preferred the room in darkness, and not just because of Edmund. She had always felt safer in the dark, cosier, more secure. Her brothers and sister had taken it in turns to fear the night, waking up and screaming at the formless, nameless terrors the darkness spawned. But she never had. Her mother hadn't allowed night lights, and it had fallen to her as the eldest to creep out of bed, first to Haydn, then later to Haydn and Eddie, to comfort and assure them that there was nothing to fear. It had been easier with Maud. They had shared the same bed.

The night had always brought other pleasures, principal among them being time to dream. Not the jumbled nightmares of sleep, but the peace and mental privacy that allowed her to refashion the events of her days into happier frameworks. Even now she was luxuriating in another world, one in which Edmund was strong, and perfect, her father was free . . . and Andrew? What did she wish for Andrew?

A tap at the door shattered the idyllic world she had created, bringing a bewildering sense of loss.

'Come in.' She hoped that whoever it was wouldn't stay long. Now she'd been rudely returned to reality she remembered her priorities, chief of which was cuddling Edmund while he could still feel her presence. She hadn't needed Trevor's diagnosis to know that very soon she wouldn't be able to.

She remained standing with her back to the door as it opened. She resented the light flooding in from the landing, and heard the unmistakable tread of masculine feet.

'Trevor?'

'It's not Trevor. It's me.'

She turned. Andrew's broad, tall frame was silhouetted in the doorway, the light behind him throwing his face into shadow.

'You didn't have to come.' Her voice was icy. Andrew didn't hear the emotional numbness that lay behind it, only the chill note that shut him out.

'I didn't have to, but I wanted to. How's the baby?' Even now he couldn't bring himself to call the child by the name she had given it.

'Have you seen Trevor?'

'Yes. He drove me here.'

'Didn't he tell you?'

The light had fallen on her face and figure, casting dark shadows. From what he could see of her above the shawl, she looked thinner, more gaunt than he remembered.

'He told me he's very ill. Bethan, won't you let me help?' Andrew pleaded. 'At least allow me to hire a night nurse so you can get a good night's sleep.'

If he had offered to sit up with the child himself she might have been kinder; as it was she saw his plea as a continuation of the demands he had made in London.

'No doubt you, like Trevor, think Edmund would be better off in the Graig Hospital,' she countered bitterly. 'Both of you have forgotten I've worked there. I *know* what it's like on the children's ward. He's my child, Andrew. I'll look after him.'

'He's my child too,' he reminded her pointedly, hurt by her rejection of his olive branch, and angry with himself for being peevish. Was it so hard for her to take help from him? She had undoubtedly accepted it from her family. Did she intend to shut him out of her life permanently? 'Can I at least look at him?' he asked when the silence in the room became too crushing for him to bear.

She unwound the shawl from her waist, removed Edmund and placed him, wrapped in his lighter shawl, in Andrew's arms. Then she switched on the light. Harsh, glaring, it shone directly down on to the baby's face.

Andrew lifted the shawl, holding it over the baby's eyes. 'He doesn't like the light,' he murmured.

'I thought you'd need it to make a medical examination.'

'I didn't want to examine him. Just hold him.'

'Trevor's told you that his bronchitis has developed into pneumonia?'

'Yes.'

She switched off the light, but not before Andrew had time to register the bluish tinge on the baby's skin as he laboured to draw breath into infected lungs. Andrew held him close to his chest. He could feel the erratic beat of the tiny heart beneath his hand. This was his child. His son, and this was the first time that he'd held him in his arms, or even looked at him for any length of time.

'Bethan I'm sorry . . .' the words sounded pitiful, shabby, totally inadequate. He wanted – no needed – to offer her more than sympathy. 'If you return to London with me, I'll find a specialist . . .'

'I think Edmund's seen enough specialists, don't you?' She held out her arms and he gently replaced the baby in them. Holding him against her shoulder she wrapped the shawl around them both. The baby cried, a thin weak wail, then recognising the smell and feel of his mother, settled again.

Andrew felt desperately tired, mentally and physically. He looked around for a chair; seeing none, he sank down on the corner of the bed.

'You're staying with your parents?'

'I hadn't really thought about it, I've only just come in on the train.'

'I'm sorry I can't offer you a bed. The house is packed. As you can see, the baby and I are both in here, and if you moved in as well, none of us would get any sleep.'

He wanted to break through the barrier of cold formality, reach out, stroke her cheek, ask her if she'd got any sleep at all the last few nights, but fear of rejection held him back, and his hands remained firmly locked in his pockets.

'The boys are sharing one bedroom,' she explained unnecessarily as though she had to justify her refusal to allow him to stay. 'Diana's in the other. Charlie's in the front room downstairs, and Phyllis Harry and her son are in the box room.'

'Phyllis Harry, do I know her?'

'Rhiannon Pugh who lived across the road died last week. This morning the bailiffs put her lodger Phyllis Harry and her baby out on the streets, so we've had to put them in the box room.'

'Wasn't she the woman who was stoned out of chapel?'

'You remember me telling you that?'

Was it his imagination or was there a glimmer of a smile on her lips? 'I do. Bethan, are you mad? Think of your reputation. Think of Diana . . .'

'She had nowhere else to go.'

'She could have gone to the Graig.'

'To the workhouse?' Bethan was speaking softly so as not to disturb the baby, but there was a venom in her voice that needed no raised tones. 'That probably seems an easy option to you, but then you've only worked in the place. You've never been under the threat of being sent there.'

He allowed the barb to pass without comment. He

thought of leaving her now, of going to his parents' house. Of relaxing with his mother, father and the inevitable after-dinner brandy in their tastefully overfurnished sitting room. His mother would no doubt fuss about Bethan living apart from him, and about Evan Powell's imprisonment, just as Mrs Llewellyn Jones had done. And if news had travelled to the Common about Bethan taking in Phyllis Harry as well . . . The thought of having to listen to more gossip decided him.

'I'll sleep downstairs in a chair in the kitchen.' He didn't frame it as a question lest she refuse him even that small privilege.

'You won't be comfortable.'

Did she really want him to leave that much? 'I'll manage,' he said testily. 'But until bedtime I'd like to stay here if I may?' He wished he could have said 'with you' so there would be no mistake, but again he choked on the words.

'There's nothing you can do.'

'I've brought my bag. It will save you sending for Trevor.'

She knew then that the end was nearer than she had thought.

'If you don't mind I'd like to rest for a while now.' She looked at him as he sat on the bed, and he rose. She didn't sit down until he was on his feet. He watched her for a moment. She was holding Edmund very close, her cheek pressed against the baby's, her hand wrapped around his tiny fingers, as though by holding him she hoped to ward off the inexorable advent of death.

'I'll go downstairs then.' He looked around the room, shadowy in the half-light, saw the cold cup of tea on the dressing table. 'Would you like me to bring you anything?'

'No thank you.'

There was nothing left for him to do there.

He had only ever been in the house once before, but he had been in a hundred like it when he had practised medicine in Pontypridd before taking up his London post. Leaving the landing light burning, he walked down to the back kitchen and opened the door. After the chill of the bedroom the room seemed hot, smoky and crowded. Charlie and William were slumped in easy chairs either side of the stove. Trevor and Eddie were sitting at the table talking, and Diana was stepping over outstretched legs and moving kitchen chairs in an effort to get near the stove. Phyllis Harry was nowhere to be seen, and Andrew was grateful. He hoped she'd gone to her room for the night. He could barely cope with the family let alone a stranger.

'Doctor John.' William was the only one to greet him as he opened the door.

'Hello William, it's good to see you,' he replied with a forced geniality.

'Wish we could say the same,' Eddie muttered audibly.

'Would you like a cup of tea, Doctor Lewis, Doctor John?' Diana asked, pushing a brown curl back from her flushed face as she lifted the boiling kettle from the hotplate.

'No thank you, Diana. I have to get back,' Trevor answered.

'On call?' Andrew asked, grateful for the one presence in the room that wasn't hostile.

'No. But I was last night and I only managed to sleep an hour. I'm whacked.'

'Who's on call tonight?' Andrew asked warily.

'Your father. But as I'm nearer Bethan knows that she only has to send and I'll come, whether I'm on duty or not.'

'I've told Bethan I'll stay.'

Trevor nodded.

Eddie stared at Andrew, dumbfounded. 'You're staying here?'

'Just for tonight,' Andrew said quietly. 'That's if it's all right with everyone.'

'We don't count,' Eddie snapped. 'It's Beth who matters.'

'It's Bethan I'm thinking of,' Andrew retorted quickly.

'Have you come straight here from London?' Diana asked.

'Yes.'

'In that case you'll be wanting more than a cup of tea.'

'Tea will be fine, thank you. I don't want to put you to any trouble.'

'No trouble. Bethan didn't eat her dinner. It will only take a moment to heat up.'

'In that case, thank you.' Andrew was too wary of offending to refuse the offer.

'I'll be off then. Remember, if you need me, send Eddie or William down. I'll be easier to get hold of than your father,' Trevor added tactfully.

Andrew followed Trevor and Eddie out into the passage. Eddie opened the door.

'It's good of you to keep calling in like this, Doctor Lewis,' Eddie said clumsily, donning the mantle of the man of the house again. 'I know our Beth appreciates it.'

'I just wish I could do more for the baby, Eddie.' Trevor held out his hand and Eddie shook it.

'I'll walk you to the car.' Andrew followed Trevor down the front steps. 'Not exactly the warmest of welcomes,' he murmured as Trevor opened the door of his car.

'They know the baby is dying. As you saw, Bethan's taking it badly, and that's put all of them under a lot of strain. They're all very fond of her,' Trevor added superfluously.

'I know,' Andrew answered irritably. 'What I can't understand is with all of this going on, why Bethan had to take someone else in today.'

'You don't understand . . .' Trevor only just stopped himself from saying 'us'. He hadn't grown up in the Graig but in a poverty-stricken household in the dock area of Cardiff. He knew better than any of the crache in Pontypridd just why the working classes needed to offer and accept support. Why they clung together more in times of stress and trouble. But he didn't know how to begin explaining it to Andrew.

'I am trying to understand,' Andrew protested.

'I know.' Trevor rubbed his eyes. He was so tired he was finding difficulty in focusing. 'But until you've gone through what these people have, it's not easy. You will send for me?'

'In the morning.'

'Either your father or I will have to sign the certificate.' Trevor climbed into his car. 'I'm sorry, Andrew.'

'I know.' Andrew turned his back and climbed the steps into the cold, unwelcoming house.

Chapter Nineteen

THE ROOM SWAM alarmingly around Charlie as he bent his head to unlace his boots. He kicked them off, then lay back on his bed without undressing. It wasn't just his arm that was throbbing, but also his head. He felt sick, tired and ill, but not all of his sickness was due to the pain that emanated from his burnt hand. He couldn't stop thinking about Alma. Her curt refusal to go to the hospital with him shouldn't have made any difference. It wasn't as if she was his . . .

Red-gold hair, green eyes, tall slim figure – so many similarities to Masha, and yet so different in disposition. Masha. A name he tried to forget, because the slightest whisper of it in his mind brought back the taste of her kisses, the feel of her body nestled close to him. Masha! Gentle yet playful. Like a kitten that hasn't yet learned to claw. Would she have turned into a shrew? Never. He smiled at the thought. Not his Masha.

'I love you, Feodor.'

She lay alongside him in the bed, the sheets and blankets billowing around their entwined bodies. Her head resting on his shoulder, her arms wrapped so tightly around his chest that he had difficulty breathing. He moved his finger over her arm, tracing on her skin the shadows that fell through the curtained window. She propped herself up on her elbows, and looked at him.

'It was more fun to be your mistress than your wife.'

The mischievous smile on her face begged for punishment. He reached out to tickle her, but she melted into his arms. He looked for her, called her name, begged her to return . . .

*

The cry woke Andrew. He had pulled the two easy chairs together fronts facing, in the kitchen, taken off his jacket and overcoat, covered himself with them as best he could, put his feet up, and slept. He hadn't meant to but the warmth of the stove, the aftermath of the tiresome journey, the strain of facing Bethan and his son, had all taken their toll. He tried to rise, got his long legs hopelessly tangled in the wooden arms of the chairs, and fell between the two seat cushions. Rising to his feet he slammed full force into the kitchen table, cursed and stood still for a moment trying to remember where he was. He saw the line of light beneath the door. Graig Avenue! William had said he would leave the lamp burning.

He stumbled against a wooden chair as he tried to negotiate the furniture. He heard the second cry as he opened the passage door. It sounded as though it had come from the room directly to his left. As he tapped lightly on the door, the stair creaked overhead.

'Are you all right?' He tried to recall just who Bethan had said slept there. The lodger, Charlie? He pushed open the door. Charlie was lying, stretched out on his bed fully clothed. His face was so white it blended with his pale hair, making him appear more phantom than living, breathing man.

'I heard a noise. If your hand is giving you a lot of pain I have something in my bag that might help.'

Charlie opened his eyes wider in an effort to focus. 'I'm fine, Doctor John,' he murmured unconvincingly.

Cold politeness again! Was that all he was ever going to get in this house?

'It's all right, Eddie. I just slept awkwardly. Rolled on my hand.'

Andrew glanced backwards. He started when he saw not only Eddie's face but William's inches away from his own.

'If you're sure you're all right?'

'I am, William,' Charlie insisted. 'Go back to bed.'

314

Andrew followed the boys out of the room but returned with his case a few moments later.

'I can give you a pill that will help you to sleep.'

Too emotionally drained to argue, Charlie nodded assent. Andrew went into the kitchen. Unable to find a glass he took a cup from the dresser and walked out to the washhouse to fill it with water. When he returned Charlie was sitting on the side of the bed, his feet resting on the floor.

'I wouldn't think of going for a walk just yet if I were you.' Andrew handed Charlie a pill and the cup of water. 'If you like I could take a look at it.'

'I have to go back to the hospital tomorrow to have it dressed again.'

'Then it must be bad.'

'It's not good.'

'How did it happen?'

'I picked up a poker by the hot end.'

'That seems a strange thing to do.'

'Someone was waving it close to a woman's face at the time.'

'I'm sorry, I didn't mean to pry. It's really none of my business.'

'You're not prying, and as it happened in Ronconi's café the story will be all over town tomorrow, if not tonight. I'm sorry Doctor John, I'm afraid I woke you.'

'I wish someone other than Bethan in this house would call me Andrew,' he said fervently as he sat on the chair in the bay. 'And I'm not tired. Not any more. I'm not even sure I was sleeping.'

'Your son won't live much longer.' It was a simple statement, spoken sympathetically.

'No he won't,' Andrew agreed dully.

'Bethan—' Charlie took a crushed packet of Players cigarettes from his top pocket and offered Andrew one. To his amazement it was accepted – 'has had a lot to do lately. Running this house, seeing to all of us, visiting her father in prison—'

'I wanted to ask you about that,' Andrew broke in quickly, hoping Charlie would answer the questions he hadn't found the courage to ask Bethan, 'and about her mother. Has Elizabeth really moved out?' He lit both their cigarettes, and Charlie sat forward, blowing smoke at the floor. 'Please,' Andrew pressed, hoping to find an ally in the Powell household. 'Bethan hasn't written about any of this to me, and I can hardly ask her what has happened now. Before I even reached Pontypridd I was given the full story of Evan's imprisonment. According to the gossips, that is,' he added caustically.

'Mrs Powell walked out the day Evan was sentenced to six months' hard labour. Eddie found out that she's living with her uncle in the Rhondda. She hasn't been back here since she left. Neither has she answered any of Bethan's letters.'

'And Evan? He struck me as being very even-tempered. I have difficulty imagining him doing anything that warranted a prison sentence, let alone hard labour.'

'Evan and I went to a Mosley meeting,' Charlie began. 'You know Bethan's father is a Communist?'

'I suspected as much from what he told me.'

'The ideology flourishes among people who have nothing to lose,' Charlie said dispassionately.

'You're Russian, you've lived in a Communist country. I take your word for it.' Andrew was left with the feeling that Charlie had said more than he'd understood, not only about Communism, but about his own history.

'Evan went to the Mosley meeting along with a lot of other miners to put forward the unemployed's point of view. Mosley brought his bodyguard. A fight broke out, Evan swung a punch, but unfortunately for him the blackshirt it was intended to land on ducked, and a policeman got it on the nose.'

Andrew laughed in spite of the misery that had settled like a black cloud over him since he had reached Wales. 'Good for Evan. Every time I see the newsreels I'd like to land a blackshirt one myself.'

'You'd probably feel differently if you were paying for the privilege with six months' hard labour.'

'I probably would,' Andrew agreed soberly. 'Has Evan appealed against his sentence?'

'He pleaded guilty. A solicitor costs money.'

'Why didn't Bethan come to me?'

'Perhaps she thought you had enough to worry about with the baby.'

'How can I worry about the baby when she took him out of our flat to bring him here?' Andrew paced uneasily to the empty fireplace.

'Bethan always does what she thinks best, not for herself, but for others.'

'You know her that well?' Andrew looked Charlie keenly in the eye.

'It's difficult not to know someone well when you live in the same back kitchen.'

Andrew was suddenly jealous. Of Charlie, Eddie, William, Diana – of all the men – and women – who were closer to his wife than he was.

'She's a very special woman,' Charlie said slowly, meeting Andrew's steady gaze. 'She has great inner strength, but that strength is being tested to the limit. She needs help . . .'

'Which you all give her.'

The irony wasn't lost on Charlie. 'When we can, and when she'll accept it,' he agreed cautiously. 'But I've never known her to forget she's married to you.'

'Pity her devotion didn't extend to sending for me herself when the baby became ill, instead of leaving it to Trevor.'

'You're here now. When it matters.'

'But I can't stay. My job, my apartment – everything's in London.'

'The one thing I've learned, Doctor John' – Andrew winced at hearing his surname yet again – 'is that places and work are unimportant. People you care about are the only things that matter in life.'

'I'm sure you're right. But I can't leave my job just like that.'

'It must be difficult, being a doctor.'

'Sometimes it is.'

'And it must be difficult being Bethan right now,' Charlie continued perceptively. 'Her father asked Eddie to keep the home going so he'd have something to come back to. She knows Eddie can't possibly earn enough to pay all the bills on his own. That's why she stayed.'

Of course! Why hadn't he thought of that? Without Evan bringing in any money, the Powells would probably lose this house. Bethan had told him that it was mortgaged. Perhaps she would have returned to him if things had been different here. If her father hadn't gone to prison, if her mother had stayed, if her elder brother hadn't been working away, if he hadn't sent her money . . .

Andrew heard the cry before Charlie, but then he'd been waiting for it. He rushed through the door and up the stairs. Eddie and William were already on the landing in their pyjamas, and Diana had opened her door. All of them were looking at Bethan as she stood in the open doorway of her bedroom. She was still holding the baby in her arms. But now his face was blue, the harsh rattling sound of laboured breathing finally quiet.

'Bethan?' Andrew called her name softly. A cold shiver ran down his spine as she looked through him as though he were invisible. Eddie stepped between them, held out his arms and she went to him.

Trevor took a death certificate from his bag on the back seat of the car, filled in the details, signed it and handed it to Andrew.

'Has the undertaker been?'

'William's gone to get him. There didn't seem much point in disturbing him last night.'

'They're used to it . . .'

'What are you saying, Trevor? That it will be better when we put the baby in a box, out of sight and out of mind?' He thrust open the passenger door of the car and walked up the street towards the mountain. Trevor waited a moment, and when Andrew didn't turn back, he climbed out. Buttoning his mac to his chin to protect himself from the downpour, he followed. His friend hadn't gone far. He'd walked past the houses, up the hill, past a levelled plot where a community club was being built, and was walking blindly along a narrow sheep track that led to the top of the mountain.

Fighting his instinct to retreat, Trevor caught up with him close to the summit.

'I want to help,' Trevor put his hand on Andrew's shoulder. 'Will you let me?'

When Andrew turned round his face was wet, but only from the rain. His eyes were wild, dry, burning in their intensity. 'I'm sorry. I just had to get away for a moment.'

'You don't have to justify yourself to me.'

'Perhaps that's the problem. I don't have to justify myself or my actions to anyone. Not you, not Bethan . . .'

'Bethan cares.'

'Not any more.'

'Not at the moment, perhaps,' Trevor conceded, 'but she will again. There's too much between you for it to be otherwise.'

'I have a lot of things to do,' Andrew said flatly. 'I have to discuss things with the undertaker when he gets here, telephone London, see my parents . . .'

'Would a car help?' Trevor asked.

'Doctors on call need them.'

'I'll be in the hospital at nine. You can have it for a couple of hours then.'

'Thank you.' Andrew reached out and clasped Trevor's arm. 'You've been a good friend, even when I've been a bloody fool.'

'Bethan does need you,' Trevor insisted as they began their descent.

When Andrew didn't answer he felt like shaking him. But Bethan had asked him to keep her secret and he had to respect her confidence, though he hated himself for doing so. 'You're right, Andrew,' he agreed as they walked into Graig Avenue.

'In what way?'

'There are times when you're a bloody fool.'

Careful to keep one step ahead of the patrolling policemen, Phyllis walked the side-streets around the workhouse. Up and down Grover Street, up and down Kirkhouse Street, all the time nursing her son in her arms. Eventually dawn would have to break. And then she'd do what she should have done when the bailiffs had knocked on Rhiannon's door the day before.

She'd heard what Doctor John had said about Bethan taking her in. She'd been putting her son to bed, and after he'd slept she'd cried herself to sleep, but not for long. She'd been awake when Charlie had shouted out in his sleep, she'd heard Bethan call Eddie, and afterwards she'd listened while Diana and Bethan had cried in Bethan's bedroom. It was then that she'd packed her son's best clothes and favourite rag dolls into a pillowcase.

If she stayed in Graig Avenue she'd focus gossip on Evan's family and she couldn't bear the thought of doing anything that would hurt him. But as she paced the cold, inhospitable streets, she wished with all her heart that there was somewhere for her and her son to go other than the workhouse.

'I've cooked all the meat that was here. I followed the recipe books, and it looks all right. But I haven't tasted any of it.'

Alma stood back doubtfully as Charlie inspected the hams, pork legs and sides of beef she'd roasted. 'William said something about pies and pastries . . .' she began, taking his silence as an ominous sign of disapproval.

'These look all right.' He slid a clean skewer into the beef and withdrew it slowly, prodding the area around the hole with the forefinger of his unbandaged hand to check the colour of the juices as they ran out. 'We'll find out what they taste like when they cool and we slice them.'

'I was going to do that after I made the pies and pasties. I've mixed the fillings.' She pointed to three huge saucepans simmering gently on the stove.

'I think we'd be taking on too much by attempting to do pastry goods as well now.' He glanced at her. She was pale and drawn, her green eyes glittering like enamel in the early morning sunlight. 'You look tired.'

'Just the after-effects of yesterday.'

'I know what you mean. Bethan Powell's baby died last night.'

'I'm so sorry.' She remembered Bethan smiling at her, and the towels she had given her as a house-warming present; she had written Bethan a note to thank her for them only yesterday. She had always found it hard to take kindness from others. Now was her chance to help someone else. 'Is there anything I can do?' she asked sincerely.

'Write to her, perhaps go and see her after the funeral.'

'You think she'd want to see me?'

'I'm sure she would. But in the meantime we're going to have our work cut out here.' He deliberately steered the conversation on to business matters. 'William has gone to fetch the undertaker, and then he and Eddie, if he can get away, are going to run the stall for me. After last night,' he held up the sling, 'I'm not going to be up to cutting meat or working on the market for a while.'

'Perhaps we could buy in pies,' Alma suggested.

He leaned heavily against the tiled wall.

'Here,' she pulled a chair out from under one of the zinc-covered tables. 'You should sit down.' Charlie took her advice, and it was then that she saw he was really ill. 'Look, the ingredients are all here. Seeing as how I've already started suppose you let me have a try.'

'You told me yourself you've never cooked pro-fessionally.'

'How hard can it be? Besides you're here to supervise.'

'I've never cooked professionally either.' He looked at her and she coloured.

'All right,' she said, lifting down a bag of flour. 'Let's give this a go.' To her surprise he made no attempt to leave, but continued to sit and watch her.

'I haven't said thank you for last night,' she said guiltily, feeling that it was her fault he was injured. 'Not only for stopping that maniac waving the poker in front of my eyes, but also for not pressing charges against him afterwards.'

He fell silent for a moment. 'I wasn't just thinking of you. He began by threatening me, remember. Then, like an idiot, I lost my temper.'

'After seeing you, I hope you never lose it with me.' She had meant it as a joke, but her words fell flat in the quiet atmosphere of the kitchen.

'Only fools lose their tempers,' he replied unequivocally. 'And all I've succeeded in doing is hurting this business before it's even opened, as well as jeopardising my job running the stall. William and I talked last night. He's going to take over the slaughterhouse and market with Eddie's help, and that, I'm afraid, leaves this place staffed with a one-armed man, and you. Unfortunately until I find out what kind of trade we're going to get here I can't afford to pay anyone else.'

'Which means?' She was terrified that he wasn't going to open the shop after all. She'd already handed in her notice to Tony.

'Which means that although William can help on the days when the market is closed once he's finished his stint in the slaughterhouse, it's mainly down to you; and if you want the job you'll have to do more than just the cooking. I know I said you could have the afternoons off, but if I can't cope, would you mind working in the shop as well? The only problem as I see it is the long hours . . .'

'You want me to serve behind the counter after what happened in the café?'

'I'll be there with you most of the time. All I need is another pair of hands to help me cut the meat and take the money.'

'But—'

'You can't allow the gossips to ruin your whole life, Alma,' he said irritably. 'If they come in, we'll just have to face them together.'

She hadn't had a chance to tell him about her mother and her trip to see the minister. But now, when he was ill, exhausted and worried, wasn't the time. He'd done so much for her.

'If you want me to serve in the shop, Charlie, I'll be happy to do it, and work whatever hours are needed to make a go of the business. I'll cope with the Marys and Fredas as best I can. And you don't have to worry about my health. I'm used to hard work and eighteen-hour days.'

He gave her one of his rare, tight smiles. 'I knew I'd picked the right girl for the job.'

'Name?'

'Phyllis Harry.'

'State your business.'

'We're homeless.' She held up her son, who was blue after the hours spent in the cold.

'Follow me.'

The lodge-keeper led her through the main gates into a small yard. To the right was the master's house; to the left, the gate lodge, both low-built and bordered by well-stocked, colourful flowerbeds. Facing her was an intimidatingly high building, a veritable wall of dour grey stone, and set in the centre of it was another set of gates, only marginally lower than the first. She walked towards them, expecting the porter to direct her into the yard she could see beyond the gates, but he halted at the entrance to the open passageway that cut through the block.

'You can wait here,' he ordered. He opened a door on her right that led into a low-ceilinged waiting room. Painted the inevitable institution shades of green and cream, it appeared to be crowded with people. Hugging her baby close she looked around warily. A whole family – mother, father and five small children – occupied one corner. A filthy old woman who stank of drink and urine sat in another, singing to herself. Three middle-aged men stood despondently close to the door. She clutched her son and crept as close as she could to the family. She stood there, leaning against the cold, stone wall for what seemed like hours, watching and waiting, fearful of what was to come because of the stories she'd heard, mainly from Mrs Richards.

'One night! That's all poor Martha lasted in there. They took her baby away from her, and she cried her eyes out. Dead of a broken heart by morning . . .'

'TB, more like it,' Harry Griffiths had contradicted. (She must have been in his corner shop.)

'You believe what you want to, Mr Griffiths. I know better,' Mrs Richards had crowed.

'Females and children follow me!'

Phyllis kissed the top of her baby's head, gripped her bundle tightly and followed a sister dressed in a dark blue uniform dress that was almost covered by a white apron, collar and cuffs. They walked through the gate into yet another yard dominated by a massive block, the largest she had yet seen.

'Males follow me,' a masculine voice commanded. 'Females to the left.'

The group Phyllis was with turned at the command. To her surprise they seemed to have picked up more children and women from somewhere. Behind her, she could hear the mother of the small children crying, her sobs accompanied by the low murmurs of her husband.

'Come on now, stop that for the children's sake. It's not for long. Only until we get on our feet again . . .'

'Males, to the right.' A male nurse directed the men away from the women. The mother lingered, clinging to her husband's arm.

'You're not doing yourself or your husband any good.' The male nurse peeled the woman's fingers away from her husband's shabby jacket.

'Females in line.' Phyllis shuffled along, taking her place in the queue that formed in front of a high, three-storey block of dressed stone. It began to rain, heavy spots that rapidly turned into a downpour. There was no shelter in the yard, and as no one had suggested walking in through the open door that faced them, Phyllis pulled Rhiannon's old shawl higher, covering her son's face and head.

'All infants under three to be handed over.'

'Your baby.'

Phyllis stared at the young nurse in front of her.

'Your baby,' she repeated. 'He can't be left out in the cold like this.' The nurse held out her arms.

'He's hungry.'

'He'll be fed and looked after.'

'When can I see him?' Phyllis shook uncontrollably as she slowly unwrapped the shawl with numbed fingers, and wrapped it around Brian.

'That will depend on you, and how you get on. If you work well and behave yourself, possibly a week Sunday,' the sister replied officiously, standing alongside the young nurse.

'Best hand him over without a fuss, love,' a woman murmured higher up the line. 'It'll go hard if you don't.'

'Infants three to eleven years of age.'

'Where are you taking them?' the woman who'd clung to her husband asked.

'Maesycoed Homes. They'll be well looked after. Eleven to sixteen, Church Village homes. Come on Sam,' the young nurse smiled at a gangling youth who was being led across the yard by a male nurse. 'You know you're only twelve.'

'I want to stay with my dad.'

'Not this time, Sam.'

'Bailiffs put us out again, Nurse Harding,' his mother said to the staff.

'Get these children out of here.'

Phyllis couldn't see where the harsh masculine voice came from, but it provoked an instant response. Brian was snatched from her arms so quickly that she barely had time to turn her head and check the direction he was being carried in.

'Name?'

'Phyllis Harry. I gave it to the porter . . .' She wouldn't have dreamed of protesting if she hadn't been so upset by the sound of Brian's screams growing fainter as he was carried from the female yard into the deeper recesses of the workhouse.

'And now you have to give it to me. Age?'

'Forty-one.' Someone had pushed her into the reception area of the female ward block. To her left was a huge tiled room with a row of baths set in the centre. She could smell the foul stink of disinfectant from where she was standing. She began to count them . . . three, four, five, six, seven . . .

'Last place of residence?'

'Danygraig Street.' She wouldn't implicate Evan, especially here.

'Reason for leaving?'

'The bailiffs evicted us.'

'Non-payment of rent?'

'No,' Phyllis replied indignantly. 'My landlady died.'

'Relatives?'

'Only my son.'

'Husband deceased or absent?'

She lowered her head. 'I'm not married.'

'I see.' The disapproving tone said it all.

'Last occupation?'

'Cinema usherette.'

'We have no cushy jobs like that here. It'll be domestic work. Plain and hard. If you prove satisfactory we may find you an outside situation. A portion of your wages will be deducted to support yourself and your son. I take it you have no money?'

Phyllis put her hand in her pocket and pulled out a threepenny piece and two pennies, all the money she had after paying for the funeral. Then she remembered her Post Office book. There was seven of the ten pounds Charlie had given her on it. She'd left it in the box room, in Rhiannon's jewellery box. How could she have been so stupid? It would have kept her and Brian for a week or two. Given her time to think of something. Now it was too late.

'Hand it over.'

'Are there any situations where I can keep my son with me?' Phyllis ventured, as she laid her pennies on the desk, hoping even at this late stage for a miracle.

'None.'

'When can I see him?'

'We'll consider a visit in a week or two. What's that you have there?'

Phyllis looked down and realised she was still holding the bundle she had made of Brian's rag doll and his clothes. 'They're my son's—'

'Inmates are not allowed personal possessions. Hand them over.'

'But . . .'

'I'll see your son gets them.' Another, younger, prettier nurse left the bathroom and took the bundle from Phyllis's hands.

'His name's Brian. Brian Harry. He's only a baby,' Phyllis called after her.

'Inmates are not allowed to speak to staff until they're spoken to,' the admitting sister admonished sternly. 'Any problems with you, woman, and you won't be seeing your child for quite some time. In there,' she indicated the bathroom. 'Next?'

'It's not so bad,' the younger nurse whispered in her ear. 'They're not all like Dragon-face. Now here's your uniform.'

She gave Phyllis a pair of wooden clogs and a long drab work dress stitched out of coarse Welsh flannel. 'Undress next to your bath. Leave your clothes in a neat pile on the floor. I'll take them.'

'But where?'

'You're not allowed to wear your own clothes in here, Phyllis isn't it?'

Phyllis shook the dress out in her hands. 'But what about underclothes?'

'You have your dress. It's modest enough.' She walked away holding the bundle out in front of her.

'It really isn't that bad when you get used to it. The first day is always the worst,' said the older woman whose son had pleaded to be allowed to stay with his father. She followed Phyllis into the bathroom with its row of waiting baths.

'No talking along there. Strip off.'

Colour flooding her cheeks, Phyllis hung her head and began to unbutton her blouse.

'They won't let you keep anything like that, love, and once they get their hands on it you'll never see it again,' the woman whispered as Phyllis fingered the gold chain with its heart-shaped locket that Evan had given her the day Brian had been born. 'Didn't you have anyone you could leave it with?'

Phyllis shook her head, tears stinging her eyes.

'Well then, you'd better hand it over first as last. Sad, but there you are. They sell things like that, you know. Set what they get against the cost of our keep, or so they say. Pity you didn't think of pawning it. You might have been able to stay out of here a bit longer if you had.'

'Hurry up there. There's others waiting to get in that bath.'

Phyllis stared down at the water, grey and scummy with something other than disinfectant.

'The inmates get to use them first, love,' the woman told her. 'New arrivals are always last in the queue.'

Phyllis felt that the final remnants of her dignity went

with her clothes. The last thing she did before stepping into the water was to unfasten the locket from around her neck and slip it into her mouth. Tucking it into the hollow of her cheek with her tongue she decided they'd have to kill her before she handed that over. As long as she held on to it, she still had Evan – and Brian. Their photographs were inside. And she had the feeling that she was going to need to look at their smiling images often in the days that lay ahead.

Chapter Twenty

'DARLING, I AM sorry,' Mrs John rang the bell for the maid and ordered an extra place to be laid at the breakfast table. 'It must have been a dreadful strain on you, and Bethan of course. How is she taking it?'

'As well as can be expected,' Andrew answered the standard question with the standard reply.

'Well, all I can say is it has to be for the best, darling. A child like that . . .'

Two days ago Andrew would have agreed with her sentiments, but after seeing the anguished expression on Bethan's face as she had nursed the child the night before he couldn't. Not any more.

'You must be absolutely worn out, all this—'

'Bethan's borne the brunt of it,' he interrupted.

'Yes, of course,' she agreed hastily. 'Being the mother, she must have.'

'How are you and Dad keeping?' He determinedly changed the subject.

'Oh, we're fine, right as rain.' She began to rearrange a posy of primroses on the side table next to her. 'Your father was upset of course when he saw Bethan's father in the police cells. And I can't say that either of us was exactly overjoyed when we heard that he'd been sent to prison. It's just like her aunt's case all over again, such a dreadful . . .'

As his mother chattered on, Andrew sat back and studied her as though she were a stranger. Peculiar really, how he'd had to leave home before he could evaluate his parents for what they really were. The foibles, the pettiness, the meticulous attention paid to dress and detail at the expense of humanity. Even the house seemed to epitomise their faults. Old-fashioned, cluttered and fussy, it grated on his nerves after the simple, clear-cut, modern lines of the furnishings he'd chosen for his own flat.

He found himself wondering what Bethan's taste was. He'd picked out all their furniture, even their cooking utensils and linen, invariably settling on the aesthetically pleasing lines of art deco. He'd asked Bethan several times if she had a preference, but as she'd constantly deferred to him and his taste, he'd taken her at her word and gone ahead and selected what he wanted for his home. Just as his mother had selected everything for this one. Was there no happy medium in marriage?

'. . . have you any idea why he did it, darling?'

'Why who did what?' He stared at his mother blankly.

'Bethan's father hit the policeman, of course,' she stressed irritably, lowering her voice as the maid came into the drawing room to announce that breakfast was waiting to be served in the dining room.

'It was an accident. He was trying to hit a blackshirt.'

'Really, dear. Are you absolutely sure?'

'Absolutely,' he echoed as he followed her into the hall.

'Andrew. Good to see you.' His father pumped his hand up and down enthusiastically. 'Sorry about the circumstances and all that.'

'Tea or coffee, darling.'

'Coffee please.'

His mother reached for the silver coffee pot on the sideboard. It stood next to the silver teapot, sugar bowl and milk jug. He found himself appraising the silverware in a way that he had never done before. The muffin-warmers, the butter dish, the cruet set, the hot-water jug, the trays, the spoons . . . how much money did they represent? For years he had taken all of this – the house, his parents, their money, the servants – for granted. How worthless it all seemed now he was faced with his son's death and Bethan's grief.

'Any chance of a job here?' he asked his father casually as he picked up his coffee and sipped it.

'What, here in Pontypridd?'

'I can't think of any other "here".'

'I thought you were settled in London.'

'I'm not.'

'But it's such a good opportunity for you. Working in the Cross with all those specialists and consultants. I would have given my eye teeth to have had the chance to do the same at your age.'

'Perhaps I'm not ambitious.'

'Bacon and kidneys, Andrew?' His mother interrupted their conversation to push the hot dish towards him.

He shook his head.

'Of course you're ambitious. It's poppycock to say you're not. Every fellow wants to get on in life. Look, I know things aren't going very well for you at the moment—'

Andrew burst out laughing. A harsh mirthless laughter as he pushed his clean plate aside. 'Not going very well,' he echoed. 'My son dies . . .'

'It's not as if it wasn't expected, or a blessing,' his father retorted angrily, retreating from what he sensed could become an 'emotional' scene. 'You're young. You can have others.'

'Having babies isn't quite like having puppies, you know. Besides, it must be obvious to everyone with eyes in their head that my marriage isn't exactly what you'd call "up to the mark".'

His parents exchanged telling looks and his mother reached out and placed her hand over his. 'We know, darling, believe me we know, but we warned you against marrying Bethan. It was obvious from the start that the two of you simply weren't suited. But it's not the end of the world,' she consoled him. 'You can divorce her. After all, this is the 1930s not the dark ages. No one thinks that badly of divorced people any more. You only have to read the papers. It happens in the best of families nowadays, even Royalty.'

'But not mine if I can help it,' he snapped. 'Well, Dad, is there any chance of a job?'

'Posts are always available in Pontypridd and the valleys, you know that,' his father replied testily. 'Doctors aren't exactly queuing up to work here. The junior working with Trevor at the moment is taking up a position in Cardiff Infirmary next month.'

'Then you'll put in a word for me?'

'Andrew really, it's what you were doing before you went to London. Four pounds a week in the hospital and whatever you can pick up from your share of the penny-a-week patients. You could do much better.'

'It's how you started out.'

'Yes and look at me now. Senior Medical Officer in a Welsh backwater.'

'If you'd wanted better or different, why didn't you try for it?'

'My father was here, and I thought my roots were. I freely admit I should have never returned to the town after college. But the last thing I want is for you to repeat my mistakes.'

'Suppose you let me run my own life.'

'Andrew!'

'Look, while we're discussing business I know Granny left me money . . .'

'You and Fiona,' his father broke in, wondering what was coming next. 'We never made any secret of it. It's invested, and the interest is added to the capital every year.'

'How much is there, and how long would it take to cash?'

'Why?' his father asked suspiciously.

'I want to buy a house.'

'Here in Pontypridd?' his mother said doubtfully. 'But that's such a final step.'

'The Hawthorns is for sale. If you're set on staying here I suppose that would do you.' His father heaped more bacon and toast on to his plate. 'Old Mrs Herbert died last month, and I happen to know that the family want a quick sale. You could probably get it for four hundred pounds.'

333

'And it's just down the road,' Mrs John smiled brightly, determinedly making the best of a bad situation. 'I could look out for Bethan, introduce her to all the right people, propose her for the Ladies' Guild . . .'

'How much did Gran leave me then, Dad?' Andrew asked, ignoring his mother's projections of his and Bethan's future. 'Is there enough to buy a house?'

'A great deal more, actually. Fifteen hundred pounds when I last looked.'

'Can you arrange for me to have access to . . .' Andrew thought for a moment. 'Six hundred.'

'But the house will . . .'

'Will need furnishing,' Andrew finished for his father. 'And I'll need to buy a car, and it wouldn't hurt to have a bit in the bank. Oh, and I'll probably need somewhere to store my things for a week or two when I give up the lease of the London flat. Can I use the rooms over the garage?'

'If you must,' his mother said. 'But darling . . .'

He looked at his watch. 'Is that the time! I have to go.'

'But you've only just got here,' his mother protested.

'Oh, and Dad could I have the second car for a couple of days? I borrowed Trevor's to get here but he needs it.'

'I suppose so,' his father consented ungraciously.

'Thank you. I'll get Trevor to drive me up later to pick it up.'

'Will you be staying?' his mother asked hopefully as he left the table.

'No, but thank you for the offer,' he called back.

He left the house through the french window in the drawing room and walked across the garden to the garage. He glanced up at the rooms he'd occupied when he'd been at home. It seemed like half a lifetime ago. He had some growing up to do, and the sooner he began the better, for him and Bethan.

Andrew had to wait for Trevor to finish his rounds in the

Graig Hospital before he could return to the Common to fetch his father's car. As a result it was midday before he arrived back at Graig Avenue. For the first time he walked straight into the house and through to the back kitchen without knocking the front door. Charlie and William were nowhere to be seen, but Eddie was there, spooning tea into the pot.

'Bethan's upstairs,' he said coldly when Andrew entered. 'Diana's with her. She's not going into work today. Do you want tea?' he asked gruffly.

'Yes please,' Andrew answered, chalking up another first. Eddie actually offering him something.

'You didn't see Phyllis Harry, did you, when you came up the hill?'

'Phyllis Harry? Oh, the woman Bethan took in yesterday. I'm sorry, I've never met her.'

'She's disappeared,' Eddie said as he poured boiling water on the tea. 'I can't find her anywhere. She would have been carrying her baby in a shawl,' he added as an afterthought, forgetting that half the women on the Graig had babies of an age to be carried in shawls.

'I didn't see anyone on the hill,' Andrew explained. 'I drove up. I've borrowed a car.'

'It must be nice to know people you can borrow things like that off,' Eddie retorted nastily.

'Well, if you'll excuse me I think I'll go and see Bethan. Shall I take her up her tea?'

'If you like. Tell Diana hers is poured down here.'

Andrew tapped quietly on the bedroom door before entering. Bethan and Diana were sitting side by side on the bed. Bethan had dressed Edmund in the suit Laura had given him and laid him out the night before. Now he was lying in a small white coffin placed on a trestle at the foot of the bed.

'I've brought you some tea, Bethan,' Andrew said, laying it down on the dressing table in front of her. 'Eddie said to tell you that yours is ready downstairs, Diana.'

'I'll be back in a few minutes, Beth.' Diana squeezed Bethan's hand before leaving the room.

'Bethan?'

She turned round slowly and faced him.

'Bethan . . .'

'You do know what the headstone and grave you agreed to this morning will cost?'

'A plot for three is always expensive,' he said pointedly.

'I haven't any money, Andrew.'

He reached out and touched her arm, gratified that she didn't shrug off his touch. 'Now is not the time or place to sort out our problems. Can't we just bury our dead—' he looked down at the tiny body in the coffin – 'and when it's all over start again?'

The eyes that looked into his were cold and spent.

'Please, Bethan.'

'There's nothing to start again, Andrew,' she said indifferently. 'Don't you realise that?'

Andrew waited until she finished her tea, then he carried both cups downstairs. Diana passed him in the hall, and he remembered hearing the boys move around the night before. There was very little privacy in a house like this. He laid the cups on the table, said goodbye to Eddie and left. As Bethan obviously didn't want him near her, there really didn't seem to be anything else for him to do. He climbed into his car, drove down the hill into town and parked in the police station yard. Both of his father's cars were well known, so no one would question the presence of this one, merely assume that his father had taken his mother shopping.

Saturday was the busiest day of the week in Pontypridd. Like Wednesday, both the indoor and outdoor markets were open, and it was traditionally the day when the whole town shopped for Sunday, their one day of rest. He knew he was unlikely to run into any of his parents' friends. The crache preferred to buy their fresh food on a Friday when only the indoor market was open.

It gave them first choice of the goods on offer, they didn't have to contend with Saturday's crowds, and although there were fewer bargains to be had and prices were higher, they didn't mind paying extra, for what they saw as better quality.

Andrew walked past the watchmaker's, down Penuel Lane, through the fruit market, bypassing the haberdashery stalls, and into the butcher's market. Bethan had mentioned that the Russian managed a stall there. He looked around, searching for a sight of his blond hair.

'After a bargain, Doctor John? Seeing as how you're almost family I can offer you a pound of rump steak at a knock-down price.'

William was standing behind one of the centre stalls watching him.

'I was looking for Charlie,' Andrew explained as he walked towards him.

'He's in his shop. He's leased the one opposite the fruit market on the corner of Penuel Lane.'

'Thanks. I'll go there.'

'Sure I can't tempt you with that steak?' William heaped a couple of bloody red pieces on to newspaper. 'One and six a pound. Go on, treat yourself, you can afford it.'

'I'd buy it if I thought you and Eddie would share it with me.'

William eyed him carefully. 'We might at that if Diana cooks it.'

'You're on.' Andrew dug in his pocket. 'Put enough in there for Charlie and the girls as well. I'll bring the beer.'

'I'm sorry about little Edmund,' William sympathised as he handed the parcel over. 'He was a nice little fellow. Quite a character in his own way, especially when he had the hiccups.'

'I'm glad he had you to care for him during his last weeks.'

Andrew walked away quickly not trusting himself to

say any more. He found the shop without any problems; the only wonder was he hadn't noticed it before, particularly as it had 'CHARLIE'S COOKED MEATS' painted in foot-high blue letters over the doors and window. He peered inside: it looked bright and clean and new. There was a small queue of customers at the counter. He pushed open the door and an attractive girl with bright, red-gold hair looked up from the till.

'Is Charlie here?' he asked.

She apologised to the woman she was serving and lifted the latch on a half-door set into the counter. 'He's in the kitchen, if you'd like to go through.' She opened a door in the back wall. 'It's Doctor John, isn't it?'

'I wish I knew everyone in Pontypridd who seems to know me.'

'I'm very sorry about your baby, Doctor.'

'Thank you,' he said awkwardly, feeling that Bethan should be receiving the condolences, not him.

In the kitchen Charlie was removing slices of beef from a cool cupboard on to a plate. As he was using only one hand it was long, slow work.

'You said last night that you had to go up to the cottage today to have your hand dressed. As it happens, I have to go that way so I wondered if you'd like a lift.'

'I went there first thing this morning.' Charlie turned to face Andrew as he spoke. He looked ghastly, even paler than usual.

'That isn't really why I called. I'd like to talk to you about Evan Powell if I may. It won't take long, only about half an hour.'

'I'll see if Alma can manage without me.' He checked that his collar was fastened and opened the door. Andrew heard him speaking to Alma through the hubbub of conversation in the shop. Then he returned.

'As long as it is only half an hour,' he said. 'We seem to be busy.'

'Business is good.'

'Too early to say. We only opened today.'

Andrew waited until he and Charlie were alone again before continuing.

'What you told me last night about Evan. Would you be prepared to sign a statement in a solicitor's office to that effect?'

'Of course. It's the truth.'

'Did anyone else see that Evan was aiming to hit a blackshirt?'

'Plenty.'

'Then why weren't they called to court?'

'The police were expecting trouble. They convened the magistrates' court at six in the morning. There wouldn't have been any time to call witnesses. Besides, Evan didn't want to incur any costs, so he pleaded guilty. All the magistrate had to do was sentence him.'

'He didn't even plead extenuating circumstances?'

'Not to my knowledge.'

'Then would you mind if we called into Spickett's the solicitor's? They're not far, only in Gelliwastad Road. I thought about it last night. There's a possibility that we may be able to get Evan out of jail before he serves his full sentence.'

Charlie looked at him, wondering if they had all misjudged Bethan's husband.

'Bethan's going to need him,' Andrew said as Charlie opened the back door of the shop. 'Now more than ever.'

'Ashes to ashes, dust to dust . . .'

To the disgust of Elizabeth and John Joseph Bull, who'd made a point of writing to Bethan to announce that they would be attending Edmund's funeral, Andrew had engaged the Anglican vicar, Tony Price, to conduct the service. Andrew had settled on Tony Price because Trevor had said he was a kindly and humane man, and because he couldn't have borne one of the hellfire and damnation services that John Joseph Bull was notorious for conducting, any more than he could have withstood one of the genteel Anglican services his mother was so enamoured of.

Organising the whole funeral had been a nightmare. Bethan was adamant that she wanted to attend the actual interment, breaking with the sacrosanct 'men only, women in the house' Welsh tradition. She'd also refused to have any food in the house, which meant that any women who wanted to pay their respects had to do so at the graveside or not at all. Elizabeth had been so appalled that she'd actually visited the house she'd sworn never to enter again in an effort to persuade Bethan to change her mind about having a 'funeral tea', but Bethan, to Andrew's admiration, had refused to be swayed. She hadn't even needed his support to face her mother, something he had mixed feelings about. Since Edmund's death he'd spent all of his days in Graig Avenue, and his nights close by in Trevor's house, in the vain hope that she would turn to him for comfort, instead of to her family.

She was standing opposite him now, flanked by her brothers and her father who'd been allowed out of prison for the occasion. Between them lay the open grave, a deep chasm that seemed to emphasise the depth and finality of their estrangement. He looked down at the small white coffin nestling in its depths and shivered despite the warm spring sunshine. It looked smaller than ever at the bottom of the dark pit, its surface overshadowed by two very separate wreaths. Bethan's simple posy of small white rosebuds set against a background of blue forget-me-nots made his expensive wreath of waxy-looking, trumpet-shaped lilies and overblown red roses appear vulgar and crass.

'In hope of the life everlasting . . .'

He had been right about his wife needing her father. Evan's arm was wrapped around her shoulder. Haydn, who'd handed his role over to his understudy for one night to be with his sister, held on to her right hand. Eddie was standing on her left, next to his father and close to William and Diana.

He wished he could see Bethan's face beneath the thick

veil she was wearing. Take some of her grief and burden himself with it. If only they were alone . . .

'Thank you, Reverend, a most moving service.' It was over. Evan was thanking the vicar while looking at Andrew, making him feel guilty for neglecting yet another duty.

'Andrew, we'll see you later?' His mother, dry-eyed, tight-lipped, tapped his arm. His father, resplendent in his dark made-to-measure suit alongside her, his uncles, his aunts, his cousins, even the Llewellyn Joneses – all here to mourn a child they had never known, because it was the 'right thing to do'; and across the other side of the grave from them, Bethan's family and friends, Laura, Trevor and Charlie firmly fixed among them. The separate halves of Pontypridd had come together at the graveside of a child who should have belonged to both worlds, yet even here they couldn't mix. Each stuck rigidly to its own side of the grave. And Eddie, big, tough, 'take on and fight the world Eddie', clutching a teddy bear Bethan had bought for the baby; holding it so tight he virtually wrenched an arm from its body before throwing it into the grave.

'So sorry, Andrew.'

'So sorry' . . . Handshakes . . . 'So sorry . . . So sorry . . .' Expressions of sympathy, but only from his own family and friends. Nothing from Bethan's side. Then his mother actually bridged the gulf, going over to Bethan.

'So sorry . . .'

Weren't there any other words in the English language?

'You and Andrew must come and dine with us soon.'

Bethan nodded her head without answering. Elizabeth moved closer, standing next to the tall, impressive figure of John Joseph Bull. Taking his courage in his hands, Andrew walked over to Bethan.

'I'll take you back. There's room for four, five at a push, in the car,' he said, looking at Eddie and Haydn.

Evan pushed Bethan gently towards Andrew.

'Go with him, love. I'll see you soon, and I'll be thinking of you.' It was only then that Andrew saw the uniformed warder standing at a discreet distance behind the funeral party. Evan stepped back and Elizabeth stepped forward.

'My sympathies and condolences, Bethan.'

There were other words in the English language after all.

'And mine.' John Joseph Bull extended his hand to his great-niece. 'But God's will be done. He finds ways of punishing the sinners and—'

'Excuse us.' Wrapping his arm round Bethan's shoulders, which were still warm from the weight of Evan's hand, Andrew led her down the long path to the cemetery gates and the car, Haydn, Eddie, William and Diana following close behind them.

'I'm not coming back, Evan.' Elizabeth confronted her husband as he stood alongside the warder. The prison officer tactfully retreated even deeper among the gravestones.

'When I heard that you'd left the house I didn't expect you to return,' Evan said flatly.

'That's just as well. I've put up with as much as I can. Uncle John Joseph is going to try and get me a teaching situation. They now allow women with widow status to teach.'

'Would it be more convenient for you if I died, Elizabeth?' Evan asked drily.

'As far as I'm concerned, Evan, you are dead.' She took her uncle's arm and followed Bethan, Andrew and the boys down the long straight path that cut across the graves to the gate.

'Ready, Evan?' the warder asked as the last of the party turned their backs on the open grave.

Evan saw the gravediggers waiting. 'As I'll ever be.' He held out his wrists in expectation of the cuffs that had been removed as a special concession.

'There's no need for that,' the man said. 'You aren't

thinking of going anywhere are you?'

'Not for a while,' Evan agreed softly. 'Not for a while.'

'Andrew, you can't leave Pontypridd. Not now!' Trevor said hotly.

'Just what are you thinking of?' Laura demanded as she slammed a steak and kidney pudding down on the table. 'Bethan needs . . .'

'Bethan has her brothers and Diana.'

'Brothers are no substitute for a husband. And don't go all big-headed on me because I said that,' Laura turned angrily on Trevor who was sitting quietly in his chair. 'They'll look after her, keep her busy, that's what she needs right now. Charlie even asked her if she'd help out in the kitchen of his shop for a week or two until his hand heals.'

'And you're happy with that?' Trevor asked, concerned for Bethan's condition, which she obviously hadn't seen fit to mention to Andrew.

'Not entirely. But then she won't be on her own, and they won't let her do too much . . .'

'And what happens when Charlie doesn't need her in the shop any more? What then?' Trevor asked.

'Then,' Andrew took the enormous serving spoon Trevor handed him and helped himself to a small portion of the pudding, 'I hope to be back. All I have to do is work my notice in the Cross and sort out the flat.'

'You're coming back to Pontypridd for good?'

'Yes.'

'To the Graig or the Common?' Laura demanded astutely.

'What would you say if I said neither?' he answered quietly.

For weeks after the funeral Bethan moved through her days like an automaton. She woke when the alarm went off on her bedside table, she called everyone in the house, she made breakfast, cooked, washed, cleaned, scarcely noticing that Eddie's working days became shorter and shorter on the three days when she didn't help out in Charlie's shop. Trevor Lewis had told everyone in the house to watch her, make sure she kept busy, but not enough to overtax herself. He made a point of calling in every day, as did Laura. And Laura took care to make sure that Bethan was never alone, not even for a minute. On the days Bethan stayed home, Eddie didn't leave the house until Laura came. If it was Laura's baking or washing day she took Bethan back down to her house with her for 'company'. It was Laura who persuaded Bethan to walk through the market with her for the first time two weeks after Edmund's death, and it was Laura who confronted embarrassed neighbours who turned their backs or went into shops when they saw her and Bethan walking together, because they didn't know quite what to say to a mother who'd lost a child who was 'different'.

Laura occasionally took Bethan to Pontypridd Park in the afternoons. They sat on benches and watched the sons and daughters of the crache play tennis, or they walked to the cricket field, or the bandstand, or along the river, but by tacit agreement they never went near the children's playground. That was perhaps the hardest thing of all for Laura, because she wanted a child so much. She would have liked nothing better than to discuss Bethan's pregnancy, to find out what it felt like to give birth to your own child, but one glance at the look of anguish that had never entirely left Bethan's face was enough. So she stuck to 'safe' topics: Haydn's career, Diana's working life, economical recipes, and the doings of her various brothers and sisters. And she continued to invite Bethan into her tiny house after their outings, making her cups of tea, insisting that she wait until Trevor arrived so he could drive her up the remainder of the Graig hill to Graig Avenue. Attentions Bethan accepted, thanked them for, and always in the same chill monotone.

When Trevor drove Bethan up the hill he asked how she felt and tried to talk to her about the coming baby, but

344

without success. After he watched her get out of the car and walk up the steps to her house, he invariably drove away cursing Andrew, who had left Pontypridd the day after the funeral and not returned. Not even sending word of when he could be expected. Nothing, in over four weeks.

'Hello, girl!'

'Dad?' Bethan whirled round, staring dumbfounded at her father standing in the washhouse doorway. 'You're here . . . you . . . how . . . you haven't . . .'

'No, love,' he smiled, as he closed the door and sat in his chair. 'I haven't escaped. I've been back a couple of hours, and I've banked up the fire and made a nice pot of tea. Take off your hat and coat, and sit down. You look worn out.'

'Oh Dad.' Bethan flung her arms around his neck. Scalding hot tears fell from her eyes – the first she had shed since Edmund had died.

'They let me out this morning. Bail, pending an appeal.'

'I didn't know you were appealing.'

'Neither did I until Mr Spickett—'

'The solicitor in Ponty?'

'Engaged by and paid for by your husband, turned up yesterday afternoon to tell me that he'd arranged it all. Andrew even posted bail. Fifty pounds. Mr Spickett seems to think there's a very good chance I won't have to go back.'

'Andrew never said a word to me.' Bethan finally released her father and pulled the pins from her hat.

'Perhaps he didn't want to say anything in case it didn't work out.'

'That would be like Andrew,' she agreed.

'I have to report to the police every morning, but at least I'm home and I can work. Is Eddie out on the round?'

'The round's had to go, Dad. Charlie hurt himself and

Eddie helped out on the stall and in the shop for a while. Now Charlie says he can't manage without him.'

'Is that the shop Charlie was thinking of opening a while back?'

'It's open now. It *is* good to have you home.' She lifted the teapot down from the range. 'Aren't you hungry?'

'I had some bread and cheese when I came in.' Evan frowned. He didn't want to ask the next question but he had to.

'Where's Phyllis Harry? I went to walk through Rhiannon's and there's new people in the house.'

'They evicted her as soon as Rhiannon was buried.'

Evan's frown became a look of anguish, and Bethan's heart went out to him. For the first time since the death of her son she found herself feeling for the suffering of another, and despite the pain it exacted, it wasn't entirely unpleasant. Something akin to the hurt that was a part of giving birth, an agony that had a purpose.

'Charlie brought her here. It was the day Edmund died. She left in the early hours of the morning without saying anything. When we found out later that she'd admitted herself and Brian to the workhouse, Charlie went down to bring her back, but she wouldn't come. She insisted that she'd bring disgrace on all of us if she lived here. Charlie offered her a job in his shop, said she could sleep in one of the spare rooms above it, but she wouldn't leave . . . Dad, where are you going?'

'To bring her and the boy back where they belong.'

'I hope she comes.'

'You know, don't you?'

'I know Brian's your son. I also know that Mam will never come back once Phyllis is here.'

'She wouldn't have come back anyway,' he said with a grim smile. 'And even if she had, I'm not entirely sure that I could have lived with her any more. Not the way we were. Prison does funny things to you. Makes you value what you've got, think of what you want to do with the rest of your life.'

'I'll sort out the beds and make the tea. She'll be sharing with you, Dad?'

He stopped in his tracks. 'I . . .' he stammered, colouring in embarrassment for the first time in his life. He had been prepared for a lot of things, but not this much understanding from his daughter.

'She can go in the box room. It is empty, isn't it?'

'I'll make up your bed, and the box-room bed. That way Phyllis can choose whether she sleeps with you or Brian. I'll move in with Diana.'

'Love, about you and Andrew . . .'

'I don't want to talk about me yet, Dad. Let's get you and Phyllis sorted first.'

'Just one thing – when is that husband of yours coming back to get you?'

'I don't know,' she said carelessly.

'He loves you, Bethan,' he said earnestly. 'Just as much as you once loved him.'

She looked at her father in amazement. 'Yes, I suppose I did love him. Didn't I?'

Chapter Twenty-One

'NAME?'
      'Evan Powell.'
'Householder?'
'Yes.'
'Occupation?'
'Rag man.'
'Relationship to the inmate?'

Evan swallowed hard. 'Miss Harry is a friend of my family,' he answered eventually.

'You intend to offer the inmate a domestic position?'
'Yes.'
'You are married?'
'Yes.'

'As the inmate is an unmarried mother and deemed to be in moral danger, your wife should be the one making this application, Mr Powell, not you.'

'My wife is not living with me.'

The thin, sharp-featured clerk laid his pen down on an adjoining chair and stared disapprovingly at Evan. 'Do you really expect the authorities to release a woman into your care, Mr Powell, when by your own admission you are living apart from your wife . . . with . . .' he glanced at the paper in front of him, 'an extremely precarious way of making a living, to say the least.'

'Miss Harry is a friend of my daughter and my niece. They are both living in my home with me, and my niece and my son both work in shops in the town.'

'I see. You may have a reasonable income going into your household, Mr Powell, but if your daughter and your niece are not married, then I hardly think Miss Harry would be a suitable person for them to associate with.'

'My daughter is married.'

'Her name?'

'Bethan John.'

'Her husband's name?'

Evan debated whether or not to tell the man. His son-in-law had already done a great deal for him. He was loath to make free with the connection and risk embarrassing him further, although he knew full well that Andrew's name would probably accomplish what he had thought impossible a few moments ago. He looked up, saw the grey walls, remembered what it had been like for him in prison, and thought of what Phyllis was going through. The sight of the bars on the windows made the decision for him. 'Andrew John. Doctor Andrew John,' he added, so there could be no mistake.

'Doctor John's son?' The clerk's tone changed immediately to one of polite deference. Evan had disliked the official on sight; now, he decided, he hated him.

'He is Doctor John's son,' Evan agreed tersely.

'Can I take it that this woman's services will be required by your daughter?'

'By all of us, to run the household. We have three lodgers.'

'I see.' The clerk tapped his nose irritatingly with the stem of his pen. 'That puts an entirely different complexion on the matter, Mr Powell. I am sorry that I had to ask you those questions earlier, but you do understand that we can't be too careful when we hand over inmates to prospective employers.'

'I understand.'

'You realise of course that you will be accountable for her welfare while she is in your employ. That you will be responsible for paying her a fair wage, and for holding back a proportion to pay for the upkeep of her child . . .'

'I intend to remove the child from here as well.'

'That is most unorthodox, Mr Powell, and something the authorities would never recommend. The child will interfere with this woman's ability to carry out her duties.'

'Until she came in here, Miss Harry was an extremely efficient housekeeper. The child lived with her then and didn't interfere with her duties. It will be welcome in my house.'

'Yes . . . well. Without referring to the records I couldn't tell you if the child is still here . . .'

'Where else would he be?' Evan demanded, his blood running cold at the thought of something happening to his son while he was here, in the hands of strangers.

'We have been fortunate in placing some of the younger babies with families who are prepared to adopt them.'

'Surely you can't do that without the mother's permission?'

'Not if the mother is capable of making her own decisions,' the clerk hedged evasively as he left his chair and headed nervously for the door. 'But then Miss Harry may have consented . . .'

'I know Miss Harry. She would never willingly give her child up for adoption.'

'In that case he's probably still here. I'll look into it for you.' He wrenched open the door and practically ran outside. 'I also have to have this application checked. Placing inmates isn't entirely up to me, you know. If you would wait here.'

The clerk closed the door behind him. Evan stood up and paced the floor uneasily, unnerved by the talk of adoption. Just what *did* go on behind these walls? He hated asking for favours, even more than he'd hated using Andrew's name, but he began to wish that he'd thought of calling in and asking for Trevor Lewis's help on the way down the hill. Like all unemployed miners he lived in fear of the workhouse, knowing just how easy it was to end up in the poor ward. Plenty of his workmates, and their wives and children, had been forced to throw themselves on the mercy of the parish. When he'd heard about their plight he'd wished them better days, but then he'd had no idea that it was so damned difficult to get out of this building once you were inside it.

He could hear hammering coming from the carpenter's shop across the male yard to his right. He walked up to the door, put his hand on the knob and hesitated, debating whether or not to go in search of the clerk. Deciding against it, he turned and walked back to his chair. Time crawled by. He waited. And waited.

'If you'd like to come this way, Mr Powell?' The clerk appeared in the doorway. He led Evan across the entrance hall into a long, thin corridor. 'There are some papers you have to sign.' He tapped a door that had MASTER'S OFFICE on it in large black letters. 'They are release papers.' The man gave him a sickly little smile.

'For both Miss Harry and her son?'

'Yes. Her son was up for adoption, but he hadn't been placed.'

Five minutes later the formalities were over. Evan only hoped that Andrew John would never have cause to regret the free use he'd made of his name. He was returned to the waiting room and left alone. Ten minutes later Phyllis appeared in the company of a nurse.

He hardly recognised her. She was wearing a long, grey, shapeless woollen smock. Her hair was straight, cut short in a most unflattering style. She hobbled with difficulty in unwieldy wooden clogs, her face downcast, her hands, redder and more work roughened than he'd ever seen them, clasped in front of her.

'Phyllis.'

She raised her head. Forgetting the nurse who was standing beside her, she ran towards him, tripping headlong over the clogs into his arms. She fell, sobbing on his shoulder.

'I'll just get your son, Phyllis. I won't be long.' The nurse retreated tactfully, but neither Evan nor Phyllis heard her. They were holding on to one another as though they intended never to let go.

William was living in almost as much of a haze as Bethan, but for a very different reason. After an adolescent awakening to the pleasures of illicit 'dirty' photographs, two quick kisses with Tina, and years of wondering, he'd finally discovered all the joy, ecstasy and passion of sex. Totally obsessed with Vera, he lived for the moments she stole from George and so generously gave to him.

He'd heard one or two of the married boys down the gym complain that fun with women wasn't all it was cracked up to be. That the craving wore off after a couple of months. That wasn't his experience. As the weeks of his affair had turned into months so their lovemaking had become increasingly adventurous, urgent and frenzied. The moments they snatched together were all the sweeter for being forbidden – and fraught with danger. He held no illusions about George's jealousy, or the wrath that George would hail down on both their heads if he should ever discover what they were up to. But fear of George didn't stop him – or Vera – from becoming bolder, more careless, or increasing the risks they took.

They made wild, abandoned naked love in George's shed every Saturday and Wednesday night. George's sherry bottle took a hammering as Vera fed as much of it to Carry Hardy as she would down. And Carrie had never disappointed them. Sometimes it was one or half-past before Vera managed to creep outside, but whatever the time he was waiting and – as spring progressed and the nights warmed – ready. On Tuesdays and Thursdays Vera did her shopping in town, slipping into the shed at the back of Charlie's shop in between calls. At William's insistence they never repeated the insanity of retreating behind the shutters of Charlie's stall.

But for all of his obsession with Vera, or to be more precise, her body, William never considered himself and Vera a couple. On the rare occasions he thought about his future he saw himself with Tina Ronconi, although his commitment to Vera meant he rarely went to the café, and never on market nights. Sometimes days at a time passed without him seeing Tina. Constantly preoccupied with scheming and planning out his next meeting with Vera, he failed to see that Tina was cool towards him on the few occasions when he did go into Ronconi's.

In public he was careful – very careful indeed. He avoided looking into Vera's eyes; he tried not to say too much, or too little when he had occasion to pass George's stall, and he believed – really believed – Vera when she assured him that they were too clever to be found out. But neither of them had reckoned with the all-seeing eye and cunning of a jealous man who'd married a woman a third of his age.

For the first time in his life, George neglected his customers, watching every move his wife made instead of attending to their needs. He didn't worry about Wednesday and Saturday nights when he joined the card school in the Queen's, because he continued to pay Carrie, and pay her well, to walk home with his wife and stay there until he arrived. And sure enough, every time he staggered into his house in the early hours Carrie was snoring in the easy chair, and Vera was sleeping like a baby in their bed.

It was then that guilt beset him most. When he watched Vera as she slept, her fair curls falling across her face, her eyes closed, her mouth relaxed in a sweet innocent smile, he wondered how he could ever believe her capable of betraying the trust he had placed in her on their wedding day. Then the next morning she'd exchange a glance with one of the handsome young assistants who worked the market, and a murderous rage of jealousy would rise to consume him all over again. And none of the assistants on the market came any more handsome, charming or amenable than young William Powell.

All Vera had to do was make a detour around Charlie's stall on her way to the 'Ladies' and swing her hips provocatively within William Powell's sights, for all George's nagging doubts to surface. Gradually he became convinced, absolutely convinced, despite Carrie Hardy's watchful eye, that William Powell had his feet under Vera's table. But conviction wasn't enough. He wanted and needed proof. And he knew just how to get it.

*

A firm pattern of trade had been established within a short time of Charlie's shop opening. Alma knew that on Wednesdays, Fridays and Saturdays she would be run off her feet, so she was grateful when Bethan John came in to give them a hand, although she would have liked to know exactly what was 'going on' between Bethan and Charlie. Mondays they had the rush of people who'd eaten their pantries and cupboards bare on Sunday, which left Tuesday and Thursday mornings as quiet times. Both days William worked the morning in the slaughterhouse and the afternoons in either the shop or the kitchen. And every Tuesday and Thursday since the week Charlie had opened, William had asked her to keep an eye on things for half an hour or so and disappeared into the old shed at the back.

She'd look up from pushing pasties on to plates in the kitchen one Thursday afternoon to see William peeking round the door into the yard. Moments later Vera Collins had tiptoed out behind him, her face flushed, her curls in disarray. He'd straightened her hat, kissed her on the lips, slipped his hand under her skirt to give her a friendly squeeze, and let her out of the side door that led into Penuel Lane. Suddenly everything that had puzzled Alma about William fell into place. His absentmindedness, the times he hadn't heard what she'd said because he'd been too busy daydreaming, the stupid mistakes he made. It was too close to what she'd been like during the early days of her affair with Ronnie Ronconi. She knew exactly what William was going through. And she felt for him. Really felt for him.

'Want to go to a party?'

Alma looked up. She was alone in the shop with Charlie. His hand had healed and he was removing the empty plates from inside the glassed counter. Eddie was out the back slicing a whole ham ready for the late-night rush which inevitably came round about six on a Saturday.

'Are you asking me?'

'Yes.' Charlie straightened up and looked across at her. 'Diana, William and Eddie are coming and, if we can, we hope to persuade Bethan to join us.'

'What kind of a party?'

'A Russian one. Down in Bute Street.'

'Cardiff docks?'

'Don't believe all the stories you've heard about the place.'

'My mother would have a fit.'

'Then don't tell her.'

'Charlie!' She pretended to be shocked and he smiled. He'd grown accustomed to working with Alma and although the atmosphere between them was always professional, it wasn't professional enough to prevent her sharing the occasional joke with Eddie, William – and him.

'I lived down there for a while when I first came to Wales, and I have a friend who's celebrating his name day.'

'What's a name day?'

'The day of the saint he's named after.'

'How are we going to get there?'

'Bus. Everyone works in the week so Sunday is the best time. It will go on all day.'

She thought for a moment: William, Diana, Eddie, Bethan . . . with that number of people around, nothing could possibly happen to incite any gossip about her and this boss.

'All right, I'll come.'

'Meet you on Broadway bus stop at ten in the morning.'

'I'll be there.'

Bethan paced uneasily from room to room in Graig Avenue. Everything was neat and tidy, clean and orderly. Phyllis had proved to be a good housekeeper, and, after a strained beginning, was proving to be a good friend. Her son filled the house with his chatter, taking to the boys and Diana, and her and, through no fault of his own, making her heart ache even more for Edmund, and everything she had lost with him.

Her only regret about Phyllis was that it had taken Evan not Charlie to persuade her to leave the workhouse. So much time had been wasted when they could have been getting to know one another. The day her father had returned to the house with Phyllis and Brian, she had helped Phyllis put Brian to bed in the box room that was now his. While they had been occupied upstairs Evan had explained to the boys and Diana exactly whose son Brian was. Eddie hadn't liked the situation at first, but Phyllis's gentle diffidence had eventually won him over, and if the neighbours tittle-tattled about the latest additions to the Powell household, or thought Evan's relationship with Phyllis strange, none of them had yet found the courage to say anything openly to their faces.

Bethan opened the door to the front parlour and stared at the spot where she had kept Edmund's pram. After the funeral Eddie and Diana had bundled up all of Edmund's things and put them in the attic, but it hadn't helped. She only had to close her eyes to picture the day cot, his teddy bear, his clothes, his frail, tiny frame . . .

She turned her back on the parlour. Desperately trying to shut out the painful memories, she gazed blindly out of the window. The street was brilliant with sunlight. It was a warm, beautiful Sunday afternoon. The sort of day she had loved to walk out in dressed in a summer frock. Just the feel of light cotton against her skin after months of serge and wool had been enough to make her happy.

Evan had taken Phyllis and Brian for a walk up Shoni's pond. They had asked her to go with them, just as Charlie, Diana and Eddie had pleaded with her to go to Cardiff. She had told them that she preferred to stay at home, and reluctantly they had been forced to take her at her word. But for the first time since Edmund had died she was beginning to regret her decision to stay in the house. Perhaps it was not too late. She could put on her shoes – go up the mountain . . .

The front door opened and she turned. Andrew was standing before her, spruce as always in an open-necked white silk shirt, navy blue blazer and grey flannels. She remembered washing and ironing the shirt and suddenly, unaccountably, tears started in her eyes.

'Can I come in?'

She nodded, a thickness in her throat preventing her from speaking.

He closed the door and walked up to her. She was wearing a loose black and white cotton frock, a shapeless overall tied over it. She had put on weight since he had last seen her, but she still looked pale, tired and strained.

'I was hoping you'd come for a ride with me.'

'You have a car?'

'Didn't you see me pull up?'

She looked out. A shining new car was parked in front of the house, its black paintwork and chrome bumper glittering in the sunshine.

'I'm sorry, I really didn't see you coming. I was miles away.'

'Please—' he held out his hand but she didn't take it. 'Will you come?'

'Where to?'

'Does it have to be anywhere special? We need to talk.'

'There really doesn't seem to be a lot to say.'

'We're still married, Bethan.'

She wondered if he wanted to ask her for a divorce. She could hardly refuse him – not when she was living in Pontypridd and he was living in London. 'Give me a few moments to get my shoes and a cardigan.' She ran up the stairs, washed her hands and face, splashed lavender water on her neck and wrists, combed her hair and spread a little powder on her cheeks. She didn't bother with lipstick; her face was so pale it would have made her look like a clown. She took off the overall and buttoned up the cardigan to conceal her thickening waistline. Andrew waited for her to leave the house and followed her down the steps, opening the passenger door of the car for her.

As she expected he turned left at the bottom of Graig Avenue, went up over Penycoedcae and took the seaside road that ran through Beddau and Llantrisant.

'Are you going to Swansea or Porthcawl?' she asked when they reached a point half-way up Penycoedcae hill.

'You'll see in a moment,' he answered mysteriously, smiling at her.

She looked away from him, out of the window. 'When did you come back?' She didn't really want to know: it was simply talk to break the silence that had fallen between them.

'Late last night. I booked into the New Inn,' he added, not wanting her to think that he'd run back to his parents.

'And when are you leaving?'

'I'm not. I've given up my job in the Cross, the lease on the flat, and moved all the furniture back. It's being stored in my father's garage.'

'What are you going to do?'

'That—' he glanced across at her – 'depends entirely on you.'

She retreated into silence again, resenting the idea that she had to take responsibility for his life as well as her own. He turned left into a drive. To their right loomed a huge house that she had seen often from the road and admired. A veritable mansion, she had equated it with the big houses Jane Austen had written about in her books, but she had never been so close to it before.

Double bays swept up either side of the pillared front door, from the ground to the second floor. Above them was a neat row of small attic windows.

'What's this?'

'A house.'

'Whose house?'

He fished a key out of his blazer pocket. 'I can hardly expect you to live on the Common, and I'd rather not live on the Graig for reasons that have nothing to do with snobbery, but with your family's well-founded dislike of me. So I thought we'd compromise and settle on Penycoedcae. This place isn't so far up the hill that your family can't walk here a couple of times a week. And if you don't like the idea of trekking up and down to see them and Laura, you'll just have to learn to drive, won't you?'

'Drive. Me drive a car?'

'Why not? I've got enough money set aside to buy another one, and driving is nowhere near as difficult as nursing.' He climbed the steps to the front door and opened it. 'Please Bethan, just take a look inside. I've taken my old job back, in the Graig,' he said as she walked slowly towards him. 'Junior doctor, working under Trevor.'

'Andrew, I know you. You won't be happy with that for long.'

'What I do know is that I can't live without you. I've found out the hard way that my happiness depends on you. Please, Bethan, take me back. I know I've behaved like a fool, especially over Edmund. But after he was born I felt so guilty . . .'

'You felt guilty!'

'If I hadn't left you when you were pregnant, you wouldn't have had to carry on working, you wouldn't have fallen down the stairs in the Graig . . . you might not have had such a rough time when he was born. And even then I could have demanded a Caesarean but I didn't until it was too late . . . Bethan please, love. What's wrong? What have I said?' He reached out hesitantly and enveloped her in his arms as tears fell silently from her eyes.

'It was my fault Edmund was the way he was,' she sobbed. 'All my fault . . .'

'How can you say that? Bethan, it wasn't. Oh God I'm sorry. I made it so difficult for you. I'm sorry, darling. But it's not your fault, it's mine. Didn't you realise he was damaged by the birth? It was my fault, not yours. All my fault. I should have seen the problems coming. I'm sorry, darling. So very, very sorry. I know I don't deserve it, but won't you please give me one more chance?'

Through the tears and half-understood words a horrible suspicion formed in her mind. She wrenched herself out of his embrace. 'I suppose Trevor told you.'

'Told me what?'

'That's why you want me back, isn't it?' she continued, too angry to listen to him. 'Why you want to start all over again. Wipe the slate clean, pretend that Edmund didn't exist. Try to blot out one baby's life by having another. Well it won't work, Andrew . . .'

'You're pregnant!'

'You didn't know?' she whispered, seeing the truth in the stunned look in his eyes.

'How could you keep something like that from me, Beth?' He sat down suddenly on the doorstep.

'I left London, after . . . after that night. I didn't find out until I'd been in Pontypridd for a couple of months.'

'You could have written.'

'Why? To give you one more excuse to put Edmund away? To tell me that I couldn't look after him and the new baby?'

'I was there when Edmund died,' he reproached her.

'And you returned to London straight after the funeral.'

'Only because you shut me out. You never once said you wanted me to stay. You turned to your brother, your family . . .'

'Because they're always there when I need someone.'

'Oh God, what a mess. What a bloody awful mess.' He covered his eyes with his hands.

'You should have listened to your parents.' Her anger died as suddenly as it had flared. 'We were never really suited. It went wrong between us from the start. Perhaps my mother and Uncle Bull were right. Edmund was the way he was because of—'

'That's rubbish Beth, and you know it.'

He lowered his hands and continued to sit on the step

staring at the trees that shaded the rolling lawn he'd envisaged sitting out on in summer, eating picnic teas, playing tennis, croquet . . . He'd been so wrapped up in his ideas of starting again, of being alone with her, making up for all the pain and loss she'd suffered that it hadn't once crossed his mind that they could have other children. Even now he didn't want to consider the strain they would put on a relationship that was so fragile, so tenuous . . .

'It doesn't matter either way now. Not really,' she murmured. 'It simply won't work. There's nothing left, Andrew.'

'Bethan, I've changed,' he protested earnestly. 'I promise you this time I've really changed.'

'So have I.'

'Please, won't you at least come inside, look at the house. Please.'

'There's no point.'

'Then what? You're leaving me?'

'I left you months ago.'

He rose to his feet and wrapped his arms around her again. This time she didn't pull away. Simply leaned her head against his shoulder, breathing in the old familiar scents she would always associate with him. Kay's soap, Andrew's cologne, tobacco . . . Standing together in this peaceful garden in the sunshine she wanted to believe that they could begin again. But then she remembered Edmund, their estrangement, the gulf between them that no amount of talking would ever bridge.

'Andrew . . .'

His mouth was on hers, silencing her. She surrendered to the magic of his touch, the sensation of his lips. It was easier to allow herself to be swept along on the tide of his passion than to resist it. After all, it was something she'd done so many, many times before.

A cloud drifted across the face of the sun, the air grew cooler, the kiss ended and the spell that had held her shattered.

'It's hopeless, Andrew,' she protested as he finally released her.

'You want me, Bethan. If you didn't you wouldn't have kissed me like that. You . . .'

'I want you.' She looked up into his dark brown eyes, tawny and gold with reflected light. 'Oh I want you, but when the kissing stops the problems start, and we can't live out the rest of our lives in bed.'

'But I love you.'

'And I love you.' She looked away from him, unable to bear the pain and hurt reflected in his eyes. 'But sometimes love simply isn't enough.'

Chapter Twenty-Two

THE HOUSES WERE small, red and yellow brick set in a typical dockside terrace of two-up, two-downs with lean-to washhouses and outside ty bachs, but the minute Alma entered the street she sensed she'd moved into an alien world. Even the smell was different: spicy food, exotic perfume, strange drink and tobacco, and judging by the widest smile she had ever seen spread across Charlie's face, she knew that somehow the foreign atmosphere held a little of the essence of Russia.

More animated than even William had seen him before, Charlie wandered up and down the street, greeting people of all races and colours, introducing them to Negroes, Russians, Chinese and Norwegians, sampling food from the tables that the women had set up on the pavements, laughing and slapping men heartily across the back; the whole time speaking in a harsh guttural language that transformed the old familiar Charlie of Pontypridd into a gregarious native of this new and outlandish place.

'Feodor! Feodor Raschenko!' A burly man built like a bull, who towered above William by a head, gave Charlie a bear hug, swinging him high off his feet.

'Was that Charlie's ribs I heard cracking?' Diana asked as Charlie's blond head almost disappeared into the man's long black hair and beard.

'You old fool, where have you been hiding yourself?' The man kissed Charlie on both cheeks before setting him down on the pavement.

'I haven't been hiding anywhere,' Charlie protested. 'Your mother always knows where to find me. Come on you old rogue, meet some friends of mine.'

'Russian?' the man beamed at Diana and Alma as he strode over to where they were standing next to William and Eddie.

'Welsh,' Charlie corrected.

'That's an unusual nationality to find in Bute Street.' He extended a hand the size of a meat plate. 'Any friend of Feodor is a friend of mine,' he shouted, pumping William's hand up and down enthusiastically then turned to Eddie. He bowed elaborately before Diana and Alma and kissed their hands. 'Especially young ladies as beautiful as you. But then, Feodor, you always have had good taste in women.' He lifted an enormous shaggy eyebrow in Charlie's direction.

'And as they're my friends,' Charlie smiled pleasantly, 'I expect you to treat them like princesses.'

'Why wouldn't I?'

'Because you're drunk, Nicky.'

'And what else would I be on my name day? Come. Come?' he beckoned them through the front door of his house and into the kitchen where the table was groaning from the weight of punch bowls, bottles and an array of odd glasses. Charlie extracted two bottles of beer from the bag he'd brought, and handed them to the boys, depositing the remainder beneath the table.

'Punch for the ladies.' Nicky slopped out the fruit-covered contents of a punch bowl into two large glasses. 'And for the men, a man's drink, eh Feo,' he said, producing a flask of clear liquid. Swigging it directly from the bottle, he downed a third before handing it over to Charlie, who did the same. 'You want some in your beer?' he asked the boys.

'Go easy,' Charlie warned William and Eddie, somewhat incongruously considering the face he was making after swallowing Nicky's vodka. 'And especially you,' he whispered to Diana and Alma. 'I know what this man puts in his drink.'

'You know nothing, Feo,' Nicky shouted at the top of his voice. 'You never have. Come on, it is time for dancing,' he cried as the sound of music drifted in from the street.

'Feodor, you have come to see us.'

'Mama Davydova!' Feodor swept a fat old lady off her feet, and kissed her soundly on the mouth.

'I have a feeling this is going to prove an interesting party,' William muttered as he sipped sparingly from his beer bottle.

'And I have the feeling that I never knew Charlie at all,' Diana echoed in bewilderment as an assortment of women dragged him away from them, out into the street.

'Come, come, you dance.' Nicky put one arm the size of a tree trunk around Alma's shoulders, the other around Diana's, then, afraid after Charlie's warning that he might have offended them, he straightened up to his full height, removed his arms and offered them a hand each.

'Princesses,' he said with a twinkle in his eye.

Alma burst out laughing. 'Princesses it is.'

'I won't give up, Bethan. I want you to know that. I won't ever give up.' The sky had darkened to a rich, dark gold in the west. Over in the woods on their left a skylark was singing its last plaintive evensong.

'I can't argue with you any more, I can't even think straight.' Bethan was sitting with her back against an enormous chestnut tree whose branches spread over a quarter of the lawn. She was annoyed with herself for breaking down and crying when Andrew had offered to drive her home an hour ago. He had tried to comfort her, but his apologetic words and gentle caresses had only served to upset her all the more. She had been unable to regain control of her emotions, crying bitter, salt tears that had left her throat burning, her eyes heavy and an after-taste of exhaustion that made her feel weak and totally unable to cope, either with Andrew's constant pleading, or with the thought of going home to face Evan and Phyllis's caring concern. 'I only know that I can't risk my own, or your, happiness again. It hurts too much when it all goes wrong.'

'And the baby?' he pressed, attempting to come to terms with the idea of becoming a father for the second time.

'I'll look after him,' she said trying not to think of Edmund, and how she had failed him.

'And me?'

'You can see him. You can . . .'

'Say hello to both of you when I pass you in the street? Think about what you're doing, Bethan. We could be a family . . .' he wanted but couldn't bring himself to say 'again'. He moved closer, sitting opposite her on the stone steps of a wooden summerhouse that had fallen into dereliction.

'A family!' She had a sudden very real image of herself and Andrew sitting out on cane chairs in this garden with babies playing on a rug at their feet. Then she thought of her life in Graig Avenue, surrounded by people yet always alone, because she missed the close, loving relationship that she and Andrew had once shared – and could share again until – until when? Until something else went wrong? She rose abruptly, dusting off the skirt of her dress with her hands.

'Look, as we're here and I have the key—' he played for time, wanting to keep her with him and prepared to go to almost any lengths to do so – 'won't you at least look around the house with me? It may save me making another trip.'

'Andrew, I'm not going to change my mind about living with you because of a house.'

'I know that.' He smiled at her, the old boyish smile that had once made her heart turn somersaults. 'But I have to live somewhere, and I rather like the look of this place.'

She reluctantly followed as he led the way through a tiled porch that was about the same size as the room Charlie lived in. The hall would have swallowed the back kitchen in Graig Avenue three times over and still had room to spare. Doors opened from it on to vast imposing room, after room . . . so many rooms.

'You're thinking of living here by yourself?' she asked in stunned amazement, taken aback by the sheer size of the place.

'I need a house.'

'But Andrew, this is ridiculous.'

'I'll grant you it needs some money spent on it, and it has to be decorated, but when it's finished it could be quite lovely.'

'It's too big for any sense.'

'That's only because it has no furniture in it at the moment.' He consulted the estate agent's sheet. 'Look at this.' He opened a door on to a huge kitchen that ran the full width of the back of the house.

'More doors?'

'Butler's pantry, ordinary pantry, dairy . . . stores . . .'

'A butler's pantry?'

'It would make a marvellous storage cupboard.'

'For what? I don't know of any housewife who makes enough jam to fill those shelves.' She left him and walked back into the hall where she sat on the bottom step of the magnificent sweeping staircase.

'I know it doesn't look too good now, but believe me it's solid, all it needs is decorating.'

'It's so isolated.'

'That's one of its attractions.' He sat beside her, careful to leave a few inches of space between them. 'I had hoped we could get to know one another again without too many distractions.'

'Junior doctors are always on call in Pontypridd. It's not like London.'

'We'll have a live-in maid so you won't be alone when I have to go out.' He sensed a yielding, but was wary of pushing too hard, too fast.

'How many bedrooms are there?'

'Four main ones, and eight smaller ones.'

'And you want one live-in maid?'

'We'll get as much help as we need.'

'On a junior doctor's salary?'

367

'I have money set aside.'

'You won't have it for long if you take this place on.'

'Bethan . . .'

'No.' She left the hall and walked outside into the garden.

'Bethan, I know I've behaved badly. I know I don't deserve another chance, but I love you. I need you. The flat, London, it was all so empty without you. I'm sorry I made such a lousy father. I'm sorry I didn't understand about Edmund. Please . . .'

'If we were going to live together again, I would want a say in where we live and how it's furnished, and that,' she pointed to the huge house behind them, 'isn't it.'

'Then you'll look at something else with me?'

She hesitated, caught in a trap of his making. 'I didn't intend to say that.'

'You still love me.'

'I loved Edmund as much.'

'I know.'

'Andrew, we could go on this way for ever, fighting all the time, hurting one another . . .'

'I promise I'll never, never hurt you again.'

'No one can make a promise like that.' She smiled despite the pain gnawing inside her. Two steps and she could be at his side. In his arms. It was that easy. Two steps . . .

'All we need is a beginning, something to build on. Beth, can you honestly say that you haven't woken up lonely in the night?'

'I've been lonely,' she admitted.

'Then give me one more chance.'

She looked up at him, her dark eyes frightened, enormous in her pale face. 'You don't know what you're asking, or what you'll be getting. I feel . . . I feel cold, Andrew. Cold and dead.'

'I want you however you are.'

'I won't be easy to live with.'

'I don't want easy, just you,' he persisted urgently, hope rising within him.

'I want a smaller house than this one.'

'You can have whatever house you like. I'll even live on the Graig if it will make you happy.'

'That would be too great a sacrifice to ask for.' He detected the glimmer of a smile. 'And if you were hoping that by offering me the Graig I'd reciprocate by agreeing to live on the Common, you're mistaken.'

'There's some nice houses in Graigwen.'

'So they say.'

'Bethan, can we try again?'

'I'll never forget Edmund.'

'I wouldn't want you to.'

'And if this one isn't perfect?'

'You'll have to teach me to love him. I don't seem to be very good at it.'

Two steps. She clung to him, her hands around his neck. 'I'm sorry, Beth,' he murmured, brushing the top of her head with his chin.

'Both of us are going to have to get into the habit of talking, of trying harder.'

'I know. Here, I have something for you.' He pulled a jeweller's box out of his pocket and opened it.

'My locket! You redeemed it.'

'I wanted to give it back to you months ago, but there never seemed to be a right time until now. Here,' he fastened it around her neck.

'What do you think of old furniture?' she asked, fingering the locket as they walked towards his car.

'What kind of old furniture?' he enquired suspiciously, wondering if she was testing him.

'Late Victorian.'

'You know I hate it.'

'I like it,' she said determinedly, thinking of Rhiannon Pugh's furniture stored in Mavis's house. She had always liked it, and if she could persuade Andrew to buy it for her, Phyllis would have some money of her own for once. 'Tell you what. How about we compromise? You can have a modern dining room and I'll have an old-fashioned parlour.'

'Fine, as long as you share your parlour with the children's toys, and we have a modern sitting room for company. There's room for both in this house, and it's going cheap too.'

'No.'

'I'll let you furnish the kitchen and bedrooms as well.'

'I'll hold you to that.'

'Does that mean you'll reconsider the house?'

'I've reconsidered enough for one day.'

'Do you want to drive around Pontypridd and look at more houses, or do you want to come back to the New Inn and have dinner with me?' He halted in front of the car and pulled her gently towards him.

'You want to show me your room?'

'It's a nice one.'

'I'm sure it is.'

As he opened the car door, he bent to kiss her. They had a long way to go, but they'd made a beginning. And he was determined that in this beginning would be the right end, for both of them.

Mama Davydova was playing an instrument that Charlie, during one of his more lucid moments had gravely informed Alma was a balalaika. The soft, haunting melody filled the street with a romantic atmosphere eminently suited to the twilight and the shadowy silhouettes of the women as they moved swiftly and silently, clearing the tables of empty plates and replacing them with full ones.

Nicky was slumped in an easy chair he'd carried outside his front door, his head resting low on his chest, his long hair falling across his face, concealing his eyes. Alma was sure he was asleep, but when the playing stopped he was the first on his feet, clapping and cheering, making more noise than half a dozen ordinary mortals. A guitar strummed somewhere behind them, another picked up the tune, and another, until a rousing Cossack dance-beat echoed through the air. Nicky looked round, saw Charlie and slapped his arm across Charlie's shoulders. Both men shed their jackets and began to dance, side by side, twisting and turning on their heels, their slow movements gradually, almost imperceptibly, growing faster and faster with the throb of the music until they whirled like dervishes, jumping higher into the air than Alma would have thought possible, to the accompaniment of resounding whoops from the crowd.

'Is that a Cossack dance?' Alma asked Mama Davydova, who'd taken Nicky's chair.

'Yes. We are all Cossacks,' she smiled. 'Nicky especially. Even here he behaves like a Cossack,' she replied a little sadly.

'And Charlie?' William asked. He'd always been curious about Charlie. After three years of living with the man, once in the same room, he knew virtually nothing about him other than that he was Russian.

'Charlie?' Mama Davydova looked puzzled.

'Feodor,' Alma, who'd made a note of the name Nicky had called him, corrected.

'No, he was a . . . how do you say it . . . he worked the land.'

'A farmer?' Alma hazarded.

'His father and grandfather were *boyars* – landowners. Their kind didn't fare too well after the Revolution.'

'Is that why he came to Wales?' Alma asked shyly.

'No.' The old woman realised that she'd said more than she'd intended. 'No that isn't why he came. You want some *blinys*? Pancakes,' she explained in answer to Alma's puzzled look. 'Come, get them with me.'

Alma followed her into the kitchen, and helped lay the ready-cooked pancakes on plates covered with hand-crocheted lace clothes.

'You love Feodor,' Mama Davydova informed her gravely.

'No.' Alma reddened in embarrassment. 'I work for him.'

'No, you love him,' the old woman repeated. 'I have seen the way you look at him, and the way he looks at you. He loves you. But it will be very difficult for him to admit that he can love again. And that will be very hard, for both of you,' she finished enigmatically, as she picked up a plate and walked down the passage.

The dance had finished and Charlie, his unbuttoned waistcoat hanging loose over his shirt, was standing with Nicky sharing the inevitable vodka bottle.

'*Blinys*, you're an angel Mama.' He planted a vodka-flavoured kiss on the old woman's cheek as he helped himself from her plate.

'You need food, otherwise you will get as drunk as my Nicky.' She pinched his cheek before sinking into the chair that stood outside the front door. 'Come you,' the old woman called to Alma, 'come and sit next to me. I will tell your fortune.'

'And mine?' Diana asked, walking over with Alma.

'It is only the truly young who want their fortune told,' the old woman said to Charlie.

'Those who have lived through more than they bargained for already know their fate,' he replied in Russian. He looked away from the girls towards the end of the street. Alma followed his line of vision. Just beyond a group of Russians, Negroes, and a stolid German shepherding his family of solemn-faced young men and pigtailed daughters, she saw a crowd of sailors.

'Russian ship's come in.' Nicky exchanged a look with Charlie and both of them moved swiftly towards the sailors, pushing their way through a noisy, dancing crowd that had gathered around a Negro jazz band.

'I had no idea Charlie knew so many people.' William looked on amazed as his red-faced boss was greeted by the sailors.

'When they speak it sounds as though they're all choking on their tongues,' Eddie commented.

'You have hard decisions facing you,' Mama Davydova said as she gripped Alma's palm tightly. 'You have the chance of happiness, but it will only come once, and like all good things it will not last. Recognise your destiny when it comes, take it and make the most of it while you can, my child.'

Alma scarcely followed what the old woman was saying. Her attention was still fixed on Charlie. Even across the length of the street she could see that he had become grave, serious, as though he had heard bad news.

'Now mine,' Diana pleaded, laughing at a joke of Eddie's as she gave the old woman her palm.

Alma left them and walked past a woman who was passing around plates of little meat and fish pies.

'Dance!'

'Come on Nicky, Feo!'

The sailors took up the cry. Someone handed Alma a cup of stew, so hot and spicy it burnt the roof of her mouth. The Negroes blasted on their brass instruments, the music grew deafening, the atmosphere more and more raucous. She gazed at Charlie, unable to reach him, only watch as he moved in a world she could never hope to understand, let alone enter. Why had it taken Mama Davydova to tell her what she should have known? Charlie loved her. Why else would he have helped her when she had most needed it? Lending her money, offering her a job, a place to live, saving her from Bobby. And she loved him. But it had taken a party that emphasised their very different worlds to make her realise just how much.

'Alma?'

The music had finished and Charlie was swaying alarmingly on his feet before her. As he staggered she caught him.

'Take him into the house,' Nicky suggested, as she almost collapsed beneath Charlie's weight. 'Splash his head with cold water.'

'I warned you, Nicky. Feodor isn't used to vodka, not the way you drink it, not any more.'

'He'll be all right Mama. You always fuss.' Nicky flipped the cork from a bottle of vodka that one of the

373

sailors had handed him and drank deeply. 'Here.' Putting his shoulder beneath Charlie's he helped Alma to half carry, half drag him into the house. 'In the front room,' he said, his voice slurring thickly. 'There on the bed.'

'You'll stay with him?' the old woman asked Alma as she walked in behind them.

'I will.' There was a flannel next to a huge ewer of cold water on the washstand. Alma wrung it out and laid it on Charlie's forehead.

'You won't be disturbed.' The door closed, and Alma sat beside Charlie who was struggling to sit up.

'Do you want water?' She poured some from a jug into a glass on the stand.

'No!' Charlie lashed out and knocked the glass from her hand. It shattered against the wall, water spraying into both their faces. She picked up the jagged pieces and heaped them in the corner. When she turned to face him again she saw pure anguish in his face.

'Charlie!' She knelt on the floor before him. 'What's the matter?' He put his hands either side of her face and ran his fingers slowly down her cheeks. She placed her hands over his and he helped her to her feet. Then he rose. Lifting her off her feet, he turned and laid her on the bed.

He was beside her, kissing her, his hands stroking her breasts beneath the flimsy fabric of her dress. He muttered a few Russian words, and she found herself hoping against hope that it wasn't another woman's name. His lip brushed lightly over her earlobes, her throat, her mouth. His weight pressed her down into the mattress as he lifted his arms and pulled off his waistcoat. His shirt was next, wrenched over his head. Then his vest.

'Alma.' This time he whispered her name clearly as he ran his fingers through her curls. 'Alma . . .'

A passion she had thought she would never experience again stirred within her. Her skin flamed where Charlie touched her. A need, a hunger, all-enveloping, all-consuming burned within her. She only knew that she

374

wanted him, here and now, as she had never wanted anything in her life before.

She had no recollection of removing her clothes, only an acute awareness of his naked body as it stretched out alongside hers. His bare thighs moved tantalisingly over her legs, his hands fondled her breasts, teasing, stroking the sensitive skin of her nipples. His tongue was in her mouth. She could taste the cool, clean flavour of vodka on his breath, as he caressed and aroused her to the point where pain and ecstasy seemed to be one and the same, before finally piercing her body with his own.

She cried out, and he thrust into her again, and again, mercilessly driving harder and harder, evoking shameless, intuitive responses. All inhibition fell away as she allowed herself to be transported into a world of sensuality where nothing mattered except the satisfaction of the urgent cravings he had kindled within her. She clawed the smooth skin on his back, trying to pin him closer to her, so close that their bodies would merge.

Lost in passion, neither Alma nor Charlie heard the door opening nor saw the look on William's face as he hastily closed it.

'I think Charlie's a little the worse for wear,' he said to Eddie and Diana. 'If we're going to take that last bus we should make a move.'

'But what about Alma?' Diana protested. 'We can't just leave her here.'

'Alma wants to stay with Charlie.'

'But her mother will worry—'

'We will get them home,' the old woman reassured Diana as she shooed them out of her passage. 'Feodor and his young lady are safe with us. My Nicky will see to it that they get home before morning.'

'His young lady?' Diana looked blankly at William. 'I didn't know Alma was Charlie's young lady?'

'She is now,' William murmured darkly.

Chapter Twenty-Three

'I'M PREGNANT, WILL.'

Vera had waited until after they'd made love to tell him. She was sitting on the floor of the shed behind the shop, stark naked except for a thick gold chain around her neck and a pair of gypsy hoop earrings. The earrings had cost William every penny of his savings, but the wild, ecstatic thank-you he had received had more than justified the expense.

'Are you sure?' His heart began to pound erratically against his ribs. This was one eventuality that hadn't crossed his mind.

'It's not George's.' She turned a miserable face to his. She hated the idea of bearing a child. For her it loomed as a watershed, the dividing line between youth and old age. She'd soon be fat and old like her mother. Vera's mother had been pregnant at sixteen and had a dozen by the time she was thirty. Vera knew all about morning sickness, varicose veins, stretch marks; bloated, swollen, heavily veined breasts, and smelly whining babies who demanded constant feeding and nappy changes.

'I know it's not George's.' William pulled on his trousers and reached for his cigarettes.

'How . . .'

'You told me when we first met that you never do it with him, not properly anyway.'

'I did?'

'Don't you remember?'

'Yes,' she lied quickly, resolving to keep a tighter rein on her mouth in future. 'What am I going to do, Will?' She rose to her feet and clung to him, genuinely frightened.

'We could go away,' he suggested in desperation.

'Where?'

'I don't know.' He drew impatiently on his cigarette. 'I'll have to think about it.'

'I know what would be easiest, Will.' Her eyes reminded him of a cornered cat's.

'What?'

'If we got rid of it. There must be ways . . .'

'If there are I don't know of any.'

'I've heard women say all you need is money. There's this man and all he wants is twenty pounds . . .'

'Twenty pounds! I can't get hold of that kind of money, Vera.'

'Oh Will!' She began to sob.

'Ssh, you don't want anyone to hear you, do you?'

'No.' She took the handkerchief he handed her and dried her tears.

'You ought to dress.' He bundled her clothes together and pushed them towards her. Her nakedness suddenly disturbed him, for a new and entirely different reason. Normally at this stage of the afternoon she would have dragged him down on top of her for second helpings, but her news had sapped all his desire. He stared at her flat stomach, imagining a baby growing in its depths – a smaller version of himself. He was beset by the oddest feeling: a peculiar mixture of tenderness and protectiveness. He didn't love Vera, at least not like he loved Tina, but she was carrying his child and that entitled her to some consideration. And then again, she was good in bed – very good. He could live with a wife who doled out what Vera did, every night of his life.

'We'll have to go away together,' he said finally. 'There's no other way out. I'll try and get hold of some money.'

'Where?'

'I don't know yet. I have to think. I don't suppose you have any ideas?'

'No.'

'Wherever we go it's bound to be hard at first, at least until I get a job, but we'll make it. Rent a room somewhere . . .'

'Oh Will,' she ran her fingers inside the waistband of his trousers and kissed him on the mouth. 'You are good to me. How soon can we go?'

'Just as soon as I can arrange it.'

'We could go to London. See all the sights. I've always wanted to, and George would never think of looking for us there.'

'My cousin Bethan says that things there are just as bad as down here. There's thousands out of work. People are even sleeping in the streets . . .'

'We wouldn't end up there, would we?' There was genuine alarm in her voice.

'Not if I can help it,' he said grimly. 'Don't worry. I'll find something. Now you'd better go, before Charlie starts looking for me.'

'All right, Will.' She clipped on her suspender belt and rolled on a stocking. Usually he liked to watch her dress. It was always suspender belt and stockings first, followed by wispy bits of lace that revealed more than they concealed. She never wore knickers, and dressed only in her underclothes as she was, to all intents and purposes, as good as naked. Then she'd slip a dress on top and look neat and demure. Every time William caught sight of her walking around the market his senses were inflamed by the thought of how she'd look if she suddenly lost her dress.

'Vera?'

'Yes, Will?' She smiled at him over her shoulder as she began rolling the second stocking on to her leg.

'You won't sleep with George any more, will you? This is my baby and if we're going away together soon . . .'

'Will, he's my husband. I live with him.'

'Couldn't you move in with your mother for a while?'

Vera thought of her mother's cramped house. She wouldn't have a bed to herself, or wardrobe space for her clothes. And she'd have to go back to eating bread and dripping instead of the best cuts of meat and cream cakes she bought with George's money. 'I can't go home Will,' she protested.

'Why?'

'Just think about it, sweetheart.' She turned to face him, her breasts and thighs still bare. 'If I moved out of George's house into my mother's he'd realise something was wrong.'

'You've been unhappy with him for a long time. Tell him you've had enough of his perverted ways.'

'Don't you see, he might suspect us if I moved out. He'd come after me and then heaven only knows what he'd do.'

'But I can't let you carry on living with him. Look if I get some money together you could go up to Ynysybwl . . .'

'Ynysybwl?' She stared at him in stunned amazement. Ynysybwl was a small, quiet village. Even more of a backwater than Pontypridd, and only a few miles up the road.

'Mate of mine lives there. If I explain to his missus he'd put you up until I arrange something. You could share a room with his kids.'

'No, Will,' she said firmly.

'I can't bear the thought of you and him . . .'

'Then I'll move into the spare room.'

'Promise?'

'I promise,' she murmured, suddenly realising just how much she'd lose if she left George. The trips to Cardiff, the clothes. The van at her disposal – and the car as soon as he got round to buying it . . .

'Vera?'

'You're right, Will. I must go.' She tweaked a clump of black curling hair on his chest.

'And George?'

'How many times do I have to tell you that I never do the things I do with you, with George.'

'You sleep in the same bed with him, that's enough.'

'For what he does he may as well be my sister.'

'He looks at you.'

'He's my husband.'

'Not for much longer.'

'Will, don't tell me you're going to get jealous like him?'

'When you're living with me,' he patted her naked buttocks, 'you bet, Vera.' He looked away quickly, as a sick feeling rose in his stomach and an image of Tina flooded into his mind.

Alma dropped the heavy tray on to the table. Thursday afternoon baking sessions had become a real chore. Charlie was already looking around for someone to help out part time with the cooking, or so he'd made a point of telling William within her earshot. He'd avoided speaking to her directly since that Sunday in Cardiff. Nicky had asked one of his friends, a taxi driver, to take them home to Pontypridd, and they had reached the shop at four in the morning. Just in time to start the baking. They had set to work, and at the end of the day he had apologised to her for his behaviour, hurrying out before she had a chance to reply. Since then he'd kept communication between them to a bare minimum, and she noticed that he went to great lengths to avoid being left alone with her, even for a moment.

She wondered just how much – if anything – he remembered of that night. She thought of it often, without any feeling of shame or embarrassment, simply a sense of loss that she would never again experience the wonder of that passionate abandon with Charlie again. The old Russian woman had been right: happiness *was* fragile, and tenuous. Every time she reached out to grasp it, it crumbled to dust in her hands.

Alma went back to the oven to bring out the second tray. Superficially her life was running smoothly for the first time since her father's death. She'd managed to put the traumatic events of last Christmas behind her. Charlie had been right: as time went on and there was no sign of her producing the bastard that half the town's population had expected, people had not only stopped talking about her but had started to give her sympathetic looks. Most went out of their way to be pleasant when they called into the shop, and even her mother had finally settled into the flat, arranging things so she could find her way around, sending for one of Betty Lane's children every day after school so she could walk in the park. Laura had been paid back, so the only money they owed was to Charlie, and although they had money enough – just – to pay him back he wouldn't take it. So she had left their small nest egg in the Post Office savings bank, and looked on the extra two shillings a week she would get in nine months' time almost as a pay rise. Both she and her mother had a warm place to live in, enough to eat, and an indoor bathroom. Outwardly life was good, so good, that occasionally she had nightmares that it was all a dream and she'd wake up back in Morgan Street, her security, her calm quiet days, her restored reputation, all taken from her.

'Hello Alma. Sorry to trouble you. Is your Mam in?'

'Upstairs.' She smiled at the minister who'd baptised Betty Lane's children. Primed by Betty's stories of Lena and Alma's misfortunes he'd welcomed both of them into his flock with open arms. 'You wouldn't like to take a couple of pasties up with you?' she asked.

'Not this time, not unless your mam wants them.' He returned her smile rather sheepishly. He was young, and unmarried, and he called in on Mrs Moore far more often than he needed to. But with a warm welcome and food guaranteed every time, it was hard to pass by. 'I've come to take your mam to the Mothers' Union lunch. The ladies have been hard at it all morning in the parish hall.'

'That is kind of you. She looks forward to chapel events.'

'We enjoy having her. I'll bring her back this afternoon, safe and sound.'

'I know you will.'

'Whisking Mrs Moore off again to the high life, Mr Jones?' William walked in with a ham on each shoulder.

'Something like that.' Will's joking always made the minister feel a little uneasy. 'Well I must be off.'

Charlie followed in behind William with a side of beef and a leg of pork.

'Thank you for your donation to the fund for the poor, Charlie,' the minister called out loudly. 'Due to the generosity of the town's traders everyone on our books will have an Easter dinner.'

'If you preach to your parishioners to shop here, trade will go up and I'll be able to donate more at Christmas,' Charlie replied drily.

'I don't think advertisements would go down very well from the pulpit, Charlie, but I'll see what I can do. Goodbye everybody.' He backed out of the door.

'Doesn't that man understand a joke?' Eddie asked as he came in with a tray full of pigs' heads and trotters.

'His heart's in the right place,' Alma said, grateful because he'd steered her mother out of the depression that had marred their early days in the flat. 'Do you want this beef spiced, pressed or roast, Charlie?'

'Roast, but as soon as the shop's closed we'll take a break, and start cooking early this afternoon.'

She nodded, served the last customer and clanged the door shut, locking it firmly and leaving the keys in the lock. William walked in through the Penuel Lane entrance with a dozen and a half baps that he'd bought from the baker.

'Make mine ham, Alma,' he called as he dumped the rolls on the shop counter.

'Eddie? Charlie?' she asked as she began cutting the bread rolls open.

'Pork,' Eddie called back.

'Beef,' Charlie replied quietly.

A picnic–style lunch had become a ritual every Thursday, the one day when all four of them could eat together. Not that William joined them often; he usually took his rolls outside to eat in the park. With Tina, Charlie presumed. Alma knew better. She lifted down three of the smallest serving plates and set out the rolls: five each for William, Eddie and Charlie, two for herself. The kettle was already boiling for tea.

'See you in half an hour, Charlie,' William murmured as he grabbed his plate of rolls. 'Mind if I listen to your radio upstairs, Alma?'

Charlie had bought two radios to pacify Frank Clayton next door. He'd put one in the back kitchen in Graig Avenue, and the other in Alma's living room, using the excuse that it would be a distraction in the shop, and Alma's mother could come down and tell them if anything important was on. It was the first time William had asked if he could use the flat. Alma suspected he wouldn't have asked at all if her mother had been in, which meant that Vera Collins would be coming through the door.

'Don't go moving anything up there, Will,' she warned sternly, 'or my mother will be falling over when she gets back.'

'I'll sit on the floor in front of the set and won't move.'

'There are chairs up there.'

He left just as Charlie and Eddie came in to wash their hands in the back.

'Want company, Will?' Eddie shouted after him.

'No thanks. I know you're bored rigid by cricket, and I want to listen to the scores, not you gabbling.'

'Since when has Will taken to listening to cricket?' Eddie asked innocently. Alma shrugged her shoulders. She heard the front door that led to the upstairs flat open and close quietly. She knew Vera only by sight, but her middle-aged husband, coupled with her flashy dress sense and thick layers of make-up, was enough to make Alma suspicious of Vera's motives for carrying on with William. And she couldn't help feeling sorry for Will; he bore all the hallmarks of a man besotted. Just like her, she thought resentfully as she sat across the table from Charlie to eat her own rolls.

They'd barely had time to take their first bite when there was an almighty hammering on the side door. George Collins's voice thundered through the letterbox.

'I know you're in there, you little slut! Open up or I'll smash the door down.'

'Quick!' Alma grabbed Charlie's hand.

'What—' he reluctantly abandoned his roll.

'Quick, don't argue!' she whispered urgently. 'Eddie, give us a couple of minutes then open the door.' She raced up the stairs pulling a bewildered Charlie in her wake. Throwing open the living-room door they saw Vera clutching her dress to her naked body, and William hopping about ineffectually trying to extract one of the two legs he'd thrust into a single trouser leg.

'Both of you, shut yourselves in the bathroom. Quick!' she commanded. 'And don't forget to lock the door. Vera, leave your coat and hat, I'll need them.'

William needed no second bidding. He grabbed his clothes, pulled Vera's wrist and dragged her behind him. Alma tossed Vera's hat and coat on to the chair. The door burst open downstairs just as she threw her arms around Charlie's neck. She kissed him soundly on the lips, expecting a hard dry response after the strained silence that had fallen between them since the weekend, but to her amazement he pressed her close, kissing her back. Locked together in one another's arms in the centre of the room they were barely conscious of the thunder of boots thumping up the stairs, accompanied by Eddie's shouted protests.

'There she is! Damned slut!' George grabbed Alma's shoulder and tore her away from Charlie, who retaliated by hitting him soundly on the jaw. George reeled backwards, looking in amazement from the coat on the settee to Alma's red hair, and to Charlie and back.

'It was her, Mr Collins. I swear it. I saw her come in here,' a small weasel-faced man protested as he hid behind Eddie's broad shoulders.

'What's going on here?' Charlie demanded sternly.

'My wife. She came in here.'

'The shop's closed.'

'I know, but she's . . . she . . . she's carrying on with that good-looking boy who works for you.'

'She isn't, Mr Collins,' Eddie protested, the picture of absolute innocence, as he realised what Alma had done.

'Not you . . . the other one, what's his name?'

'If you mean William, he's out on the meat van delivering to my boss's shops in Cardiff. Has this man done any damage, Eddie?'

'I think the lock's broken on the door downstairs, sir,' Eddie invented a humble subservience in honour of the occasion.

'I'll see it's fixed, I'll . . .' George's eyes lit up as he spotted the hat and coat on the settee. 'This is my wife's coat,' he crowed triumphantly.

'It's mine,' Alma snatched it.

'A likely story. Where did you buy it?'

'In Cardiff, in Howell's, not that it's any of your business,' she said haughtily, carrying it over to the window-seat.

'Didn't know shop-girls could afford to go to Howell's,' he commented snidely.

'I bought it for her,' Charlie said belligerently. 'Now if you don't mind, you'd better apologise and leave, before I call the police.'

'I'm sorry, the lock—'

'I'll fix the lock and send you the bill. Eddie, see them out.'

Charlie and Alma sat side by side on the settee, listening as George Collins and the detective he'd hired went down the stairs. Eddie closed the door behind them and crept back up.

'They walked off in the direction of the Fairfield.'

'Go downstairs, stay in the shop and keep an eye

open in case they come back. You've bolted both doors?'

Eddie nodded.

'Alma and her mother will just have to use the shop door until I get a chance to fix the other one. Go on boy, take a look outside, then finish your rolls.'

A very sheepish William crept out of the bathroom in response to Charlie's call. Charlie said nothing, simply sat and stared at him.

'Charlie . . .' William began hesitantly.

'Just get the young lady out of here while you still have a head on your shoulders, and you'd better get Eddie to help you, in case they're still lurking around.'

'I'll go up the lane to the library, Mr Raschenko,' Vera waved at him shyly from the landing. 'George will never think of looking for me there.'

'If I were you I'd think of sticking to the library from now on.'

Alma handed her the hat and coat. 'You'll need these.'

'It's not what you think,' William explained, red-faced. 'Vera and I are going away together . . .'

'We are not, William Powell,' she countered indignantly.

'Yes we are.' He turned to her. 'The baby—'

'Is my husband's,' she said quickly. 'Look William it was nice while it lasted, but I'm married to George.'

'You said you loved me.'

'I never did.'

'Seems to me that young lady wants to eat her cake, have it and own the baker's,' Alma said as William followed her downstairs.

'I'd better take you to Howell's some time and buy you a hat and coat,' Charlie said as the connecting door to the shop slammed shut.

'I didn't like the cloth or the style.'

'How long has that been going on?'

'I noticed it as soon as the shop opened. Probably it started some time before.'

He sat forward and rested his head in his hands. It would be so easy to reach out and touch her face as he'd done in Cardiff . . . He stretched out his hands. She looked down at his fingers, heavily scared by thick, white, heat-puckered skin.

'Alma I . . .' he left the seat and paced uneasily towards the window. 'I'm sorry,' he looked down into the street away from her.

'It seems it's my lot in life to fall in love with men who don't love me,' she said sadly. 'First Ronnie, now you.'

'Alma?' he looked round. She'd already gone. He stared out of the window until he saw Vera teetering on high heels along the pavement on the other side of the road. Then he turned and followed Alma slowly down the stairs.

'You should see the house. I never thought a daughter of mine would be living in a place like that. Phyllis was a bit upset of course, seeing all Rhiannon's bits and pieces again, but it's not as if we have anywhere for them, and our Bethan has really done them proud. Putting them in pride of place. It's so big, and it has so much land besides the garden. Two huge fields, heaven only knows what they're going to do with them. And although both of them seem a bit quiet, Andrew as well as Bethan, I think it might work out this time.'

'I hope so,' Charlie muttered mechanically.

Evan picked up his and Charlie's glasses from the table in the back room of the Graig Hotel. 'Same again?'

'Yes, thanks.' It was Charlie's round, and the fact that Evan was buying the drinks spoke volumes about Charlie's state of mind.

'All right, mate, I've said nothing up until now. But I can't stand it any more. What's up with you?'

Charlie took his fresh pint and sipped it. 'Nothing.'

'For once in my life things are working out the way I want them to. Bethan and Andrew are back together. I'm happy as a pig in muck living in sin with Phyllis and the boy. William's had his wild streak curbed for a while, but you're walking around as though the end of the world is in sight. What is it?'

Charlie looked around the rom. Fortunately they were the only ones in it.

'It's that pretty redhead you've got working for you in the shop, isn't it?'

Charlie looked at him, but didn't answer.

'Well it makes sense, doesn't it?' Evan continued. 'You make a stand against the gossips, you take her in, decorate a flat for her, give her a job, pay her debts . . . No one keeps any secrets in this town,' Evan said, in reply to the look of surprise on Charlie's face. 'You love her, don't you?'

'I'm in no position to love anyone.'

'You're a man, aren't you?'

Charlie pushed his pint glass away from him. 'Not much of one.'

'My advice, whatever it's worth, is to go and see her. Tell her what's worrying you, it can't be that bad. You only have one short life. No one knows how short. Perhaps it was the spell in prison that gave me the courage to live the way I want to – where are you going?'

'I'm taking your advice.'

'You're going to see her now? At this hour?'

'Yes.'

'Well I hope you sort it out,' Evan said. He left his chair.

'You leaving early too?'

'I've got a lot to go home to these days,' Evan smiled. 'There's nothing like a cosy kitchen, the love of a good woman and a warm bed. Why don't you try it, Charlie? Believe you me, it's everything it's cracked up to be.'

Evenings were lonely for Alma. Her mother, loath to break the habit of half a lifetime, when the cold and hunger of Morgan Street had driven her early to bed, still retired to her room before eight every evening, leaving Alma to her own devices. Alma had taken to spending most of her free time sitting alone in the living room above the shop, looking out of the window at the deserted street and listening to the radio.

The room was far more comfortable than the back kitchen of Morgan Street had ever been, even during her father's day. Light, airy, it was neatly, and thanks to some of the things Charlie had bought from Phyllis, better furnished than it would have been if they'd had to rely on their own poor sticks.

Earlier in the evening she had gone for a solitary walk in the park, where the sight of the courting couples had depressed her even more. A library book was lying open on her lap, but even that irritated her. She didn't want to read about Lucy Manet's happiness with her husband in *A Tale of Two Cities*. Besides, the book conjured up images of the film, and now she had the time and money enough to go to the cinema she resented having to sit there listening to the muffled giggles of the couples in the back row.

The whole world seemed to be pairing off, with the sole exception of her. She heard a key turn in the lock of the shop door below her. Craning her neck, she saw the crown of Charlie's blond head disappearing inside. He must have forgotten something. She glanced up at the chiming clock he had hung on the wall for her mother. Ten-thirty: she had to be up again in a few hours. She should have gone to bed hours ago instead of listening to the concert of Noel Coward songs. As she left her seat she heard Charlie's footsteps on the landing outside the room.

'Charlie, have you forgotten something?' she asked as she opened the door.

'No. I saw you sitting at the window, so I thought I'd call in.'

'Would you like a cup of tea, or cocoa?' she enquired remembering her manners.

'No.' He twisted the brim of his hat in his hand. 'I just want to talk to you.'

'About the shop?'

'No, about what you said today.'

'I spoke out of turn. I'm sorry, it was just the excitement of seeing George Collins come charging after William.'

'You weren't talking out of turn. Not after what happened in Cardiff.'

'I wondered if you remembered.'

'I was drunk, but not that drunk.' He thrust his hands into his trouser pockets as though he couldn't trust himself to keep them off her.

'I know you don't love me. Do you want me to leave here, not work for you any more? Is that it?' she sat down abruptly, hoping with all her heart that he wouldn't give her notice. She was afraid of losing her job, but not as afraid of losing all contact with him. Of walking out of the shop and never, ever seeing him again.

'It's nothing to do with work,' he said impatiently. He went to the window and looked down at the fountain. 'I like you very much Alma, you must realise that.'

'Like,' she echoed dismally.

'If it were possible, I'd say love. I wish I could marry you – but I already have a wife.'

The silence in the room was deafening. Alma felt as if the air was whirling around her, closing in, crushing.

He turned to face her. Leaning against the wall, he crossed his arms. 'I'm here because I want to explain, but now I'm not sure where to start. In the beginning, when I first saw you, I tried to tell myself that I felt sorry for you. That I wanted to help you because you reminded me so much of Masha . . .'

'Your wife?' She asked him in a small voice.

'Yes.' He resumed his study of the fountain. 'She looked a lot like you, tall, slender with pale skin, red hair and green eyes. But that's not why I wanted you to work for me. I know you're a special woman, Alma, a woman who deserves better than a man who looks at you and sees another.'

'Is that what you do, Charlie?'

'My name isn't Charlie,' he said harshly. 'It's Feodor, Feodor Raschenko.'

'If you love your Masha so much, why aren't you with her?' she was trembling, almost too afraid to listen to his answer, but she had to ask the question.

'I'm not with her because I have no idea where she is.'

'She left you?'

'Not willingly.'

Now he'd begun, he wanted to talk, to unburden himself of the events that had irrevocably changed his life, making every day a marathon in which the twin hurdles of loneliness and painful memories had to be overcome. 'I grew up in a small village near Moscow. Just distance enough to make it the country, but near enough to travel there in a day. That was the problem. It was a beautiful place. People used to say so all the time, but when you live somewhere you take it for granted. Forget its beauty as well as its faults.'

'I suppose you do,' Alma interposed, thinking of her house in Morgan Street. How she had looked on it as home for years, not realising just how uncomfortable a place it was until she'd been able to contrast it with this flat.

He hesitated for a moment, and when he spoke again his voice was harsh, rasping. 'The party leaders found out about it, saw it and wanted it. They moved everyone out.'

'Moved?' she looked at him uncomprehendingly.

'They wanted dachas, summer houses. The peasants were in the way. I lived in a house that had been my father's and his father's before him. It had been built by a Rashchenko four hundred years ago. But none of that mattered. Not to them. And they had the power and the control.' He clenched his jaw and she noticed a small pulse on his temple throbbing.

'But if it was your house and your land . . .'

'You don't understand Russia.' He shook his head at her naivety. 'We didn't know what was coming, and if we had, there would have been nothing that any of us could have done to change it.'

'But surely you have laws . . . police . . .'

'The party's laws, and the party's police. It was the police who moved everyone out. I wasn't even there. Masha was having a baby, I had walked to the next village to get a cot from her brother. When I came back there was nothing.'

'Nothing?'

'Nothing,' he repeated flatly. 'Most of the old houses had been flattened to the ground. Builders were already at work. Fires burned, fed by our furniture, clothes, things we had valued for years. I asked them where the people had gone and they told me, the East. I went to the station. It was deserted: no trains, no people. I asked questions, so many questions I was arrested, but that was what I wanted. I thought if I was sent East I would find her.'

'But you didn't?' There was the same look of pain and anguish on his face that she had seen in Cardiff.

'I was put in a prison. I escaped into the woods one day when I was sent out in a work party. It was spring, the snow had melted, there were no tracks for them to follow. I hid in the forest, lived with the nomads and looked for Masha and our child. For four years I looked for them. When the nomads were rounded up by the state militia I volunteered to be a seaman. They didn't think to check my identity, they simply assumed I was a member of the tribe I had been living with. They sent me to St Petersburg. I got a berth on a steamer to Cardiff.'

'And there you left the ship?'

'Jumped ship,' he corrected. 'So you see I am wanted for more than one crime in Russia. For escaping from prison, for jumping ship, for asking too many questions. People have been shot for less.'

'But you never found your wife?'

'I have never found anyone who knew what happened to her or the people in my village. Russia is not like here. People disappear all the time. Every time a Russian ship docks in Cardiff I try to meet it. I ask every sailor who comes in if he has any news. I have sent letters back with them to my wife's brother, but there has been no word. And now, even if I should find her, I am here and she would not be allowed to leave.' He turned his back on her and stared blindly out of the window. 'Sometimes, just sometimes I think it would have been easier if I had returned to the village and found her dead. I would have known then that I had to mourn. I almost envied Bethan when her son died. I never knew whether Masha had my son or my daughter.'

'How many years is it since you left your village to get that cot?' she asked after a long silence.

'Nine years next month.' He closed his eyes, and her heart went out to him.

'You could live out the rest of your life waiting for a reunion that may never happen.'

'I have no choice. I have nothing to give anyone I . . .'

She recalled the old woman's words: 'Recognise your destiny when it comes. Take it, and make the most of it while you can.'

'You have something to give me,' she whispered.

'You don't understand. I think of Masha all the time. I see her . . .'

'Since you met me?'

'More often since I met you,' he acknowledged honestly.

'You said yourself that you can't go back.'

'I can't,' he admitted wretchedly.

'All my life I've lived for the here and now, because I've been too afraid to look further than the present. For the first time I want to look forward. I want to live with you. Wake up beside you every morning, go to bed with you every night.'

'You'd live with me after what I've just told you?'

'I'd live with you.'

'I could marry you. No one here knows about Masha except you, but it would not be legal, and if it was discovered it would be one more crime to lay on my head.'

'It might be worth risking, especially if we had a child.'

'I love you, Alma. But you'd have to understand about Masha. She will always be the first one, and my wife.'

'You're not my first man, Charlie. There was Ronnie. You know that.'

'It doesn't matter.'

He kissed her and she kissed him back. Locking her fingers into his she led him quietly towards the door so as not to disturb her mother. They had one another. Tonight he would sleep in her bed, and tomorrow . . . tomorrow they would talk about a marriage – of sorts. Masha was as much a part of Charlie's past as Ronnie was of hers. There was no going back for either of them. When his emotions were less raw he would see that, and understand. They were going to live out the rest of their lives in Pontypridd where nothing ever happened. Masha was in Russia. Ronnie was in Italy. There was no chance of them ever meeting again. No going back . . .

The pips that preceded the news beeped on the radio. He bent his head to hers and kissed her again. She loved him; that was all that mattered. Not that he had a wife and child somewhere he would never see again. She loved him, and he loved her. There was no going back . . .

'I love you, Charlie.'

'Can you say Feodor?'

'I love you, Feodor.'

'*The Czech crisis deepens as German troops continue to mass on the Czechoslovakian border. Herr Hitler has announced that he has no aggressive intentions . . .*'

No going back . . .

Spoils of War

For Professor Norman Robbins, dramatist, actor, director, the world's most popular writer of pantomimes, and his talented and generous actress wife, Ailsa.
How much more laughter there would be in the world if everyone had such friends.

Acknowledgements

My gratitude to all those who have helped with the writing and research of *Spoils of War*.

Lindsay Morris and the staff of Pontypridd Library for their ongoing professional assistance and support, and a very special thank you to Penny Pugh, the archivist, without whose aid this book would be very much the factually poorer.

Brian Davies, David Gwyer and Ann Cleary of Pontypridd Historical Centre. The extensive collection of photographs of old Pontypridd that they have amassed and take such excellent care of have helped not only me, but the incredibly talented artist Gordon Crabb, who painted the jacket for *Spoils of War*.

My husband, John, our children, Ralph, Ross, Sophie and Nick, and my parents, Glyn and Gerda Jones, for their love and the time they gave me to write this book.

Margaret Bloomfield for her friendship and help in so many ways.

Everyone at Random House, particularly the miracle-workers Ron Beard and Mike Morgan, and my editor Kate Elton.

My manuscript editor, Mary Loring, for her encouragement, incisive insight into the human condition and for enriching my books in ways I would not have dreamed of.

My new agent, Ken Griffiths, and his wife, Marguerite – you said you wanted me but were you really sure what you were taking on?

This, like my other books, belongs as much to the people of Pontypridd as it does to me. I can't even begin to thank everyone for the stories, the hospitality, and the kindness I have experienced during the past eight years.

No writer can exist without readers. I am truly privileged to have so many sympathetic and understanding people among mine.

Catrin Collier
October 1999

Chapter One

'TIGHTENING THE BELT on your trousers only makes them look worse. Just clip on the braces.'

Charlie Raschenko glanced up and saw the reflection of his wife, Alma, staring back at him in the dressing-table mirror.

'I look enough of a clown without wearing baggy trousers,' he growled in his guttural Russian accent.

'You don't look like a clown,' Alma countered, elated by the first non-monosyllabic reply she'd extracted from him in two days. 'You've put on some weight . . .'

'Not enough to stop people staring.'

'You heard Andrew the same as me. If you rested more . . .'

'I would stop breathing.'

Anxious to avoid an argument that would result in Charlie retreating even further into the private world that she had failed to penetrate since his return from the war, Alma gritted her teeth and lifted his suit jacket from the bed. 'No one will notice how loose your trousers are once you put this on.'

'Only because they'll be too busy looking at my beautiful wife.'

Knowing the compliment was the closest she would get to an apology for snapping at her, Alma managed a smile as she helped him into the jacket. It was even worse than his trousers, hanging hopelessly loose on his emaciated frame.

'I had my old green velvet evening dress cut down,' she continued, conscious that she was talking too fast and too loud in an attempt to divert his attention from the pre-war suit that looked as though it had been measured for a man twice his size. 'You don't think it's too much for a wedding?'

I

'It's not too much,' he echoed dully.

A preoccupied, faraway look stole into his eyes. It was a look Alma had come to know well. Three years in Hitler's forced labour camps had drained Charlie of more than his health. Feeling powerless to help him and suddenly afraid, she shivered involuntarily as she touched his arm.

'You're cold?' Even his voice was distant.

'No. I'm fine. Let me look at you.' Brushing imaginary specks from his jacket, she stood back and straightened his loose collar and tie. Anything other than meet his chill, dead expression. 'I'm glad Megan and Dino decided to marry on a Saturday. With all the staff in, it's easier to leave the shops and it will be good to have a party and see everyone . . .' she faltered as Charlie gripped her hand.

'Alma – I . . .'

His eyes were no longer cold and lifeless. They were frightened, confused – those of a panic-stricken child who had witnessed unimaginable horrors.

She opened her arms and held him close. But she couldn't bring herself to hug him as fiercely as she would have in the old days before war had disrupted their lives and almost destroyed him. Careful to keep her touch light, gentle, she steeled herself to meet his fragility without flinching. Not even the suit could disguise that his skin stretched tissue-thin over bones that carried wasted muscles and not an ounce of spare flesh. Eight months hadn't been enough to accustom her to the frail being who had returned in place of her healthy, powerful, beloved husband. And moments of intimacy like this only served to highlight the difference between the old and present Charlie. His hair was as thick, even if it had changed from white blond to silver grey; his cologne smelled the same, his voice and features, albeit cracked and prematurely aged, were recognisable – but she was beginning to relinquish all hope that this invalid would ever again be the man she had married.

'Mary says if I put my coat on we can go to the park . . .' Their four-year-old son, Theo, thundered up the stairs

2

and rushed down the passage, only to freeze, wide-eyed and apprehensive outside their bedroom door.

Alma forced yet another reassuring smile as she swallowed her tears. She wasn't the only one having difficulty adjusting to Charlie's return. Charlie's homecoming was the first Theo had seen of his father and since then there had been so many changes for the small boy to adjust to. His banishment from her bedroom to one he shared with Mary, the young girl she had hired to take care of him. The advent of an invalid into their lives who was too tired to do any more than read him the occasional story – a very different being from the long-promised Daddy who would play with him and teach him rough boys' games. The constant commands to keep his voice down '*because Daddy is resting*' whereas before he had been allowed to make as much noise as he liked.

'You know Daddy and I are going out, Theo?' Alma asked.

He nodded, taking courage from her smile. 'Mary says Auntie Megan and Uncle Dino are getting married.'

Drained by the simple effort of standing, Charlie sank down on to the bed. Seeing Theo looking at him, he stretched out his arm and patted his son's cheek, wishing he could toss him high in the air and tickle him as his own father had done when he'd been Theo's age. But aside from his weakness he sensed a reserve in the boy that he was unsure how to overcome. A reserve that to his dismay occasionally appeared to border on fear.

'Can I get my coat?'

'I'll help you find it.' Alma took Theo's small hand in hers. 'Kiss Daddy goodbye.' Theo stood his ground.

Sensing the boy's reluctance, Charlie kissed his finger and planted it on Theo's forehead.

Clearly relieved, Theo ran out ahead of Alma. ''Bye. Can Mary buy me an ice cream in the café, Mam?'

'It's freezing out there.'

'But it's not freezing in my tummy,' Theo countered with unarguable logic. 'Mary says . . .'

Light-headed, Charlie slumped forward, listening to

3

Theo's prattling. Alma and Theo were his family – all he had in the world – and he loved them with every fibre of his being, but somehow that wasn't enough. He didn't know how to touch them and make them understand why he was the way he was and how deep his feelings for them ran . . .

'Charlie? Are you all right?'

Alma was beside him, an anxious frown creasing her forehead.

'Fine.' He rose slowly to his feet.

'I wish you wouldn't lie to me.'

'I'm fine,' he reiterated testily.

'Your shoelaces are undone, let me . . .'

'No.'

Alma stood back; forced to watch, while he struggled to fulfil a simple task she could have completed in seconds. His face was almost blue, as heaving for breath, he finally sat back on the bed.

'I'll get the present from the living room.'

She'd placed the silver coffee pot she'd found in a Cardiff jeweller's in layers of tissue paper in a brown cardboard box. She would have preferred to have bought Megan and Dino something more practical, but lack of coupons, rationing and empty shops had put paid to that idea. As she picked up the box, Charlie appeared in the doorway.

'Your buttonhole is slipping.'

Charlie took the box from her as she adjusted the pin behind the flower she'd fastened to his lapel. The parcel was heavy but for once Alma didn't argue. At Megan's insistence only five people had been invited to witness her second marriage, her daughter and daughter-in-law, Diana Ronconi and Tina Powell, both of whom were waiting for their husbands to be demobbed, her brother, Huw, and his wife, Myrtle, and Dino's old colonel and fellow American, David Ford. The reception – to which they'd invited practically everyone they knew – was being held across the road in Ronconi's restaurant, and Alma had spotted her closest friend, Bethan John, the ex-

4

district nurse, walking in with her husband, Andrew, the local doctor. If Charlie should collapse under the weight of the silver at least he'd be assured of prompt medical attention.

'It seems odd to go to a wedding reception without attending the ceremony,' Andrew commented as he held the restaurant door open for his wife.

'I can understand why Megan didn't want a lot of people there. Ever since I can remember she's always insisted that one husband was quite enough for her, even though they were together for only three years. And, as my father reminded me this morning, his brother did marry Megan in the same chapel.'

'She must have cared for him a great deal to have remained a widow for twenty-eight years.' He took two glasses of sherry from the tray the waitress offered them as they reached the top of the stairs and handed Bethan one.

'The Great War messed up a lot of lives.'

'This war hasn't done too badly either.'

Taking Andrew's comment as a reference to the problems they'd been having since he'd come home, Bethan turned her back on him, pushed the door open and stepped into the second-floor dining room. 'Good grief!'

'"Good grief!" indeed!' Tina Powell, née Ronconi, who managed the restaurant echoed. 'I'm not going to tell you how much Dino paid the florist to decorate this room or how much food and drink he smuggled in here in boxes marked "PROPERTY OF US ARMY" because he's paying us about the same amount to keep our mouths shut.'

'Big brother Ronnie might be mopping up after the war in Italy but I see you're working hard to keep the Ronconi business spirit alive and flourishing,' Andrew observed wryly.

'He'd sack the lot of us when he gets back if we didn't.' Tina offered them a plate of canapés. 'Try one. It's real tinned salmon, not dyed snook.'

'How did the wedding go?' Bethan asked.

'Wonderful, Megan looked regal, Dino proud, Diana, Myrtle and I cried, Huw sniffed as he gave the bride away and David Ford dropped the ring, fortunately it didn't roll too far.'

'Any sign of Will being demobbed?' Bethan asked. Her cousin William Powell had married Tina during the war but since then he had managed only two leaves, the last over three years before.

'Not that I've heard. I haven't had a letter in weeks and Diana hasn't heard a word from Ronnie either. If those two are living it up in Italy, drinking wine, chasing women and generally carrying on the way we think they are, Diana and I are agreed, we'll make them pay for it when they do finally get around to coming home.'

'Will and Ronnie have never been the best of correspondents.'

'They have been fighting a war, Bethan,' Andrew interposed, feeling he ought to say something in defence of the absent men.

'You sent enough letters to Bethan. I saw them. They filled a whole drawer.'

'Prisoners of war have nothing to do except write letters.' He noted the number of tables laid out with the Ronconis' best white linen and silverware. 'Has Dino invited the entire remaining American contingent?'

'He asked us to cater for sixty but there's not that many Americans coming. Since Dino's the bridegroom, demobbed and settling here, I don't think you can count him as American any more. There's the colonel, of course – Beth, have you heard? He's given Dino a job – well – arranged for the army to give him one. The colonel's been ordered to pick up where the major left off, in trying to track down the tons of American supplies that disappeared in Wales and Dino's helping him on a civilian basis. Not that either of them stand a snowball in hell's chance of finding a thing. I told Dino yesterday: it's all gone. The edible into people's mouths, the rest, hidden away until the last Yank sails home.'

'I look forward to meeting Colonel Ford after hearing so much about him.' Andrew's voice was casual but Bethan could sense his resentment. David Ford and four other American officers had been billeted in her house for almost a year before D-Day. She knew Andrew had heard rumours of a liaison between them even before his homecoming eight months before but what she didn't know was how much – if any – of the gossip he believed.

'I think there are a couple of other American servicemen coming but Dino wasn't sure how many. According to him they're shipping the bachelors home as fast as they can in the hope of saving a few for American girls.'

'Beth!' Abandoning her sherry on the nearest table, Alma embraced her as soon as she walked in.

Andrew studied Charlie with a professional eye as he shook his hand. 'Why don't we find a table?'

'You and Charlie find one. I need to comb my hair.'

'You've only walked across the road, Alma,' Andrew protested.

'It needs combing. The hairdresser made a mess of cutting the back.'

'I'll go with you.' Bethan followed Alma downstairs to the Ladies' Room behind the ground-floor restaurant. 'Charlie still the same?' she asked as soon as they were alone.

'As you see.' Alma opened her handbag and rummaged for cigarettes. Finding her case, she opened it, offering them to Bethan before taking one herself. 'And please don't tell me he'll be fine given time.' She bent her head to the flame as Bethan flicked her lighter. 'If I had a pound for every platitude that I've heard along those lines since he's been home, I'd be a millionaire.' Drawing the smoke deep into her lungs she leaned against the sink and looked Bethan in the eye. 'Tell me the truth, will he ever recover?'

'Physically, Andrew's promised you he will, but that's not what you're asking, is it?'

'When he first came home I thought we'd be all right. But then he used to touch me, even kiss me occasionally

7

when no one else was around. I don't know what happened or when, but some time after those first few weeks he changed. You know Charlie, he never did say much, now he hardly says a word. Half the time I feel as though I'm living with a stranger and the other half, that even the stranger isn't really there. That all I have is an empty husk. If the soul and personality can be poured out of a person, that's what's happened to Charlie, Beth. There's no spark, no feeling – nothing – and it's driving me mad. I want him back but I'm beginning to wonder if he even exists to get back.'

'As Andrew told you, no one's ever experienced what the survivors of Hitler's death camps have before. There's no medical precedents, no textbooks to guide the doctors. You saw the films.'

'Yes, and I've tried to talk to Charlie about them but every time I mention the word "camp" he walks away. I can understand him not wanting to relive what he went through but I can't just stand back and watch him disintegrate without lifting a finger either. So, I end up trying to imagine what it must have been like for him and I've no idea whether I'm close to the truth, or if it was even worse than I picture it. Whatever happened, Beth, it's eating him alive and I can't do a thing to stop it.'

'But you do talk to him about other things?'

'Oh yes,' she grimaced. 'The weather – rationing – shortages of raw materials for the shops – Theo's drawings – what he'd like for tea – not that he eats a tenth of what I cook, which is why he still looks like a walking skeleton.'

'Nothing important?'

'No.' Alma turned to the mirror. 'I've tried everything you suggested – romantic dinners, soft music, I even dragged him to the White Palace to see *Frenchman's Creek* from the back row. As a last resort I went for the more direct approach . . .' She bit her bottom lip to stop it from trembling.

'And?' Bethan pressed.

'He pretended to be asleep and when I tried to discuss

8

it in the morning, he shut himself in the kitchen with the account books.'

'Andrew sees him a couple of times a week. I could ask him –'

'No.' Alma was adamant. 'I don't want Charlie to know I've talked about this to anyone. Not even you.'

'I want to help.'

'You have, by listening. If I didn't have you to confide in, I probably would have resorted to rolling round the floor and screaming like a demented two–year–old by now.'

'That approach might even work.'

Alma smiled in spite of herself as she reached into her bag for her make-up. 'For the time being I think I'll persevere with subtlety.'

'You never know, given the amount of drink Dino's stockpiled, tonight could be the night.'

Alma pushed up a stick of lipstick that was barely a quarter of an inch high and applied it sparingly. 'What worries me is that they could have done something to him in that camp. I've read about the medical experiments the Nazis carried out. Since Charlie's come home, I haven't even seen him naked. He used to walk round half the time with nothing on, now he even wears pyjamas in bed.'

'Before the war he was a fit, healthy man and you didn't have Theo or Mary living with you.'

'I didn't think of that.'

'And Andrew has examined him, several times.'

'He hasn't said –'

'He wouldn't,' Bethan interrupted. 'Not to me, but he would to you if there was anything seriously wrong.'

'So, I'm letting my imagination run away with me.'

'On that point.' Bethan automatically checked her reflection in the mirror. Her nose needed powdering and her lipstick was smudged but, preoccupied with Alma's problems, she didn't notice.

'I'm sorry, I keep dumping all my troubles on you and it must be just as difficult for you and Andrew to adjust. I'm so wrapped up in Charlie I tend to forget that Andrew was away for even longer.'

9

'Things could be better,' Bethan conceded. 'Like you, I feel as though I'm living with a stranger. The main problem is Andrew wants everything to be perfect, especially with the children. It's worked reasonably well with the Clark girls. After being evacuated, orphaned and adopted by us in the space of two years they appreciate having a settled home and a father – even a new one – and they're prepared to meet Andrew more than halfway. It's Rachel and Eddie.'

'They can't get used to having a man around the house.'

'You've seen it with Theo.'

Alma nodded.

'Andrew expects them to love him before they know him. It's not easy for any of us after five years apart but it's hardest of all on Eddie. Ever since he was born Rachel and I have been calling him the man of the house, now someone else has taken that role. And before Andrew came home Eddie had Rachel and me all to himself. Now Rachel hardly bothers with him. She's become a real Daddy's girl, shadowing Andrew whenever he's around, and if the four of us are together Andrew always seems to want to talk to me when Eddie does. Oh, Eddie treats Andrew politely enough, but as a stranger not a father, and I can't help feeling that he resents Andrew for coming back.'

'I'm sorry.'

'There, now I've poured it all out on you, but at the risk of repeating what you don't want to hear, dare I say, neither of us has problems that time can't cure.'

'I hope you're right. There's just one more thing.'

'The house? You've taken Charlie to see it?'

'I dropped hints about how cramped the flat is for the four of us, and how Theo needs his own room. Charlie neither agreed nor disagreed with me, so I mentioned the house. I've made an appointment for both of us to view it tomorrow.'

'Good for you. You must be making some headway with Charlie if –'

'I only made the appointment because Mrs Harding won't hold it any longer without putting it on the open market and I can't blame her. It's a beautiful house, Beth, big and light and airy. The garden's not huge like yours, but it'll be fine for Theo to run around in and best of all, Tyfica Road is less than five minutes' walk from the shop.'

'You still haven't said what Charlie thinks of the idea of moving.'

'That's just it, he's said nothing – absolutely nothing. He hasn't even said he'll view it with me, but mind you, he didn't object either.'

'Do you think he'll go?'

'Possibly, if he hasn't shut himself away somewhere, and I force him.'

'Do you want me to call round some time tomorrow with the car?'

'Would you, Beth? I told Mrs Harding we'd be there at two o'clock. Charlie's always listened to you. If you tell him it's a good idea to move, between the two of us we just might persuade him.'

'I'll be there. Judging by that noise it sounds as though everyone's arriving at once, we'd better go back upstairs. It would be bad form to arrive after the bride and groom.'

Andrew sat watching the door intently; only half listening as Tina's sister, Gina, and her husband, Luke, enquired after Charlie's health and business. He tried to recall everything he'd heard about David Ford as he waited for the man himself to appear. Tall – or had he heard that from the children? – in which case tall could mean anything over five foot four. Old – or again was that Rachel? To a child anything over twenty would seem ancient.

A slim, blond man in an American officer's dress uniform of olive-drab tunic, light khaki trousers, shirt and tie walked through the door and headed straight for his table. He extended his hand.

'Dr John, forgive me for introducing myself. I recognised you right away but then I lived with your photograph for almost a year. I'm happy I finally have an opportunity to thank my absent host. I'm David Ford.'

Andrew rose to shake David's hand. He wasn't sure what he'd been expecting, but it certainly wasn't this tall, youthful, direct man with a shock of blond hair and blue eyes. Every colonel he'd met had a rather off-putting air of self-important arrogance, presumably cultivated in an attempt to communicate their superiority over lesser ranks and beings. And in the main it worked. He'd met none who could be remotely considered agreeable, charming or approachable – all adjectives he'd heard applied to David Ford and, now he'd finally met the man for himself, understandably so.

'I've heard a lot about you,' Andrew acknowledged guardedly.

'Likewise. That's quite a family you've got there. How are Bethan, Rachel, Eddie and the Clark girls?'

'Well, thank you. Bethan is around here somewhere.'

'I'd like to pay my respects.'

'As you're in Pontypridd again you must visit us.'

'I couldn't impose on your hospitality a second time.'

'Bethan would be upset if you didn't. Are you staying in town tonight?'

'No, I'm stationed in Cardiff. I have a room in the officers' club there.'

'It would be bad form to miss any of this party by returning early. The top floor of the house is still full of your furniture . . .'

'I've been meaning to contact you about that.'

'It can wait. Please, you really must stay. Bethan!' He hailed her as she returned with Alma. 'Come and help me persuade the colonel to stay the night with us.'

'My name is David.'

'And I'm Andrew, but then you'd know that.'

'It's nice to see you again, David, and looking so well.' Bethan glanced uneasily from David to Andrew. The tension between them was palpable. After a moment's hesitation she offered David her cheek, watching Andrew as the colonel stooped to kiss it. 'You've recovered from your wounds?'

'A1 fit for duty.'

'David was seriously injured during the invasion,' Bethan explained.

'Not that seriously,' he corrected, anxious to change the subject. He looked across to the top table where Diana was putting the finishing touches to a flower arrangement. 'From what I saw this morning my old army cook is settling down well here.'

'A couple more months and my Aunt Megan will have turned him into a Pontypriddian, accent and all.' Bethan's face was beginning to ache from the strain of smiling.

'He certainly looks happier than I ever recall seeing him before.'

David had meant the comment to sound light-hearted but with Andrew's attention fixated on his every word it held a wistful tinge that he realised could be open to misinterpretation.

'And I'm glad Dino finally persuaded my Aunt Megan to set a date.'

'From what he told me, he set five, and she chickened out of four,' David replied wryly.

'Ladies and gentlemen, would you please go to your tables and be upstanding for the bride and groom,' Megan's brother, Huw Davies, shouted, assuming the mantle of Master of Ceremonies.

'Won't you join us, David?'

'Thank you for the invitation, Andrew, but Dino's commanded all remaining Americans to the top table. I believe it's something to do with needing the moral support of his fellow countrymen in the face of over-whelming odds.'

'We'll see you later?'

'I'll look forward to it.' David nodded to Andrew and smiled at Bethan. His gaze met Bethan's for the briefest of moments but he saw enough to realise she was uneasy about something. And given the way Andrew was watching him he didn't need anyone to spell out what was troubling her.

*

13

'The bride and groom!' As the toast echoed around the room, Bethan lifted her glass to Megan, resplendent in a cream and lace silk costume that her newly acquired nieces-in-law had sent from America. As the guests sat down, Dino rose.

'My wife and I . . .' the laughter that greeted his opening drowned out the rest of his sentence. Shrugging his shoulders he crumpled the sheet of paper he was holding into a ball and tossed it on to the floor. 'So much for speeches,' he continued when he could finally make himself heard. 'Those of you who know Megan, also know how hard I had to work on her just so I could say those four words.' His face fell serious as he looked down at her. 'But boy, was it worth it.'

'Let's hope she still thinks so in six months,' Tina called out from the door.

'That's another thing I've learned since Uncle Sam sent me on this trip,' he retorted cheerfully. 'There are some people over here who will never accept us Yanks as the good guys. Even stepdaughters-in-law.'

'Maybe in another ten years or so.' Tina nodded to the waitress behind her. She entered the room carrying an outsize, elaborately iced cake, larger than any seen in Pontypridd since before the war.

'Ladies and gentlemen,' Tina announced, 'I give you the Ronconi family present to the bride and groom, and before the groom asks, it *is* real, not cardboard and in answer to any other questions – don't ask.'

Through the laughter and ceremony of cutting the cake that followed, Bethan's attention, like everyone else's was drawn to the top table.

'He's what you women call good-looking, isn't he?' Andrew murmured.

'Dino?' Bethan was very fond of the middle-aged, short, plump American who'd captivated her aunt, but by no stretch of the imagination could she call him good-looking.

'I was referring to the colonel.'

'David? I wouldn't know.'

'Come on, Beth, you know.'

'I suppose he is, I've never thought about it,' she lied, taking the slice of cake the waitress handed her. 'I wonder where Tina found these ingredients. I haven't seen dried fruit this quality since before the war.'

'I think it was a good idea to ask him to stay with us tonight.' Andrew refused to be fobbed off by a discussion on dried fruit.

'I don't.' The instant she'd spoken she realised her reply had been too quick, too finite.

'It would put an end to the rumours once and for all if he stayed with both of us, Beth.'

'I wasn't aware people were still talking about David and me.'

'Weren't you?'

'I have better things to do than listen to old women's gossip.'

'It's not just the old women, Beth. A lot of the men coming home are questioning what their wives did when they were away.' Crumbling his cake into small pieces he left it lying untasted on his plate.

'I told you nothing happened between David and me.'

'And I believe you.'

She looked into his deep, probing eyes and wished that she wasn't, and never had been, attracted to David Ford.

'Are Dino and Megan going on honeymoon?' Alma enquired, sensing and attempting to defuse the tension between Bethan and Andrew.

'He's booked them into a hotel in Mumbles for a week, but don't say a word. It's a surprise.'

'Lucky Megan,' Alma murmured enviously. 'It's years since I've seen the sea.'

'We still have the chalet on the Gower, why don't the four of us take the children down there for a week?' Andrew suggested.

'In winter?'

'Why not winter, Bethan? The rooms have fireplaces. There are plenty of farms we can buy wood from. The beaches will be empty, the walks glorious.'

'Is there room for all of us?' Alma asked.

'There are three bedrooms, two with double beds, one with singles and two living rooms. We could put Eddie and Theo into one bed, Rachel could have the other and there are couches for the Clark girls in the sun lounge. I can vouch for their comfort because I've slept on them myself.'

'What do you think?' Alma turned to Charlie. 'We have good staff, the business could run itself for a few days.'

'Make it a week.' Andrew moved his chair so the waitress could pour his coffee.

'What about petrol to get down there, and the practice?'

'Leave the details to me, Bethan. What do you say, Charlie?'

'If Alma wants.'

Bethan squeezed Alma's hand sympathetically beneath the tablecloth.

'Alma wants.' Alma laid her free hand on top of her husband's. 'Very much indeed.'

Constable Huw Davies helped his blind wife, Myrtle, to Bethan's table before waylaying Tina. 'Waitress just told me there's a stray soldier downstairs . . .'

'Will!' Before Huw could say another word Tina whipped off her apron and ran full pelt down the stairs.

'William's back?' Andrew asked.

'Tony,' Huw corrected.

'Given the Ronconi temper, I wouldn't like to be in your shoes when Tina sees her brother not her husband waiting to greet her.'

'Tony?' Tina looked a little uncertainly at the uniformed soldier with dark eyes and black curly hair sitting at the family table in front of the till.

'I haven't changed that much, have I?' he asked, rising from his seat.

'Of course not.' She hugged him then called to a waitress. 'Eileen, tell Mrs Grenville Mr Tony Ronconi's here.'

16

'Mrs Grenville? Mr Tony Ronconi?' Tony queried. 'That's a bit formal, isn't it?'

'Not with the staff. You home for good?'

'I hope so.'

'There's a wedding upstairs.'

'I know, your mother-in-law's marrying some Yank or other.'

'Not some Yank. Dino's nice. He gave me the chocolate and cigarettes I sent to Will, Ronnie and you.'

'And what did you give him in return?'

'One more remark like that and I'll be giving you a punch on the nose.'

'I meant café favours.'

'He's had the odd free coffee.' Tina examined her brother carefully, wondering if he'd been drinking. 'Why don't you come upstairs?' she suggested, remembering the last time he'd been home on leave. Drunk and offensive, it had taken the combined efforts of William, Ronnie, Diana and herself to calm Tony, and the damage he'd done to his relationship with Ronnie in that one afternoon had never been repaired. 'Nearly everyone's there,' she added persuasively, deciding that if he had hit the bottle he was less likely to create a scene in front of a gathering of their closest friends and family.

'I don't want to break in on a party, besides I've ordered a meal to be served here.'

'You can eat upstairs. No one will mind. I don't suppose you've heard anything of Will?'

'Or Ronnie?' Gina asked eagerly as she joined them, momentarily forgetting the fight between Tony and Ronnie the last time he'd been home, in the excitement of seeing her brother again.

'No. Mama wrote that they were in Italy. I've come from Celle.'

'Mrs Powell?' a kitchen hand called to Tina from behind the counter. 'They're asking upstairs if you want them to go round with the coffee pot a second time.'

'No peace for the wicked. I'll be back in a minute.' Tina ran back up the stairs.

'I take it Celle is in Germany.' Gina manoeuvred her swollen body into a chair beside Tony, drawing his attention to her advanced state of pregnancy.

'You and Luke didn't waste any time.'

'It's our first and we've been married five years.'

'In that case you're slow, and yes, Celle is in Germany.'

'I hope the bloody Krauts are suffering all the torments of hell,' Eileen cursed earnestly as she served Tony pie, vegetables, mashed potatoes and gravy.

'They're suffering.' Tony appreciated the irony in the waitress's outburst. He knew Eileen's family. Her father had remained in a protected job in the council offices for the duration. Her mother's war work had extended as far as a few voluntary hours for the WVS and her brother had wangled himself a safe position in an army supply office in Scotland. 'Almost as much as the Italians in the valleys who lost half their families to internment and the other half to exile in Birmingham. Not to mention the ones like my father who were killed being shipped out of the country to prison camps in Australia and Canada.'

'Well, it's no more than the Krauts deserve, I'm sure.' Eileen hesitated uncertainly, wondering why Tony was talking about his family in the same breath as the Germans.

'You're sure? All their cities and towns are flattened. Three and a half million of their soldiers have been killed, along with three million civilians, they've no food, half of them have lost their homes, their industries are wrecked and to top it all their country's full of occupying troops telling them what they can and can't do.' He sliced through the pie and poked suspiciously at the filling.

'Serve them bloody well right. If you ask me, Tony –'

'No one is asking you, Eileen,' Tina broke in abruptly as she returned to the table. 'And I'll have no swearing in here. It's time you helped upstairs. Just one more thing,' she added as the girl walked away. 'It's Mr Ronconi, to you.'

'Mr Ronconi!' Tony made a face at his sister. 'Not even *Mr Tony Ronconi* as it was earlier. Thank you for the elevation from the ranks, sister. What have I done to deserve it?'

'Nothing – yet.'

'Is there room for me at home?'

'Of course,' Gina broke in eagerly. 'The evacuees left months ago, Mama, Alfredo and Roberto came home from Birmingham last March. Maria, Theresa and Stephania stayed there with their husbands, which was hard on Mama but Angelo's back.'

'I heard. Where is he?'

'Running the Tumble café with Alfredo.'

'Alfredo's a kid.'

'Eighteen,' Tina corrected.

'You moved out of the rooms above the Tumble café, Tina?'

'No.'

'But you will be moving out when Will comes home?'

'First Gina and Luke, then Angelo, now you. Those rooms are my home and I'm hanging on to them.'

'Accommodation is a problem in the town,' Gina revealed.

'So I gathered from the conversation on the train as I came down.'

'You'll be all right at home. There's a bed in Alfredo and Roberto's room.'

'What about the boxroom?'

'Angelo grabbed it.'

'Then he can ungrab it. Where are you and Luke living?'

'We have the parlour and one of the bedrooms. We've been looking for our own place but it's hopeless. He'll be so glad to see you, Tony. I'll go upstairs and get him.'

'What about Laura and Trevor's house in Graig Street?' Tony asked, enquiring about their oldest sister's home as Gina left.

'Diana's living there with her children and it's a toss-up who'll be back first, Laura and Trevor from the hospital he's been stationed in at Portsmouth, or Ronnie. And there's no way that place is big enough for two couples and three children.'

'Well, one thing's certain. Big brother won't stand for me moving in with his wife.'

'Why are you so interested in getting your own place anyway?' Tina asked irritably. 'Now that the war's over, and you're home for good, you've plenty of time to get yourself sorted.'

'I want to sort myself out now, along with who is getting what part of the business. What's in this pie? No, don't tell me, I've a feeling I don't want to know.'

'Ronnie will decide who's going to run the cafés when he comes home.'

'Who made him Chief?'

'Mama after Papa died. Given there are eleven of us, Tony, there's no way we can all work in the business. With only three cafés . . .'

'I thought Ronnie went into some sort of partnership with Alma and Diana.'

'Diana went into business with Alma in the shop she inherited from her first husband. That's her son Billy's inheritance and nothing to do with us.'

'They used our High Street café as an extra kitchen.'

'They're still using it and they pay us rent, which I sent with what else could be spared to Mama and the younger ones in Birmingham. How else do you think they lived?'

'So what are you saying, Tina? That now I'm home for good I'm out of the business I ran before the war when Ronnie swanned off to Italy.'

'Of course not. Ronnie –'

'Ronnie hates my guts. If it was down to him I'd be put out on the streets without a penny.'

'Now you're being melodramatic as well as stupid,' Tina said uneasily. 'Tony, you should be upstairs meeting old friends not discussing things that need thrashing out at a family conference.'

'And if I'm not around for the family conference?'

'You're family, you'll be consulted,' she bit back crossly.

'Are you still running things, or has Angelo taken over?'

'Angelo's managing the café on the Tumble. I'm running this place. Gina –'

'Should be out of it, given the state of her.'

'She helped manage this place until two months ago.'

'You girls have husbands to keep you.'

'And because we have husbands you think we should move over and make room for you?'

'The war's won. A woman's place is in the home.'

'And if the woman doesn't think so?'

'I'll talk to you after Will comes home.'

'Will's my husband, not my master.'

'Tina, don't you see you won't be needed? Angelo and I as good as ran the cafés before the war.'

'Papa was in charge then and you know it. We all helped.'

'It's time to break up the inheritance, Tina.'

'Says who?'

'Me. The cafés and this restaurant are a family business.'

'Exactly, and we're family.'

'Whose family? You're a Powell, Laura's a Lewis, Gina's a Grenville. You should look to your husbands to keep you as the younger girls in Birmingham have done, and just as my wife will be looking to me.'

'You're married?' Tina stared at him incredulously.

'I will be as soon as it can be arranged.'

'Do we know her?'

'I doubt it.' He looked his sister squarely in the eye so there could be no mistake. 'She's German.'

Chapter Two

Tony laid his knife and fork on his plate, sat back and faced Tina. 'The look on your face has just destroyed my appetite.'

'A German girl! Tony, how could you! It will kill Mama.'

'As Mama raised no objection to your husband or Ronnie's wife joining the family I don't see how she can possibly object to mine.'

'And what's wrong with Will and Diana?' As Tina's voice rose precariously, the attention of all the waitresses and most of the customers within earshot focused on their table.

'Before you lose your rag, look at Will and Diana from Mama's point of view. Even forgetting they're not Catholic –'

'And this German of yours is, I suppose.'

'She is. And respectable.'

'And my Will isn't?'

'Tina – Tina . . .' he shook his head in mock despair, 'love is supposed to be blind not stupid. Will and Diana's mother has been in jail for receiving stolen goods, Diana was married to a queer before Ronnie took up with her and Will's played around with half the female population of Pontypridd . . .'

'Not since he married me.'

'Not since he married you because he's only been home twice in the last six years,' Tony murmured, deliberately keeping his voice low in contrast to her high-pitched outrage. 'But I wouldn't answer for the female population of wherever he's been stationed. You've only got to look at Vera Collins' son. He bears a closer resemblance to your William than George Collins.'

'If he is Will's son, then why did George keep him when he threw Vera out for carrying on with GIs?'

'I have no idea. All I'm saying is that if Mama can put up with Will and Diana –'

'First Will, now his sister. Are any of us good enough for you?' Tina demanded hotly, rising to her feet. 'If we were anywhere other then here, brother or not, I'd punch you into the middle of next week.'

'Thanks for the floor show,' Tony drew her attention to the people staring at them, 'and the warm welcome,' he added caustically. Tossing his napkin on to the debris on his plate he left the table.

'You're not thinking of going home.'

'Where else?'

'Do you intend to tell Mama about this woman?'

'Her name's Gabrielle.'

'Tony, how can you forget it was the Germans who killed Papa and put Angelo in a prison camp for five years?'

'Gabrielle's twenty-one. She didn't kill or imprison anyone.'

'And I suppose she didn't even know that her country declared war on the whole world.'

'Of course she knew,' he retorted impatiently, 'but she spent the war studying not fighting. She has a degree, she speaks four languages, she likes needlework and cooking and she's quiet and gentle. There's something else, Tina. Her family has suffered just as much as ours. Her two brothers died on the Russian front and her father was killed fleeing from the Russians when they invaded East Prussia. She was lucky to escape with her life.'

'How can you set our family's suffering against that of a – a – German!' Tina's indignation was superseded by shock as she realised Tony was deadly serious. 'Papa was drowned . . .'

'It was the good people of this country who interned innocent Italian businessmen, in 1940, not the Germans.'

'It was a German torpedo that sank the *Arandora Star* and killed Papa.'

'Are you absolutely sure about that, Tina? Because

I've heard different.' He walked behind the counter and picked up his kitbag.

'Tony, you're not going?' Gina called as her husband, Luke, helped her down the stairs. 'Everyone's asking about you . . .' She looked from Tina to her brother. 'Is anything wrong?'

'I've work to do.' Brushing past Luke, Tina ran back up the stairs.

'Tony?'

'You and Luke will be home later?'

'We'll be leaving as soon as we've helped Tina clear up here,' Luke answered, confused by Tina's hasty departure.

'Then I'll see you in Danycoedcae Road.' Swinging his bag over his shoulder Tony turned his back on them.

'Tony, come upstairs, just for five minutes,' Gina pleaded, as the door slammed shut behind him.

'It can't be long before Ronnie comes home,' Bethan reassured Diana as they watched Megan and Dino leave the top table.

'I hope you're right. At this rate Catrina will be celebrating her third birthday without seeing her father.'

'Knowing Ronnie, he'll make up for it when he does come home.'

'How did you and Alma cope, Beth, all those years alone? Eddie was, what, four and a half before he saw Andrew, Theo, three and a half when Charlie came home? Do you ever catch up with those missing years?'

'Truthfully?' Bethan looked across to where Andrew and Huw Davies were trying to draw Charlie into conversation. 'Not yet, and perhaps not ever, but don't forget Ronnie hasn't been away anywhere near as long.'

'Two years six months four days and,' Diana glanced at her wristwatch, 'five hours and thirty-five minutes.'

'You two didn't have that much time together, did you?'

'I just wish he'd write.'

'I'm sure you will hear soon.'

'It's not just me who misses him, Billy does. He can

just about remember what it was like to have a stepfather, but there's a world of difference between two and a half and five. I only hope Ronnie can live up to his expectations when he does finally make it back.'

'Time to wave off the bride and groom,' Andrew interrupted. 'Angelo's bringing the car round from the White Hart car park.'

'I've hardly had a minute to say a word to you, love.' Megan stopped in front of them and kissed Diana.

'Got one of those for your stepfather, Diana?' Dino asked.

'You know something, Dino,' Diana smiled, 'that stepfather bit sounds wonderful.'

'We'll be back in a week . . .'

'Mam,' Diana shook her head fondly at her mother, 'nothing is going to happen in a week.'

'I'm not so sure. That cough of Billy's . . .'

'Is something he puts on whenever you're around because he likes the taste of that syrup and vinegar medicine you make for him. I know you'll take care of her, could you try and stop her from worrying as well?' Diana planted a kiss on Dino's cheek. 'But you'd better watch that smile, if it gets any wider your face will crack in two.'

'Ronnie'll be home soon to put one just like it on yours.'

'That's what I've been telling her, Auntie Megan.' Bethan picked up her handbag. 'Come on, time to wave you off.'

'Do you two know where Dino's taking me?' Megan pumped, 'because he refuses to say a word to me.'

'Probably booked you into a dosshouse by the gas works in Cardiff,' Diana joked.

'Angelo disappeared into the car park of the White Hart for two hours first thing this morning,' Gina confided to Bethan as they followed Megan, Dino, Diana and the rest of the guests down the stairs. 'He met the colonel there but I couldn't get a thing out of either of them when they came back into the café, other than they'd been swapping the colonel's car for a Jeep so the honeymoon couple could travel in comfort. There was also talk of one of the mechanics from Ianto Myles' garage helping them to get it perfect for the bridal couple, but judging by the amount of schoolboy sniggering, it's my guess they weren't checking the engine.'

'As long as the army doesn't disapprove.'

'How will the army find out if David doesn't tell them?'

Diana peered round the crowd blocking the doorway of the restaurant and started to laugh.

'Oh my God! David Ford, are you responsible for that?' Megan demanded.

The colonel's standard, US Army-issue officer's car was virtually unrecognisable. Strings of red, white and blue paper flowers that looked suspiciously like the ones that had been made for the VJ celebrations six months before, festooned the bodywork from bumpers to roof. *'Good Luck'* and *'Just Married'* messages had been scrawled in bright pink raspberry syrup over all the windows. But the absolute crowning glory were two four-foot boards tied to the roof, decorated with expertly drawn, comically accurate cartoon images of a coy Dino and seductive Megan bearing the caption, *'FELLOW MOTORISTS BEWARE, DRIVER'S HANDS OTHERWISE OCCUPIED.'*

'I am not driving anywhere in that.' Megan glared from Dino to David. 'And I recognise the artwork, Angelo Ronconi. There isn't another man in Pontypridd who can draw like that.'

'Come on, darling,' Dino coaxed, 'just as far as our house. I'll clean it up while you change.'

'Not one yard.'

'Come on, Megan, be a sport.' To Bethan's amazement, Andrew picked up her aunt, dumping her in Dino's arms before opening the passenger door.

'As far as the house and not one yard further,' Megan relented.

'Told you I'd tame her,' Dino crowed.

After making sure Megan's coat was inside the car,

Dino climbed into the driver's side, and turned the ignition. The car inched forward to the raucous accompaniment of dozens of rattling tins that Angelo and Alfredo had filled with stones and tied to the back bumper. Unable to hear herself think, Bethan stepped back and found herself standing next to Tina.

'Anything wrong?' she asked, wondering why Tina wasn't in the forefront of the hubbub as she usually was.

'Just tired.' Tony's revelation was too new, too devastating for Tina to contemplate sharing it with anyone – even Bethan.

'Good luck,' Bethan called as Dino slid the window open and waved. 'Be happy.'

'That's an order, Morelli,' David shouted from beside her. 'I'm sorry, Bethan,' he apologised, 'I can't take your husband up on his invitation. Pressure of work. With Dino away for the next week I'll have to put in twice as many hours. You'll explain?'

'Of course.'

Sensing rather than seeing Andrew watching them, he tipped his hat to her, as though she were a stranger. 'See you around, ma'am.'

'No – no – no – no – I won't hear one more word!' Mrs Ronconi's dark eyes glittered hard with raw anger as she shook her diminutive fist at Tony. Half the height of her second son, and thinner and frailer than she'd been before the war, Mrs Ronconi still had the power to intimidate her children.

There was something ridiculous in the fierce altercation between mother and son – comic farce bordering on tragedy, worthy of Chaplin or Keaton – but neither Gina nor Luke, the only ones in the family who'd been brave enough to stay in the kitchen once the shouting had started, were laughing.

'I would rather die than accept a German into this family and that is absolutely my last word.'

'Mama –'

'Antonio,' her voice changed as her anger turned to

27

pleading, 'isn't it enough that they killed your father and made a prisoner of Angelo all these years?'

'Not all Germans are bad, Mama. Gabrielle didn't hurt anyone.'

'But she *is* a German and they start wars, force us to fight them, make us suffer and now you want to fra . . . frat . . .'

'Fraternise, Mama,' Luke supplied helpfully, unable to stand the tension a moment longer.

'That's it! Fraternise! And it is forbidden. All the newspapers say it is forbidden.'

'Not since last July, Mama,' Tony contradicted.

'So, because someone tells you it's all right to go off with enemy women, you do! What was this woman doing when all the other Germans were running around fighting, killing, looting, burning, bombing and drowning innocent people and imprisoning your brother – and Charlie – have you seen Charlie? They put a nice, quiet man like him in one of those horror camps. They made films of them and showed them in the pictures.'

'I've seen the places as well as the films, Mama.'

'And you still want to marry with the enemy.'

'The war's over, Mama. We won.'

'It's not over for me – not ever for me.' Mrs Ronconi's voice softened slightly as she gazed reverently at the photograph of her husband that dominated the chimney-breast. Rigidly posed in his best black suit, white shirt with wing collar and dark tie, his face adorned with a modest version of the luxuriant moustache he had worn in his later years, he looked younger than even she remembered him ever being. After a few moments during which neither Tony, Gina nor Luke dared speak, she turned from the photograph to confront her son. 'Antonio, you marry this girl and you will no longer be my son or a member of this family.'

The calm, quiet assertion was absolute and final. If his mother had screamed or ranted, Tony would have continued arguing, as it was he picked up his kitbag and went to the door.

28

'Tony.' Leaving her husband's side Gina went to her brother. 'Please, Mama, we need to talk about this.'

'I've said all there is to be said, Gina,' Mrs Ronconi pronounced firmly.

'But Tony's been fighting for six years. He needs to rest – to stay somewhere.'

'Not in this house.'

'Mama . . .'

''Bye, Gina.' Tony kissed her cheek and offered Luke his hand.

'You can't go like this,' Gina protested as she followed him down the passage. 'We're your family . . .'

'Are you?'

'Tony, don't be stubborn. Of course we're your family.'

For the second time that day Tony turned his back on his sister, closed the door behind him and walked away.

'That's Theo finally down. Mary wore him out in the park but the little monkey fought off sleeping until he couldn't keep his eyes open. I had to read him the *Three Little Pigs* four times. You'd think he'd know the story off by heart by now, wouldn't you?'

'He does.'

Encouraged by Charlie's response and feeling that her latest ploy of ending every communication with her husband in a question was beginning to work, Alma ventured a change of subject. 'It was a good wedding reception, wasn't it?'

He nodded briefly as he picked up the *Pontypridd Observer*.

'Did Bethan tell you she's driving us up to see the house in Tyfica Road tomorrow?'

If she hadn't been looking directly at him she would have missed his second acknowledgement.

'That's the door. I wonder who it could be at this time of night. Perhaps Mary's forgotten her key. I told her she could go to the pictures.' As she started down the stairs that led to the side door of the shop that was the flat's entrance she caught a glimpse of a uniformed figure behind the patterned glass. Tentatively opening the door, she smiled in relief when she saw Huw Davies and, standing behind him, Bethan and Andrew.

'This is a surprise, Huw. Myrtle said you had the day off.'

'Sergeant called me back. Can we come in?'

'Of course. Bethan, Andrew, it's lovely to see you.' She kissed Bethan's cheek as she stepped into the narrow hallway. 'Would you like tea or something stronger? I have a bottle of sherry. There's no beer or brandy but Charlie has some vodka hidden away . . .'

'I'm sorry, Alma, this is an official visit.'

'Official? I don't understand, Huw.'

'The sergeant knows I'm friendly with you and Charlie, that's why he sent for me.'

'Is someone hurt?' Confused, Alma looked from Huw to Bethan. She had no family other than Charlie and Theo, and they were both upstairs. Then she thought of her friends and Mary. 'There's not been an accident! Mary? Someone going home from the wedding . . . ?'

'No one's hurt, Alma.' Huw put his arm around her. 'Charlie upstairs?'

'Yes.'

'I've got some news for him. It's not bad, but it might be a bit of a shock, which is why I asked Andrew to meet me here.'

'And I came to keep you company while they're talking to Charlie,' Bethan broke in. 'Why don't we go upstairs? I'll give you a hand in the kitchen.' Bethan led the way, leaving Alma no choice but to follow with the men.

'It's Huw and Andrew to see you, Charlie.' Alma went into the living room and opened the sideboard where she kept the sherry and Charlie's vodka. 'Would you like a drink?' she asked Andrew and Huw, lifting out both bottles.

'Perhaps later,' Andrew suggested.

'I'll be in the kitchen with Bethan then.' Closing the door, Alma walked down the passage and into the kitchen where Bethan had already taken two glasses from the dresser.

'I brought sherry.' Bethan opened her handbag and lifted out a bottle.

'Snap.' Alma opened the bottle she was holding. 'What's this about, Beth?'

'I don't know. Huw telephoned us and asked if we'd meet him here. All he'd say is what he just told you, that he has some news for Charlie.'

Without thinking Alma filled the tumblers Bethan had set on the table to the brim.

'You trying to get us drunk?'

'Sorry, I was miles away.'

'I thought it might be something to do with the camp Charlie was in. The papers are full of stories about the army gathering evidence for war crimes trials. Charlie must have witnessed a lot of atrocities in three years.'

'Yes,' Alma said slowly, 'yes, that could be it. I only hope it doesn't bring it all back and make him worse than he already is.'

'Huw's good at this sort of thing,' Bethan reassured, recalling the times she had accompanied Huw when he'd been sent to tell women that their husbands and sons had been killed in pit disasters. 'Why don't we sit down?'

Alma pulled a chair from the table and sat opposite her friend.

'Is that Theo's latest drawing?' Bethan repeated the question twice, before giving up. With both of them thinking about what was going on in the living room, any attempt at conversation was pointless.

Andrew had taken it upon himself to remove one of the smallest glasses from the sideboard and pour Charlie a measure of vodka. He handed it to him before sitting down.

'You won't join me?'

'Sergeant will have my guts for garters if I start drinking on duty, Charlie,' Huw demurred, as he tried to sort out what he had to say to Charlie in his mind. It didn't help that the Russian was sitting relaxed in his chair, patiently waiting for him to begin. He cleared his throat. 'We had a communication from the Red Cross. I mean the station had a communication. They're looking for a Captain Feodor Raschenko who was liberated from Nordhausen prison camp last April.' Huw paused, but Charlie continued to sit as composed and self-possessed as when they had walked into the room. Deciding to abandon tact and diplomacy in favour of the direct approach, Huw blurted out, 'They want to know if the man in Nordhausen could be the same Feodor Raschenko who married a . . .' he pulled a crumpled telegram from his pocket and smoothed it over his knee, 'Maria Andreyeva in 1929 in a village . . . K . . . Kra . . .'

'Krasnaya-Poliana,' Charlie supplied in a voice devoid of emotion.

Huw looked at the paper doubtfully. 'Could be.'

'It's fourteen miles north of Moscow.'

'Then, this woman is your wife?' Andrew stared at him incredulously.

'Yes.'

'This is an official visit, Charlie. I could be called to give evidence if any of this reaches a court of law, so please, think carefully before you say anything else,' Huw warned solemnly. 'Did you marry Alma knowing that your first wife was alive?'

'I hoped she was.'

'And Alma?' Andrew asked.

'I told her.'

'About this Maria Andreyeva,' Huw pressed.

Charlie downed the vodka Andrew had handed him. Leaving his chair he walked to the table. Taking the bottle he refilled his glass and poured out two more measures, which he handed to Andrew and Huw.

'You're facing a bigamy charge, Charlie.' Forgetting his earlier refusal on the grounds of duty, Huw emptied his glass in a single swallow.

'I always knew it was a possibility.'

'Then why in God's name didn't you divorce her?'

'How can you divorce someone when you don't know if they're alive or dead?' Charlie focused inwards on a world that Andrew and Huw could only try to imagine. 'I was eighteen when I married Maria – Masha; she was seventeen. She disappeared a year later.'

'Ran away?'

'No, Huw.' Charlie's voice grated oddly as if it was rusty from disuse. 'To understand Masha's disappearance you must understand a little about Russia. A few months after Masha and I married, Stalin began to clear villages and set up collective farms. Anyone who owned property –' a cynical smile played at the corners of his mouth – 'a horse, a cow, a few pigs – was suspect in the eyes of the Communists. And my father had even paid others to work for him. He was the worst of the worst in Communist eyes, a Kulak – an enterprising, rich peasant in a village of rich peasants. Our entire community stood in the way of progress. You see, everyone there owned something of value – a house, furniture, land, animals, tools. All over Russia peasants started killing their live-stock and burning their crops and possessions rather than have them taken from them by the Communists. It led to a chronic food shortage – not rationing like here in the war, but famine. People started dying in their tens of thousands, the children and the elderly first. My father and the older men talked about protest but it was just talk. No one in our village had the courage to make a stand against the Communists or the heart to destroy possessions that had taken generations to acquire. In the end the inevitable happened. Everything we had was taken from us.'

'Stolen?' Huw frowned.

'If a State can steal.'

'In Russia in the early thirties individuals' property was put into a common pot for the use of the community to be taken, each according to their need.'

'I see you know your Russian propaganda, Andrew. But it wasn't quite that simple in our village. We were within a few hours' travelling distance of Moscow.

Certain party members thought our lands were just the place to build their dachas – summer houses,' he explained in reply to Huw's quizzical look. 'I wasn't there when they came.'

'They?'

'The party members – soldiers – I don't know who they were. I was away getting a cot from my brother-in-law's house fifteen miles away. Masha was having our first child. When I came back the village was empty. No – not quite empty,' he amended. 'Gangs of zeks – prisoners – had been moved in to burn the houses and outbuildings that weren't wanted, in readiness to build the new.'

'Didn't you go after your wife?'

'Not only my wife – my parents, brothers and sisters, uncles, aunts, cousins, my entire family and almost everyone I knew. I asked and was told they'd been put on trains going east. I went to the railway station, it was empty, no trains – no people – nothing.' His eyes glazed over as he retreated back to that other country, that other world.

'And then?' Andrew prompted.

'I started to walk east to look for Masha and my family. I didn't find them.'

'How long did you look?' Huw finally removed his notebook and pencil from his top pocket.

'Four years. Then I was arrested.'

'For what?'

'Asking questions.'

'No one gets arrested for that,' Huw interposed.

'Not here in peacetime.'

'But Russia is our ally, a great country . . .'

'You've been listening to the miners, Huw. I was sentenced to ten years in a prison camp – the standard time for asking questions in the Soviet Republic. I escaped after two, made my way to the coast, took a berth as a seaman, came to Cardiff – the rest you know.'

'And in all that time you've never heard from your wife?'

'I made enquiries, wrote letters to my brother-in-law

34

but no one I contacted had heard from anyone in my village. I didn't intend to marry again. I couldn't forget Masha – have never forgotten her – but I found Alma. Of course I told her about my first wife. She – we – understood that there was no going back, not for me, not for Masha wherever she was – but that was before the war.'

'How long after Masha's disappearance did you marry Alma?'

'What difference does it make?'

'How long, Charlie?'

'Nine years.'

Huw looked across at Andrew. 'It's seven years, isn't it?'

'What?'

'If you don't hear from anyone in seven years you can apply to have them legally registered dead.'

'I don't know if British law applies to Stalinist Russia, Huw.'

'Masha? She's alive?' Charlie looked at the telegram in Huw's hand.

'If this woman is your wife she's in a displaced persons' camp in Germany.'

'And she remembers me. After sixteen years she still remembers.' Charlie was more animated than Andrew had seen him since his return.

'She must have told her story and somehow, someone connected her with you. All we have is this enquiry.'

'Do you have an address where I can write?'

Huw handed him the telegram. 'I'll be honest with you, Charlie. I haven't a clue what will happen now. The sergeant assumed it was a cut-and-dried case of bigamy, that this was some woman you met during the war, took a fancy to . . .'

'In one of the Nazis' forced labour camps?'

'The sergeant doesn't always think things through, Andrew.'

'I must know how Masha is, how she survived, what happened to the rest of my family . . . our child . . .'

'And Alma?' Andrew reminded.

35

'I need to talk to her.' Charlie looked at Huw. 'That is, if you're not taking me away.'

'I'm not arresting you, Charlie. But I think it would be best if you come up to the station tomorrow. It might be easier for you to talk to us there. And in the meantime I'll see if I can find out anything else about this woman. From what you told me there's no guarantee she's your wife.'

'She knows my name, where we married . . .'

'And that you're living here. From what I've heard, most refugees will lie, steal, sell their mother and give their right arm to be allowed into this country. Who's to say that this woman didn't meet your wife somewhere and pinch her story in the hope of conning you into paying her passage over here?'

'Then you think she might not be Masha?' It was as if someone had switched the light out in his eyes.

'It has to be a possibility. We'll start our enquiries by asking for a photograph. Hopefully she'll not have changed too much.'

'After sixteen years in camps she'll have changed.'

'Do you want me to tell Alma about this?' Andrew asked.

'No, I'll tell her.'

'Would you like Bethan or me to stay here tonight?'

'Thank you, Andrew, but no.'

'If you need us, telephone, day or night, it doesn't matter, we'll come.'

Tony leaned on the bar of the Graig Hotel and ordered another pint of beer from the vaguely familiar, blowsy barmaid.

'You're Judy Crofter, aren't you?' he asked, after deciding that there was no way her brassy blonde hair could be natural.

'And you're Tony Ronconi. Your sister was in school with me.'

'Seeing as how I've six of them, it would have been difficult for you to have gone to school round here and not have had one of them in your class.'

'Just as well you're wearing uniform.' She pushed the fifth beer he'd ordered in two hours towards him. 'Orders are, two pints and over, only to be given to serving soldiers.'

'It's good to know I've given up nearly seven years of my life for something.' He lifted his pint, 'Cheers.'

'Cheers,' Judy Crofter smiled as she wiped a cloth over the bar in front of him.

'So, do you want a drink?' he asked, taking the hint.

'I wouldn't say no to a port and lemon.'

'Did I give you enough money?'

'Oh yes.' She opened the till again and tossed most of his change into it before pouring herself a drink. 'So, how much leave you got?'

'All over bar the official demob next week.'

'Nice to put your feet up and see the family.'

'Yes,' he agreed cryptically. 'Judy, you haven't got any rooms here by any chance, have you?'

'Rooms for a party, you mean?'

'For me to sleep in,' he corrected irritably.

'Why do you want to sleep here when you live in Danycoedcae Road?'

'Because the house is full with my mother and the kids home.'

'I know what you mean. I'm dreading my brothers coming back from the Far East. We've only got two rooms and a boxroom. I moved into their room when they left. My father has the other bedroom and I can't say I'm thrilled with the thought of going back into the boxroom. But there you are, I don't suppose I'll have any choice. I can't expect three great big hulking men to sleep in a single bed in a space not big enough to twirl a cat with a short tail.'

'Rooms, here?' he reminded.

'There are two but they're taken on a weekly basis. Big nobs from the pits,' she confided in an undertone.

Tony picked up his pint, wondering why he'd ordered it. The room was already wavering around him. He'd eaten hardly anything of the meal he'd ordered in the restaurant and four pints mixed with family arguments on top of an almost empty stomach didn't make for a clear head, but without thinking further than the next five minutes he took a long pull at the mug.

'Do you know anywhere else I might try?' he asked.

'Surely your mother can put you up? I know it might mean sleeping on a sofa . . .'

'I want a bed. I've slept in enough makeshift places the last six years to last me a lifetime. Leave is supposed to mean home comforts.'

'See what you mean. Well, I suppose I could let you have our boxroom. Like I said it's small but it's clean and since the munitions factory closed I've nothing else to do but work here nights and look after the house during the day so I could do your washing and feed you. You have got a ration book?'

'You live in Leyshon Street, don't you?'

'Isn't that good enough for people from Danycoedcae Road?'

'It's perfect, not so far to stagger from here but I've got someone to see first. Give me the number and a key and I'll leave my bag there.'

'Fifteen bob a week all right?'

He raised his eyebrows.

'Including breakfast and tea,' she added swiftly. 'It's number fourteen, the key is in the door because there's bugger all to steal. My father works nights, but don't worry about him, we've been short since munitions laid me off. He'll be so pleased at the thought of extra to pay the rent, he won't mind the two of us sleeping there alone.'

'You sure?' Tony asked, realising how it would look.

'I'll get us a bit of supper, shall I, from the chip shop?'

'That would be nice.' Thrusting his hand in his pocket he pulled out two shillings. 'Here you go.'

'Ta, Tony. Whoever you've got to visit don't make it too late. Seeing as how neither of us has much to get up for in the morning we could have a bit of fun before hitting the hay.' She gave him a broad wink as the landlord shouted at her to get on with serving the other customers.

38

Chapter Three

THE LIVING ROOM above Charlie and Alma's shop was quiet. So still, the tick of the mantel clock staccatoed into the chill air like rifle shots, fraying Alma's ragged nerves to breaking point. Shivering, she hunched further into her cardigan. Hoping to get Charlie to bed early, and incidentally save on severely rationed coal, she'd banked down the fire just before their visitors had arrived. But with frost icing the February night air and coating the windowpane, it hadn't taken long for the temperature of the room to drop below a comfortable level.

'Do you think this woman could be Masha?' she asked, shattering the silence that had closed in, enveloping each in their separateness since Charlie had broken the news.

'I hope so.'

Leaving her chair she walked to the fireplace and hooked the guard in front of the grate so if any coals fell out during the night they couldn't roll further than the tiled hearth. She knew what she had to say, it needed saying, but above all she needed to convince Charlie that she meant every word.

'Do you remember the night you told me about Masha?'

He looked into her eyes with such love she might have been touched if she hadn't recalled that he'd once told her it was her resemblance to Masha that had attracted him to her. She even heard his voice echoing back from that momentous night – *'She looked a lot like you, tall, slender with pale skin, red hair and green eyes.'*

'It was the same night I told you I loved you.'

She knelt before him and took his hands into hers. For the first time in months they were actually talking, but Alma was very conscious that it was the hope of

Masha re-entering his life that had wrought the miracle, not anything she had done.

'You also told me that I had to understand about Masha. That she would always be the first one – and your wife.'

'That was a long time ago, Alma.'

'Seven years and a war ago, Charlie, but I know you. Your feelings don't alter with time.'

'Masha and I were married only a few months. I haven't seen her in sixteen years. I don't even know if it is her, and even if it is, she might not recognise or want me. She could have married again. Anything could have happened to her. The fact that she is in a displaced persons' camp now suggests her life hasn't been easy. She could have been in one of the Nazis' forced labour camps like me – or, even worse, one of the death camps.' His eyes were miraculously alive – and tortured.

'First, you have to find out if it is her, Charlie,' Alma said practically. 'And if it is, chances are she'll need looking after and the best place to do that is here, in Pontypridd, where you have a home, friends and business. I'll view that house in Tyfica Road tomorrow. I've already talked to the solicitor so I have a fair idea of what it's worth. We have more than enough money saved to offer a fair price and if it's in the condition I believe it is, I think we should buy it.'

'For you and Theo?'

'No. Theo and I will stay here with Mary for the time being. If this woman is Masha you'll need somewhere to take her.'

'This flat –'

'Is too public and noisy. There are people in and out of the shop at all hours, if it's not the customers and delivery-men it's the staff. Theo, Mary and I are used to living here and it's ideally situated to run the business. Besides, if you don't mind I'd like to carry on overseeing the shops until you decide what you want to do with them.'

'I couldn't live with Masha in the same town as you.'

'Why not, Feo?' she asked, unconsciously reverting to his Russian name. 'It's not as if any of us have done anything wrong. It wasn't your fault that you two were separated. Neither of you left the other willingly.'

'Alma, I'm sorry . . .'

'There's nothing for you to be sorry about, Charlie,' she declared a little too firmly. 'Masha is your first wife, you loved her and she you. I know what it is to lose someone you love. You were missing for just over three years and it almost drove me mad. I can't begin to imagine how I'd feel after sixteen . . .' Her breath caught in her throat. Fighting to maintain her composure she murmured, 'I'm really glad she's alive, Charlie. For both of you.'

'And us?'

She turned away as she rose to her feet. 'I don't think Pontypridd is ready for a man with two wives.' She'd intended the comment to sound light-hearted but her voice cracked under the strain.

'It might be better for you and Theo if I moved out.'

She gripped the back of the chair in front of her so tightly her knuckles hurt. 'If that's what you want.'

'I could move in with Andrew and Bethan for a while. They have room.'

'I'm tired, I'm going to bed.' Alma walked quickly to the door but not quite quickly enough. Charlie left his chair, caught her by the waist and clung to her, and for a brief moment nothing else mattered. Then just as abruptly, he released her.

As Alma left the room she felt that the embrace had been his way of saying goodbye.

Tony walked down Graig Street peering at the houses until he came to the one he'd been looking for. A key protruded from the lock just as it did from every other front door he'd passed. He was surprised how odd that looked to him after six years away and eight months in post-war Germany but then the realisation came – he was home. And as Judy had so succinctly pointed out, after years of shortages and rationing people on the Graig had '*bugger all worth stealing*'.

He hesitated, debating whether or not to go in. He'd

been unsure of the welcome he'd receive at home but he was very sure of the reception he'd get in this house. As his drink-fuddled mind groped towards a decision, he recalled all the stirring speeches he'd been forced to listen to since he'd been in the army. Hadn't he and millions of others like him just finished fighting a long and bitter war to assert their own and every other man's rights? And wasn't that all he was trying to do, assert his rights?

Turning the key, he stepped into the flagstoned passage to be greeted by silence. Everything was quiet, no murmur of radio, or voices – no lights shining beneath the doors. He glanced at his watch but it was too dark to read the face. Feeling his way past the parlour door on his right and the stairs on his left, he headed for the kitchen and opened the door. It was warm – too warm after the street – and he tugged at his collar. The curtains had been opened and the moon shone silvery cold through the small back window. He could see from the muted glow of small coal smothering large that the stove had been bedded down for the night and the room tidied. As he fumbled for the light switch he heard a step on the stairs.

'Tony! What on earth are you doing here?' Dishevelled and even more beautiful and seductive than he remembered, clutching a long, bottle-green brushed cotton robe to her throat, her dark hair hanging loose around her face, his brother's wife, Diana, blinked back at him.

'Thought I'd call in on my sister-in-law,' he slurred, discovering that his voice, like the room, was wavering uncontrollably. 'Give big brother Ronnie – head of the family's wife – a chance to welcome the hero home from the war. And there's Billy, my step-nephew – only we know he's a lot closer than that, don't we, Diana? I want to see him.'

'At a quarter past ten at night?'

'Why not?' Reeling, he crashed into the table, sending the cruet rattling.

'Tony, whatever you want, it will have to wait until morning. And I'd be happier if you'd bring one of your sisters with you the next time you visit.'

'So beautiful and so heartless. You weren't always like this, Diana.'

'You're drunk.'

The disgust in her voice spawned resentment. 'Course I'm drunk. I'm home from the army. I have every right to be drunk after what I've been through and suffered for the women and children of this country – drunk as a lord . . .'

Stepping back, Diana opened the door to the passage wider. 'Out.'

'No!' Grinning inanely up at her, he fell back into the easy chair.

'Tony, don't make me throw you out.'

'I'd like to see you try.' He slid down, propped his feet on a stool and stared defiantly up at her.

'How about me doing it for her?'

Stunned, Diana stared in disbelief as the tall figure of her husband strode past the open front door and down the passage. Muffled in layers of army-issue khaki, he tossed his kitbag on to the stairs before confronting his brother.

'Ronnie! I didn't know you were back.' Tony started nervously, sending the stool crashing to the floor.

'I bet you didn't. Angelo told me you were home. I didn't think you'd be idiot enough to come here.'

'Wanted to see my sister-in-law – and Billy . . .' Tony shrank back into the chair as Ronnie drew closer. Tony was eight years younger than his brother, but he was also five inches shorter and not so drunk he'd forgotten the pain Ronnie had inflicted on him the last time they had clashed.

'Ronnie!' Diana screamed as her husband's hand closed on the front of Tony's uniform collar.

'Just helping him through the door.'

'He's drunk.'

'I noticed.'

'You can't just throw him into the street.'

'He's not bloody well staying here.'

'You're hurting him,' Diana pleaded.

'See, she still likes me.' It was one remark too many.

'But I don't!' Lifting Tony bodily from the chair, Ronnie slammed him against the wall close to the dresser.

43

The whole piece shook, sending the china juddering on the shelves. 'And how often have you called to see my wife since I've been away?'

'Ronnie, please, he hasn't been back in Pontypridd since you two fought last time.' Distraught, Diana tried to pull Ronnie off Tony but the room was crammed with overlarge pieces of furniture and the table blocked her way. 'Ronnie – please let him go,' she begged.

Grim-faced Ronnie continued to pin Tony high off his feet, watching dispassionately as his features turned blue-black.

'Ronnie you're killing him . . .'

'And you're not worth going to jail for, are you, little brother?' Ronnie finally slackened his grip enough for Tony to draw breath. He turned to look at Diana. Her eyes were damp, brimming with unshed tears.

'Ronnie . . .'

All the love, warmth and welcome Ronnie had dreamed of every night since he'd left her was mirrored on her face. But the momentary distraction was what Tony had been waiting for. Arms flailing wildly, he lashed out. Catching Ronnie unawares he sent him crashing backwards on to the table. Pressing home the unexpected advantage, Tony jumped on top of him.

'Stop it. Both of you!' Diana grabbed Tony's arm to prevent him from slamming his fist into Ronnie's nose. Striking out blindly, Tony hurled Diana aside. She screamed as she reeled over the easy chair into the window. She heard the glass shatter, felt the shards raining on to her head and body, heard Ronnie shout, saw blood . . . But strangely there was no pain – no pain at all – as tidal waves of purple twilight moved in from the shadows, enveloping everything, even Ronnie's face – fearful – and so very, very loving.

William Powell left his plate on the counter of the café, winked at Angelo, opened the kitchen door and walked straight through to the passage. Shouldering his kitbag he ran lightly up the stairs. The streetlamp shone through the lace that covered the landing window, but both rooms were in darkness. Leaving his bag in the living room, he tiptoed to the bedroom. Turning the knob he peeped round the door to be confronted by total gloom. He was momentarily disorientated before he realised that Tina hadn't replaced the blackout curtains.

'Come any closer and I'll scream.'

'Not that Angelo will run upstairs to rescue you, he's too busy throwing out the stragglers.'

'Will! Is it you? – Damn!' The lamp thudded to the floor as Tina missed the switch and knocked it over.

'Close your eyes.' He switched on the main light, smiling as she sat up, pushing her unruly mass of black curls away from her face.

'Shut the door, it's cold.' She said the first thing that came into her head as a draught of icy air whistled in from the passage.

'I know. The train Ronnie and I travelled down on from London was unheated and it took ages ...' It suddenly struck him that he was gabbling trivialities during a moment he'd been planning, waiting and longing for almost every minute since he'd left her. He continued to stare, wanting to absorb every aspect of her – her presence – her essence – the exact way she looked with her hair falling forward over her sleep- and cold-flushed cheeks. Then he realised she was scrutinising him in exactly the same way.

'I can't believe you're here. Damn it, Will, why didn't you write or send a telegram? I could have prepared a special meal or at least stayed up ...'

'There wasn't time to let you know.' Smiling at her pique, he opened his arms. Throwing back the bed-clothes, she dived to the foot of the bed and hugged him over the footboard, nestling her face against the scratchy, rough, woollen, army-issue overcoat that smelled of cold, oil, trains and the unique, mixed essence she had almost forgotten, that was her husband.

He bent his head to kiss her and she clung to him, forgetting that her feet were freezing out of the bedclothes, her hair was a mess, her face was shiny with cold cream and even for one blissful moment the old purple cardigan she was wearing over her thickest – and least glamorous – nightdress.

'So, have you missed me?' he questioned, finally releasing her.

'How can you ask?'

'I assumed you'd be lonely but then I wasn't expecting to walk into the café at this time of night and find you in bed.'

She dragged him down next to her. Unfastening his overcoat he pulled her on to his lap.

'Your mother and Dino got married today and I was feeling miserable, lonely and envious.'

'Of my mother and that fat American she sent me a picture of?' he laughed.

'Of your mother having that fat American in her bed tonight – and he's not that fat,' she contradicted, 'just cuddly.' She slid her hands beneath his coat and jacket, seeking reassurance and warmth as he kissed her a second time.

'I'll pull my vest up if you promise to keep your hands in one place. They're like two little snowballs, move them any lower and you're likely to destroy all chances of making tonight a happy one.'

'I promise.' She curled up on his knees, hooking the bottom of her nightdress over her frozen feet before unbuttoning his shirt.

'You were telling me how much you envied my mother having an American in her bed. I trust that means you wanted me, not a Yank, in yours?'

'Stop fishing for compliments. If I say any more, I'll flatter you and you've got a big enough head already.'

'Same old wife.'

'Same old husband.'

'You hungry?' She tried to climb off his lap but he tightened his grip on her waist and pulled her back against his chest.

'Not for food. Ronnie and I bullied Angelo into feeding us.'

'You've been downstairs . . .'

'Only as long as it took us to eat. Ronnie and I were starving.'

'It didn't occur to either of you that your wives would have liked to have seen you before the rest of Ponty?'

'We needed sustenance so we could concentrate on more important things than food when we greeted our women.'

'I bet Diana's happy.'

'Not as happy as her brother.' Wrapping his coat around her he drew her even closer. 'Now I know what it's like to cuddle an icicle. I hope you don't thaw, I have no idea how to clean melted woman off my uniform.'

She sat up suddenly. 'Tony!'

'Tony who?'

'My brother Tony,' she said irritably. 'Luke came down earlier looking for him. My mother threw him out of the house. He could be out there freezing to death.'

'Wise woman, your mother, but then I gather Tony's been even more stupid than usual. I hear he wants to marry a German.'

'Angelo told you?'

'Before he even said hello and welcome back. And about Tony, I know him. He'll have found a warm hole to crawl into lined with all home comforts, including a woman.'

'So that's how you soldiers behave when you're away from your wives?'

'Not me, I'm a happily married man. Tony is a bachelor.'

'For the moment. You sure I can't make you anything to eat?'

'I'm sure,' he reiterated, unfastening his buttons and pulling his shirt free. 'How about you crawl back in there and warm the sheets for me.'

'You going somewhere?' she asked as he left the bed.

'I've something for you in my kitbag.'

'I'd rather have what's under that uniform.'

'And I thought all women were mercenary.'

'We are.' Kneeling, she tugged at his overcoat.

47

'So you only want me for my body.'

'It's been so long, I think I've forgotten what to do with it.'

Peeling off his shirt and vest in one easy movement, he unbuttoned his trousers. 'It's like riding a bike: once we get started you'll remember.'

'How do you know?'

'I haven't forgotten my last leave.'

She looked down and saw her ugly nightdress and the even uglier cardigan. Throwing back the bedclothes she stepped out on to the cold linoleum.

'Where are you going, woman? You're supposed to be warming the bed for me.'

'To get this black lace thing I bought. It's guaranteed to excite you.'

Dropping his trousers to his ankles he sat on the side of the bed and started to laugh.

'What's so funny?' she demanded, annoyed, as his laughter grew louder and tears of mirth started pouring down his cheeks.

'You!' he chortled. 'After three years of living like a monk you think I need black lace to excite me.'

'William Powell . . .'

'Mrs Powell,' he whispered, forestalling her temper by sliding his hands beneath her nightdress. 'May I suggest we get under the bedclothes before we both turn to ice, and please,' he fingered the thick red flannel as he pulled it over her head, 'can we donate this nun's penance robe to the Communist relief fund for Russian refugees?'

'There was a lot of screaming and shouting, Constable Davies. I tried knocking my kitchen wall with the poker because it backs on to Mrs Ronconi's kitchen and I know she can hear it because I did just that when our Mary scalded herself. Mrs Ronconi came running to help then – but this time the shouting didn't stop. To be honest, I was too afraid to walk in afterwards – well, anyone would be, wouldn't they, because afterwards the house was that quiet. That's when I sent Alf – Alf Pickering, who lives the

48

other side of me – to the telephone box on the corner to dial 999. Normally, I wouldn't have bothered the police, but the screams – well, it sounded like someone was being murdered – and the shouting – if there hadn't been shouting I would have left well alone. But it did sound like someone was being murdered in there and that nice Mrs Ronconi normally doesn't make a sound. Quiet as the grave her and the kids are – day to day that is – except on Sundays when her mam and sister-in-laws come round – then it's nothing but women cackling. You can hear them through the wall – but then everyone has a family get-together now and again, don't they? On the whole she's just the sort of neighbour you want. But I did see a man going in there tonight. Two actually . . .'

'It's all right, Mrs Evans. You did the right thing, leave it to us.' Huw looked over her head to Hopkins, the novice constable he'd brought with him.

'The screaming's stopped now but it was terrible. Like a stuck pig being gelded and I should know. Born and bred on a farm . . .'

'Mrs Evans, why don't you make us all a nice cup of tea while I go in and see if Mrs Ronconi needs help.' Leaving Mrs Evans to Hopkins, Huw opened the door and called down the passage.

'Is that someone crying?' Hopkins asked, after he'd finally shaken Mrs Evans off so he could follow Huw.

'Don't know, boy. Shut the door and turn on the lights.'

As soon as he heard the front door click, Huw pushed open the door to the kitchen. White-faced, he gripped the sides of the doorframe and reeled back into the passage.

'Oh my God!' Hopkins turned his head and retched.

Sick to the pit of his stomach, but more experienced than Hopkins at concealing his reactions, Huw forced himself to go back into the room. Side-stepping the pools of blood he grabbed a tea towel from the back of a chair and kneeled on the floor beside Ronnie. As soon as he'd done what he could, he looked up at his colleague swaying on his feet in the doorway.

'No time to faint, boy. There's a telephone behind you. Dial 999. Tell them we need a doctor. Don't forget to give them the address and say I told you it's life or death, and we're going to need an ambulance . . .'

'Uncle Huw?'

A small boy dressed in pyjamas a couple of sizes too big for him, holding the hand of an even smaller girl, appeared behind the young policeman in the passage.

'Billy,' Huw attempted a smile as he lowered his voice, 'what are you doing up at this time of night?'

'Mam . . .'

'Everything's going to be fine, Billy.' Huw signalled to Hopkins frantically with his eyes. 'Take Catrina upstairs. I'll be there as soon as I can. After you've called 999 see they get to bed,' he murmured under his breath to the constable, as he tried to block Billy's view of Diana with his body. 'Then telephone Ronconi's Tumble café. Tell them what's happened and that we need a babysitter – urgently.'

Angelo could hear Tina giggling and William laughing as he ran up the stairs. It was obvious what they were doing but need overrode embarrassment and he hammered resolutely on their bedroom door.

'Whoever that is, go away!' Tina shouted.

'We're dead,' Will added.

'Police phoned, Diana's had an accident.'

Quicker than Will, Tina wrapped herself in the patchwork bedspread and jerked open the door.

'What kind of accident?'

'I don't know because I couldn't get much sense out of the man I spoke to. All I know is Huw said he needed both of you, quick.'

Pale and trembling, Hopkins was standing guard outside Laura's house, keeping a small crowd of neighbours at bay when Andrew slowed his car to a halt. He didn't waste time on preliminaries.

'Mrs Ronconi's in the kitchen,' he announced as Andrew and Bethan stepped out.

'The children?' Bethan asked.

'They're unhurt. Constable Davies had me telephone the café. Mr and Mrs Powell are on their way up to look after them. He thinks it best you go straight to the kitchen, Nurse John.'

Laura's normally immaculate kitchen was in uproar. The windowframe was smashed to pieces, slivers of glass and wood scattered over the sill and floor, the table was on its side, the easy chair upturned, half the crockery had fallen from the dresser and was lying, shattered on the flagstoned floor. Covered in blood, Ronnie was kneeling in the centre of the confusion, cradling Diana in his arms.

'Ronnie.' Bethan kneeled beside him, gently moving him back so Andrew could examine Diana. 'I didn't know you were home.'

Ignoring her, he continued to nurse Diana.

'Has an ambulance been sent for?'

Reading the urgency in Andrew's voice, Bethan rose to her feet. 'I'll check.'

'It's bad?' Huw asked Bethan.

'It's not good.' Bethan knew Huw too well to lie. 'We need to get her to an operating theatre as soon as we can. You've sent for an ambulance?'

He nodded, 'It'll be here in ten minutes.'

'What the hell happened?'

'I wish I knew. I only got here a few minutes ago. A neighbour heard a fracas and called the station. Ronnie hasn't said a word since I've been here.'

'He's in shock . . .'

'Bethan?'

Alerted by the alarm in Andrew's voice, she turned back to see blood pumping out of Diana's arm, soaking the rug and flagstones. Opening Andrew's bag she removed a tourniquet.

'The ambulance should be here in ten minutes.'

'Let's hope she lasts that long.'

Bethan pushed down hard on the pressure point in the crook of Diana's elbow as Andrew tied the rubber tubing tightly on Diana's upper arm. Steeling herself, Bethan cast a professional eye over her cousin. It was difficult to see past the blood and glass splinters to assess the damage. Either Ronnie or Huw had pressed a tea towel on the side of Diana's head. Seeing her looking, Andrew moved it slightly. Bethan only just managed to stop herself from crying out. There was a gap in Diana's skull, just below the hairline, that ran two inches long and half an inch wide.

'There's too much blood to see if there's glass in it.'

Taking a sterile dressing from Andrew's bag, she removed the tea towel and gently covered the wound.

'Ronnie?' Bethan called his name twice but he refused to look at her. 'The ambulance is coming.'

He continued to gaze down at Diana, holding her hand, white and very small in his own.

'It will be better if I go with her, Ronnie,' Andrew said briskly, reverting to his no–nonsense professional manner. 'You can follow with Bethan in the car.'

'You'll have to come in the car with me, Ronnie,' Bethan repeated slowly.

Huw appeared in the doorway. 'The ambulance is here, and Tina and Will have arrived.'

'Tell the driver to bring the stretcher in.' Andrew touched Ronnie's arm. 'We're going to move her now. Do you understand?'

'Why don't you take Will and Tina upstairs to the children?'

Bethan's plea fell on deaf ears. Ronnie refused to relinquish his hold on Diana's hand as the ambulance men lifted her on to their stretcher under Andrew's direction. He walked beside her as they carried her outside. Huw had moved the crowd back but Bethan could see them all craning their necks in the hope of getting a good look at Diana on the stretcher. The ambulance driver and his mate, both experienced professionals, finally managed to prise Ronnie's fingers away from Diana's as they loaded her into the back of the ambulance.

'Get him in as quickly as you can,' Andrew ordered

Bethan as he climbed up beside the stretcher. 'He's in shock.'

'I recognise it when I see it,' Bethan snapped, the strain exacting its toll on her. 'You'll see her soon, Ronnie, I promise,' she murmured in kinder tones, gripping his hand tightly, as one of the men closed the doors.

Despite all Bethan's efforts to coax him indoors and away from prying eyes, Ronnie continued to stand, watching until the ambulance drove down to the main road and turned the corner. Then he began to scream.

'Get him on the sofa and hold him still,' Bethan shouted as Huw and William struggled to push Ronnie through the door and into the parlour. After they managed to remove his overcoat she pulled up his sleeve and injected him. 'Don't let him go until his eyes close and you can feel him relaxing.'

'Remind me never to quarrel with you, Beth.' William practically sat on Ronnie as Bethan picked up the telephone to call a second ambulance.

'How is Diana?' Tina whispered from the top of the stairs as Bethan replaced the receiver.

'We'll know more after they've operated.'

Tina ran down the stairs, 'Don't give me that hospital double talk. I'm not one of your bloody patients. Diana's your cousin and my sister-in-law . . .'

'Beth knows that, Tina.' Huw laid his hand on her shoulder. 'Why don't you go back up and see to the kids?'

'They're all right for the moment, that young copper's with them.' She looked down at Ronnie, who was slumped on the parlour sofa.

'I knew he was in shock, I just didn't realise how bad he was. I'm sorry, Tina,' Bethan apologised. 'It had to be done. I had no choice.'

Tina went to the kitchen door. Transfixed by the mess of broken and upturned furniture, crockery and blood-stains she turned to Huw. 'What happened?'

'I don't know. We had a call at the station, I recognised the address . . .'

'In God's name, why won't anyone tell me what's going on?'

'Because none of us knows, love.' After verifying that Ronnie was well and truly out of it, William went to her. Pulling her head on to his shoulder, he held her tight as she started to cry. 'Try to think of the children. They need you now because with Mam away you're the one they know best.'

The shrill sound of an ambulance bell rang closer.

'You'll let us know what's happening, Beth?'

'The minute I hear, Will. You two will stay here?'

'Until morning.'

'If there's any news I'll telephone from the hospital.'

After seeing William and Tina safely upstairs and into the children's bedroom, Huw closed the door and beckoned Hopkins downstairs. They went into the kitchen.

'Domestic?' the copper asked.

Huw knew what he was suggesting because it had become an all-too-familiar scenario since the war had ended. The headlines usually read, *Soldier arrived home to find wife in arms of other man*. Much as he refused to believe it of his niece, even he had to admit all the evidence pointed that way. Ronnie still had his overcoat on; Diana was in a robe and nightdress. Blood all over the place and the smashed furniture indicated that there'd been one hell of a brawl. That was without the shouts and screams that had led the neighbours to call the police, in itself a remarkable event for Graig people. And he hadn't forgotten Mrs Evans' assertion that she had seen two men enter the house. Nosy parkers like her were a godsend to the prosecution.

'Check the wash house, the back door and the garden path – take your torch.'

'What am I looking for?'

'If I knew that, I wouldn't have asked you to make a search.'

As Hopkins opened the door that led into the wash house, Huw walked to the front. Neighbours were still

54

standing in the street, gossiping and watching the door.

'Come on now, people, it's all over. There's nothing for anyone to see and nothing anyone can do to help, so why don't you all go home?' He waited, knowing that if he stood on the doorstep long enough they'd disperse peaceably.

When the last door had closed in the street he looked up and down before walking to the main road. Everywhere, quiet streets and houses with darkened windows yawned back at him. The few people not already in bed were in their back kitchens. There wasn't a family on the Graig who wasted coals by using their front parlour in winter. And in summer the hallowed room was only opened up on high days, holidays and formal Sunday tea occasions when posh maiden aunts visited.

A dog barked from the direction of the dairy on the corner of Factory Lane. The sound cut hollowly through the frozen air as the long, low shadow of a stray cat darted back up in the direction of Leyshon Street. Not knowing what he'd been looking for, or even expecting, he returned to the house.

'There's a blood trail, Constable Davies. It goes from the kitchen to the sink in the wash house then down the garden path and over the wall on to the mountain.'

Lighting his own torch Huw followed Hopkins along the route. There was no mistaking the thin trail of blood spots.

'We don't stand a chance of tracking these on the mountain,' Huw complained more to himself than Hopkins as they stood, shining their torches over the garden wall. He turned as he heard steps in next door's garden. 'Mrs Evans, isn't it time you went to bed?'

'Yes, Constable Davies, but I couldn't sleep without knowing if you'd caught him. I didn't see him coming out of the house and I wondered if you'd got him the back way.'

'Who, Mrs Evans?'

'The other Ronconi. The one who went into the house before Mrs Ronconi's husband.'

Chapter Four

'YOU TOOK YOUR time. Is that blood on your face?'

'I had a nosebleed.' Tony squinted as he struggled to focus on Judy. There were three of them and he wasn't sure which was real.

'It's all over your coat.'

'It's had blood on it before, it'll clean off.'

'You been fighting?'

'Sort of.'

'You hurt?'

'No.'

'Anyone I know.'

'Family.' Rolling his coat into a ball, Tony dropped it on a chair.

'I put your chips in the oven, they'll be dried to a cinder by now.' Opening the door set in the side of the range Judy lifted out a stained, greasy tin and tipped a few dried chips on to a plate that didn't look much cleaner than the tin. 'Do you want salt and vinegar?'

Feeling distinctly queasy at the sight of so much burned grease, and not daring to open his mouth lest the beer that lay so heavily on his stomach spew out, he shook his head.

'If I'd known you were going to leave them I would have eaten them myself sooner than seen them go to waste.' Pushing the tin back into the oven Judy slammed the door. 'The Ty Bach's the first door on the right outside the back door. I've put a clean towel in the wash house – it's the one with blue stripes.'

Rushing through the wash house and into the yard that separated the narrow strip of garden from the house, Tony yanked open the first door he came to. He only just reached the bowl in time. Sinking to his knees he retched violently, ridding himself of most of the contents of his stomach, but seconds later the world still revolved alarmingly around him. Feeling cold, clammy and extremely sorry for himself, he wiped his mouth with the back of his hand, pulled the chain and staggered outside.

Someone – not Judy he guessed – had laid out the area in carefully measured vegetable plots. A row of bean sticks stood in readiness for spring planting, neatly stacked against the dry-stone wall that adjoined the neighbour's garden, and he could make out the frost-coated leaves of rhubarb and winter cabbage.

Leaning against the wall of the house, he looked up. The sky was a rich navy velvet, the stars glimmering, diamond pinpricks of intense light – majestic, beautiful, awesome, and sick-making. Why oh why had he drunk so much? His mouth and throat felt as if they had been packed with sewage. His head was pounding, he was incapable of stringing two coherent thoughts together and despite the ice in the air he craved to be even colder.

Was it all a nightmare? Had he really gone to Laura's house to see Diana or had he imagined it? He closed his eyes. An image of Diana sprang to mind, lying alarmingly still, her eyes closed, her head covered in blood – and Ronnie, crouched over her, his greatcoat more red than khaki. It had to be a dream. A bad dream! He couldn't have killed Diana. Not a woman! Now men, that was different – he'd killed plenty of men – but then he'd been ordered to. That was war, following orders and killing men.

He felt blood trickling down from his nose over his mouth again and wiped it away with the back of his hand. That was it! He'd had a nosebleed. He often got them when he drank more than a couple of pints. No wonder he was light-headed. He'd made it all up – Diana, Ronnie, the house, the fight – a sort of daymare as opposed to nightmare. But, dear God, it had seemed real.

He opened his eyes again. He could almost believe he'd run from the house over the mountain and back down on to the road to the telephone box to call an ambulance. Stood behind a crowd of people, watching as Diana was carried out of the house on a stretcher.

It must have been his fear of Ronnie that had done it, coupled with the drink and his nosebleed. Ever since his last leave he'd been terrified that his brother would set on him again and turn him into mincemeat.

'You all right?' Judy interrupted from the wash house.

'Looking at the sky.'

'It's warmer in the house.'

'I'm all right out here.'

'Some of us have better things to do than freeze out here, and I need to show you your bedroom.'

Hesitantly, not at all sure he could prevent his stomach from heaving again, he followed her though the wash house and kitchen to the foot of the stairs where he'd dumped his kitbag. As she led the way up the narrow staircase he caught glimpses of plump, naked pink thighs above thick, black stocking tops. Gabrielle would never allow him to follow her upstairs or precede her down, but then – he comforted himself with the thought – unlike Judy, his Gabrielle was a lady – a real lady with a title.

Tony Ronconi, younger Ronconi son, who had been forced to play second fiddle to his older brother, Ronnie, all his life had caught himself an aristocrat who worshipped the ground he walked on and he couldn't wait to show her off to the whole of Pontypridd.

'I warned you it wasn't a palace.'

'It'll do.' The door hit the side of the narrow single bed and the room was only just long enough to accommodate the bed-frame. He couldn't help thinking it would have made a better broom cupboard than bedroom. Dropping heavily on to the lumpy mattress he touched the quilt. 'It's damp.'

'It's just cold. I haven't slept in this room since the boys left in '39.'

He looked up and saw the top button of her pullover was unfastened. As he watched she deliberately moved her hand and unfastened the two below, displaying the vee of her breasts.

'Do you want to wash downstairs first?'

Thinking of his stomach he nodded assent. Pulling the drawstring on the top of his kitbag he heaved it forward and removed his wash bag. Beneath it were rows of neat little packages.

'Want a present?' On impulse he handed her a bottle of perfume he'd intended for Tina.

'Ooh, Tony. What is it?' She tore at the white paper. 'Scent!' Throwing her arms around his neck she kissed him.

Without thinking he reached up and squeezed her left breast through her woollen sweater.

'Ooh, naughty,' she squealed. 'I'll have you know I'm a respectable girl.'

'Course you are,' he mumbled, leaving his hand where it was.

'You got a girlfriend, Tony?'

Too addled and exhausted to risk explanation he shook his head.

'Shame, nice-looking boy like you.' She laid her hand over his. 'Ooh, you are cold.'

'This is a bloody cold room.'

'Mine's warmer because it's over the kitchen. Do you want to sit there a while?'

'The kitchen.'

'My bedroom, silly.' Taking his hand she led him into the back bedroom. 'See, it is warmer.'

'And the bed's bigger.' Throwing himself on top of it, he closed his eyes in the hope that everything would finally stop moving around him.

'Get your dirty boots off my best bedcover.' Judy pushed his feet aside and began fiddling with his laces. As she loosened them, she pulled off first one boot and sock then the other. 'You're not thinking of going to sleep on me are you, Tony?'

He opened his eyes to see her unbuckling her liberty bodice.

'Real scent, needs a real thank you.' Dropping her vest and liberty bodice on to a chair she unscrewed the silver cap on the bottle and sprinkled the contents liberally between her breasts and over her bra. The sickly aroma of rotting roses pervaded the air, making his stomach heave even more. There never had been much love lost between him and Tina, which was why he'd bought her the cheapest scent he could find.

Judy pushed him playfully, rolling him over to make room for herself on the bed. 'Here give me your hand, I'll warm it.' Taking his fingers she clamped it on the grubby pink, artificial silk cup of her bra. He could feel her nipples hardening beneath his touch and despite his nausea, instinct came into play. He could have been back in any one of the dozen or so brothels he'd frequented and offloaded his pay in between the Normandy coast and Germany. He hadn't come home, he hadn't had the dream about visiting Diana – he and Ronnie had never had a fight . . .

'We'll be warmer under the covers,' he suggested thickly.

'Ooh, naughty.' She breathed chip fumes over his face and into his ear. 'Only if you make me your girl. Ow . . . !' she shrieked as he tugged at her thick elastic bra strap, pinging it against her back.

'Your fault.'

'Why is it my fault?' she giggled.

'Decent girls undress before they get into bed.'

'I am your girl,' she persisted.

'Course you are.' He wondered why every girl he'd ever met wanted the promise of the world with icing sugar on before they'd perform. 'Bad' girl, that is. He'd never had to promise a decent one anything. There was no point because there was only one thing they held out for – a wedding ring – but then that was the only kind of girl to marry . . .

'If I'm going to undress, shouldn't you?' She unfastened the buttons on his blouse and unbuttoned his braces.

'You've done this before,' he slurred as she started on his fly.

'Only to my brothers when they're pissed, and I always stop at underpants.'

'Then you're in for a revelation. I ran out of clean ones.'

'You dirty beggar.'

Kicking off his trousers he lay back on the bed as she leaned over to start on his shirt. Sliding his hands around her chest he unclipped her bra, exposing her breasts. Screeching with false modesty she tried to pull it back but he proved stronger. Tossing it aside he stroked her naked breasts, weighing them in his hands and thumbing her nipples.

'Nice,' he mumbled, 'very nice.' Pushing up her skirt he tugged at her suspenders.

'Watch out, these are my last pair of stockings without a darn. Here, I'll do it.' Aware that he was watching and drooling over every inch of newly exposed flesh, she pulled up her skirt and rested one foot on the bed. Unclipping her suspenders she leisurely rolled down one stocking. She would have liked to have carried on undressing slowly, but it was too cold. Moments after divesting herself of everything except her artificial silk bloomers she was under the covers beside him.

'You're freezing.'

'Then warm me up.'

Without any further preliminaries he lay on top of her, pushing her legs apart with his knees.

'You've still got knickers on.' Diving beneath the covers he tore the elastic as he pulled them down.

'You like it rough.'

'You don't?'

'I like masterful men,' she gasped as he thrust into her, 'but not brutal,' she squeaked as his fingers closed around her nipples, pinching them.

Moments after climaxing he rolled off her.

'That's it?'

'You want more?' He snuggled beneath the covers. The bed was soft, warm and comfortable. His eyes felt unaccountably heavy. Only vaguely aware of her fingers pinching, poking and prodding, he turned his back on her.

'Tony!' There was a sharp edge to her voice that ruffled the pleasant drowsiness that was stealing his senses.

'I'm sleepy. Leave me be.' He threw off her hands. 'I'll pay whatever you want, just leave me be.'

'Pay! You bastard, Tony Ronconi! Get out of my bed this minute.' Bracing herself on the headboard she pulled up her knees, placed the soles of her feet in the small of his back and kicked with all her might, sending him sprawling out on to the bare floorboards. 'What do you think I am? You – you – filthy beast!' she shrieked as, jerked into sudden consciousness and unable to control his nausea, he retched over the chair holding her clothes.

The next few moments blurred into a cacophony of howls, screams and evasive movements on his part as he grabbed his trousers and fled down the stairs. Barefoot, braces dangling, flies undone, shirtless he found himself out on the street. Judy was still screaming obscenities from behind the closed door as she slammed it behind him.

Sinking to his knees he perched on the kerb and leaned forward, head on lap, toes in the gutter. If only he'd been able to stay in the spacious villa his unit commander had requisitioned in Celle, with the Jeep he drove parked outside the door.

At this time of night he'd be comfortably ensconced in the feather bed in the fourth largest bedroom. In the morning he'd be gently woken by the smell of freshly ground coffee and frying sausages and eggs as Gabrielle's mother, who had been given the post of unit cook, made breakfast. Just as he finished eating, Gabrielle herself, beautiful and elegant in her brown serge costume, her shining fair hair plaited back away from her face, would come in. She'd smile her special smile – the one she reserved just for him – before taking her place at her desk outside his CO's office.

Gabrielle, his Gabrielle – with her at least he would be warm and loved.

*

'Nurse John, can I get you a cup of tea?'

'Only if you're having one yourself, sister.' Bethan moved her chair closer to the couch Ronnie was lying on in the examination cubicle the porters had put him in when they'd carried him into the Graig Hospital. The same hospital Andrew had taken Diana to, simply because it was the nearest.

Ronnie'd showed no signs of stirring when she'd examined, cleaned and stitched the cuts on his hands and face. She was glad. Another half-hour – hour at the most – and the effects of the drug she had given him would begin to wear off and she was dreading him recovering consciousness before Andrew emerged from the operating theatre with news of Diana.

'Nurse John, Dr John asked me to take over here. He's in the office.'

Bethan knew better than to ask the sister if there was any news. She found Andrew, still in his theatre gown, slumped back in a chair, his feet balanced on the corner of the desk, a tray with teapot, milk and two cups set out at his side.

'There's no reason for you to have stayed. You're not a district nurse any more.'

'With you operating they were short-staffed. I was glad to help.'

'You could go home now, take the car, I'll call a taxi . . .'

'What's the news about Diana?'

'I called in one of the military surgeons from East Glamorgan to help.'

'Please, Andrew, don't spin it out.'

'You saw Diana, you're a nurse. She's still alive and that's about all I can tell you. Given care and time, her arm and the other injuries to her body will heal. There'll be scarring, of course, mostly superficial, nothing that will impede her movements and probably nothing that cosmetics and long-sleeved dresses won't hide.'

'And her head injury?'

'There were bone and glass splinters in the wound. We've cleaned it out and repaired her skull as best we can.

But I wouldn't even like to hazard a guess as to the damage. You know the options as well as I do: epilepsy, loss of the ability to reason, damage to memory or even, as my co-surgeon so cheerfully predicted, total insanity. And that's without the lesser disorders of single or double incontinence, loss of speech, limb co-ordination . . .'

'I get the picture.'

'I'm sorry, Beth. I'm as fond of Diana as you are.'

'But you do think she'll live?'

'If she doesn't get pneumonia or have a fit between now and tomorrow morning she stands a chance, but whether or not she'll be grateful that she's survived is another thing. How's Ronnie?'

'Heavily sedated. The only way we could calm him was for me to give him an injection.'

'I wouldn't have left you with him if I'd known he was that bad.'

'There wasn't time for you to think of Ronnie, only Diana.'

'I'd like to know exactly what happened in the house before we got there tonight.'

'I'm sure it's not what it looks like.' She poured out two cups of tea, added milk and handed him one.

'And what do you think it looks like?' he asked, mystified by her train of thought.

'I heard two porters talking when we brought Ronnie in. They were already gossiping about a domestic in Graig Street. "*Returning soldier catches wife in bed with other man then tries to kill her.*" You know how people love to make up stories.'

'Unfortunately.'

'But I refuse to believe it of Diana – or Ronnie.'

'The thought of Diana having an affair never crossed my mind. But then, you and I know Diana and Ronnie. Try not to think about it, or let the gossip upset you until we find out the facts. I've told the recovery room sister to call me if there's any change in Diana's condition, and no doubt the ward sister will inform me when Ronnie wakes.' Lifting his legs down he pushed his empty cup back on to the tray and reached for his cigarettes. 'So, why don't you go home, Bethan? The children –'

'Will be fine with Nessie. Tomorrow's Sunday so she doesn't even have to get them ready for school.'

'You're determined to stay.'

'You know Diana's the closest I have to a sister now, and I still think of Ronnie as my brother-in-law even though Maud is dead. He's never forgotten it or that he's Rachel and Eddie's uncle. I can't leave either of them when they might need me.'

'Then we're both in for a long night. What do you suggest? A game of snap to take our minds off things we can't do anything about?'

'Anything you want,' she replied carelessly. 'You haven't said a word about Charlie or why Huw sent for you earlier before talking to him.'

'I think it's something Alma should tell you – if she wants to.'

'Is it bad news?'

'It could be,' he replied irritatingly, but she refused to take his bait.

'I know Alma's desperately worried about Charlie.'

'I'm worried about Charlie. I'm thinking of sending him to a specialist.'

'You said he was making a good recovery.'

'He was for the first couple of months after he came home.' Flicking his lighter Andrew lit a cigarette and pulled on it, wondering why it was so much easier to talk to his wife about other people's problems than their own. 'He's slipped back.'

'Could it be his stomach? He doesn't seem to be putting on weight.'

'Only because he's not eating enough.'

'He admitted that?'

'Alma told me the last time I talked to her. Do me a favour, Beth. Call in on her tomorrow when the children are in Sunday School.'

'I don't need you to tell me to call in on Alma.'

'I didn't mean that the way it sounded . . .'

'But as I have nothing else to do . . .'

'You said you didn't mind giving up work.'

'I agreed to move over and make room for a demobbed single nurse to take my post as district nurse. That's not quite the same thing.'

'So, you resent staying home and looking after Eddie, Rachel and me?'

'Don't put words into my mouth, Andrew.'

'But you don't want to stay at home? I don't even know why I'm asking, the fact that you're here now, says it all.'

'Put it this way, I've never been much of a housewife, and with a live-in maid and both the children in school I have some free time that could be put to better use.'

'You may have to take over Billy and Catrina.'

'I doubt Auntie Megan will let me do that and she'll be back the minute she finds out about this.'

'There's always voluntary work.'

'Join the middle-aged, middle-class Mrs Llewellyn Joneses of this world in "good works", ministering to the "deserving poor" and running fêtes and bazaars. No thank you.'

'If you'd remained a district nurse I would never see you.'

'Like I hardly ever see you.' She couldn't resist the gibe, but that didn't stop her from regretting it the moment it was out of her mouth.

'I'm glad I finally met the famous David Ford,' he said evenly, deliberately changing the subject.

'And was he what you expected?'

'He didn't quite fit the mental image. I'd heard he was good-looking but I didn't expect someone so young. All I can say is, if he's typical, American brass is cut from a very different cloth to British. He's also surprisingly direct for an officer. He told me I have quite a family.'

'He was very fond of all the children, the evacuees as well as ours.' She listened hard but the corridor outside the office was deathly still.

'And you.' It was a statement, not a question.

'As a friend,' Bethan countered.

Andrew knew he should leave it there but some devil prompted him to take it further. 'Close friend.'

'I told you, Andrew, he helped all of us with our problems not to mention extra rations he and Dino –'

'Were here and I wasn't.' He didn't attempt to conceal his bitterness.

'We've been over this a dozen times. You told me you didn't believe the gossip about David and me. If something's happened to make you change your mind, why don't you just come right out and say it?'

He almost shouted, '*I want to believe you but I can't because I'm insanely jealous.*' 'He seems a nice bloke,' he finished lamely.

'He is,' Bethan agreed shortly. 'And I'm fond of him in the same way I am of my brother Haydn.' Daring Andrew to say more, she continued to watch him as he squashed his cigarette end into the ashtray on the sister's desk.

'Dr John?' A staff nurse knocked on the open door. 'Sister's asking if you could take a look at Mrs Ronconi.'

'I'm there.'

More concerned with what had been left unsaid than said about David Ford, Bethan reached into her pocket for her own cigarettes.

Too terrified to think of what was happening to Diana, she tried to concentrate on what Andrew had said. It wasn't his fault that she'd been coerced into giving up her job – and it did make sense for the time-consuming post to be filled by a single woman rather than a married one with two small children. But sense couldn't alleviate her boredom, nor dull the growing conviction that nothing she did mattered and could probably be done – and better – by any one of a number of other people. She was a good nurse, and she wanted to nurse, yet Andrew had almost sneered at her for staying with Ronnie tonight. What did he want her to do, mark time – until – when?

She hated to acknowledge it, even in her private thoughts, but there had been an edge and excitement to wartime living that she missed. Never knowing when she might be called on to deputise for the doctors as the stretched medical services were put under even more strain. Organising get-togethers and scratch meals from practically nothing for family and friends at short, and often no notice, to celebrate allied victories and unexpected leaves. Waiting for news from the various fronts along with everyone else in the town and being swept up in the universal elation when it was good . . .

'Bethan.'

She looked up to see Huw Davies, helmet in hand, standing in the doorway. 'I'm sorry, there's no real news. I would have telephoned if there had been. All I can tell you is that Diana has survived an operation and Andrew's with her now.'

'I was just passing.'

'And they let you in. Come in, sit down. I might be able to rustle up some fresh tea.'

'No thanks, love. I only wanted to know how Diana is. I saw the open wound on her head . . .'

'It's far too soon to know if there'll be any permanent damage.'

'And Ronnie?'

'Still out for the count, which is probably my fault. I think I got carried away and gave him too much.'

'He needed too much the way he was thrashing around.'

'Have you any idea what happened?'

'We picked up Tony Ronconi, drunk, in Leyshon Street. He only had on a pair of trousers, nothing else, not even underpants, and he was gabbling about killing Diana.'

'Tony! I don't believe it . . .' she faltered. It was an open secret in the family that Diana's eldest son, Billy, hadn't been fathered by her first husband, Wyn, but was the result of a fleeting and disastrous liaison with Ronnie's younger brother that had ended when Tony had left to join the army. A full two years before Ronnie had returned from Italy and fallen in love with the newly widowed Diana.

'Mrs Evans saw Tony go into Diana's house tonight.'

'He didn't go in invited, Huw. Diana would never –'

'I know that and you know that, love, but it's the rest of the world I'm concerned about. You know what the Graig is for gossip. And that's why I think I'll stay here until Ronnie comes round. The sooner I know what really happened in that house tonight, the sooner I can nip any nastiness in the bud.'

Tony was sitting at the table in the single room, which was all Gabrielle's mother had been able to rent after fleeing from East Prussia to Celle just ahead of the invading Russian Army. Originally a bedroom, the room now did service as kitchen, bathroom and living room in addition to its original function; but as Gabrielle's mother was so fond of reminding her daughter, *we might be reduced in circumstances but we are still von Stettins and – as such – have standards.*

A makeshift curtain in front of a shallow alcove hid the buckets and bowls they used for washing, along with their towels, flannels and water pitcher. A scarred, rickety old cupboard fit only for firewood, with broken doors and drawer that no one could open, held the battered pots and pans the Red Cross had given them as their share of the refugee charity handout. Their few clothes were housed in cardboard boxes but everything was spotlessly clean and there were still a few touches of elegance and style to remind them and their visitors of lost splendour.

The table in the centre of the room was always draped with a hand-embroidered linen cloth – and never the same one two days running. The rug covering the stained floorboards was handmade Bokhara. At mealtimes the silverware and porcelain were antique heirlooms, part of a small hoard of family treasure Gabrielle's mother had consigned to bunkers deep in the Hartz mountains for safekeeping, 'just in case' the war got too close to the home she always referred to as Schloss von Stettin. The single German phrase she had taken care to translate to 'Castle von Stettin' for Tony's benefit, to let him know exactly '*who*' he – a pathetic unworthy sergeant – was daring to court in her daughter.

'More coffee, Tony?' Gräfin von Stettin's voice, soft, silvery, reverberated towards him, making him feel even more ill at ease. The Gräfin's formal manners invariably made him feel like a great, clumsy oaf. Try as he may, he couldn't get used to balancing on worm-eaten chairs or sipping acorn coffee from wide, shallow Continental coffee cups, before a table laid with delicate porcelain that he was terrified of breaking.

'No, thank you, Gräfin.'

He looked to Gabrielle, cool, beautiful, desirable, and a graphic image of her naked sprang, unbidden to his mind. Her breasts, perfect, pale globes tipped with rosy pink nipples, the gentle curve of her rounded highs, the dark triangle between her legs – then, suddenly, he realised the Gräfin was reading his thoughts. Blood rushed to his face – he fought to loosen his collar – a voice interrupted. A voice that had travelled over a great distance and one that had no place in this bizarre room with its broken furniture and relics of a more leisurely and opulent lifestyle.

'Could fry eggs on his head.'

'Silly bugger, sitting out half-naked in the street at night. Serve him right.'

'We should send for the doctor.'

'He's been sent for.'

'He's not bloody well here, is he?'

Someone heaped heavy things over him – his body – his face. He felt as though he were being smothered. He fought to reach Gabrielle sitting across from him at the table but every time he took a step forward she floated backwards. He continued to struggle but it was futile – he simply couldn't get to her. She was slipping and fading away before his eyes and he was powerless to stop it. Then suddenly she wasn't Gabrielle at all, but Diana. Pale, beautiful, standing at the foot of the stairs in Graig Street in her bottle-green robe. She smiled and held out her hand to him. He went to take it, then screamed. From the crown of her head to her feet she was bathed in blood. Thick, crimson blood that welled constantly from a hole in her skull and still she continued to hold out her hand – and smile.

Alma laid her book on the bedside cabinet and checked the clock. She'd read a dozen pages in the last half-hour without a single word registering. And it had been a full hour since she'd last heard Charlie pacing around the living room, and he still hadn't come to bed. Switching off the lamp she lay back on the pillows and closed her eyes.

The first image that came to mind was Charlie's face as he'd said, '*It might be better for you and Theo if I move out.*'

Better! How could it possibly be better? Did he really believe that after all the misery of their three-year separation it would be better for them to live apart now? Didn't he realise that when it came to him and Theo she had no pride, no regard for gossips, or even the law? If a position as mistress was all he was able to offer her, then she would accept it – and to hell with gossip and convention. She wanted *him* – no one else – and if he could only give her a part of himself then that part was better than the whole of any other man.

The one, the only, thing she couldn't bear was the thought of never seeing him again because if that happened she knew she wouldn't want to live. Not even for Theo.

Before the war she had flattered herself that she understood Charlie, and the grief that had almost destroyed him when he had been forced to leave Russia and all hope of finding his family. But then, before the war they had been close. Each had known what the other would say before it was said. She had asked him not to sign up for active service and later to turn down the offer of special duties, but she had *asked* – not demanded or begged. If she had been more insistent, would he have listened? And if he had, would things have been any different? Would he have had a normal soldier's war, whatever that was? Spent five years in a POW camp, like Andrew, or fought in Italy alongside William and Ronnie – or, worse of all, died a hero's death at Dunkirk like Bethan's brother Eddie?

'What ifs?' . . . Stupid useless regrets for what might have been. Charlie was here, now, she had to talk to him before he left and it was too late.

Switching on the lamp, she slipped out of bed, wincing as her feet sought her slippers on the cold floor. Picking up her striped flannel dressing gown, she tied it around her waist and opened the door. The door to the living room was closed. She turned the knob and stepped inside. The standard lamp burned behind Charlie's chair. A notepad and pencil lay loosely on his lap between his relaxed fingers. He was asleep.

Treading softly so as not to wake him she reached for the blanket folded on the sofa intending to drape it over him. Then she saw the envelope lying on the table. It bore two addresses: one in the Cyrillic alphabet she had asked Charlie to teach her when she'd seen him use it to work out costings for the business before the war, the other in English.

There hadn't been time for her to master more than a few words of Russian and no time at all for the Russian alphabet, but there was no mistaking the addressee.

Mrs Maria (Masha) Andreyeva Raschenkova.

Alma stood and stared at it. For the first time she realised that if this woman was Charlie's legal wife, her life would change absolutely and irrevocably. Whatever else, Masha was Charlie's first love and, knowing him, he would be totally and completely faithful to her. There would be no room in his life for a mistress even if she had been a wife of sorts to him for seven years. But where did that leave her – and Theo?

Chapter Five

SLOWLY AND CAREFULLY so as not to disturb Billy, William withdrew his arm from beneath the small boy's head and shook it in an attempt to ease his cramped muscles. After glancing at his wristwatch, which was just about readable in the dim glow from the nightlight, he looked across to where Tina was cuddling Catrina and saw that although the child's eyes were closed, his wife's were open. Nodding towards the door, he crept stealthily towards it. Turning the knob quietly, he stepped through to the landing.

'It's four o'clock,' Tina whispered as she followed him.

'I know, and I haven't slept a wink, have you?'

She shook her head. 'But at least the children have.'

'Fancy some tea?'

'I don't fancy going into that kitchen. I wonder why Bethan hasn't telephoned.'

'Because she hasn't any news.'

Tina fell silent. Something in Will's tone reminded her that there was news besides good and she realised she'd been hoping – no *expecting* – to hear that Diana was going to be fine.

'The children all right?'

'Sleeping, Constable . . . ?'

'Hopkins, sir.'

'Is my uncle around?'

'Sergeant stopped by to pick him up, sir. He was needed elsewhere.'

'For something more important?' Tina enquired acidly.

'I wasn't privy to whatever it was, Mrs Powell.'

'Come on, Tina, let's sit down.'

'My orders are not to let anyone in the kitchen until after the detectives look it over in the morning, sir.'

'That's all right, we'll go into the parlour.'

'I'm sorry, I'm not even allowed in the kitchen to make tea.'

'In that case we'll have to make do with something stronger.' William produced a hip flask from his top pocket and offered it to the constable.

'Not allowed on duty, sir.'

'No one's here to see. Go on . . .'

The boy didn't need any more urging. He finished the capful William handed him and looked disappointed when William took the flask along with himself into the parlour.

'This wasn't quite what I had in mind for my first night back,' he said, sinking his face into his hands as he sat alongside Tina on the sofa.

'I still can't understand what happened. There's no way Diana could have fallen through that window. The chair was in the way.'

'There's no point talking about it . . .' He shot up as he heard voices at the door. Diving out into the passage, he looked from Huw to Bethan.

'Let's go into the parlour,' Huw suggested, sniffing the air in front of Hopkins and giving him a hard look.

'There's no real news.' Bethan covered Tina's hand with her own as she sat next to her. 'All I can tell you is that Diana's survived the operation but she has a skull fracture and we won't know the extent of her injuries until she comes round, which could take days or even, I hate to say it, weeks.'

'And Ronnie?' Tina asked.

'He came round but he became hysterical when I told him he couldn't see Diana so we had to sedate him again.'

'I'm sorry, love.' Huw patted Tina's shoulder clumsily as he looked to William. 'But we've got to be practical. Bethan and I thought it might be an idea to move the children.'

'Now?'

'It's best they leave before the neighbours are about. If you two pack their things we'll take them to my house. I

74

know Myrtle's not up to looking after them and I have to work, but we've three spare bedrooms as well as a parlour we never use, so I thought that perhaps you two could stay there with them until your mam comes back, Will. Knowing her, she'll want to take care of Billy and Catrina for the time being, and as Dino's bought that house in our street Billy and Catrina won't have far to move when Megan does come home. In my opinion, the less upset they have to cope with after this night the better.'

'They and you are welcome to stay with me,' Bethan offered.

'Thanks, Beth, but as Uncle Huw said, it makes more sense to take them to his house. Mam will be home like a shot when she hears about this and she'll want Billy and Catrina with her.'

'Are you going to telephone her?'

William looked at his watch again. 'I am, but not this early. What do you think, Uncle Huw? Eight o'clock.'

'Knowing Megan, big as you are, she'll put you over her knee if you make it any later.'

'Then we'd better get Billy and Catrina's things together,' Tina said.

'Andrew had to make a call down the police station. As soon as he's finished, he'll be here to pick us up. Could you and Will pack their clothes, Tina? You know where Diana kept – keeps them?'

'Yes, I do, and thanks, Beth,' Tina said gratefully.

'Good, the sooner we get started the sooner we can move them out of this house.'

'We tried to get you an hour ago, Dr John.'

'I was operating.' Andrew refused to elaborate further. The worst part of being a small-town doctor, and the only aspect he truly resented, was the universal assumption of Pontypridd's inhabitants that they had the right to demand his undivided attention at any hour of the day or night – and this was proving to be an exceptionally long night.

'He's in the cells. If you'd like to follow me, doctor . . .' The duty sergeant reached for the keys behind the

75

reception area and unlocked the door that led to the stairs and basement.

'Constable Davies mentioned that you'd picked up a drunk in Leyshon Street.' Andrew chose his words carefully, knowing that Huw had told him more about Tony Ronconi and his bizarre confession than he should have.

'Drunk with cuts and bruises. If he'd been the run-of-the-mill Saturday night troublemaker we wouldn't have bothered you, Dr John. To be honest there wasn't even much point going through the usual "walk the white line, touch your nose with the tip of your finger" tests. The man was almost comatose. But he looked as though he'd been in a fight and you know about the rumpus in Graig Street. We heard you'd operated on the woman,' he answered in response to Andrew's quizzical look. 'So, we decided to hold him until he sobered up to see if he could help with our inquiries.'

'What do you call cuts and bruises?' Andrew enquired.

'His nose was bleeding and he had a few scratches and bruises on his head and hands but nothing that the duty first aider couldn't cope with.'

'So why am I here?'

'When we looked in on him over an hour ago he seemed a bit more than just drunk.'

'That's hardly surprising, it's freezing down here,' Andrew remonstrated as they reached the bottom step.

'Stone basement, doctor.'

'And you keep people here?'

'It's only a holding cell, Dr John. We're not here to mollycoddle them.'

'Whatever happened to innocent until proven guilty?' Andrew ducked his head to accommodate a dip in the ceiling that dropped it a couple of inches short of six feet. He hung back as the officer unlocked the first cell they came to.

'When we noticed he was ill we gave him an extra blanket.'

'I trust he was duly grateful,' Andrew commented sarcastically as he entered the stone cell. He sniffed the air. 'It's not only cold, it's damp.'

'We're below ground level here, doctor,' the sergeant observed as Andrew went to the narrow, drop-down, steel shelf that held a spartan board bed. Tony Ronconi was lying alarmingly close to the edge, tossing restlessly beneath two grey woollen blankets.

'I'm Doctor John. Do you know where you are?' Tony's eyes were open but Andrew noted the classic symptoms of delirium and doubted he was capable of focusing. 'You're in the police station. Do you remember how you got here?' His second question elicited an incoherent mumbled response.

Andrew turned to the sergeant. 'Have you sent for an ambulance?'

'Thought it best to wait until you got here, doctor.'

'Do it now, Sergeant.'

The sergeant ran off. Andrew heard him shouting up the stairs as he removed his stethoscope from his bag, folded back the blankets, and began his examination.

'Is is bad, doctor?' The sergeant returned and hovered anxiously at the cell door, as Andrew closed his bag and replaced the blankets.

'Both lungs are infected. It looks like pneumonia and, frankly, I don't know if he'll survive. Have you contacted his family?'

'We were going to wait until morning, Dr John. It could be embarrassing for them. He only had a pair of army-issue trousers on and the flies were undone. Nothing in the pockets, no underclothes, boots or shoes. We thought it could be a domestic. Soldier home on leave, out for a good Saturday night, gets drunk, goes to see his brother's wife. Brother comes home unexpectedly – well – you've been operating on Mrs Ronconi . . .'

'And you were so busy concocting this little fairytale you didn't think to call an ambulance to get this man into hospital before he died?'

'We called you, Dr John.'

'And I can't be everywhere. Don't you people ever use your own initiative?'

'He could be connected to a potentially serious case, doctor.'

'So you decided to freeze him to death.'

'We wanted to question him. Besides, nine times out of ten, the Saturday night drunks wake in the morning, get their summonses and stagger off home.'

'This one isn't capable of staggering anywhere. Get two men to carry him upstairs. The sooner that ambulance gets here and he's admitted into the Graig, the happier I'll be. I'll go on ahead and warn them he's on his way.'

Andrew just had time to check that there was no change in Diana's condition and Ronnie was still sleeping before the ambulance bell announced Tony's arrival. Running up to the men's isolation ward, he met the porters wheeling Tony into a cubicle.

'Bronchitis?' the ward sister asked.

'Pneumonia, nurtured and helped along by exposure,' Andrew pronounced authoritatively, checking Tony's pulse.

'Staff,' the sister called. 'Prepare a cold sponge bath to bring down this patient's temperature.'

'Is there any penicillin in the pharmacy?'

'I'm not sure, Dr John. Even if there is, we'll have to wait until it opens at eight to get a script filled.'

'I'll write him up for it anyway and I'll call in again in a couple of hours to check on his progress.' Andrew walked to the sink to wash his hands.

'He's a Ronconi, isn't he?'

'You know him?'

'No, but I trained with Laura Lewis, Ronconi that was. They all have that look about them. Dark eyes, dark hair and similar features. It's peculiar, isn't it, how when you get to know one member of a family well, afterwards all the brothers and sisters look slightly odd, as if they're not quite right. But I couldn't tell you which one this is.'

'Tony.' Andrew took the towel she handed him.

'The ambulance men said they picked him up at the

police station. Do you want me to arrange for the relatives to be contacted?'

'No, I'll do it later.'

'Don't forget to warn them that there's no visiting for anyone this sick.'

'If he comes round the police will want to talk to him.'

'Not until he's well enough.' She scribbled something on Tony's chart before peering at Andrew over her glasses. 'This is my ward, Dr John, and whatever he's done, he's my patient now and no one will see him until I say so.'

'Diana?' Ronnie asked thickly. His tongue was too big for his mouth and his lips felt as though they were made of India rubber.

'We operated, but it's too early to tell if there's any permanent damage.' Andrew checked Ronnie's pulse.

'Her head . . .'

'We repaired the fracture as best we could.'

'But her brain could be affected.' Ronnie lay back on the pillows. He clearly didn't expect Andrew to answer him because he looked across to Huw, who was sitting on the only chair in the cubicle. 'Billy and Catrina?'

'They're safe in my house with William and Tina. Can you remember what happened?'

'Tony and I had a fight. Diana tried to stop us, Tony lashed out and hit her through the window.'

'We found Tony in Leyshon Street. All he had on was a pair of trousers.'

'He's in here now with pneumonia.' Andrew decided that as Ronnie was calm enough to ask lucid questions, he might as well know the worst.

'He was fully dressed when he ran out of our house. He had his greatcoat on.'

'Would you like to tell me what you and Tony were fighting about?' Huw pressed.

'No.'

'Tina said he called into the restaurant this afternoon to tell her he was marrying a German girl and wanted his share of the business.'

Ronnie remained silent.

'I'm trying to help you out here, boy,' Huw said firmly. 'Diana's my niece and I intend to find out how her head was cracked open.'

'She may be your niece but she's my wife and I just told you.'

'You and Tony were fighting, she tried to stop you and Tony flung her through the window?'

'That's right.'

'Intentionally?'

'Not even Tony's that vicious or stupid.'

'Then it was an accident?'

'I suppose so.'

'Listen, Ronnie, if you're covering up because you want to tackle Tony and pay him back yourself afterwards, I'll come down on you like a ton of bricks. There's two kids crying themselves to sleep in one of my spare bedrooms right this minute. God knows what's going to happen to their mother. They need their father and a fat lot of use he's going to be to them if he's in jail.'

'As soon as I'm out of this place, I'll take care of them, Huw.' Ronnie looked up at Andrew. 'Can I see Diana?'

'She's unconscious. Her only chance of recovery is absolute quiet and bed rest.'

'Nurses go into her room, don't they?'

'Yes.'

'I'll be as quiet as them.'

'You weren't earlier and you feel like hell now because we had to sedate you twice tonight.'

'I remember.'

'What do you remember?'

'Bethan coming at me with a needle. That's a brutal wife you've got there.'

'I'll tell her what you said.'

'She'd let me see Diana.'

'She would not.'

'She would, because she'd recognise that I've calmed down.'

'If we get caught the sister will string me higher than St

Catherine's steeple.'

'All I want to do is hold her hand and see her breathing for myself.'

'Help me get him into a wheelchair, Huw.'

Diana lay still and white under a sheet only marginally paler than her skin. A bandage covered her head and her eyes were closed.

'She looks . . .'

'She's sleeping off the effects of the anaesthetic,' Andrew reassured, keeping his concern that Diana might be already slipping into a coma to himself. He held back in the doorway until he was sure Ronnie wouldn't break down or say another word, then wheeled his chair next to her bed.

'You can take a five-minute break, nurse,' he ordered the trainee sitting at Diana's bedside. 'I'll stay with the patient.'

Ronnie sought Diana's hand. Holding it lightly in his own, he stared intently into her face.

Afterwards Huw put those five minutes down as the longest he'd ever lived through. No one spoke; no one even seemed to breathe in the room as time ticked inexorably on. The only signs of life were Ronnie's eyes, probing, burning, willing Diana to recover. The moment the nurse returned, Andrew wheeled Ronnie out.

'Can I stay with you, Huw?' Ronnie asked.

'You haven't been discharged,' Andrew pointed out mildly.

'I'm discharging myself. Just you try and stop me.'

'Then I suppose Myrtle and I'd better find you a bed, boy.'

'Upstairs, clean your teeth and straight back down to put on your coat and shoes. No squirting water,' Bethan warned Eddie, as Polly and Nell, their adopted daughters, chased him and Rachel up to the bathroom. As they left, Bethan took her hat down from the stand.

'Want a lift into town?' Andrew asked from the stairs as

she held her pearl-headed hatpins in her mouth, freeing her hands to arrange her hat.

'I'll walk in after I've taken the children to Sunday School.' Jabbing a pin into the side of her hat, she stood back to study the effect.

'We can drop them off on the way.'

'You should stay in bed. You didn't get in until after six . . .'

'I've slept enough for now. I'll have an early night. Besides I should check on Diana. You going to Alma's?'

'You're really worried about her, aren't you?'

'I think she might be in need of a friend.'

'Coat, shoes,' Bethan prompted Rachel as their maid, Nessie, hauled Eddie off the stairs and struggled to hold him still long enough to lace up his boots. 'Be good, Eddie. Look, Polly and Nell are all ready for church.'

'Joan Evans says I'm a show-off,' Rachel chanted breathlessly as Bethan stooped to fasten the buttons on her coat.

'And why are you a show-off, little miss?' Andrew asked absently, fumbling in his overcoat pocket for his car keys.

'Because Mam has a maid to do our dirty work.'

'Nessie isn't our maid, she's our friend,' Bethan said quickly, colouring as she glanced at the young girl who'd been working for them for six months. Then she remembered that Nessie's mother lived next door to Joan Evans' family in Danygraig Street. She only hoped the resentment came from the Evanses' side of the terrace, not Nessie's family. 'That's right, isn't it, Nessie?'

'Yes, Mrs John.'

'Joan says Mam's forgotten she comes from Graig Avenue. I told her that was silly. We go to Graig Avenue almost every day to see Grandad, Auntie Phyllis and Brian so if Mam had forgotten where Graig Avenue is, we wouldn't go there, would we?'

'You tell Joan Evans she's a silly little busybody.'

'Andrew!' Bethan shook her head at him.

'You cross with me, Daddy?' Rachel's bottom lip quivered.

'No, darling, of course Daddy isn't cross.' Bethan crouched down to help her with her shoe buckles.

'I'm not cross with you, sweetheart, but I am cross with Joan Evans. Now come on, or you'll be late for Sunday School, I'll be late for my patients and Mummy will be late to look at a house with Auntie Alma.' Hauling Eddie from Nessie's lap, Andrew hoisted him high in the air, swinging him up on his shoulders before opening the door.

They heard the telephone ring as Andrew drove the car out of the garage.

'If that's the hospital I can't get there any quicker, and if it's anyone else they can wait or phone my father,' he muttered, breaking his own resolution to try to answer calls personally if he could.

It was then Bethan realised that Joan Evans' tittle-tattle had annoyed him as much as her and it was entirely her fault that the children were subjected to it. It had been her idea to send their children to Maesycoed Infants, which she had attended with her brothers and sister, rather than a private school which Andrew would have undoubtedly preferred and no doubt insisted on – if he hadn't been in a POW camp and in no position to insist on anything.

Would they never move on from the same old problem that had dogged them all their married life? Her working-class roots versus his middle-class respectability. One thing was certain, if she'd remained with her own kind and not *forgotten where she'd come from* to quote Joan Evans' mother, there would be no question of her being bored. Because her days, evenings and most of her nights would be filled with the endless, cooking, cleaning and sewing needed just to keep a family clothed, presentable and fed.

'It's a lovely family home, Alma.'

'It is, isn't it?' Alma unlocked the back door that led into the kitchen of her cooked meats shop. Lifting the kettle from the hob, she filled it and put it on the gas stove.

'You going to take it?'

'Yes.'

'For Masha?'

'What else can I do, Beth?' Alma put two mugs on the long, wooden preparation table and sat opposite her. 'Charlie went to the police station first thing this morning to make a statement. He did say when he came back that the sergeant thought they wouldn't prosecute because of the time lapse and special circumstances. Apparently this doesn't come into the same category as your run-of-the-mill, average bigamy case because Charlie had no way of knowing or finding out if Masha was alive or dead. But that didn't stop Charlie packing a bag and calling a taxi. He was going to ask if he could stay with you, but thought better of the idea. He said it might make things difficult between you and me because we're such good friends so he was hoping your father would put him up for a while.'

'He and Dad were close before the war. They used to talk for hours on end. And if he's in Graig Avenue you won't have to worry. Phyllis will take good care of him,' Bethan reassured, knowing that her father's common-law wife was as fond of Charlie as the rest of the family were.

'As I said, he didn't even want to view the house in Tyfica Road with us. Just said if I think it's right to buy the place, he'll go along with it.'

'And Masha?'

'He's written to her and the Red Cross is forwarding his letter.'

'What about the shops?'

'Charlie hasn't really been strong enough to work in them since he's been back. Oh, he walks around here from time to time but the only actual work he's done is with the books, and he can do them just as well in your father's house as here.'

'What are you going to do?'

'What can I do other than stand back and let Charlie go?' Alma delved into her pocket, took out a packet of cigarettes and offered them to Bethan.

'But you're his wife.'

'And so is Masha.' The kettle whistled and she left the

84

table to wet the tea. 'I'm not the wronged woman here, Beth. He told me about her before he married me.'

'That's the whole point, he did marry you. God, just listen to me. I can't believe we're talking about Charlie.'

'If anyone is to blame for this, it's me. If I remember rightly, Charlie's proposal ran along the lines of, "*I could marry you. No one here knows about Masha except you, but it wouldn't be legal and if it was discovered it would be one more crime to lay on my head.*"'

'Crime? I know Charlie's hardly ever mentioned his past but there's no way I'll believe he's a criminal.'

'Apparently he is, in Russia. He went looking for Masha, asked too many questions, ended up in prison and escaped. So, he's not only a criminal but an escaped criminal.' Alma poured out the tea, sat back in her chair and drew heavily on her cigarette. 'Beth, promise me you'll be a friend to Charlie whatever happens?'

'I don't have to tell you how much I value Charlie's friendship and yours.'

'That's just it, Beth. I know the people in this town. Let's face it, Charlie will always be Russian Charlie – the foreigner. Once word gets out he's a bigamist, I'll get all the sympathy and he'll get the brickbats. He'll need every friend he can get. I know there's your father and Andrew but I'd like to think that he had a woman he could turn to.'

'I'll be his friend, Alma, but not at the expense of being yours.'

'Damn! That's the delivery.' Alma rose to answer a knock at the back door.

'Your ration from the slaughterhouse, Mrs Charlie.'

'Are Sunday deliveries going to be a regular thing from now on?'

'We told your boy –'

'I got the message. Well, as you're finally here you'd better bring it in.'

'It won't happen again. We've been taking stock before the new restrictions come into force. This will be your last delivery at these quantities. Manager told me to tell you, he's very sorry, but he's had to cut your ration by a third.'

'A third!'

'Government orders, Mrs Charlie. The war might be over but food shortages aren't.'

'Government orders or not, I'm sure your manager can do better than two-thirds of my usual order.'

'I'm only the messenger, Mrs Charlie.'

'Then I'd better talk to your boss.'

'Suits me, Mrs Charlie. I've had nothing but flak from the customers since the manager started cutting orders yesterday, and there's a lot worse off than you. I'm tired of it. Don't suppose there's a cuppa going?'

'Help yourself. There's even a pastie, not that you deserve it.'

'You're a life-saver, Mrs Charlie.'

'I'll get out of your way.' Bethan left her chair and pushed it under the table.

'You will give my love to Ronnie and the children, and tell your Aunt Megan if there's anything I can do, she only has to ask.'

Bethan knew it was useless to remind Alma she had enough problems of her own. 'I will.'

'Thanks, Beth, you're a real friend.'

'So are you.' Bethan hugged her. 'See you.'

Side-stepping the deliverymen and leaving through the back door, Bethan glanced at her watch. It was three o'clock. She – and Andrew if he didn't have any more calls or emergencies with his existing patients – had arranged to meet the children in her father's house for Sunday tea at four thirty, one and a half hours away. Polly and Nell enjoyed the responsibility of walking Eddie and Rachel up the Graig Hill after Sunday School and would undoubtedly see her early arrival as an indication that she didn't trust them to look after the younger two. She could go up and help Phyllis prepare the meal but what if Phyllis had already done everything? She'd only end up interrupting Charlie talking to her father. She really wanted to go to see if she could help in Huw's house, but Huw had telephoned and asked if she and Andrew could visit at seven after the children were in bed so Megan and

Ronnie could talk to them. Billy and Catrina adored Diana almost as much as she adored them. And Bethan doubted that even the support of a grandmother as loving and close as Megan would help Diana's children adjust to the sudden absence of their mother and their traumatic removal from the only home they could remember.

The Italian cafés were open but she was neither thirsty nor hungry. There was always home and housework but quite apart from the long walk up and down Penycoedcae Hill, Nessie would have finished the daily chores by now. The girl might even think she was checking up to see that her afternoon off hadn't started a couple of hours earlier than it should have, and after Rachel's comment this morning the last thing she wanted to do was upset her. She could visit her mother-in-law in her spacious villa on the Common and might have even considered it seriously if they'd got on better.

There was nothing for it but her father's. Turning right, she began to walk up Taff Street, to see David Ford handing a case and kitbag from the back of a Jeep to the doorman of the Park Hotel.

'Mrs John, out and about on this cold Sunday afternoon.'

'Colonel Ford, how nice to see you.'

'And you're probably going to see a lot more of me. As most of our equipment seems to have disappeared in the area around Pontypridd and the Rhondda Valleys, Command has moved me here.'

She looked up at the imposing façade of the hotel. 'Nice billet.'

'It'll do. Don't suppose you got time for a cup of coffee in Ronconi's?'

'And set the gossips going again?' She smiled as she offered him her arm. 'I'd love to, Colonel.'

'How are you coping?' Bethan asked Angelo, after watching him let rip at the waitress for keeping customers waiting while she chatted to a young man in uniform.

'Not very well. I can't stop thinking about Diana, and

then there's Tony. And my mother doesn't even know yet. Ronnie's coming over shortly so he, Tina, Will and me can go up Danycoedcae Road to break the news to her. I'm dreading it.'

'Bethan told me what happened. I'm very sorry. If there is anything I can do to help your brother or his wife, I would be happy to.'

'Thank you, Colonel, but this is one messy situation that the Ronconis are going to have to sort out for themselves and I know my mother, she's going to blame herself.'

'It's hardly her fault . . .'

'Didn't you know, Beth? She threw Tony out last night.'

'Whatever for?'

Angelo looked around to make sure no one was listening. 'You know Tony, once he's made up his mind to do something he does it no matter how stupid, so there's probably no point in trying to keep it quiet. He's gone and got engaged to a German.'

'From what I saw when I was over there, some of the girls are human,' David commented drily.

'I even proved it. There was a cracking little land army piece on the farm I worked on as a POW . . .' He looked at Bethan, and cut his story short. 'But there's no telling my mother any of it. She blames the entire German race for my father's death. Tony would have been better off getting engaged to a Martian.'

'If Tony really cares for this girl, your mother will come round.'

Angelo shook his head. 'It's not just her, Colonel Ford, there's Ronnie. You know as well as I do, Beth, that he blames the Germans for your sister's death, and now this business with Tony and Diana. I know the police have got it down as an accident but I can't see Ronnie ever talking to Tony again, even if Diana makes a full recovery, which from what I've heard doesn't seem likely.'

'It's too early to make a prognosis about Diana. All we can do is hope – and pray.' Bethan considered what

Angelo had said about the Germans. Ronnie had married her younger sister, Maud, before the war, only to see her die when they had been forced to take refuge in the Italian hills so Maud could escape internment when Italy joined Germany in declaring war on Britain. But surely he wouldn't be narrow-minded enough to blame Maud's death on Tony's German girlfriend?

Utilising the consummate skill all the Ronconis seemed to possess, Angelo completed his transformation from ranting café manager to conversational friend. Pulling a chair up to their table, he clicked his fingers, 'Coffee for three,' he ordered the waitress. 'You will have another?'

'No thank you, I have to get back to work.'

'It's Sunday, Colonel Ford.'

'Not in the US Army.'

'Normally we would have arranged a party, with William and Ronnie coming home together,' Bethan mused, half to herself.

'It would have had to be in your house. The restaurant is fully booked for the next two weeks with paying welcome home parties.'

'Business before brotherly love,' David smiled.

'You Americans have got it right.' Angelo agreed, moving back so the waitress could set a tray on their table. 'But at least Will being here should take Tina's mind off Tony's evil doings with Germans for five minutes.'

'Ronnie and Tina have more sense than to blame an innocent German girl for your father's and Maud's death.'

'That's if she is innocent. She must have done something in the war. The Germans had their women's army sections too. Think about it, there's hardly a family in Pontypridd that hasn't lost someone close to them in the last six years.' Angelo pushed the coffee David had refused earlier towards him. 'But then I don't need to tell you that, Beth. You lost a brother and sister. Quite apart from what Tony did in Ronnie's house last night, would you want your brother bringing a German girl into your family now it's finally over? Because I certainly don't.'

89

Chapter Six

'I KILLED THEM! I killed your Diana and my Tony, Ronnie! God forgive me, I killed them . . .' Mrs Ronconi thrust her hands upwards into her greying curls, practically tearing them out by the roots.

'Mama, no one's killed Diana or Tony because they're not dead.' Too afraid to look at Ronnie, Angelo gripped his mother's shoulders and forced her down into a chair.

'But they're dying and all because I threw him out into the cold. My son – my own flesh and blood – first he goes to your house, Ronnie, to make trouble, and your wife dies trying to stop him, then he freezes to death in the streets while I am lying safe in my warm bed . . .'

'You didn't get him drunk, send him down to Diana's or make him sit half naked in a gutter in Leyshon Street on a frosty night,' Angelo pointed out logically. He stepped back as Ronnie crossed the room and sat next to his mother.

'Diana and Tony are in the best place, Mama,' Ronnie took her hand into his. 'The doctor and nurses are doing everything they can to save both of them.'

Gina took the kettle from the stove, warmed the teapot, heaped tea leaves into it and returned the kettle to the range to boil, principally because she needed something to do rather than from any real need for tea. As Mrs Ronconi started to wail again, William hustled Roberto into Gina's room, out of sight, if not sound, of his mother-in-law's hysterics. Uncharacteristically quiet, Tina trailed back and forth from the dresser, lifting down cups and saucers.

'Diana, yes they will care for her in the hospital because everyone knows she is an angel,' Mrs Ronconi cried between sobs. 'But Tony – he threw her through a window and as if that isn't enough, he wants to marry a German. No doctor or nurse will want to care for him. He needs his mother because he has no one else. I have to go to him.' Mrs Ronconi would have left her chair if Ronnie hadn't pinned her down.

'You can't, Mama. He's resting. That's the best thing for him now. Rest, medicine and nursing care. As soon as he's conscious Andrew John promised to let us know, and then you can go and see him.'

'And if he wakes in a strange place he'll think we abandoned him. I want Laura. If Laura was here with Trevor, they'd make him better.'

'Andrew John is a perfectly good doctor,' Ronnie said brusquely, shorter with his mother than any of them had seen him before.

'But he isn't married to one of your sisters like Trevor. And Laura is a nurse. They're family, Ronnie. They would look after our Tony like family.' Mrs Ronconi dabbed her eyes with her handkerchief. 'I must see Tony, tell him I didn't mean what I said last night. That this is his home. Will always be his home if he marries fifty Germans. That I could be so cruel to my own flesh and blood . . .'

'Mama, there's no point in you even trying to see him. He won't be able to hear you, he's unconscious and the hospital won't let anyone see him until he wakes,' Ronnie's voice grew harsher as he began to lose patience.

'My son – my baby – is dying, and you're keeping him from me.'

'No one is doing anything of the kind, Mama.' Tina handed her mother the tea Gina had poured for her. 'And I agree with Angelo: whatever's happened to Tony is his own fault.'

'But we – his family – his own flesh and blood, closed our doors to him.'

'Because he wants to marry a German, Mama.'

'Is better he marries a German than he's dead, Tina!' The more agitated Mrs Ronconi became, the thicker her Italian accent became. 'I'll make a bargain with God. If

Ronnie's Diana and my Tony recover, Tony can do what he wants.'

'Even marry a German?'

'Yes, Tina, even marry a German. I swear before God, if this girl is what he wants, and Ronnie's Diana and my Tony get well, then I'll accept her as a daughter.' She glared at Tina, daring her to say otherwise. 'We will all accept her – all of us. We'll give them a wedding – a big wedding Tony can be proud of, so this German, whoever she is, will know she's not marrying just anybody off the street. She is marrying a Ronconi. Tony will have to have one of the cafés and a house – somewhere to live . . .'

Angelo rolled his eyes heavenwards. 'I'm going down the Tumble. Alfredo booked this afternoon off weeks ago. See you, Ronnie.'

'I'll be down tonight. We'll have a family conference.'

'You want to talk about the business today of all days, with Diana and Tony in hospital?'

'Seeing as how we can't do anything for either of them, I can't think of a better time.'

'When Tony's with you, not before,' Mrs Ronconi protested. 'Ronconi's is a family business, all the Ronconis need to be there to decide what's to be done with the cafés.'

'Don't worry, Mama, we won't cut Tony out.'

'If he lives, Ronnie.' As the seriousness of Diana's accident and Tony's illness finally sank in, Mrs Ronconi broke down. Covering her face with her hands, she began to cry uncontrollably. Relinquishing his place to Tina, Ronnie walked Angelo to the door.

'Café, tonight half-past eight?'

'You sure you want to do this?'

'It needs doing and the sooner the better.'

'Alfredo and I will be there. You'll tell the girls?'

'I'll get them there.'

'Ronnie, what if Tony . . .'

'Knowing that troublesome little bastard he'll live to make our lives hell another day.'

Angelo stared after his older brother as he returned to

the kitchen. He'd accompanied Ronnie to the police station earlier, heard Ronnie insist that Diana had fractured her skull as the result of horseplay between him and Tony that had got out of hand. Saw him sign statement after statement to ensure that the police wouldn't prosecute Tony or take the matter any further. Even heard him say *'accidents happen'*. And now – now – he couldn't help thinking that he'd seen Ronnie in many moods – but never quite so bitter, angry or unforgiving as this before. He'd meant it when he'd told Bethan earlier that he didn't think Ronnie would ever talk to Tony again. Now he wondered if the pneumonia didn't kill Tony, whether Ronnie would.

'I should be on my way up the Graig Hill not strolling round the park with you.'

'Come on, Bethan. A five-minute walk isn't going to make any difference to your life.'

'We've been here ten minutes already and I have things to do.'

'I wanted to explain that I didn't ask to be sent back here.'

'But you didn't refuse the posting.'

'No.' David Ford fastened the top button on his overcoat and pulled up his collar. The wind that whistled down from the snow-capped mountains that encircled Pontypridd cut sharp as it tore along the floor of the river path that linked the two main gates to Pontypridd Park. 'But I'm regular army and it doesn't pay a regular officer to question orders or a posting. Refuse Pontypridd and I could find myself cooling my heels in an Arctic training camp north of Alaska.'

'It couldn't be any colder than this.'

'But the company could be a lot worse.' He offered Bethan his arm as they came to a fork in the path.

'You have a choice: the children's playground or the sunken garden.' She pulled her royal-blue scarf higher, winding it over her mouth and nose.

'I'm a bit old for swings and roundabouts.'

'Then it's the sunken garden.' She took a deep,

satisfying breath of intoxicating fresh air that chilled her lungs and sent the blood racing to her head. 'I'd forgotten how beautiful winter can be. I love the park when it's like this.' Her eyes shone dark, flecked with wonderment as they turned towards a vista of vast lawns transformed into sheets of pure, unsullied white by frost-crimped snow. Even the shrivelled debris of last summer's blooms in the decorative beds had been changed into glittering fairy sticks by clinging snowflakes and ice.

'And I'd just love to take you to Montana. Winter there is really something. Cold clear days and nights that bring the stars so close you think you can reach right out and pick them from the sky. Snow six feet thick, mountains so high you can walk all day and never reach the top, and forests you can lose all the sheep in Wales in.'

'Then they must be huge.' She smiled at his reference to sheep. 'You go there a lot?'

'Used to when I was a kid. My mother's folks came from that way and my grandfather had a place up near the Canadian border. We spent a couple of Christmases there.' He hesitated as they reached the edge of a low dry-stone wall. 'So this is the famous sunken garden.' He peered over the top.

'It's pretty in spring and summer.'

'What I was saying about not asking to be sent here – I meant it, Bethan. The last thing I want is to make trouble between you and your husband.'

'Andrew made his feelings that obvious at the wedding yesterday?'

'Any guy with a wife like you would be worried at the thought of losing her.'

'Are you saying that he has a right to be suspicious?'

'Not of you. But an old bachelor who's been shown a glimpse of domestic bliss – now that's another thing. Just look at me, I've only been back in Pontypridd officially for a morning and so far I've lured you into taking coffee with me in Ronconi's . . .'

'With Angelo and every reprobate mitching Sunday School looking on.'

94

'And now a walk in the park.'

'There isn't a more public place in Pontypridd. And Andrew said the best way to silence the gossips would be for you to visit both of us.'

'People talk about us?'

'You didn't know?'

'No, but your husband obviously does. No wonder he looked at me the way he did yesterday.'

'He had a letter when he was in the prison camp. About us, the affair we were supposed to be having, right down to details like how Rachel and Eddie were calling you Daddy.'

David whistled. 'Bethan, I had no idea.'

'It's all right. Andrew's father helped me to convince him it was a pack of lies.'

'I shouldn't even be talking to you.'

'That would only make it look as though we had done something wrong. Andrew's right, you should visit both of us. I'm not suggesting you give up the Park Hotel for your old rooms in our attic but perhaps you could come for a meal.'

'You want me to?'

'Yes.'

'You two must have a strong marriage. I knew Andrew was a lucky guy, I didn't know just how lucky.'

'Please, David, talk like that doesn't help. You see Andrew and me – well, it's not been easy since he came back. He was gone for almost five and a half years and he seems like a stranger, almost as much of one as I must seem to him,' she qualified carefully, lest he think she was trying to heap all the blame for their problems on to her husband. 'I'm not going to lie, we're not getting on that well, but that's nothing to do with you. In fact you being here is a help. Frankly, I've never needed the support of my friends more. And this afternoon you've almost made me forget what Diana's going through for five minutes. It's been fun. In fact the most fun I've had – since . . .'

He looked into her eyes and knew that if he didn't change the subject he'd find himself on dangerous

95

ground. 'How are you at snowball fights?' He checked around to ensure there were no other uniformed officers within sight before scooping a handful of snow from the top of the wall, pressing it into a ball and throwing it at her.

She ducked and it fell wide. 'Better than you, if that's the best you can do.' Using both hands she made a snowball and threw it, catching him neatly between the eyes.

'Why haven't I discovered this talent of yours before?'

'Because we were both too busy working to have fun.' She neatly side-stepped his next three balls, while hitting him squarely in the face every time.

'Work! That reminds me . . .'

'Coward, you only want to go back to the hotel because you're losing.'

'Then I surrender.' He held up both hands as she lobbed a giant ball on to his chest.

'Unconditionally?'

'To the victor the spoils.'

'Then we'll expect you tomorrow evening, unless something happens with Diana, in which case I'll leave a message in the Park Hotel to say different. Eight o'clock for a meal and whatever drinks Andrew can find but I warn you, last time I looked we were down to rubbing alcohol.'

'How about I bring the liquor?'

'It might be safer.'

'And where can I walk you, ma'am?'

'The railway bridge. I'll see myself up the Graig Hill.' She suddenly decided that a quick detour into the Graig Hospital and up to Diana's bedside might help her, if not her cousin. 'Come here. We can't have a senior officer walking round looking as though he's rolled in snow.' As she brushed the flakes from his shoulder their gaze met again. Looking away quickly, she took his arm. 'Now tell me more about Montana. It's probably the closest I'll ever get to America.'

*

Andrew was driving back from Alma's where he'd been disappointed not to find Bethan waiting for him, when he saw them, walking arm in arm out of the mid-town entrance to the park. Engrossed in one another's conversation they had eyes for no one and nothing except one another as they trudged on up towards the Tumble, barely aware even of the dirty drifts of snow and ice piled high in the gutters by the snowplough. As he watched, Bethan's feet sank ankle-high more than once, soaking her shoes and feet, and each time, David placed his hands round her waist and swung her forward on to the nearest, comparatively dry piece of pavement.

They looked – and were behaving – like lovers. The town, the people, the cyclists pedalling slowly through the tyre tracks made by the few cars that managed to get a petrol ration didn't exist for them, just as nothing had once existed for him and Bethan outside of the love they felt for one another. He pulled his car into the kerb and parked outside the Park Hotel. Turning off the ignition he wound down the window.

Listening hard, he picked up snatches of conversation but their voices were too faint, too distant for him to catch any words. But just as they turned the corner by Rivelin's he saw Bethan fling her head back and cling even more tightly to David's arm, and a second later her laughter, light, carefree, echoed towards him.

He felt as though someone had twisted a knife into his windpipe and jumped on his chest, forcing all the breath from his body. He'd never realised that something that wasn't a physical hurt could cause so much pain. Bethan might not have made love to David Ford – yet – but she could laugh with him. Be happier in his company than she could be with him.

He continued to sit, watch and wait until only their footprints in the snow remained to show that they had walked that way. And in the five minutes it had taken them to round the corner above Rivelin's, he had pictured enough scenes of intimacy and happiness between them

97

to destroy his peace of mind – and all faith in his ability to rebuild his marriage.

'We shouldn't even be talking about the business with Tony in hospital,' Alfredo complained, as Ronnie, Tina, Gina and Angelo pulled chairs up to the preparation table in the kitchen of their Tumble café.

'We can't wait until he's out because we have no way of knowing when that might be,' Angelo filled a pitcher of water and placed it together with five cups in the centre of the table.

'If,' Alfredo corrected morbidly.

'Alfredo! How could you?' Gina brushed a tear from her cheek.

'Shall I get Luke?' Tina asked. 'He's only playing cards in the back with William and the others.'

'Gina'll be fine.'

'She's pregnant, Ronnie.'

'We've all noticed, thank you, Tina.' Ronnie sat at the head of the table. 'The latest news is, Tony's resting comfortably, breathing easier and responding to some penicillin the hospital managed to get hold of. Andrew stopped off in Huw's to tell me.'

'Does that mean he'll be all right?'

'Andrew said he's out of immediate danger, Gina, so that has to be good.'

'Perhaps now he's out of danger he'll wake up and tell us where he left the rest of his clothes and his kitbag.'

'And thank you for that, Tina.'

'Any news of Diana?' Angelo ventured, sensing that Tina and Gina wanted to know, but were too afraid to ask.

'She hasn't come round, so they can't assess the damage.'

'Ronnie . . .' Gina tried to touch his hand but he withdrew it sharply.

'Can I point out that this is supposed to be a conference about the business and Tony is not the only one who isn't here. Mama and Laura have as much say as the rest of us.'

'So why are we here?' Alfredo demanded truculently.

98

'To talk about what each of us wants, expects or hopes to gain from the business and the best way to run the cafés. As you all know, we're down to this café and the restaurant.'

'You were the one who rented out our café on High Street.'

'Right, Alfredo, let's discuss that first. I telephoned Alma this afternoon –'

'All of a sudden she has more say in the Ronconi business than the Ronconis.'

'I never had you down as quite so stupid, Alfredo. It looks like you would have been better off spending the war somewhere that taught you basic discipline and manners than Birmingham with Mama and the little ones.'

'You're not letting the rest of us get a word in edgewise, Ronnie.'

'We're all Ronconis.' Tina tapped a cigarette on the table.

'And what's that supposed to mean?'

'It means we don't allow anyone, even family, to push us around. I also used to think it meant that we possessed a certain amount of intelligence but listening to you for the last ten minutes has changed my mind. I agree with Ronnie, Alfredo, you're stupid and I have no intention of allowing you to drivel on endlessly about nothing. I for one would like to get out of here in the next half-hour.'

'So you can go back to Huw's with your Will,' he sneered.

'Now Megan's taken Catrina and Billy to her house, we're moving into Laura's to get it straight for her and Trevor. I would say you might find out what it is to be married one day but with your looks and charm –'

'Shut up, the pair of you!' Ronnie snapped. 'The only reason I'm speaking first is that I have spent the last few months thinking about all our futures and most of the afternoon looking at the current cash flow and profit of the restaurant and café. So can we please start? You mentioned the High Street café, Alfredo.' He lifted a pile of ledgers that he'd stacked on to a stool behind him on to the table. 'I know it's the first café Papa opened and of sentimental value to us all, but even before the war it was the least profitable. The rent Alma and – Diana –' he hesitated and blinked hard as he mentioned his wife – 'are paying us for the premises, is only five per cent short of the profit we made in 1938. On what I estimate the building is worth –'

'How can you possibly know what it's worth? You've been away three years.'

'Mama left me and Gina in charge. You think we're so stupid, Alfredo, we can't do accounts and evaluate our assets on an annual basis?'

'And what about Diana? She can't pay us rent now.'

A hush settled over the table. Angelo was the first to speak.

'I suggest you don't say another word, Alfredo, because if Ronnie doesn't thump you, I will.'

'The accounts of the shops Diana managed are in order. I know because I looked over them this afternoon after I looked at ours. I will take over and manage both the High Street shops Diana was running for Myrtle and Billy, and the one in the New Theatre until Huw and Myrtle decide what to do with them. And I will also see that the rent Alma and Diana have been paying us will continue to be paid,' Ronnie said heavily. 'Now to get back to Ronconi business, I don't think it's worth reopening that café.'

'Because Alma and Diana's shop is doing so well in our premises?' Alfredo chipped in, giving Angelo a defiant look.

'Because if you look at the bottom end of the High Street there are two other cafés open, one across the road and one next door to those premises. We only had five tables and twenty covers in the place and that was a squeeze. I think we should continue collecting the rent which gives us a ten per cent return on our investment in the building and, incidentally, a nice little addition to the profit on our other two places.'

'And this place and the restaurant?' Angelo asked quietly.

'It's obvious from what Tony said to Tina yesterday he wants – expects – to run one of them. And Mama won't forget her promise to God or change of heart about the German wife if Tony recovers.'

'So, you expect Angelo and me to bugger off! Just walk away and leave the restaurant free for you and Tina –'

'Tina and I want out of the business, Alfredo.'

Angelo was the first to regain his composure. 'Who's going to take over, Gina, me or Alfredo?'

'Tina, Gina and I discussed this with Mama after you left Danycoedcae Road, Angelo.'

'Without me!'

'Give it a rest for five minutes, Alfredo,' Ronnie barked.

'You even sound like Papa.'

'Shut up!'

'I wrote to Maria, Stephania and Theresa when they decided to stay in Birmingham instead of coming back here with Mama,' Tina interposed.

'They're happy there with their husbands,' Alfredo chipped in grudgingly.

'And we're pleased for them, Alfredo. They all agreed they don't want anything to do with the business, which is hardly surprising when you consider none of them ever worked in the café or restaurant.'

'They really don't want anything?' Angelo echoed incredulously.

'Papa left everything unconditionally to Mama in his will.' Tina lit her cigarette and deliberately blew smoke into Alfredo's face. 'She owns all three places, so it's up to her what she does with the business – and who she leaves it to.'

'And as it would be foolish to sell now, when prices are plummeting, it follows that we have to delegate someone in the family to run them. What Mama, Tina, Gina and I propose is that Tony take over this place with the rooms above for him and this German girl, if he insists on marrying her. That gives Tony his own little section of the business to run and separate living accommodation for the both of them at a distance from the rest of us. Which leaves you two with the restaurant.'

'But Mama will still own all three buildings and the business.'

'Would you like to suggest she hands it over to you, Alfredo?'

'We'll be doing all the work, we have to live.'

'And the three of you will be drawing wages. Mama will get her usual share, and the profits will go to the business. The account is healthy at the moment so I see no reason why we shouldn't consider opening a third Ronconi restaurant or café in a year or two, which will give you one each. I don't suggest we get into debt by doing it immediately, and that will give you a breathing space to learn a few things, Alfredo, and not just about the business. I don't envy Angelo trying to teach you.'

'What about you three, Laura and Roberto?'

'Laura'll have her hands full looking after Trevor and young John when she comes back. From what Mama and Tina told me this afternoon, Roberto's the only one of us with any brains and he wants to stay on in school. The income Mama draws from the cafés is more than enough to keep her and Roberto, even if he makes it to university, which I hope he will. With the rest of us independent, and Luke and Gina living with her, perhaps Mama can actually begin to take things easy for the first time in her life. But I warn you,' he gave Angelo and Alfredo a hard look, 'Mama's income is sacrosanct. I'll see the businesses sold off before I'll allow it to be cut. Any improvements or expansion will have to be paid for out of the profits you two and Tony generate, and don't try fiddling the books. Tina and I will be looking at them once a month.'

'So you'll still be running Ronconi's.' Alfredo kicked his chair back from the table and crossed his arms in disgust.

'No, all Tina and I will be doing is looking after Mama's interests.'

'And you two are happy to move over and make room for us after running the café and restaurant all through the war?' Angelo asked his sisters.

'We won't be just moving over,' Tina smiled, 'we're going into a new venture. Ronnie and William are setting up in business.'

'Cafés?'

'No, and before you ask with what, Will and I have our gratuities from the army and a bit set aside from Italy, money we made quite separately from the cafés. As soon as Luke can get released from the pit he'll be joining us.'

'So you've got it all worked out.'

'Any objection, Angelo?'

'Not me. You've been more than fair.'

'Alfredo?'

'Angelo and me'll still have to live at home,' he grumbled sulkily.

'Not at all, you'll be drawing wages so you can look for your own place. In fact I think it's a good idea. Give Mama a rest from cooking, washing and cleaning up after the pair of you.'

'Want us to go this week?'

'Next will do, Alfredo,' Ronnie responded caustically.

'But Tony's in no condition to take over this place.'

'Yet,' Tina broke in. 'Will and I will move out of the flat as soon as we find a house of our own. Until then, I'll do what I can to help out, but you two have to realise that Will, and the business he and Ronnie are setting up, comes first.'

'So you expect me to run this place?'

'Until Tony's fit enough to take over. What's the matter little brother, not up to it?'

'I'm up to it,' Alfredo growled.

'Good, that's settled.' Pressing the palms of his hands on to the table Ronnie rose to his feet.

'All we need now is for Diana and Tony to get better,' Gina observed.

'And this baby to be born so you'll stop crying at the drop of a hat,' Tina added.

'Just one more thing, Ronnie,' Angelo asked. 'What kind of business are you and Will setting up?'

'All in good time.'

'Cafés?'

'No, Alfredo, I told you, most definitely not cafés, so you don't have to worry about competition, at least not from us. If you run Ronconi's into the ground, it will be entirely down to your own efforts.'

'You'll be there if I come to you for advice?'

Angelo and Ronnie were sitting alone, the others had all left and the café kitchen was as quiet as it only could be after the last food orders had been cooked on a Sunday night.

'If advice is all you want, but I'm as capable of making mistakes as the next man, Angelo.'

'I know that, but face it, Ronnie, you never put a foot wrong when you and Papa built up this business before the war and we all knew it was you who made the decisions. Papa couldn't settle whether to have jam or marmalade on his toast at breakfast, let alone whether the time was right to open a new café or restaurant.'

'He could be indecisive,' Ronnie conceded, smiling at the memory.

'Look,' Angelo offered him a cigarette, 'I just want you to know that if there's anything I can do for Diana – anything at all – give blood, look after the kids, help in any way – I will. She's a fantastic woman and a great sister-in-law,' he added hastily, lest Ronnie misunderstand his meaning. 'You haven't been around since I came home but she's helped the family and just about everybody else in so many ways. Mama, Tina, Gina –'

'Thanks, Angelo.' Ronnie cut him short.

'Want a drink?' Angelo asked, embarrassed by the silence and not knowing what else to say.

'You keep drink here?'

'Tina told me it was a Ronconi tradition. Medicinal brandy, in case anyone got burned or splashed with fat.' Leaving his chair he pulled out the watch fob that had belonged to Ronnie when he had run the cafés before the war, and flicked through the keys attached to it. Finding the one he was looking for he unlocked a small cupboard at the back of the kitchen and extricated a half-empty bottle of brandy.

'Is that the one I left in '43?'

'It is. The girls never seemed to have the same number of emergencies as us when they ran the cafés.' Angelo took two teacups from the centre of the table. 'You staying with Megan and Dino?'

'For the time being. Billy didn't even recognise me, which is hardly surprising considering how long I've been away, I never saw Catrina before today and there's no way Megan will let either of them leave her house while Diana's in hospital.'

Angelo poured generous measures of brandy into both cups. 'They're bright kids.'

'I keep forgetting everyone around here knows them better than I do. I've a lot of catching up to do.' Ronnie sipped the brandy, sat back and looked at Angelo. 'Don't take this the wrong way. I know you're trying to help but we've both fought in the war. You must have seen head injury casualties.'

'Too many.'

'Then you won't mind if we talk about something else. You, for instance. You were a kid when I left for Italy before the war. I come back and you're a POW. Then I go away again and now it's –'

'Ten years later.'

'At least. You seem to have grown into a good bloke with a fair amount of common sense.'

'Compared to Alfredo?'

'Compare a rabid dog to Alfredo and the rabid dog would come out on top. What's the matter with him?'

'He's furious because he was too young to join up before the war ended. He thinks he's missed out on all the glory and medals.'

'I would have gladly given him my share.'

'POWs didn't have any to share. I think he just feels a bit useless. He couldn't stay here to help Tina and Gina when the family was sent away because everyone with the surname of Ronconi was a suspect traitor. From what

Mama told me he had a rough time in the school he was sent to in Birmingham. The kids couldn't fight the war but they could beat up the Italian fascist kid. Then he comes back here and first me, then you and now Tony return to push him around.'

'Put like that you could almost feel sorry for him – until you see him spitting and snarling like a cornered wildcat.'

'He'll calm down.'

'You'll calm him down more like. What about you? Do you really want to run the restaurant?'

'I had no choice when I came home because Gina wanted to give it up and to be fair I couldn't think of anything else I would rather do.'

'And now?'

'The work's all right.'

'And outside work?'

'You ran the cafés and restaurant, you know how little time is left.'

'A little.'

'You been talking to Tina?'

'No, but you've been a prisoner for a long time. You must have missed women.'

'There is a girl.'

'Anyone I know?'

'The eldest of the Clark girls.'

'The evacuees Bethan took in and adopted?'

'She's training to be a nurse in Cardiff Infirmary. I'm going to ask her to marry me.' It was the first time Angelo had admitted how much he loved Liza to anyone, including her.

'Will she say yes?'

'I think she might.'

Ronnie finished his brandy. 'I hope you'll be very happy.'

'If I make her as happy as you made Diana, I'll be doing all right.' Encouraged, when Ronnie didn't object to him mentioning his wife's name again, he continued. 'All Diana could talk about was you. Practically every sentence began with, *When Ronnie comes home* . . .'

'Yes, well, I made a right mess of that, didn't I?'

'As you told the police, it was an accident. The sort of thing that could happen to anyone.'

'Not everyone tries to kill their brother. If I hadn't half-strangled Tony, Diana wouldn't have been in the way when he lashed back at me.'

'I wish there was something I could do for her – and you.'

'You could do what I did this morning when I left hospital. Go to church and light a candle.'

'I haven't been in a church since before the war.'

Ronnie went to the door. 'Neither had I, Angelo. See you around.'

Chapter Seven

'THIS HILL IS endless.'

'You offered to walk me home.'

'I'd forgotten how far it was and it's cold enough to freeze a battalion of brass monkeys.'

'And your muscles are aching, you're tired and hungry, my bag is heavy . . .'

'And I'm a sensitive soul who wants to curl up and die whenever my girlfriend makes fun of me.' Angelo hugged Liza closer as they trudged towards the top of Penycoedcae Hill. All he could see of her were her eyes, sparkling icy-blue in the frosty moonlight, and the tip of her nose peeping out above her scarf.

'Who says I'm your girlfriend?'

'You are, aren't you?' he maintained apprehensively. 'You haven't been out with anyone else in months.'

'That you know about.'

'I thought you spent all your free time in Pontypridd.'

'There's always the twelve hours left after I've done my ward shift in the Infirmary. Three for studying, an hour for washing, ironing and starching my uniform, another to play with make-up and transform myself into a human being instead of staff and sister's doormat, that leaves seven for the high life – oh, and I almost forgot – sleeping.'

'I'm serious, Liza.' He stopped and drew her back, out of the slush of traffic-churned snow and ice, towards a gate set in the hedgerow. As she looked up at him he cupped her face in his gloved hands and kissed her, a slow, gentle kiss that thawed both their lips. Pulling her even closer, he wrapped his arms around her. 'I told you, it was settled last night. I'm going to run the restaurant. I'll have a good wage. We can get married.'

'Married!'

'Why not?'

'I hardly know you.'

'You've known me for nearly a year.'

'Ten months, which you've spent working day and night in the restaurant or café and I've spent training in Cardiff. Angelo, I like you –'

'That's good to know.'

'And you can snap out of that huff when you like. I'm very happy to have you for a boyfriend but I want to finish my training and then there's my sisters.'

'I thought Bethan John and Mrs Raschenko had adopted them.'

'That doesn't make them any the less my responsibility. I promised my dad before he was killed that I'd look after them. I couldn't have done it without their help, and Mary is very happy working for Mrs Raschenko but Polly and Nell are bright. They may want to stay on in school and if they do, I want to be earning a good wage so I can help them.'

'And me?'

'There'll be more nights like this. A lot more, I hope.' She locked her hands round his neck and stood on tiptoe, waiting for him to kiss her again. Refusing to be placated he pushed her away.

'The last thing I want is a long courtship, Liza. I've wasted four years of my life as a prisoner in Germany as it is. I want some fun.'

'So do I. Lots of it before I have to start cooking, cleaning, washing, scrimping and saving, and bringing up kids – and don't say it's not like that. Being the eldest, I got lumbered with most of the housework after my mother died.'

'And we're going to have loads of fun with you spending six days out of every seven in Cardiff Infirmary.'

'And you spending six out of every seven in the restaurant and the seventh in the café.'

'It'll be easier now Alfredo and I know exactly who's running what. And once Tony's recovered and running the Tumble café, I'll probably be able to wangle every Sunday off.'

'And I'll still get only one Sunday off in seven. But do we have to talk about this now, Angelo? I don't have to be back in the Infirmary until the day after tomorrow. I was hoping we could do something tomorrow night, like sitting in the back row of the pictures and finding somewhere private to talk afterwards.'

'You know what happened the last time I took you to the restaurant when it was closed.'

'You cooked me a real egg and chips.'

'And afterwards?'

'I said thank you.'

'I'd like you to say thank you properly, which is why I want us to get married.'

'And I want to get to know you better, which means a longer courtship. So, do I get the pictures and egg and chips tomorrow evening, or not?'

'I'll keep proposing.'

'I can say no nicely.'

'Come to the restaurant at half-past six,' he capitulated, unable to come up with any more forceful arguments as to why she should marry him sooner rather than later. 'All the staff will have gone by then.'

'I'll be there.'

'And I'll find something to cook.' Taking two nights off in a row would mean quarrelling with Alfredo because it was his turn to run the Tumble café, but if he offered a two-night stint in exchange for one, Alfredo would take it and it would be worth the sacrifice. He smiled down at her – definitely worth it.

'More potatoes, David?'

'No, thank you, Bethan. That was a fine meal but if I eat any more I won't fit into my uniform.'

'So, what exactly are you doing in Pontypridd, David?' Andrew handed his plate to Bethan and sat forward, anticipating David's explanation.

'Looking for some of the six million tons of equipment

our army mislaid in Wales.'

'Mislaid?' Andrew raised his eyebrows.

'The US army's not naïve, Andrew. The million or so tons of canned goods have gone for good. I have no intention of prying into the pantries of good Welsh citizens. What we're most concerned about are our missing Jeeps and,' he made a wry face, 'guns, tanks and rolling stock.'

'Tanks and rolling stock? You mean railway wagons? You can't be serious?'

'Unfortunately I am. I know how ridiculous it sounds but we can't find them anywhere.'

'I can understand why criminals would steal guns but why on earth would anyone take tanks and railway wagons?' Bethan returned from the kitchen with a gooseberry pie she'd made from home-grown and bottled fruit.

'That's what I'm here to find out.'

'At least they're big enough for you to recognise when you see them,' Andrew observed drily.

'If they haven't been repainted or broken up.'

'Gooseberry tart?' Bethan held it up in front of both men.

'Please. I remember the children picking them when I was here and Maisie and Megan teaching Dino how to bottle not only gooseberries but all the other fruit you'd grown. It seemed to involve heating the kitchen with pans of boiling water to steam bath temperature and a lot of quarrelling. You ended up sneaking into the pantry to steal a loaf of bread and jam to make the children sandwiches because there was no chance of anyone making anything other than preserves that day. What did the children call the gooseberries now – gos goggs, wasn't it?'

'That's right.' Bethan cut a large slice and lifted it carefully on to a plate. 'I've only custard, I'm afraid, no cream.'

'I love your custard.'

'You didn't when you first came here.'

'Perhaps I've learned to adapt.'

'Or be uncommonly polite,' Andrew suggested

cuttingly, furious at David's intimate knowledge of his family and their home life. If the man was out to make him feel like a stranger in his own home – and to his own wife – he was succeeding.

'David doesn't have to be polite here,' Bethan interrupted sharply, taking care to cut Andrew a slice of tart of equal size to the one she had given David. Cutting a smaller piece for herself she resumed her seat wondering why she had gone along with Andrew's suggestion that it would be a good idea to invite David for a meal. He'd done nothing but snipe at the colonel since he'd turned up. Even the bottle of bourbon David had brought had elicited only the barest and gruffest of thanks.

Silence, tense and embarrassing, closed in on the table as they passed round the custard jug.

'Bethan tells me you'll be living in the Park Hotel,' Andrew said at last.

'The brass is of the opinion that it will work out cheaper than renting rooms and an office. They've given me a kind of suite with a bedroom and a small separate room with a desk, filing cabinet and telephone, so I've nothing to complain about.'

'It *is* one of the best hotels the town has to offer.'

Bethan jumped up as she heard the front door open. 'Liza, darling,' she cried as she went into the hall, 'how lovely to see you. We weren't expecting you.'

'I swapped shifts with a girl who wanted to go to a wedding next week. I hope you don't mind, Auntie Bethan, but I asked Angelo in for a warm. He walked me up here.'

'All the way from town?'

'Unfortunately,' Angelo confirmed dolefully from the hall.

'Don't stand out there, Liza, Angelo, come in,' Andrew called, as pleased as Bethan that they'd been interrupted.

'You remember the colonel?' Bethan asked, as Liza followed her into the dining room.

'Of course. Hello, Colonel Ford.'

To Andrew's annoyance Liza kissed the colonel's

cheek, reinforcing his opinion that David Ford was far too familiar not only with Bethan but every member of his family.

'Mrs John's been telling me that you're studying nursing in Cardiff.'

'That's right, in the Royal Infirmary.'

'Hello, Bethan, Dr John, Colonel Ford. I've left your case in the hall, Liza.'

'Thank you, Angelo.'

'Come in, sit down here, close to the fire,' Andrew pulled two chairs from the table.

'Are you hungry?' Bethan asked. 'I could heat up some soup.'

'No thank you, Auntie Bethan. Angelo made me a meal in the café.'

'But you'll both have some gooseberry tart and custard?'

'With a bourbon chaser.' Andrew picked up the bottle David had brought from the sideboard.

'Just a small one, Dr John.' Angelo sat down feeling more like a gauche sixteen-year-old schoolboy than a twenty-three-year-old restaurant manager. One of the reasons he wanted to marry Liza as soon as possible was his uncertainty about courtship and all its mysterious rituals. He was never sure just how far it was permissible 'to go' with a decent girl before marriage because the years he should have spent finding out such things had been taken by the army and later the Germans.

He had known Bethan all his life, and Andrew John since their marriage, but it was the first time he had been invited into their house with Liza. And although he suspected that Bethan and Andrew knew he spent as much time with Liza as their respective jobs allowed, he was plagued by the thought that he should have formally asked for their permission to court her.

'Has Ronnie told you the latest news about Tony?' Andrew asked.

'Yes, he called in the café this afternoon with Billy and Catrina.'

'Angelo and Ronnie's brother has pneumonia. He's in the hospital,' Bethan explained hastily, hoping neither David nor Angelo would mention their conversation in the café the day before. Andrew was jealous enough of David as it was, without knowing she'd spent time with him.

'But thanks to penicillin, he's making a remarkable recovery. You can tell your mother and Ronnie that Tony can receive visitors tomorrow but no more than two, or the sister will have my head on a plate.'

'And Diana?' Angelo asked.

'There's still no change there, I'm afraid. But that goes for change for the worse as well as better.'

'We're hopeful.' Bethan passed him the whisky Andrew had poured.

Angelo glanced uneasily at Liza. 'Would it be all right if I took Liza to the pictures tomorrow night, Dr John?' he blurted out.

'As she's the one involved I think you'd better ask her.' Bethan cut the remaining tart into two pieces, lifted them on to plates and handed them to Liza and Angelo. 'You have two days off Liza?'

'I don't have to be back until late Wednesday afternoon, ready for the night shift.'

'Your sisters will be pleased.'

As the conversation moved easily into small talk about Liza's nursing training, her sisters' progress at school, and the difficulties of getting supplies of food for the cafés, Bethan frequently caught David's eye. It wasn't that he was staring at her, in fact she sensed it was rather the opposite – that he was trying to avoid looking at her. She couldn't help contrasting the strained atmosphere between the three of them, before Liza and Angelo had walked in, with the free and easy one yesterday afternoon in the park.

Was it so unreasonable of her to want to keep David as her own special friend and to enjoy his company occasionally without Andrew's presence? Then she saw Andrew watching her every move and decided that whether it was unreasonable of her or not, her husband would definitely think so.

'A pint of beer, Judy, and a drink for yourself if you want it.'

'Ta, Glan, you're a real gentleman.' She beamed at the porter from the Graig Hospital as she reached for a mug. 'You're late off shift.'

'Don't talk! I've been trying to get away for the last four hours. Two of the night porters sent round sick notes so I was "persuaded" to stay on. When I joined up I was given every promise in the world that my job would be kept open for me. Now I'm back, I'm on the same money I was before I left. Bloody juniors who weren't fit to wipe my boots then have been made supervisors over my head and they see to it that I'm given every mucky mess to clear and every twilight shift that comes up. If I refuse to sort them or work on when they want me to, I'm warned, "*It's last in, first out, Glan.*" "Land fit for heroes" my arse. If you weren't a lady I'd tell you exactly how knackered I feel.'

'Language!' the landlord shouted from the bar.

'Sorry, Dick.'

'I should think so. You just come off duty?' He joined Judy at the side hatch that opened into the corridor where Glan was standing.

'Unfortunately, but I've been here in spirit for the last couple of hours.'

'Don't suppose you know how Ronnie's wife or young Ronconi is? The missus was in the café this afternoon. From what she heard there isn't much hope for either of them. The coppers and gossips can say what they like. I think it's a crying shame to think of a young mother like that lying in hospital with her head cracked open and a young lad who's fought all through the war, upping and dying of pneumonia when it's over. Makes no sense, no sense at all.'

'From what I heard, they're both holding their own. Tony a bit better than Diana. But you know the Ronconis: they're all pretty tough.'

'Then Tony might make it?'

'Seems like there's a chance.'

'I hope so for the sake of the rest of them. Nice family.' He wandered back down the bar.

'Diana and Tony are ill?'

'Where you been for the last two days, Judy?' Glan delved into his pocket and pulled out a shilling.

'Where do you think? Cooking and cleaning up after my old man. I haven't had a minute to stick my head outside the door from Saturday night until I came here tonight. So, what happened?'

'From what I heard, Ronnie came home unexpectedly and found Tony in his house with Diana. They had a fight and either Ronnie or Tony shoved Diana through the kitchen window, breaking her head open. Tony must have run off afterwards because the police found him half-dressed – in your street as it happened. Appears he'd had one too many – not that anyone can blame him for that, seeing as how he was on leave. Anyway, they locked him in the cells for the night and by yesterday morning he was in a bad way. Sister said it was young Dr John that saved him. Got some of this new drug the papers are full of – penicillin,' he pronounced, proud that he'd remembered the word. 'After a week or two's rest they reckon he'll be as good as new.'

'I'm glad to hear it,' she muttered absently, taking his money and ringing up the price of his pint.

'You all right, love?' he asked as she returned his change.

'Fine, why?'

'You didn't get a drink for yourself.'

'I'll have one later.'

'What time do you get off?'

'I'm going straight home tonight, Glan. I'm tired.'

'I could walk you.'

'It's only across the road.' Any other night she would have jumped at the chance but all she could think of was Tony's kitbag. She'd dumped the clothes he'd left in her bedroom into it and pushed it beneath the bed in the boxroom, but it couldn't stay there. Her father rarely went in there but what if the boys came home and found it?

'Judy!'

'Mmm . . .'

'What's the matter with you? I've been talking to you for the last few minutes and you haven't said a word.'

'I told you, I'm tired.'

'Tomorrow night? You – me – walk home?'

'I'm off.'

'Even better, how about the pictures?'

'OK,' she agreed half-heartedly, still preoccupied with thoughts of the kitbag.

'Meet you outside the White Palace at six.'

'You sure you'll be able to get away tomorrow night?'

'With you waiting, love, not even matron herself will be able to stop me.'

'Thank you for a lovely evening, Bethan, Andrew.' David hesitated before deciding it would look odder if he didn't kiss Bethan's cheek. Afterwards, he held out his hand to Andrew.

'It was our pleasure, David,' Andrew replied with equal insincerity.

'Are you ready, Angelo?'

'Yes, Colonel.' Angelo gave Liza's hand one last squeeze before following David through the door.

'See you tomorrow, Angelo.' Liza waved as the two men trudged through the snow towards David's Jeep.

''Bye,' Bethan called before closing the door.

'It was good of the colonel to give Angelo a lift down the hill.' Liza returned to the dining room and began to heap dirty dishes and glasses on to a tray.

'It was good of him,' Bethan agreed. 'Leave that, Liza. You do enough work in the wards all day and don't try to tell me you don't. I was a trainee once. Now go on up and see your sisters. If they're asleep I suggest you join them.'

'You sure, Auntie Bethan?'

'I'll give Bethan a hand.' Andrew walked in from the kitchen with an empty coal bucket.

'Then I'll say good night.' She kissed Bethan.

'Liza?'

'Yes?'

'That's a nice young man you've got there.'

'Angelo? He's not bad is he, Auntie Bethan?' She laughed as she ran up the stairs.

'That girl's grown up so much since I took her in.' Bethan heaped the last of the glasses on the tray as Andrew placed the bourbon in the sideboard. 'You don't have to help me here,' she murmured, slightly unnerved by his silent presence.

'I really don't mind.'

'Togetherness is hardly washing dishes.'

'Then what is it, Bethan?'

Leaving the tray on the table she looked across at him. 'What's that supposed to mean?'

'What I said. I'm asking for your definition of togetherness.'

'It's a bit late to play games, Andrew. You have surgery first thing in the morning, I'll be up early with the children.'

'So, we carry on without talking.'

'We're talking now.' Picking up the tray she ferried it into the kitchen. She'd piled the dishes high, next to the sink. Normally she would have left them until morning and either she, or Nessie would have done them along with the breakfast things. But disturbed by Andrew's mood and wanting to delay the moment when she'd have to join him in bed, she put a spoonful of grated soap ends into the enamel bowl and ran the hot tap.

'I've taken out all the coals that can be salvaged from the dining-room fire and damped down the ashes.' Setting the metal bucket he was carrying in front of the stove, Andrew lifted the glowing embers with tongs, placing them carefully on top of the fire before shutting the stove door.

'Leave the fireplace for Nessie to do in the morning.'

'I intended to.'

'It was nice to have a fire in the dining room. We only

118

lit it there a few times during the war – once for Rachel's second birthday; then there were a couple of Christmases. Your parents spent the last one of the war with us. But I think I've told you that already.' She was conscious of gabbling, of saying anything to fill the strained atmosphere.

'Yes, you did.'

She leaned on the sink and took a deep breath as he returned the coal bucket to the wash house. She heard the cold tap running and guessed he was washing his hands out there. By the time he returned she'd finished all the glasses and laid them upside down on the draining board. She'd just begun on the plates when he brought the last of the cutlery and crockery in from the dining room.

'There's only the tablecloth.'

'It'll need washing. I'll see to it in the morning.'

'Right, you wash, I'll dry?' Taking a tea towel from a drawer in the dresser he picked up a glass.

'You don't have to do that.'

'I know I don't, Bethan, but I want to.'

Noticing that he'd called her Bethan, not Beth, all evening, something he only did when he was angry with her, she didn't argue any more. Stacking the plates in the wooden drainer she began on the cutlery. 'This silver needs polishing. After you've dried it, leave it out for Nessie.'

'I will.'

'Andrew,' unable to bear the tension generated by his absurdly polite responses a moment longer, she confronted him. 'Something is wrong. What is it?'

'Absolutely nothing.'

'Something is bothering you.'

'You think I should be bothered?'

'You've been odd all evening.'

'I apologise if I have but I assure you, if my behaviour has upset you in any way it wasn't intentional. Wasn't I good company for your colonel?'

'He's not my colonel!'

'But he'd like to be.'

'We're friends, Andrew.'

'I know, good ones.'

'You have women friends.'

'Not like David Ford.'

'They wouldn't be, would they?' she retorted tartly. 'He's a man.'

'Why so upset, Bethan?'

'Because you're being ridiculous.'

'Ridiculous.' He raised his eyebrows.

'Don't stand there looking all holier than thou. You think there's something going on between David and me. Why don't you finally come out with it?'

'Why should I, when you've already told me there's only friendship between you.' He gazed back at her, cool, self-contained and provocative. Positively daring her to say otherwise.

'If there's no trust between a husband and wife then their marriage isn't worth this much,' she burst out furiously, clicking her fingers.

'I quite agree.'

'Damn you, Andrew! You're enough to drive a saint to desperation.' Finally losing her temper she clenched her fists.

Catching her wrists before she could pound him, he pulled her close, all the while staring deep into her soft, brown eyes. She recoiled, uncertain whether he was about to hit her or push her away. In the event he did neither. Forcing her head back, he kissed her but there was no tenderness in his lips or his body as he used his weight to slam her against the wall. Everywhere he touched, his impact was savage, almost brutal in its intensity. Her wrists smarted as he finally released them to wrap his arms about her shoulders. His teeth and lips bruised hers as his tongue entered her mouth.

Suddenly afraid, she struggled to free herself but he was too strong – too determined. His fingers moved to the row of buttons at the back of her dress. He fumbled for only a few seconds before losing patience. Grasping her dress at the neck he tore it along its entire length from shoulder to hem. Ripping it from her body he tossed it to the floor and all the while he never stopped kissing her. As his fingers roamed over her flesh, brushing aside straps and snapping hooks and buttons, wrenching them from her underclothes, she shivered and not entirely from cold. Even now, with both of them angered to the point of violence he was sufficiently familiar with her body and skilled enough to evoke responses that were half pain, half pleasure.

The light burned, the door was open to the hall, but Bethan was oblivious to everything except the all-consuming, urgent hunger he'd engendered within her. But all Andrew could think of as his body finally pierced hers, was this once – maybe for the first time since his return – he would drive every thought and every consideration of David Ford from her mind.

Noticing a light burning in the room he used as an office, David opened the door to find his old cook/batman sitting at the desk scribbling a note.

'Dino, you're the last person I expected to see here at this time of night. I know you've had to cut your honeymoon short but you should be home in bed with your wife.'

'Got a tip-off in a pub that I thought might interest you. Now you're here I can destroy the evidence. The natives don't like snitches who run to the authorities with tales.' Tearing the piece of paper he'd been writing on from the pad, he shredded it into tiny pieces before consigning it to the bin. 'I've been drinking with my brother-in-law.'

'The constable?'

'Megan ordered us out of the house. She and Myrtle wanted to try to get through to Ronnie. Megan's afraid that if he doesn't talk about Diana soon he'll crack wide open.'

'So you and the constable went to one of the back rooms that are kept open twenty-four hours a day for the police?'

'In New York maybe. In Pontypridd they're more conservative.'

Knowing better than to ask, David removed a bottle of bourbon and a couple of glasses from the top drawer of the cabinet and poured out two full measures.

'To snitches.' He handed Dino one.

'You didn't hear it from me, but I think we –'

'Me until next Monday. You're on honeymoon, remember. Where you spend it is your concern.'

'All right, you should take a look at a scrap yard on a farm above Treforest run by a Ianto Myles.'

'He has our stuff?'

'He's selling guns to disgruntled ex-servicemen who are having trouble finding jobs.'

'Our guns?'

'That's what Huw and I haven't been able to find out but Huw hopes they are. He'd like nothing better than for you to nip this in the bud before anyone gets hurt.'

'And incidentally do his job for him. Anything for a quiet life, your new brother-in-law.'

'Nothing wrong with that.'

'Nothing at all, given what's happening in your family. But everyone knows a lot of guns have come back into this country with demobbed servicemen. Half the men I've talked to have souvenir Lugers.'

'I've told you what I heard.'

'And I'm grateful, Dino. So,' David sat on a chair and lifted his feet on to the desk, 'how's married life?'

'Apart from worry over Diana and Ronnie, pretty wonderful. You should try it yourself some time.'

'I have.'

'There's nothing like it when it works.'

'And there's no one so smug as a happy bridegroom.'

'Guilty, but then Megan's quite a woman, and,' he eyed David carefully as the colonel replenished both their glasses, 'so is her niece.'

'Mrs John? I've just had dinner with her – and her husband.'

'If I'm talking out of place, tell me to go to hell.'

'I haven't any authority over civilians.' David lifted his glass.

'Colonel . . .'

'Now you're a spy out of uniform perhaps you could bring yourself to call me David. I take it you brought up the subject because your wife put you up to it.'

'She's worried about Mrs John.'

'You can tell her I have no designs on my charming ex-landlady and even if I had, her husband is quite capable of punching me on the nose.'

'And she'll tell me that the way you and your ex-landlady look at one another says different.' Dino picked up his glass and stared thoughtfully at the liquor as he swirled it around. 'After living in the same house as you and Mrs John, I couldn't help feeling that if Captain John hadn't came back from the war his widow wouldn't have remained a widow for long.'

'But he did come back.'

'And people are talking.'

'So Mrs John told me yesterday.'

'I know when it's time to shut my mouth.' Dino finished his drink.

David picked up the bottle and refilled both glasses a third time. 'People here think differently to people at home.'

'Not that differently.'

'I mean about divorced men. They see us as immoral scoundrels.'

'They're revising their opinions. If the newspapers have got it right, half the returning servicemen want to get shot of their wives.'

'And your wife thinks Dr John wants to join them.'

'It's not what Megan or I think that's important, Colonel. I've said all I came to say. You won't forget the name?'

'Ianto Myles.'

'Come to dinner one night when things have settled down a bit at home and we know what's happening to Diana.'

'You'll cook Italian?'

'If you want me to.'

'I'd like to, thank you.' David poured himself another drink after Dino left but he didn't cork the bottle. Dino was right. It wasn't important what anyone else thought, only he and Bethan. Not for the first time he wondered if it might be possible to persuade her to put her own happiness above that of everyone else's for once in her life. Should she succeed, he suspected that it would go a long way to ensuring his own.

'Will.' Tina dug her elbow into William's ribs.

'More, please,' he mumbled drowsily.

'Will, wake up!'

Something of the urgency in Tina's voice percolated through his sleep-numbed brain. He sat up quickly, catching his head painfully on the headboard. 'This had better be good.'

'Someone is at the front door. I heard a scratching.'

'And I locked it, so unless they're small enough to crawl through the letter box they can't get in.' He snuggled down next to her. Pulling the sheet and blankets around his chin he punched the pillow into shape and wrapped his arm round her waist. She threw back the bedclothes. 'Tina!' he remonstrated. 'I was just getting comfy.'

'And I definitely heard something. No one knows we're staying here, but everyone knows Diana's in hospital and the children are being looked after by your mother, so it could be burglars who think the house is empty.'

'More likely a cat.'

'I heard a bang. Cats don't bang!' Picking up her nightdress from the floor, she slipped it over her head.

'Bloody women! Get back between the sheets before you freeze to death.' Stepping out of bed he fumbled for his pyjama bottoms, among the tangle of bedspread. 'I can't see a thing.'

'Then switch on the light.' Tina closed her eyes tightly against the glare.

'I was better off sleeping in a barracks full of men. At least they didn't hear bogey men at . . .' he squinted at the alarm clock, 'three in the morning.' Finally extracting his pyjama trousers he pulled them on. 'On the other hand . . .' he looked down at her pink, sleep-flushed face, 'you do have some advantages over a barracks full of men. Stay just as you are. I'll be right back.'

Padding softly out the door and down the stairs he slid back the bolt on the front door, opened it and peered into Graig Street. Frost haloed the streetlamps, the chill air nipped at the bare skin on his chest but there wasn't a sound or flicker of life to disturb the peaceful scene. He was about to close the door when he looked down.

'Who was there?' Tina asked, sitting up in bed as he trudged back up the stairs.

'Tony's kitbag. It crawled here all by itself by the look of it, but don't worry, I invited it in. It's safely bedded down on the sofa in the parlour.'

'There must have been someone there.'

'Possibly fairies.'

'Shouldn't you telephone the police?'

'It can wait until morning.' Pulling off his pyjamas he climbed back into bed.

'Ow, you're freezing!'

'That's the advantage you have over a barracks full of men. I can claim conjugal rights and demand you warm me up.' Pulling her close, he unashamedly siphoned off her warmth into his own frozen body.

'Will . . .'

'I've never known a woman like you for talking at the most inopportune moments.'

'All I did was say your name.'

'But it wasn't in a breathless, romantic way.'

'The breathless romance can wait a minute. Do you think Diana's going to be all right?'

'She'd better be, because if she isn't, I won't wait for pneumonia or Ronnie to kill Tony, I'll do it myself.'

'Do you think Tony's the reason why Ronnie's opting out of running the cafés?'

'I told you, Ronnie and I have been working on this business idea for months.'

'But the cafés and restaurant were more Ronnie's than anyone else's in the family. He helped my father set them up. Opening the restaurant was his idea.'

'You heard him, he said he was fed up with having to be polite and smile at people while serving up endless plates of beans and chips and cups of tea.'

'He never did much smiling and no serving that I remember.'

'He had to make sure you and the others bowed and scraped while you served. Now, before Ronnie and I find a new business and I work myself to the point of exhaustion in it, can I expend some of my surplus energy in a way we'll both enjoy?'

Chapter Eight

ALMA WAS READY waiting, muffled to her eyes against the cold in the doorway of the shop. Theo, wrapped in his winter coat, knitted hat, scarf and mittens, stood next to her, his small hand lost in hers, watching her face intently as she scanned the street for a sign of Charlie. Daily outings with Daddy had become part of Theo's life since Charlie had moved out. Alma had explained his absence from their lives by stressing that although Daddy loved both of them very much, he was very tired and needed more rest than he could get living over the shop, so he had moved in with Uncle Evan and Auntie Phyllis for a while.

Theo hadn't been unduly perturbed. Daddy *was* always tired, and his absence from the flat meant that he could go back to making as much noise as he liked. And the daily outings after school and at weekends with Daddy, or visits to his Uncle Evan's house with Auntie Bethan in her car to see him, had become treats that he looked forward to. Sometimes Uncle Evan's son, Brian, or Auntie Bethan's children, Eddie and Rachel, were around for him to play with, and when they weren't, Daddy was there to tell him stories about a strange country called Russia, stories that weren't like any he'd ever been read from books.

'Auntie's Bethan's car,' he cried, at the exact moment Alma saw it. Jumping up and down, he pulled at Alma's hand but she wouldn't release him until Bethan had stopped at the kerb and turned off the engine.

'Coming up to play with Eddie and Rachel, Theo?' Bethan asked, opening the door.

'Can I?' Instinctively he turned to Alma, then realised his father had stepped out of the passenger seat.

Knowing it was expected of him, he ran up and gave Charlie a cautious embrace that showed Alma just how far her son's relationship with his father had progressed since Charlie had moved out of the flat.

'You're both welcome to come back with me. There's a fire in the small sitting room, you can have it to yourselves.'

'Thank you, but we have to see the house,' Alma demurred.

'I could run you up to Tyfica Road.'

Charlie shook his head as he helped Theo into the back of the car and Bethan didn't press her invitation further.

'Don't go walking up the Graig Hill, whatever you do, Charlie. I'll pick you up when I drop Theo off. Seven all right?'

'It's fine by me,' Alma answered.

Charlie nodded again as he waved goodbye to Theo.

'You sure you're up to walking to Tyfica Road?' Alma searched Charlie's face for signs of illness and fatigue, then realised with a jolt that he looked far fitter and healthier than when he'd left.

'I've been walking over the mountain every day. Much further than from here to Tyfica Road.'

To her surprise he offered her his arm, she took it and they turned up Penuel Lane.

'I wasn't expecting you to buy the house so quickly.'

'Mrs Harding couldn't wait to get out of the place. With her husband dead and her son killed in the fall of Singapore all she could think about was making a new start in Cardiff with her daughter. I've put the house in your name. Spickett's are seeing to the contracts and there's some documents for you to sign but you can move in today if you want to.'

'It will need furniture.'

'Not much. Mrs Harding only took her personal things and a few bits and pieces that were of sentimental value, like her china cabinet, ornaments and pictures. Frankly I think the house looks better without them. Her taste isn't exactly ours . . .' She faltered, suddenly realising how inappropriate that sounded. There was no more '*ours*'. This was Charlie and Masha's house, not hers – a house she would never live in. 'What's left are the basics,' she continued quickly. 'The floor tiles and lino are in good condition, the rugs are old, but there's no holes in them, which is just as well as there's no carpeting to be had for love nor money in Ponty at the moment. The curtains are old-fashioned plush, dark and gloomy, but they'll do until better's available. All four bedrooms, dining room, parlour, living room and kitchen are furnished, unfortunately in solid pieces that were built with durability not beauty in mind. But you'll see for yourself in a minute.'

'You paid her for them?'

'One hundred pounds the lot. There's no way you could furnish a house that size for so little these days and that's supposing you could get the furniture. Even utility is strictly rationed to newly married couples and we – none of us – come into that category. Mr Spickett set the price on the basis that there are one or two valuable pieces that would fetch a good price. I believe him. You know how empty the auction rooms are these days?'

'No, I don't. But then I've had you to shield me from practical things since I came back.'

They crossed Gelliwastad Road and began walking up the hill past Tyfica Crescent and into Tyfica Road.

'This is it.'

'It's a fine big house, Alma.'

'It won't be very warm in there, but I've a fire burning at home. I thought we could look round and go back for tea.'

He nodded assent. She walked up the steps to the front door; taking the key from her pocket she pulled off her glove and slotted it in the door. She had been to the house a dozen times in the last couple of weeks, finalising plans and details about the furniture with Mrs Harding but now that Charlie was beside her, she felt strange, peculiar, almost as though she were a salesman selling it on to a third party.

'It seems a good solid house.' He glanced approvingly

at the tiled porch, the inner door with its stained-glass panels, and the ornate plasterwork on the ceiling.

'That's what Ben Davies said.'

'Do I know him?'

'He's a builder Mr Spickett recommended. I had a survey done, of course, but Mr Spickett said it was as well to call in a local builder. There are a few things that need doing but nothing urgent. A section of the dry-stone wall in the garden needs rebuilding, there are a couple of loose tiles on the roof – you can see them if you stand on the back steps – and all the exterior woodwork, especially the windows, need repainting. But as Ben Davies said, that goes for just about all the outside woodwork in Pontypridd and it won't be remedied until the paint shortage is over. He gave me an estimate of just under thirty pounds for the lot.'

'You told him to go ahead with the work?'

'When he can.'

'Good.' Charlie stepped into the front parlour. 'I think this is a good-sized room.'

'It makes a nice sitting room,' Charlie agreed, frowning at the Victorian red plush sofa, chaise longue, easy chairs and matching curtains.

'I'll look round for something to put over those marks.' Alma pointed to some lighter squares in the yellow wallpaper where Mrs Harding's pictures had hung. 'The dining room is through here.' She led Charlie back into the hall and through the door opposite, into a room filled with a heavy mahogany dining table, eight chairs, two carvers and a massive sideboard.

'As you said, good-sized rooms.'

'This is a smaller, everyday sitting room.' She walked down the passage and opened a door to the right of the staircase. 'It also leads to the kitchen and wash house. The furniture is a bit shabby.' Alma could have kicked herself. Why was she apologising for the sagging, faded chintz sofa and chairs when she was talking to her own husband?

'Good range,' Charlie commented approvingly,

walking through to the kitchen that he suspected had been, and would make, more of a living room than any of the other three rooms they had just walked through. He opened the door of the vast stove with its fireplace, water boiler, oven and hotplates.

'Mrs Harding left a gas cooker and electric clothes boiler in the wash house. Also all her everyday dishes and cutlery and enough linen to furnish the bedrooms.'

Charlie walked through to the wash house and garden. When he returned Alma took him upstairs. The principal bedroom was furnished with an enormous Victorian suite in an even darker mahogany than the dining room. Gentleman and lady's wardrobes towered either side of the bed. A massive dressing table with double the normal complement of clothes and trinket drawers stood in front of the bay window, blocking out most of the light. A tallboy and two chests of drawers placed either side of the high bed-frame swallowed up what little room remained. The two secondary bedrooms were much the same, only their suites were marginally smaller – and lighter, in oak and walnut.

'No washstands,' Charlie commented.

'There's a bathroom.' Alma showed him a white-tiled room far too large for the plain white three-piece suite it held. The bath was boxed in mahogany panels and mahogany dados ran round the room. 'Towels in the airing cupboard, here. I've had them all washed.' She showed him a stack of white towels. 'As you see, old-fashioned but serviceable.'

'It's comfortable and clean.'

'The boxroom was the maid's room.' Returning to the landing, she opened the door on a room seven feet by five, built over the hall. A narrow iron bedstead ran beneath the window. A broom handle jammed up close to the ceiling held half a dozen rusting wire coat hangers. A tiny, iron-framed travelling washstand, with waste bowl and water jug neatly shelved beneath an earthen basin with a plug, filled the rest of the space.

'The maid wasn't allowed to use the bathroom?'

'Mrs Harding made a point of telling me she was relegated to the outside Ty Bach and had to bring her washing water up from the kitchen and carry her slops down.' She closed the door on the room. 'What do you think?'

'You'd have to be hard to please to find fault with a house this size.'

'Then you think Masha will like it?'

'Bethan told you the woman is Masha?'

'She didn't have to, Charlie. She told me you wanted to talk. It's the first time since you left. I assumed you'd heard from her.'

'I have.'

'If you've seen all you want to here, let's talk in the flat. I left the fire burning. Tea's all laid.'

'Alma . . .'

'In the flat, Charlie.' She preceded him down the stairs. 'We'll talk about it there.'

'We moved one of the beds into the parlour for you, Tony. We thought you'd be more comfortable down-stairs.' Mrs Ronconi hovered in the passage as Angelo helped Tony out of the taxi and into the family home in Danycoedcae Road.

'I would have been fine upstairs, Mama,' Tony snapped. At a warning glance from Angelo, he stooped to embrace her. 'Really, Mama, I am fine,' he reiterated in softer tones. 'It's just that after having the nurses and sister in the Graig Hospital hovering over me day and night for nearly three weeks I can't stand anyone fussing.'

'You never could when you were little. But you nearly died –'

'And Dr John told us he's made a full recovery, Mama,' Angelo broke in firmly. 'Another week's rest and he'll be as fit as a fiddle.'

'A week might not be enough . . .'

'It'll be enough, Mama.' Angelo steered his brother into the parlour. The three-piece suite had been pushed against the wall to make room for a single bed. In between the bed and an easy chair, Mrs Ronconi had set out a small round table with bowls of winter apples, boiled sweets and home-made toffee. The *Pontypridd Observer* lay neatly folded under a small pile of books from the library.

'Roberto chose the novels.' Angelo drew Tony's attention to the books. 'He thought you might like to read to pass the time.'

'That was thoughtful of him.'

'And I've lit a fire in this room every day for a week so it should be well aired.'

'It's all very nice, Mama.'

'You go and see to Gina and your new granddaughter, Mama,' Angelo suggested tactfully. 'I need to talk to Tony about the business.'

'Yes – yes, Angelo, you do that. But I think everything you and Ronnie have decided is fair. Tony, I hope you'll think it's fair . . .'

'Mama,' Angelo prompted patiently.

'I must see to Gina. But you two will want tea.'

'We'll come into the kitchen for it when we're ready, Mama. In the meantime I have something stronger that might be more to Tony's taste.'

'He's been ill, Angelo. He nearly died . . .'

'Mama, please go and see Gina.'

'Your new niece, Tony, she's beautiful,' Mrs Ronconi enthused while still blocking the doorway. 'Luke and Gina named her Alice, after Luke's mother. You wait until you see her. She's just like Catrina was at that age. They could be twins.'

'Tony and I'll come in the kitchen later, Mama. You can show her to him then.'

'Yes, of course. Well, I'd better go to see to Gina.'

Angelo closed the door as his mother walked down the passage to the kitchen. 'Right, first things first. Mama's been arranging and rearranging this room for over a week, ever since Andrew John mentioned that you might be discharged. That coal fire,' he pointed to the grate, 'represents half the family's coal ration, including Luke's free allocation for working in the pit. After today, I suggest you tell Mama that you don't need a fire lit in here because you'll be happier sitting in the kitchen with the rest of the family.'

'I didn't ask for a fire.'

'No, but you know what Mama is like when one of us is ill. And the fruit and sweets on that table may not look much to you after living off loot in Germany but it represents Mama and Roberto's entire month's ration, so go easy.'

'It's bad enough having Ronnie play the big brother, I'll be damned if I'll put up with it from a kid four years younger than me.'

'As I've been running things for the last eight months I suggest you shut up and listen. About the business – Ronnie, Gina, Tina, Alfredo and I discussed it . . .'

'And surprise, surprise, decided to cut me out.'

'We hoped you'd run the Tumble café.'

'And the rooms above it?'

'Tina and Will are moving out, so you and this German girl of yours – if you insist on marrying her – can have them.'

'I would have preferred the restaurant.'

'As it's the bigger of the two places it seemed sensible for me to oversee the kitchen and tables and Alfredo the shop side of that business.'

'It's the better of the two.'

'It has no accommodation above it.'

'I don't think Gabrielle will be happy living over a café. She's used to better. She was brought up in a castle . . .'

'In which case she should have found herself a prince with more in his back pocket.'

Tony glanced round the parlour. 'We could move in here.'

'With Gina, Luke and now a new baby taking up two rooms, and Mama, Roberto, Alfredo and I filling up every other inch of space?'

'There's four bedrooms.'

'Three and a boxroom. If this girl of yours is too grand to live above a café I can hardly see her being happy with a six-foot-square boxroom, unless you expect Gina, Luke and the baby, Alfredo, Roberto and me or Mama to move in there.'

'We could move a double bed in here.'

'And if you sleep in here where would you live?'

'The kitchen with the rest of the family.'

'You'd ask Mama to share her kitchen with a German?'

'She shares it with Gina.'

'Gina's her daughter, your girl is one of the master race responsible for fifty-five million deaths in Europe in the last six years, including Papa's.'

'She's a wonderful girl. Everyone loves her . . .'

'Don't try pushing Mama any more than she's already been pushed by your pneumonia, Tony,' Angelo warned. 'When you were ill she promised God that if you and Diana recovered she'd accept your wife and pay for your wedding and that was it. And Diana's still in a coma.'

'That's not my fault,' he interposed haltingly.

'She wouldn't be in a coma if you hadn't gone where you weren't wanted, but enough's been said about that night and unfortunately none of it can undo the damage that's been done to Diana. To get back to Mama – I didn't hear her offer God, or you, any more concessions. And you know Mama, a promise to God is sacred, even one regarding an ungrateful son pushing for more than she's prepared to give, a child who needs putting in his place.'

'I can see that my family are going to give Gabrielle a great welcome.'

'We'll be polite.'

'And expect her and me to make do with two poky rooms over the café while Gina and Luke lord it here, and presumably Tina and Will have Laura's house to themselves.'

'Laura and Trevor are moving back as soon as he's

demobbed. There's a housing shortage, or haven't you noticed?'

'So where are Tina and Will going?'

'They've rented a place so you can have the rooms over the café.'

'And the business?'

'What about it?'

'I'm not stupid. If you and Alfredo are running the restaurant and me the café, it's because Ronnie and Tina have something better lined up for themselves.'

'They're opting out. Ronnie and William are setting up on their own.'

'Who's financing it?'

'They are, with their own money earned outside Ronconi's.'

'Seeing is believing.'

'You're welcome to look at the books any time. In fact it might be a good idea if you did, because apart from overseeing Mama's interest in Ronconi's, Tina, Gina and Ronnie want nothing more to do with it.' Producing a flask from his inside pocket he removed a couple of tiny glasses from his mother's 'best' china cabinet and filled them. 'Just one more thing, Tony. This might not be the best time to say it, considering you've just come out of hospital, but Ronnie and Tina asked me to remind you that they haven't forgotten the last time you were home. Or the first night of this present leave of yours.'

'I was drunk both times . . .'

'So it would appear. I don't know the details because they wouldn't tell me but I think it's just as well you realise that neither Ronnie nor Tina want to see you again. I'm prepared to go along with the public face of family unity for Mama's sake but Tina and Ronnie won't be at your wedding. And Ronnie gave me a message for you.'

Tony held out his hand.

'He didn't write it down. It's quite simple. You go near him, his wife, his stepson or daughter again and he'll kill you.'

'I was drunk . . .'

'And I saw the expression on Ronnie's face when he gave me the message. He means it, Tony.' He tossed off the drink he'd poured himself. 'Now let's go into the kitchen and see our new niece.'

Tony lifted his glass and sniffed it.

'It's best brandy, Will brought it back from Italy. Oh, and, Tony,' he murmured casually as his brother rose to his feet, 'if one word of Ronnie's message gets back to Mama, never mind Ronnie, I'll reshape your face. Apart from Ronnie and Tina not wanting to see you, we're a happy united family.'

'In front of Mama,' Tony said sourly.

Angelo clamped his arm across Tony's shoulders as they left the parlour. 'Always in front of Mama.'

Without asking what he wanted, Alma placed a cup of tea and a plate of sandwiches on a sofa table next to Charlie. He'd automatically sat in his favourite easy chair next to the fire, but already things were different. He was sitting too stiff, too upright, more like a visitor than the master of the house.

'Do you want me to do any more to the house in Tyfica Road?' she asked, deciding to deal with practical things first. 'I had it cleaned after Mrs Harding left, but if you want me to arrange a regular domestic help who'll light the fires and give the place a daily going over, I could arrange it.'

'You've done more than I had a right to expect.'

'Mrs Lane's youngest is in school now. She's looking for work and she's prepared to come early every morning and lay the fires. I didn't ask her,' she explained lest Charlie think she was trying to interfere in his life with Masha. 'She asked if I knew anyone who was looking for a cleaner.'

'If she's prepared to come in every morning, and it's no trouble to you, tell her to start immediately and keep the kitchen stove alight. The house needs airing.'

'When is Masha coming?'

'As soon she gets berths on a ship. The Red Cross said it might take a couple of weeks. Possibly less.'

'It will seem like a long time for both of you.'

'There are medical and immigration certificates to arrange and it won't be easy to book passage from Germany to here. There's a lot of pressure on transport, most of it is taken up by military personnel.' Without thinking he'd reiterated the official line given him by the Red Cross.

'Masha has written to you? You are sure it is her?' She held her breath, hating herself for daring to hope otherwise.

'She sent her photograph.'

'Can I see it?'

'Alma . . .'

'I'd like to. You told me once that I looked like her.'

'You did.'

'Not any more?'

Charlie reached into the breast pocket of his shirt – over his heart. Alma hoped she was reading more into the place he'd chosen to keep the photograph than he had intended. He removed a blue airmail letter. Unfolding it carefully he revealed two small passport-sized photographs but instead of handing them to her as she'd expected, he looked at them for a moment. Confused and more resentful than she would have believed possible, she struggled to keep her composure as she waited for him to make the next move.

'There's something else, Alma. Do you remember me telling you that Masha was pregnant?'

'Yes.'

'We have a son, Peter.'

'He survived.'

'Miraculously, and according to Masha only because he inherited my tenacity for life. When my village was emptied, everyone including Masha and my parents, brothers and sisters were sent to build a tractor factory in Stalingrad. Peter was born there. An hour after his birth Masha was sent back to work.'

'Who looked after him?'

'The state. He was brought up in nurseries and orphanages but Masha managed to keep in touch with him, right up until the war broke out. It couldn't have been easy for her. In Russia the state accepts total responsibility for the children and discourages parental contact, particularly between prisoners and their children. But she tried to instil a sense of family in him. When the Germans invaded, they were sent as slave labourers to work in a cement factory at Auschwitz. According to Masha it was Peter who kept them both alive during that time. When the Red Army advanced on Poland they were shipped west, which is why they ended up in a displaced persons' camp in the American sector at the end of the war.'

'He kept them alive – but . . .' Alma thought rapidly, 'he can't be more than fifteen?'

'Sixteen.' He finally handed her the photographs. 'But as you see, he looks older. There were boys in the camp I was in. They either learned to toughen up and survive or they went under.'

Ignoring the boy, Alma studied Masha's photograph first, tracing the lines on her face and comparing them with her own. There was no way of knowing from the black, white and grey tints if Masha had the same green eyes and auburn hair as her, or was the same height, as Charlie had once said. She could see a certain similarity in the set of their eyes and the curve of their lips, but the woman in the photograph had sunken cheeks, and wrinkles scored the skin round her mouth and on her forehead. Her eyes were tired and there were dark circles beneath them. She looked like an old woman yet Alma knew that Masha had been a year younger than Charlie when they'd married which made Masha thirty-three to his thirty-four now. Charlie's first wife was only seven years older than her, yet the photograph could have been that of a pensioner.

'The camps are brutal. Stalin's – Hitler's – it makes little difference to the inmates who runs them,' Charlie murmured, as though he'd read her thoughts.

'It could be a poor photograph.' She finally looked from Masha to the boy. A fierce jolt sent shivers down her spine. Charlie said his son was sixteen but there had to be a mistake. This photograph could have been taken of Charlie when they'd first met.

'This is you. The face, the features . . .'

'That's what Evan, Phyllis and Bethan said.'

'He's coming with Masha?'

'Yes.'

'Have you told them about me and Theo?'

'No, but I will the night they arrive. The Red Cross liaison officer thought Masha might not come if she knew I had married again.'

'Masha never married a second time?' Alma finally found the courage to voice her secret hope.

'She's spent all the time since we were separated in camps.'

'And people in camps don't marry.'

'Zeks – prisoners don't marry.'

'You'll move into the house with her?'

'I don't know, Alma. I won't know anything until I see and talk to her – and Peter. It will be strange for all of us.'

'At least the house will be big enough for the three of you.'

He sank his head in his hands. Needing something to do she removed his untouched teacup and placed it on the table.

'I do understand, Charlie, I really do.' After a moment's hesitation she brushed her fingers against his cheek. Grasping her hand, he held it close to his face, kissing her palm. 'You don't have to tell Masha about us on my account, Charlie.'

'That wouldn't be fair on you.'

'She has nothing and no one but you. You were forced to part once, she wouldn't understand if you abandoned her again. And there's Peter; he has never known what it is to have a father. Theo and I are so much luckier than them. We have good friends, a nice home, and while I work here a good income. When you meet Masha I want you to think only of her, Charlie, and not worry about us. We have everything we need.'

'The shops . . .'

'Now is not the time to talk about the shops. I ran them for you during the war; I can carry on doing it for a while longer. Meet your Masha when she comes. Talk to her, then settle with her what you want to do with them and this place. I'll go along with whatever you decide.' Picking up the teapot she muttered something about making fresh tea and went to the kitchen. Closing the door behind her, she leaned against it and finally allowed the tears she'd been struggling to keep in check to fall. But silently – there was no way she could allow herself to add to Charlie's anguish by letting him know just how heartbroken she was at the prospect of losing him – this time for ever.

'What are you doing, Tony?' Mrs Ronconi asked as she hauled a wicker basket of ironing into the kitchen from the wash house.

Tony gritted his teeth. After six years of army orders, when his off-duty moments had been entirely his own and he could have spent them drunk, insensible or brawling for all anyone cared, he resented his mother's constant prying into his private life.

'Writing a letter,' he growled, hunching further over the kitchen table.

'To your girlfriend?' Was it his imagination or was there a condemnatory tone in her voice.

'No.'

'Then who are you writing to?'

'Arthur Pearson.'

'I don't know him.'

Finally giving up on his letter, Tony put down his pen and looked at her. 'You should, he's our MP.'

'You're writing to our MP? Tony, if you're making trouble –'

'I am not making trouble, Mama.'

'Then why write to an important man? After what happened to your father it's better that we don't draw attention to ourselves. An MP, Tony . . .'

'I want Gabrielle to come over here so I can marry her before I turn grey.'

'And you expect him to bring her from Germany?'

'I'm asking him to help us get the permits she needs. I'm not the only British soldier waiting for a German bride. And it's not as if others aren't coming over. What I'd like to know is why they're being allowed in and there's a delay with Gabrielle's papers. Gina told me that the *Pontypridd Observer* reported a wedding last December between a Ponty boy and a girl from Hanover.'

'I heard.' Tight-lipped, his mother dropped the basket on the opposite end of the table to where he was sitting.

'What did you hear, Mama?' he asked, instantly on the defensive.

'You know how people talk.'

'No, I don't know. I've been away six years.'

'It's what we've all tried to tell you, Tony. People don't like it. We fight these Germans for six years, they kill us and now they're coming to Ponty to marry our boys and live here as if nothing has happened.'

'So, people are giving this German girl a hard time, is that what you're saying?'

'A hard time! Haven't we all had hard times enough with the war and this never-ending rationing?'

'But she's having a harder time than most. People won't talk to her, no one's friendly, she's getting the cold shoulder. Am I right?'

'How would I know? I hardly leave this house.'

'But you're saying that when Gabrielle comes she'll be treated like this girl?'

'I told you. I will give you a wedding, you have the rooms over the shop, they are furnished with good things that Tina took from this house so you'll have a roof over your heads and food in your stomachs.'

'And you'll treat Gabrielle like a daughter?'

'How do I know? I'll have to meet her first.' Mrs

Ronconi pulled Angelo's linen shirt from the pile of ironing in the basket, sprinkled it with water and rolled it into a sausage.

'Mama, I know you . . .'

'Write your letter, Tony. Let me know when she is coming and I will arrange the wedding.'

'I spoke to Father McNamara. He needs at least three weeks' notice to call the banns. Gabrielle is going to have to live somewhere before the wedding.'

'In the café.'

'You can't ask a girl like Gabrielle to live over the café by herself.'

'Why not? It was good enough for our Tina.'

'Tina was married and . . .'

'Be very careful what you say about our Tina, young man.'

'She can look after herself,' he finished lamely.

'And this German girl of yours can't?'

'Mama, everything will be strange. The country, the people, the language – you can't ask her to live alone.'

'You'll be in the café all day and every evening.'

'She can hardly sit in the café.'

'Too grand, is she?'

'And she can hardly sleep there alone,' he continued, ignoring his mother's last question.

'So where do you suggest she go?'

'I thought I could sleep in the café and she could have the boxroom.'

'You expect Angelo to move out?'

'It will only be for three weeks.'

'Gina has the new baby, I have enough work to do with the boys. I am not going to run round after a German.'

'Then I'll ask Laura to take her when she comes back.'

'I wouldn't count on that if I were you. She's having another baby.'

Taking his letter, he folded it, pushed it into an envelope and sealed it. Leaving the table, he opened the door to the passage.

'You going out?'

'To post my letter.'

'Wrap up warm.'

Mrs Ronconi shook her head as he slammed the door behind him. Of her eleven children Tony had been the most difficult. Until he was eighteen she had made allowances for him because he had been put under pressure by his father to become a priest. But ever since he had convinced his father to allow him to work in the business instead of going to the seminary, he had been trouble – nothing but trouble all the way, especially with girls. He had almost married that nice Diana Powell . . .

She smiled to herself as she realised what she was thinking. That nice Diana Powell had married her Ronnie. And didn't he deserve happiness more than Tony after the way his first wife had died? It was a bad thing for any mother to admit that she had a favourite among her children, but Ronnie – he was more of a man and husband than Tony ever could be. It was better Diana was married to her Ronnie. If only her head would mend quicker . . . But Tony?

She dipped her fingers into the bowl of water on the table and liberally damped a tablecloth. Only a few more things to do. Time to set the irons on the fire. As she lifted the cover on the hob and laid the flat irons on it to heat up she tried to recall the features of the girl she preferred to think of as 'the German' rather than 'Gabrielle' in the photograph Tony had shown her. She remembered pale eyes, glossy hair coiled in plaits, her chin – was it weak? That would be a bad sign. And her mouth – hadn't it been on the small side? Everyone knew that indicated a mean nature.

Perhaps it was just as well that this girl hadn't got her papers. It gave Tony more time to change his mind – and find himself a nice Welsh-Italian girl.

Chapter Nine

'WILLIAM, IT'S FOUR in the morning,' Tina laughed, as he dropped a line of kisses from the back of her neck to the base of her spine. 'You promised to meet Ronnie at seven.'

'Just celebrating our first night in our new house. You know something; I might put Ronnie off. It's been all go ever since I got home. Staying in Huw and Myrtle's, looking after the kids, taking them to my mother's, cleaning Laura and Trevor's house, moving Ronnie and Diana's stuff to my mother's, moving into the rooms above the shop, then out of them – now this house. I think I need a good rest. I'm not feeling at all well and a day in bed may be just what I need to set me up.'

'I'll bring you hot drinks every half-hour.'

'I'll need more personal attention than that.' Pulling her even closer he sighed contentedly. 'Skin is a marvellous invention. I think I'll begin an in-depth study of yours.'

'I really would like to get this house sorted tomorrow. Your Uncle Huw is a lovely man but when he lived here, he lived like a bachelor.'

'He was one before he married Myrtle,' he agreed drily.

'I gathered that. I doubt he decorated this place after your grandmother died.'

'As she went before my time, I wouldn't know.'

'I wouldn't say no to some help.'

'Ronnie and I have things to do.'

'You were talking about putting him off.'

'Tina, much as I love and adore you, to be honest, I'm fed up of cleaning. First Laura and Trevor's place then the rooms above the café, now this one.'

'But we're going to live in this one until we can afford to buy our own.'

'If you like it enough to clean it, we could buy it off Uncle Huw if he's prepared to sell.'

'With what? Buttons?'

'I don't think Uncle Huw collects buttons.'

'Have you any idea what houses go for these days? I've saved some money from my wages for running the café and my soldier's wife's allowance but nowhere near enough to buy a house. Let's face it, until you and Ronnie find a business to set up and it starts making a profit, or you go back to work for Alma –'

'We've quite a few actually.'

'A few what?'

'Buttons in the bank.'

'The river bank?'

'I told you, Ronnie and I did a bit of wheeler–dealing in Italy.'

'You said. Enough to put a deposit on a business?'

'Oh, we made a bit more than that. There'll be enough left over to buy this place.'

'Outright, without a mortgage?'

'Of course.'

She sat up suddenly. 'I know you and Ronnie. What kind of business, because if –'

'Ssh, woman. Nothing illegal.'

'William!'

'We sold a few things.'

'What kind of things?'

'I've never known a woman with so many questions. Useless things that were lying around.'

'No one buys useless things and in my experience nothing is ever "*lying around*". It always belongs to someone.'

'I suppose you could argue that some of the stuff we sold belonged to the German Army but they didn't seem to want it. And . . .' he pulled her back under the eiderdown, 'as I said, there's enough for us to buy a half-share in a business and put a deposit on a big house or buy a small one outright.'

'I don't believe it.'

'I promised you when we married that when the war was over we'd live happily ever after.' Pulling the sheet over both their heads he kissed her again – and again – until she decided that all her other questions about money, work, businesses and houses could wait.

'Well?' Megan looked up from the flour and salt she was sieving into a bowl as Ronnie walked through the door.

'Your son, William Powell, Esquire, and son-in-law Ronnie Ronconi, Esquire, are now the proud owners of Powell and Ronconi, scrap yard and garage.' Taking the tea she poured for him, Ronnie dropped into the easy chair next to the range.

'Why Powell first?'

'In case anyone saw Ronconi and expected tea, beans and chips.'

'I hope you've done the right thing.'

'And I hope we've bought the right things. They cost us almost twice as much as we wanted to pay.'

'You're both broke?'

'Not quite.' He winked at her as he looked down at Catrina, who was playing at her feet. 'I stopped by the hospital. Andrew was there, so I got to see Diana for a few seconds.'

'Still no change?' she asked anxiously.

'That's the official line but I thought her colour was better. No one else seemed to have noticed it and just as I started to point it out to Andrew, the sister swept in, and us out of Diana's cubicle. I swear if that woman comes out with one more, "*Your wife's doing as well as can be expected, Mr Ronconi. We're making her as comfortable as we can,*" I'll take one of those great big enema syringes they keep in the sluice room and give her a good dose of what she's so fond of doling out.'

'Ronnie!' Megan tried to look disapproving but couldn't help laughing.

'Daddy,' Catrina chattered, looking up at him from

the hearthrug where she'd laid out a family of tiny rag dolls.

Megan smiled triumphantly. She'd spent all morning coaching her granddaughter to accept the stranger who'd suddenly walked into their lives as her often spoken of, but never seen father. Ronnie gave the first real smile Megan had seen since he'd moved in with her and Dino.

'Yes, darling, Daddy's home. Come on my lap.' He sat patiently, arms extended until she'd gathered all nine of the dolls Diana had made her into her arms before climbing on to his knees.

'Diana's got to come round sooner or later,' Megan said firmly, cracking an egg into a basin and beating it with a fork before adding it to the milk she'd measured into a jug.

'And if she doesn't?'

'You don't know my daughter, Ronnie Ronconi.'

'Yes I do, and it's slow murder trying to live without her.' He hesitated for a moment, 'Megan – you've never really asked me what happened that night.'

'You and Tony were messing about and accidentally pushed Diana through the window.'

'Megan –'

'There's been too much talk about that night, Ronnie, and none of it is helping Diana. Thanks to Wyn Rees stepping in and marrying Diana, Billy's got a dead hero for a father and all the stepfather he needs in you.'

'You know.'

'That Tony's Billy's father? Diana told me years ago and I'm glad she had the sense not to chase after him and demand he marry her. It would have been a disaster. Wyn Rees was a good man and good to Diana but no husband, through no fault of his own, bless him. Some men are just cut out to like men not women, but as my grandmother used to say, everyone's different and thank God for it. I know you two weren't together that long before you had to go off to Italy but you made Diana happy, Ronnie, probably for the first time since she was a child. She lived for the day you'd come home. You do know that, don't you?'

Too choked to answer her, he nodded as he bent to pick up one of the dolls that had fallen on to the rug, and tickled Catrina's tummy with it. She giggled, throwing her small arms round his neck as he hugged her tight.

'And you do know Diana never saw Tony alone from the time you left until that night?'

'I don't need any convincing on that score, Megan. I heard them talking before I tried to throw him out. If only I hadn't tackled him . . .'

'And we'll have less of that blaming yourself. It's not your fault. What happened, happened. We have enough to do to get Diana well without dwelling on things that can't be changed.'

'Now I know where Diana gets her attitude to life from, and why I love her so much.'

'You'll get her back, Ronnie.'

'Billy go to school all right?' he asked, needing to change the subject.

'Yes, Dino took him. I think he's missing Diana more than any of us.'

'I don't think that's possible. I was wondering: do you think it would be a good idea if I took him to the pictures on Friday night? Just the two of us? Tina was saying that there's a special showing of *Snow White and the Seven Dwarfs* on in the White Palace. If I picked Billy up from school, I could take him to the restaurant for tea before the five o'clock show. We wouldn't be out much before nine so it would mean he wouldn't get to bed before ten, but he could have a lie-in on Saturday.'

'Diana'd have a fit at the thought. She insisted on regular meal and bed times, but,' Megan smiled broadly, 'I think it's a great idea, and I'm sure so will Billy.'

It was an unprepossessing sight by any standards. Three acres of barren, black-silted mountainside almost completely covered by rusting pieces of unidentifiable machinery and scrap cars that didn't even warrant the effort of cannibalising their interiors to turn them into chicken coops. Here and there, occasional unstable pyramids of shiny, bald tyres threatened to topple over on to the debris below. As Tina walked towards the low, rickety farm gate that served as entrance to the yard, a flock of crows fluttered upwards from the roof of a ramshackle shack alongside it, squawking in indignation at being disturbed.

'What do you think?' Will asked disarmingly.

'As an act of mercy, you and Ronnie are going to bury the dead?'

'There's money in that dead.'

'Money! No one with any sense would go near that disgusting pile of junk with a septic barge pole. For once, I think you and Ronnie have found an even bigger mess than you could have made on your own.' As realisation dawned, Tina stared at him, horrified. 'Don't tell me you paid out good money for this place?'

'One week from today you won't recognise it.'

'A week! It'll take a couple of bulldozers, a fleet of lorries and a month of Sundays to clear that, and even then you'll have to pay for somewhere to clear it to. And what will you do with the land afterwards? Start a slag farm? Last I heard, even the coal owners didn't know what to do with the stuff.'

'You're missing the point, Tina,' William said impatiently. 'Most of this is metal.'

'Rust,' Tina corrected sharply.

'Salvageable rust. And at the moment the price of scrap metal is low –'

'I can understand why, there seems to be a lot of it about.'

'Only because the war is over,' William explained as if he were a headmaster, and Tina the class dunce. 'So, we buy cheap now and sell when the price goes up, which it's bound to do as soon as this country gets back on its feet and starts manufacturing domestic goods again.'

'Even supposing this ridiculous plan of yours works, what will we live on until then, fresh air?'

'We have some money set aside, and there's the garage.'

Tina narrowed her eyes. 'What garage?'

'The one on Broadway. Ronnie's looking at it right now. We bought it along with this field from Ianto Myles' widow.'

'What did he die of? Blood poisoning after taking a walk through this.'

'A heart attack.'

'I'm not surprised. He probably checked his assets against his overdraft.'

'The garage is a going concern. We saw certified accounts.'

'And you took the word of an accountant and a solicitor! You two are insane. Even if people had the money to buy cars, there are none and there's no petrol.'

'But there will be, sweetheart.' William put his arm around Tina's waist. She shrugged it off.

'I suppose you want me to start tightening my belt and teaching Billy and Catrina to do the same. It's a bit hard on a two-year-old, but Billy might just be old enough to understand that he has an insane uncle and stepfather.'

'There are enough business people in the town, like the doctors and shop owners, who have cars and vans and need them serviced every couple of months, for the garage to tick over nicely until the boom starts.'

'Tick over enough to keep us and Ronnie's children?'

'As I said, we have a bit put by for emergencies.'

'And to think I let you two talk me into giving up the café for this! What did you have in mind for me, dusting and polishing the scrap iron?'

'Ronnie and I are going to do that.'

'Diana would never have let Ronnie buy this.'

'Yes, she would have, because unlike you she believes in her husband.'

'You'd need fairy dust in your eyes to believe in this.'

'We were hoping you'd run the garage for us,' Will ventured.

'Run it!' she reiterated scathingly. 'You've booked me on a crash course in mechanics?'

'We have a mechanic. He worked for Ianto for years and

if we need another, there's thousands being demobbed.'

'It's reassuring to know that you don't want me to look under a bonnet.'

'There's a nice little room at the front of the garage that Ronnie and I are going to clean up and turn into an office and reception area where people can sit and wait while their cars are being serviced. We were hoping that you would do the accounts there, man the telephone, book cars in . . .'

'Can you see me in a garage?'

'We would pay you,' William said carefully.

'And you and Ronnie?'

'Would set up this scrap yard. I grant you it doesn't look promising at the moment but once we've sorted the metal that's only fit for meltdown from the bits that can be cleaned up and reclaimed, we'll soon start making money. Spare parts for cars and machinery are almost impossible to get these days.'

'Run it? The two of you together?'

'We were hoping Luke would do that for us when he's released from the pit.'

'No doubt, while you two sit on your rear ends living off the fat of the land.'

'We'll be attending auctions.'

'You what . . . ?'

'Before you explode, Tina, give this business idea of ours a chance. Petrol won't always be rationed. We're going to buy up cars and lorries, do them up and sell them on at a profit. Ronnie thinks we can't lose if we get into the garage business before the boom.' Wary of the look in Tina's eyes, Will gave up on the sales pitch he and Ronnie had devised in Italy to convince their wives that their plan would work.

'Ronnie is crazy and you're even crazier for listening to him. Pontypridd is a working-class town. The ordinary people here will never be able to afford cars.'

'Yes they will. Ronnie says –'

'Ronnie says! Well I'm having no part of it. As soon as the house is straight I'm going to look for a job.'

'Tina . . .' William chased after her as she stalked back towards the ancient Trojan van they'd borrowed from Angelo.

'Drive me home, right this minute.'

'Tina . . .'

'Not one more word, Will. If you've any sense you'll go looking for Ronnie and back out of this deal before it's too late.'

As William drove away he didn't have the heart to tell her that it was already too late, and he and Ronnie had deposited the deeds to the scrap yard and garage in the bank before he'd met her.

'Charlie, you didn't have to come down here. I would have called to see you, if you'd let me know something was wrong.'

'I've had enough preferential medical treatment as a friend of the family.'

'Not at all. You're looking better.' For once Andrew didn't have to lie. Charlie was still a long way from the man he had been before the war, but he had put on some weight, his face had lost its cadaverous, drawn look and his eyes were alert. More like those of a live man than the ex-death-camp inmate he had travelled home with from Germany nine months before.

'I'm fine.'

'You always say that.'

'I'd like to talk to you about my wife.'

'Your Russian wife?' Andrew asked carefully.

'It must be difficult for a man like yourself to understand how someone can acquire two.' There was no humour in Charlie's statement.

Andrew glanced at his watch. 'Is there anyone else in the waiting room?'

'No.'

'How about we go for a drink in the New Inn and talk there. The bar is always quiet this early in the evening and there's a few secluded corners where we won't be disturbed.'

'What are you drinking?'

'Pints with brandy chasers,' Andrew suggested. 'The first for nourishment, the second for medicinal qualities.'

'First round on me.'

Andrew slung his stethoscope and a few boxes of pills from the desk into his bag. Snapping it shut, he followed Charlie out. After locking the surgery door, they walked the short distance to the best hotel Pontypridd had to offer. As Andrew had predicted, it was empty and he commandeered a private table while Charlie went to the bar.

'You've heard from the Red Cross?' Andrew asked as Charlie set the drinks before him.

'Masha is leaving Hamburg on Monday night. She'll be in Tilbury early on Wednesday morning.'

'I don't know what to say. You and Alma are good friends, I've always thought you belong together. I have difficulty imagining you married to someone else.'

'Alma understands about Masha.'

'I've talked to her, she seems to understand a great deal more than most wives would under similar circumstances. Are you going to Tilbury to meet . . . ?' Andrew only just stopped himself from saying 'this woman' but he couldn't bring himself to say 'your wife'. As far as he was concerned Charlie only had one wife and she wasn't Russian.

'Meet them,' Charlie finished for him. 'Yes.'

'Them? She's bringing someone?'

'Our son.'

'I had no idea you had another child.'

'Masha was pregnant when she disappeared. I hoped but I didn't really expect the child to survive. The Red Cross sent me two railway warrants because they thought I might need the support of a friend when I meet Masha and Peter at Tilbury. Masha's spent years in camps. She's ill, weak, and although I'm her husband, after sixteen years, I doubt we'll even recognise one another. You saw what I was like after only three years in Nordhausen. We're bound to be more like strangers than man and wife.'

'You'd like me to go with you?'

'I was thinking of Bethan. Masha may need the help of another woman, especially a nurse on the journey back here.'

'Have you asked her?'

'No. It's difficult. You and Bethan are Alma's friends as much as mine. If you don't want to meet Masha I would understand and respect your decision.'

'Have you talked to Alma about this?'

'Not about meeting Masha. But you know Alma has insisted that Masha move into the house she bought in Tyfica Road.'

Andrew finished his brandy and lifted his pint on to the mat in front of him. 'I'm sure Bethan would be happy to go to Tilbury with you. So would I, for that matter. I can always get my father to take care of the practice for a day or two but there's one thing you'll have to understand, Charlie. I can't see Bethan befriending Masha at the expense of her relationship with Alma and I certainly won't. If possible we'd like to be friends with all of you but if ever there's a conflict, Bethan will side with Alma, you do know that.'

'There won't be a conflict.'

'Alma may feel differently when your first wife and son are actually living round the corner from her and Theo. Have you thought of taking Masha elsewhere?'

'Alma wouldn't hear of it. As she pointed out, everything I have is in Pontypridd. All my friends, the business – her.'

'But you're abandoning her for this other woman.'

'I won't desert her.'

'But you've already moved out of the shop.'

'Masha is my wife, my first wife,' Charlie muttered hoarsely. 'And if I live with her it won't stop me from loving Alma.' He slouched over his brandy. 'I could sooner stop breathing than loving Alma. She brought me happiness when I had given up hope of even finding contentment again. She married me knowing I had another wife who might be alive. She waited for me all through the war, refusing to believe that I'd been killed when everyone with better sense told her there wasn't the remotest possibility I'd survive. She built my single shop into a chain of twelve that's making more money than even I dreamed of. She gave me a wonderful son . . .'

'Are you saying you don't want to take this Russian wife of yours back, Charlie? Because if you are, there are people who can help.'

'It's not that simple.'

'Why not? We have one life. What's the point of living if we don't make at least one person happy, if only ourselves. No man talks about a woman the way you're talking about Alma only to walk away from her.'

'You know how I was.'

'You were suffering from depression. It was only natural after what you'd been through. It takes time for the body and mind to adjust.'

'Depression? You think that was natural?'

'Perhaps natural isn't the right word. I knew something went wrong a couple of months after we came back. Was it you and Alma?'

'No – perhaps in a way – it's not easy to explain. But I felt as though I was slipping back, away from everyone. I was there and I wasn't. Even everyday living demanded more from me than I had to give. I could hear people talking but it was too much effort to answer their questions. I could see that Alma – Theo – all the people who cared about the man they knew as "Russian Charlie" were fine. They didn't need anything from me – Feodor Raschenko – the man who should have, and perhaps did, die in the camps. I had come back to a town that barely accepted me before the war, to a wife who had waited, and a son. But even Theo wasn't really mine. He was Alma's and Mary's. It wasn't their fault. It was just the way it was. I hadn't been there for Theo when he was born and they were. I was a stranger foisted on him, someone for him to resent because I came between him and his mother. I'd spoiled his safe, happy, childhood world.'

Andrew suppressed his instinct to tell Charlie he was wrong, because for the first time since he'd discovered him in a corner of a stinking typhus hut in Nordhausen the Russian was actually talking about himself and his feelings. And he sensed there was more to come.

'The camps . . .' Charlie looked into Andrew's eyes. 'You saw them, but not when the Germans were there and no one who saw them after the SS left can have any idea of what it was like to exist in them day after decaying, rotting day. I survived because I learned to look on things no man should without lifting a finger to help. And I did things that I will never tell a living soul about. Even now, just thinking about them is enough to make me wish that I'd died of shame. You found a dead man, Andrew. When you came into that hut, looked at me and gave me your hand, you helped a corpse from my grave and that's what you brought back to Alma.'

He drank his brandy and Andrew signalled to the barman to bring two more.

'All I could think was: why me? Why had I survived when so many so much worthier had died? I didn't deserve to live any more than they but they were the ones whose bodies had been thrown into the pits and burned in the crematoria. I came back, looked at Alma and Theo and saw that they had led a happy, well-ordered existence without me. They didn't need a dead man weighing down their lives.'

'You can't blame yourself for surviving, Charlie.' Andrew paid the barman who brought the brandies to their table.

'I can blame myself for sinking lower than the level of an animal to survive, and for making Alma unhappy when I came back. She doesn't need me.'

'But Masha does?'

'She has no one and nothing else. She has spent sixteen years in camps, I was in them for three and I can't imagine longer. And my son – he was born in the camps. Did you see the boys at Nordhausen? Children with the faces of old men, or worse, evil, cunning wolves. Masha and Peter need me because I am all they have. Me – Feodor Raschenko – a Russian who like them no longer has a country to call his own.'

Andrew took his brandy and sat back in his chair. He'd watched Charlie give up on life when he'd been surrounded by kindness and the love of a woman who had fought hard to be strong for him. How could any of them have known that all he'd needed to give him the will to live was the simple human condition of being needed?

'If you want us to, Bethan and I will travel up to Tilbury with you next Wednesday.'

'Thank you.' Charlie picked up his brandy.

'You do realise Masha might be as weak as you were when you left the camp?'

'I have her letter.' He removed it from his pocket; slipped out the photographs it contained and opened it. Like Alma, Andrew noticed that he kept it in the pocket closest to his heart. 'She writes that she is glad I am alive and that I didn't have to live in the work camps like her. My parents, three brothers and two of my sisters died not long after I last saw them.'

'I'm very sorry.' As Andrew murmured the hackneyed phrase of condolence he realised that Charlie hadn't looked at the letter once.

'They were among the lucky ones. From what I heard at Nordhausen, conditions in Stalin's camps weren't any better than Hitler's – just different.'

'Did anyone from your family survive apart from Masha and Peter?'

'No.' Andrew was not a sensitive man yet even he could hear the anguish behind the single word. 'Masha writes that Peter is strong and clever and that it was he, not she, who scavenged the food and privileges that kept them alive after they were taken by the Germans.'

'He's sixteen?'

'Yes.'

'You'll have to find something for him to do.'

'I'll ask him what he wants.' Charlie looked down at his untouched beer. 'Shall we have another brandy?'

'Why not, and why don't you come back with me for dinner?'

'Thank you, but no.'

'That way you can ask Bethan to come to Tilbury yourself. I have a house call to make in town later, I'll bring you back then.'

'Evan and Phyllis are expecting me.'

'Then I'll drop you off on my way up the hill. Look, I can always find something to do in the surgery, why don't you call and see Alma and tell her some of the things you have just told me?'

'No.' Charlie's reply was harsh, finite. 'It would only make things more difficult for her if I did.'

'Perhaps you're right, Charlie. But at the moment I don't think things can be any more difficult for her than they already are.'

'Look, Ronnie, I'd like to help you, but money is tight right now. Ianto never expected me to pay my bills in cash, and certainly not the minute the van was fixed. He always gave me time.'

'How much time?' Ronnie asked, glancing at William who was standing, arms folded, leaning against the door of the filthy, grease-stained cabin they'd promised Tina they would transform into an office.

'If you'll only take cash – at least a month or two. Times are hard, very hard.'

'For all of us, Gwilym.'

'There's nothing I can do about it, Ronnie. I haven't a penny to my name. All the farmers round here live hand to mouth in winter. I've nothing but a few cold weather greens and the wife's faggots and stuffing mix to sell on the market, and they don't bring in enough to pay the coal bill.'

'Butter, cheese, eggs?'

'I can see it's been a long time since you've walked round the market. They haven't appeared on any stall since the beginning of the war. They're strictly rationed and no sign of a let-up. The government fixes the price and they take all we can produce for a pittance. The money I get for my eggs doesn't cover the cost of the chicken feed. This war's not just been hard on you soldiers, those of us on the home front have suffered something terrible too.'

'And you're going to suffer some more, Gwilym. No money no van.' Ronnie capped his fountain pen and laid it across the invoice pad on the grubby, finger-marked, steel table in front of him.

'You can't do that!'

'I just did.' Ronnie pocketed the van keys to drive his point home.

'How am I going to get to market?'

'You just said there was no point in going there because you've next to nothing to sell.'

'I've always got a bit – like I said the winter greens and the wife's faggots . . .'

'And the black market eggs, butter, milk and cheese you deliver to your special customers on the way, Gwilym,' Ronnie suggested quietly.

'Talk like that could get me into trouble and there's no truth in it. Not a word!'

'You denying you used to pay Ianto in goods?'

'Now and again, I used to give him a bit on the side when it suited us both. But nothing illegal, mind. Just a bit I saved from my own personal stock. I'm a patriot through and through, me.'

'How much is the bill, Ronnie?' William asked.

'Ten pounds fifteen shillings and sixpence, parts; six pounds two and fourpence labour, and a pound towing charge, which makes, seventeen pounds, seventeen shillings and tenpence.'

'You're bloody thieves, that's what you are. Over six pounds' labour! The wife and me work from dawn to dusk for a month and don't see anywhere near that kind of money.'

'The wife and you aren't skilled mechanics, Gwilym. A trained man and boy worked on your van for three days and nights, including Sunday and that's double time.

You were the one who told us it was a rush job. "*Couldn't be without it for Wednesday market*" was what I believe you said on Sunday when the mechanic picked it up from your place.'

Seeing he was beaten, Gwilym eyed Ronnie sideways, then scratched his head thoughtfully. 'Tell you what, seeing as how it's you, and you were so good about fixing it in time for tomorrow morning, how about I give you half a cow. I've got a bit of a thing going with the slaughterhouse and they'll always kill the odd animal for me as a favour when I've a few unexpected bills to pay.'

'We're not into the black market, Gwilym.'

'I'm not saying you are, but like everyone else, you've got family.'

'Not one big enough to eat half a cow before it goes off.'

'Make it a whole cow and you have a deal, Gwilym.' William said suddenly.

'Will . . .'

'That's daylight robbery!' Gwilym exclaimed indignantly.

'A whole cow or we keep the van.' William deliberately refused to meet Ronnie's eye. 'And,' he smiled, 'not an odd cow either, Gwilym. One of your best beef bullocks will do.'

'I can sell those for twenty-five guineas.'

'In that case sell it and give us the money,' Ronnie interrupted.

'You have to be careful these days. There's people watching all the time. Jealous buggers who won't think twice about shopping a mate if there's a reward in it for them.'

'Exactly, and if we're running the risk of getting caught we'll need extra to cover that risk,' William stated firmly.

'You'll not be wanting the head and the innards?'

'The whole cow, Gwilym, or the deal's off. How soon can you deliver?'

'To here?'

'The slaughterhouse. We'll take it from there.'

'They do their specials on Thursday night.'

'In that case, I'll expect to go to the slaughterhouse on Friday morning and arrange delivery of my meat.'

'That's a lot of meat. If you need any help to get it off your hands –'

'No help, Gwilym. Here.' William stepped forward and picked up the invoice. Unscrewing the cap from Ronnie's pen he wrote, *Full payment to be received in cash by the first Saturday after the above date or van to be repossessed in lieu of payment.*

'There, that makes it nice and legal, now all you have to do is sign that and you can drive away.'

'Bloody highway robbery, that's what this is,' Gwilym grumbled, but he took the pen.

'We'll still take cash on Saturday.'

'Your cow will be there, first thing Friday morning but they'll be wanting it out of the slaughterhouse quick. The meat inspector's no fool and he never lets on when he's coming.'

'We'll take it out, don't worry. Ronnie, give the man his keys. Nice doing business with you, Gwilym.' William offered his hand. Still grumbling the farmer hesitated before taking it and walking through the door.

William went to the window. Taking his handkerchief from his pocket he cleaned a small hole in the grimy glass and watched Gwilym drive away. 'We're going to do it, Ronnie. We're going to catch up with all the bastards who've been sitting nice and safe and cosy in Pontypridd making a fortune on the black market while the Nazis have been using us as live targets. There may be quick money to be made during a war but there's still some to be made in reconstruction. This is going even better than I thought it would.'

'Better!' Ronnie brushed the horsehair stuffing off his trousers that had leaked out of the chair he'd been sitting on, and joined William at the window. 'What are we going to do with a whole cow including head and innards?'

'Think about it, Ronnie. Who do we know who sells food and can cook it on the premises?'

'The cafés and Alma, but the girls ran the café and restaurant legally during the war and Angelo hasn't put a foot wrong since he's come back. I'll not have my brothers running the risk of prosecution just because you've done a dodgy deal, Will.'

'I thought you'd opted out of running the cafés.'

'I'm still head of the family. If Angelo takes any of your meat I'll take a walk up to the police station myself.'

'You weren't so fussy in Italy . . .'

'Because Italy was a bloody shambles. There weren't any police to chase up black marketeers and even if there had been, there weren't any prosecutors to prosecute. Haven't you read the *Pontypridd Observer* since we've come back? At least half a dozen cases of black market dabblers are tried every week.'

'That doesn't mean we're going to be one.'

'You not me. I've two kids and a sick wife to think about. I'm having nothing to do with this.'

'You'll take half the profits.'

'I'll take no more than what it takes to clear Gwilym's bill.'

'Not even if I sell at double the price of the bill to Alma?'

'Not even if you sell at ten times the price. But I warn you now, Will, Alma hasn't got where she is by bucking the system. You start poking around in Gwilym and the slaughterhouse manager's *"special business"*, and you'll find yourself standing in the dock alongside them.'

Chapter Ten

'MY LETTER TO the MP worked,' Tony announced as he sat down to tea with Gina, Luke, Roberto and his mother. 'He must have moved Gabrielle's name up one of the lists because she's arriving in London next Wednesday.'

His mother paled as she picked up a tureen from the table. 'Mashed potato?' She dolloped a large spoonful on Tony's plate.

'Did you hear what I said, Mama? Gabrielle –'

'We all heard, Tony. Luke, take three sausages not two. You need your strength working down that pit.'

'I'll be going up to London to meet her.'

'As long as you don't expect any of us to go with you. We can't afford train tickets let alone the waste of good working time.' Mrs Ronconi forked three sausages on to Tony's plate. 'Pass Luke the gravy boat, Roberto.'

'The wedding –'

'I said I would arrange it and I will; a beautiful one you can be proud of. Do you know if she has a dress and a veil, or will we have to find one? Perhaps Laura's would fit her. You poor girl,' Mrs Ronconi looked down fondly on Gina, 'getting married in that terrible registry office on the day I took the little ones to Birmingham. You had to make do with that awful costume.'

'It wasn't awful, Mama, it was new.'

'Wartime!' Mrs Ronconi scoffed. 'Poor you and poor Tina. Both married in ordinary clothes in an office, not a church, and Tina without a soul from her family except you and Luke there. And now here I am arranging a beautiful wedding for a German. But you don't have to remind me, Tony. I promised God, you and this German a beautiful wedding and you will have one. I only hope Diana's head will mend in time for her to see it.'

Tony had the grace to stare down at his plate as Gina and Luke exchanged glances.

'You'll have to clean the rooms above the café, Tony,' Gina murmured, in an attempt to fill the awkward silence that had fallen over the table.

'I think the German can clean them herself. After all, she has them for nothing.'

Hoping for a favour, Tony allowed his mother's disparaging observations to pass without comment for once. 'Please, Mama, won't you reconsider allowing Gabrielle to stay here?'

'There's no room. Roberto, stop poking at that cabbage. Eat it at once, before it gets cold.'

The entirely blameless Roberto stopped forking potatoes into his mouth and switched to cabbage.

'There will be room if I move into the café,' Tony persevered.

'So, you want this German of yours to sleep with your brothers in Alfredo and Roberto's room.'

'Of course not, but Angelo could move out of the box-room and in with them.'

'I'm not asking Angelo to move anywhere.'

'Then I will.'

'What's the difference between you or the German sleeping in the rooms above the café?' his mother demanded fractiously.

'I've told you, they're not suitable.'

'Not suitable!' Mrs Ronconi left her chair and drew herself up to her full height of four feet ten inches. 'They were suitable for our Tina and her William. Anyone would think this German of yours is Princess Elizabeth.'

'All I'm asking is that you let her stay here for three weeks until the banns are read and we can get married.' Pushing his chair back, Tony left the table. 'But it appears that is too much to ask you to do for your new daughter-in-law.'

'And where are you going in the middle of a meal?'

'Down to the café.'

'It is your day off. If you don't rest or eat properly you will be ill again.'

'I'll have to do something with the rooms, seeing as how no one in the family will help me.'

'Tony . . .'

'Let him go, Gina. You have enough to do to see to your husband and your baby. Why should you run round for a woman who is too good to live in the rooms our Tina made into a home?'

'Tell you what, Mama,' Tony opened the door, 'why don't I move into them right away, seeing as how William and Tina have already moved out?'

'Suit yourself. What do I care if you want to live in sin with a German. She is only a German. But there'll be no big wedding if you do.'

'Given the attitude of this family you can keep your bloody wedding.'

'See what she is making you do. Swearing at your own mother – I told you that you can have a beautiful wedding and a place to live, Antonio,' his mother called after him as he stormed through the door and down the passage. 'I didn't promise God anything about having Germans in my house. And I won't. Not while I have breath in my body and strength in my arms to shut them out.'

'Andrew, is that you?' Bethan called from the kitchen as she heard the front door open and close.

'You expecting anyone else at this time of night?'

Steeling herself for yet another bout of bickering and wounding remarks, she called back, 'Of course not. I've kept your supper warm.'

'What is it?'

'Welsh rarebit.'

'I've forgotten what meat tastes like.'

'So have we all since the war started,' she bit back more harshly than she'd intended.

He remained in the hall a moment longer than it took to divest himself of his coat, hat, gloves and scarf. Their lovemaking had become more intense and frequent since the disastrous dinner with David Ford but once they had their clothes on, the sniping began. Principally because he simply couldn't stop thinking about her relationship with David and – he suspected – neither could she.

All reason dictated that she had every right to seek out and enjoy the company of a man who had proved such a good friend to her and their children through a difficult year of war. But reason couldn't stop jealousy gnawing every time he caught sight of the colonel's tall, slim uniformed figure walking purposefully along Taff Street. Or wanting to lash out every time one of their acquaintances made a snide comment along the lines of, '*Saw your wife out walking in the park with that nice American colonel the other day, Dr John. Bet he sees you all right for a few parcels of tinned food.*' Or worse of all – remembered her laughter the day he had seen them walk out of the park gates together.

'Sorry, I'm late.' He would have kissed Bethan's cheek when he entered the kitchen if she hadn't been crouching over the stove. 'I had a drink with Charlie,' he added by way of an explanation.

She pushed her hands into a pair of oven mitts. 'How is he?' There was real concern in her voice as she removed the plate from the rack where it had been warming and laid it on the wooden tray she'd placed on the table in front of his chair.

He went to the sink to wash his hands. 'Better than I've seen him in months. His wife – Russian wife,' he amended, 'is arriving in Tilbury next Wednesday.'

'That is going to be hard on Alma.'

'And you. He asked if you'd travel up with him to meet her. The Red Cross sent an extra travel warrant for him to take a friend. Apparently his wife is very weak and they thought he might need help with her on the journey.'

'And he asked you, not me, if I would go with him?'

'He's going to ask you himself but first he wanted to know how I'd feel about you meeting Masha. After all, we're Alma's friends as much as his and he didn't want to risk complicating our friendship.'

'So, if you'd objected to my going to Tilbury with him he wouldn't have asked me?'

'It wasn't like that, Bethan.'

'It sounds like it to me. Dear God, we women ran things perfectly well without you men interfering all through the war and now you're back, you're deciding where we should go and who we should meet without consulting us. We're not children or idiots.'

He finished drying his hands on the kitchen towel and pulled his chair out from the table. 'I know you're not,' he agreed quietly.

'So what did you tell him?' she demanded in exaspera- tion as he prodded the dried up cheese with his fork.

'I told him I'd try to get some time off and go with you.'

'A family outing! That's all the woman needs – to be confronted with a mass of strangers when she arrives in a foreign country after travelling across Europe from a displaced persons' camp.'

'Two of us hardly constitutes a mass.'

'And Charlie? She hasn't seen him in sixteen years.'

'I said I'd talk it over with you.'

'No you didn't,' she challenged.

He laid down his knife and fork, 'All right, I didn't, but I didn't think you'd be so opposed to my going with you.'

'You did say Charlie has only one extra travel warrant.'

'I could buy a ticket. Charlie's a good friend, he needs help.'

'And our loyalty to Alma?'

'Apparently she's being so civilised about Charlie's other wife, he's sure she wouldn't mind us going up to London with him.'

'You took Charlie's word for it, or you stopped off on the way back and asked her?'

'I took his word.'

'I see.'

'Bethan, I'll go along with whatever you think best, but please, consider Charlie. He's still weak. He may be taken ill – anything could happen between here and London. Even if the train's on time and all the connections go smoothly it's a twelve-hour journey. To go there and back in this freezing weather without taking a break is exhausting for a fit man, let alone someone like him.'

'You think he'll need a doctor?'

'He'll need a friend more, which is why I thought both of us should go. If you don't want to, I will, and if you do, the two of us might be more help to him and his wife. If you're worried about Alma, and I can see why you should be, then perhaps you could talk over the situation with her.'

'I already have.'

'Then why are we arguing?'

Ignoring his question, she poured herself a cup of tea and sat opposite him at the table. 'Alma asked me to help Charlie, and I told her I would, but only if it didn't affect our friendship.'

'Then you will go to London with him?'

'Yes, as he wants me to. Will you?'

'If you have no objection, and I can persuade my father and old Dr Evans to look after things here.'

'I'll tell Alma I'm going with him tomorrow.' Bethan reached for the cigarettes in her apron pocket.

'I wish you wouldn't smoke so much.'

'Why?'

'Because of the Reinkoff report. He believes it is one of the causes of cancer.'

'So it's all right for you to smoke and not me?'

'I don't smoke anywhere near as much as you. And I don't smoke American cigarettes.'

'They're so much stronger than British? Or is it the person who gives them to me that you object to?' Bethan lit her cigarette and drew on it defiantly as he pushed his meal aside. 'If it's dried up it's your fault.'

'I'm not hungry.'

'Do you want tea?'

'Please.'

He wanted to reach across the table, grasp her hand and force her to look at him – really look at him – the way she used to before the war – and David Ford had driven them apart. Instead he took the tea she offered and stirred it.

'The main reason I'm late is Charlie started talking about the camps, the war, Alma and his Russian wife. And once he started I didn't want to stop him. You know how reticent he's been.'

'What did he say about his first wife?'

'That's difficult.'

'Because he asked you not to tell anyone?'

'No, because he feels that he's only just recovering emotionally after his experience in the camps. The one thing he is certain of is that his first wife has more right and claim to him as a husband than Alma.'

'Alma would agree with him there.'

'Really?' He stared at her in amazement.

'Alma feels that as he told her about Masha before they married, and warned her that Masha would have first claim if she ever turned up, she has nothing to complain about.'

'But surely Alma didn't think this Masha was still alive?'

'I rather think events have proved there was no way of anyone knowing that, one way or the other.' Clearing her cup and saucer into the sink, she picked up his plate. Taking his knife, she scraped off the cheese into the pigs swill bin.

'What did you do today?'

'I went to town and queued for three hours to get our groceries and an hour and a half to get our ration of fruit. No doubt you heard I also ran into David Ford.'

'As a matter of fact I did. You two seem to "run into" one another quite often.'

'And what's that supposed to mean?'

'That Pontypridd is a small town,' he replied, deciding she could take his comment anyway she wanted.

'It's all the smaller for people like Mrs Richards and her daughter. I doubt they wasted any time in telling you that David and I went to Ronconi's together. If you'd rather I didn't see him, why don't you come right out and say it, Andrew.'

'So you can play the injured, indignant wife? He's your friend . . .'

'Shouldn't that be "our", considering he's had dinner with us.'

'Beth . . .'

'I'm too tired to argue, Andrew. The children will be up early, I'm going to bed.'

Stifling the urge to call out *'What's happening to us?'* he watched her walk out of the room and listened as she ran lightly up the stairs. Moving from the table he sat in the comfortable chair in front of the range, leaned back and gazed up blindly at the ceiling. His head was still swimming from the after-effects of too much brandy and beer on an empty stomach. It wasn't the right time to think about anything serious, certainly not Bethan and their problems, but he couldn't help himself.

The only time they ever talked rationally and seriously was when they discussed other people's problems. As soon as they touched on their own situation, reason gave way to a ludicrous game of one-upmanship played out at the expense of their marriage.

Where did they go from here? Carry on as they were 'for the sake of the children', rubbing along as best they could until they ended up like most of the *'respectable'* middle-class couples who formed the backbone of the town, polite and deferential to one another in public, and barely communicating in private.

He could go upstairs now, climb into bed beside her – even make love – for want of a better word because for all its intensity, their physical relationship had lost something. Perhaps a sense of themselves as people who truly cared for one another; all technique and no emotion like a Beethoven concerto played on a pianola.

Bethan had never refused him anything physical because she had never pretended that their sex life was any the less important or enjoyable for her than him, but he couldn't help wondering if she thought of him or David when they switched off the bedroom lights. Skilled but perfunctory – that was the best description. Who had coined the phrase 'intimate strangers'?

Their lovemaking, like their relationship, wasn't what

it had been before the war. Or was it his memory that was defective? Was his present disillusionment the result of their long separation? Had he remembered their marriage as it had never been, during all those long years in the prison camp? Had he woven dreams into a reality that had never existed outside his own mind, or had it simply turned sour between them like so many couples he saw in his surgery? Men who asked if there was any way to find out if the child born during the war was the result of a brief leave or '*a fling between the wife and a Yank*'. Because they'd heard rumours – there were always rumours. And it wasn't just the men. There were women who wanted to know the symptoms of venereal disease because they were convinced that their husbands had strayed in the forces and passed it on to them. And there were others who asked if their husbands had it – and if they did, was that why they hadn't touched them since their return?

He left the chair and switched off the light. So many unhappy couples and miserable people, why did he and Bethan have to be among them? He climbed the stairs, looked in on his sleeping son and daughter, and decided that when the weather broke and the first signs of spring appeared, he would drag Bethan and their family off to the chalet on the Gower. Away from everything and everybody including David Ford. There he'd finally have it out with her and force her to face the deterioration in their relationship, because he'd rather risk what was left of their marriage in the hope of recapturing what he believed they'd lost than go on the way they were.

'You seem to be having difficulty in understanding the word no, Will.'

'Where's the risk, Alma? You'll be getting your "off the ration" meat delivered along with your regular order. Long before any inspector can catch up with it, you will have cooked and sliced it, or baked it into pies and pasties. And who's to say what's in the pies you sell?'

'I say, Will. One of the reasons the shops are doing so well is that I list all the ingredients including the percentage of meat in all our products. If I suddenly start selling double the poundage of cold, sliced beef or twice the number of pies, the inspectors will want to know where the meat came from. And there's no point in my increasing the percentage of meat in the fillings because the customers won't pay any more for our pies and pasties.'

'But I'm offering you a chance to double your turnover.'

'Plus a ride to the local police station, a visit to the magistrates' court and a prison sentence. I have Theo to think about, Will. I've gone through the war without dabbling in the black market, and I've done all right. I'm not about to start risking everything I've built up now.'

'You won't even consider my offer?'

'I have considered it.' She picked up the teapot and refilled both their mugs. 'But that's not to say I won't put some legal business your and Ronnie's way. I've got one van on the road and the driver's always being asked if he can supply other shops with our products. Sooner or later this rationing is going to ease and I'll be able to get the supplies to fulfil all the potential orders – legally.' She gave him a ghost of a smile. 'When that happens I'll need another vehicle. I've applied for permits and extra petrol coupons and I wouldn't mind buying another van ready for when they come. So if anything suitable comes up, you'll let me know?'

'New or second-hand?'

'Preferably new, but I wouldn't turn my nose up at a relatively new ex-army vehicle – as long as it is above board,' she added emphatically. 'David Ford and Dino were in here yesterday. They've succeeded in tracking down a couple of missing US army vehicles and mentioned that they will probably go for auction.'

'Thanks for the tip. I'll go and see them.'

'And . . .' she looked around to make sure none of her staff were within earshot, 'if you ever have smaller quantities of anything off the ration –'

'Like?' he broke in quickly.

'A pound of cheese, butter or bacon, or a couple of pounds of sugar, I'd be interested.'

'In other words you wouldn't say no to any extras you can put on your own table?'

She thought of another table she'd soon have to fill as well, 'Exactly.'

'I see, you're like everyone else I've talked to this morning, won't turn down the offer of more than your allotted rations but you're not prepared to run any risks to get them.'

'You wouldn't be running any risks if you'd been around the last couple of years and read the court reports in the *Pontypridd Observer*. Some of the magistrates can be savage.'

'So I'm finding out.'

'It's not worth taking a chance, Will.'

'That's what Ronnie said.'

'You should have listened to him.'

'It's funny to think you once worked for him as a waitress, then Charlie as a shop assistant and now you're not only handing out advice on how to live and run a business but also managing the most successful shop chain in the area. This war's turned everything topsy-turvy.'

'A lot of water has flowed under the Old Bridge since I worked for Ronnie Ronconi,' she said easily. What seemed even odder to her was that while she'd been Ronnie's waitress she'd also been his mistress. But then that had been before either of them had married. Looking back now, it was almost as though it hadn't been her but some other woman who'd waited tables in Ronconi's, cleaned and locked up every night and climbed the stairs to the small cold room on the first floor to make love to him afterwards.

'I heard about Charlie's first wife.'

'I expect the whole town has by now, Will. Please, don't tell me how sorry you are.'

'I'm too fond of you as an ex-employer and friend to pretend I'm delighted.'

'And I can't be sorry the poor woman survived.'

'You're one tough woman, Alma. And not only in business.'

'I had a good teacher, and not only in business.'

'Ronnie?'

'No, Charlie, but they're not unlike one another in some ways. The quality I've always admired in both of them is their single-mindedness. If they want something, they go for it whether it's business, pleasure or family, and to hell with the consequences. If I've been successful it's because I've tried to foster that attitude in myself. But single-mindedness doesn't mean being downright reckless.'

'I get the message: no black market goods through the back door of Charlie's cooked meats and pies.'

'None, but thank you for thinking of me.'

William finished his tea. 'In that case I'd best be on my way. I only hope Angelo and Alfredo can use a whole cow in the restaurant and café.'

'People talk, Will. A sudden glut of meat will get noticed and Ronnie won't like it.'

'He's already told me he won't. Any suggestions?'

'Be cautious. What Angelo can't lose in Ronconi's normal turnover, chop into manageable pieces and spread around. I'll take four pounds, your mother will take another couple, and then there's your Uncle Huw, your Uncle Evan . . .'

'And no one will notice I'm humping meat around my family?'

'Not if you borrow Angelo's Trojan. He goes up the Graig Hill at least once a day.'

'Thanks for the advice. And I won't forget about the van.'

'Ianto used to service the one I've got. Did you keep his mechanic on?'

'Afraid Ronnie or I might try our hand at fixing things we know nothing about?'

'Not Ronnie – you. And I'm still smarting because you didn't come back to work for Charlie. You could have taken your pick of the shops. Managed any one you liked. You're a good worker, Will.'

'It's time to move on. I have a wife to support.'

'If I was the betting sort, I'd back Tina on keeping you rather than the other way round any day.'

'Don't tell Ronnie that or he'll go into partnership with

his sister instead of his brother-in-law.' He kissed her cheek. 'Take care of yourself, and if you want to waste an evening bring Theo over to Bonvilston Road. Tina and I've moved into my Uncle Huw's old house.'

'For good?'

'If Tina decides she wants it we'll buy it, but you know what women are like.'

'Kinder, sweeter, gentler and far more sensible and reliable than men.'

'That doesn't deserve an answer.' He turned round as the back door opened and Bethan walked into the kitchen. 'Cold enough for you, Beth?'

'I thought you'd be wishing it colder.'

'Not me. After Italy I like it warm enough to bake bread.'

'But meat keeps better in cold weather and I've heard you've got a whole cow's worth.'

'Is there anyone in this town who doesn't know everyone else's business?'

'You're back in Ponty, boyo,' she joked.

'So I've discovered. Well, if I'm going to get rid of my ill-gotten gains before the coppers catch up with me I'd better go out there and start selling.'

'You can put me down for a couple of pounds and my father – oh and my father-in-law.'

'The upright Dr and Mrs John from the Common?'

'We'll take it up as a present.'

Will kissed her cheek. 'I'll drop six pounds off in your house.'

'Thanks, Will, and be careful,' she warned.

'It's all right, I've had the full lecture from this one.' He gave Alma a brief hug. 'She needs looking after.'

'What is it with the men since they've come back,' Bethan grumbled as he left. 'They seem to think we need instructions on how to behave towards one another all of a sudden.' She saw the expression change on Alma's face. 'I'm sorry, that was tactless of me. I don't know how you're managing to keep going without Charlie.'

'Perfectly well,' Alma lied unconvincingly. 'Tea's still warm, want a cup?'

'Just a quick one. I came to see if there's anything I can do to help in the house.'

Alma shook her head. 'Mrs Lane was putting the finishing touches to it this morning. I'm going over there now to give it one final check-over before they . . .' She faltered, then smiled determinedly. But Bethan knew her too well. She was aware just how much of a struggle it was for Alma to retain her composure. 'Move in.'

'Would you like company?'

'No, thank you. As I said, it's just going to be a quick in-and-out. And shouldn't you be preparing for your journey? You are still travelling down to Tilbury with Charlie?'

'Late Tuesday, Andrew's booked us berths on an overnight sleeper.'

'Sleeping on a train sounds like fun. I haven't done much travelling. Charlie always said we would after the war . . .'

'Alma . . .' Bethan hugged her.

'I'm all right, Beth. Really. Just finding it a bit difficult to organise my life without him but I'll get used to it. I'll have to, seeing as how I have no other option. Now if you'll excuse me, I really do have to go if I'm going to be out of the place before Charlie arrives.'

'You'll be up for tea on Sunday with Theo?'

'Of course, and I'll see you then.' She gave Bethan a brittle smile, leaving her no option but to walk away.

'It happened about half an hour ago, Dr John. I thought you'd want to know right away as you've taken such an interest in the case.'

'Have you informed the family?' Andrew asked the sister.

'No, I assumed you'd want to do a full examination first.'

'And she's conscious now?'

'She was when I left. We called Dr John senior as well. He's with her now.'

Irritated by the sister's officiousness, Andrew ran ahead, down the corridor and into the ward to Diana's cubicle. He could hear the soft murmur of voices and recognised Diana's voice – weak and subdued – responding to his father's gruffer tones.

'Sleeping Beauty's finally decided to join the land of the living,' his father said as he pushed open the door.

Andrew nodded to the nurse standing in front of the window, before turning to the bed. Diana was lying back, thin, pale and drawn, but her eyes were open. Gleaming brown pools in a pinched, bleached face.

'Well, hello there. You had us all worried for a while.'

Diana looked at him blankly for a moment, then murmured. 'Andrew.'

'How are you feeling?'

'My head hurts.'

'That's hardly surprising.'

'That's what I said, and she's having problems moving her left leg and arm but I told her not to worry.' Andrew's father smiled down at Diana. 'She's been in bed a long time. I doubt there's anything that exercise, care and rest won't cure.'

'Do you remember what happened?' Andrew asked.

'No.'

'But you do know where you are?'

'Dr John told me, I'm in hospital.' She looked from Andrew's father to Andrew. 'How long have I been here?'

'Over seven weeks.'

'Seven weeks! Billy . . .'

'Hey, young lady, no moving until we say you can.' Andrew's father pushed her gently back on to the pillows.

'Your mother is looking after both the children,' Andrew reassured.

'Both?' She looked at him in bewilderment.

'Billy and Catrina.'

'Who's Catrina?'

Andrew's father gave him a warning glance and shook his head.

'You know your mother,' Andrew chose his words carefully. 'Apart from missing you, Billy's having the time of his life.'

178

'That's good. Does Wyn know I'm here?'

Andrew struggled to control his features and keep the shock from registering on his face. Diana's first husband, Wyn Rees, had been killed in a munitions' factory explosion in December 1941.

'Everyone knows you're here,' he replied cautiously.

'But you've been very ill, my dear,' Andrew's father murmured soothingly. 'We've had to restrict your visitors.'

'But I must see Wyn. He'll be so worried . . .'

'First, I think we'd better send for a specialist and see what he says. We don't want you slipping back into another coma.' He pulled a prescription pad from the pocket of his white coat and scribbled on it. 'Nurse, would you get these from the pharmacy for Mrs . . . this patient's headache.'

'Yes, Dr John.'

'And ask sister to make sure that someone sits with the patient at all times. That's an order.'

'Yes, Dr John.'

'How's Bethan?' Diana asked Andrew.

'Well. Everyone's well.'

'And William? Mam is always so worried about him. The war . . .'

'Don't you go worrying about the war, young lady. We're winning it on all fronts.'

'You're not just saying that, Dr John?'

'Would I lie to you?'

'Yes. Both of you would. It's what doctors do when they're worried about their patients. Bethan told me.'

'Then I'll have to tell Bethan off for giving away trade secrets.' Andrew heard the squeak of a rubber-soled shoe behind him as a replacement nurse walked into the cubicle. 'You get some rest, Diana. I'll be back in a little while.'

'But I will be able to see Wyn and Mam?'

'As soon as the specialist has taken a look at you and given his permission.'

'They send their love, Diana. Everyone sends their love,' Andrew reassured as he followed his father out of the cubicle.

Chapter Eleven

Charlie paid the taxi driver, picked up his case and looked up at the front door of the house in Tyfica Road. He tried to view the house dispassionately, as if he were a stranger and a foreigner seeing it for the first time – as Masha would on Wednesday. But all he could see was their house in Russia. He didn't even have to close his eyes to recall every detail of the farm he had been born in, grown through babyhood and childhood to adulthood in, and carried his bride into. The home he'd expected his eldest son to inherit after his death just as he'd expected to inherit it from his father.

Two storeys high with gabled windows on all four sides that curved the roof into the gentle, rolling lines that he had since come to recognise as uniquely Eastern European. Solid walls and deep-set windows crafted from oak planking, weathered grey by more than four hundred hot, dry Russian summers and sub-zero, snow-filled winters. The windows of the two principal rooms on the ground floor thrown out into bays that opened into the garden – vast by Pontypridd standards – and lush and green in spring and summer. There had been an orchard of cherry, apple, plum and walnut trees and a fruit garden crammed with raspberry canes and black, white and red currant bushes. Closer to the house were flowerbeds filled with bulbs, and great clumps of perennial flowers that his mother and grandmother had lovingly nurtured from seed. And at the back, behind the kitchen door, neatly tilled, carefully weeded lines of vegetables and salad that his father had taught him to tend, separated from the geese and chicken runs by a fence of close-nailed palings.

And here! Apart from a square of grass the size of an average tablecloth, there was no garden to break the line of steep concrete steps that led up to the front door. But there was the small back garden, terraced in three layers, each higher than the last and none large enough to hold more than a single cherry or apple tree.

He walked slowly up to the door and unlocked it with one of the keys Alma had given Bethan to pass on to him. The tiled porch had been cleaned, the stained glass in the door polished, the floor disinfected. He could smell it. Unlocking the inner door he stepped into the hall. He found himself enveloped in unexpected warmth that was all the more welcoming after the frost outside. The stairs and passage stretched before him, sterile, dead areas wallpapered in an uninviting dull tan and dark brown abstract pattern, and carpeted in a vile weave of brown and beige leaves and pink and orange roses that he couldn't imagine anyone selecting from free choice.

The front door at home in Russia had opened directly into the large, comfortable room his family had lived in for twelve generations. Like the outside of the house, the walls had been lined with oak planking, oiled and polished by scores of Raschenko women until it gleamed, rich and dark, cool in summer and warm in winter. Opposite the door the stairs led upward to the second storey, an integral part of the room that lent height and an extra display area for family pictures and portraits. Paintings had been hung on every available inch of space, some expertly executed, most not, and one or two unashamedly childish. By-products of lessons in the village school to be framed by proud parents.

Here and there, they'd been interspersed with newer photographs of his parents, grandparents and even one of his own wedding. Him standing proud and erect in a sober dark suit and new shirt Masha had stitched for the occasion. And Masha beside him in a simple, calf-length white dress carrying a posy of flowers from her garden. Both impossibly young, bright and hopeful, looking to a future together after a public secular service and a clandestine one with a priest arranged by his mother-in-law who refused to give up her religion even after the state had outlawed it. Recalling the photograph, he reflected that it had been as well neither he nor Masha had been able to see exactly what that future held in store for them.

Aside from the pictures, colours sprang to mind. A veritable rainbow of vivid, beautiful shades. Rich red, sea green, gold, turquoise and deep sapphire blue – like that of the eyes set in the Icon of the Virgin in the village church before it had been taken down and stripped of its jewels and gold frame by order of the party. All those colours and more had been woven into the wool rugs that covered the wooden floor, one wall and the three vast couches, every one of them large enough to serve as a bed. A massive square table filled the centre of the room. There must have been many tablecloths but the one he remembered was dark green cotton, embroidered with a border of red and cream roses.

An enormous stove dominated the north-east corner of the room, large enough for the entire extended family to sleep on when winter set in and finished in blue-and-white Delft tiles that his grandfather insisted had been carried all the way from the Netherlands by a well-travelled Raschenko son in the eighteenth century. But that room – that house – was lost. He hadn't dared think of it for sixteen years. Did Masha regret it? Was she hoping, even now, that he'd recreated it here? Would she be disappointed?

He pushed open the door to the parlour Alma had shown him, expecting the same red-plush-upholstered, dark wood furniture, unfashionable reminders of some-one else's taste and memories. But the red plush had been hidden by throws in a colourful red and green print that looked suspiciously Russian. There were plants in beaten brass bowls and Alma had found pictures to replace those Mrs Harding had taken – prints of her favourite Pre-Raphaelite painters that he suspected hadn't been too hard to track down in the pawnshops of Pontypridd. He recognised a Burne-Jones and a Mucha; then as he turned to the fireplace he stopped in his tracks. He was looking at the work of Elena Polenova, a copy of an illustration from his favourite childhood book – *The Little White Duck*. This hadn't been something Alma had picked up by chance.

'I intended to be gone before you came.' Alma stood beside him. 'Do you like it?'

He nodded, not trusting himself to speak.

'Your friends in Cardiff heard about Masha. They visited the shop and asked if there was anything they could do to help. They supplied the material and prints and some Russian books and magazines for your son and Masha. I put them in the kitchen. As you'll have to keep the stove alight there for cooking and hot water, I thought you might want to use it as a living room until the warmer weather.'

'Thank you.'

'Thank your friends, Charlie. They gave me all sorts of other things – spices for cooking, glass jars of salted cucumbers and herrings – and vodka. If you look around and in the cupboards you'll find them. Are you moving in now?'

'I thought I'd familiarise myself with the place before Masha comes.'

'Bethan told me she's arriving on Wednesday.'

He took her hand. 'I'm glad you're here.'

'The chimneys have been swept,' she continued quickly, conscious of the warmth and pressure of his fingers on hers. 'The kitchen stove's been lit for over a week so the downstairs is well aired. We lit fires in the bedrooms for the first time today but the beds have been aired with warming pans and Mrs Lane made up all of them this morning because I wasn't sure where you'd want to sleep. Mrs Lane will be in every day to see to anything that needs doing. I told her to treat the place as her own in the sense of look round and do what needs doing, unless of course, Masha orders her to do something different.'

'Alma . . .'

'There's a good stock of coal in the coal-house but it won't last more than a week or two if you light all the fires

183

every day and you won't get a ration big enough to keep everything going. I suggest you keep the range in the kitchen alight and, as I said, use that as a living room and light the fires in whichever bedrooms you are using for no more than an hour or two every evening. The pantry's stocked with enough food for a week and there's soap, shampoo, toothpaste and brushes in the bathroom. I've tried to think of everything but that doesn't mean I have. If there's anything you need I'll be in the shop.'

Relinquishing her hand he reached out and gripped her shoulders. She was trembling and it wasn't from cold. Instinctively he pulled her close, wrapping his arms around her. She tried to move away but his touch was so warm, so familiar she succumbed to temptation and rested her head on his shoulder.

'I know I told you Masha would always come first, Alma, but please, believe me, I never thought I'd find her again.'

'I know.'

'I've hurt you and Theo.'

'Theo's young, he accepts things easily and he'll be fine as long as there's enough people to love and look after him. It's you I'm worried about, Charlie. You always want to do the right thing, putting everyone else first and yourself last. You have given Theo and me all we could possibly want. A nice flat to live in, more than enough money to buy whatever we need. Please, for your own sake, concentrate on Masha and Peter for a while.' Pushing him away from her, somehow she found the strength to extricate herself from his arms. 'Now, if you don't mind I'll leave you to look around by yourself. I'd rather not come here again.'

'You don't want to meet Masha?'

'No.'

'After she hears about you and realises how hard you worked on this house she may want to meet you – and Theo.'

'You can bring Theo here, Charlie, but I'd prefer to stay away.'

'I understand.'

'I don't think you do. I don't want to meet Masha because I rather suspect I'll end up liking her and, given the circumstances, we can hardly be friends.'

'No.'

'Unless you turn Muslim and set us up in a harem. That was a joke,' she explained swiftly when he didn't smile.

'After Masha and Peter have settled I'd like to come back to work. I thought I could manage the Treforest shop.'

'Or the Pontypridd one. I spend most of my time travelling between the others but we can sort out the details in a week or two.'

'You won't mind working with me?'

'We're working together now. You do the books.'

'Hardly a full-time job.' He watched her button her coat. 'You know Andrew and Bethan are travelling with me?'

'Bethan told me. I'm glad you'll have company. It's a long journey.'

'I'll be round before we go, to see Theo.'

'He'll look forward to whatever time you can spare. When Masha is with you, it won't matter if it's every day or not.' Winding her scarf around her neck, she pulled on her gloves and adjusted her hat. 'You will remember what I said about taking care of yourself,' she pressed earnestly.

'I will.'

She turned her back on him and walked to the front door. He followed. Opening the inner door she slipped her hand into her pocket. 'I almost forgot.' Taking his hand she pressed her set of keys to the house into his palm and closed his fingers over them. ''Bye, Charlie.' Unable to bear the pain in his eyes she ran down the steps.

He continued to stand in the porch watching, as she walked down the road. She didn't see him looking after her – she didn't have to. She knew he was there. She could sense his presence.

He waited until she rounded the corner. Closing the

door, he locked it. The house was ready, waiting expectantly – for what? Picking up his case, he looked up the stairs. Time to move in and begin a new life, or perhaps simply pick up the threads of an old one he had assumed had been broken for ever.

Andrew drove slowly down Broadway. Seeing the sign for Myles' Garage he slowed his car, turned right and parked on the forecourt. He must have passed the place hundreds of times without noticing it, but then no one he knew had owned it before. Opening his door, he stepped out and walked across a concrete parking area littered with cars in various stages of disrepair. A mechanic stood in front of the open bonnet of an Austin, cleaning a lump of metal with an oily rag, while two boys watched disinterestedly.

'Mr Ronconi?' he asked.

'The office.' The older of the two boys pointed to a ramshackle shack that stood behind a couple of dilapidated petrol pumps. Home-made, spidery lettering on a wooden board that hadn't even been cut straight, grandly proclaimed 'OFFICE'. Andrew decided he could be forgiven for missing it. He knocked at the door and pushed it wide.

'Ronnie?'

'Here.'

'So this is your new business?'

'Andrew, nice of you to call in. Grab a chair if you can find one that's safe to sit on. Frankly, I'd rather you'd waited until Will and I had a chance to clean this place up before paying a call.'

'It could do with some sorting.'

'Not burning down, which some people have suggested? So, how can I help you? Your car needs servicing or, better still, you want to buy a new one, or a good second-hand one for Bethan?' Ronnie glanced up from the stack of unpaid bills he'd been wading through. 'Ianto wasn't good on paperwork. It's a miracle the audited accounts showed a profit . . .' He studied Andrew's face. 'You haven't come here to support the business, have you?'

'Diana came round a couple of hours ago.'

Ronnie left his chair and reached for his overcoat.

'Ronnie, sit down.'

'I have to see her.'

'Please, sit down!'

'What's wrong?' Ronnie perched on the edge of the steel table and looked Andrew in the eye. 'Whatever it is, tell me. I'd rather hear the truth than any number of "*don't worry, it will be all rights*". You know me. Know what I went through with Maud. Please . . .'

'The absolute truth is, we don't know exactly what Diana's mental and physical condition is – yet. We called in a specialist. He examined her this afternoon but he says, and my father and I agree with him, that it's too early to predict the full extent of the damage that has been done to her brain or if the damage that we can assess is permanent. What I can tell you is that she has lost some control over the left-hand side of her body.'

'She's paralysed.'

'At this moment she has little control over the movement in her left arm and leg. But, as I said, it is far too soon to predict whether that condition is permanent or not.'

Ronnie took a deep breath. 'So she's going to need a lot of help to adjust and someone to come in and run the house and look after Billy and Catrina. She may need a wheelchair – constant attention. I can cope with that.' He reached for his cigarettes and pushed one into his mouth. 'But that's not all – I can see it in your face.'

'She's also lost her memory. It's hardly surprising after a trauma like the one she sustained.'

'She doesn't know who she is?'

'She hasn't lost it completely.'

'So, she does know who she is?'

'She knows her name. She remembers Billy, her mother, me, Bethan – basically everyone including Wyn, but she thinks he's still alive and she's married to him. As far as my father and I can work out she's stuck somewhere in 1940 or '41. She doesn't even know the war is over.'

'You haven't told her?'

'It's not simply a question of filling in the blanks between what she can remember and the present, Ronnie. Should she suffer another shock on top of the last one – even mental as opposed to physical – she could regress, possibly into another coma. Frankly, the brain is the last great medical mystery. We can draw maps of the skull to indicate the exact areas responsible for specific functions. If a man sustains an injury to one part as opposed to another of the brain, we can predict with a certain amount of accuracy whether he's going to be blind or lose control of his legs. But when it comes to the memory we haven't a clue.'

'So where do we go from here.'

'I wish I knew.'

'You're the doctor, Andrew. You must have an opinion.'

Andrew could only admire Ronnie's self-control. If the situation had been reversed and it had been Bethan emerging from a seven-week coma, he suspected he'd be ranting like a lunatic.

'Diana's asking for Wyn and her mother.'

'Her mother can visit. Wyn we can't conjure up.'

'Quite.'

'And if I walk in?'

'For obvious reasons we haven't dared mention you. She may remember you coming back in 1941, she may even remember that Maud is dead but . . .'

'She won't remember we're married.'

'Precisely.'

'Have you seen Megan?'

'She told me where you were.'

'She knows?'

'As much as I've just told you.'

'If Diana were Bethan, Andrew, what would you do?'

'Take it easy, very easy. In my opinion, and it is only an opinion, I think Megan should go in first but not until tomorrow and then only once or twice a week. Give Diana a month or two –'

'Month!'

'The one thing I can confidently predict is that her recovery is going to be painfully slow. Apart from the missing years there's the loss of limb control. She needs rehabilitation, exercises, help and tests to determine if the left-hand side of her body is going to be permanently affected.'

'What's Megan going to tell her when she goes in? That Wyn is working late and can't come and see her?'

'No, of course not. But I don't think we can plan what Megan's going to say until we know what kind of questions Diana's going to ask. And Megan won't be able to see Diana alone. All visits will be carefully monitored by doctors.'

'You'll keep the dragon witch at bay?'

'That I can promise you.' Andrew smiled at Ronnie's description of the ward sister.

'And Billy?'

'You know the dragon witch's opinion on child visitors.'

'Germ-laden insects to be squashed.'

'There's another aspect. If Diana thinks Billy's a baby we can hardly take a five-year-old in to see her.'

'Will could go in, tell her he's on leave.'

'One at a time, Ronnie.'

'And in the meantime I have to sit back and do nothing.'

'For a few days at least,' Andrew concurred.

'That is going to be hard.'

'If I come up with a cast-iron way for you to see Diana, without her seeing you, I'll take you in. But I won't risk a setback, not even for your peace of mind.'

'I wouldn't want you to.'

'I know it's going to be difficult for you, but we have to think of Diana and put her first, and the good news is she's finally out of the coma.'

'She will remember, though, Andrew, in time? She will remember me, our marriage, Catrina?'

Andrew forced himself to meet Ronnie's searching gaze. 'The absolute truth, Ronnie. I simply don't know. I only wish I did.'

'One, I'm not working for any man who talks to me the way you just did, and two, I've been hired as a waitress not a bloody cleaner!' Maggie Evans was shouting at Tony but she was playing for all she was worth to an attentive audience of customers.

'One, I don't know how you're used to behaving but I'll have no swearing in here, especially from staff and women, and two, you've been hired to work in the café,' Tony responded firmly. 'And the rooms upstairs are part of the café.'

'I've never seen any customers walk up there.'

Determined to stand his ground, Tony dropped the towel he'd been using to polish the steamer, walked out from behind the counter and confronted Maggie. She was thirty-eight, a lot older than most of the young girls the Ronconis usually employed as waitresses, and three years in munitions, two of them as a line supervisor, had given her an air of authority that intimidated a lot of people. Including him – although he would have been loath to admit it. 'I've taken over the running of this café,' he began heavily.

'You've been here five b . . . minutes.'

Encouraged by her last-minute concession to his admonishment about swearing, he continued, 'I ran this place before the war. I'm doing it again now and I'm ordering you to go upstairs and clean those rooms. Thoroughly,' he added emphatically.

She hesitated and for about thirty seconds he thought she was going to capitulate. Instead, she pulled at the bow that fastened her apron and yanked it from her waist. 'Stuff your café! Stuff your rooms! Stuff your job! And stuff your orders!'

Scarcely believing what she'd said or the way she'd said it, he looked around. A couple of bus crews sitting close to the fire in the back were sniggering. At him! Losing his temper, he bellowed, 'Out!'

'I'm going down the restaurant. Mr Angelo knows how to treat people who work for him. No wonder the rest of your family hate your guts. Bloody Nazi lover! You even behave like Hitler. Well, I'm no Eva Braun or Nazi minion –'

'Don't think for one minute that Angelo will take you on in the restaurant after I've fired you.'

'You've fired no one, Mr high and mighty bloody Tony Ronconi. I quit.' Pushing him aside she snatched her handbag from beneath the counter and stalked out of the door to the accompaniment of a smattering of applause, catcalls and whistles from the customers.

Stunned, Tony stood in the middle of the front room of the café. Fortunately the midday rush was over. But there'd soon be a spate of afternoon shoppers wanting tea, coffee and snacks, and after that the post-work, pre-theatre and picture crowds. Maggie had covered the two till late-night-closing shift, hours that few women were prepared to work, especially women who could be trusted to man the till without dipping their fingers into it. What did he do for staff now?

Opening the swing door that led into the kitchen he saw the cook reading the paper, and the boy who helped him flicking through a comic. The sight irritated him, but after the spat with Maggie he was more cautious.

'Watch the front for me for ten minutes?' he asked the cook.

The cook folded his paper and walked out. As soon as he'd taken the station behind the till, Tony ran upstairs. For the first time he was beginning to understand why Ronnie and Tina had given up the café so easily. It demanded total commitment from half-past five in the morning, when the first buses began ferrying early shift workers to the mines and factories, until half-past twelve at night when the late-night bus crews called in for their post-shift tea and toast. Without his brothers or sisters to help on a regular basis, as they had done before the war, he'd be behind the counter for the best part of nineteen hours a day except for the odd day when he could persuade Angelo or Alfredo to give him a break. And Gabrielle – what would she be doing while he was working? Sitting upstairs in the dismal rooms he'd be lucky to see for a couple of hours' sleeping time?

He pushed open the doors to the two rooms Tina had set out as sitting and bedroom. Small, poky, dark, furnished in cast-offs from his mother's house, they looked sad and dingy to him. How would they look to Gabrielle, who'd regaled him with stories of the magnificently furnished castle she and her mother had been forced to leave behind in East Prussia, with its fourteen bedrooms, six sitting rooms, bathrooms tiled in Italian marble and acres of formal gardens?

How could he offer her two first-floor rooms, a kitchen shared with a café and an outside Ty Bach housed in a rickety wooden shed . . . ?

'Hiding?'

He turned to see Angelo climbing the stairs behind him.

'Just looking to see what, if anything, can be done to make these rooms more comfortable.'

'And the café?'

'The cook's watching the till. He knows where I am if he needs me.'

'I've brought you another waitress.'

'You've not taken Maggie on in the restaurant after I fired her?'

'Too true, I have. Grafters like her are hard to come by and her version is she walked out before she was sacked.'

'She refused –'

'To clean up here. We employ her as a waitress, Tony.'

'Exactly. *We* employ her and she talked to me as though I was dirt.'

'Maggie's not daft. It's all over town that you're marrying a German girl. She probably realised you'd be bringing her here and she wanted to make it clear that she's not prepared to clean for her.'

'Gabrielle wouldn't want her to once she arrived.'

'You sure of that?' Angelo leaned against the banister.

'I'm sure that a decent girl like Gabrielle wouldn't want anything to do with a common-as-muck woman like Maggie.'

Angelo shook his head. 'I don't know what's happened to you, Tony.'

'The war happened to me.'

'The war happened to all of us,' Angelo pointed out mildly. 'You don't see Ronnie and me putting on airs and graces with the staff.'

'I can do without a bloody lecture from you. I run this place, you run the restaurant. That was the deal, wasn't it?' he demanded belligerently.

'It was.'

'Then I'd appreciate you backing me when I sack a woman for giving me a mouthful.'

'As you said, Tony, you run this place, we run the restaurant, that means we each run our own staff.'

'You won't sack her?'

'No.' Angelo stepped on to the stairs. 'Oh, that waitress I brought up has already started work. We only took her on in the restaurant last week but she's quick, clean and prepared to do the late shift, so she should suit you.'

'Do I know her?'

'Should do. She's from Leyshon Street – Judy Crofter.'

'I don't want her.'

'Yes, you do. After Maggie told the entire staff of the restaurant about the argument you two had, Judy was the only one prepared to come up here and the only one who volunteered to work until midnight.'

'And I'm telling you I don't want her!'

'Because she comes from Leyshon Street?'

'What are you getting at?'

'You were picked up half-naked in Leyshon Street . . .'

'And, as I told the police and everyone else, I don't remember a thing about that night.'

'Very convenient. Just like the convenient reappearance of your kitbag.'

'I must have taken digs somewhere and they dropped it off outside Laura's when they heard I was in hospital.'

'This is me, your brother Angelo you're talking to, Tony, not the police. I don't believe in stories just because they clear the record and keep the paperwork to a minimum.'

'And I don't want Judy Crofter working here,' Tony repeated forcefully.

'You ever heard the expression "beggars can't be choosers"? First Maggie, now Judy. You want to try living in the real world for a week or two. Waitresses – good waitresses, that is – are hard to come by.'

'I'll find my own.'

'Please yourself. We can always use an extra pair of hands in the restaurant. I take it you can manage tonight?'

'You know damn well I won't get anyone at this short notice.'

'In that case take Judy for now and find someone else tomorrow.'

'You'll send another girl up in the morning?'

'No.'

'I thought there was a shortage of jobs.'

'Not waitressing, and certainly not the hours and wages we're paying. And although the tips up here might be more regular than in the restaurant, they're generally a lot smaller.'

'So I don't even get a say who I employ here.'

'I don't know what the hell's got into you. Sack Judy by all means, but it seems to me that whatever went on between you two – and before you explode, I don't want to know – she's more forgiving about it than you are. Oh, and when you do sack her send her back down to us. We can always use a willing worker.'

'You would and all, wouldn't you?'

'Too royal. You want to run this place entirely separate from the restaurant, carry on, find your own staff and sack them six times a day if you want, but do me a favour, clear it with Ronnie first.'

'Ronnie doesn't run the business any more.'

'But he does watch over Mama's interests and she owns it.'

'Look, Angelo, I don't want to run this place separate from the restaurant,' Tony murmured in a conciliatory attempt to cool their argument. 'In fact I was hoping you'd cover for me from about four this afternoon. I need to sort these rooms. They need decorating and new furniture. You know Gabrielle's arriving on Wednesday. I won't have –'

'No chance. I'm off from three o'clock this afternoon. I arranged it with Alfredo over a week ago.'

'What do I do?'

'I thought you'd arranged to take Tuesday evening and all day Wednesday off.'

'To meet Gabrielle. I told you, I need time to sort these rooms.'

'Then do it tonight.'

'When? After twelve thirty?'

'If that's all the time you've got.'

'And what furniture shops are open then?'

'Tony, I hate to say it but you've obviously forgotten what it's like to work in the family business.'

'Be a sport, Angelo,' Tony pleaded, trying the soft approach. 'What have you got to do that's more important than straightening out these rooms for Gabrielle?'

'Got a girl to see.'

'And mine is coming.'

'And she's agreed to marry you. So, who's more important? Your girl who loves you enough to give up everything to be with you, or mine who has to be coaxed and cajoled into spending an evening with me?'

'Are you saying you won't cover for me for a measly couple of hours?'

'Yes.'

'You bastard!'

'Calling me names won't help change my mind. If you want more time off, talk to Alfredo. Got to get back to the restaurant. See you.'

Muttering under his breath Tony followed him down the stairs. He walked back through the kitchen into the café. The cook was still at the till, his newspaper rolled under his arm, watching Judy clean a table. As she leaned over, her short black skirt rode up, showing a strip of coarse, unbleached cotton stocking top and a lot of white thigh.

'Judy,' Tony nodded curtly. 'I'm surprised you want to work here.'

'I prefer the hours, Mr Ronconi. They're more what I was used to in the pub.' She gave him a smile that made his blood run cold. Most girls would have gone out of their way to avoid him after what had happened between them on the night of his homecoming. He knew she wanted something from him. The question was, what?

Chapter Twelve

'I HAVE *NEVER* EATEN a meal like that in my life.' Liza slumped back in her chair in the basement kitchen of the restaurant and beamed at Angelo.

'Neither have I. When brother-in-law number two goes black marketing he goes the whole hog – or should it be cow? I think I had steak once, years ago, but it was stewing steak and it didn't taste anything like that.'

'I feel so guilty.' Liza looked down at her plate, scraped clean of the half a pound of steak, chips and tinned peas Angelo had served up such a short time before. 'That was probably double the meat ration for a family of eight for a week.'

'Another shandy?' Angelo held up the beer bottle.

'Only if you put in twice as much lemonade as you did last time.'

'There's no chance of you getting squiffy after what you've eaten.'

'I still have to walk up the hill.'

'I've got the Trojan.'

'Great, no walking. I think I must have done about twenty miles round the wards last night. All the night sister could say was "*Trainee Clark get me this, Trainee Clark get me that.*" I don't think she knows any of the other girls' names.'

'She picks on you?' He gazed into her eyes as he topped up the lemonade in her glass.

'No more than one or two of the others, to be fair, and that's going to overflow in a minute.'

Still staring at her, he stopped pouring and handed her the glass. 'You thought any more about what I said?'

'I haven't changed my mind about marrying you as soon as you can get the banns called, if that's what you mean.'

'One more evening like last time we met and I might not stop in time for you to wear a white wedding dress.'

'So?'

'Liza, I love you. I want you to be my wife, not fancy woman.'

'I'm not pretty enough to be anyone's fancy woman.'

'Fishing for compliments.'

'I'd settle for a kiss.' Leaning across the table, she touched her lips to his. 'Shall we move up to the sofa on the landing outside the function room?'

'I'm weak enough to say yes, although Alfredo was complaining the other day that the springs are about to give way.'

'That's you, not me.' She smiled mischievously. 'We'd better clear up first.'

'Dump your plate alongside the frying pan in the sink. The boy who washes the dishes will see to them in the morning.'

'But it's full of water. Everything will get horribly cold and greasy.'

'Exactly, so no one will be able to see what we ate.' Dropping their cutlery into the basin he pushed her plate sideways into the water besides his. 'I'll take the beer and glasses.' He led the way to the foot of the stairs and switched off the kitchen light. A faint glow shone down from the bulb they'd left burning in the upper stairwell.

'Seduction lighting,' she murmured, kissing him again.

'Where do you get your words from?'

'The other trainees. Most of them were in the ATS.'

'Seems to me you're training alongside some pretty loose women.'

She laughed softly. 'And it seems to me you're horribly old-fashioned.'

'What's that supposed to mean?'

'Race you upstairs.'

'Too many cakes and not enough exercise,' she teased as he reached the sofa a full minute after her.

'Unlike you, I had my hands full.' He pushed the

glasses, beer and lemonade into the corner, where there was no danger of either of them kicking them over, before falling on to the sofa beside her. Staring unashamedly into his eyes, she unfastened the buttons on her cardigan, then began on her blouse.

'Liza,' he protested thickly, 'I told you what this does to me.'

'Promise you won't be angry.'

'About what.'

She opened her fingers.

He looked down at the palm of her hand and frowned. 'Is that what I think it is?'

'The girls call them French letters, although some of them say American might be a more apt description.'

'How in hell did you get hold of it?'

'One of the girls is going out with a doctor, he gave her a pile to keep for when he comes round to visit. She knows we've been courting a while and thought we might like some.'

'Some!'

She opened her handbag and handed him half a dozen.

'Liza, no decent girl should even know what these are for.'

'You think decent girls should get pregnant before they're married?'

'I think decent girls shouldn't sleep with men before they get married.'

'Even men they've been going out with for a year who want to marry them?'

He swallowed hard, 'I don't want . . .'

'To make love to me?'

'You to talk this way.'

'You'd rather we stripped off and made love without talking about it?'

'I want it to be special between us.'

'It *is* special. Have you ever made love to a woman?'

'You can't expect me to answer that.'

'You want to marry me, but you won't talk about lovemaking.'

'Is this your way of telling me that you've made love to another man?' he demanded hotly.

'And if it is?'

'I heard about you and an American – Maurice somebody or other – Colonel Ford's driver.'

'Maurice Duval. He was killed not long after D-Day, months before I met you.'

'And you slept with him?'

'Would it make any difference to you if I had? Would it?' she repeated when he remained silent.

'I don't know.'

'Well it shouldn't. I'd feel the same way and I'd be the same person if I'd slept with a hundred other men before I met you and you still haven't answered me. Have you ever made love with another girl?'

'One,' he admitted, flustered by her directness.

'Here in Pontypridd?'

'Not that it's any of your business, but no. It happened on a farm in Germany Glan Richards and I worked on when we were POWs. She'd been drafted into the Land Army.'

'You loved her?'

'Liza . . .'

'Did you love her?' she repeated forcefully, driven by a sudden and unexpected jealousy.

'No. Glan thought she looked like a right tart so we both tried our luck.'

'And you were successful?' His silence told her what she wanted to know. 'So, you lost your virginity in a really "special" way,' she derided scathingly.

'I'm a man,' he retorted defensively.

'Don't you dare spout that rubbish to me about it "being different for men".'

'Well, it is, isn't it?'

She moved as far away from him as the sofa would allow. 'Why?'

'We *are* different. We have different needs – more drive – we can't control ourselves as well as women. Women don't . . . I mean they . . . decent girls that is . . .'

'Don't like sex, and have to stay pure to please the worldly-wise experienced man who sweeps her off her feet,' she finished for him, realising that he was too disconcerted by her blunt approach to say another word. 'What have you been reading, Angelo, *Snow White* or *Cinderella*?'

'You have a way of making me feel a fool.'

'I'm glad, because you're behaving like one. For your information, most girls are just as curious about boys as boys are about girls. And most mothers talk to their daughters about sex.'

'Did yours?'

'Before she died, yes. And I talk to Auntie Bethan about it, and we both talk to my sisters. In fact women discuss it all the time. You should have heard some of the things your sister Tina said to Auntie Bethan and Mrs Raschenko about how much she was missing William in bed, when he was away fighting.'

'Trust Tina – and I don't want to hear the details,' he added quickly before she could start. He reached for his beer glass. 'I never thought I'd be talking to any girl like this.'

'You'd prefer kisses and fumbles in the dark. Or a quick roll in the hay with a "*right tart*"?' Her smile diffused his embarrassment – and anger.

'It wasn't good,' he admitted. 'And afterwards it was downright humiliating. A couple of the other men caught us before we were dressed. She didn't seem to mind that much.'

'But you did?'

'And you and this American. It was "special"?' he asked, avoiding her question.

'You and your "special". No it wasn't,' she conceded, 'because he wouldn't let it be. I wanted him to make love to me. I even undressed – completely – but all he would do was hold me. Like you, he wanted to wait until we were married. So he died a virgin.'

'You loved him?'

'Very much.'

'As much as you love me?'

'In a different way, because you're you, and he was him.'

'And if he'd come back?'

'How can you expect me to answer that? He didn't and you're here and I do love you. Very much. Enough to hand you these,' she pressed the entire bundle of French letters into his hands, 'to undress completely in front of you and make love for the very first time. Not "let you" make love to me, but make love right back, the way my mother told me it should be between a man and a woman.'

'And marriage?'

'One step at a time.'

'But you will marry me?'

'When I'm ready, after I'm qualified, and if we both feel the same way we do now.' He opened his mouth but she laid her finger across his lips. 'All my life I've been told men are only after one thing. It's women who are supposed to want security. You're turning everything upside down.'

'Only because I love you.' He watched as she removed her cardigan. 'You're going to catch cold.'

'Not with you to keep me warm.'

'We'll be even warmer if we use our overcoats as blankets.' Suddenly embarrassed, he ran down to the coat rack on the ground floor. When he returned she was completely naked. He stood for a moment, thinking he had never seen anything more beautiful – but it was only a moment. Even as he carried his overcoat over to her she kneeled on the cushions and pulled off his jacket and pullover before starting on the buttons on his shirt. They kissed, breaking apart so he could slip his vest over his head.

Finally, when their clothes lay in a single heap and they were exploring one another's bodies with their lips and fingers, he realised that it had only been fear of a repeat of the disaster with the Land Army girl that had led him to want to delay this moment. No ceremony could have made it any more than it already was. Liza was right: they loved one another – nothing else was needed to make it absolutely perfect.

'Mr Tony.'

Tony turned to see the cook standing in the kitchen doorway. 'We've scrubbed the ovens, hobs, tables and sink for the morning and put the rubbish out.'

'You want a medal for doing your job?'

'Just an idea of what time we can go.'

'When the café closes.'

'You expect us to work an eighteen-hour shift?'

'So, what hours do you usually work?'

'Mr Angelo stops all kitchen food orders after half-past five.'

'And if someone wants a meal after that.'

'They have sandwiches, or toast, food that can be prepared at the counter unless it's quiet enough for the waitress to go into the kitchen and heat up some beans. All the customers know that.'

'Then why didn't you tell me?'

'I thought Mr Angelo would have mentioned it.'

'Well he didn't,' Tony retorted brusquely, knowing full well he couldn't blame Angelo. His younger brother had tried to discuss his taking over the running of the café but he had brushed aside all advice by sternly reminding him that he had managed the place before the war.

'You'll have to pay us double time for the last two hours.'

Too exhausted to argue, Tony nodded agreement as the cook and boy exchanged their whites for overcoats and caps. He locked the outside kitchen door after they'd left and returned to the café where Judy was ringing up their only customer's payment.

'Waitresses don't work the till.'

'I couldn't find you, *Mr* Ronconi, and the gentleman wanted to go. Thank you, sir.' She pocketed the twopence the man handed her as she held open the door for him to leave.

'Next time, call.' Tony looked around. The place was

deserted, unusual even for the quiet hour which was too late for shoppers and too early for evening revellers.

'I've washed down the tables and chairs and swept the floor in the back ready for the evening trade. Is there anything else that you want me to do, Mr Ronconi?' She adopted a false air of meek subservience as she picked up the brush and bowl of soapy water she'd used on the furniture and carried them through to the kitchen.

'Yes, you can make us both a cup of coffee, take them to the family table,' he indicated the one directly behind the door, 'and tell me why you volunteered to work here.'

'Very good, Mr Ronconi.'

He watched her every move as she prepared the coffee, and much as he would have liked to, he couldn't fault her methods. She levelled the measuring spoon off with a knife to get exactly the right quantity as she mixed the milk powder with water. She polished the cups with a clean tea towel before filling them with coffee essence. She heated the milk mix in the steamer for the correct time and even remembered to wipe the rod with the steamer cloth afterwards.

'So, why are you here?' he asked as she served him his coffee and laid hers in front of the chair opposite his.

'Because Mr Angelo said I was free to negotiate my wages with you,' she answered pertly, waiting to be invited to sit down.

'I'm sure he told you no such thing. All our waitresses get standard rate.'

'One pound ten shillings for six shifts – in my case two in the afternoon until gone midnight six days a week – with one twenty-minute main meal and two ten-minute tea breaks. Food and drink provided but no choice offered.'

'That's right.'

'Last pay packet I had from munitions was seven pounds nineteen shillings and sixpence.'

'Then you must be sorry the war's over.'

'Not that sorry, because you're going to make up my pay.'

'I'll make it up as far as one pound ten shillings.'

'Can't keep a dog on that.'

'Then look elsewhere for something better.'

'If I did that I might have to tell people about the night you came home.' She narrowed her eyes, reminding him of a cat. A hungry, predatory alley cat.

'How you dumped me drunk and half naked in the street to get pneumonia?'

'More like how I offered you a room out of pure kindness when you told me you had nowhere to go. And how you raped me.'

'And after I raped you I ran no further than your doorstep to sit in the gutter and almost freeze to death? And you were so upset at being raped, you waited until now to complain? A likely story?'

'We fought, you were so drunk I managed to throw you out and I didn't complain because I was too ashamed of what you'd done to me but then you tried to do it again when we were alone in the café – now. That's not so far from the truth and you were found in Leyshon Street.'

'I wandered there in a drunken stupor.'

'And left your property in my bedroom?'

'You dumped my kitbag on my sister's doorstep.'

'Your kitbag, not your underwear, and they have your name-tape sewn into them. I wonder how your German wife-to-be would react to the news that her fiancé is a rapist.'

'Or your father, brothers and neighbours to the news that you're a prostitute.'

'No one who knows me would believe that.'

'No?' He pushed his chair back from the table and propped his feet on the chair in front of her coffee. 'The landlord saw you talking to me in the Graig Hotel. And you were *very* friendly, so friendly in fact he had to remind you that you had other customers to serve. Something in his attitude towards you that evening suggests that you might not have left that job of your own accord. After all, a barmaid makes a fair number of tips in free drinks. I'd say about double what the average waitress

205

gets in this café. So all I have to do is go to the police, say you offered to have sex with me, and when I refused to pay, threw me out.'

'You wouldn't dare.'

'Why not?'

'Everyone would think you were looking for a prostitute – your mother, your sisters – your fiancée . . .'

'And I would remind them I'm a normal red-blooded male who stooped uncharacteristically low after six hard years of war.'

Bringing her hand back hard she slapped him soundly across the face, sending his chair rocking. He grabbed her wrist.

'You little bitch!'

'And you're a bastard.'

'Looks like we're well matched. You're fired.'

'Two waitresses in one day?' she jeered. 'Everyone knows you and your brothers don't get on. All I have to do is go back to the restaurant like Maggie and they'll give me a job just to annoy you.'

'Not if I tell them I found a pound note from the till in the pocket of your overcoat after I caught you taking money from a customer.' He flicked a note from the side pocket of his khaki work coat and held it up in front of her.

'I'd tell them the truth.'

'What truth, Judy? You'd protest your innocence and I'd point out I have no reason to lie. Then I'd hint that a woman used to earning seven pounds nineteen shillings and sixpence a week in munitions would undoubtedly have difficulties managing on one pound ten shillings, which is all we can afford to pay our waitresses. It would look as though the temptation of the unguarded till and me out of the way in the kitchen was too much. And if you bring up that night in Leyshon Street it would only succeed in spicing your motive for stealing with a touch of revenge. After all, no tart likes giving it away for nothing. Believe me, my brothers would see it my way – and so would the police – if I chose to take the matter to court.'

'You'd do it and all, wouldn't you?'

'To a stupid bitch who tried to blackmail me, yes. You've only worked in the restaurant a week, don't bother to go there or come in here tomorrow.'

'I'm entitled to wages . . .'

'Here,' he tossed her the pound he was holding, 'and . . .' he dug into his pocket again, 'a ten-shilling note and half a crown, bonus. Don't bother to return my underclothes. You can keep them in return for the two shillings' worth of exercise I got out of you. That *is* the going rate for a woman of your class, isn't it?'

Cheeks burning, she went to the coat rack in the front of the café. Ripping her coat from the peg she ran to the door.

'Here!' He was there before her, flinging it wide and holding it open, 'and don't ever come into any of our premises again or rumours might start flying.'

'I won't forget this, Tony Ronconi. I'll pay you back if it's the last thing I do.'

'I think not, Judy, not if you want to find yourself another job in this town. It's surprising just how fast gossip can spread, especially when it comes from the horse's mouth.'

'So.' Ronnie shivered in Megan and Dino's unheated parlour as he poured himself and William two small whiskies from the bottle he had brought back from Europe, which was diminishing far too rapidly for his liking. 'Why the insistence that we have to talk business in private?'

'Because I do need to talk business with you.'

'You could have done it over tea.'

'I don't want my mother, Tina or Dino hearing what I have to say.'

'We've been working together all day.'

'I've been hauling meat around all morning and sorting the scrap yard all afternoon. I haven't seen you for longer than a minute or two at a time.'

'True. Well, make it short. I want to get a full day in the garage tomorrow. Those accounts are in a hell of a mess.'

'Anything to stop thinking about Diana. When Mam sees her tomorrow –'

'Business, Will, before I freeze to death.'

'It's the scrap yard. I cleared the bottom end.'

'Well done you. Want a pat on the head?'

'Forget the sarky remarks, Ronnie. I found some things.'

'Saleable things, I hope.'

'All right, I know we're down about a fiver on that bloody cow Gwilym talked us into taking.'

'You talked Gwilym into giving us.'

'Whatever, either way. It's not good business to sell to family. They expect rock-bottom prices and if you ask for enough to cover costs they think you're trying to rip them off,' William said quickly, not wanting to dwell on his mistake.

'Out with it, what "things" did you find?'

'Three US Army Jeeps, two lorries . . .'

'That's crazy. I walked all over that field . . .'

'They've been stripped down but they're all there, all right.'

'You took the mechanic up from the garage to check?'

'You think I'm stupid? No, I checked everything myself. Some of the parts were hidden under the tyre mountains, some under rusting piles of junk, and a couple of the more vital pieces were in the shed by the gate.'

Ronnie let out a long low whistle.

'And there's more.'

'More Jeeps and trucks?'

'Boxes of uniforms. I haven't checked through everything but there does seem to be a hell of a lot of stuff there. Do you think Ianto's widow knew they were there?'

'I don't know.'

'Could be someone hid the lot there after he died and they'll come back looking for it. Ronnie, what do we do? Go to Dino and David Ford? Everyone knows we've only just bought the yard . . .'

'And if someone has hidden the stuff, comes back for it and discovers we've handed it to the Yanks?'

'It'll be tough on them.'

'And us. It doesn't pay to have too honest a name in the scrap trade.'

'So what do you think we should do?'

'We're partners, aren't we? You've had more time to think about this than me. What do you suggest?' Ronnie finished his drink, corked the bottle and replaced it in the sideboard.

'Sell it on quickly and if someone turns up looking for it, offer them half of whatever we get.'

'That's not a bad idea. You got a buyer in mind?'

'I had a word with the landlord in the back bar of the Horse and Groom early this evening. Mentioned that I might be in the market for an American Jeep. He suggested a scrap yard down the estate on the left-hand side as you're going towards Cardiff. They don't hold anything long, but he said they take orders. On that basis I reckon they might take some, if not all of what we've got off our hands.'

'Did he pass on any names?'

'All he said was *ask for Jerry*.'

'Don't know any Jerry's, do you?'

William shook his head.

'Perhaps we should take a trip down the estate tomorrow morning. On the other hand it might be more sensible to go there after we've walked around the scrap yard. You might have missed something.' He picked up their empty glasses. 'You were right not to mention this to Megan and Tina. They'd only worry.'

'Not to mention nag us into an early grave. All I've been hearing from Tina since I've got back is how this or that bloke has been sent down for dodgy dealing.'

'Like me, she's worried about your business ideas.' Ronnie opened the door.

'Tina, what are you doing?' William demanded furiously, when he saw her standing in the passage.

'Getting our coats, it's time to go.'

'I would have got them,' he snapped, knowing full well she'd been trying to eavesdrop.

'You and Ronnie are up to no good, aren't you?'

'This is where I go into the kitchen.' Ronnie kissed Tina's cheek. 'Good night, little sister. Thanks for the visit and the children's sweets.'

'You stay where you are.'

'You can order your husband about, sweetheart, but not me.'

'It comes to something when Ronnie and I can't have a word in private about the business, without you sticking your ear against the door . . .'

'You're up to more black market dealings, aren't you? The pair of you!' She blocked Ronnie's passage to the kitchen. 'Go on, admit it.'

'Will's the expert on that subject, not me.'

'I've been talking to Megan and we're agreed we're not putting up with it.'

'Putting up with what?' William questioned innocently.

'You and Ronnie breaking the law.'

'I give you my word, Tina,' Ronnie said, 'my days as a lawbreaker are over, not that there were ever that many of them. Now, with your permission, I'll take these glasses into the wash house before I drop them.'

'It's you, isn't it, Will?' Tina asked as Ronnie closed the kitchen door behind him. 'You were the one who wanted to talk in private, not Ronnie. You've done a deal with some idiot who thinks he can outwit the police. What is it this time? More meat? Cheese? Eggs? Clothes? Shoes? You'd flog anything on, if you thought you could make a pound or two out of it.'

'I would not. And I give you my word, you don't have to worry. It's the straight and narrow for me from now on.'

'Why don't I believe you?'

'Sometimes I think those two have only stayed married six years because they've spent less than six weeks together since their wedding day,' Megan said softly as Tina and William's high-pitched argument echoed into the kitchen.

'They'll sort it out, Megan.' Ronnie took the cigarette Dino offered him.

'As long as they don't wake the children with their sorting.'

'Young love. What it is to have the energy to quarrel.'

'Jealous, Dino?' Megan asked.

'Not me, honey. I've reached the age where I appreciate the benefits of a quiet life, especially a good woman who's prepared to make all my decisions for me.'

'Trying to quarrel with you is like trying to punch water.' Megan set aside her knitting and studied Ronnie, who was standing in front of the stove, staring at the fire.

'You'll have Catrina for me tomorrow when I go up to the hospital, Ronnie?'

'I'll take her to Diana and Alma's shop in High Street. I want to check it's being run properly.'

'And you'll be close enough to pounce on me the minute I walk out of the gate.'

'I need to know Diana's well.'

'Andrew's optimistic and he's not one to get people's hopes up for no reason.'

'I can't imagine Diana not knowing she's married to me.'

'Give her time, she'll remember,' Megan patted his shoulder as she left her chair. 'Anyone for a last cuppa?'

'Tea, please, honey, and a piece of that apple pie if there's any left.'

'You'll look like a barrage balloon if you carry on eating the way you are, Dino,' Megan remonstrated.

'A happily married man should look contented.'

'Ronnie?'

'Nothing thanks, Megan.' Ronnie drew heavily on his cigarette. 'I think I'll go on up to bed.'

'If I were you I'd hold on for a few minutes. Judging by the noise Will is making I've a feeling my daughter-in-law has just told him something he didn't want to hear.'

'And I'm telling you that no wife of mine is going out to work!' William slammed his fist into the wall and glared at Tina.

'You and Ronnie wanted me to work in your grubby little garage.'

'That was different. The garage is a family business.'

'Too royal it's different from the Park Hotel, and I know which I'd prefer to work in.'

'You'll be next door to the man's bedroom. I won't let you do it, Tina, and that's final.'

'Won't let me! Won't let me!' she repeated furiously. 'Just who do you think you are, William Powell? A bloody staff sergeant dealing with a conscript?'

'And I won't have any wife of mine swearing.'

'Any wife? How many do you have?'

'It's not ladylike,' he retorted wondering how she'd managed to switch the argument from a serious matter like her wanting to work for David Ford to women swearing.

'Ladylike! What do ladies have to do with anything? It wasn't ladies who kept the home fires burning while you men were gadding about in Africa and Italy.'

'Gadding! I was bloody well fighting and I've the bullet holes to prove it.'

'And I heard you were shot by a sentry on our own side. What were you doing, Will? Crawling back through the lines after a night drinking and carousing with the women of the town?'

She'd hit so close to the truth William didn't answer for a moment, and when he did it was to steer the argument back on the course he wanted it to take.

'I won't have you working for a Yank and certainly not in the Park Hotel.'

'What do you object to? The Park Hotel or the Yank?'

'Both. The Park Hotel is full of bedrooms.'

'That's why it's called a hotel. People stay there and sleep overnight when they're away from home.'

'And that's not all they do. Everyone in town is talking about David Ford and Bethan.'

'And you believe them?'

'I believe Andrew John's a fool for putting up with it. If Bethan was my wife she wouldn't be allowed to give David Ford the time of day.'

'Perhaps, unlike you, Andrew realises a wife is a human being with her own opinions, not a dog to be brought to heel.'

'I'll not have the town gossiping about you too.'

'I'll be working in an office that's open to the public.'

'Tina, you're no clerk . . .'

'You think I can get something better? The man's offered to pay me three pounds a week to type his letters, man the telephone –'

'You can't even type,' William broke in heatedly.

'How do you know what I can and can't do. You've been away for the last six years.'

'Tina –'

'And don't try soft-soaping me. I've told David Ford and Dino I'm taking the job and that is exactly what I'm doing. Taking it. If you don't like it, you can damn well lump it.'

'I told you two not to get married.' Ronnie stuck his head around the door.

'And you can stay out of our business!' Picking up the nearest thing to hand, which happened to be a clothes brush, Tina flung it at Ronnie's head. He only just managed to close the door in time. The brush hit the door, denting one of the panels.

'Why don't you two go home and do your arguing in your own house?' Megan called from behind the closed door.

William picked up his hat. 'I mean it, Tina. You work for David Ford and I'll . . .' His voice trailed when he realised he couldn't think of a single thing he could do if she defied him.

'You'll?' She stood arms folded, coolly waiting for his reply.

'You'll be sorry,' he warned, his temper rising again.

'Talk to me like that and you won't have a wife to come home to.'

'You'll move into the Park Hotel?'

'I might just do that. On the other hand I could always rent rooms somewhere.'

'Leave our house and you needn't bother to come back.'

'I'm going to say goodbye to your mam and Dino.' She tried to pass him.

'Tina . . .' He grabbed her arm.

'Let me go!' Struggling violently, she kicked him in the shins.

'That bloody well hurt.'

'It was bloody well meant to.'

'Why have you got to be so stubborn?'

'Why have you got to be so stupid?'

They faced one another for what could have been one minute or ten, both of them wondering how they had reached this impasse.

'Why can't it be like it was when I came home on leave?'

'Because when you came home on leave it was such a rare event everyone was prepared to rally round so I could drop everything to be with you. Now everyone's home they have their own problems, which take precedence over ours.'

'I won't stop you working –'

'You can't stop me working,' she broke in forcefully.

'But does it have to be for an American?'

'Are you concerned because of the Yanks' reputation with women or because he's looking for things that you and Ronnie are stockpiling in your scrap yard?'

Again she'd stumbled so close to the truth, he couldn't answer for a moment. 'I wish we had half a dozen kids to keep you busy,' he said when he could finally speak.

'When you give me one, I'll consider giving up work, not before.'

'You're really going to take this job?'

'Yes.' She opened the kitchen door and pushed past Ronnie.

'Told you before, Will, and I'll tell you again,' Ronnie advised as he joined him in the passage, 'there's no point in quarrelling with women. The secret is to let them think they're running the marriage.'

'And how do you do that?' William asked sourly, lifting

his overcoat from the row of pegs behind the door.

'Give them everything they ask for while doing exactly what you want.'

'So you think I should smile sweetly at Tina, and say, "*Marvellous, I'm so pleased you've found yourself a job. Go ahead and work for David Ford with my blessing*"?'

'What!' Ronnie dropped his cigarette on to the doormat. Stamping on it before it burned the bristles, he turned to Will. 'Please tell me I didn't hear that properly.'

'You did. My wife, your sister, is working for the Yank who's been ordered to look for what we've got hidden in our scrap yard.'

'Will, you're hopeless. If I'd been around I would never have let you marry Tina. You haven't a clue how to keep her under control.'

Chapter Thirteen

ANDREW DECIDED THAT there was nothing quite like a bleak dockside at dawn on a winter morning, especially after a long night spent on a freezing, unheated train, that for all it's 'sleeper' status had afforded very little opportunity to actually sleep. Bethan had been hustled off to a 'Ladies Only' carriage, but from the numb and exhausted look on her face, it had been no better than the one he and Charlie had shared with two doleful Tommies returning to Germany to finish their last tour of duty before demob.

The beds had been nothing more than narrow boards let down from the carriage walls and covered with the thinnest possible straw mattresses, a single rock-hard pillow, rough, unbleached calico sheets that itched, and a solitary grey blanket. All of which had been pitifully inadequate to offer either comfort or warmth. But Charlie hadn't complained. Andrew suspected that the Russian hadn't slept either but every time he had looked across at him lying on his back on the top tier bunk opposite his own, his eyes had been closed.

Possibly it had been a trick of the light – only a single lamp had been left burning in the corridor outside their compartment – but he thought he'd seen evidence of tension beneath the outwardly stoic exterior. A deepening of the frown marks above Charlie's eyes, a sharpening of the lines around his mouth, a slow tightening of his fists.

Perhaps Bethan had been right. He shouldn't have insisted on travelling up with them. He probably would have been more use staying in the Graig Hospital, within easy distance of Diana should there be any further change in her condition. Bethan was well able to cope with anything that happened to Masha or Charlie. And she would cope – that much he was sure of. She was a competent and experienced nurse, more experienced than some doctors, although it was hard for him to admit it after he had insisted she give up work.

He looked across at her, pallid and wan in the leaden grey, early morning light. She was standing slightly apart from Charlie, as self-contained as the Russian, as they both gazed straight ahead towards the towering, rusting hulk of the great ship, gigantic and forbidding in the chill dawn. Rain was falling – a light, steady drizzle that soaked into their overcoats and trickled down their necks, dampening their faces and making them feel even more miserable than they already were.

The gangplank had been dropped and, as Andrew watched, uniformed sailors bolted it to a sloping, metal walkway that had been hauled up to meet it from the dockside. Murmurs of anticipation rippled through the crowd beside and behind them as figures began to line up on deck. But Charlie continued to watch as silent and impassive as if he were waiting in a mundane queue for rations, rather than for the first glimpse of a wife he hadn't seen in sixteen years.

Andrew glanced behind him to check on the position of the taxi rank. Only two cabs were waiting. He debated whether or not to walk over and engage one, and decided against it. There was no way of knowing how long Masha and Peter would be, and even after they disembarked there would still be all the formalities of immigration and the driver would be bound to start the clock the minute he spoke to him.

He went over the journey ahead in his mind. A taxi to the station, an uncomfortable, crowded regional train to London then another taxi to take them across London to Paddington. They could hardly expect Charlie's wife and son, frail and delicate after their years in camps, to take the underground as they had done. He checked his watch again. They had reservations for the nine o'clock train out of Paddington to Cardiff, three hours away. Bethan had ordered a hamper to be delivered to their seats from a grocer's the stationmaster had recommended because she'd been concerned that there'd be no time to eat, even supposing they could find a decent café or restaurant. Unfortunately station buffets and dining cars had long been consigned to memory and he was beginning to wonder if the country would ever get back to what it had been in 1939. After the full day's journey it would take them to get to Cardiff they'd finally be able to pick up his car to transport them the last twelve miles to Pontypridd.

'They're beginning to disembark,' Bethan murmured, her breath clouding in the cold air as the first figures appeared on the gangplank.

Fifty yards from where Charlie, Bethan and Andrew waited, and oblivious to their presence, Tony waved as a trim figure in a familiar brown suit and hat emerged on to the deck of the ship. She stood for a moment looking lost and confused as she scanned the sea of upturned faces. He waved even more frantically. Pushing his way through to the barrier that separated the welcoming crowds from the passengers, he had a sudden brainwave. Putting two fingers into his mouth, he whistled. Gabrielle stopped so he knew she had heard him but it took an age for her to walk the hundred yards from the ship to where he was standing.

'Tony, darling.' She rushed over to him, hugging him across the waist-high barrier. 'You came to meet me.'

'I wrote I would,' he murmured, holding her as close as the barricade would allow. All his problems dwindled into insignificance as he finally embraced the one person in the world he felt truly understood him.

'I know but it's so far. I looked in an atlas, you travelled hundreds of miles to be here . . .' She was crying and laughing at the same time. 'My luggage, my box . . .'

'Keep going. Straight on to Immigration and Customs, miss.'

Tony glared at the Customs officer. Had he been unduly abrupt with Gabrielle, or was it his imagination?

'This way, miss.' The officer held out his hand and helped a girl behind Gabrielle who was struggling with a bag. 'Here, I'll get a trolley for you, miss.'

'Thank you so very much, officer. You are so very kind,' The girl gushed in a French accent.

'Anything for our allied war brides, miss.'

And nothing for our enemy war brides, Tony thought bitterly as he watched Gabrielle struggle towards the immigration shed with a case that was larger and very obviously heavier than the French girl's.

Masha and Peter were the last to leave the ship, a frail, hunched, elderly looking woman who stumbled along as though she were crippled, helped by a tall, thickset man with a shock of white hair escaping from beneath a peaked, navy workman's cap. Andrew looked and looked again. This couldn't possibly be Charlie's son, the feeble, starved child they'd been expecting – the product of years of deprivation and harsh, brutal upbringing in labour and death camps.

Bethan reached out and touched Charlie's arm as he leaned against the barrier, but he continued to stare straight ahead, unaware of anyone's presence except Masha's. Slowly, infinitely slowly, the woman continued to totter towards them, hand on rail, half carried, half supported by the man at her side.

As she stepped down on to the dock she looked across at Charlie, and Bethan felt as though an electric spark had sprung between them. There was instant and soul piercing recognition. Like Alma, Masha's eyes were green, a deep, true, emerald green that carried within them a hint of the beauty she had been. Her features were finely drawn, but her skin was creased like that of an old woman. And not even the shapeless brown overcoat she was wearing could disguise her painfully emaciated figure.

'Feodor!' was the only intelligible word Bethan made out in the outpouring of incomprehensible Russian that flooded from Masha along with tears as, to her consternation, Charlie breached the barrier and ran to meet his wife. As they clung to one another, an official marched towards them but, too embarrassed by the display of emotion to admonish Charlie for contravening dock regulations, he contented himself with a discreet, if loud cough.

Bethan looked around for Andrew and saw him talking to an officer at the door of the immigration shed. She smiled at the boy who was standing behind Masha but the smile died on her lips and she shivered as though someone had walked over her grave. He *was* Charlie. The lodger who had moved into her Aunt Megan's house when he'd come to run a market stall for a Cardiff butcher ten years before. A Russian who had yet to be christened 'Charlie' by a fellow stallholder who couldn't get his tongue around 'Feodor Raschenko'.

Tall, powerfully muscled, with chiselled features, white hair and ice-blue eyes, so familiar – and so frightening – for all his similarity to his father. She reminded herself that before she had come to know Charlie, she had been terrified of him too. Self-possessed, taciturn, the Russian's overt strength coupled with his protracted silences and habit of never speaking until spoken to had once unnerved her. But this boy was something else – just as powerful, just as self-assured as his father, but there was no underlying humanity or warmth in the expression on his face, only hostility. And she was left with the uncomfortable feeling that he would think no more of killing a man – or woman – than he would of swatting a fly.

Disconcerted by his stare, she pointed to herself. 'Bethan John. I know your father.' She spoke slowly in the hope that he'd understand friendship was intended behind the gesture.

'Peter,' he answered briefly without offering his hand.

'Your father has been so looking forward to you and your mother's arrival.' She watched as Charlie finally managed to untangle himself from Masha's arms and lead her towards the immigration shed where Andrew stood waiting.

'Why has he been looking forward to it, Mrs John?' Peter enquired in English. 'Guilt from abandoning us? Or perhaps he would like to divorce my mother so that he can carry on living with his second wife?'

To Bethan's astonishment his English was impeccable, his accent as refined as if he'd attended one of the top public schools.

'Are you surprised that I knew my father had married again, Mrs John?'

'I'm sorry, you startled me. I wasn't expecting you to speak English – and so well.'

'There were many opportunities to learn languages in the camps.'

'Bethan.' Andrew signalled for them to come forward. He held out his hand to Peter, who ignored it. 'Hello, I'm Andrew John, a friend of your father. I see you've met my wife, Bethan. Shall I take the bag, young man?' He took the weight of the rucksack on Peter's back.

'Don't you dare touch that!'

'As you wish.' Andrew was as taken aback as Bethan by Peter's animosity and perfect command of English, but unlike her, he managed to conceal his surprise. 'I've arranged for us to wait in an office until your luggage has been passed by Customs.'

'The bag you just tried to take from me is our luggage, Mr John.'

'Dr John,' Andrew corrected automatically. 'In that case I'll see if I can get us a taxi.'

Bethan didn't ask how Andrew managed to bypass the queue at the taxi rank. She was only grateful that he managed it. As the cab drew up next to the shed, Andrew opened the door and Charlie helped Masha into the back. Folding down the seats that backed on to the partition that separated driver from passengers, Andrew took one and offered the other to Peter. Bethan sat alongside Masha, who was still tearfully clinging to Charlie.

As soon as Peter closed the door the driver set off. As he drove along the quayside Bethan reflected that it was going to be a very long journey to Pontypridd – quite possibly the longest she had ever experienced.

'Diana,' Dr John senior looked round the door of her room, 'you have a visitor.'

Diana turned her head and held out her right hand as Megan walked through the door, loaded with a box of chocolates Dino had scavenged and an enormous bunch of hot-house flowers that Ronnie had insisted on buying, although in her opinion they were wickedly expensive.

'Mam, what beautiful flowers!' Diana exclaimed.

'I'll put them in water.' The nurse took them from Megan.

'They're from all of us.' Megan took the chair Dr John pulled up to the right side of the bed for her.

'Wyn?'

'Everyone.' Megan struggled to maintain her composure in the face of Dr John's warning look. 'Now tell me, because everyone will want to know, how are you feeling? The truth mind.' She tried not to look at Diana's left hand lying, twitching uncontrollably on the bedcover.

'Billy . . .'

'Is well and as happy as he can be without you to look after him.' She glanced up at Dr John, seeking his approval. She had spent the last half-hour sitting in the ward office, listening to him lecture her on what she could and could not say to her daughter. 'You're the one we've all been worrying about. You're so thin and white. Are they giving you enough to eat?' She squeezed Diana's right hand as she sat down.

'They've done nothing but bring me food since I woke up.'

'Only because you need it. Are you in pain?'

'I have a bit of a headache, that's all. And they're giving me tablets for it.' Diana looked to Dr John. 'But Billy . . .'

'Is fine.' Megan only just stopped herself from adding, *'and working hard in school.'* It was all very well Andrew's father warning her to keep the conversation general and not to mention the last five years but with Diana looking at her she was finding it a lot harder than he had suggested it would be.

'And Wyn? Why hasn't he come in to see me?'

Megan looked to Dr John for guidance.

'Because we thought it best that you see your mother

first, Diana,' he said quietly. 'As I explained to you earlier, we can't risk you getting upset or excited. Not so soon after coming out of a coma.'

'But Wyn's the last person to upset me. He's quiet and kind . . .' She looked from the doctor to Megan and back. 'Something has happened to him. I know it. Otherwise you'd tell me how he is. What are you keeping from me, Mam? Is Wyn hurt – ill . . . ?'

'Everyone's fine, Diana.' Dr John moved to the other side of her bed and patted her shoulder in a futile attempt to calm her.

'Then why isn't Wyn here?'

'I think it's time for you to go, Mrs Morelli. We can't have our patient getting upset.'

'Mrs Morelli? Mam – what's going on? Don't go. Don't leave me. Mam, please tell me what's going on.'

'I'm going to give you something to make you sleep, Diana.'

'I don't want to sleep. Mam, stop him!'

'You need to rest, Diana.'

'And when I wake up I'll still want to know where my husband is . . .'

'One thing at a time, young lady.' Dr John picked up a syringe from a sterile tray laid out on the windowsill.

'I don't know anything about doctoring, but I do know a girl at the end of her tether when I see one and I think it's time someone told my daughter the truth,' Megan interrupted. 'Because if we don't, she's only going to fret about it and make herself worse.'

Andrew stood in the corridor and looked through the high window of the train; watching acre after acre of snow-blanketed countryside roll past. The gentle sweep of the hills and sloping fields hedged with iced thorn bushes looked unbelievably beautiful after the grimy, bombed-out suburbs of London. He glanced at his watch. Another hour and they'd be entering the West Country.

It was freezing in the corridor but he needed time to himself without the strain of looking into either Charlie or Masha's tormented eyes. Or facing Charlie's son's unwavering, antagonistic glare.

The carriage door slid open and closed behind him, and Bethan joined him.

'Do you have a light?' She held out her cigarette.

'Forgotten your lighter.'

'It's in my bag on the rack. I didn't want to disturb Masha and Charlie by lifting it down.'

Taking his lighter from his pocket he flicked it. 'What do you think of Masha?'

'I think she needs a full medical and a great deal of care. Charlie's going to have his work cut out nursing that one back to health.'

'I have a feeling she'll be less work than that boy.'

'I can't believe he's only sixteen.'

'Charlie said something to me when he'd heard they'd survived. About camp children having the faces of old men or even worse, evil cunning wolves. I hate to make snap judgements but I think I know which of the two is sitting in there.'

'He's obviously very protective towards his mother.'

'Obviously.' Andrew glanced back into the carriage. 'How about we give them some privacy to get to know one another and take a walk up the train to see if there are any empty seats further on? I don't know about you but I'm beginning to feel the after-effects of a sleepless night and a long cold morning's wait.'

'And if Charlie needs us?'

'I'll ask the guard to tell him where we are.' He saw Bethan turn back. 'There's nothing we can do there for the moment, Beth,' he said gently. 'They need to be alone.'

'I've been in a coma for six years?'

'No – seven weeks.' A few times during his long career as General Practitioner and Medical Officer of Pontypridd and District Hospital Board Dr John had felt useless, for all his training, and this was proving to be another of them. 'Nurse?' he bellowed, wishing he hadn't allowed the woman to go off and arrange the flowers Megan had brought in.

'Dr John.' She appeared in the doorway.

'Tell sister to get Cardiff Infirmary on the telephone and ask Mr Manning to come back here as soon as he can.'

'I don't understand.' Diana looked from her mother to Dr John in bewilderment as the nurse left the cubicle.

'It's quite simple.' Megan turned her back on Dr John so he couldn't give her any more hard looks. 'You had a knock on your head, you slept for seven weeks and now you've woken up, you seem to have forgotten the last six years.'

'Forgotten . . .'

'As far as I can make out, although it's not easy trying to make anything out with all these doctors trying to help.'

Diana sank back on the pillows. 'And in the meantime you married.'

'Dino Morelli. He's an American, but he's living here now. You were at our wedding but there's all the time in the world for you to meet him again.'

'And Billy and Wyn and Will . . .'

'Mrs Morelli, I must protest.'

'Please, Dr John. Let my mother stay just a little while longer,' Diana begged. 'You can see I'm not upset.'

'I've already told you, Billy is fine, and Will is too.'

'Andrew yesterday – he said something about two children.'

'You've a lovely little girl, Diana. She'll be three in a few months.'

'And Billy is?'

'Just six. They're both missing you but I'm looking after them and keeping them busy.'

'And Wyn?'

'It's definitely time for you to go now, Mrs Morelli.'

'Please, Dr John, I promise not to get hysterical or start shouting again. But I know Wyn. He'd be here if he could. He's dead, isn't he? Please, just tell me the truth.'

'He was killed in an explosion in the munitions factory five years ago, love. You were terribly upset at the time but you were very brave. You had to be for

Billy's sake.' She held Diana tightly as tears started in the corner of her eyes.

'Now that really is enough.' Dr John tried to hold Diana's left hand down to stop it from flailing wildly as it had done since Megan had mentioned Wyn's death. 'Any more and there really will be a setback.'

'I'm all right, Dr John. It's just a shock, that's all.'

'Can I give her the good news, Dr John?' Megan asked.

'I think Diana has enough changes to adjust to for the moment.'

'We won the war, Diana.'

'Will?'

'He came back safe and sound.'

'Of course – how stupid of me,' Diana spoke slowly as she tried to think things through and sort them in her own mind. 'Andrew – he was in a prison camp. What about –'

'What about no one,' Dr John said firmly. 'That's it.'

'Dr John, Mr Manning said he'll be here after his clinic.'

'Very good, nurse. Tell sister you gave me the message. Mr Manning's the specialist, Mrs Morelli,' he explained to Megan, 'and he's going to be furious with me for allowing the patient to get into this state.' He shook his head as Diana began to cry again. 'I really do have to ask you to go.'

'One more thing, Dr John,' Diana pleaded tearfully. 'Can my mother come again, and bring my brother?'

'In a few days.'

'*Days!* Please –'

'Visiting is twice a week only. There are signs all over the hospital to that effect and the sister will make my life a misery if I try to overrule her.'

'He's right, love.' Megan reluctantly left the chair. 'You're the important one now. You have to rest, eat properly and try to regain your strength. Remember, you have two gorgeous children waiting for you to come home.' She dropped a kiss on to Diana's forehead and squeezed her right hand.

'Photographs – you must have some of the children?'

'I'll bring some in next time.'

'Promise?'

'I promise. Look after yourself, love.'

'Mrs Morelli, you won't bring photographs or anything else into this hospital without my express permission,' Dr John reprimanded as he and Megan reached the end of the corridor.

'Don't you think it would help her remember if she saw her children? She doted on them.'

'I'm sure she did but you've covered more ground in ten minutes than Mr Manning intended to in six months. You should never have told her that her first husband was dead.'

'I should have let her think he'd deserted her?'

'No.'

'Then what?' Megan looked at him. 'I'm an uneducated woman, Dr John, but I do know my daughter and I want what's best for her. And in my opinion lying to her now, when she's in that state, will do more harm than good.'

'And you have to realise, Mrs Morelli, that Diana's brain has been damaged. When my son and the surgeon from East Glamorgan Hospital operated they had no choice but to remove some of the tissue. Your daughter's in a delicate state. She may never recover any more than she already has and the odds are she may even get worse. I think you should prepare yourself and your family for the very real possibility that she may never remember those missing years, or even the conversation you had with her today. Good day, Mrs Morelli.'

Charlie shifted further into the corner seat and adjusted his arm so Masha's head could rest more easily on his shoulder. She was unconscious more than asleep, worn out by the journey and a life of privation he didn't want to think about or imagine. He looked across at his son, sitting bolt upright, stern and resolute on the bench seat opposite.

'You have done a fine job of looking after your mother,' he said softly in Russian.

'One of us had to,' the boy replied flatly in English.

'When did you learn English?'

'I can't remember.'

'Russia – Germany?'

'One camp or another, one language or another, what's the difference?'

'You do speak Russian.'

'And Polish, German, French, Dutch, Finnish and Norwegian. Why do you want to know? You thinking of sending me to an academy?'

'Did your mother tell you how we were separated?' Giving up on Russian, Charlie reverted to English.

'She told me that the village you lived in was razed to the ground and all the people moved out and on to the site of the tractor factory in Stalingrad. And how you never even came looking for us.'

'She didn't tell you that I never came looking for you,' Charlie contradicted quietly.

'Only because she wanted to believe that you cared for us. I know better.'

'I did look for you.'

'Not hard enough.'

'No,' Charlie conceded. 'Not hard enough.'

'Or long enough. You have another wife and son.'

'Who told you?'

'The English officer who visited our camp. He said you'd been a prisoner of the Germans too.'

'Yes.' Charlie looked into his son's eyes hoping to find a spark of empathy. There was none.

'Pity they didn't kill you. If I'd been in the same camp and known who you were I might have. But then, perhaps not. The best die first, the worst – like you – always find ways to survive.'

'You're right.' Charlie looked at his son. He'd met so many boys like him in the camps. Always boys, never men. Those old enough to have memories of a family life and love and kindness had clung to them. The boys who had been born into the barbaric world of camps and zeks spawned by Hitler and Stalin had grown up devoid of human emotion, especially pity, love and compassion. It was as if all capacity for affection had been drained out of them and replaced by a cold, hard cynicism that prevented them from forming bonds with other human beings.

'This other woman of yours, I won't let my mother live with her.'

'She won't meet her. I have a house all ready for you.'

'You're not living with us.' It was a threat not a question, and Charlie recognised it as such. He hadn't thought much about what Peter was carrying in the rucksack that he refused to allow out of his sight and Customs hadn't seen fit to search, but he guessed there was at least one knife, its blade honed razor sharp. He only hoped there wasn't a gun. He wasn't sure Pontypridd was ready for Peter unarmed; Peter armed was a terrifying prospect and one he felt certain would end up in the cells under the police station.

'I will do whatever your mother wants me to. Have you told her that I remarried?'

'She didn't need to know.' Peter turned away and looked out of the window.

'I will tell her.'

'You can't hurt her any more than you already have. Did you even think of her when you left Russia?'

'I never stopped thinking about her – or the child she was carrying.'

'I won't listen to your lies. The English officer said you lived in this country before the war. When did you come? A week or a month after they took my mother to Stalingrad?'

'I looked for your mother in Russia for four years. I asked so many questions I was arrested and sent to Siberia.'

'I don't believe you.'

'You don't have to, Pasha.'

'Only my mother calls me that.'

'I will call you Peter if that is what you want.'

'I'd rather you didn't call me anything.'

Charlie pointed to the hamper Bethan had left on the

seat. 'Would you like something to eat?'

Peter was ravenous but his pride wouldn't allow him to admit it. 'No.'

Masha stirred at the harsh sound of her son's voice. She opened her eyes and her wasted, old woman's face broke into a smile. 'I thought I was dreaming but I'm not. You're really here, with me, Feodor.'

'I'm really here,' Charlie smiled back at her. 'Are you hungry?'

'I think so.'

Gently lifting her head from his arm Charlie went across to the other seat and opened the hamper. There were packets of sandwiches, a slab of fruitcake, half a dozen apples, a tube of oatmeal biscuits and chunks of cheese. Beneath them were five plates, knives and five bottles of lemonade. He preferred not to think how much it had cost Bethan.

'There's nothing hot to drink, only lemonade,' he apologised to Masha 'but we may be able to buy tea if there's a stall at the next railway station.'

'Lemonade would be good.'

He handed her a bottle before unwrapping the sandwiches, coarse slices of national loaf filled with improbably pink slices of Spam, and margarine. Placing two on a plate, together with some of the biscuits and a couple of pieces of cheese, he handed it to her.

'Would you cut a slice of cake for your mother?' he asked Peter in English, passing him a knife.

'Do you want a piece of cake, Mother?' Peter asked in Russian, ignoring his father.

'Perhaps later, Pasha. There's enough food on this plate to feed the three of us for a week.' She looked up at Charlie. 'That sounds so good, "the three of us".'

Charlie looked across at his troubled son and nodded agreement. 'It does,' he said in Russian. 'It really does.' And shifting his gaze to Masha he tried to believe it.

'You told her Wyn is dead.'

'I had no choice, Ronnie.' Megan peeled off Catrina's

coat and handed her back to Ronnie. They were sitting at the family table in the Tumble café, a place she knew Ronnie wouldn't have walked into if he hadn't been absolutely certain that Tony was stuck on a train somewhere between Pontypridd and London.

'Even though Dr John warned you that telling her about Wyn's death could cause a setback.'

'I was afraid that the idea of Wyn deserting her could cause a bigger setback. If you'd been in my place what would you have said? He's busy? Working late? Out with the boys? All excuses guaranteed to make a woman feel her husband thinks no more of her than the cat.'

'She never mentioned me. She never –'

'For the tenth time, no. I've told you everything Dr John, I and she said, twice over.'

'Here you go, Catrina, two slices of Mars Bar and no telling anyone that your Uncle Angelo slipped them to you.'

'Thanks, Angelo.' Ronnie hid the slices in front of his teacup.

'Anything I can do?' Encouraged by Catrina's smile, Angelo pulled a chair out from the table and joined them.

'Not unless you've taken up brain surgery lately,' Ronnie responded sourly.

'From what I heard Diana's not too bad, just missing six years of her life.'

'And paralysed down one side of her body,' Megan added, tensing her fists as she recalled Diana's useless, twitching arm.

'Tell me to mind my own business if you like, but if she's forgotten the last six years, wouldn't it help to find out the last thing she can remember and take it slowly from there?'

'Perhaps you should try talking to Dr John instead of me, Angelo.'

'No, Megan, Angelo's right. Something must have happened six years ago.'

'Wyn was killed.'

'That's it,' Ronnie said excitedly. 'We all know Diana was devastated. It's understandable she wouldn't want to remember that. Now you've told her –'

'Ronnie, you didn't see her, I did. Dr John explained that her brain's been damaged. The last thing he said to me before I left was to prepare the family for the prospect that she may never recall those missing years.'

'Daddy!' Catrina tried to wriggle off Ronnie's lap as he tightened his grip round her waist.

'Come with Uncle Angelo, sweetheart.' Angelo lifted her off Ronnie's lap. 'Let's go and see what we can find under the counter for good little nieces.' He looked back at Megan and Ronnie as he led Catrina away. It was difficult to judge who looked the more shattered, husband or mother.

Chapter Fourteen

'A LETTER CAME FOR Tony.' Gina pulled the pram into the café behind her and perched on a stool in front of the counter where Angelo was pretending to polish the café's cutlery, but actually reading the newspaper he'd spread it out on.

'And you brought it down here knowing he'd be in London. What is this? Tony shunning? First Ronnie and Tina, now you. Are the family only going to come in here from now on when he's away?'

'I don't care whether he's away or not. The baby needed a walk.'

'I can see she ran all the way down the hill. Month–old babies tire so easily, it looks as though you've exhausted her.' He leaned over the counter and pushed back the wad of knitted blankets that covered his diminutive niece.

'Don't, you'll wake her and I could do with a couple of minutes' peace to drink the cup of chocolate you're going to make me.'

'You know where everything is.'

'My memory's gone terrible since I had the baby.'

'Women! They're never happier than when they've got a man running round after them,' he griped, pushing the cutlery to one side and lifting down a mug.

'So, did Tony do anything to those rooms afterwards?'

'He was too busy sacking waitresses to do anything else before he caught the train.'

'Who did he sack?'

'Maggie. Don't worry,' he forestalled her indignation, 'Alfredo and I kept her on in the restaurant.'

'I should think so too. She's a fantastic worker. There aren't many like her.'

'The other one was Judy Crofter. I asked what had

happened between them, but all he would say is that she won't be around any more and not to worry because she wouldn't be down the restaurant looking for work.'

'So, who've you got here now?'

'Maggie. She's in the back room but only because I'm running the place. There's no way she'll work here tomorrow when Tony's in charge. Do you think this high-falutin' German of Tony's would waitress?'

'After the way he's been talking about her I wouldn't try asking him if I were you. Surely you can get someone to come up here?'

'They've all heard about the German girl who's going to be living upstairs and none of them wants to come near the place.'

'The war's over . . .'

'And some people will need time to forget. Personally, I can't say as how I blame them.'

'And I think it's time that everyone in the family realised that this girl of Tony's must love him very much.'

'What makes you say that?'

'Just look what she's giving up to be with him. Her country, her family, friends, language – everything she knows to come here and make a new life among strangers. It won't be easy for her.'

'I sometimes wonder if the devil himself walked in here and asked to borrow a pan of hot coals, you'd believe he wanted them to make toast not roast sinners. You sure you're not an angel come to earth by mistake, Gina?'

'Don't be silly.' Sitting on a stool she took the chocolate he'd mixed and steamed for her and stirred it. 'I just think we should give Tony's fiancée a chance.'

'You know as well as I do there's no way Mama will have her in the house.'

'Yet – and while she's changing her mind there's no reason why the rest of us can't welcome her to the family.'

'Don't tell me you walked down the Graig Hill in a snowstorm to scrub out the upstairs?' When she didn't answer him, he tackled her again. 'If you've walked a mile in temperatures below freezing with your baby to get things ready for this girl, there's no hope for you, Gina. You do know everyone regards you as the family doormat, don't you?'

'I wasn't doing anything else this afternoon and she is going to be my sister-in-law.'

'She's going to be mine but you don't see me reaching for the scrubbing brush.'

'But you could,' she smiled.

'The hell I will.'

'All of you have been so kind to Luke since we married – you and Tina and Ronnie and Diana and Mama . . .'

'If you punched Luke between the eyes he'd think you were doing him a favour by swatting a louse off his eyebrow. He's like you, Gina, a sweet kid who's not quite of this world.'

'Luke's not a kid any more,' she protested indignantly, 'and neither am I. He's twenty-two, which makes him only a year younger than you.'

'That's just years. Sometimes I feel like his grandfather – and yours.'

'He's been down the pit four years and it's rough down there.'

'And you've been married for four years and you're so sweet and naïve I wonder if you and Luke found this baby under a gooseberry bush.'

'Angelo!'

'Sorry,' he grinned. 'I'm just trying to tell you that this woman of Tony's –'

'Her name is Gabrielle.'

'Is a refugee, so don't go thinking that she's giving up everything for Tony. Refugees have lost everything – home, country, belongings, the lot. She'll not be like you or even think like you. She is going to be hard, mercenary, grabbing and bitter.'

'How can you possibly know that?'

'You're forgetting that Glan and I were in Germany when the war ended. Those last months when the Russians were closing in from the East and the French, British and Americans from just about every other direction, there were loads of homeless German girls who'd been bombed out or forced to flee from the Russians. They did everything they could to persuade us to take them to the American and British lines to escape the Russians.'

'Really?' Her eyes widened.

'They were terrified of them.'

'But the Russians were our allies.'

'Raping, pillaging allies who didn't much like what the Germans had done when they'd invaded their country. I probably shouldn't say this to you, but most of those German girls would sell themselves for a loaf of bread and their younger sisters and grandmothers for a ticket out of Germany.'

'Come on, Tony wants to marry Gabrielle. She has to be nice.'

'And seeing as how she *wants* to marry Tony, as you put it, I'd say she has to be insane. He's the most selfish one of the lot of us, and his temper's worse than Ronnie's ever was.' He watched Gina finish her chocolate. 'You're still determined to go up and clean those rooms, aren't you?'

'I'd like them to look nice for the family's sake, that's all.' She lifted two bulging shopping bags out from underneath the pram.

'What have you got there?' he asked suspiciously.

'A few bits and pieces.'

'Does Mama know what you're up to.'

'She knows I'm in town.'

'And Luke?'

'Luke knows what it is to come to a strange place where no one wants to talk to you. You wouldn't believe how badly the miners treated him and the other Bevin boys when they first turned up to work in the pits.'

'Probably on a par with the treatment meted out to the first British POWs to be sent to German farms.'

'Well, there you are then. You understand why I want to welcome Gabrielle. As the café's quiet why don't you nip out and get a bunch of flowers? I know there'll only be hot-house ones and they're expensive but Luke and I will go halves with you. Then, when you come back, you can put Maggie in charge here and come up and give me a hand.'

'You poor things you must be starving and freezing.' Mrs Lane bustled down the passage as soon as she heard the key turn in the front door of the house in Tyfica Road. 'I've got tea all ready and waiting in the kitchen. I laid the table in front of the stove. It's nice and warm in there. It won't take a moment to heat up the stew – beef stew,' she gave Bethan a sly smile, suspecting that she too had benefited from William's foray into the black market, 'and the kettle's only just gone off the boil so you can have a cup in two ticks.'

'Thank you, Mrs Lane, that sounds just what Mr and Mrs Raschenko need.' Andrew stepped into the hall and dropped Charlie's overnight bag at the foot of the stairs.

'It was good of you to wait. You must be anxious to get back to your husband and children,' Bethan hinted tactfully.

'Not that anxious. If there's anything I can do, I'll be only too happy to do it.'

Bethan looked behind her and saw Charlie trying to help Masha from the car. Pushing him aside, Peter lifted Masha out, carrying her up the steps as if she weighed no more than a rag doll.

'Perhaps you could run a bath for Mrs Raschenko,' Bethan suggested, deciding it might be best to get Mrs Lane out of the way when Masha came into the house for the first time.

'But her tea . . .'

'She should eat it in bed.'

'Of course, Dr John.' Mrs Lane dragged her feet as she walked up the stairs in the hope of catching a glimpse of Mr Charlie's 'other' wife, so she could be the first in the town to tell everyone what she looked like. But she was disappointed. Realising what she was doing, Bethan ran up the stairs behind her, hurrying her up.

'You've aired the nightgown?'

'Yes, Mrs John. And ironed and put away the new clothes Mrs Raschenko . . .' she paused, 'the other Mrs

Raschenko gave me, in the wardrobe in the biggest bedroom. Oh, and Mrs Raschenko gave me some clothing coupons. I've put them in the top drawer of the dressing table. She thought as we weren't sure of Mrs Raschenko and her son's size they might want to choose their own clothes. Not that there's that much in the shops. I was in Leslie's last week –'

'Thank you, Mrs Lane. I'll take over from you in the bathroom as soon as I've turned down the bed.'

'It's no trouble, Mrs John.'

'I'll do it, Mrs Lane,' Bethan said in her best no-nonsense nurse's voice. 'You'll be in tomorrow?'

'First thing, like the other Mrs Raschenko told me to.'

'Perhaps for the time being we could call her Mrs Alma.'

'Well, I've known her since she was Alma Moore . . .' she began doubtfully.

'I'm sure she wouldn't think it was disrespectful.' After checking the bedroom, Bethan went into the bathroom. Mrs Lane had set the plug in the bath and hot water was gushing out of the tap with great clouds of steam. Taking a handful of precious bath salts from a jar Alma had hoarded through the war, Bethan scattered them thinly into the water. 'Thank you for everything, Mrs Lane. I'd appreciate it if you'd tell Dr John the bath is ready on your way out. He'll be in the kitchen.'

'Yes, Mrs John.' To Mrs Lane's acute disappointment all the bustle was over by the time she went downstairs. Hearing voices she knocked on the kitchen door, fully intending to walk in, but before she could open it, Andrew emerged.

'Mrs John said to tell you everything's ready upstairs and the bath is run.'

'Thank you, Mrs Lane. And everything looks wonder-ful in the kitchen. Mr Raschenko is very appreciative. Here, let me help you on with your coat.'

After closing the front door behind Mrs Lane Andrew returned to the kitchen. Masha was lying back in a chair, white-faced and exhausted. Charlie was making tea and Peter was prowling around from kitchen to pantry, wash house and back, lifting up objects and examining them, prising lids from jars and sniffing the contents, opening pots and pans and fingering the insides. He reminded Andrew of a predatory beast investigating new quarters.

'Bethan's got everything ready for you upstairs,' Andrew spoke directly to Masha, knowing Charlie would translate for him.

She murmured something that sounded like a protest but Charlie calmed her.

'I can carry her up if she's tired,' Andrew offered.

'I brought her in, I'll do it.' Elbowing Charlie and Andrew aside, Peter swept his mother up in his arms in a proficient way that suggested he had done so many times before. Andrew opened the door and Peter carried her out of the room and up the stairs. Hearing water running and smelling the bath salts he walked straight into the bathroom where Bethan was laying out warm towels from the airing cupboard. Setting Masha into a wickerwork chair he looked around the room as Masha spoke rapidly in Russian. Bethan smiled at Masha, pointed to the towels, nightgown and dressing gown she had laid out, and turned to Peter.

'Please, tell your mother if there's anything else she needs I'll be outside the door.'

'There is one thing my mother and I would like to know, Mrs John. How many people besides yourself, your husband, the woman we saw and my father live in this house?'

'This house is yours, Peter, yours and your mother's. Dr John and I live a few miles away. The woman you saw will keep house and cook and clean for you as long as you want her to, but she only comes in during the day. She lives with her own family a short distance away.'

'This is for my mother?' His tone was incredulous.

'Your father bought this house for your mother and you,' she emphasised, stretching the truth because she knew Alma would have wished her to.

'And my father. He lives here too?'

'Why don't you look at the bedrooms,' she suggested, not knowing where Charlie had decided to live and deciding if Peter should hear it from anyone, it should be

Charlie. 'Your father thought your mother would like to have the largest because it has a fine view over the town and hills opposite but there are three others. I'm sure he would be happy to let you have whichever you want.'

She waited while Peter translated her reply to his mother.

'My mother finds it as difficult, as I do, to believe that my father owns this house.'

'Your father has worked very hard to earn the money to buy it.'

'Doing what, Mrs John?'

'I'm sure he'll tell you everything in good time.'

'The only rich people I've ever met are thieves.'

'Your father is the most honest man I know,' Bethan countered, finding it difficult to control her dislike of this blatantly hostile young man. 'Can I do any more for your mother?'

Turning to Masha he spoke rapidly in Russian. 'She can manage. She doesn't need to be bathed like a baby,' he added churlishly.

'I didn't think she did, but I would appreciate it if you told her that I am a nurse and my husband is a doctor.' Without waiting for his reply she left the bathroom and went out on to the landing. When he closed the door to the bathroom she beckoned him forward. 'Perhaps you would like this bedroom. It looks out over the garden.'

'Show me the room you have prepared for my mother.'

She took him into the principal bedroom. He said nothing, but just like downstairs he paced from one end of the room to the other. Fingering the drapes and satin bedspread, opening the wardrobe doors, touching the new clothes with their labels still attached, clothes Bethan suspected had cost Alma a fortune either on the black market or in buying people's clothing coupons. Nothing escaped his scrutiny – the perfume and box of face powder and lipstick on the dressing table, the Russian books and magazines on the bedside table, the prints on the wall. Finally he turned to her again.

'There are more bedrooms?'

She showed him the second and third bedroom and the

boxroom. He walked into the boxroom and tested the thin camp bed.

'This room used to be the maid's – the maid of the last owner that is. It's very small.'

'It's like a cell, Mrs John, and I'm used to cells.'

'You want to sleep here?'

'Yes. For the first time in my life I will have a cell of my own, one I won't have to share with anyone.' Finally removing his rucksack from his shoulders he laid it on the bed. Then kneeling carefully so as not to topple the lightweight bedframe he looked out of the window, down at the steps and the road beneath. Sensing she'd been dismissed, Bethan returned downstairs.

Andrew and Charlie were in the kitchen, Andrew standing, smoking, watching while Charlie set out a tray for Masha.

'Masha's having a bath. She's tired, Charlie, and I think she should have a medical check-up but not until she's settled in.'

He nodded. 'Thank you, Bethan.'

'If there's anything else we can do –'

'Especially with Peter,' Andrew broke in undiplomatically.

'You don't like my son?'

'Charlie . . .'

Bethan had almost forgotten Charlie's smile. Just like spring sun touching a withered winter landscape it illuminated his entire face. 'I rather think this son of mine is beyond our help, don't you?'

'I think he's behaving the way he is because he's unsure of himself,' Bethan suggested, choosing her words carefully. 'Everything's strange. He needs time to adjust.'

'I wish I could agree with you. But he doesn't understand your concept of "strange" because his whole life has been strange. Can you imagine moving from one camp to another, one children's institute to another and always having to fight to ensure your place in the pecking order? That boy probably learned to raise his fists and punch, and punch hard, in a camp nursery.'

'He survived and that has to be to his credit, Charlie.'

'Yes, Andrew, he survived and he looked after his mother. I doubt she'd be here now if it wasn't for him.'

'And now he has you,' Bethan said encouragingly.

'He hates me.'

'You're his father. He'll change now he has you to guide and help him.'

'No he won't, Bethan. Andrew said it all. He's a survivor but he's also a thug. I may not have brought him up but I've been in the camps, I know him and I understand him. If either of you show him the slightest kindness he'll take it as a sign of weakness. Please, remember I said that and warn everyone he's likely to meet. I'll do what I can but I doubt I'll be able to influence him.'

'He does love his mother,' Bethan broke in swiftly.

'Yes,' Charlie mused. 'That I believe, but then she looked out for him and protected him when he was a helpless baby. I think he cares for her only because the situation is now reversed.'

'And from a sense of duty,' Andrew suggested.

'He doesn't know the meaning of the word.'

'Masha has memories of her life with you. Perhaps she'll be able to help Peter to adjust to a normal life.' Andrew finished his tea and placed his cup on the table. 'You can help her, Charlie, and through her, the boy.'

'I hope you're right, Andrew.'

'So do I because I'm not sure that Pontypridd is ready for Peter Raschenko as he is.'

Gabrielle shivered as she stole closer to Tony, who was sitting in the corner seat of the train. All she could think about, all she could hear, were her mother's interminable warnings ringing through her mind. She knew she had hurt her in wanting to leave Germany after they had lost everything, but she had tried to make her mother understand she loved Tony and could only see a future for herself with him, and that meant moving to his country. But instead of accepting that her daughter loved Tony, Gräfin von Stettin had done everything she could to try to dissuade her from going to him.

Her mother had constantly reminded her that life in Britain would be strange, every person she met hostile, and although she hated to acknowledge that her mother had been right, so far she had seen nothing to prove otherwise. London could have been any one of the dozen German cities she had visited since the end of the war. Blanket-bombed into rubble that even looters and scavengers could no longer be bothered to comb through.

And London had been only the beginning. As far as she had been able to make out from the streets and houses visible from the train before daylight had faded, Britain was a poor country. Strips of small, mean houses, so different from the big, airy apartment blocks with neat tiers of balconies that she'd been used to, and everything needed cleaning, tidying, painting and rebuilding – so much rebuilding. She clutched Tony's hand tighter as she gazed up into his face. Had she done the right thing in leaving Germany and coming here? It had seemed the only thing to do when he had asked her to marry him but that night in the park had been so wonderful – and now – now he looked so different out of uniform.

She closed her eyes and relived the most romantic night of her life. A band had been playing in the pavilion, couples had danced on the paved area in the centre of the lawns, all the men were in uniform – British – American – French. There had been wine – so much wine brought by the French soldiers and the Americans had brought food hampers from their PX. She and Tony had waltzed and afterwards he had led her away from the lights into the shadows. Not too far – she would never go out of sight or earshot of other people with any man – and after kissing her very lightly on the mouth he had proposed.

Looking back she wondered if she had been slightly drunk as that entire evening had taken on a surreal tinge, like a scene viewed through tinted glass. The sky had been too blue, the stars too bright, the shadows too purple – and there had been the sudden prospect of leaving Germany for ever – exciting and a little frightening. But then that had been something she – and almost every other refugee – had wanted to do since the Russians had invaded the eastern part of Germany. And not only the refugees. It was almost every German girl's dream to hook an American or British serviceman. Even a Frenchman was better than the prospect of trying to find a husband among the broken-spirited, cowed and beaten remnants of their own armies.

Britain, America and France weren't suffering under the heel of the conqueror, they were free, and there was more chance of finding happiness out of the mess that was defeated Germany. And as if the prospect of a glittering future in a foreign land wasn't enough, there was Tony, dark, dashing and handsome in the sergeant's uniform that had so upset her mother.

The first time Gräfin von Stettin had seen her sitting next to him in the garden of the billet where they both worked, she had screamed that she would sooner allow her daughter to be courted by a monkey than a non-commissioned officer. The second time, she had taken Gabrielle to one side and asked outright if Tony was a Jew. It had taken three months of coaxing on Gabrielle's part before her mother would allow her to invite Tony to the shabby room they called home. And then, only after Tony's fellow servicemen had confirmed that his family were important business people in Wales, who owned a chain of fine restaurants and hotels, a fact Tony had modestly endorsed when her mother had challenged him outright. Although, as befitting an unassuming man born to wealth and position he'd refused to elaborate or add to the information her mother had gleaned.

And six months later, here she was, sitting in a dirty, cold, unheated train next to the man she had fallen in love with one magical summer night. Only Tony didn't look in the least like the man who had kissed her then. He looked completely different from the dashing sergeant who had left her in Celle. Civilian clothes made him look smaller, shabbier somehow, and she couldn't help noticing that his suit was creased, his overcoat stained with tea, and his shirt collar grubby. But then everyone on the trains and stations appeared filthy. They all looked as if they could do with a good wash because everything was covered with smuts. What had her mother called Wales – a 'coal pot'. That was it. Like Silesia – a filthy area where coal was dug out of the ground and the dust filled the air, making everything dirty.

'You warm enough?'

'Yes, thank you, Tony.' She was freezing but even if she'd told him the truth there wouldn't have been anything he could have done about it other than give her his own overcoat.

'As soon as we get in I'll make you something to eat in the café.'

'Café? I thought you owned restaurants, hotels . . .'

'We're going to live above one of the cafés. I run it.' Tony looked out of the window to avoid any more explanation. He recognised the houses behind the street-lights. They were coming into Treforest. Another ten minutes and they'd be at Pontypridd station. He hadn't even asked Angelo to light the fire in the sitting room and bedroom. He and Gabrielle would have to sit in public in the café or the less congenial surroundings of the kitchen.

'Everything is all right, isn't it, Tony?'

'Everything's fine.' He tried to smile at her as he lifted her case from the overhead rack. 'The next stop is ours. If we move up to the door I'll see if I can find a guard and make arrangements to have your trunk taken off the train.'

'She's just tired,' Peter protested as Bethan tucked the sheets and blankets around Masha.

'She needs to rest,' Bethan replied.

'I've brought you some food,' Charlie murmured in Russian as he walked in with a tray set out with a bowl of bread, another of stew and a glass of water.

'You want my mother to eat in here?' Peter asked from the doorway.

'Just for tonight because she is tired. Ours is down-stairs. Will you join me?'

Peter spoke rapidly to his mother in Russian. As she answered, Bethan wished, and not for the first time, that she could understand what they were saying. The very few times she had heard Charlie speaking his native language he had made it sound soft, almost musical, just like Masha's intonation. Peter's Russian reminded her of the rattle of a machine-gun – loud, angry and terrifying.

Charlie murmured something to Masha, smiled and left. Bethan helped her to spread a napkin over her nightdress and sheet.

'I will sit with my mother while she eats.'

Bethan nodded agreement. 'Would you please tell her that my husband and I are leaving but we will be back tomorrow and if she feels in the slightest unwell, either I or my husband will come down to see her.'

'She won't need you, Mrs John.'

'Your father has our telephone number.'

Bethan walked downstairs to where Andrew was waiting in the hall. 'Peter's staying with his mother while she eats,' she announced to Charlie.

'You will be all right . . .'

'I'll be fine, Andrew. Do you think my son will knife me in the night?'

'The thought had crossed my mind,' Andrew said flatly.

'Bethan . . .'

'You want me to call in on Alma, Charlie?'

'I know you've had a long day but I would be grateful.'

'I intended to, anyway. See you tomorrow.'

'That's the train pulling in.' Gina went to the window of the café. 'They'll be here any minute. Perhaps you should go and see if they need help with the luggage, Luke.'

'Tony will have a porter bring it across.' Angelo continued to polish the glasses behind the counter although he was as curious as Gina to see Tony's fiancée.

'I should go up and check the fires.'

'Gina, it looks like a palace up there and you know it. Sit down and wait for them to come to us,' Angelo ordered, spotting Tony's dark figure at the foot of the steps that led up to the platform.

'And here they are,' Luke opened the door to a porter who was wheeling the most enormous wooden trunk.

'Where do you want it, Angelo?' he asked, heaving for breath.

'Stick it in the corner of the kitchen. Will it go behind the counter?'

'Just about.' The porter heaved it round the corner and through the door that led into the kitchen.

'Thanks, Dai.'

'Don't envy you trying to get that upstairs.'

'When we try I'll give you a shout.'

'Shout all you like, I still won't come.' Dai pocketed the shilling Tony handed him.

'Welcoming committee?' Tony asked as he walked in, arm in arm with Gabrielle.

'We thought we'd stop by to say hello.' Gina smiled at the woman who was going to be her sister-in-law. 'Hello, I'm Tony's sister Gina.'

'How do you do? I am Gabrielle von Stettin and I am pleased to meet you.' Gabrielle's handshake was firm, her returning smile cautious, but friendly.

Gina studied her as Tony introduced her to Angelo and Luke. There seemed to be something old-fashioned about her manners. An excessive, almost formal, civility for someone who was about to join the family but then perhaps that was the German way. She couldn't help thinking of the war as she watched her shake Angelo's hand. This woman was one of the same people who had been trying to kill British soldiers, overrun the whole of Europe, make it bow to German supremacy . . .

'Gina?'

'Sorry, Angelo, I was miles away.'

'I was telling Tony how hard you've been working on the rooms upstairs.'

'Not that hard. Here, I'll take you up, Gabrielle,' she offered, stressing the last syllable of her name as Gabrielle herself had done when she'd introduced herself. As Gina led the way through the kitchen to the stairs, Tony was overwhelmed by the smell of beeswax polish and washing soda, and realised Angelo hadn't exaggerated. His sister really had spent most of the day cleaning the rooms.

'This is the living room, Gabrielle.' Suddenly shy, Gina opened the door wide. A fire burned in the hearth, new covers had been slipped on to the cushions on the two easy chairs, the wooden arm rests gleamed, newly buffed and polished. A dark red chenille tablecloth had been thrown over the table to hide its scarred surface and a vase Tony didn't recognise stood in the centre filled with greenhouse-forced daffodils.

'The flowers are beautiful!' Gabrielle exclaimed, walking into the room and smelling them.

'The national flower of Wales,' Angelo said proudly.

'It is a pity they have no perfume.'

Gina took the remark personally as though she should have ensured better – and perfumed – flowers.

'The bedroom is next door.' Luke led the way.

Tony sensed Gabrielle's disappointment – and disgust – as they looked at the washstand with its chipped toilet set and cheap deal bedroom suite, so discoloured by age and mistreatment that no amount of polishing could disguise the abuse it had been subjected to by eleven Ronconi children.

'It's a start, Gabrielle,' he ventured.

'Am I going to live here?'

'Until we are married, and then I'll move in.'

She turned and smiled at Gina. 'Thank you for the flowers.'

Upset by the lack of mention of the rooms, it was as much as Gina could do to mutter, 'That's all right.'

'Where are the bathroom and kitchen?' Gabrielle asked Tony.

'The toilet is outside and the kitchen is in the café.'

'Tony, we should talk about this place. Perhaps we could sell it and buy something with better living accommodation.'

'I'll get your supper.' Angelo ran down the stairs. Gina and Luke followed, leaving Tony to explain to his fiancée that the café wasn't even his to sell.

Chapter Fifteen

'WHAT DO YOU suggest I do while you talk to Alma – alone. Sit in the car and freeze. Or would you prefer me to disappear into thin air until such time you decide you're ready for a lift home?' Andrew negotiated the narrow bend out of Penuel Lane into Taff Street and pulled into the kerb outside Charlie's shop.

'I'm not expecting you to do anything, Andrew, but as you're obviously niggly after your long day, it might be best if you go home.'

'And if I do that, how are you going to get up Penycoedcae hill. Fly?'

'Taxi.'

'As if you'll find one at this time of night.' He glanced at his watch. 'I'll have a swift half in the New Inn and be back here in a quarter of an hour. Will that be enough time for all the private, "women only" things you want to say to Alma?'

Bethan didn't answer him. Slamming the passenger door, she left the car and walked up to Alma's door. He slid back the window.

'Fifteen minutes,' he called after her.

'I haven't a stop watch.'

'Now you're being ridiculous.'

'*I* am!'

'If you're not out, I'll knock the door.' Grinding the gears, he drove away.

'I heard the car.' Alma had appeared on her doorstep.

'I should think just about the whole of Taff Street did the way Andrew's driving, and you're a fibber. You didn't hear anything, you've been looking out the window for us.'

'Guilty. I've got sandwiches, sherry and coffee all

ready. Tell me,' she demanded, before they even reached the top of the stairs, 'what is Masha like?'

'Tired, old, worn out before her time.'

'Does she look like me?'

Bethan waved her hand from side to side. 'Difficult to say. Her eyes are the same colour.'

'And her hair?'

'Grey.'

'You must have talked.'

'She only speaks Russian.'

'And Charlie? How did he look at her when they met? Could you tell if he still loves her? Is he moving in with her? Did he speak Russian to her? Of course, he must have if she doesn't speak English. His son? What is his son like . . . ?'

'One question at a time,' Bethan pleaded as she led the way into Alma's living room. 'You know Charlie far better than I do. I find it impossible to work out what he thinks about anything unless he tells me outright but he did ask me to call and see you now.'

'You're not just saying that?'

'Would I do that to you?' Bethan hugged her before sitting down.

'Did he give you any messages for me?' Alma poured two sherries and handed Bethan one.

'He just said he'd be grateful if I called in on you.'

'He knew I'd be worried about him travelling up to London and back without a break.'

'Alma, I've been watching you and Charlie ever since he heard Masha was alive. Hasn't it occurred to you that you're being just a bit too calm and rational about his leaving? Haven't you even thought of fighting back?'

'Fighting who, Beth? The man I love, or a woman who on your own admittance is "*tired, old, and worn out before her time*".'

'Charlie's given her the house; he's prepared to support her. After sixteen years apart I can't see that she has the right to demand any more from him. From what you've told me, he was eighteen and Masha seventeen when they were separated. That's barely out of childhood. I remember that age. You think you know what you want but you haven't a clue what life is about.'

'How old were you when you met Andrew?'

'Nineteen, which proves my point. I thought I couldn't live without him but I managed very well for six years. Charlie was twenty-eight when he married you. He was a man, not a boy, and you've only got to look at him whenever your name is mentioned. He loves you, Alma, I'm sure of it.'

'And you don't think he loves Masha?'

Bethan fell silent as she recalled that first look between them on the quayside. Was it possible for a man to love two women at the same time? 'I can't read his mind. If you want to know who he loves more, Masha or you, you'll have to ask him.'

'Is that what you think I should do?'

'I think you should demand that he stay with you and Theo. You've made it too easy for him to leave. It occurred to me tonight when I was showing his son around the house . . .'

'Peter. What is he like, Beth?'

'An absolute monster.' Bethan saw the look of confusion on Alma's face. 'I'm sorry, I shouldn't have blurted it out like that but even Charlie agreed with Andrew when he warned the boy was trouble. He's aggressive, rude, made absolutely no effort to hide his hatred of Charlie . . .'

'How can he possibly hate Charlie? He's his father!'

'He's very attached to his mother. I'm guessing that he blames Charlie for deserting her before he was born.'

'But Charlie didn't walk away from her willingly. Hasn't anyone told him what happened?'

'Believe you me, there's no telling that boy anything. But I shouldn't be talking about him like this. As far as looks go, be warned, he's a mirror image of Charlie when he first came to Pontypridd. Line him, Theo and Charlie up and they could be the same person at different ages.'

'Poor Charlie, having to cope with a difficult son on top

of everything else.' Alma sat at the table and picked up her sherry.

'Poor Alma, more like.'

'Beth, I know you're only thinking of me and Theo, but please, don't suggest I complicate the situation by making demands of Charlie that he won't be able to meet. Things are difficult enough for him as it is. I know it must have been hard for you and Andrew to see him with another woman . . .'

'Dear God! You are the most unselfish person I've ever met.'

'Try and put yourself in my place, Beth. What would you do if Andrew had another wife?'

'Put the flags out and give her a month's rations to take him away.'

'You would not.' Alma laughed as she brushed a tear from the corner of her eye.

'Try me. Find a woman who claims to have married him before me, and I'll pack his bag for him.'

'Things still difficult between you two?'

'Impossible.'

'I asked you earlier what you'd do if you were me, I know what I'd do if I were you. Hold on to Andrew with everything I have.'

Bethan glanced at her watch. 'I have to go, Andrew only gave me fifteen minutes.'

'I'm sorry, I've been keeping you talking when you must be exhausted from travelling.'

'I'll be down tomorrow for a longer chat.'

'Promise?'

'I promise.' As Bethan ran down the stairs she couldn't help thinking of her instinctive reply to Alma's advice, one that fortunately had gone no further than being phrased in her own mind. She didn't want to hold on to Andrew with everything she had, because she no longer loved him. It was as simple and final as that.

Charlie picked up one of the bowls Mrs Lane had set out on the kitchen table and ladled stew into it. Taking a piece of the bread she had cut and laid out on the breadboard, he placed it on a side plate next to the bowl. He looked up as his son walked into the room carrying Masha's tray.

'Would you like me to serve you some stew?'

'No.' Peter set the tray on the table. Half of one slice of bread had gone and about a quarter of the stew.

'Your mother didn't eat very much.'

'We didn't get this much food in any of the camps in a week. It's going to take her time to learn to live off the fat of the land.'

Allowing his son's sniping to pass without comment, Charlie took the tray and carried it into the wash house. Returning to the table he was surprised to see Peter helping himself to the stew. After his refusal to eat anything from the hamper in the train he'd begun to wonder if the boy was prepared to starve himself as a matter of pride.

Sitting opposite Peter, Charlie began to eat. The stew was good and the quality of meat better than he'd tasted in years but he couldn't help contrasting it with Alma's. She had a way with herbs, of adding sprinklings of flavourings that most housewives didn't think of. Probably tips learned during her childhood and adolescence when her widowed mother didn't have the money to buy good-quality food. He could recall sage, mint, dill and thyme growing in the pots she kept on the kitchen windowsill, but there were probably others. In comparison, Mrs Lane's stew was bland and tasteless.

He broke his bread carefully into four symmetrical pieces, then poured himself a glass of water, all the while taking sly glances at Peter, who was eating as though he hadn't seen food in a month.

'We should talk tomorrow,' he suggested, realising that Peter wouldn't speak again until spoken to.

'Why?'

'Now you're here, you have to do something.'

'What do you mean?' The boy pushed his bowl away and glared at Charlie.

'School – work – something.'

'What do you do?' Peter crossed his arms and stared belligerently.

'Work in a shop – a cooked meat and pie shop. I could find you something there or in the kitchens where they make the pies.'

'Women's work,' Peter dismissed scornfully.

'There must be something you want to do. You speak so many languages, perhaps you should study.'

'I was a *Kapo* in the Portland Cement factory at Auschwitz.' When Peter saw Charlie wince at the word '*Kapo*' he allowed himself a small smile of triumph. He had finally succeeded in hurting this apparently imperturbable man. 'They gave me a whip.'

'I do know how the Germans treated *Kapos* and how they ordered the *Kapos* to treat their fellow prisoners. I'm surprised they considered you old enough for the responsibility.'

'I told them I was twenty.'

'And they believed you?'

'I was bigger than most of the men and being a *Kapo* meant I could make things easier for my mother.'

'Well, there are no openings for *Kapos* with whips in Pontypridd. So, you'll have to think of something else.'

'You're a rich man, you can keep me.'

'What gave you the idea I was rich?'

'This house. Bethan John said you bought it for my mother and me. And now all this food.'

'This stew was made with meat a friend donated,' Charlie informed him, twisting the truth about William and the black market meat. 'Don't think we'll be eating like this every day. There's food rationing in this country. And this house took ten years' savings.'

'Money you earned working in a shop?' Peter asked contemptuously.

'Yes.'

'I won't work in a shop.'

'Then we'll have to find you something else.'

'I'll find my own work and my own way of making money.' Lifting his foot on to the chair next to him he pulled a stiletto from the back of the heel of his shoe. As Charlie watched, he drew his thumb down the edge of the long blade. A thin red line opened up and blood welled out. He sucked it from his hand, all the while staring into Charlie's eyes.

'If your own work and way of making money involves stealing or knifing people you'll end up in prison.'

'I've heard about British prisons. They are like Russian rest homes.'

'Possibly, but for you prison won't be the end of it. You will be sent back.'

'To Russia?'

For the first time Charlie saw a trace of fear in the boy's eyes. 'I doubt any other country will have you.'

'But you're here.'

'And I had to sign a document stating I'd guarantee you and your mother's good behaviour and ensure that you both observed the laws of the land which basically means you forgetting everything you've learned about life in the camps. You give the police reason to think you're a criminal or a danger to others and they'll lock you up, then deport you.'

'And my mother. If that happened? If I was deported, you'd look after her?'

'I'd prefer to do it with your help.'

Peter returned his knife to his boot, concealing the handle beneath his trouser turn-up. Sitting back at the table, he picked up his spoon and proceeded to finish what was left of his stew.

'Would you like to go out tomorrow, take a look at the town, perhaps buy some clothes for yourself?'

'I'm going out tonight.'

'Would you like me to come with you?'

'No.' Cleaning the last vestiges of stew from his bowl with a piece of bread, Peter pushed it to one side; Charlie picked up the dirty dishes and carried them into the wash house.

'Would you like some tea? I can make it Russian style,' Charlie offered when he returned.

'Have you got vodka?'

'No,' Charlie lied.

'Then I don't want anything. I am going to see my mother.' Leaving the table, he ran upstairs. Charlie waited until he heard Masha's bedroom door close then he went into the hall, picked up the telephone receiver, and dialled the number of Pontypridd police station.

'Did you have enough time to say all you wanted to Alma?' Andrew enquired a little shame-faced, as he pulled up outside Charlie's shop to see Bethan waiting in the doorway.

'Yes, thank you,' she replied frostily. 'Did you enjoy your swift half in the New Inn?'

'Not really. Bethan . . .'

'Andrew, I'm exhausted, do you mind if we just go up to Graig Avenue, pick up the children and go straight home?'

'If that's what you want.'

'That's what I want,' she echoed dismally as he drove up Taff Street.

'Hello. How's the baby?' Liza kissed Gina's cheek as she bumped into her and Luke leaving the café.

'The baby's fine, Liza.' Gina managed a small smile. 'It's nice to see you. Angelo didn't mention that you had a day off.'

'It's tomorrow, but I thought I'd catch the last bus up tonight and surprise Angelo.'

'He could do with some cheering up,' Luke said, as an angry argument resounded from the kitchen.

'Angelo and Tony?'

'Like cat and dog. But as Angelo's in charge for the rest of the night, Maggie's serving, so if you want anything, ask her. I have to get Luke home. He's on early shift in the morning.'

'Luke is not a baby to be "got" anywhere,' Luke protested, his nerves, like Gina's, stretched to breaking point by the tension generated from Gabrielle's arrival.

'What's going on?'

'Tony's German fiancée has arrived, but don't worry, she's upstairs and not likely to come down again tonight, so you should be safe enough. See you, Liza.' Gina closed the café door behind her.

'Any chance of a coffee, Maggie?' Liza asked as she sat at the family table.

'For you, love? Anything.'

'Don't suppose you want to tell me what's going on?' Liza winced as Tony's shouting escalated to a new high.

'Boyfriend's privilege, love, but if I were you I'd think long and hard about carrying on courting Angelo.'

'Angelo's a nice boy,' Liza smiled, thinking Maggie was pulling her leg.

'He's a lovely boy and a darling, but he's got a swine of a brother.'

'Now that Tony's running this place, Angelo doesn't have to come up here again and the chances are they won't see that much of one another.'

'Now that Tony's running this place none of us have to come up here again,' Maggie muttered darkly, 'and I've a feeling that goes twice over for the customers. You mark my words, Liza. Lord Tony Ronconi's grand ideas will drive people away and close this place in a fortnight. I only hope he doesn't bankrupt the restaurant while he's doing it.'

'Mother, do you have everything you need?' Peter asked Masha, who lay propped up on pillows in bed, looking through one of the Russian magazines she had found on her bedside table.

'Everything I could possibly want and more, thank you, Pasha.'

He slipped on his short blue workman's jacket and matching cap – the only coat and cap he possessed. 'If you don't need me, I will take a look around the town.'

'Pasha, you're not used to towns. It's late. You're tired . . .'

'The boy will be fine, Masha. Let him go.' Charlie

walked in carrying two cups of tea with sugar lumps in the saucers. 'Pontypridd's a quiet place. It's not as if he wants to explore the middle of Moscow.'

'But he's not used to being out on his own.'

'Nothing will happen to him. Here,' Charlie set the tea down on the bedside cabinet, put his hand in his pocket and pulled out two half-crowns.

'I don't want your money.' Peter backed towards the door.

'And I'm not giving it to you. Only lending it until you find work. You can't do anything in this or any other town without money.'

'The shops are open?'

'No, but there are bars that serve beer. You'll recognise them by the signs over the door and the noise inside.'

'Do they serve vodka too?' Peter demanded truculently.

'You have to be eighteen before they'll serve you beer or vodka. But you can buy an orange juice or lemonade.'

'I don't drink children's slops. And I won't have any trouble convincing anyone I'm eighteen.'

Recognising the futility of argument Charlie didn't try to contradict him. 'You'll also find cafés that serve coffee, tea and food. But neither the bars nor the cafés give anything away without money.'

Peter reluctantly stepped forward and took the coins Charlie offered.

'Just so you know, that's about a day's pay. There's a key to the front door in the top drawer of the small chest in the hall. Take it; I don't want you waking your mother when you come in.'

'You're staying here, in this house, with us?' Peter squared up to his father.

'That is up to your mother.'

Peter hesitated for a fraction of a second and for the first time Charlie caught a glimpse of how thin his son's veneer of bravado really was. He had done a good job of convincing Andrew, Bethan and him that he was a dangerous thug, and perhaps he had been – in the camps. But the camps were a closed domain. Peter had been born into them, grown to manhood – of sorts – in them but he clearly had no idea of the world outside. Charlie had a feeling that tonight would not only be his first taste of Pontypridd but his first taste of freedom. The first time he would walk down a street in an ordinary town as an ordinary person.

Feeling sorry for the boy Charlie was prompted to repeat his offer. 'If you're tired, Peter, I would be happy to show you round tomorrow.'

'I'm not tired.' Turning on his heel, Peter ran down the stairs. Charlie heard him opening and shutting the drawer in the hall, then the front door closed.

'He will be all right, Feo?' Masha asked anxiously.

Charlie thought of the telephone call he had made earlier. 'Yes, Masha, he will be fine. Nothing can happen to him here.' Pulling a button-back Victorian chair up to the bed, he sat on it, wishing the seat was higher and it wasn't quite so small and dainty. 'Are you too tired to talk?'

'No, but after sixteen years, Feo, I should warn you that I have a lot of things to say.'

'We both have a lot of things to say.' He handed her the tea he had made for her.

'Where shall we begin, Feo?'

'How about me saying "welcome home, Masha"?' he smiled.

Peter had always prided himself on his sense of direction. He had often boasted that if he were sent to a new camp, within a few hours he would have orientated himself not only within the camp but outside it. Instinctively, he sensed which was south, north, east and west, even on a cloudy moonless night. Besides, tonight he had taken the precaution of looking out of his bedroom window and studying the town spread out in the valley below. He had noted a ribbon of lights shining marginally brighter than the ones on the periphery. All he had to do was walk down the steps on to the street – he remembered to turn back when he was on the pavement and take a good look at the house, memorising the distinctive stained glass in the front door. Then with his heart beating more erratically than it had done since the Americans had arrived in Buchenwald and announced all the inmates were free, he set his face to the town.

The street was silent; no one stirred, no noise came from behind the closed doors. Silent people living silent lives so as not to disturb their neighbours, he decided scornfully, hating them because like his father they didn't appreciate how well off they were.

Turning left, he crossed the road and turned right down a hill, constantly bearing in mind that he needed to head straight ahead from the house. Ignoring turnings to the left, he halted at a crossroads at the bottom of the hill. A huge church loomed on his right, larger than any he had ever seen, and he recalled someone telling him that religion wasn't outlawed in Britain. On the opposite side of the road was a lane, dark and narrow. The sort of place thieves would hide out in. Deciding to explore it, he closed his hand round the knife he had transferred to his pocket and walked on, emerging in what he suspected was the main street of the town.

Ribbons of shops stretched either side of him on both sides of the road as far as he could see. Most were closed, their doors locked and canopies folded back. A crowd of about a dozen boys stood grouped around an elaborately carved stone fountain on his left. They were laughing and joking, making a lot of useless noise. Clutching his concealed knife he stared at them, daring them to approach him. They glanced at him, then turned away, carrying on as if he wasn't there.

Relaxing his hold on his knife, he pulled his cap down further on his head, shading his eyes with the peak. The larger, more imposing shops seemed to loom ahead on his right. He set off that way, walking slowly, looking in windows as he passed. None had their lights on. Someone – had it been Dr John or his father? – had said something about fuel restrictions being in force, but occasionally a streetlight shone close enough to a display window to illuminate the wares. One window was filled with pianos, another with hats and umbrellas, the next with shoes – he stood, gazing for five full minutes at a time. He had never seen such luxuries, so many clothes. He walked on down the street in bewildered wonderment, so engrossed he didn't notice the man walking just as leisurely as himself, twenty paces behind.

A burly man, older than his father, in a uniform with a helmet that he would have recognised from the photographs of Britain he'd studied so avidly in the displaced persons' camp when he'd first been told that his father was prepared to offer his mother – and him – a home.

'Feodor, we both know what happened to me in the last sixteen years. I don't want to talk about it.' Taking his big hand into her small one, Masha kissed the tips of his fingers. 'But you – you have changed so much.'

'You expected me to still look eighteen?'

'We weren't allowed to take anything from the house – not even a photograph. At first – in Stalingrad – all I had to treasure of yours were my memories. Then, as Pasha grew older and began to look more and more like you, I could see you in him, as you were that last time when you kissed me goodbye and set off to get the cot. I no longer had to close my eyes to see you in my mind. I only had to look at Pasha. So, to me, you were always young – unchanging – the boy I fell in love with . . .'

'And now my hair is silver, my face wrinkled, my strength half of what it was.'

'You were in a camp too.'

'They told you about that?'

'And that you had made a life for yourself here before the war. Tell me about that, Feo. How did you get enough money to buy this great big house?'

'I set up shops. Cooked meat and pie shops.'

'You have more than one?'

'Twelve –'

'Then you can find a job for Pasha,' she broke in eagerly.

'I have already offered. He doesn't want one.'

'He doesn't know what he wants, Feo. I'm worried about him. He has done things – things that may have been necessary in the camps,' she qualified carefully, refusing to be disloyal to her son. 'But he knows nothing of life. Ordinary life, like it was for us when we were growing up and first married.'

'You don't have to worry about Pasha, or look after him any more, Masha. He may not know what he wants – yet. But I will take care of him, whether he wants me to or not.'

'He gets into fights.'

'All boys of his age do. It's not serious.'

'It is when Pasha fights. He has killed and not just once, Feo. He knifed a man because he refused to put me on the list of prisoners to be transferred from Auschwitz when the Russian army was about to overrun the camp. Then when we arrived in Buchenwald –'

'Everyone kills in a war, and life in the camps is a kind of war,' Charlie interrupted, preferring not to hear about the things his son had done to ensure his mother's and his own survival, before he'd had time to complete his own judgement of the boy. 'With us to help him, he'll get used to life on the outside.'

'I do hope you are right, Feo. He is so like you and not just in the way he looks. He has your heart, your soul, your goodness, please give him a chance . . .'

'Have I changed so much, Masha, that you think you have to plead with me to love our son the way a father should?'

'You were my husband,' she touched his fingers, 'but I was taken from a boy. Now I see a man.'

'And you are disappointed.'

'Not disappointed, shy. Which is stupid for a woman my age. I have to tell you something, Feo –'

'Masha,' Charlie interrupted, 'please let me speak first.'

'You want to tell me that you have another wife and son.'

'You know. Peter said you didn't.'

'What would Peter know about it?'

'He said the English officer who told him I was alive mentioned that I had another wife. Peter said he didn't translate everything the officer said because he didn't want to hurt you.' Charlie sat back in his chair and reached for his cigarettes. 'You knew I had married again, Masha, and yet you still came.'

'I wanted to see you because sixteen years hadn't changed my feelings for you. And I thought that if you had made a new life for yourself with no room in it for us, you wouldn't have sent the money for Pasha and me to come here.'

'You still love me.'

'Feo, I'm not what I was.'

'Neither am I.'

'Things happened to the women in the camps.'

'I saw. You don't have to tell me about it.'

'I want to. I was luckier than most. After Pasha was born there was a man who looked after me and helped me and Pasha. He was a sergeant in charge of the guards and he took care that I was never sent to the guards or men's barracks to be raped like the other women. I was still pretty then. But I never loved him as I loved you, Feo. I need you to know that.'

'You left him to come here?'

'The Germans killed him before they sent us to Auschwitz. And by then I was too old to attract any man. That's when Pasha started looking after me.'

'I can't bear to think that all the time I was living here in comfort, you were suffering in the camps.'

'Do you love your other wife, Feo?'

'Not like I love you,' he replied truthfully, hoping she wouldn't ask him to explain any further.

'Did you live here, in this house, with her?'

'No.' He left the chair and walked to the window. 'She bought it for you with my money when I told her that you and Peter had been found.'

'And she doesn't mind you living here with us?'

'When I heard that you were alive I left her.'

'Because of me?'

'Because of you, and because with you alive my marriage to her wasn't legal.'

'And now I'm here, you have two wives to choose from. Which one of us do you want, Feo?'

'I have friends I could live with.' He deliberately avoided answering her question. 'The same ones I have been living with since I was told you had survived.'

'There are a lot of bedrooms in this house.'

'Four.'

'You are my husband, your place is here.' She patted the bed beside her, 'but I have just told you that I haven't been faithful and I have grown old – and ugly.'

'No, Masha.' He turned to her and smiled. 'To me you can never be old or less than the beautiful angel I fell in love with.'

'I never thought I'd hear you call me that again.'

'So, my beautiful angel, do you remember the first time I kissed you?'

'On top of the hay we were stacking in my father's barn. I thought you would never let me go.'

'And the harvest dance that followed.'

'When we danced until dawn and you took me home and kissed me again. My father nearly disinherited me because you'd unfastened all the buttons on my blouse and I hadn't noticed. But it wouldn't have made any difference if he had disinherited me, because in the end we lost everything . . .' Her eyes were dry but they held more misery than if they'd been filled with tears.

'Not everything, Masha. We have our son, Pasha – not that he allows me to call him that – and one another.'

'Pasha is not a bad boy, Feo, just tough and frightened – a dangerous mixture but I couldn't always be with him to teach him better.'

'You kept him alive and that in itself is a miracle. Remember our wedding?' he continued, wanting to bring the smile back to her face.

'I prefer to remember another night, six months before

our wedding when we were back in my father's hayloft. I was sixteen, you were seventeen and the months to your eighteenth birthday that your father and mine insisted we wait to get married seemed half a lifetime away. We undressed and made love for the first time like no one else ever made love before.'

'That night I felt as though we invented love.'

'You made me so very happy. And I was lucky because I had that happiness to cling to in the camps. I tried to talk to Pasha about you; to explain how life should be, but it was like trying to teach a blind man about colour. I couldn't make him understand. When he was little he thought my stories about you were fairytales like *The Little White Duck* and when he was older, instead of liking you and wanting to know more about you as I'd hoped and intended, he hated you for not rescuing us.'

'He's young, he needs time and that's one thing we have plenty of.'

'Come to bed.'

'Just like that?'

'You are my husband.'

'It's been sixteen years.'

'Switch out the light and pretend they never happened, Feodor.'

She was delicate, fragile, her fleshless bones light and frail like those of a young bird. Almost afraid to touch her lest he inadvertently hurt her, Charlie moved, slowly, gently, too concerned that he might be causing her pain to think about his own pleasure.

Her lips were dry; her body as unsubstantial as that of a child's as he lifted her on to him; her hair, thinner than he remembered. But as she drew closer and covered his body with hers the years rolled back in a way he would never have believed possible. Once again they were in her father's hayloft. He a young man, and she a girl, two virgins about to invent lovemaking, with their whole lives ahead of them to enjoy one another – and life.

Chapter Sixteen

As Peter walked slowly up Taff Street, he saw the bars Feodor – he was making a conscious effort not to think of the man who had deserted his mother before his birth as his father – had mentioned. He even went into one. The air was blue with cigarette smoke, the lighting dim and the walls yellowed by nicotine. A dozen or so rickety tables set in an undulating sea of spit-blackened sawdust were surrounded by stools occupied by shouting, cursing men who looked as though they were in competition with their neighbours to see who could make the most noise. Overwhelmed by the unfamiliar scene, he set his features into his most intimidating expression, as he continued to stand by the door waiting for an opening between the men standing around a long, high, dark wood counter drinking large glasses of beer.

Just as one man left and he stepped forward, someone walking in behind him knocked his shoulder – hard. Turning, he fled back out on to the street, telling himself that he didn't want to drink in a bar that had such a sour, acrid smell. Besides, the only woman in the place had been serving. A heavily painted, hard-faced, improbable redhead who looked even older than his mother.

More than anything else, he wanted to talk to girls – young and preferably pretty ones. He had seen a few he would have liked to approach on the train but he hadn't dared go near them in front of Feodor and Andrew and Bethan John in case they laughed at him. Girls were something of a mystery. Ever since he could remember, his mother had told him tales about love. Stories featuring beautiful princesses and handsome princes who lived in magnificent castles and dark forests, who only had to look into one another's eyes a single time to fall in love and live happily ever after. And every time his mother had begun the tales, her eyes had misted over and he had known that it was not handsome princes or beautiful princesses she had been thinking of but his father.

There'd been women prisoners in every camp he'd been incarcerated in. They'd had their own barracks and working areas, usually kept exclusively female. Newcomers among the common zeks soon learned, some the hard way, that the young and pretty women were the property of the guards and an ordinary prisoner touched them at his peril. However, the clever and fortunate male prisoners inevitably found a way round the segregation to gain access to the women, and as soon as he'd reached the age of sexual curiosity he had fought to be numbered among the fortunate. He had even lain with a woman once, in a waterlogged ditch behind her barracks. It had been cold, dirty and uncomfortable, and too dark to see her face. And she hadn't even been his. One of the older guards had whispered in his ear that he knew a woman prepared to open her legs for any man who had something to give her – and him. He had handed the guard a gold coin he had found in the boot of a fellow prisoner who had died in the bunk next to his and 'paid' the woman in apples scrounged from the guards' kitchen in return for a couple of pints of stolen petrol.

He had seen her close up in the kitchens the next day and to his dismay discovered she was downright ugly, wrinkled, toothless and old. He had gone with her because he had burned to know what it was like to lie with a woman but although he had nothing to compare the experience with, he sensed that there had to be more. A lot more, otherwise why would people make up stories about perfect love, like the ones his mother had told him?

Perhaps tonight he would find a girl – a pretty one with teeth – who'd be prepared to belong to him and no other man. A woman he could lie naked with who would help him discover if this love that his mother talked about was as wonderful and perfect as she had promised it would be.

*

The road began to slope upwards, narrowing as it was carried over a bridge. Peter leaned on the metal parapet and stared down at the river beneath, its dark waters gleaming with gold and silver puddles of reflected light. A bus rattled past, stirring him from his reverie, and he walked on, past an enormous building pasted with film posters of cowboys embracing women with perfectly waved hair and red, Cupid's bow lips. Then suddenly, the road opened on to a square. A train thundered over a high bridge ahead, lights shone from a window on his left and he smelled coffee. Good, strong, appetising, real coffee, like that the kitchen orderlies had brewed for 'staff only' in the displaced persons' camp.

His taste buds burst into life. He couldn't remember ever drinking real coffee, only acorn coffee, and he wanted to find out if the taste was as wonderful as the smell promised it would be. Pushing open the door he went inside.

There was a wooden bar with stools set in front of it like the drinking bar he had looked into, but the place was cleaner, brighter – and quieter. Behind the counter were shelves of white pottery jars decorated with black letters, glass bottles of gleaming boiled sugar sweets and pastel-coloured syrups, and a massive polished steamer and brass till. Several people, some dressed in blue serge uniforms with peaked caps, sat at tables spread out between two rooms separated by a partition that fell a door's width short of the wall.

'Can I help you?' A stout, middle-aged woman in a black dress, white apron and cap asked from behind the counter.

'Coffee.'

'Milk, sugar?'

He hesitated before deciding to take everything on offer. 'Yes.'

'Only one sugar mind. I'll bring it to your table. Where are you sitting?'

A young girl sat alone at a table squeezed in between the counter and the front door, a pretty, young girl with glossy, brown hair and brown eyes who smiled when he looked at her.

'Here.' He pointed to the table.

'That's the family table, sir.'

'What family?'

'It's all right, Maggie.' Liza lifted up the newspaper she'd been reading to make room for him. 'Angelo will probably be arguing with Tony in the back for the next half-hour. You know what they're like.'

'It'll be your funeral if Angelo's the jealous sort. One coffee coming up.' Maggie banged the metal jug against the steamer to show her disapproval as she mixed the milk.

'You look exactly like Uncle Charlie,' Liza said as Peter unbuttoned his jacket and shifted the knife in his pocket before sitting down, 'so I'm guessing you're the son he's been expecting.'

'Who is this Charlie?' he demanded truculently, sounding angrier than he'd intended.

'Charlie Raschenko.'

'I only know Feodor Raschenko.'

'When he first came to Pontypridd people couldn't get their tongues around "Feodor" so someone called him Charlie and the name stuck.'

'"Tongues around"?'

'It's slang, it means that people here found it difficult to say Feodor.'

'Then they're stupid. Feodor's not difficult to say.'

'Not if you're Russian but it's different for the Welsh. It's like "tongues around". If you're not used to the way people speak in a place, even though you know all the words you still might misunderstand the meaning. Every area in Britain has its own slang. Take me, for instance, I don't come from round here and when I first arrived I couldn't understand half of what people said to me. I'm Liza Clark by the way and I take it you are something Raschenko?'

'Peter.'

'I never thought a Russian would speak such good English.'

269

'Because you think Russians are stupid?'

'No more than people in Pontypridd. You get clever and stupid everywhere you go, don't you? What I meant was, it's not easy to learn languages. I can't speak one single word of Russian or any language besides English, although plenty of people here have tried to teach me Welsh.'

'Languages are easy to learn.'

'Not for me. When did you arrive?'

'Today.'

'And you're out tonight.'

'I wanted to see what the town was like.'

'So, what do you think of Pontypridd?'

'It's a town like any other,' he answered in an off-hand way, hoping the comment would make him sound well travelled and worldly-wise. 'How do you know so much about me?'

'Because my adoptive mother, Mrs John, went to London to get you and your mother with your father.'

'Bethan John is your mother?'

'She adopted me and my sisters after my father was killed in the war.'

'Why did she do that?'

'That's an odd question. I suppose because she's kind.'

'You're very pretty,' he said suddenly, earning a black look from Maggie as she dumped his coffee on the table in front of him. He put his hand in his pocket and offered her one of the half-crowns.

'You pay before you leave.'

'But I could leave any time.'

'And if you don't pay your bill before you go I'll chase after you.'

Peter looked Maggie up and down. 'You wouldn't catch me.'

'Less of your lip, young man,' she retorted tartly, returning to the counter.

He looked at Liza. ' "Lip" . . . ?'

'You settle your bill as you leave the café in case you want anything else after your first order. Another coffee or a piece of toast or cake,' Liza explained. 'If you do, it will be added to your bill, then you pay for everything in one go when you finally leave.'

'It's not like that anywhere else I've been.'

'Pontypridd may take a bit of getting used to. As I said, I had trouble when I first came here. I'm from London.'

'I saw London today.'

'Not the London I knew. That's been flattened in the bombing.'

The door opened and closed behind him but Peter couldn't stop looking at Liza long enough to check out the newcomer. 'You really are very beautiful.'

'I'm not, just average really.'

'I would like to go to bed with you.'

'Hey, young man, that's no way to talk to a lady.'

'Uncle Huw?' Liza smiled up at the policeman. 'Have you met Charlie's son?'

'Not yet. What was it that you just said to this lady, young man?'

'That she's very beautiful and I would like to go to bed with her.' Peter's face reddened as he realised that most of the people in the café were staring at him.

'He's having trouble with his English, Uncle Huw,' Liza explained. 'What he really meant is he would like to ask me out. Isn't that right, Peter?'

'I hope that's what he meant.' Angelo had left the back room and was standing behind the counter next to them.

'Of course it is, Angelo. Meet Peter Raschenko, Charlie's son. In Britain we shake hands,' she whispered in Peter's ear.

Peter stood up and took Angelo's hand, shaking it firmly. 'Hello.'

'Hello, I'm Angelo Ronconi, and she,' he pointed at Liza, 'is my girlfriend, which means she doesn't go out with anyone except me.'

'You're going to marry her?'

'As soon as she'll have me. And that coffee is on the house. A welcome to Pontypridd present,' he clarified, as a mystified expression crossed Peter's face. 'Liza, I didn't know you were here but seeing as how you are, I'm taking you home. I've had just about all I can take of this place for one day.'

'That's me finished if his Lordship is taking over.' Maggie unfastened her apron and dropped it on the counter.

'Maggie, please, finish the shift. For me,' Angelo pleaded.

'Not for six months' wages. Enough is enough. I'm going.'

'We still going home?' Liza asked Angelo.

'We most certainly are. Good night, Huw, good night, Peter, it was nice to meet you.' He opened the door to the kitchen; Tony was nowhere in sight. 'Tony,' he called out loudly, 'I'm leaving. The café is all yours and as you're the only one in, I suggest you take over.' His conscience kept him at the foot of the stairs until he heard Tony moving about, but he carried his coat outside, and put it on in the street lest Tony call him back.

Wrapping his arm around Liza, he pulled her close. 'Home straight away or the sofa outside the function room in the restaurant for half an hour first?'

'The sofa.' She kissed his cheek. 'I've missed you.'

'Not one tenth as much as I've missed you. Did I ever tell you how beautiful you are, or how much I want to marry you?'

'I think we've just proved that sixteen years isn't that long.' Charlie sat up in bed and lit a cigarette.

'I never thought I'd see you again . . .'

'No tears.' Charlie lifted the edge of the sheet and blotted them gently away.

'You have always made me so very, very happy – then – and now.'

'And you me.' He tried not to think of Alma as he pulled Masha's head down on to his shoulder. 'I thought I had lost you for ever.'

'It's a miracle I found you again and when we go back to Russia –'

'Go back!' He switched on the bedside light and stared at her. 'You want to go back to Russia after the camps – after everything that happened to you and Peter?'

'But of course we're going back.' She stared up at him in bewilderment. 'We can't live here, Feo. We are Russians, this isn't our country. We need to hear our language, to breathe Russian air, to feel Russian soil beneath our feet, to feast our eyes on the woods, sink our hands into the lakes . . .'

'Masha, this is where I live now.'

'No Russian can live outside Russia. He can barely exist.'

'So the poets say, but I have been existing well enough for the last twelve years to want to stay here.'

'You don't understand. The man who told me you were married –'

'The British officer.'

'No, the politruk.'

Charlie's mind worked feverishly. 'A Communist commissar told you I had another wife?'

'Yes. He came to see me in the displaced persons' camp in Germany.'

'Did he talk to Peter as well?'

'No, he said he had no reason to talk to Peter. You're an important man now, Feodor. That's why the politruk came looking for me and why he told the British about me so you could be found. You are needed in Russia, Feo, to help rebuild the country after the war. The politruk warned that you might not want to go back but it is our duty to repay the debt we owe to Mother Russia . . .'

'You and Peter paid any debt we owed to Mother Russia ten times over, Masha.'

'Please, Feo, don't be angry about the past, not now. The politruk promised that we could move back to our village. Have our old house . . .'

'On condition you asked me to go back to Russia?' Charlie could hardly believe what Masha was saying. That twelve years and a world war after he had left the Soviet Union the government was still concerned enough about him to find his wife and use her to get him to return to his homeland. This had nothing to do with him being imprisoned for asking questions and looking for Masha, or even escaping and taking a job as a seaman and jumping ship in Cardiff. This was something far more.

'Yes, of course he asked me to persuade you to return. But what kind of Russian doesn't want to live in his own country?'

'And Pasha?'

'Pasha is just a boy, Feo. He is not important like you but he is our son, so of course he will go back with us.'

'Did the politruk tell you what I did in the war?'

'He said you were a hero. That you fought with our British allies but you never forgot that you are a Russian.'

'There isn't a Russian born who can forget that. Masha, I love Russia, it's my country, will always be my country but I am not going back.'

'A Russian is nothing without his country.'

'This Russian would be dead back in his country and without Pasha to look after you, so would you.'

'You're talking nonsense. They explained it all. The village had to go for the collective good. But it is done now. There are no more kulaks, no more individuals who think only of themselves and their families. Now everything is different and it will be different for us. As an important man you would be given your own house, Feo. Just think, your – our – old house. Remember the garden – the woods behind – the fields? Think of it, Feo, the three of us living together in your father's house. The Raschenko house once again full of family. Peter will find himself a girl, bring her home just as you brought me and carried me over the threshold. His children will be born in the bedroom where we made him. We will have grandchildren . . .'

'Whatever the politruk told you, whatever he promised, I – and you, Masha – would be sent to the camps.' He knew it was far more likely that both of them, and Pasha, would have bullets pumped into the back of their skulls the moment they stepped across the Russian border, but he kept that thought to himself.

'But I thought you knew. That you understood that was why I came here, to explain that you don't have to stay away any longer. That you can go home.' Weak, exhausted, both physically and emotionally, she began to cry.

Charlie took her in his arms again and pulled her back beneath the covers. 'Hush, Masha, hush. We don't have to talk about this now. Come now, it's time to sleep. We'll speak in the morning.'

As his soft words gradually took effect, her eyes closed, and her sobs subsided. He lay, cradling her, pacing his own breaths to her shallow ones – and thinking. He had been a fool to believe that the re-emergence of Masha into his life after so many years had been down to mere coincidence. That out of all the displaced millions of slave labourers from Hitler's Reich – Jews, Russians, Poles, Eastern Europeans of every nationality and creed – someone had 'by chance' connected him with Masha.

Tomorrow he would make a telephone call, and arrange to talk to a senior officer in the section that had employed him during the war. If there were any decisions to be made, he would need help from them. But even more he needed all the assistance he could get to convince Masha that Russia was the last place either of them – or Pasha – should return to.

'You don't like the coffee, boy?'

Peter made a wry face. 'It doesn't taste the way I expected it to.'

'It never does,' Huw revealed. 'Coffee always smells better than it tastes. Is this your first cup?'

'I've had coffee plenty of times,' Peter boasted unconvincingly.

'So have I, but a wartime coffee isn't as good as a peacetime and I have a longer memory than you to remember what peacetime coffee was like.' He sat back in his chair. 'So what do you think of Pontypridd?'

'That is what Liza asked me. I haven't been here long enough to find out.'

'Tell you what, why don't I walk you back to your father's house and show you some of the sights along the way.'

'You know where my father lives?'

'Everyone in town knows Russian Charlie. Your father is a well-respected and important businessman.'

'He works in a shop,' Peter sneered.

'He owns the shop.'

'He has bought it, like the house?'

'Come on, I'll show you where it is.' Leaving his chair he nodded to Tony, who was standing, scowling behind the till, and opened the door.

'Can you smell it, boy?' he asked as they stepped out into the cold.

'What?' Peter asked suspiciously, watching as Huw stood tall and straight, sniffing the air.

'Spring. And after the long winter we've had, we need it.'

'It's not so cold today,' Peter answered dismissively.

'Cold enough for me, although you are probably used to colder.'

'In Russia we have snow six feet deep and the temperature drops so low the rivers freeze over.'

'After weather that cold, you'll have no trouble adjusting to our winters. But still, it will be nicer for you to get to know the town in the warm weather. See that lane up there?' He pointed out an opening between two shops. 'That's one of the entrances to the park. Everyone in town goes there in spring and summer. There's tennis courts, swimming pools, football and cricket pitches. If you like sport, that's the place to go. And if you just like sitting around taking in the sun and doing nothing in particular, it is still the place to go. You'll come across all the young people in town there. And that is the New Inn.' He indicated an imposing façade across the road. 'It's one of the oldest buildings in Pontypridd and most people think the best hotel in town. I'll take you for a drink in there some time.'

'Vodka?' Peter asked.

Huw laughed.

'That's funny?' Peter was instantly on the defensive.

'No, I was just thinking you're your father's son all right. When he first came to Pontypridd that was all he used to drink and because you can't smell it on a man's breath, most people didn't think he drank at all. But my sister – Charlie lodged with her at the time – soon cottoned on. She said she didn't need to smell drink to know a man had been at the bottle, just look in his eyes.'

'My father gets drunk?'

'Never that I've seen,' Huw lied stoutly. 'Up there,' he pointed left, 'is Market Street. Markets are held there every Wednesday and Saturday and people come from miles around to shop there. I'm a policeman and I shouldn't say it, but if you want clothes, food – anything off the ration book – that's the place to get it.'

'You buy there?'

'Sometimes. Come on, we'll walk up this way, then I'll take you past your father's shop and home.'

'Your brothers never close the café at twelve sharp. They always wait until the last customers are ready to leave.'

'And I'm telling you that you are ready to leave, Dai,' Tony ushered the railway worker to the door.

'But my shift doesn't start for another half-hour. Where am I supposed to go until then?'

'The waiting room.'

'Real bloody joker, aren't you?'

Closing the door behind Dai, Tony rammed the bolts home and turned down the lights. Running lightly up the stairs, he tapped at the bedroom door. He had to knock three times before Gabrielle answered and he could have sworn she sounded tearful more than sleepy.

'It's me, Tony.'

'Go away, you can't come into my bedroom before we are married.'

'I have to talk to you – explain about tonight. The café . . .'

'I'm tired.'

'I'll be back in the morning. You'll be all right?'

'As you can't stay here before we are married, Tony, I will have to be.'

Tony ran back down the stairs, checked all the windows and doors on the ground floor, then double locked the front door and began the long walk up the Graig Hill.

Gabrielle turned her tear-soaked pillow over to the dry side and lay back staring at the pattern drawn by the streetlights on the ceiling. She had come to Britain prepared to help her husband. To work alongside him in a fine hotel or restaurant. She had imagined herself dressed in a white blouse and dark skirt behind a desk, greeting people as they came to stay. Ringing the bell to call the porter to carry their bags to their rooms, typing polite letters to suppliers as she'd typed letters for Tony's commanding officer, arranging flowers on the reception desk and in the dining room. But never working in a dirty little café across the road from a railway station, with a flat above it that didn't even have a bathroom or kitchen.

But what could she do? Write to her mother to beg her to borrow money for a ticket home – no, not home – the Russians had taken her home. So it would have to be that one horrible little room in Celle. And to do that she would have to admit that coming to Britain and getting engaged to Tony had been a terrible mistake. That her mother had been right and she had been wrong about Tony and she should never have agreed to marry a man who hadn't made higher rank than sergeant.

She had her pride. She would die sooner than admit her mother had been right all along. But neither would she stay in these dreadful rooms over a nasty little café that catered for workmen of a type she would never have spoken to before the war. Tomorrow . . . she'd think of something tomorrow – when she wasn't so exhausted and tired by the journey – and all the lies Tony had told her.

Unable to sleep, Charlie left Masha's bed, pulled on his

pyjama trousers and dressing gown and went downstairs. The kitchen was warm and cosy and he set the kettle on the stove to boil. He'd just wet the tea and reached for the vodka bottle he'd hidden behind the books Alma had found, when the key turned in the door.

'Peter?' he called.

'And Huw,' Huw answered. 'Is that tea I smell?'

'I've never known a man with a nose like yours.' Charlie opened the door to the passage. 'I've just made it. Would you like a cup, Peter?'

'No.'

Charlie looked at the boy. He was quieter, more subdued than he'd expected him to be after his first foray into the outside world, and Huw was smiling. So, the outing hadn't turned into the disaster Masha had been afraid of and he'd feared, for all the reassurance he'd given her.

'I found some vodka to spice it up.' He held up the bottle.

'Make mine without your firewater. I'm on duty.' Huw walked through to the kitchen. 'Nice place you got here.'

'Thank you.' Charlie reached for two more cups and filled both to the brim with milk and tea before handing Peter the vodka bottle but Peter forestalled him by taking a great gulp of tea to make more room in the cup.

'I found this one,' Huw slapped Peter's shoulders, 'in Ronconi's chatting up Liza Clark, much to Angelo's disgust.'

'I was just being friendly. Huw showed me your shop. You didn't say you owned it.'

'You didn't ask.'

'Is my mother well?'

'She's sleeping.'

'Peter was telling me that he is something of a mechanic.'

'I didn't know.' Charlie looked at his son, not sure whether to believe his bragging to Huw, or not.

'It was my job to make sure all the lorries in the cement factory worked. I stripped down and cleaned the engines when they wouldn't and later on I showed other men how to do it.'

'And repaired them?' Huw asked.

'When the Germans had parts to give us to replace the broken ones.'

'Ronnie was only saying tonight in Megan's that he and Will were thinking of looking round for another mechanic. If you want a job, Peter, you could do worse than work for them.'

'They are more friends of yours?' Peter glowered at Charlie.

'You'll soon find out that everyone knows everyone else in Pontypridd,' Huw explained. 'They're either friends or not so friendly, but in this case, yes, William and Ronnie are friends of your father's. Good ones. I'll mention you to Ronnie if you like.'

'Can I see him tomorrow?'

'He'll be in the garage on Broadway. That's the street straight on from the café you were in tonight. It's on the right-hand side of the road. You can't miss it.'

'I'll find it.'

'Well, much as I hate working cold winter nights, this town won't look after itself.' Huw handed Charlie his cup and rose to his feet. 'Thanks for the tea.'

'And thank you for looking after him,' Charlie whispered, as he walked Huw to the front door.

'He's not a bad boy, your Peter, but you need to work on his English. He asked Liza to sleep with him.'

'He what?'

'She said it was just a language problem, but I'm not so sure.'

'Neither am I.' Locking and bolting the door behind Huw, Charlie returned to the kitchen where Peter was uncorking the vodka. Taking the bottle from him, he put it on the sideboard, out of reach.

'So, what do you think of Pontypridd?'

'I think everyone in Pontypridd asks the same question.'

'You think you'll be able to live here?' Charlie enquired cautiously.

'You thinking of sending me somewhere else,' Peter probed warily.

The boy's answer told Charlie all he wanted to know. 'You don't want to go back to Russia.'

'Would you want to go back to a camp?'

'No.'

'Then why do you think I want to go back to one?'

'Have you talked to your mother about where she wants to live?'

'All she has ever talked about was being with you.'

'She never said anything about wanting to go back to Russia?'

Peter pushed his teacup across the table and glared at his father. 'If you want to go back there, you can go alone. And I'll kill you before I'll let you take my mother or me with you.' Leaving his chair, he slammed the table with his fist. 'I won't let you! I won't –'

'Quiet! You'll wake your mother. The last thing I want to do is go back to Russia.'

'Then why are you talking about it?'

'I'll tell you in the morning.'

'You'll tell me now.'

'Your mother said tonight that she wants us all to go back there.'

The coal settled in the stove, crackling like machine-gun fire as the embers fell through the grating at the bottom of the oven. Peter jumped instinctively.

'You didn't understand her . . .'

'I understood but I needed to know what you thought about going back. And now I know, it's time for bed.' Charlie pushed the chair he'd been sitting on under the table, gathered the cups on to a tray and took them into the wash house. On his return he picked up the vodka.

'Afraid I'll drink all of it?'

'Yes.'

'I would too.' For the first time the boy smiled.

'I know you would. I remember what I was like at your age. Just one more thing: I'm aware that camp life is different and that you grew up in them and haven't had a chance to find out what life is like on the outside. But when you meet young girls for the first time, may I suggest that you don't ask them to go to bed with you.'

'Huw told you.'

'Only because he's afraid you'll get into trouble. If Liza Clark hadn't known who you were and had made a formal complaint you could have been taken into the police station and charged with disturbing the peace.'

'And be deported?'

Once again Charlie saw fear in Peter's eyes, confirming that any thoughts of returning to Russia were entirely Masha's idea and not the boy's.

'Yes, and the least you'll risk if you try it again with someone else is a punch on the nose from an irate boy-friend, brother or father.'

'I've never been beaten in a fight.'

The look in Peter's eyes told Charlie he was lying but he let it pass. 'And if you beat someone here, the police may arrest you for assault. Next time you meet a girl you like, try saying, *Can I buy you a coffee and talk to you?* or *Would you like to come for a walk in the park with me?* or *May I take you to the pictures?*'

'And afterwards the girl will go to bed?'

'No, it doesn't work that way. Most couples in this country only go to bed together after they're married.'

'Then I'll have to ask a girl to marry me.'

'Not until you know her really well and never the first time you meet her. Courtship takes a long time. If you go too fast with the right kind of girl, you'll frighten her off.'

'I didn't frighten Liza Clark.'

'Because she's a nice girl who knows you've been in camps all your life and made allowances for your behaviour. You were very lucky to choose her out of all the women in the town to talk to tonight.' Checking round the room Charlie opened the door. 'Coming to bed?'

'Later. I want to read a magazine.' Peter felt he had to make a stand for independence.

'See you in the morning.'

Peter sat in his chair and listened as his father walked

up the stairs, he heard the floorboards creak on the landing, looked up at the ceiling and knew with absolute certainty that his father had gone into his mother's bedroom.

All he could think of was, she couldn't have any pride. To take him back into her life – and her bed – the very first night in his house. No pride at all.

Chapter Seventeen

TONY SPENT ALL morning leaning against the wall that separated the café from the kitchen. One half of it backed on to the staircase that led upstairs, and he listened intently for the sound of Gabrielle stirring. As soon as he heard the creak of a tread, he heated up the coffee he'd prepared for her, flung open the door and picked up the breakfast tray he'd set out with bread, a sliver of real butter, jam, coffee jug and cup and saucer.

She was just walking back into the kitchen from the outside Ty Bach. A light sprinkling of raindrops glistening on her long, red woollen dressing gown and fair hair, plaited loosely into a rope that fell almost to her waist. She looked tired, sleepy and to his eyes – very beautiful.

'Good morning, Gabrielle,' he murmured, not at all sure of the reception she'd give him after the arguments of the previous night.

'Good morning, Tony.' Her reply was terse. Any frostier and he'd have turned to ice.

'Here you go, miss, hot water.' The cook handed her a china jug full of hot water.

'I've made you breakfast,' Tony held up the tray.

'I prefer to eat breakfast after I've washed and dressed.'

'Of course. I'll bring it up later. When would you like it? In ten minutes, quarter of an hour or do you need more time?'

Taking the jug she turned and walked back up the stairs without answering him. Hearing shouting, Tony rushed into the café.

'Be glad we're honest,' a bus conductor griped. 'We could have walked off with everything behind here, including the till if we'd wanted.'

'You wouldn't have found much in it if you had.'

Taking the money the man offered, Tony rang up the cash register. The conductor was right, there was no way he could manage the café without a waitress. Opening the door into the kitchen he called to the cook's boy, 'Run down to the restaurant and ask Mr Angelo if he's had any luck finding a replacement waitress for this place.'

'Still can't get anyone to work for you, Tony.'

He turned to see Judy Crofter sitting on a stool she'd pulled up to the counter, her dyed blonde hair scraped back under a black beret, her pale face highlighted with layers of garishly coloured face paint.

'I told you not to come back in here,' he said, very conscious of Gabrielle upstairs.

'You did, but I've been to see a solicitor since then.' She smiled and nodded to a railway porter as he came up to pay for his second breakfast. 'I'll have a tea, please, Tony, weak and black and a slice of toast and Marmite.' There was a quiet confidence in her demeanour that unnerved Tony. He took the porter's money, rang it into the till and poured her tea.

'Are you going to tell me why you went to see a solicitor or do I have to drag it out of you?'

'I'm pregnant and I'm naming you as the father.'

'A likely bloody story.' His face darkened as he confronted her.

'All I have to do after the baby's born is demand a blood test. It is yours, Tony.' Her voice was low but it held more menace than if she'd screamed and shouted at the top of her voice. 'Since you, I've only gone out with Glan Richards, and there's been no hanky-panky there. He'd swear it on a stack of Bibles because although he's tried every trick in the book to get my knickers down I wouldn't play with him. You see, Tony, you've ruined it for me with every other man.' She reached for her handkerchief.

'You can stop the theatricals, you silly cow. And what about before Glan? How many were there then?'

'I'll not lie. There were a couple of Yanks, nice lads, but they went back months ago. Before you, Tony, there

285

wasn't a soul for six months. I told the solicitor about your small-minded threat to tell the police that I'm a prostitute but he said you'd have to find half a dozen men who'd paid to have sex with me, and your brothers wouldn't do. The police are getting a bit wary of men denouncing their girlfriends as prostitutes when they get pregnant. And let's face it, when the baby comes I'll be able to prove you're the father.'

'No you won't. All a blood test can prove is that someone is not the father.'

'There's too much evidence against you, Tony. You said it yourself. Everyone in the Graig Hotel knows you took me home that night. You were found drunk and naked outside my door. I showed my father your underwear . . .'

'You what!'

'I had no choice; he's seen me being sick in the morning. He wanted to know who the father was. I told him.'

'Great, now it will be all over the bloody Graig that I slept with you.'

'My father doesn't want the news broadcast any more than I do. It's a disgrace enough having a bastard, without it being fathered by a Nazi lover who wants to marry a German. But my father has agreed that I can carry on living at home and bring the baby up there if I keep house for him and my brothers.'

'They're home?' Tony's blood ran cold. He was acquainted with two of Judy's brothers, burly six-footers who'd been local heavyweight boxing champions before the war.

'They will be soon. As the solicitor told me, and as I see it, you can go one of two ways. Either you accept this baby as yours, and pay me maintenance or I'll take you to court and drag your name through the mud. One thing's for sure: I'm not footing the bill for bringing your brat up on my own. And I'm not going into no workhouse either. You had your fun, I don't see why you shouldn't pay for it.' Taking a cigarette from her handbag she lit it. 'Are you going to make me my toast and Marmite?'

Tony reached for the bread. 'How much maintenance do you want?'

'Fifteen bob a week.'

'I can't afford that. I'm getting married.'

'You should have thought about that before you put it about with me. Poor bitch, even if she is German. I feel sorry for her getting lumbered with a swine like you.'

'Look, tell you what I'll do. I'll give you your old job back.'

'Twilight shift, thanks but no thanks.'

'You can have the daytime shift here. I'll pay . . .' he made a few rapid calculations, 'one pound fifteen shillings a week. That's five bob above the odds.'

'Haven't you heard a word I've said? I'm having your baby. I should be taking it easy, not working.'

Gabrielle opened the connecting door and joined Tony behind the counter. She was wearing a knitted, belted brown dress embellished with circles of embroidered yellow daisies at the yoke and hem. It accentuated her bust, trim waist and smoothly rounded hips. With her hair neatly coiled into a plaited bun at the nape of her neck, she looked cool, elegant, and in comparison to Judy, a lady who'd inadvertently wandered into the company of a chorus girl.

'Good morning.' She smiled at Judy. 'Would you introduce me to your friend please, Tony?'

'Judy Crofter, she used to waitress here.'

'And you must be Tony's German fiancée.'

'Gabrielle von Stettin, I am pleased to meet you.' Gabrielle held out her hand and Judy touched the tips of her fingers.

'Judy Crofter and I'm pleased to meet you too, I'm sure. Well, Tony, seeing as how you've no one here at the moment, I'll start back immediately but it will be an extra ten bob a week not five. What do you say?'

'Five,' he growled.

'I don't see anyone else here who can do the job.'

'Ten for this week, we'll discuss it again before Sunday.'

'Too true, I don't work Sundays.' She smiled at Gabrielle. 'I hope you will be very happy, Fräulein von Stettin. Would you like me to get you breakfast?'

'Did you enjoy your lie-in?'

'It was absolute heaven. Although Polly and Nell complained when my alarm went off at six.'

'You set it?' Bethan asked in surprise.

'Always when I have a day off so I can switch it off and turn over. An extra couple of hours in bed is my idea of absolute bliss, and there's no point in having them unless you're aware of the luxury. Shall I make some tea?'

'Yes, please, and some breakfast for yourself.'

'Toast will be fine. I'm meeting Angelo in the restaurant at one when it closes for the afternoon. He's going to cook for me.'

'You're lucky he and Alfredo are running the restaurant, not the café.'

'Angelo warned that he won't get every Thursday afternoon and Sunday off. Although the restaurant keeps to shop hours, Tony will expect him and Alfredo to relieve him now and again.'

'Tony will need it. Tina was always complaining about being on call eighteen hours a day when she lived over the café.'

'And Tony's girlfriend arrived last night.'

'What is she like?'

'I didn't see her but there was a big row between Gina, Angelo and Tony. Angelo didn't say much about it but I gather Tony had told the girl that he, not the family, owned the café. Angelo said she took one look at the rooms Gina had worked hard on all day and asked Tony if they could sell the place and buy something better.'

'Poor girl.' Bethan pushed a pin into the hem of a skirt she'd cut for Rachel from one of her old ones.

'Why poor girl? Angelo said she was stuck up.'

'She might have been exhausted rather than stuck up, considering she'd just travelled for days to get here.'

'I suppose so. As I said I didn't see her, only heard the

row between Angelo and Tony.' Liza went to the pantry and opened the bread bin. Taking out a loaf she cut two neat slices and speared one on a toasting fork before filling the kettle. 'Auntie Beth, when did you know that you were in love with Dr John?'

Taken aback by the question, Bethan wondered if the gossip about her and David Ford had reached Liza, then realised the girl was probably talking about her own relationship with Angelo.

'I've never really thought about it.'

'You must have.'

'I'm not trying to avoid answering,' she said quickly, suspecting that it couldn't have been easy for Liza to ask such a personal question. 'I suppose I just accepted the way things worked out between us. He came to the Graig Hospital when I was training. He was young, newly qualified, and by far and away the best-looking doctor in Pontypridd. He'd also lived in London, had a car and his own flat. And those things alone were enough to set every nurse in the hospital after him.'

'So you chased him?'

'No, oddly enough I didn't. Not because I didn't like the look of him but because I assumed he wouldn't want to know me. Our families and backgrounds were completely different. When Andrew noticed me at the hospital dance and asked me to go out with him, I did, but only because all the other nurses persuaded me I would have had to be mad to refuse. I never thought for one minute that it would last longer than that first outing. But Andrew put up with a lot – not just from me, but my family. Once we started going out together on a regular basis my mother, father and brothers assumed he was only after one thing.'

'Your body.' Liza spooned tea into the pot.

Bethan smiled. 'Definitely my body, not that my figure was ever that wonderful.'

'So you only went out with him at first because he was young, handsome, had a car, flat and a good job?'

'That makes me sound like a gold-digger. I went out

with him because he asked me, was prepared to organise outings on my days off, and because by then I liked him and we had fun together. He took me to places few people could afford to go to in those days – theatres, circuses, drives in his car. The pits were closed; no one had any money. I handed most of my wages over to my father to keep the family, not that I'm complaining – nearly all the nurses in the Graig had to do the same. I was no different or any harder done by. It was just a bad time.'

'But there must have been one moment, one special moment when you realised you wanted to spend the rest of your life with him?' Liza urged.

'Have you had that moment with Angelo?' Bethan asked intuitively, deliberately turning the conversation around.

'No, that's why I'm asking. Like you with Dr John, when we first started going out together, I liked him a lot. He's young, handsome, earns good money, takes me places – when we both can get time off . . .'

'And he makes you wonderful meals in the restaurant.'

'Yes.' Liza laughed as she poured boiling water on to the leaves in the pot. 'And given the food in the nurses' hostel and Royal Infirmary, that's something not to be sneezed at. I admit it, Angelo's a fantastic cook and I enjoy eating the meals he makes for me.'

'More than his company?'

'No.'

'But something's not right.'

'It's probably me. I always thought that when I fell in love it would be momentous, huge, like Cinderella at the ball.'

'And it was like that between you and Maurice?'

'You saw me, Auntie Beth, you know what I was like. I couldn't breathe when he was around. I couldn't wait to see him and when I did, all I wanted to do – all I was capable of doing, was just sitting and staring at him.'

'We all noticed. But both of you were very young.'

'So, was it that way between us because we were young and it was the first time either of us had felt that way? Or

290

was it because of the war and we both knew that he could be killed as soon as he got sent overseas? Or was it because I loved him more than I do Angelo?'

'That's a lot of questions and I can't help you on the last one. Only you can know whether you loved Maurice more than you do Angelo. But I do know that when you're young everything seems that much more intense. Everything is new, not just each other but even the idea that you can fall in love . . .' Bethan paused, remembering what it had been like when she and Andrew had first begun to make love. She looked across at Liza. 'Are you and Angelo . . . ?'

'You won't be angry if I tell you we have – are.'

'I'm not angry. You're nineteen, Liza. You've been going out with Angelo for nearly a year.'

'And I'm very careful. A girl doesn't have to get pregnant these days.'

'No. One good thing that came out of the war was all the publicity about French letters. Before the war doctors would only prescribe them to married couples, and then only if the woman's health would be endangered by pregnancy.' Bethan couldn't help recalling her hasty, hole-in-the-corner, registry office wedding in London when she had been six months pregnant with her first child.

'And I do like Angelo very much. He's asked me to marry him but . . .'

'You're not sure.'

'I can't stop thinking about Maurice and wishing we'd made love just once, and then there's my training. I want to finish it and become a nurse.'

'That, I think, is a very good idea. You're too bright to hide all that talent away in domestic drudgery just yet.'

'That's what I keep telling Angelo. The problem is –' she looked at the toast she was browning over the fire, pulled it from the fork and turned it over to toast the other side – 'I want you to tell me if Angelo is my Mr Right when, as you said, no one can possibly know the answer to that question except me.'

'Have you considered the reason you're asking is that you already know Angelo isn't the one for you?'

'Or is he, and I'm crying for the moon because I want Maurice back and I can't have him?'

'Have you met anyone else?' Bethan asked perceptively.

'Where would I meet someone else?'

'In the hospital. You're a nurse, you must meet lots of young doctors, just as I met Dr John.'

'The doctors in Cardiff Infirmary treat nurses like lepers. They'd never dream of considering any of us as human, let alone women with feelings.'

'Come on . . .'

'Have you ever picked a towel up off the floor after a doctor's dried his hands on it in front of you and dropped it, sooner than contaminate his fingers by touching yours?'

'Unfortunately, yes. And now you mention it I can even remember what it felt like.'

'And every free moment I get away from the hospital I spend in Pontypridd, and as Angelo's here, there's no chance of meeting anyone else.' She slipped the first piece of toast from the fork on to a plate and buttered it.

'Perhaps you should make a point of going to other places.'

'If I did that I wouldn't see you and my sisters. But what if Angelo *is* the right man for me, Auntie Beth, and I'm looking for something that doesn't exist? That's why I wanted to know the exact moment you realised you were in love with Dr John and he was the only man for you.'

'I'm not sure I'm the best person to talk to about this, Liza. You see, looking back I don't think there ever was such a moment. And my relationship with Andrew hasn't been all red roses and romance, not in the picture-book sense. It's no secret in Pontypridd that he only married me because I was pregnant.'

'I'm sorry, I didn't mean to pry.'

'It's not a good beginning for a marriage. I loved him, but when we married I couldn't be sure he was marrying me because he wanted to and he loved me, or out of a sense of duty to me and the baby. Then we set up home in London.' Bethan laid the sewing on her lap, picked up the tea Liza had poured for her and hunched over, staring into the fire. 'It was awful. I didn't know a soul apart from Andrew. We lived in a poky little flat, and the baby was ill.'

'Rachel?'

'No. His name was Edmund. He died not long after he was born.'

'I'm so sorry, Auntie Beth. I shouldn't have asked you all these questions.'

'I'm glad you did in a way, because in asking the questions you might be able to learn from my mistakes. And it's ancient history now.' Bethan tried to smile and failed. 'I have Rachel, Eddie, and you and Polly and Nell and half-shares in Mary. Six, happy healthy children.'

'And Dr John.'

'And Dr John,' Bethan echoed, 'but remember what I said, Liza, and be careful. Making love is wonderful, and especially wonderful when it's with the one person you love and value above all others. But having to marry because a baby is on the way is no way to begin life together, because you can never be sure of one another's motives for marrying, or whether your husband resents you for pushing him into taking responsibility he didn't want or wasn't ready for. If you're not sure Angelo is the right one for you, perhaps it might be an idea for you to stop seeing him for a while. Take a break, meet other boys. In a month or two you may feel differently about Angelo or find someone else. Who knows, maybe even another Maurice?'

'There'll never be another Maurice, Auntie Beth, perhaps that's the problem. One of the girls in the hostel thinks that everyone has only one soul mate. If you don't meet him, or he ups and dies on you, that's it. You have to wait until you're reunited in heaven.'

'And I think she's had a sad experience in the war.'

The door slammed and Andrew shouted from the hall. Liza jumped out of her chair.

'Hello, Dr John,' she greeted Andrew as he walked in. 'Would you like a cup of tea?'

'That would be lovely, thank you, Liza, and as you're

my adopted daughter do you think you can bring yourself to call me Uncle Andrew like Polly and Nell?'

'I'll try but it won't be easy. All through the war Auntie Bethan and everyone else referred to you as Dr John and that's how I always think of you. Is that the time?' She looked at the clock as she gave him his tea. 'I must run down the hill or the dinner Angelo is cooking for me will be burned. 'Bye, Auntie Beth.' She kissed Bethan's cheek. ''Bye, Uncle Andrew.' To Andrew's amazement she offered him a kiss as well. 'See you later.' Charging into the hall, she picked up her coat and dashed through the front door.

'I wasn't expecting you back.'

'I had a heavy surgery, then I called into the hospital.' He sugared the tea Liza had poured for him. 'Diana's had her second session with the physiotherapist and although it's early days, the specialist and my father are cautiously optimistic that she'll regain some, if not all the movement in her left arm and leg.'

'And her memory?'

'It's early days.'

'But the specialist still thinks it could be gone for good?'

'There's tissue damage. You know as well as I do, Bethan, that compared to some of the options, memory damage is not that dreadful.'

'Try telling that to Ronnie.'

'I may have to.' He settled in the chair opposite hers and pulled out the pipe that he had bought himself a few days before as part of his drive to cut back on smoking, on the premise that a pipe was more fiddly than cigarettes and he'd be less inclined to indulge. 'So, after my full morning, I thought I'd come home for some lunch with my wife.'

Resting the skirt she'd been hemming on her lap she looked up at him. 'How long were you out in the hall?'

'Long enough,' he replied quietly.

'You heard me talking to Liza?'

'You never told me you weren't sure whether I'd

married you because of the baby. For the record I loved you, Beth, and I would have married you whether there'd been a baby or not, and even if you hadn't been able to have a baby. But tell me, would you have married me?'

'If you heard me talking to Liza you must have heard me tell her that I loved you.'

'Loved – the past tense. And you still haven't answered my question. Did you feel trapped into marrying me? I am doctor and man enough to know that in that situation women can feel just as trapped as men.'

'I married you and you married me because given your sense of responsibility and mine, there wasn't any other real option open to either of us at the time. There's no point in raking it over now. We both know that a free choice later on, without a pregnancy, would almost certainly have given us a better start.'

'And we both know that if there hadn't been a baby, or a quick and shabby registry office wedding, you would have been free to love David Ford.'

'Not David again . . .'

'Please, Bethan. I'm not shouting, I'm talking, because there are several things that need saying. Ever since I came home there's been this strain between us. I've been trying to convince myself that it's only to be expected after over five years away. In that time Rachel's grown from a baby into a proper little girl – some would even say madam. Eddie was born and reached the ripe age of four and a half before I saw him, and both of them have done very well without a father meddling in their lives. I knew when I came home – perhaps better than most of the men who came back – that nothing can ever recapture those missing years. But what I wasn't prepared for was the loss of everything we had before. The closeness – the intimacy – the shared smiles . . . Am I wrong or was there really a time when I could look into your eyes and you in mine and we'd know without saying a single word, no matter how many people were in the room, just what the other was thinking?'

When she didn't reply he pushed tobacco into his pipe, struck a match and lit it.

'A man came into the surgery today. He and his wife had quarrelled. It would be laughable if it wasn't so tragic. He was a territorial, one of the first to be called up in '39. They married because they were in love and terrified at the thought of never seeing one another again. They had a twenty-four-hour honeymoon in the back bedroom of her mother's house, then he went to France. Like me he was taken prisoner at Dunkirk. Since he's been home they've done nothing but fight. Last week she took the poker to him and broke his arm.'

'A bit excessive.'

'Some would say she suffered extreme provocation. All he's called her since he got home, is "old hag". He keeps complaining that he left behind a pretty young girl and came back to an old woman who'd lost her looks working long hours in a munitions factory. I didn't help when I suggested he look in a mirror. Six years can wreak havoc. The difference between a fresh-faced, rosy-cheeked nineteen-year-old girl and a worked-out, exhausted, twenty-five-year-old woman is considerable in his eyes. But saying that, he's lost half his hair and all his teeth. The poker incident was the last straw. Both of them have given up. They're getting a divorce.'

'Read the papers; it's happening all over the country.' The words came out easily enough but her heart was thundering when she said them. Was that what he was leading up to? A request for a divorce? Wasn't that what she wanted?

He slammed his fist down on the arm of his chair. 'Not to us, Beth. I'll be damned if I'm going to sit back and let it happen to us! Do you think I don't know how unhappy you've been since I've come home? Do you think it's been easy for me, living with you day after day, climbing into the same bed as you night after night, watching you run the house, play with the children, and never once smile at me. Oh, the children – yes, you smile at them and our friends, your father, Ronnie, Alma, Charlie, David Ford . . .'

'That's it, isn't it, Andrew? David Ford.'

'Yes,' he admitted finally, deciding that even if she walked away from him, for once he was going to tell her exactly how he felt. 'But before you say another word I know you've never made love to him and probably only kissed him once or twice and then no more passionately than you've kissed Charlie.'

'How do you know?'

'Because if you two had ever jumped into bed together he would never have come up here for dinner. He's far too much of an officer and a gentleman for that,' he derided, unable to resist the gibe.

'Then, if you know we've never slept together why are you always talking about him and why are you so jealous?'

'Because he can make you smile and laugh, and I can't. Because when I was away, he was here, making the children and you like and even love him. Because he shares memories with you that I played no part in. Maybe you didn't mean to shut me out when I came back, Beth, but I felt that you did and maybe – just maybe – that's entirely my own fault.'

'Do you realise this is the first time you've called me Beth in months? It's always been Bethan.' Her eyes were bright, but he couldn't tell whether it was from emotion or anger.

'What I'm trying to say is, will you give me and us another chance, Beth? I know what you feel for David Ford and I suspect he'd take you on tomorrow if you asked him. God! It makes my head spin to think how fast he'd take you and the children on if you told him we were getting a divorce. The stupid thing is, I've nothing against him apart from the fact that he's rather obviously fallen in love with you. He's a good man, and no doubt he'd give you and the children everything you want – in America. But I can't bear the thought of my children growing up without me, much less in another country, and I have no idea how I'd live without you. So I'm asking you to let me try and make you fall in love with me again.'

'No one can control their emotions, Andrew.'

'But we can control our lives, and it seems to me that we've both been working far too hard since I came home.'

'I haven't been working at all.'

'Yes you have – boring tedious work, running the house, trying to cope with Alma, Masha and Charlie, Ronnie and Diana's, and now Liza's problems. So many problems that have no solutions. I'll go and see my father this afternoon and ask him to take over the practice next week or bring in a locum. I know there's no way to tell, but as far as I can forecast nothing much should happen and if it does, tough. I won't be around. We'll pile the kids in the car and take them down to the chalet.'

'We were going to go down the Gower with Charlie and Alma.'

'Not this time. For once I want you to put me and us before everyone else. Will you come away with me for a week?'

'The children have school, there's the house . . .'

'The children will always have school, there's always the house. Yes or no, Beth?'

'Yes.'

'Your waitress is very efficient,' Gabrielle commented, sitting with her back to the window. She was beginning to understand why Tony had taken her breakfast tray upstairs. Every time the door clanged open she sensed another pair of eyes staring at her. The café was positively buzzing with excited whisperings.

'She's done the job before.'

'Perhaps I should hang a board around my neck: "*Genuine German girl, and former enemy.*" She tried to smile when two men who came to pay their bill stared blatantly at her.

'They'll get used to you.'

'I feel like an animal in a zoo.'

'Gabrielle, about last night,' he returned to where she was sitting on a stool at the counter. 'I'm sorry you got the wrong impression about the café.'

'You told me that you owned part of your family's

business. I assumed, as owner, you could do whatever you wanted with this place.'

'I'm sure I said I managed it. It must have been a language thing.'

'Your colonel used to tell me that my English, written and spoken, was better than that of most of the English secretaries he'd employed.'

'My mother owns everything. I work here for a wage.'

'Like the waitress.'

'I earn more than the waitress and when my mother dies . . .'

'Is your mother old or ill?'

There was a strange expression on her face making it difficult for him to decipher her train of thought. 'No.'

'You told me you have several brothers and sisters.'

'There are eleven of us.'

'Your brother Angelo mentioned last night that your family run this café and one restaurant. Are there any hotels, Tony?'

'Not yet – no,' he admitted, wishing he'd never suggested otherwise. 'But there was another café. It's rented out.'

'So, even if your mother is about to die, which I sincerely hope she isn't, there is no reason for her to leave this café to you, any more than any of your other brothers and sisters. She may even think it more sensible to leave everything she owns to all of you. In which case this café and the restaurant could be sold off to realise the money, or alternatively you could carry on working here at a wage for your family for the rest of your life.'

'You're angry with me?'

'Very angry, Tony.'

'I know this café isn't much –'

'It's not the café, Tony. It's your lies. When you asked me to be your wife I told you I loved you, but you didn't love me.'

'Of course I did.'

'Not enough to tell me the truth. You deliberately made me believe that you owned fine hotels and restaurants.'

299

'We do own a restaurant.'

'One that your brothers manage. And you promised me that we'd live in a comfortable apartment, not two rooms without a bath, a toilet in a wooden hut outside and a kitchen shared with a café, where I'd have to ask a strange man's permission every time I wanted hot water to wash myself.'

'It's not easy to find accommodation in the town at the moment with everyone coming back from the war, but I'll look. I promise you I'll try and find something better. Yes?' he snapped as a bus conductor walked up to the counter.

'When you've finished talking to your Nazi girlfriend perhaps you'd like to serve us?'

Drawing back his fist Tony punched him soundly on the nose.

Chapter Eighteen

'How's my favourite girlfriend?' Angelo asked Liza as he rang up the till, and transferred the cash already bagged in paper envelopes into a canvas sack.

'Tired after walking down the hill.' She leaned over the counter so he could kiss her.

'Will you look at that,' Maggie shouted to the other waitresses as they collected their coats and handbags, 'and it's barely dinnertime. Imagine what they'll be like after dark.'

''Bye, girls,' Angelo prompted. 'Enjoy your afternoon off. Don't do anything I wouldn't do, and shut the door behind you.'

'I haven't got the energy to do what you're doing, let alone think of things that you wouldn't, Angelo.' Maggie winked at Liza as she headed out through the door.

'Here you are, Alfredo.' Angelo tossed him the sack. 'Straight to the bank and if you're feeling generous, you could offer to take over the café for Tony this afternoon and evening so he can spend time with his girlfriend.'

'I'm not that generous,' Alfredo growled.

'Where's your heart?'

'Beating beneath my empty wallet.'

'If that's a hint for extra or an advance on wages I'm not biting.'

'Then I'm not going near the café.'

'Poor Tony.'

'Seeing as how you're the one who suggested it, why don't you take over?'

'Because I'm here, and I need him,' Liza smiled.

Alfredo picked up the sack and stuffed it in his pocket. 'And I'm going to the pictures. There's a cowboy matinée on in the Palladium.'

'Charming little brother I've got there to go with my immediate older one,' Angelo complained as Alfredo left. 'Now, what would you like to eat – or shall we go up to the landing first to whip up an appetite?'

'I would like to talk –' The telephone interrupted her. 'Shouldn't you answer that?'

'No, because it will only be someone wanting me to do something and seeing as how we both have an afternoon off I don't want to do anything that doesn't involve you.'

'It sounds urgent.'

'How can a telephone sound urgent? It's the same ringing tone if a rep's trying to sell me the latest thing in dried peas or if someone in the family has had a heart attack.'

'Angelo, I can't hear myself think.'

'Ronconi's,' he barked, finally picking up the receiver. He listened intently for a few seconds then cried, 'I'm there!' down the line. Grabbing his coat he threw the keys to Liza. 'Lock up for me.'

'Where are you going?'

'The café. Tony's been arrested. Find Alfredo and tell him I need him.'

'Hello, stranger.'

'Bethan.' Diana sat up in bed and extended her right arm to her cousin. 'I was hoping Dr John would let you come. He promised he would, but the doctors here promise a lot of things and then forget about them.'

'Mrs John, you do realise that we can't extend any privileges to you in this hospital. You might be a doctor's wife but you are no longer on staff . . .'

'I know, sister, but Dr John – senior, that is – telephoned and suggested I visit my cousin this afternoon.'

'And I've been advised that this patient is to have no unsupervised visits. As there is no doctor on this ward at present, I am afraid I will have to ask you to leave.'

'It's all right, sister, I'm here.' Andrew's father walked into the cubicle. 'You're never able to stop work on a busy ward like this for a moment, are you, sister?' he murmured sympathetically. 'Well, why don't you take the opportunity to make yourself a cup of tea and put your feet up for five minutes now. I'll let you know when we leave.'

Giving Dr John a stern look, the sister left the room.

'No extra cups of tea for me on this ward for the next year or two,' he said, not entirely humorously. 'Thanks for coming, Beth.'

'Yes, thank you.' Diana gave Bethan an enormous hug as she leaned over the bed to kiss her cheek. 'See, I can move both arms now. You will tell Mam? They won't let her back in again until Saturday.'

'Which is why I allowed Bethan in this afternoon. But I warn you, she knows she's here to calm you down and stop you asking so many questions.'

'I promised I'd be good if you allowed her to come, didn't I?'

'And I'll hold you to that promise, young lady.'

'I'll tell your mother.' Bethan sat on a chair next to the bed. 'How are you? The truth, mind.'

'Worn to a frazzle, whatever one of those is. A woman comes in three times a day to pummel me and make me do more exercises than anyone in their right mind would want to.'

'But that "woman", as you call her, has helped you to regain some control over your left arm and leg.'

'I know, Dr John, and I'm grateful. Really I am,' Diana conceded. 'But I have a million and one questions and no one will give me any answers.'

'I'm not surprised. From what I've heard your number one question is, "when can I go home?" and you're asking it ten times an hour.'

'More like twenty,' she corrected, and Bethan saw a trace of the old mischievous Diana.

'You remember home?'

'Wyn's house. Do I still live there?'

'Don't answer that, Bethan,' Dr John ordered.

'When can I see Will?'

'On Saturday, with your mother.'

'Promise?'

'You heard it from the horse's mouth.' Bethan grasped Diana's right hand. 'I've missed you and our talks.'

'Sorry I can't say the same but it would sound peculiar under the circumstances. I don't think you can miss anyone when you're in a coma. Although I really do miss Billy, and I can't begin to imagine him as a five-year-old. The doctors and nurses,' she glanced at Dr John, 'won't even let me have a photograph of him.'

'All in good time.'

'You're beginning to sound like a cracked record, Dr John.'

'And patients should show more respect to their doctor.'

Diana turned back to Bethan. 'William really has come through the war all right?'

'You know your brother, Will is more than all right. He's absolutely fine. He even made some money in Italy.'

'He was in Italy?'

Bethan looked apologetically at her father-in-law, 'Sorry, that just slipped out.'

'Make sure nothing else does.'

'What does it matter where Will was in the war, now he's back home?' Diana said, determined to be both casual and cheerful because she suspected if she showed the slightest emotion, she'd lose not only the prospective visit from her mother and William, but have this one curtailed. 'Is he working for Charlie again?'

'He's got a new job but he'll tell you all about it himself.'

'And Mam is married. What is my stepfather like, Beth?'

'Can I show Diana a photograph of Dino and Megan, Dr John?' Bethan asked.

He glanced over her shoulder as she pulled it from her bag to make sure it was just of Dino and Megan and no one else. 'That one and no others.'

Bethan handed it to Diana.

'He must be short.'

'He's taller than your mother.'

'Not by much that I can see and she's five foot nothing, although he is a whole lot wider. Mam said Billy's living with them.'

'Yes, and they're looking after him beautifully.'

'And I have a daughter?'

'You're moving on to dangerous ground, Diana,' Dr John warned.

'How am I ever going to remember the last six years if people won't talk to me about the things I've forgotten? Mam said I named her Catrina after our grandmother.'

'You did, and she's going to be a beauty.'

'She's two?'

'Yes, she's just beginning to talk in sentences and she loves playing with Billy, Eddie and Rachel –'

'Bethan, we have to go.' Dr John had suddenly realised where Diana was leading the conversation but Bethan was ahead of him and had already left her chair. 'And you, young lady,' he admonished Diana, 'were warned not to ask questions by the specialist, who only agreed Bethan could visit you on condition you kept the conversation fixed on events that you can remember.'

'If Wyn's been dead for over four years, who's Catrina's father?' Diana blurted out impatiently.

'One thing at a time, Diana.'

'She does have a father?'

'Of course she has a father,' Bethan reassured.

'I married again after Wyn was killed?'

'Yes.'

'That's a relief. At least she's not a bastard. But I can't remember . . .'

'Which is why you have to take things easy. Bethan, we really do have to go.'

'Here,' Bethan handed Diana the photograph. 'Why don't you look at this to see if it helps jog your memory. You went to your mother's wedding. She wouldn't have many people in the church but afterwards there was a big party in Ronconi's restaurant.' She didn't dare look her father-in-law in the eye as she mentioned 'Ronconi'. 'Practically everyone we know was there.'

'Will?'

'No, he came home later that night.'

'Does my husband live with me?'

'Not during the war, but he's back safely now and he can't wait to be with you when you leave here.' Bethan looked helplessly at Dr John.

'Then why hasn't he been to see me?'

'Because, young lady, we're afraid what the shock might do to you if he does,' Dr John broke in.

'So he's happy to stay away because you say so?'

'He's not happy, Di,' Bethan gave her hand one last squeeze.

'Now why don't you lie back on those pillows, and try to get some sleep?'

'I slept for weeks, Dr John.'

'That was a coma.'

'If my husband wants to see me and I want to see him, what's the problem?'

'The problem is you don't remember him.'

'At least tell me his name,' Diana pleaded.

'Not one word, Bethan.'

'I'll go and see him, Di, and tell him you were asking about him.' It wasn't much of a consolation but it was all Bethan was able to offer before Dr John pushed her out of the cubicle.

'Judy, what are you doing here?' Angelo asked in bewilderment as he burst through the door of the café.

'What does it look like? I'm working.'

'Tony took you back?'

'It's just as well he did.' She jerked her head towards the back room, which had been emptied of customers by two policemen, who were questioning Tony and Gabrielle.

'Angelo,' the younger of the two policemen called to him, 'sorry about the circumstances.'

'I came as soon as I got the call.'

'I'm afraid we're going to have to arrest your brother for assault.'

Angelo glanced from Tony, who was sitting, sullen and wretched, staring down at the table in front of him, to Gabrielle who was very close to tears. 'What happened?'

'Fred Jones –' the policeman began.

'The bus conductor, that Fred Jones.'

'That's the one. He made a crack about Miss von Stettin here; your brother took it personally and hit him. Unfortunately Mr Jones banged his head on a table on the way down. We don't know the extent of his injuries but he's been taken to hospital and his companions made a formal complaint. Even if they hadn't, with Mr Jones hospitalised we have no choice but to arrest and charge your brother. Depending on Mr Jones' recovery the charge may become more or less serious.'

'Can Tony get bail?'

'Not until the magistrates' court convenes tomorrow morning. By then we should have the medical reports on Mr Jones and we'll be better placed to know how your brother stands. Come on, Tony. We gave you ten minutes' grace for Angelo to get here. Now he's arrived it's time to go.'

'I'm sorry, Gabrielle,' Tony mumbled as the police constables closed in either side of him. 'I'm sorry for everything, for lying to you, for –'

'Don't worry about Gabrielle, I'll look after her,' Angelo shouted after him more for Gabrielle's benefit than Tony's, as the police escorted Tony through the door. Moments after they left, Liza rushed in with Alfredo.

'We saw Tony with the police.' Alfredo made a face as he looked around. 'I suppose you want me to take over.'

'For the moment.' Angelo shook his head at Liza. 'I'm sorry. You said you wanted to talk to me.' He drew her into the back room away from the crowd in the front room of the café.

'It can wait.' She looked at Gabrielle who was still sitting alone at the table the constables had used to interview Tony. 'As you've got your hands full here, I'll meet my sisters from school and spend some time with them this afternoon.'

'If you're going back home, I'll telephone you later.'

'There's no need. You just take care of things here. I'll write to you tomorrow.' Liza kissed him on the cheek.

'And I suppose I can kiss the pictures goodbye,' Alfredo grumbled, slopping the cup of sweet tea he'd made for Gabrielle on his own initiative, as he plonked it in front of her.

'Good boy,' Angelo patted his back. 'I'll talk to Gabrielle.' He glanced to where she was still sitting, crestfallen and forlorn. 'Until we know one way or the other what's going to happen to Tony, I suppose one of us had better move into the rooms upstairs.'

'With Gabrielle?'

'Don't be an idiot. I'm taking her up to the house.'

'What about Mama?'

'With Tony in jail we can hardly leave his girlfriend here,' he countered irritably.

'I suppose not. If you like, I'll move in here, but only on condition I have three nights off a week.' When Angelo stared at him, he mumbled. 'I was getting sick of sharing a room with Roberto and Tony anyway.'

Charlie put down the telephone and turned to see Masha standing behind him.

'Who were you talking to?'

'A friend, from the war. You slept a long time.'

'I am very lazy.'

'Exhausted, more like it. Did you sleep well?'

'How can you ask that when I slept in your arms for the first time in sixteen years?'

'Mrs Lane has made food in the kitchen. Peter and I have already eaten.'

'The second meal of the day?'

'We're greedy.'

'I'd like to see the house.'

'I would have shown it to you last night but you were tired and it was so late by the time we got here. How about doing it after you've eaten?' he suggested, unnerved by her fragility which was even more obvious now she was dressed in one of the new frocks Alma had bought for her. It was pretty, blue wool with a green trim, but it was at least two sizes too large, and Masha's face was just as pale, lined and exhausted as it had been the night before.

'It's such a big house,' she commented as they passed the sitting- and dining-room doors and walked through the second sitting-room into the kitchen.

'And in summer we'll live in every room of it.'

They entered the kitchen to see Peter sitting at the table, finishing a meal of fried potatoes, beans and salt fish.

'The tea's all ready but I haven't wet it, Mr Charlie. There's a fruit semolina in the small top oven that needs taking out in ten minutes. If you want anything else I'd be happy to oblige.'

'You've done everything there is to be done, thank you, Mrs Lane. We'll see you tomorrow.'

'As you wish, Mr Charlie. What about the dishes and your tea?'

'We'll do the dishes ourselves and with all the food in the cupboards tea won't be a problem.' He pulled a chair out from the table for Masha.

'You're looking smart, Peter,' Masha commented. He was wearing a new shirt Charlie had given him, with a collar and tie.

'I am going to see about a job. As a mechanic. A policeman told me about it last night.'

'A policeman? What were you doing talking to a policeman?' Her voice rose precariously.

'He's a friend of mine.'

'You have a friend who's a policeman. Feo, they are dangerous . . .'

'Not in Pontypridd. Huw's a nice man, Masha; you'll like him. He saw Peter in town last night, recognised him because he looks like me, and told Peter about this job.'

'See, I told you not to worry about me, Mama.'

'Fish and fried potatoes?' Charlie passed the bowls to Masha so she could help herself.

'Thank you. It's so strange to be here sitting in this lovely house in the middle of the day, eating, all three of us, and me having just got out of bed. I am used to working.'

'Not today. If you want anything done in the house, ask me and I will ask Mrs Lane to do it for you tomorrow.'

'You will have to learn English, Mama. I will teach you.' Peter took the pudding out of the oven and spooned a sizeable portion into a bowl for himself.

'We will not be here long enough for me to learn English.'

Charlie gave Peter a warning glance. 'First you eat and then I will take you round the house, Masha, so you can tell me what changes you would like to make. And if you wrap up warm we can go outside. There's a garden, it's small but there are a few things growing there.'

'Cherry trees?'

'I'm afraid not.'

'I so loved the cherry trees in spring, Feo. Do you remember the blossoms the year we married? People said there would be such a crop but we weren't there to harvest it. I wonder if anyone did or if they were left to rot and fall off the trees. Or even if the cherry trees survived. Once you helped my father replace half the stock in his orchard – cherry, apple, pear . . .'

Neither interested nor embarrassed, Peter continued eating and Charlie realised just how much of the sixteen years since they'd been separated Masha had spent in the past – probably even more than him.

'I can't meet your mother for the first time like this,' Gabrielle protested tearfully. 'Not with Tony in jail.'

'Don't you see that because Tony is in jail and we have no idea how long he is going to be there, someone else in the family is going to have to run the café? And as that someone is going to be either me or Alfredo it would be better if one of us slept in the café and you stayed with my mother.'

'I have made such a mess of everything. I wanted

people to like me but no one does. Your mother doesn't even want to meet me . . .'

'Tony's the one who's made the mess, not you,' Angelo contradicted vehemently, deliberately ignoring her comment about his mother. 'Him and his fists, he's always making trouble.'

'He has hit people before?'

'Didn't he hit anyone in Germany?'

'No.' Wide-eyed, she shook her head.

'Then you must have been a good influence on him,' Angelo replied shortly, not wanting to lie to her, but not wanting to elaborate about Diana either. 'Why don't you go upstairs and pack, and I'll bring round the Trojan to take you, your case and that enormous box to my mother's house?'

'You'll come with me?' she asked anxiously.

'Yes, I'll drive you,' he replied, thinking of Liza and the afternoon he had been looking forward to. Ronnie wasn't the only brother Tony had annoyed to the point of never wanting to see his face again. He was beginning to think that if Tony wanted to disappear into the Foreign Legion, he'd buy the boat ticket to North Africa.

'Well?' Ronnie pushed his rickety chair back from the steel table in the garage office and looked to his mechanic.

'The truth?'

'He's all shit and bull, as we used to say in the army.'

'He knows more than me.'

'No kidding!' Ronnie almost dropped the pen he was holding.

'Straight up. But there's no way he's sixteen,' he said flatly. 'It takes years to learn what he knows about cars. And he's no Russian either.'

'What do you think he is, then?' William closed the auction catalogue he'd been studying.

'He's a bloody toff. I've met them, even driven their cars for them once or twice and he talks just like them. And another thing, he's an odd bastard and I don't know if I'll get on with him.'

'If we keep you both busy you won't have to get on with him,' William suggested.

'Suppose so,' the mechanic admitted grudgingly. 'Since you two bought this place the work has been coming in non-stop. I told you, I can't cope . . .'

'And now you won't have to. With Peter taking some of the load you might even find the time to train the apprentices,' Ronnie hinted heavily.

'Not if they're like the dull buggers we got now. Can't even train them to pee straight, out back. It was like wading through a bloody swimming pool in the Ty Bach this morning –'

'Send Peter in.' Ronnie cut the man short, knowing he would complain all day – and night – if he let him. 'What do you think?' he asked William, who had walked over to the window.

'I can't get over how much he looks like Charlie.'

'But, to quote our employee, he's an odd bastard.'

'Can't get any odder than that mechanic and, as Huw said, the boy's had a tough time being brought up the way he has.'

'By the look of him he knows how to take care of himself.'

'All the better for us. No one will try to pull a fast one with him around.'

'You like him, don't you, Will?'

'I owe Charlie big time for giving me a job in the depression. And you heard, the kid's good with engines, even if he does ask girls to go to bed with him.'

'That really tickled you.'

'I wish I'd thought of that approach when I was his age. I might not have had to wait so long.'

'From what I heard about you and Vera Collins you didn't.'

'Don't go saying that in front of Tina.'

'She doesn't know?'

'Let's say she's forgiven me now I've promised to stay on the straight and narrow and come home nights.'

'Man said you wanted to see me, Mr Ronconi.'

312

'Yes, Peter. If you want a job it's yours.'

'How much?'

'Eight-hour day, five-and-a-half-day week, four pounds. If there's overtime at night or Sunday you can either take time off or I'll pay you two shillings an hour.'

Peter frowned.

'You got a problem with that?' William asked.

'How many half a crowns in a pound?'

'Eight, why?'

Peter remembered what Feodor had said about two being a day's wages and decided he was being offered better pay than his father would have given him to work in his shop. 'I'll work for you.'

'Good.' Ronnie looked carefully at him. 'I'm now going to tell you what we tell everyone who works for us, but first a warning: you'll get no special or different treatment because we're friends of your father.'

'I understand.'

'We're paying you good wages, we expect your total loyalty and honesty. You steal from us we go to the police and prosecute you. You want to borrow anything from the garage – a car – a tool – anything – you ask. If we say no, that's it. If you take it without permission we'll go to the police and tell them you stole it. If we agree you can borrow something we'll expect whatever it is back the next day in the same condition you borrowed it in or we'll dock the damage or loss from your wages.'

'Dock?'

'Take.'

'I understand.'

'And there's dirty jobs in every place. Everyone here takes a turn at them and that includes cleaning the toilets.'

'I've cleaned toilets before.'

'You buy your own overalls. Here,' Ronnie pulled two pounds from his pocket. 'That's an advance on your first week's wages. You'll need two pairs and a pair of good water- and greaseproof boots. You can buy them in town. We'll expect you first thing Monday morning.'

'If I started tomorrow I could have that blue lorry fixed by the afternoon.'

'It needs a new gearbox.'

'There's a good one on the green lorry you've got for sale. Wouldn't it be better to get the lorry that's in for repair working and wait for the new part for the one you want to sell?'

'Yes, it would. Tell you what, Peter, come in tomorrow after you've picked up your work clothes.'

'I'll get them today.'

'No you won't,' William warned. 'The shops are closed for half-day. How long do you reckon it will take you to swap over those gearboxes?'

'A few hours, why?'

'There's a scrap yard I'd like to show you. It's full of broken-down cars. Do you think you could sort out what's usable from what's not?'

'I think so.'

'Hello, Peter,' Bethan smiled warily at him as she walked into the office. 'Nice to see you again.'

'You know Mr Ronconi and Mr Powell?' he asked in surprise as she kissed Ronnie's and William's cheeks.

'My brother-in-law and my cousin. Half the people in Pontypridd are related. I've been to see Diana, Ronnie.'

'She's all right?' Ronnie and William asked in unison.

'Getting better all the time physically, and looking forward to seeing you and your mother on Saturday, Will, if the ward sister will let you in.'

'From what my mother said, she's an old cow.'

'Language,' Bethan warned, looking at Peter.

'Old cow is not so bad, Mrs John.'

'It's not a description I think you should learn to apply to any woman, Peter.'

'Come on, Peter, show me what you have in mind for that gearbox.' William led him out on to the forecourt, sensing that Bethan wanted to have a word with Ronnie in private.

'Is he going to work for you?' Bethan asked Ronnie as soon as Peter and William were out of earshot.

'Would you believe the boy's a wonder mechanic?'

'I'd believe just about anything of him. It will be good for him to have something to do. I'm not sure Charlie is up to coping with him and his mother right now. She's not very strong.'

'No one can say that about Peter.' He joined her at the window. 'Just look at him lifting that engine. You hear about a boy who's been brought up in prison and labour camps and you think of a half-starved weakling – well, I did – and in walks this –'

'Thug.'

'That's a bit harsh, Beth. Give him a chance.'

'I suppose I should.'

He grinned. 'Liza told you what he said to her.'

'Liza? I didn't even know they'd met.'

'According to Huw, they met last night in Ronconi's café. Peter told her she was pretty then asked her to go to bed with him.'

'The –'

'Liza told Huw it was a language difficulty and got him off the hook.'

'The only problem that boy has with language is he uses too much.'

'You didn't drive all the way out here to talk about Peter, did you?'

'I didn't even know he'd be here.'

'That's what I thought.'

'Diana asked about you today.'

'She remembers me?'

'No, but she has nothing to do except lie in bed, do her exercises and think. She recalled Megan telling her that she has a two-year-old daughter; we've told her it's 1946 not 1941, she knows Wyn is dead so she asked about the father of her child.'

'You told her we're married.'

'I told her she was married but I didn't dare mention your name. Dr John would have banished me from the hospital if I had.'

'She's going to have to find out sooner or later.'

'The doctors are only thinking of Diana, Ronnie, and it's the way she finds out that's concerning them. The safest option would be to wait until she remembers without any prompting.'

'That could take for ever.'

'And it could happen tomorrow. You have to understand that when it comes to the mind, doctors are fumbling in the dark.'

'And while they fumble I live in limbo land with the kids, Megan and Dino.'

'I know it's difficult . . .'

'Between you and me, Beth, I'm going round the bend. First they tell me she may never remember, now they won't tell her who I am. What do they want? To keep her in hospital for the next sixty years!'

'If it's any consolation I told her that her husband is someone who loves her very much and wants to be with her.'

'And what did she say?'

'She asked why you hadn't been to see her. Dr John told her they were afraid of what the shock might do to her if you did. I told her you weren't happy with the situation.'

'That's the understatement of the century.' He shook his head as he went back to the desk. 'Sometimes I feel like walking up to that damned hospital, battering down the door and demanding they let me see her.'

'Now that Diana's making good progress with her physical injuries, I'll have a word with Andrew. Perhaps he can persuade the specialist to fix a date for Diana to leave hospital, if only for a day's home visit. It's not much but it's the best I can do.'

'But would they let her visit Megan's, knowing I'm there.'

Bethan hesitated. 'You wouldn't do anything stupid?'

'Diana's my wife, Beth. The person I care most about in the world. She wants to see her husband; I want my wife back.'

'Then perhaps the specialist wouldn't have to know

who exactly is in the house. With the housing shortage, people have all kinds of lodgers these days.'

'I really don't want to go inside if your mother doesn't want to meet me,' Gabrielle demurred as Angelo drew up outside his mother's house in Danycoedcae Road.

'She'll be fine once you're in there, and my sister will be there with her new baby. You met her last night.'

'She didn't like me either.'

'Only because Tony got you off on the wrong foot.' He jumped out and walked around to the passenger side. 'Come on, Gabrielle, my mother would be more upset at the thought of you standing outside in the street for all the neighbours to see than you in her kitchen. God, I hope Luke's home, I'll never shift this box by myself,' he gasped, giving up on trying to lift the wooden crate that held all Gabrielle's worldly goods. Taking her suitcase, he opened the door. 'Mama?'

'In the kitchen, Angelo,' a voice called back.

'Follow me.' Sensing Gabrielle's reluctance he led the way down the passage and opened the door. 'Mama, I've brought someone to stay.' He pushed the door wider. 'This is Gabrielle von Stettin, Tony's fiancée.'

Chapter Nineteen

As BETHAN TURNED out of the garage she saw the thickset figure of Peter Raschenko swaggering down Broadway, hands pushed deep into the pockets of his short navy workman's coat, cap pushed to the back of his head, his mop of white-blond hair falling low over his eyes. Even from a distance of fifty yards he exuded a confidence bordering on belligerence. Slowing the car, she pulled up ahead of him and slid back the window on the passenger side.

'If you are going into town, Peter, I can give you a lift,' she called out.

'I am used to walking.'

'It is absolutely no trouble as I'm going that way. And you can be home that much sooner to tell your mother and father that you have a job.'

He hesitated, then opened the passenger door and climbed in.

'So, how do you like Pontypridd?' she asked when he didn't even murmur a 'thank you'.

'I will tell you what I told my father last night, Mrs John. I think everyone in Pontypridd asks the same question. And as I haven't been in the town for a day I am not sure what I think of it.' He looked out of the window as they drove past a picturesque row of cottages with long narrow front gardens.

Peter's reticence reminded Bethan of several silences she had endured with Charlie when she had first met him. She wondered what quality enabled father and son to sit easily and unembarrassed through a lack of conversation when she felt driven to say almost anything to fill the lull. Was it the difference between Welsh and Russian cultures, self-assurance learned during childhood, or simply a personality trait shared by both father and son? But there was one subject that did need broaching.

'You met my foster daughter last night.'

'Liza, and there she is,' he shouted excitedly, making Bethan turn her head sharply as Liza crossed the road in front of them and walked towards the bus stop under the railway bridge. Turning left, Bethan drew to a halt ahead of the bus queue. Leaning across Peter she opened the window again.

'I thought you were spending the afternoon with Angelo, Liza.'

'There's been a crisis in the café. Angelo will be busy for the rest of the day so I thought I'd meet the children from school.'

'I'm on my way to the hospital to fetch Andrew. We've arranged to meet the children together as we promised Andrew's parents we'd take them up to the Common for tea. Dr John has just bought a cine-camera and projector. He has a few cartoons but I think his real object is to take some moving pictures of the children. Why don't you come with us and allow him to film you for posterity?'

'Or you could come with me.' Peter stepped out of the car and walked towards her. Mindful of his father's advice, he blurted, 'I would like to buy you a coffee and talk to you, or take you for a walk in the park, or to the pictures.'

His words tumbled out so quickly that Bethan had to turn her head to hide a smile that was in serious danger of erupting into laughter.

'What do you think, Auntie Bethan?' Liza asked. 'I have nothing else planned and Dr and Mrs John aren't expecting me, are they?'

'No, we thought you'd be with Angelo but –'

For the first time Liza didn't wait for her foster mother to finish a sentence. 'Then I'd be happy to have a coffee, go for a walk or to the pictures with you, Peter. Or even,' she smiled, 'all three.'

'Would you come and meet my mother first? I want to tell her I have a job. A good one that pays more money than my father thinks is a day's pay.'

'I'm not sure I understood that, but yes, I'd like to meet your mother. You don't mind, do you, Auntie Beth?'

Concerned by the thought of Liza spending time with Peter – possibly alone – and irritated because Liza had left her absolutely no room for manoeuvre, discussion or dissuasion, Bethan replied, 'Your sisters will be disappointed.'

'But they weren't expecting to see me,' Liza reminded mildly.

'No – no, I suppose not.'

'I will take good care of her, Mrs John,' Peter's quick assurance only served to worry Bethan even more.

'You see that you do, Peter. Don't be late, Liza, and don't you dare walk up from town by yourself. Telephone and either Andrew or I will come and fetch you.'

'I will walk her home, Mrs John.'

'There's no need, Peter. We'll pick her up in the car. I'll see you later, Liza.'

'It might be a while later if we go to the pictures.'

Despite her anxiety at the prospect of Liza spending time with Peter, Bethan had to suppress another smile as Peter offered Liza his arm in blatant imitation of a couple at the bus stop. Then she looked at Liza's face and took a deep, deep breath. No – it couldn't be – it had to be her imagination. Peter was only sixteen, Liza nineteen, and at that age a three-year gap the wrong way between a girl and boy was enormous. Besides, Liza was going out with Angelo.

Then she remembered all the questions Liza had raised earlier that morning. Pushing the car into gear she drove on up the hill thinking of Andrew and what he had said about 'other people's problems'. She had a feeling she had just witnessed one in the making. An enormous one she sincerely hoped Liza wouldn't live to regret.

Mrs Ronconi retreated to the wash house and covered her eyes with her apron. 'I told Tony I didn't want Germans in my house and now you bring one in, Angelo. Isn't it enough that they killed your father, started a war and

Gina doesn't like her, without you bringing her here – into my home?'

'Mama, I had no choice. I couldn't leave her in the café by herself.'

'Tony –'

'Tony has been arrested.'

She dropped her apron. 'What has he done now?' she demanded furiously.

'Punched a man for calling Gabrielle a Nazi.'

'But she is a Nazi.'

'There are no more Nazis, Mama. We won the war and finished them off.'

'She's a German and Germans are Nazis.'

'She's a young girl who's been lied to. Tony told her that he owned a chain of hotels and fine restaurants.'

'So, she was going to marry him for his money. He fooled her! Serves her right, the – the – gold digger.'

'Mama, she has no one to turn to now Tony is locked up. Can't you feel even a little bit sorry for her?'

'Why? Because she thought she could make money from our Tony and now she can't?'

'Because she's alone in a foreign country with people she knows don't want or like her, and hate her for being German. And because Tony is in jail and might be there for a long time if the man he thumped doesn't recover.'

'So, she's suffering. Good!'

'Mama, please, just come into the kitchen to meet her. Talk to her. I promise you she is just an ordinary girl. Are Roberto and Luke at home?'

'Why?' she asked suspiciously.

'Because I need help to carry Gabrielle's box upstairs.'

'She can't move in. There is nowhere for her to sleep.'

'She can have my boxroom.'

'And where will you sleep. The street?'

'Either in Roberto's room, in Alfredo's bed, or the café. As Alfredo and I are going to have to run the restaurant and café between us until we know what is going to happen to Tony, it will be easier if one of us sleeps in the café to be there for the six o'clock morning opening.'

'You expect me to put the entire house in uproar for a German. You expect me to change the bedclothes on your bed, clean and dust the room, allow her sit with us at table . . .'

'If anyone's created uproar, Mama, it's Tony. Please, try and be nice to Gabrielle. She's been through a lot the last couple of days.'

'You can be nice to her.'

'As soon as I've carried Gabrielle's box in, I have to find Ronnie and ask him what he wants to do about Tony.' Giving up on his mother, he returned to the kitchen. He was surprised to see Gabrielle sitting at the table, nursing Gina's baby while his sister made tea.

'Want a cup?' Gina asked.

'If it's quick.'

'It will be. The kettle's almost boiled. Gabrielle's a dab hand at calming babies with colic. Mama and I haven't been able to do a thing with her all day and now look at the little angel, butter wouldn't melt in her mouth.' Gina glanced fondly over Gabrielle's shoulder at her daughter swathed in a shawl, eyes open, toothless mouth gaping in a grin.

'It is luck.' Gabrielle smiled shyly. 'And a little bit of practice. I used to help my mother take care of my twin brothers when they were babies.'

'Twins, that must have been nice.' Gina did a quick count in her head and began lifting cups down from the dresser. 'Are they in Germany?'

'They were killed in the war.'

'A lot of people were killed in the war.' Mrs Ronconi stood in the doorway. 'You must be Gabrielle.'

'Yes, Mrs Ronconi. I realise it must be very hard for you to have me in your house. I am sorry to be so much trouble.'

'Well, that can't be helped. Now you're here you'd better stay,' she sniffed. 'I don't need Angelo to tell me that this is all Tony's fault. He has always been a hothead. Nothing but trouble ever since he persuaded his Papa that he didn't want to be the priest everyone in the family wanted him to be. Not that he would have been a good priest. He would have been a terrible one. Giving people punches instead of the holy sacrament and confession. If his Papa was alive he would thrash him; as it is,' she shrugged her shoulders, 'Tony carries on punching people. You were a fool to get engaged to him. A nice-looking girl like you could have done better for herself. Angelo, what are you doing standing around here with your mouth open? I thought you were going to see Ronnie about getting Tony out of jail.'

Masha spoke rapidly to Peter in Russian. Charlie looked at Liza and translated.

'My wife would like to know if she can give you something else. Another cup of tea or a second piece of cake perhaps?'

'No thank you,' Liza replied, almost choking as Charlie said 'my wife'. It was extremely odd to be sitting in this kitchen with him and Peter's mother, who seemed so much older than the youthful and beautiful Alma Raschenko. Also, she wasn't quite sure what to call him, so she left off his name altogether. 'Uncle Charlie' didn't sound right in Peter and Masha's presence, and plain 'Charlie' positively disrespectful, but she couldn't remember hearing anyone in Pontypridd ever calling him anything else.

'Thank your mother for the tea and cake, and tell her this is a lovely house, Peter.'

Peter obediently translated, triggering another torrent of words from Masha. 'My mother says you are a nice girl.'

'So where are you two going?' Charlie asked.

'I've persuaded Peter to take me to see *Frenchman's Creek*. There's a special showing in the Park Cinema. I've seen it before but it's a lovely film and it's in colour.'

'My wife . . . I've seen it,' he said quickly, looking at Masha although he knew she couldn't understand a word of English. 'It's a good film. Enjoy yourselves.'

Peter left the table. 'I have something to do, Liza. I will be back soon.'

She sipped her tea and smiled at Peter's mother as Charlie made his excuses and followed his son up the stairs to the boxroom.

'Why are you watching me?' Peter questioned angrily, palming the pound notes Ronnie had given him that he'd been pushing under his mattress.

'I came up to ask if you had enough money but I see you have some.'

'Two pounds.' Peter held them up. 'Mr Ronconi gave me an advance on my wages to buy overalls and good strong waterproof boots. Will it be enough?'

'If it isn't I'll lend you some until your first pay day,' Charlie said, recognising his son's need to pay his own way. 'What about tonight?'

'I have the money you gave me yesterday.'

'You didn't spend any?'

'The coffee I bought was on the house.'

'Five shillings should be enough to buy two tickets to the pictures and a couple of coffees afterwards. Get the ninepenny not the sixpenny tickets. That way you can sit upstairs in the balcony, you'll get better seats and a clearer view of the screen. Oh, and you do know that men pay for women when they take them out?'

'Why?' Peter frowned.

'Because they do.' Charlie was unable to think of a single reason that sounded even remotely sensible.

'But Liza is a nurse. She earns money, she told me. Why does she need mine?'

'Because it's what's done in this country. A gentleman asks a lady out, the lady does him the favour by going with him, so the gentleman pays for the evening.'

'Then gentlemen are stupid in this country.'

'They probably are,' Charlie agreed, unable to combat Peter's basic logic. 'But you should still pay for her ticket, ice cream and anything else she wants, and at the end of the evening walk her home to make sure she gets there safely.'

'Ah, I understand, then she sleeps with you.' Peter's smile broadened as he thought of the woman he had bought in the camp with apples. Liza would be so much better. She was younger and prettier. 'Now that makes sense. Men have to pay for everything and then the women –'

'That is not the way it works at all,' Charlie stressed, struggling to keep his exasperation in check. 'Try to sleep with a girl the first time you go out with her and you will end up in prison.'

'It's a crime to sleep with a woman here?'

'If the lady complains it's called rape.'

'I would never force any woman to sleep with me.'

'That's reassuring to hear. Now listen, no lady sleeps with a man after he's taken her out just once. I explained that last night. Most people wait until they're married before sleeping together.'

'You didn't with my mother.'

'How do you know that?'

'I heard her talking to some other women about wedding nights when I was young. They thought I didn't understand but I did. Mother said her wedding night happened before she was married to you and it was the most wonderful night of her life – then all the women laughed.'

'Can we get back to tonight,' Charlie asked, infuriated by Peter's twisted understanding and obsession with sex. 'A man walks a lady home after they have been out together to make sure that she gets there safely and for no other reason. Liza lives a long way out of town but if you're lucky you might catch a bus. In fact, given your ideas about women it might be better if you do catch a bus so the driver can keep an eye on you.'

'I'll walk her home.' Conveniently forgetting Bethan's instruction to Liza to telephone her for a lift, Peter pulled a comb from his pocket and ran it through his hair.

'And if she allows it, you may kiss her. One small kiss on the cheek not on the lips and absolutely no more. No touching – no fondling – no sleeping – nothing! That is the way things are done in this country. Liza is a lady not a camp trollop. She is also Mrs John's daughter.'

'Adopted daughter.'

'Same thing. I don't want any complaints. Here,' he put his hand in his pocket and pulled out another two half-crowns. 'Just in case. Bus fares, coffee, ice creams – they can all add up.'

'You will look after Mama?'

'You don't have to ask. And Peter, remember, no touching Liza.'

'What if she touches me?'

'She won't, she has a boyfriend.'

'A new one,' Peter muttered darkly, jingling the coins in his pocket as he ran down the stairs.

'So what do you want to do, Ronnie?'

'I *want* to do nothing. I'd like nothing better than to see that runt of a brother of ours rot in jail for the next fifty years but I suppose you had better go down Spickett's first thing tomorrow to see if they can arrange bail for him. I dread to think what it's going to cost. After all the warnings you and I have given him, I thought he'd have had the sense to keep his fists to himself.'

'Me go to Spickett's, not you?'

'It's quite simple, just ask for Mr Spickett, explain the situation and he will deal with everything.'

'And the café?'

'You'd better keep Tony out of there for the time being. In fact if you can't find him a job in either of the kitchens away from the public, tell him to lie low until this is cleared up one way or another.'

'You don't want to see him?'

'If I saw him, I'd hit his head off his shoulders.'

'That leaves only two of us running the restaurant and café.'

'I'm aware of that.'

'You did say I could come to you for advice.'

'All right,' Ronnie softened his tone as he realised he was taking his anger out on Angelo, who was entirely innocent. 'In my opinion you should run the restaurant because it takes a bit of panache to serve the crache with their meat and two veg lunches, and morning and afternoon teas. Let Alfredo handle the café. And before you say another word I know both of you are going to be working flat out, but short of pulling Roberto from school, which you'll do over my dead body, I can't think of any other solution. In the meantime, look around the staff, pick out the ones you think you can trust and watch them closely. Maybe – just maybe – you'll strike lucky and find one up to managing the café one or two nights a week to give you and Alfredo a break.'

'You and Will still intent on giving Luke a job when he comes out of the pit because if you aren't, perhaps he and Gina can help out.'

'Ask him what he wants to do. Now he's a family man I can't see him eager to work evenings.'

'I'll do that, Ronnie.'

'Is that it?' Ronnie pulled a packet of cigarettes from his shirt pocket and offered Angelo one.

'Apart from Mama. When are you going to call up and see her? She talks about you and Billy and Catrina all the time. She thinks about Diana and she wants to help . . .'

'And she comes to see us here twice a week. I meant it when I said I didn't want to see Tony again, Angelo. I'll never forgive him for what he did to Diana. And while he's still living with Mama I won't visit Danycoedcae Road.'

Angelo gripped his brother's shoulder as he left the table. 'Do you want me to let you know what's happening with Spickett's and Tony.'

'You can telephone the garage. I'll be there all day tomorrow.'

'How's it going?'

'Better than the café business, by the look of things.' Ronnie left his chair. 'Do me a favour, go in the kitchen and say hello to Dino and Megan so Megan can give you a slice of the cake she's been hoarding for visitors.'

'Pleased to, then I'll relieve Alfredo in the café.'

'Life's all go, isn't it?'

'Especially when you don't want it to be,' Angelo agreed thinking of Liza and their ruined afternoon.

'You're sure you'll be all right?'

'Feo, I have eaten more than any person has a right to in the last two days. I am tucked up in a comfortable, clean bed, I have a fire and a book and you have told me three times that you will be back soon. What more can I want?'

'I love you.' Taking Masha's hand, he looked into her eyes, stooped and kissed her forehead.

'You are going to see your other wife.'

'She is not my wife any more and I only need to see her for a few minutes. I have some papers for her.'

'I understand.'

'It is only business, Masha. She knows that now you are here, there can be no going back for either of us but I can't simply walk away from my responsibilities. She has my son to bring up and it is my place to make sure they have enough money to live on.'

'Your other son, how old is he?'

'Four.'

'Would this other wife of yours think it strange if I wanted to meet him?'

'No. She told me before you came that I could bring Theo here, but she wouldn't come herself. She's too afraid that she'll like you. And as she said it would be strange for you to be friends.'

'Theo – it is English for Feodor?'

'It's short for Theodore, almost the same. We haven't talked much about my life here, Masha, but I own some shops as well as this house. That's how I made my money.'

'Peter said when he saw this house that you were rich.'

'Not rich, but I have enough to keep both my families,' he murmured wryly, 'and I have made a will dividing everything I own between you and Peter and my other son. Should anything happen to me this house is in your and Peter's name and there will be enough money for you to live on.'

'What will we do with a house here when we go back to

Russia?' She saw him hesitate. 'We are going back – you promised . . .'

'I promised that we would talk about going back to Russia, Masha, and we will.'

'You will come back with me? You must, I gave my word to the politruk . . .'

'I won't lie to you, Masha. I don't want to go back because I am sure they would put me in a camp. You and Peter too if you came with me.'

'You wouldn't think that if you'd met the politruk. He spoke so well of you, Feodor. He knew everything you had done in the war, how brave you'd been, all about the medals you won . . .'

'I'm sure he did, but I have a lot to do at the moment, Masha, with the business and the house. Your idea of returning to Russia needs more thought and discussion than I can give it at the moment but I will promise you one thing. By all that is holy to me, I swear, Masha, I will never allow us to be separated again.'

Contented she lay back on the pillows. He picked up her book from the bedside table and smiled as he handed it to her. 'You and your fairytales. I might have known. *Stepan Timofeyevich Razin and the Peasant Revolt*. And how many witches, hobgoblins, giants and monsters is he going to meet in these stories?'

'I don't know because I am only halfway through the first and he has only met evil boyars and corrupt henchmen of the Tsar.'

'I will return very soon.' Looking back at her, he closed the door softly, walked down the stairs and picked up his keys from the chest of drawers. Looking around, he decided to check the kitchen. The guard was in front of the stove and the back door was locked. He pushed aside the curtains in every downstairs room and rattled the window catches. They were all fast. There was nothing wrong. Everything was neat, clean, tidy and in its allotted place, yet he still felt uneasy. As if something was about to happen – something bad. But what?

'Masha,' he climbed halfway up the stairs and called to

her. 'I could ask Mrs Lane to sit with you.'

'You think I'm a baby that can't stay alone for a moment? When you come back, please bring me tea.'

'Would you like a cup now?'

'No, but it would be nice in an hour or two.'

Running back down the stairs he stood in the hall. He couldn't control his feelings; they were frightening – and oddly familiar. Then he remembered. He had felt this way once before. When Masha had told him she was pregnant. He had confided in his mother who had always taken such feelings as portents of disaster. Both of them had been concerned that something would happen to Masha when she was giving birth. That either she or the baby, or both, would die. But instead of the tragic scenarios they'd envisaged, the entire village had been razed and he and Masha had been separated. An event totally beyond the realms of anything he or his mother had been able to conceive.

Trembling, he steadied himself on the newel of the stair post. It was only a feeling and probably the result of coming to terms with Masha and Peter's reappearance in his life. He wasn't used to good fortune – or happiness – that was all. Checking that he had his keys he left the house and locked the door securely.

Five minutes later he stood outside his shop at the foot of Penuel Lane and looked up. A light was burning in the living room of the flat. He pictured Alma there, reading a book or listening to the radio, the slow soft smile he loved playing at the corners of her mouth.

He looked down at his key ring, singling out the key to the front door, but he couldn't bring himself to use it. Lifting his hand he closed it into a fist and knocked hard. Moments later he heard a door opening and a familiar light step run down the stairs.

'Charlie?' Alma smiled as she brushed her thick red curls away from her face with her fingers, her green eyes glowing with surprise – and love – at the sight of him on the doorstep. 'Have you forgotten your key?'

'I couldn't bring myself to use it.'

She ran up to the flat ahead of him. 'Mary, Mr Raschenko's here, would you mind sitting in the kitchen for a while?'

'Of course not, Mrs Raschenko.'

'If you'd like some tea, I could ask Mary to make it,' Alma suggested as the girl left them. She couldn't believe how much progress Charlie had made in such a short time. He looked well and strong, almost the man she had married before the war.

'No, no tea thank you.'

She opened the sideboard and pulled out a bottle of vodka.

'You kept it?'

'For visitors.' She turned and looked at him as if she hadn't seen him in years rather than days. 'Bethan told me about your wife, and I have seen your son.'

'You've met Pasha?'

'Not met, seen, and only from a distance. I was driving back from the Treforest shop in the van with the driver. He almost collided with the car in front of us when he saw him. Charlie, you must be so proud. Such a fine tall boy and he looks so much like you.'

'Yes, he does, but he doesn't think like me.' There was a hint of warning in the throwaway remark. 'How is Theo?'

'Well, happy, busy, looking forward to seeing you whenever you can spare the time, and that isn't a complaint.'

He sat as he had done once before, on the edge of the chair that had been his, formal and upright, like a guest.

'You've come to tell me that you can't leave Masha.'

'How do you know?'

'I knew before she came, Charlie. It's like I said, she has no one except you and you would never leave her, not now you've found her again after so many years.'

'She has suffered so much pain, so much hurt, I couldn't add to that by leaving her a second time.'

'And I wouldn't want you to.' She looked into his eyes,

ice blue – sometimes cold but now warm with love. 'What kind of a life could we have together knowing that it would be at the expense of Masha's happiness?'

'You understand. I knew you would.'

'I love you, Charlie, I'll never stop loving you or love anyone else . . .'

'But I want you to . . .'

'No! I won't and I don't want to.' There was finality in her voice that brooked no argument and he respected it. 'And I promise that I will bring Theo up to love and respect you – and Masha – as your wife.'

Leaving the chair he walked over to the window. Turning his back on her he opened the curtains and looked down on the elaborately carved fountain in front of the shop, consolidating his thoughts into words as he traced out the curves and lines in the stone.

'I didn't only come to say goodbye but to talk about the business. I know you haven't wanted to but I have done some things that you need to know about. When I went to the solicitor's to sign the papers for the house I made a new will and a settlement. Seventy per cent of the business is now yours, including the freehold of this flat and the shop.'

'No, Charlie, that is too much.'

'It is not enough. I may have started the business but you were the one who built it up during the war into what it is today. I looked at the bank statements. Alma, I had no idea that you had made so much money. By right you should have all of it but I have kept back thirty per cent to keep Masha and myself. Mr Spickett has drawn up the papers and you have to sign them. Seventy per cent is yours but there is a condition. I haven't put it in any of the documents but I want you to make a new will cutting me out and leaving everything to Theo. Promise me you'll do that? Without a father living with him he will need all the security money can give him.'

She nodded dumbly.

'The house in Tyfica Road, the remaining thirty per cent of the business and a third of the money in the savings account I have kept and willed to Masha and Peter on my death. Don't worry, I am in very good health,' he said drily, 'and I have no intention of dying just yet but with a family as complicated as the one I've made for myself, it's as well to take precautions. Mr Spickett has been very helpful; he has given me his word that there are no legal loopholes in the arrangements. No one can alter anything if I should die, and it doesn't matter that our marriage wasn't legal as I made you a full business partner before the war.'

'Will you still work in the business?'

'I thought the Cardiff shop could be expanded. If you don't mind I could manage that and leave everything else to you.'

'So, we'll still see each other?'

'Not if you don't want to.'

'There's Theo.'

'If we do see one another, Alma, it can't be alone, and not like this. I couldn't trust myself . . .' His breath caught in his throat and she realised that despite whatever comfort Masha could offer him, he was suffering just as much as she was.

'Charlie.' She went to him. Nestling her head between his shoulder blades, she wrapped her arms round his waist, pulling him tightly to her. 'Please, kiss me.'

'Alma . . .'

'Please, it will be the very last time.'

He turned, and she was in his arms. Bending his head to hers he kissed her hard, lovingly and longingly.

'I love you.'

'And I will always love you, Charlie, even if we can only be business partners from now on.'

'Please, don't come to the door. I will lock it.'

She heard him walk down the stairs, heard him close the door but she didn't see him in the street. A few seconds later she realised why. The letterbox clattered and there was a quiet rattle as first one key, then another was pushed through the flap.

She waited, straining her neck to catch a last glimpse of

him as he walked round the corner towards Penuel Lane. She opened the window so she could hear his footsteps die away. Then there was only silence.

Hooking the guard in front of the fire she left the room and went into the bedroom they had shared. Opening the wardrobe that had been his, she lifted out the one personal thing he hadn't taken – because she had hidden it. A black, heavy-knit Aran sweater.

Curling into a ball on the bed she hugged it close, breathing in his scent and thinking how very lucky she had been to have had him for a husband and the father of her son, if only for a little while.

Chapter Twenty

'DID YOU LIKE the film?'

'The sword fights were all right but the rest was stupid.'

'I'm beginning to think stupid is your favourite word.'

'Well, it was stupid.'

'Why?' Liza asked Peter, as they walked slowly up the hill, side by side, eating chips from newspaper cones that she'd suggested they buy as an alternative to going to the café.

'Because the pirate wanted the woman and didn't take her. He was strong, he had lots of men, he should have carried her off.'

'It was obvious that, much as she loved him, she didn't go with him because she couldn't leave her children.'

'There were plenty of servants to care for them so they would have been happy without her. And her fat, stupid husband with the silly hair would have bought them everything they wanted.'

'You're missing the point. She wouldn't have been happy without them.'

'If I'd been the pirate I would have made her sail away with me.'

'Then maybe it's just as well you weren't the pirate because you would have ended up with a miserable woman who spent all her time crying over her children.'

'I would have made her stop.'

'How? By beating her?'

'Only weak and pathetic men hit women and children.' There was an edge to his voice that suggested he wasn't trotting out a platitude he'd heard somewhere but speaking from experience. He looked at the hill in front of them. 'You live at the top of this?'

'For the one or two nights a week I can come home.'

'Do you have to live away from home when you want to become a nurse?'

'Yes, it's three years' training and I've only been doing it for six months.'

He made a face. 'Two and a half years is a long time. Why won't they let you come home more than two days a week?'

'It's one mostly, and they won't let me come home more often because I have to live in a nurses' home at the hospital. Auntie Bethan says it soon goes, and she should know: she did her initial training in Cardiff then came back to the Graig to do midwifery.'

'Are your sisters nurses too?'

'No. Two of them, Polly and Nell, are still in school and live with Auntie Bethan. The third, the next one down from me, Mary, works for – a family in town,' she explained hurriedly, not wanting to go into details about his father's other wife. 'She helps look after a home and a small boy so his mother can work in a shop.'

'Everything is different here from what I am used to.'

'Not bad different, I hope?'

'Just different. That man yesterday in the café, he said he was your boyfriend.'

'We've been going out together for nearly a year.'

'And if I want to be your boyfriend?'

'It's better we're just friends. You're years younger than me, but I enjoyed tonight, the pictures, the ice cream . . .'

'My father said I should pay for you. Why didn't you let me?'

'Your father is old-fashioned. These days most girls pay half when they go out with a boy because they don't want to feel they owe the boy anything. Besides, since the war, most girls as well as boys work so they have their own money.'

'Girls didn't work in this country before the war?'

'Those who could afford to stayed at home to help their mothers run the house.'

'I'm glad you're working and earn your own money because I want to save all I can of mine.'

'What for?'

'Mr Ronconi is prepared to pay me more money than most people earn in a day to work in his garage. That means he expects me to make a lot of money for him, but if I save enough to buy my own garage I will be able to keep everything I earn for myself.'

She shook her head. 'You're the oddest mixture, Peter. Sometimes you sound as though you're sixty years old, and at other times six. I can't make you out.'

'I love you.'

'No you don't, you've just met me.'

'My mother told me one day I would look into a girl's eyes and recognise in that one single moment I'd met the person I'd want to spend the rest of my life with. It happened last night. I want to marry you.'

'No one gets married just like that and especially not at sixteen.'

'I'd be happy just to sleep with you but my father said most people here only do that after they're married.'

'He's right.'

'He also said I should take things slowly. One kiss on the cheek tonight and only if you let me. He didn't want any complaints from Mrs John.'

'Then I'll have to make sure you behave like a gentleman, won't I? This is Auntie Bethan's house.' She turned off the lane into the driveway.

He peered ahead. 'I don't see a house.'

'It's best seen from the front. Here, I'll show you.' She led him round the curving drive until they stood in front of the three-storeyed villa. 'Would you like to come in?'

'No, I want to go home and make sure my mother is resting. She's not very strong.' He looked up at the house, outlined in the moonlight. 'How many people live here?'

'Dr and Mrs John, their two children, my sisters, me when I'm home and the maid.'

'That's all?'

'That's enough.'

'It's as big as a hotel I saw in Germany. Doesn't anyone live in small houses in Pontypridd?'

'Plenty of people. Didn't you see the two-bedroomed terraces when we walked up the hill?'

'No, because I was looking at you. Can I have my one kiss?'

'Boys don't usually ask.'

'My father said I was only to kiss you if you let me. How am I supposed to find out if you'll let me, if I don't ask?'

'Peter . . .'

'Don't laugh at me!'

'Who's laughing?' Standing on tiptoe she cupped his face in her hands and kissed him on the lips. A second later his hands locked round her waist like a vice, his tongue was in her mouth and she was fighting for air.

'My God!' she gasped, when he finally released her. 'Where did you learn to kiss like that?'

'I didn't learn, it came from my love for you. I told you one day we'll be married. Look into my eyes the next time you see me, then you'll know it too. Good night, Liza.'

'Good night, Peter.'

'Call me Pasha,' he whispered back from the gate. 'Like my mother. That will bring us nearer to being husband and wife.'

'So,' Mrs Ronconi looked over her reading glasses at Gabrielle, 'you love my son Tony.'

'Yes, Mrs Ronconi,' Gabrielle acknowledged.

'Even now, when he's in jail for attacking a man?'

'He only hit him because he called me a Nazi – and – and because we'd quarrelled,' she admitted in a smaller voice.

'You quarrelled with him because he told you a pack of lies.'

'Perhaps I misunderstood him.'

'Angelo told me that you expected a big hotel and a lot of restaurants. Did you make that up, or Tony?'

'My English has improved since I met Tony. Perhaps I didn't quite grasp what he was trying to tell me when we

338

were in Germany,' she answered, bending the truth.

'But you don't like the rooms above the café?'

'The rooms above the café are very comfortable.' Gabrielle glanced around the homely kitchen, with its patchwork cushion covers and home-made rag rugs, and realised that if anything, the living room above the café was better furnished than Mrs Ronconi's home. 'I was tired after the journey, there were so many people around. I didn't know what I was saying. The rooms are much better than the one room in Celle my mother and I have lived in since we lost our house in Prussia.'

'House . . . but your family had a castle, so Tony said. Or was that another of his lies?'

'No, that's not a lie. We did own a castle, an old one. It wasn't in very good condition – part of it was little more than ruins – and the Russians have it now. But my past is behind me, Mrs Ronconi. I came to this country to marry Tony and work hard beside him to build a life for both of us – together. I knew it wasn't going to be easy because of all the terrible things the Germans did during the war but I thought – I hoped – that . . .'

'We'd forget.'

'No, not forget. To forget would be to deny that all the people who have been killed in the war had lived. No . . .' Gabrielle struggled to find the right words. 'To accept me for who I am,' she said slowly. 'To realise that not all German people are bad.'

'You know Tony was very ill when he came home?'

'He wrote that he had pneumonia.'

'I promised God that if he recovered I would give him – and you – a big white church wedding.'

'We would be happier with a small one,' Gabrielle ventured, hoping not to offend her prospective mother-in-law.

'Do you have a wedding dress?'

'I have an elegant brown costume.'

'You girls and your costumes. You are just like my Gina and Tina – they married during the war and both in costumes.'

339

'I think a marriage is more important than a wedding, Mrs Ronconi, and I will do everything in my power to make your Tony happy.'

'That's a lot more than he deserves.'

'It is good of you to allow me to live here, in your home, but I don't expect you to keep me. I could pay for my food and rent. I have some money that I saved from the wages I earned working for the British Army in Germany. Or, if you have any work that I can do in return for my room and board I would be happy to do it. I can cook, clean, type and keep books and until I marry Tony I would like to do something.'

'And after you marry Tony?'

'I will help my husband in whatever he wants to do.'

The door opened and Angelo walked in.

'Hello.' He looked from his mother to Gabrielle, surprised to see them sitting together in the kitchen. 'Where is everyone?'

'Luke and Gina are in their parlour. Roberto's upstairs. He's supposed to be having an early night but knowing him he'll have his nose in a book. And we're here. Where's Alfredo?'

'Staying in the café.'

'Weren't you supposed to be going out with Liza?'

'I tried telephoning her from the café. Bethan said she'd gone to the pictures with a friend so I thought I'd come up here and see how you two are getting on.'

'Gabrielle's been telling me a bit about herself. Did you know she could type, keep books, cook and clean?'

'No I didn't.' He sat at the table and took a wizened winter apple from the bowl in the centre.

'I thought maybe you could find her something to do in the restaurant.'

'With Tony in jail we can do with all the help we can get.'

'What if someone calls me a Nazi again?'

'We keep our tempers and get someone else to serve them.'

'You would really let me work for you?'

'We're so short-staffed I'd take on a two-headed monkey if it could work the till. Do you understand our money?'

'Yes, I helped out in the NAAFI.'

'Be up early; we'll get you started on the counter before I go up to Spickett's to see if there's any chance of getting Tony out.'

'You think Tony could be released?' she asked excitedly.

'Ronnie – that's my eldest brother, you haven't met him – seems to think there's a possibility.'

'And if he comes out we can go to the priest and set the date for our wedding?'

'You still want to marry him?' Angelo asked in surprise.

'Of course. Tony is the only reason I came to this country. I love him,' she added firmly, 'very much indeed.'

'You didn't telephone,' Bethan reprimanded as Liza walked into the kitchen.

'Peter walked me all the way home, Auntie Beth.'

'Did he behave himself?' Andrew knocked the ashes from his pipe on the side of the stove.

'Like a gentleman.' Liza smiled. 'I think his father gave him a lecture before we went out. He even asked permission to kiss me good night.'

'You let him!'

'His father told him he could expect a kiss on the cheek, Auntie Beth,' Liza answered, stretching the truth.

'Angelo's a nice boy.'

'So is Peter.'

'He hasn't been brought up like you.'

'From what little he's said about himself I don't think he's been brought up like anyone I know, but he means well and he's good and kind at heart.'

'Liza . . .'

'I like him, Auntie Beth.'

'If you two ladies are going to argue, I'm going to bed.' Andrew left his chair.

'Haven't you got anything to say about this?'

'Plenty, Beth, but nothing Liza will want to hear or take any notice of. Just promise me one thing, Liza, don't rush into anything you may regret later.'

'I won't, Uncle Andrew, and thank you.'

'Don't thank me, I'm leaving you to face Bethan alone. If that isn't cowardly behaviour, I don't know what is.'

'Liza, Peter's sixteen, you're nineteen . . .' Bethan began as Andrew left the room.

'And I've only met him twice but . . .' She took Andrew's chair and looked across at her adoptive mother. 'It's what I was talking about this morning. Imagining that when I fell in love it would be momentous, huge, like Cinderella at the ball.'

'And it's like that with Peter?'

'Something happened between us the first moment we looked at one another.'

'But Liza, he doesn't care about anything or anyone.'

'That's not true. He loves his mother very much.'

'Only because she looked after him when he was a baby and he couldn't look after himself.'

'It's more than that. He thinks he has to act tough because that's what was expected of him when he was growing up. Once he settles down here and gets used to this country he'll change.'

'You really believe that?'

'I had tea with Peter and his parents. Peter may not show what he feels but he listens to everything his father tells him and follows his advice.'

'Like the kiss.'

'Like the kiss,' Liza laughed.

'But you will remember your promise to Andrew?'

'Of course, and as you reminded me, Peter is only sixteen. We have all the time in the world to get to know one another.'

'And Angelo?'

'You were right, I was asking you all those questions this morning because I already knew that Angelo wasn't the one for me.'

342

'Poor Angelo.'

'He'll find someone else, Auntie Beth. No one dies of a broken heart these days, and it would have been far worse for him if I had married him out of habit.'

Bethan grasped the hand Liza had laid on her shoulder. 'Take it very slowly with Peter. I'm not at all sure you're doing the right thing in giving up Angelo for that boy after seeing him only twice.'

'But I am, Auntie Beth, and don't worry about me. Give Peter a chance and he'll prove himself to you, as he has to me.'

'I will, if only for Charlie's and your sake.'

'Thank you.' Liza hugged her as she left her chair.

'For what?'

'Not shouting at me or forbidding me to see Peter.'

'As if it would have made the slightest difference. But if you have any problems – anything at all . . .'

'I'll come straight to you, Auntie Beth. I promise.'

The house was quiet when Charlie unlocked the door. As quiet as it had been when he had left. The loudest noise came from the carriage clock ticking on the mantelpiece in the kitchen. After switching on the lights in every downstairs room and checking behind the furniture and curtains, he felt foolish. What was he looking for? What on earth was he expecting to find?

Climbing the stairs he crept quietly into the bedroom. Masha was lying asleep in bed, her head on the pillows, her book lying loosely between her fingers. Taking it from her he placed it on the bedside cabinet.

'Oh, Feo, I meant to stay awake for you,' she mumbled, struggling to open her eyes.

'Go back to sleep, Masha. I will come to bed in a few minutes. Would you still like some tea?'

'No, thank you.' She snuggled down. He pulled the eiderdown over her and turned off all the lights except the bedside lamp before going downstairs. He still felt uneasy, as if something dreadful was about to happen, but whatever it was, it wasn't connected to the house. He filled the kettle in the wash house, then dismissed the idea of tea. Returning to the kitchen he sat in front of the range and reached for the bottle of vodka he'd hidden down the side of the chair.

He was still sitting there, deep in thought and well into his third glass when Peter walked in.

'I hope you behaved yourself.'

'I had a good time,' Peter replied answering him in Russian for the first time. 'And I kissed Liza. I asked first and she let me.'

'Then I can see why you had a good time, and judging by the smile on your face the good time had nothing to do with the film.'

'I love her and I am going to marry her.'

'Peter, you're sixteen!'

'You asked my mother to marry you when you were fifteen and she was fourteen. On top of a haystack on her father's farm.'

Charlie smiled at the memory before he remembered he was talking to his son. 'Your mother has told you far too much about me.'

'She used to say she could never tell me enough. Did you ask her to marry you when you were fifteen?'

'Yes,' Charlie admitted reluctantly.

'Liza is nineteen not fourteen, and old enough to make up her own mind.'

'Like you at sixteen?' Charlie mocked gently.

'Boys grow up quickly in the camps and don't laugh at me for asking a girl to marry me. I'm earning a good wage, I can keep a wife.'

'I'm not laughing, and there are plenty of men keeping a wife and family on less than Ronnie Ronconi has agreed to pay you.' Charlie held up the bottle. 'One vodka?'

'Only one?'

'That's all I'm offering. Peter, you have your whole life ahead of you; I don't want you to take things too quickly.'

'Like you. One wife at eighteen and another at . . . ?' He looked quizzically at Charlie.

'Twenty-eight, and only because I thought your

mother – and you – were dead.'

'How old is my brother?'

'Four. I'm glad you mentioned him because although my marriage to his mother has been annulled, I intend to continue seeing him. I couldn't help you when you were growing up, and I am sorry about that. I wish I could have at least seen you every day as I try to see Theo so you could have known who your father was.'

'My mother told me.'

Given Masha and Peter's differences in opinion on his worth, Charlie had no wish to pursue that line of conversation. 'I hope you will like Theo, Peter. He looks a lot like you and, I'm sure he would like an older brother if you can bring yourself to be one.'

'I would have to think about it.'

'I also made your mother a promise tonight. That I will never leave her, nor will I ever see my other wife alone again.'

'So what are you telling me? That you want me to be grateful because you have decided to be kind to your wife and son?'

'No, I'm asking you for your help to persuade your mother to forget about going back to Russia. If we can convince her to look forward to a future here – as a family – we may stand a chance of building a life for all of us in this country.'

'She's still talking about going back to Russia?'

'Yes.'

'I will do what I can to stop her from even thinking of going back there.' Peter finished his vodka, abandoned the glass on the table and went to the door. 'What time do the shops open in the morning?'

'Nine o'clock.'

'None earlier?'

'If Ronnie told you to buy overalls and boots he won't expect you any earlier. Come into town with me at half-past eight and we will see what we can find, and not just work clothes. You need underclothes, socks, shoes, a suit and trousers and shirts for going out.'

'Thank you – Father.'

Charlie sat back in his chair as Peter closed the door. As he poured himself another vodka he wondered if he'd heard him correctly – or if it had just been wishful thinking, and the drink.

'You can have him, take him away.'

'There's no charge?' Angelo stared at Mr Spickett in disbelief.

'The police questioned Fred Jones when he came round. He admitted calling Miss von Stettin a Nazi and he wasn't too keen to be called as a witness in court. Something to do with a fracas in the Two Foot Nine a couple of months ago and him being bound over to keep the peace for a year. So, tell your brother he's one very lucky man and get him out of here before the police change their mind or find something else to charge him with.'

'I will, Mr Spickett, and thank you.'

'Don't thank me, boy, just make sure Ronnie pays my bill on time.'

'I will, and it will be me, not Ronnie, who pays it,' he called after him.

He walked into the police station in time to see the desk sergeant tipping the contents of Tony's pockets out of a brown paper envelope.

'You look like hell,' he commented, as Tony rummaged through a mixture of coins, notes, train tickets, pens, bottle opener and penknife.

'And you'd look a lot better, after spending a night in the cells, I suppose?' Tony rubbed his unwashed, unshaven face. 'I'm bloody freezing.'

'Come on, I'll buy you a drink, then you can clean up above the café.'

'Where we going?'

'I'll tell you where we're not going, and that's the New Inn. They'd take one look at you and have you arrested for vagrancy.'

*

'You here to sell me a car, Ronnie, or do you want to see me professionally?' Andrew set aside the paper on the New National Health Service his father had given him, along with a warning that it might be necessary for all the doctors in the country to strike to teach the new Labour Government that they couldn't dictate policy to professional physicians.

'I'm here to see you, but not about me. Cigarette?'

'I've switched to a pipe.' Andrew pulled it out of his pocket and looked at it.

'A cigarette is quicker, safer, cleaner and a lot cheaper if you're going to use that excuse to cadge off other people.'

'You're right. It does look disgusting and it tastes even worse.' Andrew took one of Ronnie's cigarettes. 'I take it you want to talk about Diana?'

'I want her home. I've spoken to Bethan. I know Diana realises she's married. She may not know who she's married to, but once she sees me, I'm sure it will come back.'

'And if it doesn't?'

'I'll make her fall in love with me all over again.'

'Ronnie . . .'

'I've listened to all the arguments and stood aside while you, your father and that damned specialist have lectured me on what's best for me and my wife. But no more. Diana's conscious, restless, anxious to be home – not that we've got one I can take her to – she's making progress and she can do the exercises to strengthen her left side just as well in Megan and Dino's spare bedroom as she can in hospital. I telephoned the physiotherapists to ask,' he admitted sheepishly.

'I'm surprised they talked to you.'

'I told them I was you.'

'Thank you very much, Dr Ronconi.'

'I want her home, Andrew. And if you won't let her out of that hospital I'll sign her out as next of kin. And I can do that. After I telephoned the physiotherapist I phoned Spickett's.'

'I bet they didn't advise you to go ahead.'

'I didn't ask for their advice, just a ruling on a point of law. I've just spent three years fighting for everyone else's freedom. Now I'm fighting for my wife's.'

'I understand your frustration.'

'No you don't. You came home and found Bethan there, waiting for you. What did it take – ten minutes to get her into bed? Well, ten minutes after I walked through the front door my wife was lying in a pool of blood on the kitchen floor with me hoping she'd live long enough for the ambulance to arrive.'

'The specialist –'

'Hang the specialist.'

Recalling Bethan's plea that he do all he could to help Diana go home, if only for a day, Andrew relented. 'Look, I'll compromise with you. If I ask the specialist to allow Diana home to spend a weekend with her mother and children under my supervision – just to see how it goes – will you agree not to sign her out?'

'This weekend?'

Andrew thought of his ultimatum to Bethan that they spend the week in Gower. But Diana was her cousin – if anyone would understand it would be her.

'This weekend,' he agreed. 'Ask Megan to bring some clothes in for Diana. If the specialist doesn't give his permission I'll waylay her –'

'And I'll sign Diana out.'

'I'll do my best to get permission.'

'Please, Andrew, I'm not very good at throwing my weight around.'

'Frankly, Ronnie, I think you're a past master at it. But whatever you do, don't come to the hospital. Stay at home with the children and wait for Diana there. If my father or the specialist get one whiff of what we're up to it will be my head on the chopping block along with yours. I only hope it won't be Diana's.'

'So, I've decided,' Tony's hand shook as he lifted the pint to his lips in the back room of the White Hart. 'I'm going.'

348

'When?'

'Soon as I've washed and changed and packed my bags.'

'Where?'

'What does that matter?'

'Soldiers are being demobbed all the time, some are finding it difficult to get jobs.'

'They're always looking for sailors.'

'Will said you were seasick crossing the Channel.'

'Will talks too much. If I can't go to sea, I'll go back into the army. What does it matter what I do?'

'And Gabrielle?'

'Tell her I'm sorry.'

'You're sorry. Just like that. You ask the girl to come over here at her own expense. You fill her full of lies about hotels and chains of fancy restaurants. You hit a bloke out cold in front of her, get yourself thrown in jail and expect me to go and say sorry for you when you run off and abandon her in a strange country where she hardly knows a soul. You've got the wrong brother, Tony. Try one of the others – but not Ronnie. He still wants to separate your head from your shoulders for what you did to Diana.'

'I've made a mess of everything.' Tony took another swig of beer and reached for his cigarettes.

'And you're feeling sorry for yourself. Well, what about Gabrielle? Try thinking of someone besides yourself for five minutes.'

'I've got some savings, I'll give her the fare home.'

'And that will make it all right?'

'No, it won't, but you've seen her. She'll be better off without me. She'll soon find someone else. Someone with more money and better prospects.'

'And if she doesn't want this mythical someone with more money and better prospects?'

'Come on, Angelo, she'd have to be an idiot to want me after the way I've behaved.'

'I tried telling her that last night but she wouldn't listen. Come on, finish that pint. Your clothes are back at

349

the house but I brought Alfredo's clothes down to the café this morning. You can borrow his razor and a clean shirt, wash, change and go down to the restaurant. Gabrielle's working there.'

'What?'

'You heard.'

'Gabrielle? You made her –'

'I didn't make her do anything. She wants to pay her way and she jumped at the chance of earning some money. There's no one in the function room, the two of you can go up there, then if you still want to tell her to go back to Germany, you can tell her yourself.'

'There's more.'

'More what?' Angelo looked at him mystified.

'Judy Crofter's having my baby.'

'What!' Angelo dropped his pint. Fortunately it didn't fall further than the table and the glass remained intact.

'Hey . . .'

'Sorry,' Angelo shouted to the barman. 'There's nothing broken, just a bit spilled. I'll clear it up.'

'Here you go.' He threw a cloth over and Angelo mopped up the beer, glad to do something that gave him an excuse not to look at Tony's face.

'Judy wants me to pay maintenance. Ten bob a week. That's why I gave her her old job back. I agreed to give her two quid a week.'

'You agreed to pay her two quid when every other waitress gets thirty bob. You trying to bankrupt us?'

'Gabrielle was there, I didn't want her to find out.'

'I was right all along. That first night you were home – the night you knocked Diana through the window and were found in Leyshon Street in your trousers with your flies open – you'd been in Judy Crofter's.'

'I was drunk.'

'Christ, Tony, I'm fed up with hearing you say that. It's no bloody excuse for anything.'

'Judy threw me out, that's why I was sitting in the gutter.'

'Judy might not have Gabrielle's looks or education but

it seems to me she has more sense when it comes to picking men.'

Tony looked up at Angelo. 'What am I going to do?'

'I haven't a clue but I can understand why you considered going to sea.'

'Be serious, Angelo. What would you do in my place?'

'Go and see Gabrielle and tell her everything you've just told me. Then, if she still wants you, we'll know for certain that she needs to be certified.'

'William, if you've come here to tell me to go home, I'm not going. This is a good job and I'm staying –'

'Tina, sweetheart.' William planted a kiss on his wife's mouth to stop her from talking. 'I thought we settled the argument about your job days ago.'

'Your idea of settling something is to crawl between the sheets.'

'Can you think of a better way?' He glanced around. 'Ronnie here?'

'No, and neither am I expecting him.'

'I telephoned the garage and left a message for him to meet me here. Where's Dino and David?'

'God only knows where those two get to half the time. Somewhere up the Rhondda, I think. Why?'

'I need to talk to them. If I leave a letter here, you'll steam it open, won't you?'

'I would not. I'm a responsible secretary.'

'That's what I thought.' He took an envelope out of his pocket and scribbled across the address panel.

'I'll see the colonel gets it as soon as he walks in. Where are you going?' she asked as he walked away.

'Down to the front desk to leave it at reception. And don't try picking it up, it's got strictly personal written across the top.'

'Will, what's this about?'

He stuck his head back round the door. 'I don't know how to tell you this, darling, but he's got me pregnant.'

He shut the door just in time to avoid the brass paperweight she flung at his head.

Chapter Twenty-one

ANGELO LED TONY towards the window of the restaurant and pointed to the counter inside. Dressed in a neat black skirt and freshly ironed, pristine white blouse, her fair hair tied back, away from her face in a perfect, black bow, Gabrielle manned the till station. She smiled as a customer approached, greeting her with a polite bow of the head as she took the offered bill and money.

'No one's called her a Nazi?'

'Not yet, but then we cater for the crache up here and they're politer,' Angelo reminded.

'And the waitresses are prepared to work with her?'

'I brought Gabrielle in early this morning. After all the waitresses had clocked in she gave a short speech. She began by apologising for German barbarity during the war, then went on to say how she hopes that given time the people of Pontypridd will accept her and allow her to make a new life with you in Wales. Maggie was the first to say she didn't hold her personally responsible for Hitler's actions.'

'Maggie! After what she said to me?'

'It takes a lot of guts to do what that girl is doing for you, Tony. And it's not been plain sailing. She's had a few snubs, one or two people wouldn't let her serve them, but she passed them on to Chrissie. And,' he eyed his brother sternly, 'we all managed to keep our tempers.'

'I'll try.'

'Trying might not be good enough. I suggest you do better. Gabrielle's not stupid. She knows what she's up against – the whispers – the people pretending she's not there – and they will be the kind ones. For everyone in the town who'll give her the time of day it's my guess there'll be at least one if not two Fred Joneses. But she's prepared to work at it. She spent yesterday evening in Mama's kitchen and she slept in the boxroom and if she can win Mama round, I'd take bets on her winning over anyone.'

'Mama let her stay!'

'Mama said she felt sorry for her because she'd been taken in by you. I'm afraid you're right down there with the worms in Mama's estimation right now.'

'Am I in anyone's good books?'

'Gabrielle's. I don't know what you've got that's made that girl fall in love with you but I wish I had an ounce or two of it to sprinkle in Liza's eyes.'

'Yesterday, Gabrielle told me to go to hell.'

'And last night she was discussing wedding preparations with Mama. Now, are you going to go in there to tell her that you're running away on the first ship, train or whatever out of here? Or are you going to sit down quietly with her upstairs and catalogue your sins before throwing yourself on her mercy in the hope that she might forgive you?'

'She won't.'

'Not if she's got any sense. But we agreed earlier she can't have much of that because she got engaged to you in the first place.'

'I've been looking for you everywhere,' William charged into the garage to see Ronnie standing staring at the walls in the middle of the cabin they intended to transform into a reception area and office.

'I had something to do in town.'

'And I've found out who dumped all that American equipment in our scrap yard. They came looking for it today.'

Ronnie turned to him. 'You sure you got the right ones?'

'Put it this way, they were searching all the areas we found it in.'

'Did they see you?'

'No, I stayed in the hut.'

'Did they find anything?'

'No, because the boys and I finished moving the last of it yesterday. One of the Jeeps couldn't have been more than a foot away from them at one point but I swear they didn't see a thing. Aren't you going to ask who came looking?'

Ronnie moved back from the centre of the room, sat on the edge of the table, crossed his arms and twisted his mouth into a thin, hard line. 'Why have I got the feeling that I'm not going to like what you're about to tell me?'

'Because we're related to one of them. I'm sorry, Ronnie, I wish it had been anyone else.'

'Alfredo.'

'You know!'

'I suspected. That boy's been like a fighting cock without a fight to go to ever since I came home. No wonder Angelo's been complaining that he's hard-pushed to cope with the café and restaurant. He's been trying to do everything himself by the look of things. Why, oh why have I got so many downright stupid brothers?'

'Angelo and Roberto are all right.'

'And Tony and Alfredo are right pains in the arse.'

'You've got some great sisters.'

'Sticking up for your wife again?'

'I'd stick up for her more if she didn't have such a foul temper.'

'If you wanted a sweet, compliant, submissive woman to soothe your brow and warm your slippers in front of the fire, you shouldn't have married an Italian. Why do you think I bypassed my own kind and went after your sister?' Ronnie looked around the room again. 'The only paint I've been offered is institution green or grey. Both on the black market and both at an exorbitant price.'

'We could try mixing it.'

'Pay twice the price to get institution puke colour.' Ronnie slid off the table. 'I suppose I had better go into town and see what little brother has to say for himself. He should be running the café – that's if he hasn't skived off

354

to do anything else illegal. What time did you see him in the yard?'

'Around eight this morning.'

'What's the matter, you and Tina can't sleep?'

'We had a few words.'

'I take it they weren't good ones. Don't tell me – I don't want to know about your private ups and downs, or downs and downs. Eight o'clock – eight o'clock – the cook starts at half-past seven. Alfredo must have left him to run the café. Oh hell!' He stopped and looked at Will. 'If Dino and David Ford have already caught wind of this, what are they going to think of me – and you. After all, Dino's your stepfather and I'm living in the same house . . .'

'They're going to think we're honest citizens. I left a note for David Ford listing the time, place and names of everyone I saw in the yard this morning, including Alfredo. I figured it was too late to try and cover up his involvement,' he apologised as Ronnie smashed his fist into the palm of his hand.

'You're right. The others would shop him the minute they saw the inside of a police station. Did you leave it with Tina?'

'I'm not a complete idiot. I knew if I handed it to her we'd leave ourselves open to the charge that we gave it to her weeks ago to cover ourselves in case we were implicated in the thefts. Tina almost knocked my brains out in an attempt to get at it when I went to the office to look for David Ford, who needless to say wasn't there. Nosy creature, your sister.'

'Your wife.'

'I left the note at the desk and I got the receptionist in the Park Hotel to stamp it with the date and write the exact time on the envelope. All we have to do is wait for David to contact us and arrange to have the whole lot cleared from the yard.'

'Anyone else we know with Alfredo?'

'Glan Richards.'

'Why him? He went back to his job in the Graig Hospital.'

'But he lost pay and seniority. He was as bitter as hell about it the last time I had a pint with him.'

'And the others?'

'Most of them just lads. I hate to say it but Alfredo, Glan and Ianto Myles' son looked about the oldest.'

'Great, so those three will carry the can. All I seem to be doing these days is trying to keep my brothers out of jail.'

'Would you like me to come down to the café with you?'

'You're the one who saw them, not me.' Ronnie stepped back from the door and held out his hand. 'After you.'

'I'm sorry about yesterday, Gabrielle. I shouldn't have lost my temper.'

'And I shouldn't have said the things I did about the rooms and the lies you told me. If I hadn't made you angry, you would never have hit that man.'

'Angelo told me you stayed in my mother's house last night.'

'She is a wonderful woman, Tony, and so kind. We had a long talk. I am sorry I behaved so badly . . .'

'You didn't behave badly. Let's face it, everything that went wrong was my fault.' He led her to a table set in front of a window in the empty, second-floor function room, deliberately choosing one that was situated at the furthest possible point from the door so they wouldn't be overheard even if someone did break in on them. Gabrielle sat on the chair he pulled out for her, and he sat opposite. They looked down over Taff Street. The thoroughfare was packed with shoppers buying provisions for the weekend ahead. The sun was shining and although there was still a nip in the air, Gabrielle could feel the warmth of its rays through the glass.

'It's almost spring,' she smiled.

'Almost,' he echoed dolefully, dreading her reaction to what he was about to tell her.

'We will begin our new life together at the beginning of

summer. And it will be a wonderful summer, Tony. The best one of our lives.'

'I don't think so, Gabrielle, because I don't think you'll want to be starting anything with me after what I have to tell you.'

'Oh no!' She covered her mouth with her hands. 'You are going to be sent to jail. Tony . . .'

'I'm not going to jail but only because of a technicality. Mr Jones won't make a formal complaint so nothing is going to happen about yesterday.'

'He told the police he started the fight?'

'No. He was caught fighting with someone else not so long ago so he won't make a complaint because he's afraid the magistrates will go hard on him.'

'Then he is obviously a troublemaker and I am glad you hit him. And that is wonderful for us. We can start our life together without any problems.' She covered his hand with both of hers. 'Your mother will be pleased. She has already begun to organise our wedding. We talked about it last night. She wanted us to have a big one but I think I succeeded in convincing her that we would prefer a small one. I told her I have a smart costume but she said one of your sisters – Laura – has a white wedding dress that I can borrow . . .'

'Please, Gabrielle.' Extricating his hand from hers, he pushed his chair away from the table. 'This is not just about what happened in the café yesterday. It's about everything. Me deliberately leading you on to believe that my family was rich, that we had chains of hotels and restaurants and that you were coming to something so much better than you were.'

'I am as much to blame for that as you, Tony. Have you ever considered that I wanted to be rich again enough not only to believe but also exaggerate what you told me?'

'From that first day I saw you and sat next to you in the garden of the billet in Celle your mother made me feel that I wasn't good enough for you.'

'Tony –'

'Please, Gabrielle, let me finish. Yesterday wasn't the

first time I've lost my temper since I've come home.'

'Angelo told me last night.'

'You know about Ronnie's wife.'

'I know that she is very ill in hospital.'

'That's why Ronnie isn't speaking to me and why you haven't met him and aren't likely to. Diana's badly hurt, no one knows how badly. And it's my fault. I should never have gone to Ronnie's house that night. If I hadn't, she'd be fine.'

'Have you tried to tell Ronnie how you feel?'

'He wouldn't listen.'

'Then you must write to tell him how sorry you are, even if he doesn't read your letter you must still try.'

'You haven't heard the worst of it.' He moved even further back until the empty table stretched between them like a barren no man's land. 'When I left Ronnie's that night I telephoned for an ambulance. If I'd been thinking straight I wouldn't have gone to the telephone box because there's a telephone in the house. But afterwards, instead of returning to see if I could help, I went to the house of a woman I had picked up earlier in a pub.' He forced himself to look at her. 'I went to bed with her, had sex with her,' he said harshly so there could be no mistake. 'But I want you to know she meant nothing to me – nothing. She was no different from any of the other loose women I picked up when I was in the army. Afterwards, we quarrelled; she threw me out of her house. She didn't even give me time to pick my clothes up off the floor and I was too drunk to look for somewhere warm to sleep so I sat out in the freezing cold street. That's how I got pneumonia.'

'You went looking for a woman to have sex with on your first night home?'

'I'm not proud of it.'

'But all the time we were together in Germany, you never tried to do anything more than kiss me. If you couldn't wait to make love, why didn't you ask me?'

'Because I wanted to marry you.'

'Are you saying you preferred to make love to a

358

stranger than me – the woman you had asked to be your wife?'

'You're a lady. I didn't want to turn you into a prostitute. I wanted our wedding night to be perfect.' The excuses sounded lame and pathetic, even as he came out with them.

'But you never even asked me,' she repeated in bewilderment.

'You would have been horrified if I had.'

'Perhaps, but we could have talked about it. Marriage means partnership. Being able to talk to one another about anything and everything, even embarrassing things.'

'I'm sorry, Gabrielle. I've hurt you and that's the last thing I wanted to do.'

'But you intend to be honest with me from now on?'

'This isn't coming from honesty. I don't know if I would have found the courage to say as much as I have if something worse hadn't happened as the result of that night. The girl – the one I slept with – is Judy Crofter. You met her in the café.'

'Your waitress, the girl with the dyed hair! Her! Are you still sleeping with her?' She left her chair and backed towards the wall.

'I only slept with her the once but that's all it takes. She says – and she's probably telling the truth –' he added, refusing to make any more excuses for himself – 'that she's having my baby. She wants maintenance so she can bring it up. Ten shillings a week.'

'Do you have enough money to pay her?'

'No, but if I have to, I'll find it.'

'Do you . . .' the question was choking her but it had to be asked, 'do you want to marry her for the child's sake?'

'God, no! I could never marry Judy Crofter. You saw her: she's a soldier's mattress – a prostitute,' he explained when he saw the puzzlement on her face.

'So, you won't marry her but you will climb into her bed and lie naked with her?'

'Put like that, it sounds disgusting.'

'It is disgusting, Tony.'

'But no matter what you say or what you think of me or even what I think of myself, the fact remains. The child is mine, my responsibility and I have to accept that it is down to me to pay for its keep.'

'And Judy Crofter?'

'I never want to see her again.'

'But she works for you.'

'Not for long.'

'You will have to see the child.'

'No I won't.'

'But it is yours. Children ask questions, they want to know who their parents are, and in this case why they aren't married to one another.'

'I told you, I'll accept responsibility and that's the end of it.'

'That cannot be the end of it when you are a father, Tony. It is not enough to pay ten shillings a week and say, "*I am sorry, child, I made a mistake but it is all right I will give you some money before I walk away.*"' As she looked at him a cold claw of fear closed around her throat. 'You have something more to tell me.'

'This is not the first time this has happened. Just before the war, when I received my call-up papers I asked Diana – the girl who is married to my brother Ronnie now – to marry me. She didn't even know Ronnie then; he was living in Italy. Diana agreed and – I – she – because I was going away, she went to bed with me on condition we married on my first leave. We slept together – just one night – and she got pregnant with my baby. She never told me. When I next came home she was married to someone else but her baby was mine.'

'She married your brother?'

'Not then, years later after his wife died and her husband was killed in an accident.'

'I don't understand, Tony. If she agreed to marry you, why didn't she tell you about the baby?'

'Because we quarrelled. You see, that night I found out that she wasn't a virgin and I thought it important that a woman should be untouched on her wedding night.'

'But you had made love, so she would not have been "untouched".'

'But I would have been the first.'

'Do you still think it is important for a woman to be a virgin on her wedding night?'

'I have two children, one of which my brother is bringing up and won't even let me see. Now another by a woman I can't stand the sight of. I've spent the whole of my adult life behaving like a fool. To be honest I don't even like myself.'

'In that case, I think it's time you changed and you can begin by keeping your trousers buttoned up.'

'Gabrielle!'

'What is the matter? Virginal brides don't tell their future husbands to keep their – things in their pants?'

'What's the point of telling me anything?' he muttered mournfully. 'Now you know all there is to know about me, you won't want to marry a man who has fathered two bastards, picks up prostitutes and has caused nothing but trouble to you and his family.'

'I told you I loved you in Germany, Tony, and those are not words I say lightly. Oh, perhaps in the beginning it was the moonlight, your dark, curly hair and handsome eyes. But not later, after we had spent time together, and you told me your plans for the future. How you wanted a family life with a home and a wife who would be your partner in every way, not just a woman to do the cooking, cleaning and laundry. But then, I didn't know you saw me as your virginal bride.'

Leaning back against the wall she looked down on the sea of bobbing heads below. The workmen's caps she had already learned to call 'Dai Caps' from Angelo, the bank clerks' trilbys, the women's felt hats with feather and ribbon trims, the crowns and brims punched with holes she could make out even at this distance, evidence of successive years of seasonal trimmings.

'If you want a virginal bride, Tony, you will have to look elsewhere,' she said quietly. 'Didn't you ever wonder why my mother and I couldn't look one another in the eye? Why we quarrelled all the time? We are Germans. Do you know what the Russian troops did to German women when they caught them?'

'I don't want to know.'

'I listened to you, although I didn't want to hear what you had to say. Now it is your turn to listen to me,' she countered angrily. 'They raped us. When we met other women afterwards the question was not, "*Have you been raped?*" but "*How many times?*" My father tried to stop them, so they killed him. Shot him and left his body at the side of the road. There was nothing my mother or I could do about it. The Russians wouldn't even give us one minute's peace to bury him. When we reached the American sector, all the Germans – men and women – knew. They saw the shame on our faces and they knew. My mother refused to speak about it. All she could think of was getting a job with the British or the Americans. She kept saying we needed to be among civilised people but what she meant was she needed to be among people who didn't know what had happened to us. She wanted me to find an officer who would marry me and take me – and her – away from Germany so she would never have to think about what happened to us again. But even if she had come here it would have made no difference because what happened is now a part of us. We may hate it, we may want to forget about it, but we'll never escape it.' She looked across at Tony, who refused to meet her steady gaze. 'You told me your secrets, Tony, I have now told you mine. You can decide which is worse. If you ever saw a German looking at me as if I was dirt, you now know it was not because I was with a British soldier but because that German knew I was a woman who had been used by Russian troops. You lied about the hotels and restaurants, you've fathered a bastard with a woman whose bed you slept in for one night and another with someone you wouldn't marry because she wasn't a virgin. How do you feel about marrying a woman who was used by so many men, she lost count after two hundred? When you know the answer to that, tell me if you want me to stay here or go back to Germany.'

David Ford stood on the stone veranda that overlooked the sunken garden and gazed down at the central, heart-shaped, raised flowerbed. Niches set back from the walkway that surrounded the bed were filled with wooden benches, all empty except one at the far end. Walking quickly, he made his way down to the lower level.

'I got your message.' He smiled as he approached Bethan.

'Thank you for coming.'

'Didn't you think I would?'

'I wasn't sure. I know how busy you are. Dino told me you spend most days rushing from one end of the county to the other.'

'If you've been talking to Dino, you also know that we're not much further forward than we were when we started looking for our mislaid property. So, it really won't make a difference if I take the rest of the most beautiful day that we've had this year off and spend it with my favourite woman. Have you seen the bulbs over there? The daffodils . . .'

'David, do you remember what you said at Megan's wedding about Andrew being jealous of you and our friendship?'

'Yes, but that was at the wedding. Since then I've had dinner with you and we've met so often in town I assumed he no longer minded me seeing you.'

'He does.'

'I take it things are no better between you two?' He sat beside her, seeking her hand beneath the cover of his greatcoat.

'If anything, they're worse because he spends most of his time trying to analyse exactly what our problems are.'

'I can tell you what your problems are. He was away a long time, and while he was locked up in a prison camp you got used to running the show, and not only at home. Five and a half years down the line you're different people.'

'You think we don't know that.'

'There's no shame in doing what I did when my marriage went wrong. I know the moralists and Church people tell couples to work at their relationship until they get it right, but what if a couple have changed too much from the people they were on their wedding day to ever get it right again. Do they have to spend the rest of their lives trying to mend something that's broken beyond repair?'

'We have the children to think about.'

'If your only reason for staying with Andrew is the children, Rachel, Eddie, Polly and Nell won't thank you for it. All they'll get out of the arrangement is an upbringing with warring parents.'

'We try not to quarrel in front of them.'

'And while you two suppress your anger, they have to cope with restrained politeness and silences.'

'It's not as black as you're painting it.'

'I had dinner with you two, remember.'

'Andrew was being particularly difficult that night because he was suspicious of you.'

'Normally he's a happy, bubbling fountain of joy?'

She laughed. 'Not many people are. But what choice do I have, David, except to carry on as I am?'

'You can come to America with me.'

She held her breath as she looked into his eyes. 'Just like that? Pack my bags and go to America?'

'Bethan, we've been fooling ourselves with this friendship thing. We've told so many people we're "only friends" I think we even began to believe it ourselves. But we're not, are we?'

'We agreed during the war that it wasn't our time or place.'

'It wasn't then, but it could be now. Leave Andrew. Pack your bags, bring the children and come to America with me. It's a beautiful country; you can have no idea how beautiful, especially when you compare it to bombed-out, reduced-to-rubble Europe. I'll retire from the army; we'll buy a house anywhere you like. You want sunshine – we'll go to Florida or California. You want snow – we'll go to the Rockies. I'll use my savings to buy a small business, a farm perhaps. We can get some horses, I'll teach the girls and Eddie to ride. You can go back to nursing if you want to. If you don't, you can help me in whatever I do. What do you say?'

'It sounds wonderful but I can't go with you.'

'Why? You love me, I know you do . . .'

'Oh, I could so very, very easily do that.'

'Then do it.'

'And you'd never wonder if it was you I loved, or the prospect of America and the escape you offered me from a marriage that needed more work than I was prepared to put into it.'

'I'd be so glad you came, I wouldn't wonder anything.'

'Thank you.' She returned the pressure of his fingers, then released his hand. 'For being a good friend when I needed one, for saying wonderful things and offering to share your life with me but I asked you to meet me here so I could say goodbye.'

'You're leaving Pontypridd?'

'Only for a week. But I promised Andrew I'd work with him to try to save our marriage and it wouldn't be fair on him – or you – if I kept "bumping into" you like this.'

'But our meetings are perfectly innocent.'

'Innocent – after the conversation we've just had?'

'What I said about America –'

'I'll never forget it, David. You've just paid me the greatest compliment a man can pay a woman and I've behaved like a foolish, romantic girl. I was lonely, I wanted Prince Charming to come along, and I fitted you into the role.'

'It's a part I've loved playing.'

'And I've put off playing the grown-up for too long.'

'Is there nothing I can say that will change your mind?'

She shook her head.

'No regrets?'

She smiled. 'One great big enormous one and a bucketful of smaller ones. You?'

'The same.'

'But at least I can go to Andrew with a clear conscience.'

'If it doesn't work out between you two, you'll write to me?'

'No, David, because that would be too tempting and too easy, and I owe it to Andrew and the children to put every single thing I've got into what's left of my marriage.' She left the seat and held out her hand. 'Goodbye, Colonel Ford. It was wonderful knowing you.'

'Goodbye, Mrs John, it was wonderful knowing you too. And as your husband has got the girl, I hope he won't mind me stealing one last kiss.'

She expected him to kiss her on the mouth. He didn't. He brushed her cheek lightly with his lips. His moustache grazed her skin, she smelled the sharp, clean, astringent scent of his tooth powder, mixed together with the fragrances of his hair oil and cologne, then she put her head down and walked away – quickly – so he wouldn't see the tears in her eyes.

'Hello, Maggie. Angelo treating you right?'

'Hello, beautiful.' Maggie blew Ronnie a kiss as he walked into the restaurant. 'Angelo's OK but the others you can forget.'

'Where is Angelo?' he asked, looking around.

'In the kitchen.'

'Do me a favour, get him for me. I'm outside in the white van.'

'For you, Ronnie, anything.'

Closing the door Ronnie walked back to the van William had taken from the garage. A couple of minutes later Angelo walked out of the restaurant in shirtsleeves, a white apron tied over his black trousers.

'Ronnie, there was no need for you to come down here. I've sorted everything. Mr Spickett assured me Tony's case is closed for good and we won't hear any more about it. I telephoned the garage to tell you but they said you weren't there.'

'I'm not here about Tony.'

'More trouble. Not Diana . . . ?'

'Try our other brother.'

366

'Alfredo!'

'It might be an idea if you come up to the café with us, if you can spare a couple of minutes. He is in the café.'

'Where else would he be? He'll be there until six o'clock, when I've arranged to relieve him.'

'Are you coming?'

'Right now? But I'm running the restaurant.'

'I think you should be there when we talk to him.'

'If you give me a couple of minutes I'll check if Tony can take over. He's upstairs with Gabrielle. I'm not sure how it's going to work out there. He's telling her that Judy's having his baby.'

'I'm so glad I've only one sister and no brothers,' William smirked.

'It happened the night Tony came home?' Ronnie asked.

'It explains everything, doesn't it? Him disappearing from Graig Street, then being found later in the gutter outside Judy's house . . .'

'The walking kitbag,' William chipped in.

'Forget Tony, ask Maggie to take over.'

'You sure, Ronnie?'

'Absolutely. In fact the more I think about it, the more convinced I am that she should take over either the café or the restaurant – permanently. I can't see her hitting customers out cold, or impregnating waitresses, can you?'

'So, Alfredo, what are you doing tonight after the café closes?' Judy wriggled her stool closer to where he was standing studying the race predictions in the *Daily Mirror*.

'Ask Angelo. It's his night to take over.'

'Even better. Seeing as how I've been moved to the nine-till-five shift and you have a free evening we could go to the pictures.'

'No chance, Judy,' Ronnie interrupted as he breezed through the door, 'Alfredo's got a prior engagement.'

'No I haven't.' Alfredo rolled up his paper and stuffed it into his pocket as William and Angelo followed Ronnie into the front room of the café. 'What is this? You three look like gangsters.'

'And we just might start behaving like them too. Anyone in the back room?'

'No, you should know this is the quiet time.'

'Get the cook out of the kitchen and ask him to man the till. Tell him to call if he needs help.'

'I can look after things out here, Mr Ronconi,' Judy volunteered.

'I've no doubt you can,' Ronnie looked her up and down, 'but I don't like the way you look after "things" so I'd prefer the cook to do it. I'll see you after I've spoken to Alfredo.'

'What's this about?' Alfredo tried to look nonchalant as he reached for a packet of cigarettes but his hands shook when he attempted to shake one free.

'You don't know?' Ronnie walked to a table set far enough round the corner to be invisible from anyone sitting in the front room, and pulled out chairs for Alfredo and himself.

'No.'

'Where were you at eight o'clock this morning?'

'Here.'

'I'm going to ask again.'

Alfredo looked from William to Angelo as they took the two outside chairs, effectively pinning him into the corner.

'I may have gone for a walk.'

'Up the mountain?'

'It gets stuffy in here. I need fresh air –'

'And everyone knows there's plenty of that in a scrap yard,' William interrupted. 'I know exactly where you were, brother-in-law, because I saw you along with Glan Richards, Ianto Myles' son, and all your other little friends, and I know what you were looking for.'

'There was no one there –'

'Where, Alfredo? Where you hid all the lorries, Jeeps and other American Army stuff you stole?'

'We didn't steal it – I didn't – we were only setting

things straight, that's all.'

'Straight?' Ronnie lit Alfredo's cigarette and took one for himself.

'It's like Glan said. The men who've been off fighting have had a rough time getting killed and wounded and they've come home to find all the good jobs taken by cowards who pulled strings to avoid the call-up. Stay-at-home boys who've made a fortune on the black market on the backs of those who risked their lives to keep this country safe. All we wanted was a cut to make up for it.'

'Slightly flawed logic there, little brother. You weren't away fighting.'

'I had a rough time in Birmingham. You should have tried living there with a Welsh accent and an Italian name. I got beaten up all the time.'

'So you thought you'd do some major stealing to make up for it,' Angelo suggested cuttingly.

'Angelo's right.' Ronnie removed a notebook from his top pocket. 'You're involved in big-time stuff, and as you're over eighteen you'll be considered old enough to go to prison.'

'Prison! No . . .'

Leisurely unscrewing the cap from his fountain pen, Ronnie laid it and the notebook on the table in front of Alfredo. 'I want you to list the names of everyone involved in this little scam of yours, especially the people you were going to offload the goods on to.' He held up his hand to stop Alfredo from speaking. 'Then I want you to write down the precise location of any other American equipment you've stolen or know the whereabouts of. If you do that, I might – just might – be able to have a word with Dino and Colonel Ford on your behalf. And who knows, we may even come up with a compromise that won't mean you spending the next ten years looking at the four walls of a cell.'

Chapter Twenty-two

'SIT THERE UNTIL we help you out of the car.'

'Yes, Dr John.'

'And less of your cheek.'

'Yes, Nurse John.' Diana's eyes were bright with excitement as she sat back in the passenger seat of Andrew's car and waited for Andrew to walk round to open the door for her.

'Slowly, one step at a time, and use your crutches because you're not used to walking.' Andrew was almost bowled over by William, who ran out of the house to meet them.

'I could carry you, Di.'

'You most certainly will not. Come here.' Balancing on one crutch she pulled William's head down and kissed his cheek.

William bit his lower lip to control his emotion as he slipped his arm round Diana's waist to support her as she tackled the steps. Andrew glanced up at Dino, who was holding the front door open. The American nodded almost imperceptibly and Andrew saw a curtain move in the front parlour window.

'You take care with your sister,' Megan cautioned William as Diana finally made it to the doorstep.

'He is Mam.' Turning, Diana looked out over the town. 'Everything is so big, so clear, so strange, so –'

'Bloody cold when I'm standing out here in shirt-sleeves,' William complained, 'and it must feel like an ice box to someone who has just come out of a baking hot hospital.' Wrapping his arm round her shoulders, he led her into the hall and down the passage to the kitchen.

*

Ronnie held his finger to his lips as he looked from Billy to Catrina. As soon as he heard voices raised in the kitchen he lifted Catrina down from the sofa in the bay and set her on the rug next to her family of rag dolls.

'Mam looked funny.' Billy crouched next to his sister and handed her one of the dolls. 'She is going to be all right, isn't she, Daddy?'

'The doctors think so. That's why they've let her visit us. But it may be only a visit. You do remember me telling you that she might not be able to stay with us all the time just yet?'

'Yes.' Billy's bottom lip trembled.

'But it will only be for a little while. Sometime soon she'll be home for good and then we'll be able to look after her.'

'I'll help.'

'Course you will, darling.' He dropped a kiss on Catrina's head. 'But you both have to remember that Mam was asleep for a long time.'

Billy looked solemnly up at Ronnie, obviously expecting more.

'Her head is a bit fuzzy, like yours when you wake up first thing in the morning and she's forgotten some things, so we'll have to remind her about them. And while she was sleeping she couldn't eat, so she lost some weight. But we can fatten her up by giving her lots of biscuits and slices of Granny's cake.'

'Will there still be enough for me?'

'I should think so, Billy,' Ronnie smiled. 'How would you like a game of tiddlywinks until Mam has settled in enough to see us?'

'Catrina doesn't play it properly.'

'And she isn't going to learn if we don't teach her to play it with us.' Ronnie opened the box and tipped the counters out. 'What colour do you want?'

'Red.' Catrina grabbed the large red bone disc and eight smaller ones while Ronnie set the pot and cardboard scoreboard on the lino at the edge of the rug.

'Can I have blue, Dad?' Billy asked.

Ronnie nodded absently, not even thinking about the game. Like Billy he had noticed that Diana had lost weight. The only time he had seen her in two and a half years were the few minutes on the night of his arrival, and although she had been wrapped in her dressing gown he was sure she hadn't looked quite so thin and gaunt then. The navy serge suit she was wearing – one he remembered – had hung loose on her slight frame, the white blouse under the jacket positively baggy at the collar. He felt a tug at his hand and looked down. Catrina handed him the die and Bakelite shaker cup.

'Play!'

'Of course, darling.' He stretched out on the rug between the children. 'It's a real treat to have a fire in here, isn't it?' he enthused in an effort to convince them that the unusual activity in the house was all for their benefit. Catrina tipped the die out on the lino.

'You're supposed to shake it, Cat,' Billy reprimanded crossly.

Ronnie slipped the die back into the cup. 'Try again, sunshine.'

Jumping to his feet, Billy shouted, 'I don't want to play, I want to see Mam.'

'Ssh, keep your voice down. You will see her, Billy, I promise, and in a very few minutes.' Ronnie pulled him back on to the rug. 'But she's been very ill and needs to rest after her journey here.'

'And she doesn't want to see me and Catrina because she's resting?'

'Of course she'll want to see you.' Rolling on his back, Ronnie lifted him high in his arms. 'And when Granny comes to get you, you can give Mam the flowers we bought on the market and Catrina can give her the bar of chocolate.'

'Granny's never coming.'

'Roll the die, start playing and I bet you . . .' Ronnie pulled the change from his pocket and laid two silver threepences on the tiled hearth. 'Those two joeys that Granny will come to get you before the game is over.'

*

'I'm not an invalid, Mam.'

'Yes, you are, and you'll do as you're told.' Megan bustled Diana into one of the easy chairs placed next to the range. Pulling a blanket from beneath a cushion on the sofa she unfolded it and tucked it around her daughter's legs.

'Now I'm going to roast.'

'Quiet, or I'll set Andrew on you.'

'Great, now I'm the bogeyman.' Andrew carried Diana's case in, and left it by the door.

'If you don't do as you're told, he'll have you straight back in hospital.'

'All you've succeeded in doing is swapping one dragon witch sister for another, Di,' Bethan cautioned.

'Tea's ready when you are,' Tina called from the wash house.

'Come and meet the invalid before you lay it,' Bethan suggested.

'I thought we weren't supposed to overwhelm her all at once.' Picking up a towel, Tina dried her hands on it before joining the others. Megan was hovering anxiously over Diana, Andrew had sat next to Bethan on the sofa but William and Dino were standing at the door like sentinels.

'Hello, Di.' She bent to kiss her. 'Nice to see you up and about and looking so well. Boy, your hair looks great.'

'One of the nurses cut and shaped it for me.'

'Any chance of her coming to the house to do mine?' She looked across at William and Dino. 'You two standing guard, or what?'

Diana looked at them and laughed. 'Little and large.'

'Who's the large?' Megan asked.

'That depends on whether you're looking sideways or head on,' Tina teased.

'You're my stepfather?'

'You recognise me, Diana?' Dino asked hopefully.

'From a photograph Bethan gave me of you and Mam that had been taken on your wedding day. Apparently I was there but I don't remember a thing about it. You're

373

even wider than Mam said and I thought you would be.'

'Diana! I said no such thing,' Megan exclaimed.

'It's all right, I grew a skin like a rhinoceros when I married into this family,' Dino grinned, 'but only because I had to.'

'I think I'm going to like you, Dino. Did I before?'

'Glad to see you've lost none of your tact and diplomacy along with your memory, sis.' William perched on the other chair and looked up at Tina. 'Tea, woman.'

'No ordering me about to show off in front of Diana or I'll hit you.'

'See how cruelly she treats me? She needs you to set a good wifely example . . .' He stooped to rub his ankle where Andrew had kicked him.

'Where are the children?' Diana asked.

'In the parlour. We lit the fire so they could play in there.'

'That's my fault, not Megan's,' Andrew explained. 'I thought you shouldn't be bombarded with too many people at once.'

'And I'd like this to be a normal day and a normal family teatime. You should have invited Uncle Evan and Phyllis . . .'

'And all my brothers and sisters.' Tina carried an enormous oval meat plate piled high with Welsh cakes into the kitchen and set it in the middle of the table, 'including my mother and Gina, who's just had a baby.'

'Boy or girl?'

'Girl. Sorry, Andrew,' she apologised as he shook his head at her. 'I didn't think.'

'But I remember Gina marrying Luke,' Diana protested. Tired of the strained atmosphere that was the result of everyone trying too hard, she looked from Andrew to her mother. 'I want to see the children.'

'Andrew?' Megan asked.

'I want to see them, not him.' Reaching for her crutches, she heaved herself to her feet.

'I'll go and check the fire in the parlour.'

'There's no need, Beth. It will be fine.'

374

'How do you know?'

'Because there's no way you lot would leave a five-year-old and a two-year-old alone in a room with a fire. I know their father's with them and I think it's time I made his acquaintance.'

'Peter, what on earth are you doing here?' Liza stared in amazement as she walked into the lobby of the nurses' home and saw Peter standing in the foyer.

'I'm here because they told me I couldn't wait anywhere else.'

'But how did you find me?'

'You told me you worked in Cardiff Royal Infirmary. Today's my half-day in the garage, I caught a bus into Cardiff found it, and asked for you.'

'Someone in the Infirmary told you I was here?' She pulled her nurse's cloak closer to her body, holding the edges together with her fingers. She'd been fast asleep after her night shift when one of the other trainees had woken her with the news that there was a young man waiting to see her. She'd thrown on a few clothes and run down expecting to see Angelo, but Peter's white-blond head shining like a beacon in the tiled gloom of the hostel foyer had taken her breath away.

'You're angry with me.'

'Just surprised.'

'I wanted to see you.'

'I'm on night shift for the next three days.'

'The nurse I spoke to told me.'

'But I have next Thursday off.' Try as she may she simply couldn't stop looking into his eyes. Blue – deep blue – so unlike Angelo's dark brown ones.

'I have to work in the day, but I could meet you here in the evening, or if you come to Pontypridd I could see you there.'

'I'm going home to see my sisters.'

'Then we'll go out on Thursday night.' She suddenly realised he hadn't asked but told her. 'Do you have some free time now?'

She looked at her watch. 'A couple of hours. I intended to spend them sleeping.'

'But you're awake now. I could take you . . .'

'For a coffee, a walk, or to the pictures.' She expected him to accuse her of making fun of him but he smiled.

'Any or all of those things.'

'Give me a quarter of an hour to get ready.'

'You are ready.'

'Not if you look at what I'm wearing under this cloak.'

'I could help you dress.'

'Say that within earshot of the warden of this hostel and you'll never have any children. Fifteen minutes, no more, I promise.' She ran back up the stairs.

'Liza, he's gorgeous.'

'Where have you been hiding him?'

'Who is he?'

'He looks Scandinavian.'

'I thought you were going out with that Italian boy.'

'I am,' Liza mumbled, remembering that she still hadn't had time to tell Angelo of her change of heart, and he deserved to hear about it before a crowd of her fellow trainees.

'Does he know about this one?'

'Peter's a friend of the family.'

'I wish my family had friends who looked like him.'

'He's only sixteen.'

'Now we know you're lying. If you get fed up of him you know where to send him.'

As Liza finally managed to push her way back up the stairs, she stole another glance at Peter in the foyer and knew with absolute certainty that she didn't want to send him anywhere – especially away from her.

The door to the parlour opened and Megan beckoned to Billy and Catrina. 'Better get the flowers and chocolate, she's coming.'

Billy rushed to the table to pick up the bunch of daffodils and tulips he had helped Ronnie pick out earlier that morning, while Ronnie handed Catrina the chocolate that had used up his month's sweet rations.

Diana hobbled round the corner.

'Sit down before you try to hug them,' Megan advised.

Diana almost fell into the nearest chair and opened her arms. Billy stood still for a moment then, clutching the flowers, he hurtled at top speed on to her lap throwing his arms round her neck.

'Steady now, Billy. Remember Mam has been very ill.' Megan brushed a tear from the corner of her eye.

'But I'm fine now.' Sitting back, Diana held her son away from her with both hands and looked at him. 'You've grown into a fine boy.'

'You home for good, Mam?'

'I hope so, darling. If it was up to me I would be but I still have to do what the doctors say.' She looked across the room to see Ronnie struggling to hold Catrina, who was fighting to climb off his lap.

'She knows her mother,' he said quietly.

'Here, Billy, shift over.' Diana made room on her lap and Ronnie lifted Catrina gently on to her. 'Chocolate, flowers, for me?' She kissed both of them. 'Thank you so very much. Now I want you to tell me everything that you've been doing since I've been away.'

Ronnie moved closer to Megan as the children began babbling.

'Do you think she remembers?' he whispered, hoping, although he already knew the answer to his question.

'Well prepared. She's been pumping Bethan all morning,' Megan muttered under her breath.

'Me and Daddy saw you coming.'

'Did you, darling?' Diana kissed Billy's cheek.

'And we bought you flowers. I chose them.'

'They're lovely.'

'And chocolate.'

'You're spoiling me.' She handed Megan her presents. 'Don't you think it's time I saw this mystery Daddy?'

'Perhaps when the children go into the kitchen for tea.' Megan looked away, unable to meet Ronnie's eyes.

'Daddy's no mystery,' Billy giggled.

'Billy, why don't you take Catrina into the kitchen and see if Auntie Tina's set out those iced biscuits we made this morning? If she has, pick out the two nicest and put them on a plate for Mam,' Megan suggested.

'Mam . . .'

'I'm not going away just yet, Billy.' Diana allowed Megan to lift the children from her lap.

'They're quite a handful,' she said, as Ronnie closed the door behind Megan, before sitting in the chair opposite hers.

'Most children are.'

'Tina said something about having a party and inviting all her brothers and sisters; I had no idea she was serious.'

'How are you feeling?'

'Fed up with no one telling me anything. Overwhelmed at seeing two grown children, one I can't even remember. Annoyed at missing four years.' She looked at him, saw the way he was looking at her. 'I married you!'

'I wish that hadn't sounded as though you were quite so shocked – or sorry.'

'I don't remember enough to be sorry. This is awful, like walking through a thick fog and not knowing who you're going to meet when it lifts enough to see your hand in front of your face.'

'How about we sit here quietly in front of the fire and I tell you everything so you don't have to remember.'

'You'd do that? The doctors –'

'Have admitted they haven't a clue what to do with you.' Leaving his chair he kneeled on the hearthrug in front of her. Lifting back her hair, he ran his fingers lightly over the scar on her temple. 'That must hurt.'

'Not any more, although I sometimes get headaches. God, this is strange!'

'Let's see if we can make it any the less strange. Where do you want me to start?'

'It still has to be uniform, I'm afraid. I might not have time to change later.'

378

'Your hair looks tidier.'

'You're lucky I had time to comb it. You can't just turn up at the nurses' hostel like this, Peter. I could have been working, I could have been studying – and you can't take my arm.' She moved away from him as one of the staff nurses walked into the foyer. 'I'm in uniform and shouldn't even be with a boy.'

'But you were sleeping?' He followed her as she left the building.

'I was.'

'If you had been busy or I hadn't found you I would have got back on the bus and gone home.'

'Won't your mother and father be worried about you?'

'I am not a child.'

'I'm beginning to realise that.'

'What is this place?'

'A teashop.' She opened the door and looked around. There were half a dozen empty tables and she chose one by the window.

'Nurses come to drink tea here when they don't have to work?'

'And eat,' she said earnestly. 'The food in the hostel is very bad.'

'I have some money, what can I buy you?'

'You want to save all your money. I can buy my own food and drink.'

'I think,' he rested his head on his hands and looked at her, 'that very soon your money and my money will be the same.'

'What would you like, sir, miss?' The waitress pulled a notepad from her belt.

'I'd like whatever is good, two of everything.'

'Sir?'

'Never mind him, he's in a funny mood.' Liza looked at the counter behind the girl. 'Two hot chocolates, and are those fresh Chelseas?'

'Made this morning.'

'And two of those please.'

*

Ronnie sat back in his chair. 'Have I said too much for you to take in?'

'I think I've followed you.'

'You have to bear in mind that I've only given the sketchiest outline of what your life has been like for the last two and a half years because I wasn't here and I only have your letters and other people's accounts to go on.'

'I still can't believe I married you. Of all the men in Pontypridd – you!' She continued to sit staring at him with the same expression of blank incomprehension on her face that had set in when she had realised why he'd stayed in the room after the children had left.

'Any reason in particular why you can't believe it?'

'You are so much older than me. You were always shouting and grumpy when you ran the café when I was growing up . . .'

'You made the same objections when I first suggested we get married.'

'I did?'

'Yes.'

'And you were married to Maud. I remember your wedding.'

'You married Wyn.'

'I know they've both died. Bethan told me. I wish they hadn't.'

'We both did a lot of grieving at the time.'

'This is so peculiar.'

'The first thing I have to do is convince you how much I've changed from the Ronnie you remember, but it's not my shouting and moods you're thinking about, is it?'

'No.'

'You're trying to imagine making love to me and you can't, because you married Wyn in the hope that you'd never have to sleep with another man again.'

'How did you know that?'

'Because we've never kept secrets from one another. Because I'm your husband and because I've made it my business to know your every mood and thoughts. We were together for over a year before I had to leave and I used that time to study you. I was a very attentive student.'

'I remember asking Maud once if she was afraid of you.'

'And what did she say?'

'Not after she got to know you.'

'We have all the time in the world to get to know one another again, Diana.'

'What if I never remember that you're my husband?'

'We'll have to make a whole lot of new memories for you to think about.'

'It doesn't worry you?'

'The only thing that concerns me at the moment is how I'm going to keep you out of the clutches of the doctors and that hospital. Do you want to go back?'

She shook her head vigorously. 'Absolutely not.'

'Then, we'll have to make sure you don't. Come on, Di.' He left his seat and helped her out of her chair. 'The others will be wondering what's become of us, and if I don't get you back in the kitchen for tea, Andrew's going to batter down that door to get at you. Oh, and by the way, your mother has insisted we have separate bedrooms until you do remember me.' He raised his eyebrows. 'Which is such a pity. I don't know if you'll take my word for it, but the one thing we are really good at is making love. You used to insist on practising every chance we got.'

'That was good.' Peter laid a neat pile of coins on top of the bill, stacked his cup, saucer and plate and leaned over the table closer to Liza. 'And if I hadn't come, you would have slept and not eaten and gone straight to the ward.'

'Yes, and I'll probably curse you at the end of my shift when I'm worn out, but right now, thank you, Peter.' She looked at her watch. 'I have to go.'

'I'll walk you back.' He held out his hand, and this time she took it.

'Can't I come to your room, even for a moment?'

'Girls have been thrown out the Infirmary for less.'

'But I want to kiss you.'

'In broad daylight?'

'If I can't see you later, yes, in broad daylight.'

As they reached the gates of the hostel she took him to the side, into the shrubbery. As soon as the bushes screened them, he closed his hands round her waist and, almost lifting off her feet, kissed her.

'You'll be my girl?' he asked when he released her. 'You'll be my girl, Liza?'

It was almost a command. She thought about Angelo and the well-meaning lecture Bethan had given her about Peter's peculiar upbringing and how he had no experience of normal, family life and relationships with women. But the more she considered it, the more she realised that she'd meant every word she'd said. There was simply no decision for her to make.

'I can't be your girl until I tell Angelo that I can't go out with him any more.'

Wrapping his arms round her, he pulled her close. 'And then you'll marry me?'

'Not until I finish my training.'

'And if I can't wait that long?'

'Peter, I hardly know you,' she murmured, using Bethan's argument. He continued to gaze into her eyes. 'Your mother was right,' she whispered. 'You do only have to look into someone's eyes to know that you love them.'

'I hear you won't have a job for too much longer, Dino.' Andrew couldn't hide his delight at the thought, and Bethan knew he was anticipating David's imminent departure.

'Not after what these two uncovered.' He nodded to William, who'd left his seat at the table to give Ronnie a hand to help Diana through the door.

'You told her?' Andrew looked to Ronnie.

'Yes,' Diana answered, 'and as you see, Dr John, I've survived the experience.'

'Did you find everything you were looking for in the scrap yard, Dino?' Ronnie asked, eyeing the children who were busy playing with Megan's animal-shaped iced biscuits – but, he suspected, still listening in on the conversation.

'Our men are still out. We called for reinforcements, they're starting again at first light, but the colonel seems to think we're well on the way to recovering a good third of our missing property.'

'Who would have thought that Glan and Alfredo had it in them?'

'That's my brother you're talking about, Will.'

'Ours, Tina, but that doesn't make him any the less guilty.' Ronnie helped Diana into a chair. 'Sorry to have to tell you this, love, but it appears that my brother Alfredo is something of a wide boy.'

'What's going to happen to him?' Megan asked.

'We'll work something out,' Dino said airily.

'I seem to remember occasions when you weren't that far off being a wide boy, Will, or you.' Diana looked at Ronnie.

'We're both as respectable as they come these days,' Will protested.

'I've been out of it that long?'

'I keep them respectable.' Tina picked up the teapot. 'You two want tea?'

'Please.' Ronnie grabbed Billy, who'd just received Megan's permission to leave the table, and tickled him.

'Don't, Daddy. Mam – tell him.'

'Tell him what, darling?' She took Catrina, who'd held out her arms to be picked up as soon as she sat at the table.

'To stop.'

'Do you want him to?' She smiled as Ronnie swung Billy down on to his foot and lifted him back up to table level.

'Sometimes.' Billy started laughing again.

'You look exhausted, Di.' Ronnie set Billy down on the floor. 'You could have your tea in bed.'

'That would be a good idea,' Andrew concurred drily, 'if you were going to stay the night.'

'You will let me?' Diana begged.

'You can't be thinking of taking her back to that hospital?' Megan protested. 'The poor girl needs rest and a fat lot she'll get there with that dragon witch stomping around.'

'I should have known better than to think you'd let her leave once she came over the doorstep. All right, if she goes to bed right this minute and you promise to telephone me the second there's any change or if she gets ill, feverish or faints . . .'

'None of which I intend doing,' Diana maintained.

'I promise,' Ronnie interrupted.

'Then she can stay. Just for tonight. I'll be round first thing in the morning.'

'Not to take her back.'

'One thing at a time, Megan. I'll only let her stay now if Bethan sees her safely between the sheets.'

'Bully,' Diana grumbled, but both Ronnie and Andrew noticed she didn't need any further coaxing to leave her chair.

'Read us a story, Mam?' Billy pleaded.

'Not Mam, Daddy,' Ronnie said firmly, 'and it's too early. How about we go in the parlour and finish our game of tiddlywinks first?'

'Catrina's thrown the counters everywhere.'

'Then we'll have to pick them up, won't we, young man?'

'And Catrina won't be playing with you, because she's coming to her Auntie Tina, aren't you poppet, and we're going to look at a picture book?'

'I forgot, you haven't been in this house before.'

'I haven't?' Diana looked at Bethan and they both burst out laughing.

'This is the bedroom your mother made up for you.'

'It's lovely.' Diana ran her hands over the beechwood suite. 'Is this new?'

'Dino had the money and the contacts to buy it. The bathroom's next door. You can have a bath if you like. Andrew and I aren't in a hurry and I'll stay here, so you

384

can shout if you need me. Look, your mother's bought you a new nightdress and – trust Ronnie.'

'What?' Diana looked at the book Bethan had picked up.

'Some bedtime reading. It's a photograph album.' Bethan opened it; the first picture was of Ronnie and Diana on their wedding day. 'You've got quite a husband, Diana.'

'It's a pity I can't remember being married to him. He says we were happy.'

'You were, blissfully. And if he has his way I've a feeling you soon will be again.'

'I'm sorry about this weekend,' Andrew apologised as they closed the door of the children's bedroom after reading Rachel and Eddie two more stories than they'd originally been promised and conceding Polly and Nell an extra half-hour reading time.

'Can't be helped. Patients, especially my cousin, come first.'

'That's the problem, Beth, with all our relatives and friends, three-quarters of the population of this town come before us.' He opened the door to the small sitting room next to the bedroom and started in surprise.

'I asked Nessie to light a fire in here before she left for her father's house.'

'And the sandwiches and brandy?'

'Nessie made the sandwiches. I've been hoarding a tin of American ham Dino gave me for months, and I cadged the brandy off your father.'

'Grown-up time.'

'Our time. The children are in bed; the girls won't disturb us unless there's an earthquake. I've told Nessie she can stay home until Monday morning. It's not the chalet on the Gower, Andrew, but we are together and I thought that we might try to pretend.'

'Drink?' He held up the brandy.

'A small one.'

'Did something happen that I missed?' he asked as he wrestled with the cork.

'I told David Ford I wouldn't be around town to bump into him any more.'

'And you told me there wasn't anything between you.'

'There wasn't, Andrew. And now there never will be.'

'And you're sorry.'

'You told me before we married that you'd had – and I mean literally – other girls.'

'One staff nurse who was so large she was known as Two–Ton Tompkins. I got drunk at a party and she took advantage, pinning me down so she could have her evil way with me before I could put up an effective resistance. Another, I'm ashamed to say, was one of my professor's wives, who, unfortunately for him, poor soul, had an insatiable appetite for her husband's male students. I was weak and frustrated but it was a cold and embarrassing experience.'

'Were there more?'

'A few passing encounters.'

'Is that your way of telling me they didn't mean anything.'

'It was sex. Which is rarely pure and never simple. You know boys, Beth, or you should. You were fighting them off when I met you. The first Pontypridd hospital ball I went to I watched you tip a glass of orange juice over Glan Richards to cool his ardour.'

'That was an accident.'

'Neither he, nor I believed you.'

'Whether you did or didn't, it's the truth.'

He sat down and took out his pipe but made no attempt to fill it. She sat on the floor in front of the fire and leaned back against his legs.

'But you wanted to sleep with those women.'

'Apart from Two–Ton Tompkins, I thought so at the time.'

'And since you married me? The truth, Andrew. Have you ever looked at another woman and thought, yes, I'd like to know what she looks like naked, smell her perfume, find out how she makes love?'

'Beth, why are you asking me this?'

'Because I want to know.'

'I admit, occasionally I fantasise. I'm no different to any other man in that respect.'

'Would it surprise you to know that women do it too. Clark Gable, Robert Taylor, David Niven . . .'

'David Ford?'

'If we hadn't married or had the children, I might have been tempted to have had a fling with him. But the one thing I've discovered in the last few years is that you can't live your life backwards. You were the first and you're still the only man I've ever slept with. For five and a half years I missed you and sometimes – just occasionally during that time and before, if I'm totally honest – I wondered what it would be like to sleep with another man. To be truthful, I still do but that doesn't mean I want to or will. Because I know it would hurt you and the guilt would destroy me and what's left of our marriage.'

'So you'd sleep with David Ford if you could manage it without hurting me or feeling guilty?'

'You've missed the point. I would have had an affair with him if there hadn't been a you and the children but there is a you and the children. I've been selfish, Andrew. Most days during the war I was so damned tired after nursing all day, coming home and spending time with the children and doing everything else that needed to be done, fantasising about making love was the last thing on my mind. But if I needed someone to talk to – always late at night or early in the morning because that was the only time I had – David was around, making tea. Like me, drinking anything non-alcoholic to keep himself awake so he could finish his paperwork just as I was trying to finish mine. And I think one of the reasons I wanted to keep on seeing him was because he reminded me of those times when I felt important. I was doing a job, a responsible job, then, bam, you come home, I lose the job, my feelings of importance, we have a brief honeymoon . . .'

'And it's back to the grind. No wonder you fantasise.'

'We're going to have to learn to be selfish, you and I.' She unfastened her blouse and slipped it from her shoulders. 'This rug is thick and the fire is warm.' Reaching up, she unbuttoned his fly.

'Is the door locked?'

'Yes, and it's going to be locked at least two evenings a week from now on.'

'Beth,' he gripped her hand as she slipped his belt from its loop, 'am I second best?'

'Never,' she lied. She lay back, pulling him towards her. 'We have a lot of work to do, you and I, but if we try very hard perhaps we can transform some of it into pleasure.'

'I love you, Beth.'

'And I love you, Andrew. No more jealousy?'

'That, my love, is one thing I can't promise you.'

Chapter Twenty-three

'THEY'VE COME TO say good night.' Holding Billy and Catrina's hands firmly so they wouldn't jump on the bed, Ronnie led them to Diana's bedside. Setting aside the photograph album she'd been studying, Diana held out her arms as Ronnie lifted them one at a time to kiss her.

'Daddy reads stories faster than you,' Billy complained. 'And he tries to leave out bits.'

'And he goes to sleep and snores.'

'I didn't tonight, Catrina,' Ronnie protested mildly.

'You do most nights.' Billy crossed his arms mutinously.

'I'll take over.'

'Not for a week or two you won't. Right you two snitching little menaces, you've had your kiss and cuddle, off you go to your own room. Granny is waiting.' Ronnie hugged them before they scampered down the landing to where Megan was standing with hot-water bottles tucked under her arm.

'Time to sleep, sweetheart.' He smoothed the hair away from Diana's forehead and dropped a kiss on the scar on her temple.

Diana stared up at him; he seemed so tall, so strong and so incongruous and out of place in the intimate setting of her bedroom, she couldn't begin to imagine living in the same house as him, let alone lying beside him every night. 'Where are you sleeping?'

'The boxroom. If I wasn't, I think Andrew would fly down Penycoedcae Hill and drag you back into the Graig Hospital even at this time of night.'

'But we can talk for a while.'

'Andrew warned us that you've had more than enough

excitement for one day. Besides, much as I hate to admit it, you look exhausted.'

'That's because I can't stop thinking about all the things you haven't told me.'

'Di, the only thing you have to worry about is getting better.'

'I won't sleep until I get a few more answers.'

He hesitated for a moment. 'All right, you can have ten minutes.' She winced as he sat at the foot of the bed. 'Oh God! I hurt you!'

'No. It was only a shooting pain in my arm; I get them once in a while. We don't live here, do we?'

'No. We moved into Laura's house after we married and you carried on living there while I was in the army but we can't go back there. Laura and Trevor will be home soon and the children need to be looked after . . .'

'I'll soon be able to do that.'

'Not yet. I've talked to your mother and Dino, and although they're practically honeymooners they insist they're happy for us to stay here until you're on your feet. They must really enjoy having the children to put up with me living here as well but then they're nice people.'

'So we're going to stay here?'

'Only until you're well enough to move out. I've been on the lookout for a house to buy but I admit I haven't put much effort into hunting one down because I wanted you to choose it with me.'

'We have enough money to buy a house?'

'For anything you want – within reason.'

'Something close to here. I wouldn't like to move too far away from my mother.'

'I'll start knocking doors in the street tomorrow to see if I can persuade someone to move out.' He glanced down at the album. 'Bethan had a word with me about that.'

'We looked so happy.'

'We are so happy.'

'I can't –'

He laid his finger over her lips. '"Remember." Stop saying that. You should be happy now. What more could a woman want than flowers, chocolates, a doting mother, beautiful children, caring friends and family and an extremely loving husband – or one who will be when he gets the chance to show it.'

'It must be just as odd for you, having a wife who can't remember marrying you.'

'I'm so grateful that I still have you, I couldn't care less whether all the pieces in your brain are working or not.' Reaching out he ran his fingers lightly along the contour of her face from her eye to her jaw. She clamped her hand over his. 'That feels familiar.'

'I promise you, there will be all sorts of other things that will seem familiar too.'

'Such as?'

'It's easier to show you.' Kicking off his shoes, he moved up the bed and lay on top of the bedclothes next to her. Sliding his arm beneath her, he pillowed her head on his shoulder. 'You're trembling. I'm sorry, I shouldn't be here, I'm going too quickly.' He moved to sit up.

'Please, don't . . .'

'Di, it's obvious you're uncomfortable with me.'

'I'm not used to having strange men in my bed.'

'I thought you might remember – there's that word again and now it's me who's using it.'

'What sort of things did we do when we were married?'

'Lie like this for hours, just talking, which is why I thought it was a good idea to come down here. And please note we're on different levels. I'm not in your bed but on it.'

Feeling distinctly uneasy she had to make a conscious effort to keep her voice steady. 'What sort of things did we talk about?'

'Billy, what his future would be, and later, when you were pregnant, what Catrina would be like. You wanted another boy but I think only because you'd decided I did. I wanted a girl and I was so angry when I was conscripted a couple of weeks before she was born. But,' he smiled wryly, 'nowhere near as angry as you.' He stroked her hair as he smiled at the memory. 'And after we finished planning the children's lives we'd start on our own. We never envisaged anything spectacular happening, just talked about what it would be like when the war was finally over and everything was back to normal so we could get on with family life – doing family things together – being happy.'

'Like now.'

'Our lives are hardly normal now, Di.'

'No, I suppose they aren't.' Reassured, because he hadn't tried to kiss her or make love to her, she dared to rest her hand on his chest, feeling his heart beating beneath her palm. 'I do remember a few things that we haven't talked about.'

'Such as.'

'Billy's real father. That fight you had with Tony before my accident, it was because of me, wasn't it?'

'No, I was furious with him for being in our house and refusing to go when you asked him to. I wish to God I'd never laid a hand on him,' he murmured fervently. 'If I hadn't you wouldn't have gone through that window . . .'

'He must feel awful about it.'

'He! Tony! Are you insane? He could have killed you, Diana, and damned near did. The fact that you're alive is solely down to Andrew and Bethan's skill and their quick thinking. Have you any idea how close you came to dying?' He snapped his fingers. 'That close, and can you imagine what that was like for me, your mother and Billy? Catrina's too young to know what went on but Billy isn't. No matter how careful Megan and I were, he heard snatches of conversation no boy his age should, and he was petrified of losing you – so don't come to me with any cock-eyed ideas of feeling sorry for my damned brother.' He sat up furiously. Swinging his legs over the edge of the bed, he reached for his cigarettes.

'He's still your brother, Ronnie.'

'Not any more he isn't.'

'Ronnie, I could have died but I didn't. Whatever happened that night, and I'm beginning to face up to the fact that I may never remember, can't be worth bearing that kind of grudge.'

'I don't want to talk about it.'

'I do, because I can't understand why you married me knowing Billy was Tony's son. Or did you know?' she asked quietly.

'I knew.'

'I told you?'

'Diana, we fell in love. You adored me.' His tone was flippant but there was an underlying seriousness that sent her heart racing and the blood coursing headily through her veins.

'And you,' she tried to adopt his teasing tone, 'did you adore me?'

'Absolutely and completely, which is why I nearly went mad when you went through that window and probably would have if it hadn't been for Billy and Catrina.'

'Did I tell you about Billy before we got married?'

'Long before.'

'I remember Wyn saying it didn't matter to him.'

'And it didn't – doesn't – to me. No matter how many other children we have, and I hope there'll be some, none of them could possibly be any more my son than Billy is.'

'Some?'

'One or two. I have no intention of following my parents' example and having eleven. But all of that is in the future. For now,' he rose from the bed, 'you need to get your beauty sleep.'

'Don't leave just yet, Ronnie.'

'And don't do that to me.'

'What?'

'Put temptation my way. I've lived like a monk for two and a half years. I can't trust myself to stay here, alone in a bedroom with you, without things happening that the doctors have warned me to leave well alone for the time being.' He kissed her lightly on the lips.

'That's another thing . . .'

'You married Wyn because you were terrified of

making love and you knew he'd never touch you. I changed your mind about lovemaking, Di, and I'm not ashamed to say, before we were married.'

'I wish –'

'Look at Catrina. If ever a child was conceived in love, it was that one, once I let you have your wicked way with me.'

'You joke a lot.'

'Only about serious things. You'll get used to it again. And just so you know, it was you who came to my bed, not the other way round and, before I went away, you told me you'd never regretted it.'

'I'm beginning to believe you.'

'It wasn't easy to find the patience to court you slowly, Di, but last time I did it the rewards went way beyond my expectations. I'll find that same patience again if it kills me.'

'Bethan told me I had quite a husband.' She gripped his hand. 'Thank you for wanting to pick up the pieces.'

'We'll put a few more in place tomorrow, but now,' he smiled at her as he moved to the door, 'I'd better go downstairs before your mother chases me out of here with a broom handle.' He looked back at her. 'We have a whole lot of tomorrows to be happy in, Diana, that I thought we weren't going to have.'

'And Tony?'

'I'll think about what you said. I can't promise to do any more. But trust me, Di, we were happy and we will be again.'

Leaving the breakfast dishes to Mrs Lane, Masha took one of the cinnamon sticks she'd found in a jar in the store cupboard and grated it over the biscuit dough she had rolled out on the kitchen table. Sorting through the cutters she'd discovered in a drawer, she studied them carefully. It had been so long since she had made biscuits. She had vague memories of the points of the star shape browning before the body of the biscuit and burning. Similarly the points of the half-moon. Eventually she

394

settled on a round moon shape. Picking up the circular cutter she began punching biscuits, brushing them with a sugar glaze before lifting them carefully with a palette knife on to a greased baking tray.

Charlie walked in, rolling down the sleeves of his shirt. 'Easter biscuits? It's not Easter yet, Masha,' he smiled, kissing her withered cheek.

'It will be soon, and you used to say they were the best things I made.'

'They were.'

'I hope your other son thinks so, and that policeman who went with Pasha to the park. He might like a biscuit and a cup of tea when they return.'

'I'm sure he will. I won't be long. I'm just going down to get Theo, I'll be straight back.' Shrugging his arms into his jacket, he suddenly realised it didn't feel quite so loose on him. He was beginning to put on weight.

'How many potatoes would you like me to do, Mr Raschenko?'

'Enough for three adults and one child please, Mrs Lane.' He bent and kissed the top of Masha's head. 'I love you, Masha,' he murmured in Russian.

'And this evening we'll talk about going back home?'

'Pasha and I promised, but not until after I take Theo back. 'Bye, Mrs Lane.'

''Bye, Mr Raschenko. Oh, before you go, would you ask your wife if she'd like me to put those biscuits into the oven for her?'

'Mrs Lane wants to know if the biscuits are ready for the oven, Masha,' he asked in Russian.

'Please, tell her they have to cook slowly. Very slowly indeed.'

Charlie translated.

'I'll see to it, Mr Raschenko, don't mind me asking but what's in that sugar glaze? It smells wonderful and your wife seems to have made it from next to nothing.'

'Ordinary sugar and water, Mrs Lane with a sprinkling of cinnamon.'

'It looks good.'

'You'll see how good when you taste it.' It had been over sixteen years since he had eaten Masha's Easter biscuits and he could hardly wait.

'God has been good to you, Tony. You have a very beautiful bride. You must be feeling proud.'

'Yes, Father,' Tony mumbled, not daring to look at Gabrielle.

'I'll see you both for instruction on Tuesday evening at seven, and we will start calling the banns next week.'

'Thank you, Father.'

Tony reflected that it was just as well his mother had stepped in to thank the priest, as Gabrielle appeared to be as dumbstruck as he was. Moving aside, he made room for the rest of the congregation to congratulate the father on the sermon he'd tactfully based on the theme of 'reconciliation' while his mother took Gabrielle back inside the church to light candles. He wondered whether he could reasonably plead pressing duty in the café to opt out of escorting his mother and Gabrielle home. He wouldn't have even considered going to church that morning if Angelo hadn't arrived at the café before six to roust him out of bed with strict orders from their mother that he attend eight o'clock Mass. The first person he'd seen as he'd approached the church at ten to eight was his mother, busily introducing Gabrielle to the priest and as many of the congregation as would acknowledge them.

'Tony!'

'Mama.' He tried to look as though he'd been listening to every word she'd been saying.

'I am going to Mrs Servini's for coffee, her son will drive me home. You will walk Gabrielle back to the house?'

'Yes, Mama.'

'Tell Gina not to overcook the meat. It should come out of the oven at a quarter past twelve. I will be home to make the gravy.'

'I'll tell her.' He held back from reminding her that Gina had cooked perfect Sunday dinners throughout the war in Danycoedcae Road without help from anyone. After Gabrielle had finished shaking hands again with every single person Father McNamara and his mother had introduced her to, Tony offered her his arm and led her away from the church down Broadway.

'Do you want the banns called next week?' he asked as soon as the crowd was safely behind them.

'Do you?' She glanced timorously up at him from beneath the brim of her hat. 'After what I told you –'

'I think I should be the one putting that question to you after all the appalling things I told you about myself,' he interrupted.

'Nothing you told me has stopped me from loving you, Tony. But I would understand it if you wanted me to go back to Germany.'

'I don't deserve you.'

'I see.'

'Look, Gabrielle, I have some money. Not a lot, just my army gratuity and a few pounds I saved before the war. I was keeping it back to help us set up home. If you want to return to Germany you can have it.'

'So you do want me to go back?'

'No. I want you to stay here.' To his amazement he realised he'd never meant anything quite so much in his life before.

'To help your brother in the restaurant?'

'To be my wife.'

'In that case, perhaps we should call in and take another look at the rooms above the café on the way back to your mother's house. Who knows, maybe I could make them even more comfortable than they already are.'

He gripped the hand she'd tucked in the crook of his elbow. 'Angelo said you must be mad to even consider marrying me.'

'Perhaps I am mad – just a little bit.' Her face fell serious. 'We will be happy, Tony?' It was a plea more than a question.

'We will be happy,' he replied, hoping that after everything she'd been through and everything he had put her through, she'd take his words as he had meant them – an absolute promise.

The short walk between Tyfica Road and the Taff Street end of Penuel Lane was becoming familiar to Charlie. If it hadn't been for thoughts of Alma and what she was suffering behind the brave face she'd adopted to conceal her feelings he might have almost enjoyed it. A single knock at the side door brought Mary down with Theo. The boy was holding a ball almost as big as himself.

As Charlie lifted Theo on to his shoulders he glanced up. Alma was standing at the window, she moved back when she saw him looking at her but there had been time for him to read the expression in her eyes.

'Mam says I'm going to meet your new wife and my big brother, Daddy. And that my big brother might teach me to play football if I ask nicely.'

'You brought your ball in case.'

'Mam bought it for me. She said I can leave it at your house so I'll always have something to play with there.'

'Won't you miss it?'

'No, Mam bought two and my brother can look after this one for me.'

So like Alma, Charlie thought. She had promised him she would do all she could to bring Theo up to respect him and his new wife and had even included Peter.

'Right after we've eaten some very special biscuits you and I and your brother Peter will go down the park to see who can teach who how to play football. But after all those games with Uncle Evan and Uncle Andrew I have a feeling that it is going to be you who teaches us.'

'Please, come up to the house with me,' Bethan begged as Alma drew away from the window. 'We can get out that box of knitting patterns and –'

'Thanks, Beth, I know you mean well but I really would prefer to stay here.' Alma picked up a basketful of darning and carried it closer to her chair.

'Theo won't be back until seven. Mary's coming with

me to visit her sisters. I hate to think of you sitting here all alone.'

'Alone sounds good after the madhouse of the shops all week.'

'So you can think about Charlie.'

'I can't stop thinking about him, Beth. And I'm better off alone with my thoughts here than I would be making you, Andrew and the children miserable on my account. I know you want me to be angry with Charlie . . .'

'Only because of what he's putting you through. I can't believe how insensitive he's being. Asking you to allow him to take Theo to meet Masha.'

'And Peter – don't forget he's Theo's brother and probably the only one he'll ever have. I saw him, Beth. You were right when you said he looks just like Charlie and Theo.'

'He doesn't behave like either of them.'

'William was in here yesterday. He not only said Peter's a genius with car engines but he has the making of a good bloke. And you know Will. Coming from him, that's high praise.'

'It doesn't matter what I think of Peter. I'm being overruled at every turn. Liza is convinced she's in love with him.'

'Surely she hardly knows him?'

'I tried telling her that, she wouldn't listen. She insists something happened between them the moment they looked into one another's eyes. Along with love at first sight, there was even mention of the ballroom scene in *Cinderella*.'

'It can happen that way, Beth.'

'Perhaps, but that doesn't mean Peter is right for her. He's only sixteen – a child – and he's different . . .'

'If he is different from other sixteen-year-olds it's because of the camps. You know what Charlie was like when he came back. No matter what I did, I couldn't get close to him. It says something for Liza that she's been able to reach Peter.'

'It's more likely he's been able to reach her,' Bethan

retorted drily. 'She's already decided to tell Angelo that she can't see him any more.'

'I know I'm biased, but Peter is Charlie's son and if he has half Charlie's sense of duty and honour and a tenth of his capacity for love, Liza will be fine.'

'How can you say that when Charlie has left you?'

'Because he gave me the happiest years of my life, because he loved me and because he never lied to me. I have my memories and the knowledge that he still loves Theo and me, and will care for us until the day he dies. I wouldn't exchange those few years we shared for a lifetime with any other man.'

'Don't you ever think of him now, sitting night after night with Masha, living with her, sleeping in her bed – making love to her? If I cared for a man as much as you care for Charlie the thought would drive me crazy.'

'She is his rightful wife.'

'And old and weak before her time,' Bethan murmured, unthinkingly.

'Beth!'

'I'm sorry, I didn't mean that the way it came out. It's just that you and Charlie belong together.'

'And if Masha died tomorrow or thirty years from now he wouldn't come back to me.'

'You just said he loves you.'

'He does and he has always been totally honest with me. When we met the guilt he felt over losing Masha had almost destroyed him. Even after searching all over Russia for her for four years he remained convinced that he had abandoned her. I tried to persuade him it wasn't true but I never succeeded. When we married I knew that all he offered – all he could ever offer me – was the small part of him that wasn't Masha's. I realised that, yet I grasped it because I loved him and I didn't want to live without him. But when Huw broke the news that Masha was alive I had no choice but to accept that it was over between us. Charlie belongs to Masha, has always belonged to her. All I was able to do was borrow him for a while. And for that I'm grateful. So, please,' she turned to Bethan, 'don't feel sorry for me, or wish Masha anywhere but well and in Charlie's house because he gave me more happiness than any woman has a right to expect.'

'And now?'

'I have Theo, the business, my memories.'

'And the future?'

'That is my future, Beth. Please, accept it, because I have.'

'Liza!' Angelo beamed at her as she walked into the café. 'I thought you weren't off again until Thursday.'

'I changed with one of the other girls.' She didn't tell him that the short notice coupled with it being a Sunday had cost her two extra shifts. 'I was hoping you'd be here.'

'Unfortunately, for the day, but I can get the cook to take over for an hour.'

'I'd appreciate it if you would.'

'Something wrong?'

'I have to talk to you.'

'You're not –'

'Please, Angelo, not here. Can we go to the park?'

'Give me five minutes.'

'I'll meet you on the bridge.' Unable to sit and look at him a moment longer she turned and fled.

Charlie and Theo were chanting nonsense rhymes and laughing as they rounded the corner of Tyfica Road. Charlie looked ahead and saw Huw and Peter standing waiting at the foot of the steps. He pointed out Peter to Theo, then froze as three men in uniform stepped out of a car parked in front of his house. He recognised one of them, a slightly built, foreign-looking captain with dark hair and skin.

Suddenly he realised why he'd been feeling uneasy. It wasn't the house, or even his separation from Alma, devastating as that was. It was something far worse. The fear of losing control over his own and his family's lives, just as he had sixteen years before.

'You don't have to talk to them.'

'Yes I do, Huw. Peter, take Theo,' lifting Theo from his shoulders he handed him to his brother, 'into the kitchen and introduce him to your mother. Then ask Mrs Lane to make tea, or would you gentlemen prefer coffee?' He turned to the officers.

'We've travelled some distance so coffee would be most welcome, Feo,' Captain Melerski answered flatly, but politely. He looked to his companions. 'I would like to talk to Captain Raschenko alone.'

'Peter, the kitchen,' Charlie prompted.

'Not until I know what's going on,' Peter bit back belligerently.

'And none of us will find that out until I've had a chance to talk to Captain Melerski. Perhaps you gentlemen would like to wait in here.' Charlie opened the door to the dining-room as Peter capitulated and carried Theo into the kitchen.

One of the officers looked to the captain. 'Captain Melerski . . .'

'It's quite all right –' Charlie checked the man's insignia – 'Lieutenant. I have no intention of bolting anywhere.'

'Captain Raschenko and I·are old friends, we have a lot of catching up to do,' Edmund Melerski murmured.

'We are here –'

'I know why we are here, Lieutenant, and I am the senior officer present.' The captain held the dining-room door open, closing it firmly when the lieutenant reluctantly joined his companion.

'Police Constable Huw Davies,' Huw introduced himself. 'Do you mind telling me what this is about, sir?'

'I have some confidential information for Captain Raschenko.'

'Shall we go in here?' Charlie opened the door to the parlour. 'Huw is a friend, Edmund,' he explained as Huw followed them into the room. Taking one of the chairs that flanked the cold, empty fireplace he sat back and waited, just as he'd done the night Huw had brought the news that Masha was alive.

Setting the briefcase he was holding on to the chaise longue, Edmund paced to the window as Huw moved a chair protectively close to where Charlie was sitting.

'Feo, I don't know where to begin. When they asked me to do this I refused. Then they warned they'd ask someone who didn't know you to come here and I thought that would be even worse . . .'

'Sit down, Edmund.'

The captain obediently took the chair opposite Charlie's but Huw noticed he was unable to look Charlie in the eye. 'It's the Yalta agreement, Feo. The allies have made a lot of concessions to the Soviets.'

'When do they want me back?'

'Immediately. It's happening everywhere, even America. The Soviet Government has supplied the allied countries with lists of Russian citizens known to be living abroad. Some of the people left during the revolution in 1917, but the Soviets are demanding immediate repatriation of every one of their nationals, irrespective of how many years ago they left Russia or how long they've lived in their adoptive countries. The allies signed the agreement in the hope of avoiding future difficulties with Stalin. There is no doubt that it is legally binding and all the signatory countries regard it as so, but that doesn't mean nothing can be done in your case. You have friends, Feo. A lot of friends prepared to help you in any way they can. Just say the word and we'll –'

Huw frowned as comprehension dawned. 'Are you saying that the Russians want Charlie to go back there? After taking his home, his wife, arresting him . . . ?'

'Huw, thank you for trying to help, but nothing you say will alter this situation.'

'You can't go back, Charlie. You're as Welsh as I am now. You fought for us during the war. You're married to Alma . . .'

'A bigamous marriage,' Edmund reminded sadly. 'Feo, why didn't you take out British citizenship when you jumped ship in Cardiff dock before the war? The Soviet Government would still want you back but at least we could have put up a better legal argument for keeping you here.'

'Because I was an illegal immigrant. Because I didn't want to draw attention to myself and risk being sent back. Because I just wanted to get on with what was left of my life as best I could.'

'We looked at every legal angle when we got the demand. There are no loopholes.'

'And Masha?'

'A Soviet national. We might be able to put up an argument for you on the basis of your war service but not her.'

'Peter?'

'He is your son. His name is on the list of Russian nationals for repatriation, but he is not important in the scheme of things. It is you they want. We both know what you did in the war. It is your knowledge, your training and your expertise they are after.'

'How soon is immediate?'

'There's a Russian ship leaving Cardiff dock on the morning tide tomorrow. They want you on it.'

'In God's name, Charlie!' Huw leaped to his feet. 'You can't possibly consider going. You have to fight this. You –'

Ignoring Huw, Charlie looked to the captain. 'You have bargaining powers?'

'I can contact my superior.'

'There is a telephone in the hall. Tell them Masha and I will leave with you – quietly – without causing any trouble, but only on condition Peter is allowed to remain behind as a future British citizen. Tell them – tell them – I need someone to look after my business interests and act as guardian to my British-born son.'

'Feo, your friend is right, we could fight this.'

'As you've pointed out, I could, but not Masha, and I'll not leave her to face Soviet justice alone a second time. We'll meet our Russian destiny together but not

404

Peter. You said he's not important to them. Please, Edmund, for the sake of our friendship do whatever needs doing. The boy deserves a future he can believe in.'

'I swear, Feodor, I'll do everything I can for him.'

'One more thing before you telephone. We both know what's been happening to repatriated Russians since the Yalta agreement. The shootings, the ten- and fifteen-year sentences, the show trials and hangings.'

'How –'

'News travels, even to Pontypridd. Tell whoever's at the end of the line that I won't leave Masha and neither of us will walk through the gates of another camp again.'

'They've promised you will be honoured. Given a house, a good position.'

'We both know the value of Soviet promises.'

'Please, at least consider fighting this.'

'Not at the cost of abandoning Masha. And even if I did fight, Edmund, then what? You might succeed in delaying the inevitable for a week, a month – who knows – even a year. But they'll win in the end. Far more important people than me have been sent back and we both know it. Send Peter in here when you make the call. Huw, you won't mind if I talk to my son in private.'

Chapter Twenty-four

ANGELO RAN BREATHLESSLY over the Park Bridge, waving frantically when he saw Liza leaning on the parapet at the far end. Charging towards her, he wrapped his arms round her waist.

'I got Tony to take over.'

'I'm not pregnant, Angelo.'

He took a deep breath. 'I won't pretend I'm not relieved. I'd much rather marry you properly in a church than carry on the way we are.'

'There's no easy way to say this. I like you, Angelo. I respect you. You're a wonderful man but I won't be seeing you any more.'

He stared at her in total disbelief. 'Liza – what's happened – what . . . ?'

'It's not you. It's me. That's why I'm here. I wanted to tell you before you heard it from someone else.'

'But I love you. You love me.' He stood before her bewildered, uncomprehending, and she had to force herself to continue.

'I'm sorry, Angelo. I only thought I loved you.'

'I should never have made love to you.'

'It's not that.' Unable to cope with the pain mirrored in his eyes, she stared down at the pools and eddies of swirling, coal-blackened water. 'I've met someone else. I wasn't looking for it to happen but it did. I hate myself for hurting you but I can't see any way out for either of us other than this. I can't live a lie and in the end you wouldn't want me to.' She tried to touch his hand but he pulled it back. 'I know it's no consolation but I really thought that you were the one. Then I met this other man and he made me realise you weren't.'

'How long has it been going on between you?' he demanded hoarsely.

'Not long. I've only met him three times.'

'Then you can't possibly know him.'

'I don't, at least not everything about him. But I know enough to realise that I love him.'

'More than me?'

'I think so.'

'That's it, "*you think so*". You can't possibly know, Liza . . .'

'I shouldn't have said that, Angelo. I do love him. With all my heart. You'll always be a very special person but –'

'Not special enough for you to marry,' he broke in contemptuously.

'I can't, Angelo, not now.'

'But you will marry this other person?'

'Yes.'

'He's already asked you?'

'Yes.'

'And you've told him you will.'

'Not yet, because I wanted to see you first.'

'Who is he, Liza? Do I know him?' His voice was cold but his eyes burned feverishly as he glared at her.

'Peter Raschenko.'

'Peter! That kid! You can't possibly be serious. He's a lunatic. He asked you to sleep with him. He's –'

'I've heard all the arguments, Angelo. Auntie Bethan went through every one.'

'I can't believe that you'd throw yourself away on that boy. He's sixteen, for God's sake. Liza, think about what you're doing.'

'I have, Angelo. I'm sorry. Really, really sorry. I hope you'll find someone else. A girl who deserves you.'

'Spare me the hypocrisy, Liza.' He looked hard at her. 'You're determined to marry him.'

'Yes.'

'Then there's nothing more for me to say, is there?' Turning on his heel he walked away.

She continued to stare down at the river, shedding

tears for Angelo, the misery she had caused him, and finally a few of relief that she was free to offer Peter her heart – and whatever else he should want of her.

'I told you I'd never go back.' Peter stared implacably at his father. 'And I meant it.'

'I know you did, Peter, which is why I'm doing all I can to ensure that you stay in this country.'

'Safe in this house, while you take my mother back to Russia and the camps?'

'They have promised your mother that we can return to our old house.'

'And you believe them?'

'I believe your mother believes them. And I believe she will never be truly happy outside Russia. I also know that they will never forget about me or leave me alone until I do go back.'

'So you will allow them to cart you off like a piece of dirt – like an animal!'

'Shouting will only upset your mother. You have to help me, Peter. We haven't much time. Your mother and I will be leaving in less than an hour. There is a Russian ship in Cardiff; we'll be sailing first thing tomorrow. What I want you to do, what you have to do, is convince your mother that you will follow us as soon as you have sold the house and my businesses here. She doesn't need to know that will never happen.'

'And when I don't arrive?'

'I will never leave her. I have promised her and I promise you that. But whatever happens, whatever letters come back here I want you to swear that you will stay in this country. That you will never – never – try to follow us. That you will look after your brother and help his mother all you can.'

Peter leaned against the wall. 'I won't leave my mother to go back to the camps alone.'

'She won't be alone, she will be with me. You have looked after her long enough, it is my turn now.' Charlie heard footsteps outside the door. 'And you have Liza to think about. If you love her as you say you do, then your place is with her.'

'Feo?' Edmund knocked at the door and opened it.

'Can Peter stay?' Charlie demanded urgently.

'He can remain here to look after your business interests for two years and I have my superior's word that he will be given a temporary visa for that length of time. But I promise you, Feodor, by all that is holy, I will do everything in my power to ensure that he becomes a British citizen before the two years are up.'

'A lot can happen in two years.' Charlie smiled at Peter. 'You could be married by then.'

'When I suggested it, you laughed at me.'

'Not laughed. Said you were too young. I am sorry. Even in this country you couldn't be a boy for long.'

'They want you on board the ship as soon as I can get you there, Feo.'

'I have people to see.'

'No people, Feo, and no letters. No scenes, no crowds and no last words that can be misinterpreted later and lead to political demonstrations, those are my orders. But you have your friend in the house.'

'And both my sons.' Charlie thought rapidly. 'Peter, ask Mrs Lane to help your mother to pack our clothes – especially the warm ones. There are suitcases on top of the wardrobe in the spare bedroom. And food, we'll need food and drink.. Everything that won't spoil that can be spared from the cupboards. Go and help them. Your mother will want to say goodbye and remember what I said about you following us.'

'I will,' Peter muttered sullenly.

'And send Theo in with Huw.'

'Father –'

'Just do it, boy.' Charlie softened his voice when he saw the expression on Peter's face. 'Pasha, you must have learned in the camps that there are some things that cannot be changed. I need you to be strong, to look after Theo, to help his mother manage the business you own a part of. And I want you to tell everyone I know here that if I can, I will write, and if I can't, they can still write to me care of the Russian Embassy. Whatever the future holds for us, your mother and I would like to know that we aren't forgotten.'

'You'll remember that, Huw?'

'Tell Alma you love her, you'll never forget her or Theo, and you want her to look after Peter.'

'And my fond affection, lifelong friendship and good wishes to everyone else. I wish I could have stayed in Pontypridd to grow old with them.'

'I still think you're mad not to fight this.'

'If there was a way to fight and win, I would, but there's no way I can go up against the full might of the Soviet Government.'

Charlie turned to Theo, who was unnaturally quiet and subdued. The presence of strange men in uniform coupled with the serious expression on his father's face had made him forget all about football. He longed for the security of the flat above the shop and his mother's reassuring presence but he held back, feeling that it would be disloyal to his father even to ask.

'Theo.' Charlie lifted him up and held him close. 'You'll look after your mother and be a good boy?'

Theo returned Charlie's hug because he felt it was expected of him. On impulse Charlie emptied his pocket of all his money and pressed it into Theo's hand. The small boy's eyes grew round in wonderment.

'For me?' he asked as Charlie set him down.

'Your money box.'

'Father,' Peter opened the door, 'Mrs Lane's asking if you want the food packed in the hamper.'

'Whatever she thinks best. Pasha, my important papers are locked in a box in my bedside cabinet, the key's on this ring.' He handed over all his keys. 'There's also a bank safety deposit box; Theo's mother knows the number. If you don't understand something or want to know anything about my business affairs, go to her, Huw,' he looked to Huw, who nodded silent agreement, 'or Andrew John.'

'But –'

'I won't need them any more, Pasha. This house is yours now. Take Theo back to his mother with Huw after we've gone. Tell her what has happened and tell her no tears.'

Lost for words, Peter threw his arms round his father's neck and hugged him for the first time.

'It's time, Feo.' Edmund Melerski was standing in the doorway.

'You're coming with us?'

'Following in the car behind.'

'Pasha, get my overcoat and hat and tell your mother I'll meet her at the car.'

Huw picked up Theo and went to the door. He turned back in time to see the captain slip Charlie a small box as he shook his hand. Anyone without a policeman's eye and training might have missed the changeover. Charlie slid the box into his sleeve, almost as though he'd been expecting it, before embracing the captain.

Huw set Theo down and the child went running into the kitchen.

'You told them I'd prefer a bullet in the back of the skull to a camp, Edmund. Masha then myself so she wouldn't suffer seeing me go first,' Charlie whispered in Russian.

'I told them, Feo, the pills are just insurance.'

Charlie looked up, expecting to see Huw standing alone in the doorway but Peter was behind him, tears frozen in the corner of his eyes.

'We'll be together, Pasha. It's what we both want.' He gripped his son's shoulder hard as Peter handed him his coat. 'Goodbye, Huw, take care of yourself and your family and thank you for all I know you'll do for my sons,' he called back as Captain Melerski escorted him through the front door and down the steps. The lieutenant was holding the car door open. Charlie stepped in first, turning to Masha as she clung to Peter.

'We'll soon be together again, Masha,' he murmured.

'Just think,' he smiled as he reached out and gripped her hand. 'We're finally going home.'

'Alma asleep?' Megan asked Bethan as she walked downstairs.

'No, but she's curled up on Theo's bed. He's the only comfort she wants.'

'I can't believe I'll never see Charlie again.'

'None of us can believe it, Auntie Megan.'

'How is Peter taking it?'

'He refuses to leave the spare room. Uncle Huw's sitting with him in case he wants to talk. How about some tea?'

'I've made it. That poor boy, seeing his mother and father carted off like that without being able to lift a finger to help. I thought we'd fought a war to put an end to injustice. When it comes down to it we're no better than the Germans.'

Huw opened the kitchen door and walked in. 'Peter's eyes are closed but he's not asleep.'

'How can you tell?' Megan asked.

'By his breathing.'

'Can I get you anything, Uncle Huw?'

'Tea please, Bethan.' He sank on to an easy chair and buried his face in his hands. 'I've never felt so bloody useless in all my life. Just standing there, hopeless and helpless while they drove Charlie away to God knows what.'

'What else could you have done?' Bethan questioned logically. 'Arrested an official military delegation?' She took the bottle of brandy she had coaxed from Andrew's father and poured two measures for Megan and Huw.

'I checked their orders. I didn't even have the right to do that, but there must have been something I could have done to delay them, at least until Alma had a chance to say goodbye. Hopeless and bloody helpless.' He downed the measure of brandy in one gulp.

The front door opened. Bethan went into the hall as Andrew dropped a suitcase on to a chair.

412

'We brought all the clothes we found in Peter's room.'

'Where is he?' Liza followed, cradling Peter's rucksack as though it held the crown jewels.

'The spare bedroom.'

'Can I go to him, Auntie Beth?'

Bethan nodded, 'But he hasn't said a word since he walked through the door.'

'He'll be all right now I'm here. You'll see. I'll make him all right.'

Peter was lying stretched out on his back on the bed, his eyes open, staring upwards at the ceiling. Closing the door, Liza crept close to the bed. Slipping off her coat and shoes she lay beside him, wrapping her arms round his chest.

'Pasha, I am so sorry.'

'You don't have to be. I am used to being alone.'

'But you're not alone and you won't be ever again now we have one another.'

'You'll leave me.'

'No I won't,' she countered fiercely. 'Not ever.' She continued to hold him until slowly, very slowly, a tear trickled from his eye, then another and another, until the dam finally burst.

She continued to hold him all through the night, bracing her body against the shuddering of his, stroking his hair away from his face, blotting his tears with her handkerchief. Oblivious to the footsteps that hesitated outside the door, and the whisperings in the corridor, she continued to lie there all through sunset and the long cold hours. When dawn finally broke he turned to her and she kissed him, a light, delicate, chaste kiss that he returned with a passion that bordered on savagery.

There was no pretence at tenderness. His lovemaking was cruel, with none of the gentleness and consideration she had come to expect from Angelo. But she recognised his brutality for what it was. An assertion of his need to be recognised as a man, rather than a pawn in a prison system that destroyed humanity, family and all the love and

413

compassion that concept stood for. It didn't matter that his kisses bruised and his caresses raised welts on her skin. The price was small, and one she gladly paid, in the hope that it would give him a reason to trust her to take the place of the only people who had ever loved and cared for him.

'Don't you see, I have to marry him, Auntie Beth?'

'Have to!' Andrew almost dropped his coffee cup.

'Think, Andrew, they haven't known one another that long,' Bethan interrupted impatiently.

'I will marry him, Auntie Bethan; if I have to go to the courts to ask permission I will. And they'll give it to me, you'll see.'

'Liza, in all the time you've been with us I've never seen you like this. I know Peter's devastated but it's dreadful for all of us. We loved Charlie.'

'As a friend, but Charlie and Masha were Peter's mother and father and that makes all the difference.'

'I know, darling.'

'No you don't. Your father is living down the road. You can see him whenever you want. I heard what Uncle Huw said. Peter will never see Charlie or Masha again.'

Bethan looked to Andrew for support but he shook his head. She knew what he was thinking: she knew Liza better than he did, she was the one who had adopted her. This was her problem.

'I'm not saying don't marry Peter, all I'm suggesting is that you wait a while. I just don't want you to make any mistakes that you'll regret later.'

'Marrying Peter won't be a mistake. He has a bigger house than we'll ever need, all paid for. He's earning good money, more than enough to keep the both of us and my sisters if you'll let them live with us.'

'Money and a comfortable home isn't everything, Liza.'

'It's a lot.'

'What about your nursing career? You can't be thinking of giving that up?'

'I have to, Auntie Beth, if I'm going to look after him.'

'I agree with Bethan,' Andrew chipped in, galvanised by Liza's declaration that she intended to abandon her training. 'The last thing you should do is rush into anything.'

'But Peter needs to know that he has someone who loves him.'

'He can stay with us as long as he likes.'

'But staying here won't make me his. You don't understand Pasha. He's never had anything or anyone except his mother until he came here. I know his father meant well but even I could see that Pasha was suspicious of him. He simply couldn't understand why Uncle Charlie wanted to give so much and not take anything in exchange. Through no fault of his own he doesn't understand kindness – family – or unselfish love. And just as he'd found a job and was beginning to meet and talk to people like Uncle Huw and me, he has lost not only his father but his mother – the mainstay of his life. He has nothing left, Uncle Andrew, and he needs something to hold on to.'

'And that something has to be you.'

'I love him. He needs me.'

Bethan recalled the stunned, dead look in Peter's eyes as he'd climbed into Andrew's car. The warm and caring embrace he'd given Alma as she broke down when Theo asked when he'd see his Daddy again. The way he'd carried Theo upstairs for Alma, soothing the child with the assertion that they were brothers and nothing would separate them or alter that fact. Alma telling her that Will had insisted Peter had the makings of an all right bloke. Peter was odd, different, set apart from ordinary people by his upbringing but no one knew better than Liza just how different.

'I've heard worse reasons for a marriage. All right.'

'Bethan, have you gone mad?' Andrew asked, horrified.

'You heard her. We won't stop her from marrying Peter so she may as well do it with our blessing as without it. Ask Peter when he wants the wedding and what sort.'

'A registry office as soon as it can be arranged.'

'You've already talked about it.'

'This morning.'

'I love you, Liza, and I only hope that you're not taking too much on those thin shoulders of yours.'

'I'm not. I'll go and see Peter.'

'He's in my study writing a letter to the Russian Embassy in the hope they'll send him a forwarding address for Charlie and Masha. He may not want to be disturbed.'

'You don't understand, Uncle Andrew, that's just why I have to go to him. Pasha speaks something like ten languages but he can't read or write in any of them.' She closed the door behind her.

'He needs her, Andrew. He may not be the kind of boy we're used to but I believe he loves her in his way. And for her, being needed is a kind of love in itself.'

'I hope you're right.'

'So do I, Andrew, because the alternative doesn't bear thinking about.'

'The bride and groom.'

'Weddings are getting to be a habit around here.' Tina lifted her glass along with the other guests.

'And the bride is more than Tony deserves,' Angelo complained with a touch of bitterness. He glanced towards the top table where Gabrielle was seated between Tony and his mother, with Luke and Gina standing in for Gabrielle's absent family and Roberto as best man. Gabrielle had succeeded in her wish for a small wedding but, like Megan and Dino's wedding, the reception was considerably larger.

'And amen to that.' Tina handed William her sherry. 'It only seems like the other day you were getting married, Megan.'

'Which isn't bad for a soon-to-be-third-time Granny.'

'How did you . . . ?' Tina looked at the glass she'd pushed in William's direction. 'I see.'

'I couldn't be more pleased, love.'

416

'Neither can I, but not a single word to my mother until I begin to show, or my life won't be worth living. She'll make me give up work for a start.'

'And quite right too. You shouldn't be working in your condition.'

'Gina did and it didn't do her any harm. Besides, only six weeks until the last Yank leaves Ponty.'

'Except Dino.'

'Dino is no longer a Yank, Mam,' William chipped in, abandoning the conversation on the other side of the table in favour of theirs.

'Haven't you heard,' Dino boasted to his wife, 'my stepson, stepson-in-law and Angelo here have voted me an honorary Pontypriddian.'

'Which probably means they intend to drag you round the pubs every Saturday night and get you drunk, so I'd refuse the title if I were you.'

'You going?' Angelo asked as Ronnie helped Diana from the table.

'We've done what we set out to do, drink a toast to the bride and groom for Mama's sake.'

Angelo nodded. He'd been amazed that Ronnie, Megan, Huw and Tina had consented to come to the wedding and bring their respective husbands and wives. But he hadn't been surprised at Ronnie's stipulation that they would only attend on condition that the bridegroom didn't talk to any of their party.

'Gabrielle does make a beautiful bride. You will tell her that from me, Angelo?' Megan picked up Diana's handbag for her.

'Of course.'

'Laura's dress again?' Diana asked Tina, looking enviously at Gabrielle's white veil and lace and satin dress.

'Never mind, Di, we had smashing costumes.' Tina buttoned her costume jacket.

'Seeing as how you don't remember it, we could get married again,' Ronnie suggested.

'At my age, after having two children?'

'To me, fair wife, you will never be old.'

'Misquoting Shakespeare, is not romantic, Ronnie.'

'She may not remember putting me down before, but she's lost none of the knack,' he laughed, as Dino offered Diana his arm.

'You going across the road?' Angelo asked.

Ronnie nodded.

'Wish Liza well from me.'

'Do you mean that?'

'I love her. I wouldn't wish her anything else.'

'I'll tell her.'

'Not that I love her.'

'I'm not stupid, Angelo.' He looked across the room. 'There's plenty of other fish in the sea.'

'It's not a fish I want.'

'The right one for you is out there somewhere. Trouble is, you're too picky. Now take Maggie.'

'She's older than Mama.'

'Not quite. And what a personality.'

'Ronnie!'

'Sorry, bad joke, Not funny.' He watched Diana hobbling down the stairs. 'Not funny at all, because if I lost that one I don't know how I'd survive.'

'The bride and groom.' Andrew raised his glass and Bethan, Alma and Theo – looking very small and very solemn – followed suit. After their glasses had been drained they looked to the two that remained untouched on the table; both filled to the brim. Peter took one and smashed it in the hearth. The glass shattered at the back of the fire, the flame crackled and hissed, burning bright blue and green where the alcohol ran over the hot coals. He handed the second glass to Alma. She threw it but her aim wasn't as steady. Some of the glass shards fell into the hearth, hitting the tiles.

'I think you have visitors,' Andrew said, hearing a knock at the door.

'Fugitives from the wedding across the road,' Bethan predicted, recognising Ronnie's voice.

He was the first to walk into Alma's living room, which suddenly looked very small and overcrowded with an influx of eight extra people.

'We know you wanted a quiet wedding, Peter,' Huw helped Myrtle into the nearest chair, 'but we wanted to pay our respects.'

'And drink a toast.' Alma reached for another bottle.

'No, really . . .'

'Please, you have to drink the health of my bride,' Peter insisted, taking the bottle from Alma.

As toasts were drunk and Alma, who'd been tipped off by William that they might call in, handed round the extra sandwiches she'd made, Ronnie cornered Liza and handed her an envelope.

'Money's not romantic, but it's the best we could come up with.'

'You shouldn't have.'

'What, for my new partner?' He kissed her cheek. 'There's something else. Angelo said he wishes you well. I didn't make it up,' he protested as disbelief crossed her face. 'You'll take some getting over, but he'll do it.'

'I'm glad.'

'Who is Mary courting these days?'

'Mr Ronconi, you're incorrigible.'

'If love at first sight can happen to you, it can happen to anyone.'

'But Peter's wonderful.'

'I agree with that. Back first thing Monday morning to rebuild that engine, Peter,' he teased.

'Two weeks Monday, Mr Ronconi.'

'Ronnie – remember, we're business partners now. Where you going on honeymoon?'

'Our Gower chalet. They're going to tell us if it's still standing,' Andrew grimaced.

'You'll get there one day, darling.' Bethan handed him a sandwich.

'When I'm old, bald and toothless.'

'You poor hard-done-by doctor.'

Ronnie watched Bethan carefully. There seemed to be

more of a smile on her face than he'd seen for quite a while.

'You or William have any regrets about taking Peter as a full partner?'

'None, Alma. I only hope he doesn't have any when he learns that you bought the Cardiff Garage and handed it over to us as full partnership price. On my reckoning he's put twice as much cash into the business as William or I.'

'You're older, you've both got good business heads, or –' she glanced sideways at William to make sure he wasn't listening – 'at least you have. Peter needs guidance and he won't take it from me.'

'Which is strange seeing how well you've done for yourself. What's this I hear about Liza taking over the shop?'

'She insists she needs to do something, especially as she hasn't the heart to tell Mrs Lane she isn't needed any more. And as Liza is taking over both the management of the shop and the overseeing of the baking, I've rented this flat to Gina and Luke. They were pretty desperate. This place is ideal for them: two bedrooms, central, a marvellous place for a couple with a young baby . . .' Her voice caught and he put his arm around her. 'Have you heard that Theo and I are moving to Cardiff?' she continued brightly. 'With Mary of course. I couldn't stay here any more – too many memories. And Charlie was right: the Cardiff shop is ripe for expansion. And I've bought six more shops down towards Penarth.'

'Good God, woman, you're going to end up as Business Queen of South Wales.'

'That's the plan but I've a long way to go. I've taken out some hefty mortgages. I only hope everything works out in the long term. It had better. I have two sons to look out for now.'

'You don't have to look out for Peter. It seems to me he's doing all right. Beautiful wife, ready-made business, non-wicked stepmother.'

'He's very young.'

'No, he's not. Not after what he's been through.'

'To be honest, I need him more than he needs me, Ronnie. He's like Charlie in so many ways and he can help me with Theo.'

'And you?'

'You just said it, Business Queen of South Wales – sounds all right to me.'

'Woman cannot live by business alone.'

'Watch me, Ronnie, because I don't want anything else.'

'Thank you for a wonderful wedding, Auntie Bethan,' Liza hugged her. 'And you, Auntie Alma, thank you for everything.' She began to cry as she kissed both women again. 'And you three.' She kissed each of her sisters in turn. 'Look after Polly and Nell until I get back, Mary, and be extra good for Auntie Bethan,' she warned the two youngest.

'And you, look after your wife.' Andrew shook Peter's hand.

To Huw's amazement, embarrassment and pride, Peter kissed him on both cheeks.

'Thank you, all of you.' Peter helped Liza into the car Ronnie had allowed him to borrow from the garage, then walked round to the driver's side.

Alma pressed a small package into Liza's hand. 'Something from a mother to a daughter. It's the engagement ring Charlie bought me. It seems right that you have it.'

'Is Peter old enough to drive?' Andrew asked Bethan as they waved the couple off.

'No, but who is going to stop him?'

'No one,' Huw assured them.

'Why don't you all come back in for a drink?'

'One quick one, Alma.' Ronnie accepted for everyone, recognising her need for company for just a little while longer. He looked across the street.

'The other bride and groom are leaving,' Alma shaded her eyes from the sun. 'Doesn't she look beautiful?'

'Very.' Diana hesitated for a fraction of a second.

'Di, where are you going?' Ronnie followed, catching up with her at the taxi that had been hired to take Tony and Gabrielle to the station on the first leg of their journey to their honeymoon guesthouse in Porthcawl.

'Gabrielle,' Diana held out her hand to the bride, 'we haven't met but I'm your sister-in-law Diana. Welcome to Pontypridd and the Ronconi family.'

Notes

The forcible repatriation of Soviet Nationals from the allied states to the USSR at the end of the war is a matter of public record. During May 1945 tens of thousands of Cossack and Caucasian men, women and children were shepherded under British guard across the Austrian bridge of Judenburg which marked the frontier between the British and Russian zones.

Soviet NKVD commissioners travelled through France from the time of the German retreat until as late as May 1946 in search of Soviet 'non-returners', some of whom had left Russia three decades before during the revolution. Soviet citizens were rounded up and sent back from countries as far afield as the USA and Sweden, as well as areas of Europe under allied control.

The fate of thousands remains uncertain. Some officers, such as General Vlasov returned to 'show trials' and a hangman's rope, hundreds of other officers were simply shot within hours of repatriation, their families sent to Siberia for terms varying from five to fifteen years.

The historians David Dallin, Boris Nicolaevsky, Nikolai Tolstoy and Martin Gilbert have all written in depth about this tragedy. I am indebted to them for their accounts.